THE MOB 2: SHIO CUPPACIO

LISA AUSTIN

Edited by: NekeReads® Editing Service

SYNOPSIS

Pretty Little Sinner

Solana Ledesma is everything Shio Cuppacio prayed against. She lives her life without direction, routine, restrictions, or discipline. When the reckless beauty is suddenly dumped into his world, Shio believes he'll send her on her way without a second thought. Instead, he finds himself falling for the beautiful hot mess he never saw coming.

Certain God wouldn't have crossed their paths if she wasn't meant to be his, Shio vows to eliminate every man standing in his way before fully immersing himself in all things Solana Ledesma.

Until the past crashes into the present.

One phone call changes everything, revealing the existence of a daughter Shio never knew he had. Watching Solana battle the same demons that once destroyed his father forces Shio to face a truth he's been avoiding. He and Solana had been living inside a bubble—one built on temptation, obsession, delusion, and sin. A cycle that tested his control, his beliefs, and the discipline he built his entire life around. He broke every rule he ever stood on for his *Pretty Little Sinner*, only to realize her sins may be far too grave to overlook.

Now his enemies want a trade.

A girl for a girl.

Solana for his long-lost daughter.

The choice should be obvious. A man chooses his child... right?

But a child also comes with the child's mother—a woman Shio failed to eliminate years ago. And with two women hanging in the balance, there's still one obligation he can't escape: honoring his family and the mob by taking a **wife**.

But Shio refuses to give his child's mother his last name.

And his Pretty Little Sinner may not deserve it either.

A King needs a Queen, but what happens when the man who is always seventeen steps ahead is finally forced into a corner where every choice costs him something?

ORDER OF THE MOB

If you're new here, heyyy! Thank you for giving me a chance! Welcome to the Rinaldi Mob. In order to get the full reading experience, you'll need to start from the beginning. The reading order is listed below. Enjoy!

Humbled on Christmas Day
Daddy's lil Baby
Big Boss
Pregnant by a muthafuckin' Don 1
Pregnant by a muthafuckin' Don 2
Put it on the mob
Put it on the mob 2
On the mob: The Cuppacio twins
On the mob 2: The Cuppacio twins
On the mob 3: The Cuppacio twins
Blake University: Leader & Calista
The Mob: Shio Cuppacio

THE MOB2

Shio Cuppacio

LISA AUSTIN

PROLOGUE

Staring down at the white, powdery line next to the tightly rolled American bill, I felt my tongue grow heavy with saliva. Before I could swallow it down, more spit flooded my mouth. Being out with the girls last night made me feel *imparable* (unstoppable). I'd never had *amigas* (friends). I never knew I'd desired them until meeting these ladies.

Back home, my nights were spent partying with locals, people I'd never see again. But being with the girls made me feel like I belonged. They made me feel seen and accepted. With skin resembling a dark chocolate bar, I'd never felt like a member of my family, especially with my stepmother reminding me at every turn that I wasn't her child. The wives, though, came in all shapes, sizes, and shades. They not only showed me a good time, but being out with them made me feel alive. And although I'd embarrassed myself with my vocals in the studio, the night had gone on without a hitch—or so I'd thought it would.

Then we entered the club.

Then I saw *him*.

I hadn't danced with the devil in a while until I spotted him under the strobe lights, and I knew there was no way I wasn't getting what I needed. It was the one thing that would turn a good night into a *great* one. The high I felt when the candy hit my system made my body tingle every time I thought about it. It did more than make me feel weightless; it made me careless.

I didn't care that my fiancé popped up. I didn't care that my brother had accompanied him. All I cared about was how I would feel wrapped in Shio's arms. He'd done what no one had ever done: stand up for me. Everyone was afraid of the Rodríguezes.

Not Shio.

He stood in the line of fire. He went against the most feared—the untouchables.

That alone spoke volumes to me and those watching from México.

That night had done more than cement my feelings for him. It was the one night I'd finally done something for myself. I'd chosen what I wanted. Despite my knowing life was only going to get worse for me by going against my father, I still chose him. At the time, it felt good. It felt like the right thing to do. Why? Because not only was I insanely attracted to Shio, but I was dancing with the devil in the clouds. I was careless. I was weightless. I was downright out of my fucking mind. Now that the high had worn off and my sanity was intact, I was feeling what I should have been feeling at the club: *asustada* (afraid).

Shifting my eyes from the one thing that I knew would take me back to the state of euphoria, I focused on the length of my body in the ten-foot mirror wedged in between the wooden shelves of the closet. Once again, Shio had the glam team come fix me up for the evening. I didn't know what it was with Lunar and my natural *cabello* (hair), but this was his second time doing my tresses, and, like the first time, he didn't press it out. My entire life, I'd had it worked to be silky straight. Dark skin and coarse hair were not ideal where I was from. Because I had both, I stood out amongst my people. It's why I straightened it so much, and now I didn't know how to manage it in its natural state. I'd never been ashamed of my blackness, even though my mother was taboo in our home. I loved the features she'd passed down to me, but those features made me an outcast.

Fluffy, spiral-like curls framed my round face and cascaded to the top half of my back. My hair was so full and shiny, smelling like a cross between mint and berries. I even liked the baby hairs he'd gelled to rest along my hairline. The makeup looked as if it had melted into my pores. We'd decided on a full glam look, yet the application still had a softness, making me appear innocent. Back in México, I'd mostly done my own makeup because no one could match my foundation when I tried to hire an artist. Yet, Bruna had me looking like a *muneca* (doll).

Running my hand down the curve of my hips, the material of the dress felt good against my skin. There was no doubt that it was expensive. I'd quickly learned that where *pesos* were concerned, Shio didn't care. I hadn't heard him question the price of anything yet. Whatever I thought I needed, it appeared in the room I'd been sleeping in without me asking, making me wonder if he'd planted a chip inside my brain.

The olive-colored dress clung to my frame as if it were a part of my genetic makeup. It was long-sleeved and had a plunging neckline that still allowed me to wear a bra. The dress was simple, but its shape made it a showstopper. It stopped a few inches under my butt, hugging my thighs and making my hips appear even rounder. On my feet were a pair of Christian Louboutin Cassia Lace Up's that wrapped around my ankles. I loved how they resembled ballerina shoes.

As my hands continued to explore the fabric, I caught a glimpse of the oversized gold ring on my middle finger. It complemented the gold oval earrings dangling from my ears. The radio played a soft hum, but hearing one of my favorite songs from back home prompted me to stretch toward the shelf it rested on and turn the volume up as loud as it could go. Holding my hand out in front of me, I tilted my head to admire the simple gold jewelry. It wasn't the Cartier Love bracelets or the gold Rolex that had my attention. Those were gifts from the king of the castle. *Shio*. It was the gaudy ring, which had to be costume jewelry, that my eyes were zeroed on.

He wouldn't have the glam squad provide me with a real gold ring.

Or would he?

Removing it from my middle finger, I placed it on my ring finger and held my hand back out.

"Solana Rodríguez-Ledesma," I recited.

A frown creased my face as soon as the words left my lips, leaving a bitter taste on my tongue. Of all the men my father could have bargained with, he had gone and promised me to the devil. Felipe had money, power, and even looks, but he was the worst of the worst. Not only did he have no regard for his own people, but he was a known racist. His wanting a wife who was part African American was beyond me, but I had no interest in being his punching bag and blow-up doll for the rest of my days.

My cheeks rose in satisfaction as I thought back to the anger Shio had incited in Felipe. No man in my country would ever go against Felipe, not even his own father. It was the reason he turned their cartel into his own human trafficking ring. No one had the guts to tell him no. Yet, Shio stood in the line of fire, ready to go to war—*over me.*

Tilting my head in admiration, I pictured a diamond instead of a round chunk of gold. A GIA-certified, VVS diamond surrounded by princess-cut stones, just like the rest of the mob women, was now on my finger. Shio was the type of man who wouldn't spare a single expense on a ring. Everything he did was perfect. He was so calm, yet assertive and dominant. Last night, when he stumbled into the house with eyes as murky as an abandoned pond, I thought the Rodríguezes had done something to him. His clothes were torn, and he smelled like heat, sweat, and mildew. Although he looked like he'd been through hell and back, Shio still looked so damn good.

Lying in the tub on his chest, with his erection poking me and cutting through the water, I tried my hardest to focus on just being with him. He made it clear that he wouldn't touch me until he was the last man standing, and even though that sounded good, it also sounded like a horror film. Shio had won at the club, but Felipe had only stood down momentarily. He was going to come back strong. Whatever he had up his sleeves, I knew an army would follow.

"Solana Damita Cuppacio-Ledesma," I whispered.

It sounded perfect. The only man I could see as my husband was Shio. Not only was he a protector, but he was also a leader. He was a part of a mob, but he stood on his own. He proved that at the club. I wanted to be his everything. I wanted to rock his ring, wear his last name, and have all of his beautiful chocolate babies. I wanted to spend my mornings in that sweatshop he called a home gym, and my evenings with his tool sliding down my throat, like Uriah had done for him. I wanted to be the peace that he came home to at the end of the day. I wanted him to admire me as I nurtured our children. And when I wasn't being Shio's wife, I wanted to spend my free time with the American mob wives.

Before meeting the ladies, before meeting Shio, and before coming to the States, I thought the lives they lived were only for the movies. No one was really in love for real, in the real world. Couples were married either out of obligation, familiarity, or an urge to settle. Men ran the home, the marriage, and the money, and women stayed home and bore the children. That's what marriage was to me. Anything else was all fake. But seeing the way the American men in the Rinaldi Mob treated their gorgeous wives showed me a different way.

These wives did whatever they wanted. They wore whatever they pleased and had the world at their fingertips. When Shio told me last night that I could get anything out of him, I believed it. I believed it because of his actions and those of his peers. He hardly knew me and had given me an entire wardrobe. He'd made sure all my native perfumes and lotions that I loved were in the closet. His thoughtfulness and quiet care warmed me. How could a girl not fall in love with a man like Shio?

I still did not understand the dynamics between him and Glow, but since I remained in his home and he kissed me last night like it was the last time, I knew she was a non-factor. With Shio, I could have it all—love, freedom, protection, and happiness. But I knew there would be a cost. How much of the wives' happiness would I sacrifice if their men went to war because of me? I had no right to come along and ruin their happiness. I wasn't doubting the Rinaldis and the Cuppacios, but *I* wasn't worth the aftermath of a cartel war. Lives would be lost on both sides. And although nothing made me happier than the thought of the Rodríguezes dying, the American mob wives being affected caused a pang in my chest.

But I couldn't stop thinking about what being Shio's wife would do for me. My entire life, I'd been told what I could and could not do. I could party with the locals, but only because my father kept a close watch on me. I could flirt with a guy here and there, but I was never allowed to give them my number. I had never even been on a date, and I was certainty not allowed to let any man too close. My monthly appointments to check my hymen were done religiously since I could remember. I couldn't wear tampons because my father said so. I'm sure it would not be the most comfortable since I had not been with a man, but the truth was, I had no say in the matter either way. I had no choice, ever. My life was decided for me. Arranged marriage was inevitable. I had known that since I was a young girl, and I was okay with it up until a year ago when I was promised to the worst man on earth.

The imaginary diamond I had been staring at vanished, and now I was back to looking at the gold ring. It was an illusion, just like me thinking I could ever get out of this arrangement. It was all smoke and mirrors, and when it was all said and done, I'd have to face the music.

Scoffing, I switched the ring back to the middle finger.

A man who sent his own daughter to be poked and prodded every thirty days wasn't the kind of man who would just let me run off into the sunset with Shio. He'd made a deal, and if I didn't go through with it, Shio and the rest of the mob would suffer. I didn't care how carefree my life was here. There was no way I was letting that happen.

Just thinking of Shio made butterflies swarm in my belly. He was such a beautiful man. Even last night with his damaged eyes, scarred body, and sweaty pores, he was nothing short of perfection. He deserved a perfect wife. He deserved someone who didn't come with all the issues I did. I refused to bring anguish to the one man who had come along and hadn't let me down.

No.

I knew what I had to do. I was giving in—*tirar la toalla* (throwing in the towel). But my father would not win that easily. If I were going to sell my soul to the devil, I'd have my fun first. I'd been deemed a virgin this morning after my doctor's appointment, but tonight, that would be no more.

Taking a deep, agonizing breath, I closed my eyes. There was a pain in the back of my throat, and the turning of my stomach gave way to the fact that my appetite had diminished. Knowing what I had to do made me physically and mentally ill. He'd made a promise to me last night that he'd fight for me, and I agreed in that moment when we were body to body in the bathtub. But I was reneging. Against Shio's wishes, I was going back to México.

My chin dipped into my chest as my posture slumped. My skin felt itchy and hot. I couldn't face Shio right now, but if I was going to get through the night and let him have me, I would have to stop hiding in this closet like a child. I did not want to go back home. God, no. My decision to do so was spineless, but I knew it was the right thing to do for everyone. Felipe did not deserve a pure woman. No. After our date tonight, I would allow Shio to deflower me.

I wasn't sure how he would fit inside of me, but if Uriah could handle him, I could too. I planned to let Shio have his way with me, and once he was asleep, I'd call my Papa to fly me back home so we could arrange the marriage. I did not want to give Felipe more time to come after the Rinaldi Mob. The sooner he could become my husband, the sooner all this would end. I loved it here, but the idea of Shio getting caught in the crossfire was enough to kill me. Those women—I couldn't ruin their lives. So, here I was...

Standing over the one thing that had kept me sane these past few years.

Cocaína (cocaine).

White. Powdery. Potent. Pure bliss.

Picking up the rolled bill, I held it to my nostrils and inhaled deeply. My eyes bucked, my nose burned, and my throat tickled. The powder nearly made me choke, but I swallowed it down. Closing my eyes, I let the drug settle in. My heart began to drum, syncing with the loud music. Standing up straight, I dropped the bill on the island. Opening my mouth, I bared my teeth back as my gums began to tingle.

Staring back at my reflection, I hardly recognized myself. Aside from the white powder on my nose, I looked like something out of a magazine. Shio had turned me into a supermodel. My abs were visibly firm through the dress, my legs were toned, and the glam team had done their job well. There was nothing in this closet that wasn't expensive. The color of my dress was even more vibrant as the drug settled in my veins. Tilting my head, my curls bounced with animation, making me laugh out loud. My senses were sharpened, and every hair on my body stood to attention. This was the rush I needed to get through the next few hours. I was about to pull a cowardly move and leave like a thief in the night, but not before my consolation prize for the heartbreak I was giving myself.

I was giving my virginity to a man who deserved it. I couldn't wait to be stuffed with all things Shio after dinner. I wanted to feel him in every hole. He could even put it in my ears if he wanted, and I knew that was impossible.

My mouth watered with satisfaction as my *coño* (pussy) thudded along with my heart and the music. That man, that man. Everything about that man turned me on. I told myself I was done with the drugs after last night. I was going to be Shio's woman, and he needed a clean lady. He was a *hombre temeroso de Dios* (God-fearing man). There was no way he could be attached to a girl who liked to get high like that private jet that brought me to the States. No, Shio needed a delicate lady like his mother, the First Lady.

I told myself I was done, and I was done until I wasn't.

Being void of the drug, the worry started, the fear surfaced, and I found myself pacing until Shio came home blind. We had a moment in the tub. He told me there were no secrets, and even though I agreed, I knew there was no way I could honor it and tell him my choices. Seeing him vulnerable and willing to risk it all for me, I knew what I had to do. I had to leave. I had to give him his life back. But selfishly, I had to have him in some capacity. I owed that to myself.

Warmth infused my body as I thrust my chest out. Shio would be taking my virginity tonight, and even though I was entering a high, I couldn't wait to feel every inch of him. During my visit, the doctor alerted me that I was ovulating, so, prayerfully, he didn't use protection. The biggest fuck you to the Rodríguezes would be if my father delivered a pregnant "virgin" to them. Just the thought had me tossing my head back in laughter.

¡Un virgen embarazada! (A pregnant virgin!)

I nearly stumbled in the six-inch heels but caught myself using the edge of the island. The speaker changed to another one of my favorite songs, so I began to sway with the beat.

"*Sí, eso es lo que haré. ¡Dejaré que me embarace!* (Yes, that's what I'll do. I'll let him get me pregnant!)"

Once they found out, I knew they wouldn't let me have the child, but just the look on my fiancé's face would be enough for me. Carrying a piece of Shio while I married another man would still make me feel protected in a sick, twisted way. I'd feel like he was right there with me as I sealed my fate with *el diablo* (the devil). Still dancing, I picked up the rolled bill again and hit another line. My shoulders shook, and my eyes rolled back. There was one line left.

Twisting my body seductively, I alternated between laughing, singing, and talking to myself. Outside of *cocaína* (cocaine), Shio was the only other thing that made me feel like this.

Weightless. Lighthearted. Carefree.

My fingernails began to prickle as every neuron in my body fired. *Cocaína* (cocaine) made me feel unstoppable. When I was one with the drug, I no longer dreaded my past, present, or future. I loved my father with everything in me, but there were days when I wished I'd been born to a different family. I often wondered what my life would have looked like if my mother hadn't been deceased. How would I have turned out as an Afro-Mexican living in the States? Would I still have run into Shio... Or a man like him, as the other mob wives had? Would I have found a man to love me and protect me and sex me? I'd wished it had been that way, but this was my life, and I had to take it into my own hands. Getting high and making love to Shio would be the first step in doing so.

Abruptly, I stopped dancing. I could feel my eyes well up as I stood and stared at my reflection. My lips were parted, involuntarily, and thick saliva was flooding my mouth. Still, I made no move to swallow it. My mind was racing a mile a minute. I wasn't going to cry. Snorting this drug was supposed to ensure that I didn't cry—that I didn't feel. I just wanted to be happy and worry-free. Before I could stop myself, spit dripped down my lips, and without thinking, I used the back of my hand to wipe it away, taking some of my lip combo with it. They'd left the liner and lipstick behind, so I would touch up before Shio was ready to go.

Not feeling high enough, since thoughts of my current predicament were still on the surface, I placed the dollar bill to my nostril and took a long whiff at the last line.

"Oh fuuuuuck, papi," I moaned as my eyes rolled to the back of my head.

It felt too good, too right, and I rejoiced at what was to come.

Finishing the three lines, I knew tonight would go off without me being in my head or my feelings. Shio could have me every which way, and although I was certain it would be painful, at least guilt wouldn't consume me.

Running my hand down my hips, I felt electric currents flow through me as the strings of the Mexican vihuela strummed through the track. When the trumpet blared, I held my hands out and rolled my hips as I moved in a rhythm that mixed salsa and cumbia. I felt light as a feather, and as I engaged my core, the soreness from my workout the other day didn't bother me one bit.

As a matter of fact, it felt good. I felt good. Life felt good.

I'd reached a flow state where I was no longer worrying. I didn't care about my pending doom. I didn't care about the monster of the man I was going to marry. I didn't care that my future husband would probably kill me once he discovered I was impure.

Weightless. Lighthearted. Carefree.

Shio deserved me. He was the first person who had come along and had truly seen me. He'd been so generous and asked for nothing in return. Being without him was going to break me. I didn't know how I was going to live without being under his roof, but it had to be done. I wouldn't bring a war to his turf. The wives, Neltz, the other Cuppacio men—they didn't deserve to get caught up in my mess. Shio deserved me, but he didn't deserve that.

"Baby, tú eres para un loco!" I sang forcefully.

My voice cracked as Fuerza Regida's "Tu Sancho" blared. I could feel the burn in my calf muscles as I danced harder than I ever had. Crossing my right foot over my left, I spun, then spun again, then again. My curls bounced in the wind as I twirled. All of the colors around me blurred together. This was what life was about. Living without worry—without regret and fear. Before Shio, *cocaína* (cocaine) was the only thing that gave me this feeling. And I loved it.

Forgetting that I was in six-inch pumps, I took a wrong step and went crashing into the shelf next to me.

"Bwahahaha!"

I tossed my head back in laughter, my chest shaking as I reached for the center dresser to help myself up. Instead of fixing my lipstick and pulling myself together, I continued to sway my hips once I was back upright. The laughter hadn't stopped and had become uncontrollable. I didn't know what was so funny, but tears stung my eyes as I giggled harder.

Deciding the three lines weren't enough, I picked up the clothing tag I'd used to cut the drugs. The baggie sat, waiting for me, and I scooped out a bit more, thanking it for its patience. I was in way over my head already, but losing my virginity was no big feat. I needed to be as high as I could go without losing my cognizance. Once my line was spread, I said fuck it and divided out another. These would be the last two. Five lines were a bit excessive, but I had much to celebrate.

Tonight, I'd be a woman. Tonight, I'd finally do something I wanted. I'd defy my father with a man who made my toes curl just by looking at me. And that kiss? That kiss we shared last night was like no other. It wasn't my first kiss; I'd had a few with tourists just for the hell of it, but it was the first one that rendered me speechless. It was passionate, it was hungry, it was lustful, it was fulfilling, it was Shio. I couldn't wait to see where else he put his mouth tonight, and hopefully, he'd teach me how to use mine just as that *puta* (whore) had done him the day he found me in his home.

My face heated remembering that day. I was jealous, and I had no right to be. I still found myself upset anytime my mind went to that day. Picking up the bill, I placed my thumb over my left nostril and inhaled through the money with my right. My eyes fluttered, and it seemed as though the music sped up. I began dancing in the mirror as I went higher. Felipe was going to be so pissed once he realized I was no longer a virgin. I tried to suppress my giggle at the thought, but I was no longer the pilot in my body.

¡Yo tendría la última palabra! (I'd get the last laugh!)

Deciding the last line would finally be enough, I bent down to the table to hit it. I didn't know when I'd be able to get more drugs once I was in Rodríguezes possession. He'd done *cocaína* (cocaine) freely; his entire family did. But I didn't know if they would allow me to. I'd hope they would. I was going to need to be high to stay sane as Mrs. Rodríguez.

Before I could take a whiff, it felt like my hair was being pulled from its follicles. I was so high that it took me a minute to process what was going on. Dropping the dollar bill, I reached back to free my hair, but when I smelled his cologne and felt his warmth against my backside, I stilled. He smelled clean, like soap, but also the tonka beans and the gourmand of his cologne evaded my stinging nostrils. His abs were hard against my back, and I could feel the gun tucked on his waist. I was trapped between him and the island where the last line rested. Tears stung my eyes, and my limbs began to tremble. He snatched me up and shoved me forward, walking me to the mirror that I'd just been dancing in front of. I could no longer hear the music, although no one had adjusted the volume. My back was resting against his chest, his fingers tangled in my tresses, holding on for dear life as he stood us in front of the mirror. He smelled warm, rich, and nutty, but his look was cold, menacing, and sinister.

"Solana..."

I froze. His voice wasn't his own. It wasn't the caring voice I'd come to like or the stern one I'd come to appreciate. It was disturbing. It was horrific. It made my eyes bulge and my shoulders tense as my heart raced uncontrollably. Shame flooded through my nervous system as I raised my palms. I slackened my mouth as we stared at each other in the mirror. My face flushed plum, and the makeup couldn't hide my defeat. I was still high, but humiliation had a way of sobering me up.

"Shio, I can explain..." I found myself saying, although I'd been caught red-handed.

His glare sliced through me while we stood there for a beat, both of our breaths racing against each other. His eyes glossed over, and I saw something familiar in them. Hurt. I knew the look because it was something I carried every day. As quickly as he'd shown the emotion, he blinked it down and pulled me away from the mirror and turned our bodies in the opposite direction.

"Shut the fuck up. Let's go."

He wasn't yelling, but he was harsh and didn't ease his grip on my hair. He began walking us out of the closet, and panic began to seep in. He had a gun. He'd told me there were no secrets, and he'd caught me in the act of my biggest one. I didn't know what he was going to do with me, but I was defenseless. I couldn't fight him off if I wanted to. I wasn't coherent. I was aware of what was going on, but I was still very intoxicated. Even if I was sober, I was no match for a grown man who worked out religiously and lifted double my body weight. But he wouldn't hurt me.

Or would he?

Closing my eyes as he ushered us forward, his front still pressed into my back and my hair still in his grip, I tried to reach down and pull a sober Solana up. The drugs I'd consumed were pure. It actually surprised me because it was more potent than that from back home. My high would last at least another thirty minutes, so trying to snap out of it was useless. The dealer I'd copped from had an excellent plug. It was the reason I'd been so eager to keep using.

"What... Wh... Where are we going?" I asked as we exited the bathroom and walked through the room I'd probably never see again.

Shio lowered his face near mine, his facial hair tickling my skin and making my panties flood. I had to close my eyes again because I wanted to turn and *comételo* (eat him). I needed him badly, and it outweighed the shame I felt being caught getting high off *cocaína* (cocaine). I knew it was just the drugs, though, feeding my sexual desires.

It was as if Shio could sense that I needed him in the worst way because his moist lips pressed against my jaw, making me moan. My legs quaked and my belly cramped, causing me to stumble, but he held me upright and kept pushing me forward. The same feeling came over me as it did that night in the car. He'd successfully made me orgasm. I didn't know what an orgasm truly felt like, but this had to be it. My vagina thudded hard in my now milky panties.

He pulled his face back from mine and pressed his lips against my ear. The next words he spoke were enough to produce real tears down my face.

"*Para recuperar a mi maldita hija.* (To get my fucking daughter back.)"

CHAPTER 1

SOLANA DAMITA LEDESMA

I gasped as he pushed us forward, tears blurring my vision.

¿Hija? (Daughter?) *When did he acquire a hija* (daughter)? *Was it Glow's?*

"*¡Espera! ¡Tú no tienes una hija!* (Wait! You don't have a daughter!)" I screamed.

We entered the garage where his Maybach was already running, the exhaust from the pipe making me choke on my tears. The night was eerily still, and the aroma of damp soil and fresh-cut grass distracted me from the fact that Shio had me in his grasp. Shio shoved me into the car; the caring hands I'd felt last night were gone. It wasn't until my ass hit the leather seat and the slamming of the door that I was brought back to my current predicament.

Shio was in the driver's seat in a flash, reversing with such force that it nearly sent me headfirst into the dashboard.

"Shio… You don't have a daughter!" I screamed as he drove like a madman out of his neighborhood.

"Put your fucking seat belt on."

His jaw flexed as he drove over a speed bump as if it were a rock in a road and not designed to slow a vehicle. He steered the car with one hand while scrolling through his phone with the other. When he held the phone up to my face, I saw that it was mine and that he had used it for face recognition so it would unlock. Panic surged inside me. I tried to reach over to grab it, but he used his forearm to block me.

"Man, watch out!" He spat out harshly.

My breathing hitched as I watched him press the call log button and press the last number that had called. He held the phone up to his ear, and when the person didn't pick up, he tried again and again and again.

"What the fuck is your brother's number?"

I opened my mouth to reply, but giggles came out instead. Shio looked so flustered and sexy, and I don't know why, but it was funny. There was a voice in me telling me to sober up, that I was in danger, and that Shio was upset with me, but the drugs were driving my body, my actions, and my emotions.

"Shits crazy..." Shio grumbled as he went through my phone until he found what he was looking for as I gyrated in my seat. There was no music playing, but I still had the tunes from the closet in my head.

He dialed that number a few more times before tossing my phone in the back seat and pulling out his own. We were now at a red light, and I was throwing my head as I shook my ass in the seat. I felt amazing.

"Aye..." His deep voice boomed, but I couldn't stop dancing.

His scent invaded my space first, and then I felt his body heat. He was close, and it was sending my body into overdrive. His face met mine, and without thinking, I tried to grab him. He jerked his head back, leaving his body close as he leaned over me. It wasn't until I heard the loud click that I realized he was securing my seat belt. My eyes watered at the rejection, but he simply looked away and sped through the red light.

Placing his phone on speaker, he continued defying the law and going past the speed limit. His phone rang three times before the FaceTime call connected. I had gone back to twirling in my seat and was now snapping my fingers. The *cocaína* (cocaine) here would make the people back home crazy.

"Fuck you want, Moses? I ain't fucking with yo' biblical ass—"

"Nel."

"Yo..." I could hear Nel shuffling through the phone and started rolling my hips to the rustling. "Aye, you good?"

"Nah..."—Shio rubbed his hand down his face—"But I will be. Aye, look... I'll be out of pocket for a bit. I need you to make sure you check in on Hobo. I would say the nigga can croak over and starve to fuckin' death, but I made Neltz a promise."

Nel was quiet for a beat until he sighed. "Fuck that nigga! Come scoop me, and we can handle whatever got you tight in the chest together—"

"Nah, this ain't yo' problem, G." Shio stressed to him. I wanted to stop my dancing and caress him, but the drugs gave my body nothing but energy to burn off.

"Nigga, we family. Cousins—nah! Fuck that. We brothers. Yo' problem is my problem, and you 'bout the only one of us who don't have too many problems, Shio, so that means this shit, whatever it is, is serious. Come scoop me."

Shio quieted and made a merge onto the interstate. His words were low when he finally said into the phone, "Nel, handle Hobo."

He ended the call and began typing on his screen. When I heard more ringing, I knew he was making another call. I had calmed down some, no longer dancing, and was now trying to focus on Shio.

"Wassup?"

Soft baby cries were in the background before shuffling, and then the call grew quiet.

"I ain't gone be long, so you can get back to your jits. But I need you to make the drops tomorrow and for the foreseeable future. Ezio, he still off, and I know you just had babies, too, but I really ain't tryna have him—"

"What the fuck Sabrina done did?"

"My name is Solanaaaaaa," I sang out before huffing and throwing my body back into the seat.

I could feel myself bounce a bit before settling from the force. Shio cut his eyes at me, making me clamp my mouth shut. He turned back to look at the road as the car continued its speed down the road.

"Just do that for me," he said into the phone. "And make sure yo' hard-headed-ass brother handles what I told him to as well."

I could hear the man suck his teeth and mumble before saying, "Shio?"

"Yeah?"

"You'll call us if shit gets too crazy... Right? Cuz you know how we coming behind you."

"Yeah, I know."

Vello—he's Nel's brother, so that's who's on the phone, I said to myself as my brain was working overtime to function.

"These fucking women gone be the death of us," Vello said.

"Wrong. They gone be the death of *y'all*. I'll hit you."

Shio switched lanes and placed another call after sending out what appeared to be text messages. I wanted to see what he was saying and if any of them were about me. When the third call connected, I looked over and saw a bright face with colored eyes.

Ezio, I think...

The extra line had sent me beyond my limits, and I giggled when I thought about what might have happened if I'd done the fifth. Shio had saved me again.

"Who the fuck we gotta kill?"

"I'm about to be out of pocket for a bit," was Shio's reply.

I found it interesting that Shio had said very little to his family members, but they automatically knew something was wrong with him. My father and brothers were not like that with me, and I could feel my emotions taking over. The *cocaína* (cocaine) was too strong. I tuned back into the music in my head to fight off the tears. I let my body sway as if I were back in the club with the American mob wives in the quiet car, nothing but silence from the phone.

Ezio was quiet, just as the other men, until he finally said, "What happened?"

His tone was rougher than I expected. He seemed nice when we met.

"Solana's bitch-made fiancé got Bahati."

"*And*? If it's the Bahati we used to cop from, what the fuck that shit got to do with you? You ain't checking for that hoe... Unless..."

"I slipped up. And I ain't allowed to slip up, Ezio. I think shit through." He pressed a finger into his temple. "I sit back, and I aces shit. I never get into a blind situation. Before shit goes down, I already have sixteen different solutions to get us out of it. Having shit figured out is what makes me rise every fucking morning. A nigga ain't never had one up on us, one up on me. Because I'm always fifty steps ahead. But, this time, I fucked up."

"Bruh. It don't matter how much you meditate, how much you train, how much you study—you are fucking human. I know... I know sometimes we put weight on you that I'm supposed to carry but you allowed to slip up, G. As long as we rectify that shit, that's all that matters."

"I got a daughter... With Bahati. She gotta be 'bout two, Ezio. Solana's nigga done snatched them both up."

I grinned and choked on giggles.

"You think that shit funny?" Shio's eyes glossed over as his gaze shifted to me.

Instead of responding, I kept dancing. My brain would not let me accept what he was saying. There was no *hija* (daughter).

"You talking to Solana? What's happening right now? Where y'all headed? I'll meet you there—"

"They won't answer the fucking phone, Ezio. I don't fuckin' know. But I do know, I should never have let them put this girl on me. From the jump, it didn't feel right. Fuck her pops wants to give his precious daughter to a savage-ass nigga like me? Shit was flaw from the beginning. And if Don in on this shit, your wife may as well pick out her good-fucking dress because I'm murking his bitch ass too! You think I give a fuck about this mob shit? Nigga, I despise the fucking mob! The mob changed my fucking daddy—" Shio stopped his sentence and took a deep breath. His voice cracked when he said, "She on that shit, Ezee."

It was then that my upturned lips fell, and my face started to burn. The cloud that was underneath my feet was starting to descend, and my heart rate began to slow. The colors faded, the music went mute again, and my hands that were once rubbing all over my body were now shaking.

"I opened the fuckin' door to a broad that was doing cocaine as a fucking pregamer. Shit, she barely fuckin' eats, so she's probably havin' that shit for breakfast, lunch, and dinner.""Fuuuuuck."

"Yeah..." Shio spewed. "Shits a no-go."

"We beat addiction before. You helped me. We can help her. All we gotta do is get Don to get that knizzy shit again. Then we send her ass to rehab first and—"

"Nah. Her nigga wants to trade. A bitch for a bitch, so that's what the fuck I'm doing."

Sweat slicked my palms as my hearing cleared. The word "bitch" rolled off his tongue as if it were my first name instead of Solana.

"But you just said he wasn't answering the phone."

"Yeah, well... I'm 'bout to return this lil' nose picker back to sender. I'll find my family."

Shio's eyes darkened dangerously, causing me to tremor. My heart shattered into a trillion pieces seeing his lack of care for me. I had to swallow down the sob that crept up my throat.

"Shio—"

"Fuck her, Ezio! Don't you fuckin' try to sympathize with her. You were addicted to pills. Shit, we all popped them. But you still got your ass up and got to it every day. You did what the fuck you had to do to ensure that we all ate... That we all got rich! Yeah, you were getting high, but you were still making fuckin' moves. Making fuckin' money. Making shit happen.

"I worked too hard, Ezio. I worked too hard mentally, physically, and spiritually to settle for somebody who is too coked out to wash their fuckin' ass! I thought maybe she was homesick! Whole time, she locked in the room getting high. Nah, fuck nah! I need a queen! A fuckin' queen, Ezio! I got one fuckin' daughter that I just found out about, ion need another one. I don't give a fuck how pretty she is. Her sins are far too fuckin' gone for my spiritual welfare. I can't fuckin' do it, Ezio."

I faced Shio and cringed at the fire in his eyes as he looked at the screen.

"I'm gone die behind my fuckin' daughter, Ezee, and if I'm willing to die, then any muthafucka around me can die too. That's why I gotta do this shit alone."

The tears poured down my face, burning my lids due to the liner and mascara. Shio's words sliced through me like a razor blade. *Coked* out. *Daughter*. Me not being a *queen*. All three swirled around in my head like a puzzle I couldn't figure out.

Ezio was quiet again, and I could feel the pity through the phone. Using the back of my hand, I wiped my face, probably smearing my makeup even more than it already was. I was hurt, yes, but I was no one's charity case. I'd get through this as I maneuvered through everything else I'd been through. I wanted to at least get a farewell fuck from Shio, but hearing how he really felt had me feeling grateful that he'd caught me.

Yeah, I don't need him.

Ezio sighed. "Just let me know the play."

"I'm good. I just wanted to let you know what was up. I gotta go."

Shio ended the call and, at the same time, pulled through the massive iron gates. This place was familiar. It was where my feet first touched American soil. The low lights inside his luxury vehicle were no match for the runway's bright lights, which lined the sleek plane. It sat as if it were waiting for us, its open door and stairs leading inside. He'd chartered a jet, and I didn't know if he'd already done it for our date or if this was something he'd just set up. Either way, it was evident that he was trading me for his family as he'd said to Ezio.

Realization set in, and the brief, brave front that I'd put on vanished. I knew the plan was to sleep with Shio and have my father hand me over to the Rodríguezes, but hearing the disgust in Shio's voice and seeing how he'd instantly resorted to putting me on a plane without question had me ready to beg him to let me stay.

"Shio—"

"Get the fuck out the car, Solana!"

I was too ashamed to look in his face, so I stared ahead at the plane. Swallowing the saliva that my tears had produced, I pulled at the door handle and stepped out of the car. A shiver ran down my spine, so I rubbed my arm after closing the door behind me. My face felt gooey, indicating that my makeup had indeed run and smeared. The soft whirring of the plane's engine filled the night's air, and since I was still outside of Shio's car and hadn't traveled further than the passenger door, I could hear him on another call.

"Mama. You around the pastor?" His words were muffled, but I could still interpret them clearly.

The phone was still on speaker, and I could hear his mother reply, "Baby, what happened?"

"Nothing. I just... I may not... need y'all to pray for me."

I could no longer listen. I ran toward the plane, forgetting I was in heels. The tears blurred my vision, and I missed a step, which caused me to crash down on my knees. The feeling hadn't come back to the rest of my body just yet, so my knees were numb while my hands burned. I stayed on the ground, hands planted on the tar while huffing out a cry.

My chest shook, and I heaved while tears continued to flood my face. Strong arms pulled me up by my waist, and when I thought

Shio was going to coddle me, he used the strength that he trained for every morning and tossed me over his shoulder. My ass was right next to his face, and the cool air against my damp panties made me tremble, but the tears hadn't stopped.

Shio ascended the stairs, walking up each one as his shoes clank with every step. The world was upside down from this view, but I could see that his car was no longer running and was parked at an angle in the dark. He boarded the plane, with me in tow, ignoring the greeting from what I assumed was the flight crew. I could feel the blood rush to the top of my head. Balling my fists, I began beating his back. My fists were no match for his iron-like muscles, but I kept beating anyway.

"Let me fucking go! Put me down! Put me down now!"

Shio threw me into a chair, and it felt like I was on a rollercoaster. My eyes widened as I faced him directly. He leaned in to meet my gaze, and only then could I see how good he looked. His jacket was made of the finest leather, and beneath it, he wore a black designer shirt with a Jesus chain resting on it. His matching pants completed his outfit, and Prada boots covered his feet. He looked like wealth dipped in chocolate and smelled just as good.

Instead of words, he glared at me, which had me cowering in my seat.

Taking in a breath, I squinted at him and leaned back in the chair. I was so turned on and knew it had everything to do with the drugs. His eyes shifted from my face to my lap before he snarled at me.

His expression was stone-cold. The emotion he'd shown earlier in the car was gone, and he looked at me as if I were nothing. That didn't stop my body from responding to his touch, even though it hadn't been one of affection. Just last night, Shio looked at me with eyes full of longing, lust, and care. Now, as I sat in the plush, leather seat, squirming and trying to get rid of the high, I saw nothing in his gaze.

Using his thumb, he flicked the tip of his nose, shifted his eyes, and stood in place, looking out the window at nothing.

"Shio..."

Shio didn't spare me a second glance as he took the seat across from me. There were at least twenty other seats on this plane, and he chose the one closest to me. A part of me wanted to think it was because he still cared, but knowing Shio, he was probably for a reason I wouldn't think of unless he told me.

"Buckle up," was all he said in response, still keeping his gaze off of me.

I secured my seat belt at the same time as him. With his phone in his hand, he began typing, and I nearly broke my neck trying to stretch it to see who it was he was texting. When I couldn't make it out, I pushed my back further into my seat and let out a breath. Just as quick as he'd ignited a flame inside of my body, it had been put out.

A baby? A family? Who is Bahati?

I had so many questions, and it was taking everything inside of me not to ask them.

"Mr. Cuppacio?"

I snapped my head toward a middle-aged black man dressed as the pilot. His uniform was crisp, and the pins on his white shirt confirmed that he'd checked off all of the requirements to be able to operate this plane.

"Yeah?" Shio answered as he stood to face the man.

"Without your passports being aboard, in order for me to safely get you into CDMX with everything going on between us here, in the States, and them... I need you both to sign this waiver before takeoff."

"A waiver? I sent you pictures of both our passports," Shio replied.

He had a picture of my passport?

"Yes, and I have them. They will do for us to leave, but I also need you to sign here—"

"I'm not signing shit without reading it."

Shio picked up the tablet covered in a black case. His eyes examined the iPad, and after a few minutes, he swiped the screen. A few seconds later, he signed the screen with his index finger. He tapped the iPad and flipped the screen so I could see it. The words were so small that they looked like a foreign language, which they were, since it was in English. I lifted my finger to sign, but Shio pulled the tablet back.

"Don't sign shit without reading, Solana..."

"*¿Otra lecciíon?* (Another lesson?)" My attitude was there, but I was still in a semi-euphoric state, so it may have come out as a moan.

"Read the fuckin' form, Solana."

Rolling my eyes, I snatched the tablet from his hand, nearly dropping it, but it fell into my lap. I read as much as I could understand. It was something about customs and being a U.S. citizen, and a whole bunch of big words that I didn't know, so after figuring it was safe to sign since Shio had signed it, I signed my name. Shio took the tablet from my lap, his knuckles brushing my thigh, and handed it to the pilot.

Taking his seat across from me again, Shio had his head in his phone as the pilot announced we were preparing for takeoff. Shio kept typing away, and since I couldn't see what he was saying, I let my eyes wander from his hand to his neck. The diamonds in his necklace shone beneath the cabinet lights. Each time he moved a finger, the stones in his watch gleamed as well. Even though he was acting as if I didn't exist outside his instructions, he looked so damn edible. His dark chocolate skin was glowing, his low haircut was freshly lined, and his facial hair was trimmed to perfection. As he clenched his jaw while giving his phone all of his attention, he was the finest man alive, and I'd bet my next high on it.

Looking around the empty cabin, since the stewardess had disappeared behind a curtain, my brows furrowed. My heart jolted in my chest, forcing me to reach up and rub it. My breathing shortened, and I could feel sweat forming at my hairline, possibly curling my baby hairs. I was leaving America. I was leaving a place I'd wanted to come to for my entire life. I was leaving Shio. I'd planned to do so anyway, to keep Shio and his people safe, but the thought of being forced to do something while I had no clue what we were about to walk into was frightening.

The thought of Shio hating me and his last interaction with me being one that was in a negative light made me want to vomit. I couldn't breathe, or at least, I felt like I couldn't.

"Shio..."

He paused his fingers but continued to look down at his phone.

"Shio," I said, removing my seat belt.

I dropped to my knees and crawled to him. His long legs were spread wide, so I crawled between them. His signature scent engulfed me as my cry made its way up my esophagus. Gripping his thighs, I looked up at him through wet lashes and a racing heart.

"Get up." His words weren't stern. They weren't angry either. They were flat, and that was worse. Here I was, at his mercy, and he couldn't even look at me.

"Shio. Please!"

His eyes slowly lifted from his phone to my face. I sputtered a cry as tears fell.

"Don't. Don't fuckin' beg."

"But... but. Say something."

He stared into my eyes, showing no signs of remorse, yet I stayed on my knees with his muscular thighs underneath my palms.

"Fuck you want me to say?" He blinked, his wild lashes brushing against his cheeks as his thick brows slightly folded.

His silence was unnerving. I would have preferred it if he yelled at me, cursed at me, questioned me, or even took a page out of my father's book and slapped me. But, outside of him pushing me out of the house and lifting me onto the plane, nothing. That scared me more than being handed over to the Rodríguezes. The thought of him truly no longer caring for me made me ill.

"Say... Say... something. *¡Cualquier cosa!* (Anything!)"

His pink tongue slid across his bottom lip as his eyes moved from my face to my hands. It was as if his gaze were scorching because I immediately let him go. At the same time, the plane shook, sending me tipping backward. Before I could fall, he was up in a flash, his seat belt removed, and he caught me by the arm. I blinked repeatedly, nervous because I might've been injured, but happy to feel his touch. He tucked his phone in his pocket and then pulled me upward. The plane was still going through turbulence, but he was steady enough to guide me.

"No worries, we are just bypassing a storm coming through Jagoda Bay. Please fasten your seat belts."

Shio bent, his necklace hitting me in the face as he pushed me into my seat. Knowing I wouldn't get this close to him again, I grabbed his face in the palm of my hand, even though I knew I was no match for his strength and he could easily snatch away. He didn't, though. Our eyes locked on one another as he stayed hunched over, his chain dangling, and our noses brushing. Without hesitation, I pressed my lips against his as he remained stone. I pulled back slightly and pressed my lips to his again and again and again and again. Shio didn't return my advances, though. He just shot me a stale look instead. Not only was I defeated by his lack of response, but embarrassment washed over me for being so forward.

"Stay in your seat." His lips brushed against mine as he spoke, his minty breath tickling my cheeks.

He pulled away and sat back in his seat, his eyes finding the window. I ran my tongue over my lips to savor his taste, then wiped the tears from my face. There was no sense in crying. There was no sense in feeling sorry for myself. I knew, no matter what Shio had promised me, that this day would come.

He said he had a daughter. I didn't know what Felipe had told him over the phone, and I wasn't a mother, but I understood that he was trading me for his child. Even though the thought of Shio procreating with another woman gutted me like the fish at the coastal markets, there was nothing I could do about it. I sat back and accepted defeat as we flew into the night's sky. My only regret was that I didn't snatch my drugs on the way out. I needed to be high to deal with what was to come since the high had now officially worn off.

CHAPTER 2

TUNAN "TUNE" PAYNE

"Uncle Tunan, you cannot pick up your phone. Your nails are still wet."

Athena glared at me with what she thought was a menacing stare, but in reality, she looked like a baby doll. Her eyes were round and sparkled, and her cheeks were soft and blushed. The diamond earrings in her earlobes were as blinding as the ring light she had pointed directly at my face. Using the back of her hand, she swiped her braids out of her face, and because of the design, the two-beaded braids fell right back in place.

Beep Beep

"All dry. See?"

I removed my hands from under the UV light. I held them up so she could inspect them. My phone kept ringing, but I knew better than to touch it until Athena gave me the okay. My ass was numb from sitting on the small, pink furry stool, and my fucking back was burning from hunching over the small vanity table that had been converted into a nail tech's station. Or maybe it was an actual nail tech's station since there was a vanity tucked in the corner, filled with too many makeup products for a seven-year-old. Athena had everything a child could ask for. For the last couple of months, she'd been on a nail journey, filming herself on her private page, where she had only her family members as followers.

Using her index finger, she carefully tapped each one of my nails.

I waited patiently as she did her examination. My phone had stopped ringing, but the missed call notification flashed across the screen.

"You're dry. But I really think you should let me add a color like last time." She beamed.

The last time she painted my nails, she went back home to her mama and her stepfather without taking the color off. I bought every product at Walgreens to remove black polish, but the shit wouldn't budge. When I showed my sister, she laughed herself to tears for at least ten minutes straight. She was giggling so fucking hard she had to run to the bathroom so she wouldn't piss on herself. Tuscany had to take me to the nail salon up the street to get that polish drilled off. Apparently, Athena had used shellac and didn't have the tools in her kit to remove it. I told myself that was the last time I was letting her practice on me, but here I was again. This time, I only allowed her to use clear products.

Instead of telling her hell no, I smiled at my pretty niece and stood.

"Next time, Thena."

Reaching into my pocket, I pulled out a fifty-dollar bill and set it on her table. She grinned toothlessly, since she was missing both of her front teeth, and tucked the money into her little pink smock.

"See you in two weeks."

Grabbing my phone, I repeated it in my head to see if the number that had called me was one I recognized as I left her room. As I drew a blank, it rang again.

"Wassup?" I answered.

I could hear loud chatter and what sounded like fingers snapping. I took the phone away from my face to check the number again, then put it back to my ear as I navigated through my sister's hallway, stepping over my nephew's Paw Patrol ride-on truck.

"Tell this goofy-ass nigga, Gotti was having money before the rap."

The accent was Chicago—that much I knew, but it wasn't my brother, Nel, Vello, or Ezio. I pretty much knew them niggas voices, especially after spending time in that hot-ass desert together.

"Nigga, Gotti got money from rap. I give'm that!" I heard in the background.

"Yeah, he got richer with the rap, but him and his people was gettin' money in the streets. Shut yo' slow ass up. You from Jagoda Bay. How you gone speak on Memphis business?"

"Aye, who dis is?" I asked as the two bickered in my ear.

I grabbed my keys from the table, jutted my chin at my sister and her husband, who were lying on the couch, giggling at a movie, while my nephew was knocked out in his bouncer.

"You gone?" Baguette asked.

"Yeah."

He nodded and went right back to the movie. Baguette didn't trip on me staying here, but I knew he and Tuscany needed their privacy. I was in the mob now, but I still hadn't been put on any money yet, so I didn't need to be moving recklessly with my cash. I knew it was only a matter of time, though, before I had to get my own place. If push came to shove, I could get me a pack and bring in enough to keep my head above water without spending the stash I had. I'd gone from a hundred thousand to seventy, and I didn't need my funds to keep going down. I'd started with eight fresh out, so I was grateful to even have what I had. Still, I wasn't the type of dude who sat around twiddling my thumbs. Something would have to shake, and real soon.

"Aye, what you on, mane?"

By the time I was planted behind the wheel of the Infiniti, I'd figured out the identity of the caller. Italian—one of the badass little Cuppacios. I'd given them my number the other day, but hadn't expected them to use it. However, Italian hadn't wasted much time at all before ringing my line.

"I'm just saying... I told this nigga I got folks that's from the M. He really salty cuz I'm breakin' his ass in the dice game."

Pulling out of the driveway with no real destination in mind, I chuckled. "Yeah. Gotti 'nem been havin' paper."

"Told you, bitch-ass nigga."

"Aye, where you?" I asked Italian.

"Breakin' niggas pockets? Why, you tryna get yours emptied?"

Gambling was the last thing I needed to be doing, especially with some young niggas, but it had been a while since I came up on the dice.

"Yeah, I can come through and take y'all's lunch money."

"Yeah, we gone see... I'm 'bout to send you the lo'."

Italian disconnected the call first, and a few seconds later, I received his location. From where my sister lived, there was about a thirty-five-minute drive to Italian. The plan was for me to chill today and give Glow some time to get her mind right. When I left her house, I went to the mall for Athena and took my ass home to sleep. I'd stayed longer than I planned with the baby until Glee woke me up, telling me she had to change her diaper.

It was then that I got a good look at Glee. She was pretty as hell, so I could see why Leader was going insane about her. The baby was so young, but I could see both her and Leader's features in her face. Knowing that Leader had been looking for Glee and knowing he wasn't privy to impregnating her felt heavy as fuck to carry. Glow and I were married, even if it was just some on-paper shit, but Leader was my nigga. My loyalty had to be with Glow now, despite her thinking I wasn't shit to her.

Realizing I couldn't say shit to my nigga had me running out of that house so fast like it was fire under my fucking shoes. I wasn't no talkin' ass nigga, and my name wasn't DNA. I was about ninety-nine percent sure Leader was the daddy, but that was Glee's story to tell. Plus, when Glow found out her sister had been fucking a young kingpin, she was going to be ready to kill her. I needed to stay my ass on my side of town and let them sort that shit out. Hopefully, Glow wasn't going upside that damn girl's head. I knew she loved her sister despite the disappointment, so they would be all right. But shit was going to hit the fucking fan real soon, and I didn't want to be caught in the middle of it. It was only so much that my dick could do to settle Glow down. Eventually, Glee was going to have to face up to the consequences of her actions and tell her sister to stand the fuck down. After all, Glee was well over the age of eighteen or nineteen, if I could remember correctly.

"The fuck dese lil' niggas got goin' on?"

Parking my car, I pulled my Glock from under the seat and tucked it in my waistband before getting out. A group of girls switched by, with shorts so small, they looked like panties. One was eating a red pickle that stained her lips, another stood with a blue freeze cup, and a third was scrolling on her phone. The fourth, who was the thickest of them all and damn sure shouldn't be dressed in anything that small, argued on the phone, screaming so loudly that her voice was cracking. They all eyed me, and although they were straight in the face, all I offered them was a head nod. Though I was a married man, Glow and I's shit wasn't solid. I wasn't interested in fucking on shit if it wasn't her, though. Women were still at the back of my mind, with getting my shit together in the front. Glow wasn't even supposed to happen, but she had. Thankfully, she had her own motion and didn't require too much from me outside of a nut she swore she didn't want, but that wet-ass pussy begged to differ every time.

The row houses that sat in the street weren't the best, but they weren't the worst I'd seen either. Kids were running in the yards, some of them only had patches of grass. Old heads were on their porches, and there was another group of teenage girls doing TikToks in front of a pale blue house. The street was in full swing, and I hadn't caught any bad vibes in the wind yet. I hadn't visited this side of Jagoda Bay yet, but I was good in any fucking hood.

"Who dat?"

Four heads popped up from being crouched down on the porch of the watermelon-colored house I'd parked in front of. When Italian's thick brow rose, he waved the dude who was inquiring off.

"That's my people. Keep yo' fuckin' eyes on the dice cuz you gone swear a nigga cheatin' in a minute."

Jogging up the concrete stairs that led to the porch, I spoke because I'd been raised up right. I stood near the little Cuppacios and took in the scenery. It was too open out here, so I wouldn't be participating, but I'd watch their backs and kick shit.

Italian's young ass talked shit as he rolled all the right numbers, making everyone empty their fucking pockets.

"This nigga be cheating so bad," the one whom he'd been having the conversation about Yo Gotti with said as he shook his head and stood.

"On foe 'nem! I ain't gotta cheat. Just admit this nigga is the truth. Y'all may as well give it up unless y'all want to play for that costume-ass jewelry."

Italian pointed to a bystander, who was wearing a thin diamond chain. It wasn't the best quality of diamonds, but it was worth gambling for, depending on who you were.

"Shit, leggo!" He squatted, accepting Italian's challenge.

"Ro!"

My neck cracked when I turned as if the woman had been calling my name. There was a thick, pretty, peanut butter-hued beauty standing on the porch of a cream-colored house that was in better condition than the rest of the row houses. Not by much, but enough to show whoever lived there cared enough to make it look presentable as best they could. With her hand on her hip, she ran her free one through her short, blunt bob as she waited for a response from whoever Ro was.

"Roooo!"

She was in scrubs with the bottoms slightly discolored due to excessive washing, and her top had Tweety Bird all over it. I could see the stress lines in the crease of her eyes, even though she didn't look too much older than my sister, Tuscany. She was fine as fuck with her slim waist and slick curves, and she had the face to match, but her looks weren't what had me fixated on her. There was a familiarity about her. I knew it was because I'd seen the same look on my sister's and my mama's faces. She was a black woman who was tired and trying to make do with what life had given her, yet it still wasn't enough.

Her eyes were fixated on the group around me. I did a quick sweep of the porch to see who she was talking to as the guys simply ignored her.

"Aye!" Italian shook the dice in his fist. "Tell dat nigga, Ro, his fine-ass sister on her good bullshit again."

One of the little Cuppacios kicked off the wall and opened the door. The smell of bleach, Windex, and Pine-Sol spilled onto the porch. From where I stood, I could see a couch, a TV, and a gaming system, but the space was sparse, although it was clean.

"Aye, Ro... Your sis want you," he called into the house before letting the door close.

Ro's sister continued to stand on her porch, leaning on the railing, which made her hips spread even more. With the way she was squinting and tapping her Crocs against the concrete, she was most definitely on good bullshit.

Seconds later, the door opened, and a tall, lanky dude who looked exactly like Ms. Peanut Butter over there appeared. He pulled at his sweats and groaned. When a girl walked from behind him in a little-ass dress that showed her ass cheeks as she walked by, I chuckled. I remembered those days. The shit used to drive Tuscany crazy, and when my mama finally got her right mind, she used to be pissed too. It was a blessing that five boys had made it into adulthood without any pregnancies.

"Fuck!" he complained out loud.

As the girl switched down the porch steps, his sister glared at her, turning her lip up in disapproval. He looked over at me, paused, and then jutted his chin. I returned the gesture.

"You still breaking niggas, I see," he said to Italian, like his sister wasn't ready to tear his ass open.

"You know it."

"Aye! You got another job coming up soon?" he asked low enough for only Italian's ears since everyone else were in side conversations.

"Yeah... I think so. I'ma talk to my people, and then I'ma hit you up."

Visual relief expelled from his chest. "'Preciate that."

Ro left the porch without saying anything else and jogged toward his sister. I watched as she talked her shit, in which all he did was rub his hand down his waves and then pull her into his side, leading her into the house.

"His sister is so fucking fine! My brother said she been fine since they was kids. He also said her ass been stuck up since then too. I think she gay," the nigga, who was playing for his chain, gossiped.

"She gay cuz she not paying yo' young ass no mind?" Italian retorted.

"Nah, she's gay cuz she ain't giving no nigga out here no play. She been in the hood her whole life and can't nobody say they fucked."

"That just means she's selective about who she fuck with," one of Italian's friend's spoke up. I didn't think he was a Cuppacio, but he may as well have been. "Don't nobody want no ran-through-ass girl."

"Shit, speak for yourself. As a matter fact, Porsha can bring her good pussy ass right the fuck back when I'm done with this game."

"Nigga, Ro just slutted the bitch out. Give the pussy some time to cool down!" Italian clowned.

"Hell nawl! I ain't no fuckin' mechanic. Her pussy maintenance ain't got shit to do with me."

I shook my head because these young niggas were wild. I didn't judge since my brothers and I had taken plenty of bitches down together.

"And why you always giving Ro jobs and shit?" the same nigga complained. "We like money too. That nigga don't need it... He be slanging."

"Gossiping don't look good on a hard leg. It's the reason I don't offer you shit. Plus, you ain't got no fuckin' license, nigga." Italian rolled the dice, ending the game. "Now, come clean, chatty-patty-ass bitch."

Italian reached up and snatched the chain off ole boy's neck, not giving him a chance to remove it himself. The whole porch roared in laughter, while I shook my head for the umpteenth time.

Face red with embarrassment, the youngin' held up the middle finger. "Fuck y'all. Aye, Porsha! Bring yo' hot pussy ass back here."

He ran off the porch in the direction the girl Ro had just come out of the house with. It then dawned on me why Ro's sister looked so familiar. I'd seen Ro at the engagement party. He was one of the valet tenants. I nodded at the fact that he was at least trying to get some money out here.

Italian held the chain up to inspect it. "Come on. I'm done here, big cuz. And we need a ride." He grinned at me.

"Lemme find out dat's why you called me, youngin'. Come on."

It was three of them in total who followed me off the porch. Italian got in the passenger and the other two sat against a door in the back.

"Bust this right," Italian instructed as he counted the earnings crumbled up in his lap. "I'm 'bout to pawn this shit right here, and then we going to the mall."

"I'll take y'all ass to da pawn shop, but den I'm droppin' you off to yo' car. Dis ain't fuckin' Lyft."

"Shit, I can do you one even better. You can take us to the pawn shop, and we can catch a ride from there..." He grinned mischievously.

I knew a car thief when I saw one, and I knew that's what Italian was insinuating. My car-stealing days were behind me, but if the situation called for it, I'd do what the fuck I had to do to get around too.

"Aye, Gal... You know if Bella 'nem got them shoes that came out?" Italian asked with a raise of his neck.

"Nigga, ion know. That's yo' fuckin' cousin," Gal replied, all calm and shit.

"Yeah, but you watch her every fuckin' move, so I thought you knew. That's my bad." Italian smirked. "I'll just call Pearla. This their shoe money."

The other little Cuppacio snickered. "You just tryna buy some shit for Mahzeyah, but you'n wanna look like a trick."

"I ain't no trick. But if I'm gone buy my cousins some shoes, why would I leave their friend out? I'ma nice guy." Italian grinned with a shrug.

"Who Mahzeyah?" I asked.

"She a year older than him, and her daddy is that nigga, Millionaire. That man is filthy rich, and he doesn't play about his daughter. Plus, if you tryna get her attention away from Flexer, you gotta buy more than a hundred-and-fifty-dollar pair of shoes."

The boys laughed at Italian's expense.

"Flexer? Da rapper?" I asked, my tone curious. If Italian was trying to bag a rapper's girl, they weren't lying.

"Man, fuck y'all! Ion give a fuck 'bout that nigga. It ain't even like that with Mahzeyah and me."

"But you like her?" I asked.

"It's beyond like, that nigga love her."

Everyone laughed at Gal, and even Italian grinned.

"She pretty. She spoiled. She soft. She smell good. She different. I fuck with her, but ion wanna touch her. One day, I'ma be larger than life. I wanna fuck all the model bitches and shit first. I gotta get all that outta my system, and then I'ma go at her. I know if I get her right now, I ain't going to do right, so I'd rather just be cool with her," Italian said with some sound reason.

"Yeah. Dat's da best thang you can do. If it's meant to be, it will. Don't drag her into some shit when you know you ain't gone do right by her. Plus, y'all young as fuck. But if she fuckin' with a rapper, by da time you get yo' shit together, she either gone be madly in love with da nigga or severely damaged from da nigga. You gonna be ready for dat?"

Italian folded his money into one big stack while letting my words linger. He looked up at me and smirked. "If we take it there, I'ma want everything that Mahzeyah gone come with. I'm patient."

"Yeah, and you see what that patient shit got Grind... Barely hangin' on to life 'fore he could even bag his dream girl. Got Pearla walkin' around this bitch, not even acting or looking the same. Time don't wait for nobody," Gal murmured.

The car went silent, everyone mulling over his words. I'd been privy to Grind and Pearla, and it was an unfortunate situation. I felt like a fish out of water being thrown into the mix because there was so much going on. The Rinaldi Mob was like an urban soap opera. Even the little niggas were going through it.

"Even if I don't get her, I just..."

"You just wanna take care of her," I said, finishing his thoughts.

Italian lifted his head as I pulled in front of the pawn shop. It had been a straight shot after the first turn.

"Yeah, sum'n like that," he replied.

Parking, I pressed my back into the seat. With all of the brothers I had, girl talk was a fucking constant.

"Ain't nun wrong with makin' a girl feel good. Fuckin' and bustin' a nut is cool, but unless you're doing da shit right, da girl ain't gettin' too much from it. Most women only be down with da shit cuz dey know dat's what you want, and since she likes you so much, she does it. But da man who leaves a lastin' impression without even touchin' a girl... He da one she gonna think 'bout when shit is all said and done."

The car went quiet again.

"Well, shit. If that's the case..." Gal reached into his pocket and pulled out his own knot. "I'll buy the matching outfits."

We all laughed while climbing out of the car. I was simply dressed, especially since I'd been in the house, but these little niggas were fresh to death. Diamond earrings, Amiri jean shorts, crisp Air Force Ones, and designer graphic tees. They stood out like sore thumbs amongst the other boys in the hood. Still, they all commanded respect and attention, just like all of the Cuppacio men I'd come to know.

Italian's left arm was already marked up in tattoos, and I was sure that by the time he turned eighteen, he would be covered in them. You wouldn't even know these little niggas were minors unless you knew them. It was good that they had enough sense to stay the fuck away from the girls, knowing they weren't going to do right by them at their young ages. My brothers and I had led many girls on in our youth and had broken numerous hearts into a million pieces. But Italian and 'nem were living grown-ass-man lives and had access to money and real niggas in their ear to guide them. Plus, every man in their family was married or engaged, except for Shio, and looking at that fine-ass Black Mexican he had, it wouldn't be long for him either. They had good examples of Black love, so it wasn't surprising that they wanted that, too, eventually. Plus, they'd have to get married if they wanted to be in the mob when they came of age anyway. It would be interesting to see who they ended up with because, in theory, their plans sounded good, but those girls weren't going to sit around and wait on their young asses to slang dick from here to overseas.

"Yooooo!" Italian called out as the bell dinged above our heads.

The pawn shop looked like a vintage junk yard. A glass casing wrapped around the room, and it was so full of jewels and guns that it was hard to focus on one thing. On the walls, behind the casing that doubled as a counter, were an array of vintage jerseys, rims, albums, trophies, and even wallpaper rolls. A tall Iranian man with a turban circling his head pushed through a doorway that had beads hanging from it. The strong smell of incense and cleaning solution permeated the air, and a hint of man's funk followed.

"Italian... My main man. What you coming to buy today?" He grinned while assessing all of us. He looked Afghan but didn't have an accent and spoke perfect English.

"Ain't buying shit today. I'm tryna cash in."

"What about your friends? I have new jewels."

Gal pulled his phone out in response, and the other little Cuppacio was looking at vintage jerseys.

Rubbing my hand down my mouth, I nodded. "Yeah, lemme see what you got."

"And while you back there gettin' that other shit, gone look at this." Italian put the necklace on the glass. "Don't try to cheat me either, or I'ma air this bitch out."

The man grabbed the necklace with a scoff and disappeared behind the beads. I needed to be apartment hunting instead of copping new ice, but since Stella had taken all my shit with the exception of what I'd gotten from the cleaners, I could use some new pieces if the price was right.

Whether I made a purchase or not, I needed to sit down with Shio. As much as I told myself he wasn't my mother's son, the fact still remained that I took a woman he'd been interested in without being man enough to consult with him first. That was busta shit, even though it wasn't intentional. I was just thinking about the money, solidifying my position with Don Demise, and Glow's pretty ass. I had to apologize for backdooring him because I wasn't even that type of nigga. I was just trying to do what the fuck I had to do and living in the moment. On top of hashing this marriage shit out, we needed to talk about the fucking pyramid. I needed to make sure that nigga was no longer blind, and he needed to let me know what the fuck was up with these challenges. If this was what we had to do, the money needed to match it. With that smoldering heat we had to endure, marriage had been the easiest thing I'd done since coming to Jagoda Bay.

"Here we are."

The owner came back holding out a huge black binder. He set it in front of me to inspect and pulled Italian to the side to discuss the necklace. Opening it, my brows furrowed instantly at the jewelry sitting in transparent paper dividers. Reaching for my waistband, I pointed the gun and fired off a shot, shattering a section of the casing and sending glass flying. Italian jumped back, and Gal 'nem reached for their pieces until they noticed I'd been the one holding the smoking gun.

"What the fuck?" The owner's hands shot up, dropping the necklace next to the money on the counter.

"I ain't never stepped foot in dis bitch. And since I never stepped foot in dis bitch, I know it ain't no reason for my shit to be in yo' possession."

Waving the gun over every single one of my stolen pieces of jewelry, fire burned in my chest. This was the reason why my brothers couldn't locate my jewelry when they searched every shop in Atlanta. It had been pawned, states away.

"I... I... I'm just the seller. Tell him, my friend!"

Italian shook his head. "Nah, this grown-man business. I think

I'ma stay in a child's place."

"Who da fuck pawned dis shit?"

"I... I... I don't know! It was a long time ago."

I gritted my teeth, not liking his response. "How long?"

The owner's eyes shifted from me to the ancient computer he had sitting on the corner of the counter.

"I got it." Gal pulled his jean shorts up to his waist and climbed over the casing.

I kept my gun raised as the man pleaded for his life. My eyes were back on my jewelry. I couldn't believe I was looking at my shit. I just knew this hoe had slung my shit all through the A. Jewelry could be replaced, but Stella had taken everything from me. My freedom, my credit, my possessions, and a piece of my fucking heart. I'd nursed that sour-ass hoe to health, and she had fucked me over. I had no business being in jail because the ass-whooping she'd gotten was well deserved. She'd fucked me over and had the nerve to do it again when the cuffs hit my wrists.

Gal clicked and clacked on the old-ass computer like this was his shit. "Aite, he got this shit categorized by sections. I'm in the jewelry. How far you need me to look back, Tunan?"

"Dis past year, give or take." I kept my eyes on the owner, who still had his palms raised.

Gal clicked away some more before saying, "Aite. I see a Joshua Numb... a Paria Carl... Stella Wade—"

Just hearing her name had me ready to unload the clip.

"Stella. Address."

Gal pressed a button, and a receipt paper rolled out. Grabbing a pen, he wrote down the address and climbed back over the counter.

"Now, was that shit so hard?" Italian taunted.

Picking up the binder, I tucked it under my arm and put my gun back in my waistband.

"Wait! You have to pay!"

"Pay? We ain't payin' for shit. You better be glad you ain't payin' with your fuckin' life. As a matter of fact, I'll take this." Italian snatched the necklace and the money. "Nice doing business with ya."

Gal handed me the paper, and seeing Stella's address, damn near had me foaming at the mouth. Leaving the shop with our possessions in hand, I stood outside the car as the boys filed in, laughing at what had just transpired.

Stella
5469 Pineroads Blvd Apt 3165
Jagoda Bay

This bitch had been under my fucking nose this whole time.

CHAPTER 3
SHIO CUPPACIO

As soon as the wheels were down, I was waking Solana up and ushering her out of the plane. The flight was only four hours, so it was still deep in the night when we landed. I didn't give her a chance to wipe the crust from her eyes before we exited the plane. There was a car waiting for me, but nothing fancy. The Infiniti would do since it was all I could get at the last minute. The car wasn't important anyway. What was tucked under the seats mattered most.

Four hours in the sky, and by the time we were on Mexico's soil, I'd set shit in motion.

Guns. Grenades. Bulletproof vests.

Speeding down the dark streets of México City, I didn't give Solana a second glance as she looked out the window at her hometown. I couldn't even process what I felt toward Solana. I'd been feeling her. I'd thought that maybe, despite the circumstances of how she was placed in my path, we could build something. I cared for her and felt I could fall in love with her. But the minute I saw that powder residue on her nostrils, all that shit was dead. I was off that with the quickness. I was off her, and I realized I shouldn't have been *on her* to begin with. The facts surrounding her being in my possession were still so cloudy. My daughter and the good bullshit Bahati was on, by hiding her whereabouts, were my only priorities now. Don could eat a dick if he thought I was going to continue to play his games. Whatever he had going on with the Ledesma Cartel was his business—not mine.

Solana's coked-out ass wouldn't take up more space than she already had in my world. I'd fucked up and let a pretty face, rounded doe eyes, and a fat ass cloud my judgment. I knew her being sent to my home was straight-up bullshit and completely unorthodox. Her father wanted her to learn how to be a wife, which was dumb because I'd never been married, nor did I have a pussy in between my legs to train a woman to be a wife. All that bullshit was a red flag. His motive didn't matter, though, because I was done with his daughter. She'd run her course in my presence.

It took us approximately twenty-nine-and-a-half minutes to pull up to her modest casita. By the time we arrived, it was midnight, but I didn't give a fuck if it was five in the morning. I wanted answers. I came for my fucking daughter, and I wasn't leaving without her. Parking behind a black truck and two Mercedes, one older and the other brand-new, I looked over at Solana. She was whimpering and shaking, but I gave zero fucks.

I didn't have to tell her to get out, which was good because I wasn't above dragging her by her ankles from this car. I stood outside the driver's door, waiting for her to walk up the pavement. When she exited the car and looked over at me, I noticed her makeup again, the first time being on the plane. It was completely ruined, black streaks staining her cheeks and lipstick smeared all across her mouth. One side of her curls was drooping while the back and other side was smooshed into her head. She pulled her dress down, closed the car door, and circled the Infinity. Her heels were now in her hands as she walked barefoot across her father's property. She'd nearly collapsed on nothing but caught herself before she could hit the cobblestone. She shot me a look as if I were the one who had made her stumble.

Solana, even in this state—coming down from a nasty high, hair ruined, makeup tarnished, and scared for her life—was still a fucking ten. Biting down on my molars, I discreetly inspected her as she sucked her teeth and continued her walk of shame. The way the dress hugged her hips and ass was sickening. To think that tonight was supposed to end with me peeling the thin fabric off by the skin of my teeth had me heated. Shaking my head, I ran my hand over my mouth and squared my shoulders. I could never wife a fucking coke-head. That shit was dead. And the fact that she was able to hide it from me for weeks was not only dangerous but telling. It told me everything I needed to know about her: she couldn't be trusted.

Solana didn't give me another backward glance as she sauntered through the wooden door, granting us entry to her parents' dwelling. With my long legs, there were maybe a few inches between us now as I entered the house. The scents of spices and cleaning solutions in the air couldn't compete with the perfume she was wearing. How a girl as pretty as Solana could indulge in such a nasty habit was beyond me. Hours ago, being this close to her and smelling her pores would have made my dick stiff. Now, the mere sight of her pissed me off to no end.

The walls were made of thick stucco, and from the front entry, we could see straight through the living area to the courtyard. Their hacienda featured vibrant colors, stone floors, traditional wall paintings, and large windows. Archways instead of doors led to each room, making it easy for me to look in all directions.

"Señorita!" A short and stubby, round-faced housemaid grinned at Solana. Her eyes lit up at the sight of the fucking druggie.

Solana placed a kiss on her cheek. "Hola, Mirna."

When her eyes moved past Solana and landed on me, her smile faded, and she took a step back. I guess she recognized me from my last visit, which was good. She had every right to be afraid because this visit wasn't friendly.

"Aye." Solana's shoulders tensed at the sound of my voice, but she kept her face on Mirna.

"Move," I said, giving her a few seconds to peck Mirna's cheek again before moving around her.

The middle-aged woman dropped her head and scattered off, mumbling a Spanish prayer. It was going to take more than God's covering for everyone in this household if I didn't get what the fuck I came for. I'd already made peace with the Most High, so I was good with however this shit turned out.

Solana's bare feet slapped against the stone flooring as she switched with an attitude that I didn't give a fuck about. I'd already wasted too much fucking time by having to drive to the jet and fly to this country. I needed a location on my daughter immediately.

Reaching over her head, I pushed the door to the yard open. She sucked in her breath, and I inhaled that damn scent of hers. Humid night air that tasted like summer, bugs, and fertilizer floated around us. Stringed lights outlined the perimeter of the paved courtyard, and on the sofa, her stepmother sat at the far end. Maura was sipping from a glass of wine, wearing a dark green gown, which accentuated her boob job and stopped at her crossed knees.

"Where is Papa?" I didn't miss the shakiness in Solana's breath.

Maura did a double-take before her face went stoic. "Why the fuck are you here? I thought we'd gotten rid of you?"

"Maura, please. I need my father—"

"Aye, where the fuck is yo' husband?"

I didn't have time for this evil stepmother bullshit. The more time that passed and I didn't have my baby, the more deadly my thoughts became.

"How the fuck did you get in my home, and why the fuck is she here? My husband will not be taking her back, so you may as well leave. She's your problem now."

Maura's English was ass, all of her sentences running together with her Hispanic accent. It didn't help that she had probably had several glasses of wine, causing a noticeable slur.

I was out of fucking patience, and evil stepmommy had struck my last nerve. Reaching for my waistband, I pulled out my gun, aimed it at the target, and fired. Screams pierced the air, but my attention was on the sting in my hand. This gun had some power.

Two sets of feet approached, and I turned my gun in the direction of the newcomers. Ines shot his hands up, but the man beside him stood there, wearing a menacing grin.

"What is the meaning of this?" Ines screamed.

His attention went from his daughter to his wife, and then back to his daughter. With Solana's appearance, one would think she'd been dragged through the mud. Just hours ago, she'd looked like the best thing to grace this God-forsaken earth. But now, she was from a scene right out of *What's Love Got To Do With It*. Solana was Ike, however, with the way she'd been stuffing her fucking nose. Besides those little hits, as I carried her onto the jet, she knew better than to try to make me Tina.

Solana's sad demeanor didn't help as Ines eyes continued to shift between the two women. Maura's frail ass was screaming as if I'd killed her. Ines didn't know what to do or who to attend to first.

"What the fuck have you done to my daughter?" His face turned a reddish-orange hue as spit flew from his mouth.

He hadn't run to his wife, like I would've thought, and instead grabbed Solana's face.

She turned her head, removing it from his grasp. "I'm fine, Papa. He did nothing."

It was true. I hadn't done shit to Solana besides get her the fuck out of my crib, but if this nigga didn't believe that, I had no problem putting a hot one in his ass too.

"Arrrrgh!"

Maura's screams prompted Ines to move past his daughter to his wife. Kneeling beside her, he grabbed the blanket from the outdoor furniture and pressed it into her knee. It was no use, though, because the cartilage in her knee was shattered. The bitch would need a knee replacement if she didn't want to hop around this bitch looking deformed.

"What is the meaning of this, Shio? You shot my wife. You harm my daughter! Demise, this is the man you speak so highly of?"

Maura was now gasping, sweat dripping down her face, while her husband assured her that everything would be fine. I could feel Don's glare, but my focus was on what the hell I came here for.

"Yeah, Shio. Fuck you out here, blowing bitches legs off for?" Don derided.

I hadn't expected Don to be here, but when it came to him, I'd learned to expect the unexpected. Cracking my neck, I lowered my gun, folded my hands at my waistline, and continued to give Ines my undivided attention.

Look a man in the eyes. That was one of the few things my daddy taught me growing up when he wasn't too busy cosplaying an angry mobster.

"I didn't do shit to your daughter. The question you asking me, you should be asking yourself."

He drew his head back, glared at Solana, who was standing there without an ounce of shame. I knew she was no longer high, but the glossiness in her eyes told me that she was itching for another line or ten.

"What?" he asked, confused.

"Don't worry about it. Look... I need you to get your hoe-ass son on the phone. He's in the company of a muthafucka that has something that belongs to me."

Solana scoffed but looked off before I could shoot her ass a glance. She was on thin fucking ice, so it was in her best interest that she stood the fuck down.

"Hunh?" Don asked as he placed himself into my line of sight.

"Mr. Cuppacio, let's talk this out like gentlemen..." Ines bargained.

"Fuck being a gentleman! I tried that. I did that. Being a gentleman makes muthafuckas believe they can play with you. Do it look like I got Fisher Price stamped across my fuckin' forehead?"

"Shio..." Don rubbed his temple with his free hand while his other was tucked in the pocket of his suit pants.

"*Papá. Solo díselo. ¡Dile lo que sea que le estés ocultando! ¡Díselo! No más mentiras. No más secretos.* (Papa. Just tell him. Tell him whatever it is you're withholding! Tell him! No more lies. No more secrets.)"

"*Solana! ¡Soy tu padre!* (Solana! I am your father!)"

"What the fuck is these muthafuckas saying?" Don whipped his head back and forth between Solana and her father.

Solana trembled. "I'm more your property than I am your daughter." She continued shaking, her movements reflective of her pent-up frustrations. "You are my owner! You own me! You own me and use me as a pawn! But there's no need to get into that. Tell him! If not him, tell me! Because I'm done for, either way! I was done the day my mother died!"

"Fuck *tu madre* (your mother)!" Maura spit on the ground next to her.

She still found time to insult Solana, even with her kneecap shot off.

"I thought we had some family shit going on... This shit is unreal." Don ran his hand down his face as if his being in the Ledesma courtyard was a regular occurrence—a normal one.

"Can I at least get my wife some help?"

"Muthafucka, talk!" I pointed my gun, ready to push one in the dome of his Mexican ass.

"Okay, okay!" Ines gestured for me to put the gun down, but I left it aimed.

One wrong word, and I was turning this nigga into a fucking bowling ball—three shots to the fucking dome.

"I owe your Don."

"What?" Solana gasped, but I wasn't too surprised.

"I got in over my head. Many years ago, the Rodríguezes demanded that I pay them, even though no business was done with them. At first, I refused. Then, I began to notice my loved ones would either turn up dead or incarcerated. So, I gave in. I went with it, paying millions of pesos every month, and for what? Because they said so. But it was fine. I paid what I was told to pay for years. Things were tight, but I made it work."

Solana watched her father in disbelief. I honestly didn't give a fuck about the back story. I was just wanting him to call his bitch boy and tell me where my child was. However, he continued.

"Then, the eldest son of the Rodríguezes stepped into his role as the leader, and he raised the prices. I didn't know what to do. I have a family. I have people who depend on me to feed their families. I needed help. With what he was asking, had I continued to comply, I'd have nothing. I'd done business with Demise's father back then, so I reached out only to find out he'd passed on. Demise let me borrow the money, but I was to hand over something valuable in return. So, Shio... you were sent here to confirm if one of my sons was deemed valuable to your organization. If one was, they'd join you until my debt was paid."

I grunted, gaining Don's attention.

"You could have saved that story, Ledesma, because he knew all that. Ain't that right, Shio Cuppacio? Always ten fucking steps ahead." Don taunted.

"I saw the look on your face at the dinner table. My sons... They were worthless," Ines said, his tone a mix of shame and anger.

"Ines!" Maura shrieked.

"They are! They are spoiled and entitled. There is nothing they could do for anyone. I panicked, realizing Shio could see their lack. Then, Solana walked in. She walked in, and I just knew... I knew that it had to be *her*. I could tell by the way you was looking at her. I knew because—"

"Arrrghhh!" Maura's wailing ass stopped Ines from continuing his weak-ass testimony.

"You knew?" Solana gasped, hurt evident in her voice.

"I ain't know shit." I spat out, gun still drawn on Ines weak ass.

Don cackled. "Lying is a sin."

"Yeah, well, it's muthafuckas in here whose sins are greater than mine."

"So, that's what I am to everyone? A pawn? A whore?"

Using my top teeth, I scraped my bottom lip. "I need a fucking address. Now."

"Are you fucking serious?" Solana closed the gap between us, and though I towered over her, she was all in my space with her chest poked out. "You fucking knew? So what am I? The charity case. The fucking collateral?"

Her glossy eyes were now wide and wild with pain. "I… I was willing to give myself to you! I was going to! Tonight! I'd planned on letting you have me, and just to keep you safe—to keep you from going into a war that you didn't deserve, that the wives didn't deserve… I was going to surrender myself to the Rodríguezes! But that would have been unwise…"

She placed her hand on her chest as if she were catching her breath. "So if my father had come up with the money, you would have just taken… Taken my virtue from me… And… and sent me back? If he hadn't come up with the money, what would I do? Die? After… after everything? I just mean nothing, Shio?"

My muscles hardened in my face while Solana processed her words. She blinked, looked off, and then blinked again. "How fucking dare you?"

Don laughed before walking over and sitting down. "This shit is better than reality TV."

Solana balled her fist, and before she could pound my chest, I grabbed her wrists, pulling her so close to my chest that our bodies were welded.

"I'd just found out about Ines and Don's deal mere hours before our date. Still, I was willing to take yo' ass out. Still, I was willing to figure shit out and let you choose if you wanted to be married to Felipe or me… Because, as you know, this shit was going to end with you being married, whether you like that shit or not. If not me, if not Felipe, then maybe some other muthafucka on the other side of the world. The nigga whose nutsack you come from has only one fucking thing that is valuable. *One.*" I applied pressure to her wrists so that she understood what that one thing was—who that one person was.

"Don, Ines may have had hope for his bitch-made spawns, but you knew. You knew when I came here that his sons were a lost fucking cause. You sent me here just to lay eyes on Solana. I did a background check on Ines, and a daughter never came up. But you knew. You set her in my path in hopes that it all would work out. You set the trap and released the fucking wild."

Don began picking invisible lint from his tuxedo before looking up without a care in the world.

"But what I can't understand is, why the fuck would you give me a muthafucka that's already promised to somebody? I know why Ines did it. He did it as a last resort—he needed the money. But why did you do it? I know it wasn't just to play matchmaker."

Solana and I were still caught in each other's gazes, neither exchanging looks of pleasantry. I'd been talking to Don, but I needed her to feel everything I was saying. What the fuck had it been about this one fucking girl, with her soft fucking flesh? How the fuck did she hold so much power when she didn't realize the shit herself?

"Ines..." Don called out.

"You were never intended to marry Felipe. Yes, you were to be arranged in a marriage, but never with him. It's why I hide you from the world, Damita. I never even propositioned you to them... As far as they knew, you were a ghost. But on a night out, they found you. You think I would want you married off to a man of his caliber? A monster? I wouldn't do that to you, *hija* (daughter).

"So, when I saw the way Shio looked at you, I ran to him and begged him to teach you. It was the first thing that came to mind. He refused to take you with him, so I went over his head. I asked Don Demise to protect you... Just until I could find you a new husband. A husband that was more powerful than the Rodríguezes. He would protect you, and he would get one of my children to hold until I paid my debt. It wasn't supposed to be that way, but that's how it happened."

"As collateral, Papa? You could have told me. You could have told me! What if they had been worse? What if they'd been sexually assaulting me? Beating me? But I guess that's why you continued the doctors' visits." She scoffed. "You know how many days I found myself depressed, thinking about my impending doom? I thought my life was over!" Solana broke our gaze and was now glaring at her father.

"I'm sorry, *hija* (daughter). I couldn't risk it. They'd kill you if my plan got out."

"Let me ask you one question, father. Why didn't you just make a deal with Shio for me? He has money. He has status. He isn't afraid of the Rodríguezes. I saw it! You could have arranged for me to be married to him."

"Yeah, tell her why, Ledesma." Don pushed with a menacing smile on his face.

"Because he's a nigger! He's a nigger like your *madre* (mom)! He doesn't want you with a nigger, which I don't understand because you're a nigger yourself!" Maura yelled while groaning.

"There we go, peg leg!" Don whistled. "It's because he's a nigger, Solana. The Rinaldi organization—*my organization*—is good for lending money. The Rinaldi Mob is good for protecting daughters, but were not good enough for Mexican pussy? Shits foul, Ledesma. And that"—Don pointed—"That's gone cost ya. I want an extra twenty percent on top of what you owe."

"Is that true, father? I mean... You are aware you made me with a Black woman, right?"

"I'm not a racist! I just... I didn't want you to keep going through what you've gone through your entire life. I wanted... I wanted you to be accepted. To belong, Damita."

"I'll never belong! Not here anyway..." Solana turned to Don. "How much does he owe?"

"1,421,732,000.00 pesos. Whatever that is in USD. Oh, and the twenty percent too."

I could see Solana trying to convert the pesos into dollars, her body still sealed to mine. "Sixty? Sixty million American dollars?"

"Eighty," I corrected. "But the number changes by the day. Currency is unpredictable."

Solana shifted when I spoke, as if she remembered her hands were in my grasp, before she snatched away.

"I need a fucking address. Her bitch-ass fiancée has my daughter. Or did you already know that, too, Don?"

"That's why I'm here. I got the call from Ines about five hours ago. Though, I gotta admit... I'm impressed by your resourcefulness to get here so quickly, and I'm not impressed easily. I didn't think you'd let some shit like this slide by you, though, Shio. Hell, I'm trying to figure out how it slid by me. You must have a baby by Invisigal. Ines hasn't given me the address yet, though." Don glared up at the man who had caused so many issues with his dishonesty and bullshit.

"I'll give you the address, Don Demise. I have no idea what Felipe has going on, Shio. But my son is not a part of it. He's only there so that we can try and get some insight. It wasn't easy getting him in. I'm risking my son's life. Do you think I'd conspire on anything while you have my daughter in your possession?"

"Had. Had your daughter in my possession. You risking your son is for your benefit, not mine. Once I get what's mine, whoever dies, dies. Whoever doesn't, don't. Y'all can deal with your own beef."

This shit was too much. I don't know why Don's nice ass let Ledesma borrow that type of money, but knowing Don, there was some underlying shit he hadn't divulged.

"Whatever the fuck you and Don giggle about behind closed doors can continue as long as you remove me from the fucking equation. Fuck you and your high-ass daughter."

"High?"

"Ah, Don... You ain't know that either? Princess here powders her fuckin' nose! The fuck can I do with a cokehead? Fuck outta here."

If looks could kill, Solana would have shot my ass down.

"Shio... She needs your help!" Ines rasped in a plea.

I laughed and looked at his ass like the dumb nigga he was. "She needs fuckin' rehab! Ain't shit I can do for her. All this shit was stupid to agree with from the jump. Poor fucking planning. How the fuck I'm gone teach her how to be a wife? I don't have a fucking wife myself. Oh, my bad... That was just some made-up shit... Hunh, Don?

"And you... You want me to protect her, but you don't want her with a nigga like me? Nah! You wanted protection, and since I'm the only nigga that doesn't have a bitch at the crib, I was the fucking chosen one. And stop fuckin' saying I looked at her a certain type of way. I'm a man. Solana ain't shit special! I looked at her the same way I'd look at any fuckin' pretty girl. Do I look like a bitch-ass nigga to you? To any of you? This ain't Rosetta Stone! The only thing I could teach her gullible ass is how to take long dick, but with the way you check her fuckin' hymen every three to four business days, that shits impossible.

"Ion want Cocaine Barbie. What's the fucking address?"

Solana took a step back, chest heaving. Ines stood, blood on his hands, leaving his wife to cry and nurse her own wound.

"My phone... It's there." He pointed to a table that was near Don.

Don grabbed the phone and opened it with a few swipes. My fucking head was spinning from all of this shit being brought out into the opening. No matter how Don looked at it or tried to flip it, he'd set me up.

Crossing the room in a fury, gun in hand, I placed it under Ines' chin before he saw it coming. "You think this shit is a fuckin' game?"

"Wh... Wh... What?" The metallic smell of blood on Ines' hands was heavy.

"Make me fall in love with the pretty girl who belongs to another nigga... Have us two cartels go at it. With both organizations out of the way, you couldn't do nothing but win. No debt owed. A fuckin' clean slate."

Don chuckled. "Awl, shit. See... That's why you my favorite Cuppacio. I ain't even think of that."

I watched as he scrolled through Ines' phone while his phone was in his other hand. Pussy has been men's downfall for millions of years, but me—I wasn't so easily fucking fooled. I could feel Solana boring a hole into me with her eyes.

"Shio!" she yelled after I wouldn't look at her.

I gritted my teeth, tired of her fucking voice and her fucking smell. She'd stepped paces away, and I could still smell her scent. "Shut the fuck up, Solana!"

Sweat formed at Ines' hairline, but he kept his composure with my gun ready to blow his head off. Swallowing, he held his hand up to silence his daughter as if I already hadn't.

"Lesson eight, when two men are talking, don't insert yourself. Stand... the... fuck... down," I addressed Solana but kept my eyes fixed on her father and Don.

Lifting his chin with my gun, he held his hands up as I spoke. "You wanted us to take each other out? You trying to get out of your debt with the Rodríguez Cartel?"

"No... No!"

I hooked my hand around the trigger.

"Shio!" Don spoke quickly, tone even but urgent.

"Nigga, what?" I snapped at him, my eyes not leaving Ines.

"There's sum'n else..."

There was always something else with Don. It wouldn't be the fucking Rinaldi Mob if there wasn't something else.

"The Rodríguezes, as you know, are into trafficking. What those niggas do to make their money isn't my concern, but it is when it's on *my* turf. Law enforcement came knocking, asking me if I knew anything."

That was news to me. I tuned in, but I kept my gun on the flesh of Ine's esophagus.

"The laws coming to me is some shit ion fuck with. As you know, we can't afford that. I did eight years... I ain't doing another muthafuckin' day. So I did some digging, and the shit them cops was talking... It leads back puntas—"

"Perras, Don." I corrected him. He was trying to call the Rodríguezes bitches in Spanish but was saying it all wrong.

"You know what the hell I'm sayin', nigga. Anyways, them *bitches* hard to catch. They hadn't come to Jagoda Bay themselves until..."

Solana and I popped out.

Don let the realization hit me before continuing. "I have a duty to keep the Jagodians safe, and now, you do too. If anybody terrorizing my people, it's going to be me, and I ain't even on that type of time. So, the war was bound to happen anyway. This ain't a war over pussy, it's bigger than that, Cuppacio.

"Jagoda Bay wasn't random either. They been trafficking in Atlanta, New York, Cali, *and* Chicago. But it looks like the big Cuppacios were eliminated only for a knockoff El Paso brand to take over... I got the address."

Ignoring the questions swirling around in my brain, I moistened my lips. Sniffles could be heard from Solana, but I kept my eyes on her father. "Keep your fuckin' daughter away from me, Ines!"

"If you leave her here, Shio, they will get her. I will die to protect my daughter, but then I'll just be dead, and she will be taken. My debt will never be paid. You undermined him in the States; my son told me about it. I had no idea he was taking something from you, and my son couldn't have known because he would have told me ahead of time. He just told me hours ago. I called Don Demise the moment I found out."

"What part of 'I don't give a fuck about your daughter' don't you understand?"

"Okay, she stays. She stays, they take her, and they kill her. You were able to flip my army, so that tells you that I don't have the manpower to keep her safe. Demise, is that what you want? Not to get paid? For my entire family to die and the Rodríguezes' take over my operation and business?"

"Papa!" Solana shrilled at his words.

"No! You need to hear this. My biggest regret is having you tied up in this life. It's why every time Maura got pregnant with a girl, we ended the pregnancy. I didn't want another daughter and having to play politics. When they take you, Solana, Felipe won't marry you. That's off the table now. They will sell you, make money from you, and then they will kill you. That's a fact. *Lo siento nena.* (I'm sorry, baby girl.)"

Shifting my eyes from Ines to Solana, I gave her a once-over before zoning back in on Ines. Solana wasn't crying, but the look on her face was of a woman who had accepted defeat.

"We keep Solana," Don disclosed, interrupting Ines' pleas of forgiveness.

When Ines' eyes fell as if he was questioning why I still held the gun to him, I raised the gun and hit his ass across the head. Maura shrieked like she wasn't bleeding to death as I grabbed him by his shirt and held him back upright.

I kissed my teeth. "Well, you take her to the *big house*. I'm done with her. Y'all think I'm gone keep entertaining a cokehead?"

"She was stressed here. It was harmless. I had a handle on it!" Ines yelled out.

"She's a fuckin' cokehead! A young, fuckin' cokehead that loves to party and sleep all fuckin' day! How the fuck you got a handle on some shit, and she was with me still doing the shit?"

"I didn't think she'd be able to get drugs in your care!"

"Nigga, I sell drugs! She ain't get the shit from me, but how the fuck did you think it was smart, handing your daughter to a fuckin' coke dealer? *The* fuckin' coke dealer of Jagoda Bay."

"I wasn't thinking," Ines said with blood now staining his teeth and dripping from his nose. "I just needed her safe."

"Ines, you didn't tell me she was a young Whitney. That's an extra ten percent," Don said nonchalantly, adding to the Ledesma debt.

We'd been here too long, and this wasn't what I'd come here for. I was aggravated to the max, or so I thought, before Don opened his mouth and said, "She stays... With you. Trust me on this, Shio."

Pushing Ines, he stumbled over the sofa and landed beside his wife. Solana was rubbing her arm up and down, heels still in hand, her expression blank.

"You're not mine. You will never fucking be mine. Know that. Understand that. Plant that shit in your fucking brain, Solana." I snarled toward her. "You got one hundred and eighty seconds to put some shoes on and meet me at the fucking car."

Blinking, Solana nodded and rushed past me. Before she could get out of reach, I grabbed her arm, halting her steps.

"You're going to wish *like hell* you stayed here with your people, Solana. I ain't the nigga you ever want to play with, and you most definitely fuckin' played. Hurry the fuck up."

Letting her go, I watched as she ran across the courtyard, ass spilling out of her dress. Not sparing Ines and his whore of a wife another glance, I headed out the same way I came in, leaving Don there too. Once I was seated in the rental, my cell phone in the cup holder beside Solana's started buzzing. Don had sent me the address, and it was forty minutes away. Once Solana made it to the car, I was aiming to make it in ten.

It still baffled me how they knew I had a kid before I even knew myself. Honestly, that's what fucks with me the most. I pride myself on thinking through all possible scenarios, but in just forty-eight hours, I had been blindsided by four unexpected twists: The Rodríguezes showing up at the club, Don dropping us in the middle of Egypt, Solana's drug problem, and me being an absent father. Then, there was the feeling brewing within me that Ines was cooking some shit up. Don could believe he was just this helpless motherfucker, but I didn't.

Things were spiraling, and I didn't handle chaos well. If things couldn't be handled with planning and precision, then I typically resorted to killing whatever that *thing* was—people included.

CHAPTER 4

SHIO CUPPACIO

Solana came out of the house different than when she went in. Her hair was now pulled in a big ball on the top of her head. Her makeup had been scrubbed away, leaving her face bare and her nose shiny. The smeared tint on her pouty lips had been replaced with clear gloss, and the green dress she had worn previously had been exchanged for black athletic leggings and a matching jacket that she had zipped up to the neck. On her feet were a pair of black Crocs. The outfit looked like she would have to cut herself out of it. Snapping my head from her fucked up ass, I put the car in reverse before she could hop in since I'd already opened the door.

The softness of her perfume as she closed herself inside the car made me want to tell her to go back in the house and rub it off. I didn't want her in my fucking head, and there was something about her scent that put her there. I didn't know what Don had going on and didn't care; I needed to get to my child.

I had a daughter.

I couldn't help but wonder what she looked like, what her name was, what her birthday was, or what she was like. Was she more like her mother or me? Bahati and I had some good times, even though I wouldn't call what we had a relationship. Her father was our connect, and she was convenient pussy. Our arrangement should have never ended with us sharing a child. I wanted to wring Bahati's neck, but this time, I would succeed in actually killing her ass for hiding my daughter. I'd hear her out, but only because our last encounter didn't go so well. I couldn't say I blamed her for hiding our child away. The shit was fucked up, though.

The drive was silent, but internally, my thoughts were loud. I did one hundred miles per hour the entire way there and couldn't remember most of the drive. I put everything I'd just learned at Ines' crib in the last hour to the back of my mind. None of that was important right now. By the time we made it to what looked like an abandoned shopping plaza, Solana's sleepy, tweaking ass had dozed off again. Instead of waking her, I hopped out of the car and grabbed the vests from the duffel bag from the back seat. By the time I rounded the car and tossed the duffel on the hood, Solana was popping her head up from the passenger seat. Her eyes were red, and for the life of me, I couldn't understand how she was tired after sleeping the whole fucking flight. If it had been me that my father admitted to auctioning off, I'd be spitting nails. She exited the car, standing a small distance away from me with her arms folded underneath her breast. Her eyes scanned the parking lot, which was void of cars or pedestrians. There must've been nine storefronts connected in the plaza, and all of them had boarded windows and chained doors.

Unzipping the duffel, I removed the Draco resting on top and set it on the warm hood. Underneath the gun were two vests. Turning to Solana, I opened the vest and jutted my chin. I could see the fear in her eyes, but she knew better than to speak. She spread her arms, and I slid the vest on. Once it was secured, I added my own, removing the leather jacket intended for date night. I checked my gun and rested it on my shoulder. With the duffel in hand, I walked up the cracked concrete of the plaza.

Since my legs were longer, Solana had to skip in order to keep up. The brisk movement stirred her scent, and my aggravation peaked. I needed to be focused on what I was about to do. I started to turn to her and tell her to wait in the car, but she beat me to speaking.

"Umm... Do you know which one to go in?" she asked.

Clenching my jaw, I walked past the first two doors that were chained before cutting my eyes toward her. "The one that doesn't have chained doors."

From the plaza's layout, it was obvious that it was the biggest store, sitting dead in the center of all the surrounding stores. There wasn't but one light pole in the parking lot, and the stars and moon above guided us.

"So, you don't have any backup? Just us... Walking in the doors that aren't chained? We go in there and what? Shio, this is suicide."

Grinding my teeth together, I let Solana's words go over my head. I knew this plan wasn't the wisest, but it was what I had. I could have easily had her father's guards accompany us, but if they flipped on Ines, they could very well flip on me. The most I used them for was to get me these weapons and the car.

"Stay behind me, Solana."

"You're not giving me a gun?"

"Can you shoot?" I asked, keeping my stride, and my head swiveled. "Thought so. Here."

Sticking my hand into the duffel, I pulled out the tool and handed it to her.

"*¿En realidad?* (Really?)"

Instead of replying, I checked our surroundings again as we neared the entrance.

"*¿Una linterna, Shio?* (A flashlight, Shio?)"

Approaching the door, which was worn down wood and burgundy in color, I said in a whisper, "Point it when I say so."

She couldn't shoot, and she was coming off a cocaine high. If I handed her a gun, she'd fuck around and shoot her damn self. I wasn't the slightest bit worried about her shooting me. Solana would never point no toolie at me, and I could bet on that.

Lifting my foot, I rammed it into the door, knocking it off the hinges. The smell of water, sewage, and something dead hung in the air as I let the gun lead the way. It was pitch dark inside, but I could sense bodies. I hadn't seen the blueprints to know the lay out—another thing that had me feeling off my square.

"Turn on the flashlight."

I could hear Solana's breathing as I focused on everything around us.

The flashlight clicked and when she lifted it, I pulled Solana behind me, rotating my gun.

"*Cuando mi hermano me dijo que eras valiente, no podía creerlo. Tenía que verlo con mis propios ojos.* (When my brother told me you were brave, I couldn't believe it. I had to see it with my own eyes.)"

The voice got closer, and we came face-to-face with a stockier Felipe. He looked a year or two younger but just as bitch-ass as his brother. He wasn't alone, though. My eyes trailed the appearing bodies. We were surrounded by about fifty armed Hispanics, give or take a few. I was outnumbered, as I expected, but I held my head high, kept my spine straight, and my chest out. I aimed my gun at the ringleader and his weak-ass crew. Every time I moved my gun, Solana moved the flashlight while staying behind my back. Looking around, I was pissed that I hadn't let my team accompany me, but this was my mess. I just needed to figure out how to clean it up without dying and getting Solana killed.

Pointing my gun back to this chubby, 6ix9ine-looking nigga, I grinned. Felipe's brother was at least a whole foot shorter than me, with a buzz cut and tattoos all over his face. All he needed was the colored lace front and he'd be closer in resemblance to the rapper than Felipe.

"Me no speak no Espanol, bitch-ass nigga."

He chuckled, lifted his hand, and snapped his finger. The lights came on with a low rumble, and I immediately scanned the space to see if I could find Bahati. Having no sight of her, I mapped out the visible exits. There was a long hall to the left with closed doors, so I assumed that's where Bahati and our child were. Now that there was light, it was easy to see this place had been a restaurant once upon a time. There were tables with chairs stacked on top of them in a far right corner, and there was a bar behind me to the left. I could also see a kitchen beyond the bar.

There is an exit in the kitchen. Has to be.

He stared at me with amusement, like I wouldn't pull this trigger even with fifty other guns pointed at me. That shit didn't move me one way or another. I noticed when his attention moved from me to Solana. She still had the flashlight pointed at him, and his smile fell.

"*Sabes, ¿verdad? Que mi hermano se case contigo no va a impedir que todos te follemos por todos los agujeros, ¿verdad?* (You do know, my brother marrying you isn't going to stop us all from fucking you in every hole. Right?)"

I didn't take my eyes off him, even though he was staring at Solana as if she were fresh meat. Her body was still protected by me, but she had her head curled around my shoulder so she could follow me with the flashlight.

"¿Eliges a este negro de mierda por encima de nosotros? Vas a desear no haberlo hecho. (You choose this piece-of-shit black nigger over us? You're going to wish you hadn't.)"

I could feel Solana tense, so I used my free hand to pull her from my back and brought her to my front, keeping my gun aimed. The duffel was crossed over my chest, so she wasn't being used as a shield. I needed her to stay focused. If she succumbed to her fear, she'd die in this building today.

"Where they at?" I said before tapping Solana's hip so that she could translate. His brother didn't know I could speak Spanish, and I didn't want his fat ass to know either.

She shuddered, swallowed, and tilted her head as I watched chubster becoming infuriated about our closeness.

"*¿Dónde están su hija y su madre?* (Where is his daughter and her mother?)"

His grin spread again, revealing two open-faced gold teeth. "*Solana, esta es tu última oportunidad para venir. De lo contrario, morirás esta noche.* (Solana, this is your last chance to come. Otherwise, you'll die tonight.)"

"What he say?" I asked.

Solana cleared her throat. "Nothing... But they are indeed alive."

"Eres una puta estúpida. ¿Qué coño quieres con un negro americano? Somos los Rodríguez. Nuestra familia controla México. Podrías haber vivido bien. Ahora, sufrirás y te follarán hasta que sangres. Tu padre no puede salvarte. Tus hermanos no pueden salvarte. Este negro del ejército no puede salvarte... Quizás te quite la virginidad primero. Hace tiempo que no me follo a una virgen. (You stupid fucking whore. What the fuck do you want with a Black American man? We are the Rodríguez family. Our family runs Mexico. You could have lived well. Now, you'll suffer and get fucked until you bleed. Your father can't save you. Your brothers can't save you. This one army nigger can't save you... Maybe I'll take your virginity first. It's been a long time since I fucked a virgin.)

Running my tongue over my teeth, I huffed. "Maybe in another life, bitch-ass nigga."

Pushing Solana to the ground, I covered her just as shots were let off. My gun hadn't let off a shot, so the men were caught off guard, and that shit cost them.

"Andale! Andale! All this fuckin' quesadilla talk got a nigga hungry."

Nel's stupid ass came through the door, blasting and running to shield himself behind the concrete wall.

"Why the fuck yo' hardheaded ass leave us?" I heard Vello say somewhere close, but bullets were flying, men were dropping, and glass was shattering.

I was trying to get eyes on big 6ix9ine, but a pipe above us began gushing water from a bullet piercing it.

"Shio, you straight?" Ezio asked. His voice shook, but it wasn't because of fear; the power of the gun vibrating against his body had him physically shake as the bullet shot out.

I yelled back, "Yeah, I'm good," as I looked down for Solana.

Her face was contorted as she looked up at me, but I didn't have time to decipher it.

"Aye. You good?" I asked her, and she nodded, still clutching the flashlight.

Lifting my gun, I fired at the remaining soldiers. It was still about thirty of them, but they were now in an assembly line with shields. These niggas were acting like they were in Iraq at war, but then again, this was no doubt a war.

"Why in the fuck you run yo' ass out here without a plan?"

That was Matteo. He had flipped a table over and was shooting over it. I'd seen the four of them when they first came through the door after the initial bullet flew. Don had to have given them the drop on me, which meant when we were in the sky, so were they. Even though I was grateful to have backup, it was still fuck that nigga, Don. He was playing too many games, and dumping a coked-out Solana on me was no fucking training assimilation. Ole girl could've died in my house if I hadn't caught her dancing with the devil.

"Stay low," I said to Solana, pushing Don's fucked-up ways and her nasty habits to the back of my mind.

Since the men were gathered in the opposite direction, and the squad was holding their position, I managed to crouch to the back, pushing Solana along in front of me. We were soaked and wet, and my feet crunched on broken glass with each step, but I kept letting off shots as we disappeared down the hall. She slipped, and I caught her mid-fall before we kept going forward. Gun drawn, I stood, kicked in the first door, and saw it was an empty supply closet. The next door was a bathroom. Holding my breath, I kicked the last door and froze. Lying on a dirty mattress was a toddler, whose face I couldn't see because her hair was bigger than her head. My heart raced, my knees buckled, and my left eye twitched.

"Shio! Someone is coming!" Solana screamed as quietly as she could.

I pulled her into the room and stuck my head out of it. A bullet whipped past, missing me by an inch.

Blaow Blaow

Two shots to the dome removed his head completely from his body. I made sure no one else was coming but didn't move from the door.

Mmmm! Mmmmm!

We could hear muffled screams, but that wasn't my concern.

"Get the baby, Solana!"

She froze. "S-Somebody is in the closet..."

Instead of doing what the fuck I instructed, Solana went to the closet, revealing Bahati, who was duct-taped and on the floor. Her skin was sweaty, and each time she moved, a braid fell into her face.

Removing a piece of glass from her pocket that I didn't even see her slick ass pick up, Solana ran into the closet and began cutting the tape. Bahati was tearing up and still crying while I stared her down. Even roughed up, she was still fine as the last time I saw her ass over three years ago.

Once Bahati's hands were free, Solana slowly peeled the tape from Bahati's mouth, who jerked back away from her. Solana stood from crouching and moved to the bed to get the baby just as I shot another trooper coming down the hall.

"Aye, college boy! We gotta fuckin' go!" I heard Nel yell.

Solana unzipped her jacket, revealing a black sports bra. She tucked the toddler inside and then zipped the jacket back up as much as she could. That fucking jacket must've had the stretch of a Laffy Taffy because if it wasn't for the toddler's head, she would've been able to zip her completely inside. The toddler's bare feet dangled at Solana's back as her legs wrapped around Solana's stomach. Her not crying had my stomach dipping, but I couldn't focus on that right now, though. Bahati ran past Solana with the little girl and into my arms, wrapping one around my waist, dangling from me unnaturally. Her body shook as she cried into my chest.

"Shhh... Stay behind me, Bahati. We gotta move."

Not giving her time to respond, I pushed her behind me and shot two more troops coming our way. There was a black shoe sticking from under one of the dead troopers, so I snatched it.

"Solana."

She rushed to my side. I glanced at the little girl, whose face I still couldn't see due to her hair. Bending, I lifted Solana's wet, bare foot and slid her Croc back on, making sure to flip it in sports mode. When that one was back on the ground, I lifted her other leg, removed the sandal, and put that one on sports mode too.

I could feel Bahati's eyes on us, but I ignored her and asked, "You wasn't gone say shit about your shoe?"

Not waiting for an answer, I led us down the hall. By the time we got back to the battlefield, there were still at least fifteen of the Rodríguezes' men.

What the fuck had these niggas been shooting at?

I pushed the girls toward the exit and then covered for my niggas as they kept shooting and ran out the door. Once we were all on the other side, I reached into the duffel bag, pulled out my weapon, snatched off the pin, and tossed it.

"Everybody run!"

Boooom!

The building shook, nearly blowing a few of us backward. My ears were ringing, but everyone made it to an extended black truck and quickly filed inside. I pivoted and jogged to the rental, tossing the duffel inside and grabbing Solana's phone from the cupholder. The car would be taken care of by Ledesma's guards. I ran back to the black truck, which was already running and slowly moving, and hopped inside. Bahati immediately grabbed my neck, her sniffles becoming louder and louder. Once the door was closed, Matteo accelerated, burning rubber while the deserted shopping plaza went up in flames.

"Aye! Anybody hit?" Ezio turned from the front seat, scanning everyone.

Bahati was next to me in the first row, her head on my shoulder, now crying hysterically. Nel and Vello were in the back row, catching their breath. Solana was in the middle row, her seat directly behind mine. Turning around, I looked at Solana as best as I could with Bahati practically in my lap. She was rubbing the baby's back, still zipped inside her jacket, while she hummed. I slanted my eyes at her, and when she nodded, I sighed in relief.

"Naw, nigga! We ain't hit. By the grace of fuckin' God, though. Had I died back there, Pia was gone kill everybody in this fucking car!"

"Why the fuck you pull a suicide mission like this, stupid nigga? I told Don to leave your ass out here. I don't know why he got a soft spot for you incompetent niggas!" Matteo argued as he sped down the dirt road.

"I didn't ask you niggas to come. I had the shit handled."

"Speaking of handled..." Vello leaned over Solana's seat. "Where the fuck you get grenades from?"

"On foe 'nem!" Nel shouted. "This nigga thinks he's Osama bin Laden. Grenades, nigga? Damn near blew all our asses to smithereens. My fuckin' ears still ringing."

"Aye! Shut the fuck up with all that fucking crying! I'm tryna drive and get the fuck outta this country before these Mexican cops get on our asses," Matteo barked out before catching my eyes in the rearview mirror. "Shio, getcha hoe... We know she can't go on no mo' missions. Making my fuckin' head hurt."

Matteo cut a sharp left, nearly flipping the truck over and making Vello scream. "Fuck, Teo! I got kids, witcho mean ass. Don't kill us 'cause Shio baby mama won't stop blubbering."

Nel and Ezio laughed before Nel leaned over Solana's seat and said, "That's the power of that fucking grenade that got your head 'bout to explode, Matteo. Aye, as a matter of fact, you got some more of them bitches? I'm dropping a few in Preston's sick-ass simulations. Ending that psychotic-ass training once and for all."

Opting to stay silent, I let my thoughts rest until my body was alerted to the familiarity. In a truck full of sweaty niggas, gun powder, and Bahati's snotty tears, I could still smell Solana. I closed my eyes and inhaled as I tried to come down from the adrenaline rush of trying to keep myself and three others alive. Bahati and the baby were safe, Solana wasn't taken by them fuck niggas, so now it was time for me to face the music. Surviving the bullets had been one thing, but what came next would be a different kind of war for me.

Fatherhood.

~

Bahati had cried the whole ride up until we got to the hangar. Everyone except for Solana, Bahati, and me had filed out of the truck quickly, all of them eager to no longer be in the confined space. Bahati was still sniffing as she clung to my arm, not caring that she'd pissed almost everyone in the truck off. I turned and faced Solana, finding her eyes were on the little girl as she rubbed her hair and back.

"Aye."

Solana's gaze shot up and then trailed to Bahati's head on my shoulder.

"Take her up."

Bringing her eyes back to me, she climbed out of the truck, and I watched as she walked up the stairs to the jet.

"Bahati."

She popped her head up and faced me. Her face was rounder than I remembered, or it could have been swollen from all the crying. Worse, it could've been from whatever they'd done to her.

"Did they touch you?" I asked.

Fat tears rolled from her eyes as she shook her head. "No," she responded, her Kenyan accent was still heavy.

"But when one pushed me, my arm..."

I looked down and noticed that she'd been clutching her right arm this entire time. That explained why she'd cried the whole way here. Taking a look at it, I knew it was broken, but we didn't have time to do anything about it right now. Hopefully, there was a brace or something on the plane we could put on her arm until we got to Jagoda Bay.

"Aite. We gone get on the jet, and once we touch down, I'll have a doctor check you out."

"Shio. I can explain—"

"Bahati. We'll talk after the flight."

As if she were just now aware of her surroundings, she sat up fully and looked out of the window. "A private Jet?"

"Come on, Bahati. They ready for takeoff."

Climbing out of the truck, I held my hand out and helped her get out as well. I could tell she was more than likely home lounging when they snatched her because she was in brown leggings that almost looked like they matched her skin and a blue graphic T-shirt. Her T-shirt and leggings were both dirty and dingy, and her house shoes were soiled like my clothing. My eyes zeroed in on her ass as we approached the stairs. She'd done good to keep her same shape through pregnancy. She actually looked like she didn't even have a child, and I knew then that was her African genetics were showing up.

Don appeared at the jet's entrance, and I was beginning to think this nigga was using a time machine. Ain't no way he was conveniently everywhere.

"I guess you were right. You did get more money than my papa," Bahati murmured.

Don moved from the opening and went into the cockpit to speak with the pilot.

Solana had set up away from the guys, who were at the back of the plane. The toddler was lying on the extended couch near the window, and she took a seat not far from it. Nel was standing over the middle-aged stewardess, a different one from when I flew in. This was a different and much bigger plane than my solo trip. When she handed him a plate of hot wings, I grunted. Only that nigga was hungry after a whole damn war.

I took my seat, and instead of Bahati sitting with her child, she sat right next to me. Her hands were still slightly shaking, and I somewhat felt bad about her experiencing this. I was going to have to have a long talk with her. She'd witness my folks and me kill, and with the way she was acting, I wasn't too confident in her knowing what we were really into. This was a lot, but it was nothing in comparison to what we'd faced. These boys and I were built Ford fucking tough. I closed my eyes, grabbed my chain, and said a silent prayer to God for covering us. We didn't deserve His mercy, but I was grateful as fuck for it.

The baby began crying, and everyone looked to me, including

Bahati. When I looked at her right the fuck back, Solana stood and went to pick her up.

"Uhh, no. Who the fuck are you, and why do you keep picking up my child?"

"Awl shit!" Nel smacked on a chicken bone, still standing.

Solana ignored her and began to soothe the baby.

"Put my fucking daughter down, bitch!"

"Aye! Your arm fucked up!" I boasted, making Bahati jump. "She's helping because your shit broke."

"I... I have to use the restroom." Bahati stood, and the stewardess guided her to the full bathroom on board.

Once the door shut, all eyes went to me.

"You know how you always saying your house is a place of peace?" Vello stretched his arms and snatched a wing off his brother's plate. "Yeah, that shit dead. Bahati 'bout to shake all that shit up."

Vello laughed while chewing the chicken wing as I shook my head. Knowing the jokes were about to start.

"Nigga been a daddy ten minutes and already got baby mama drama!" Matteo mocked.

"But on to you..." Nel pointed a chicken bone at Solana. "We all in Mexico, in shootouts and shit. What the fuck did you do? Nigga called me on ten, dishing out orders."

"Nel, sit down," Ezio said, knowing the reason everyone had gotten frantic calls from me this morning.

"Fuck you, Bobby! I know you know. This nigga tells your pretty ass everything."

Ezio waved him off.

"Now..." He ate another wing. "You fucked another nigga, hunh? One of them Mexicans that's tatted up, hunh? Is them the same niggas from the club? I can't understand all that taquito shit, but I know when niggas tight about a bitch, respectfully."

Solana continued to soothe the toddler, who was probably hungry and wet if she was still in diapers. I had a whole child, one that I didn't know anything about. My child was in the same space as me. I'd procreated and felt like shit for not knowing. There was so much I wanted to know, and oddly, I didn't want to get the answers from Bahati.

Fuck. This was all fucked up.

"Felipe was a man I was promised to. That arrangement no longer stands. That was his brother back there. I have sex with no one." She looked at me. "Ever."

Matteo's head snapped up. "*Ever*... A virgin, nigga?" He threw the question at me.

"So that's why y'all was locked up in that house playing boot-camp," Nel said with a chicken wing hanging from his mouth. "You done stumbled upon some untouched coochie. No wonder you walked in that bitch ready to die."

"How the fuck this nigga be the last man standing to get married and get the virgin?" Vello said, almost sounding as if he was really mad about it.

Ezio snickered. "'Cause my nigga is God's favorite... Get off his nuts."

Leaving them to bicker, I stood, feeling Solana's eyes on me. She hadn't folded in battle, but my sentiments remained. These niggas could glorify her pureness all they fucking wanted. Her being a virgin didn't hold any merit when she was strung the fuck out.

Opening the door, Bahati was resting against the sink with a tissue pressed against her nose. I closed the door behind us, shutting us in.

"Shio. What is going on?"

"Let me see your arm."

She shook her head, keeping it pressed against her chest. She wouldn't be able to sit through the flight for four hours with a broken arm. If there were no strong enough pain meds on board, she would have to load up on liquor to at least put her to sleep.

She reached up and grabbed my diamond chain. "Who are you now?"

"Bahati."

"No. I was snatched from my bed. My daughter and I! Then, I was in a shootout! Now I'm on a jet, being whisked off to God knows where, and you have a bitch touching my daughter as if she is hers! She's been touched enough by strangers during this whole ordeal! You won't even look at her. You won't even touch her!"

"Bahati..." I rubbed my hand down my face. "I just killed over two dozen men. I just walked in a situation that I didn't know if I was going to make it out of just to get y'all. I literally have blood on my fuckin' hands." I held my hands out, dried blood coating my fingers. "I'm trying to process this shit and plan accordingly. You didn't want to get her, so she did."

"Don't do that! Don't make it seem like I'm a bad mother. I've been the one raising her."

"I'm not making it seem like nothing, Bahati. But did you come find me? You knew I would have taken care of mine."

"Did you forget that you tried to kill me the last time I was in your presence?!"

"If I wanted you dead, Bahati, you wouldn't be standing here."

"I wasn't about to come after someone who looked me in the eyes while his dick was still inside of me and squeezed the life out of me. My vocal cords were damaged for a month! When I found out I was pregnant, I attempted to abort four times but could never do it. I cried my entire pregnancy! I was perfectly fine with raising her and never seeing you again. I looked at you as a monster. And with us being kidnapped, it seems my assumptions were right!"

"Solana—"

"Bahati! My fucking name is Bahati!" She pushed against my chest with her good shoulder. "As a matter of fact, let me get my baby from that bitch!"

I blocked her path. "Aye. What the fuck I say? When we touch down, you'll get looked over, and then we will figure this shit out. But all that rah rah shit? Nah. You can dead it. I ain't the Shio you once knew."

She tried to step around me again, but I blocked her advancement, raising my brows.

"Shio, I'm not going to bother your girlfriend," she finally said after a brief stare-off. "I'm about to see if the stewardess has something me and my bebe can change into. We are both wet and dirty."

The way Bahati said "baby" sounded like baybay; that much hadn't changed. Waiting a beat, I moved out of the way and opened the door. Don appeared again, standing in a doorway of what appeared to be a conference room.

"Shio. Come talk to me."

Not in the mood for his bullshit, I entered the room.

He shut the door and sat at the table. "Beautiful daughter."

"Don, what is it?"

"Straight to business? Aite, cool." He pulled on his suit jacket, grinning.

We were all wet and dirty, and had neared death, and he was looking as if he stepped out of a GQ magazine shoot.

"Good job today."

"Don..."

"Aite, G.I Joe. Damn... So, look... I know you processing a lot, but time is ticking. I only allow one person to be brought into my organization, especially now with the police sniffing, even if it's because of another cartel."

Don sighed as if what he was about to say frustrated him. "Your brother, your Mexicansita, your long-lost baby mama... You got too many newcomers, Cuppacio. And I'm throwing a flag on the play. You, my boy, are at yo' newbie limit."

"Solana ain't on me. That shit is on you. Fuck I gotta do with the shit you and her sperm donor cooked up?"

"Did I ask you to fall for her? Fuck no. You was supposed to house her until I got my fucking money. You did more than give the girl a roof. You fell in love, so now that counts as one of yo' newbies.

"Despite what you niggas think, I ain't interested in playing cupid. I tricked my own wife. The fuck I look like going out my way to secure one for y'all?"

"I didn't fall in love, Don."

"Well, nigga... You fell in like. Either way, you over your limit."

"Okay, so what you saying?"

"I'm saying, Sid the Science Kid, that you gotta marry one of them." He jutted his chin at the door.

"Hell nah! Did you not just hear what I said about Solana? She's a fucking cocaine addict."

"How you know? She might've just wanted to take the edge off at the time. She said she was about to *give herself to you*. Maybe she was scared. And if you don't want to marry her, cool, you got Tems in there. Put a ring on it."

"Man, I haven't seen Bahati in years."

"Shio. You have thirty days. I've been gracious. I've been patient. I allowed your brother to come in, and even though he missed his deadline, he did his part. He did in a few weeks what you Cuppacio niggas couldn't do in months. Then, to play in my face even further, you let him steal your *own* potential wife from under your nose. I don't have no more free women. I'm not willing to bring any more muthafuckas from the outside in. Not until this trafficking shit is halted and the police not tryna get close to my shit. By then, you'll be a doting husband. So..." Don stood and grinned.

"You either gonna clean the crackhead up, like you did my sister's husband... Or you gone rock with the blast from the past. Either way, don't make me no difference. Thirty days. You decide, or I'll decide for you."

Don opened the door, and Bahati stood there with her good hand raised in a knocking motion. He excused himself and walked around her.

"Wassup, Bahati?"

"I didn't mean to interrupt. I just remembered I didn't tell you her name."

"Okay..."

"It's Shya."

God first
Make sure the family good
Eye them Cuppacio boys, the little and the big ones
Build a relationship with my brother
Get my brother rich
Health and wellness
~~*Stay on top of my mob shit*~~
Keep Hobo alive (ON PAUSE)
~~*Get through the meeting with Ines Ledesma*~~
~~*House a random*~~
~~*Find the true reason Solana is here*~~
~~*Figure out if Solana is supposed to be my wife, again*~~
~~*Find a wife that isn't Solana*~~
Kill every breathing Rodríguez Cartel member (URGENT)
Fuck Bahati up (TBD)
~~*Get my fucking daughter*~~
Get Bahati's arm fixed
Get to know my daughter

THE MOB 2: SHIO CUPPACIO

Figure out what the fuck I'm going to do with Solana
Leave the mob entirely or marry Bahati or Solana

THIS SHIT COULDN'T GET any more hectic.

CHAPTER 5
GLOW

For the life of me, I couldn't understand how I was in the most comfortable spot in the house, but I was still somehow uncomfortable. With my eyes closed, I'd been tossing and turning for the last few hours. It wasn't because I was restless. No, I'd been resting just fine for the last few days. It was the call I ignored from my mama, and then the text she sent right after that unnerved me.

Every limb in my body ached, and the thought of continuing to lie in bed made me sick to my stomach. Just thinking the word "sick" made me sit up, my back popping due to the sudden movement. Swinging my legs over the side of my bed, I nearly fell from the tangled sheets as I ran to the bathroom. Hitting the light on the wall so that I could see, I fell to my knees, face in the toilet, and released.

Bwaaaaaaaahh!

Gripping the sides of the commode, my knees throbbed against the cold tile flooring. I'd shed my clothes a day or so ago, so I was in a tank top and panties. Now, on the cool floor, I was regretting not having anything on. Sucking in air, my face was back inside the toilet before I could exhale.

Bwaaaaaahhhhh!

Tears burned my eyes as the vomit violently ejected from my body.

Glee.

Bwaaaah! Bwaaaah!

A baby.

Bwahhhh!

Marriage.

Bwaaahhh!

Every time a thought came to mind, puke followed. When nothing else came out, I flushed the toilet, wiped my mouth with the back of my hand, and stood on shaky legs. Gripping the vanity, I squinted with disgust and tried not to jump out of my skin as I stared back at my reflection. My skin was pale, my lips were dry and cracked, and the extensions on my head needed shampooing , deep conditioning, and some styling. I licked my lips for a quick fix, noticing the bags under my eyes even though I'd slept enough to last me a week. I was so frail that just standing hurt, and my arms felt as if I'd been doing pull-ups.

The plus side to looking like death was that I felt lighter. A smile spread across my brittle lips before the internal disgust reared its head. Ignoring that feeling of disappointment, I turned around and grabbed the knob of the shower, placing the handle exactly where I knew the temperature would be just right for my shower. While waiting for the water to warm, I peeled my clothing off my weakened body. When my underwear hit the floor, my lip curled at the sight of the crusty discharge in the seat. No pungent smell hit me, letting me know my girl was appropriately self-cleaning during my hibernation.

After tossing my clothes in the hamper, I ventured to the wall where my best friend and worst enemy were. Stepping onto the cold glass, I backed off as the numbers appeared, waking the device. Holding my breath and then exhaling so that I wouldn't add any extra ounces, I stepped onto the scale. The numbers were calculated for a few seconds until settling on the final ones. My smile broadened, and only then could I feel a split in my cracked lips, which I knew produced blood.

One hundred and fifteen pounds. In three days, I'd lost seven pounds.

Now, with more pep in my step, even in my weakened state, I stepped into the shower and grabbed my exfoliating gloves. Once they were lathered in antibacterial soap, I scrubbed my body from neck to foot, excluding my intimate parts. I repeated the wash twice, and by the time I removed the gloves and grabbed my loofah to add the Dove Sensitive Skin Body Wash, steam was floating around me. The antibacterial soap left me feeling squeaky clean, but it stripped all the natural oils from my skin. Many forgot the importance of replenishing your skin's natural microbiome, and that's why Dove was needed in the soap market. Once I felt good about cleansing and moisturizing, I grabbed the gentle terry cloth and feminine wash to clean my girl down below. It had taken me years to figure out what worked for my body. Thankfully, the internet and brand deals had come along, making it easier for me to discover new products. From the amount I received for free alone, I was able to find a lineup that worked for me. Bacterial vaginosis wasn't fun, and I'd gone through a phase where it seemed like it would never disappear.

With my shower finished, I tied a robe around my waist and started on my oral hygiene. Instead of the two minutes required to brush, I did it for five. Tongue scraping, flossing, and mouthwash followed, then it was time for my skincare routine. Luckily, no pimples had appeared during my slumber, but my facial skin was extremely dehydrated, just like my body. By the time I was done, it felt like I'd been at a five-star spa thanks to the products and my regimen. The thirty minutes I'd taken to care for my skin were too long, and once I started feeling lightheaded, I left the bathroom still wearing the final mask. It had to sit on my face for another fifteen minutes anyway.

Grabbing a cracker from my nightstand, I nearly swallowed it whole and then ate another. There were six empty bottles of water on my dresser, with the seventh half full. I grabbed it and gulped it down before adding it to its empty friends. The next thing to tackle was the bed. My hair was still a mess, but it needed professional care, so that would be a problem for another day. Going into my closet, I grabbed fresh linen and redressed my bed and pillows. The dirty linen couldn't fit into my hamper since I'd changed the comforter as well, so I left it in a pile on the side of my bed until I was ready to wash it later.

Sitting on the cool, crisp sheets with my back against the headboard, I began to close my eyes when my phone vibrated on the nightstand. Seeing that it was a Ring camera notification, I picked up the phone. When I saw it was just Glee getting a delivery, I locked my phone screen and tossed it on the bed. I had over a hundred messages in the group chat with the mob wives, and I felt terrible about ignoring them. Mr. Joe, our neighbor who lived across from us, also called. Jisei had called me twice, and I knew that if I didn't return her call soon, she would be popping up. Though she lived in a mansion with her husband, she still owned her townhome next door, and Mr. Joe would also emerge if I didn't show my face soon. I was actually surprised he hadn't walked across the lawn by now. I made a mental note to call her and Mr. Joe back today because I didn't want to alarm anyone with my hiatus.

Along with the unopened messages, I had hundreds of social media notifications and an overwhelming number of emails to go through. I'd received so many inquiries from management firms, and initially, the idea of giving a percentage of my earnings to a firm seemed diabolical. I was now considering listening to some of their offers. Management could mean more opportunities, and my workload would ease with a team handling the backend conversations. I had been handling everything myself and paying my contractual attorneys to review all my contracts. On the days when I just wanted to shut the world out—something I hadn't done in a very long time—management might have been either a blessing or a curse. Shaking off business thoughts from my mind, I pulled up the face mask that felt like it was beginning to slide.

Knock Knock

I bit down on my molars as the doorknob turned. It had been three days since Tunan had come over, and even with the mortgage payment handed over and his version of putting me in my place done, the situation between us hadn't changed. The dick was good, but no amount of orgasms could change how I felt. Still, it was time to face the music because I was acting like a teenager by hiding out in my bedroom and spiraling over everything.

Glee peeked in with skepticism on her face. Her thick hair was pulled back into a sleek ponytail, and although her face was clear of blemishes, her nose was wide, and her lips looked larger than usual. I knew both were from the baby weight she'd gained without it being overly obvious. As I looked at my baby sister, I couldn't believe I'd missed the signs. She'd been at my house for a few days, and I hadn't even realized she was pregnant. I was so caught up in Tunan that I missed her cry for help, and before him, I had been distracted by my influencer grind. A sob escaped from my lips, and Glee hurried inside. She set a bag on the nightstand and sat on the bed, wrapping her arms around me.

"Gleeeee... I'm so fucking mad at you!" I cried harder and louder.

Tunan was right about one thing: once I'd calmed down, I would be so ashamed of my behavior. All I ever wanted for my little sister was the best of everything. If I had known she wouldn't make it through her first semester without getting pregnant, I would have chosen for her to stay home or stay with me to attend Jagoda Bay University. But JBU wasn't an HBCU, and Blake University had been Glee's dream. I didn't understand what she saw in the small town that I thought was boring. That was one thing I'd been right about because Calista Glee had resorted to screwing at Blake after leaving so focused and ready to start her journey to medical school.

"I know. I know, sis. I'm mad at myself," she mumbled.

"You are... so... youuung, Glee. You're so young! I didn't want this for you! I don't even want it for myself."

She squeezed me tighter, smelling like my Miu Miu Fleur de Lait Eau de Parfum with Coconut Milk that she'd stolen from my room last time she visited. At least, unlike me, she'd pulled herself together. She was dressed in a mint-green Aeropostale shirt with matching sweatpants that scrunched at the calves. Pulling away from her embrace, I dabbed my eyes with the sleeves of my terrycloth robe. Looking at my sister, I immediately noticed her hair was longer than I remembered, and the scent of jasmine flowers wafted around us when I ran my fingers through it. Even with her enhanced features, my sister was so damn pretty, looking every bit like our father.

I still needed to moisturize my body and take off the mask, but Glee and I needed to really talk now that life would be new for us both. I pressed my back further into the tufted headboard and crossed my feet at my ankles. I let the silence linger for a moment longer because once I said the words out loud they would be real, no takebacks.

"You look like you had a baby," I finally said. "In the face, your lips look like they've been injected. You look good, though." I continued, truthfully complimenting the changes.

Her breasts were larger, but as my eyes moved to her waist, I saw that in the few days I'd been in my room, it had shrunk and was now nearly nonexistent. There were no signs of pregnancy or a baby around her middle, but even while she sat on the bed, I could tell her hips and backside had widened. My baby sister had given birth to a whole baby, and she was now a young woman who had proof of the fact. I hoped she wouldn't gain any more weight while breastfeeding.

"I'm sorry!"

"I'm so sorry!"

We both blurted out at the same time.

Glee rubbed her arm and scooted to the headboard beside me.

"Glee, I was out of pocket."

"No, it's fine. You were right—"

"I was wrong. You were scared, and when I should've been a big sister, I was a monster. I should have been there for you. It's just... I saw you in the hospital, then blood, then the belly, and... I didn't send you to school to have some fuck boy put your life in danger by getting you pregnant. The closest a woman is to death is childbirth.

"I was scared, Glee. I was scared I was going to lose you, and I lashed out. Then, you wouldn't tell me who the father was, and I—I realize that doesn't matter. I'm sorry, Glee. I'm sorry I wasn't there for you. I'm sorry for trying to fight you. I'm sorry for going against you and my niece. I hope you can accept my apology because God knows I am so sick about how I've treated you.

Glee smiled and nodded. "Of course, I forgive you—"

Before she could say more, I cut in and asked, "Where is she? I've been so out of pocket that I haven't officially met her."

Glee's smile widened. "She's asleep in my room. I'll go get her after I say this.

"I 100% forgive you, Glow, and I'm sorry too. You were helping me out, made it so that I didn't have to work. Then I go off to school and shut you out, not answering your calls, all because I was caught up in... a situation. I should have answered the phone. I should've told you what was going on while it was going on. But I got caught up, sis. I... I fell for someone who I should have been running the opposite way from."

She blinked back tears, and my heart broke all over again.

My baby sister was going through her first heartbreak, and I was too caught up in my own head to be the sibling and friend she needed. Meanwhile, she had to handle a newborn on her own while mending herself. Glee was handling the stress, all while still looking put together. I couldn't say the same. Just an hour ago, I looked like walking death.

"If you want to talk about it, I'm here. If not, I'm still here..."

I wanted her to talk about it. I wanted his first name, last name, and social security number. I needed to know everything about him so I could curse his motherfucking ass out, but I'd already crossed boundaries with my sister. Even though I saw her as my baby, Glee was an adult and had lived on her own for a year.

Her glassy eyes looked away. "I thought he was everything, Glow. He *was* everything. Attractive, attentive, arrogant..." She chuckled while I scoffed.

Weren't they all that way in the beginning?

"It happened fast. One minute, we were talking, and the next, he was taking my virginity."

It was a struggle to avoid voicing my opinion or showing my emotions, but I kept my expression neutral. I opted to hide how I truly felt so she could feel comfortable venting to me. She had a mother, one we shared. Right now, she needed her sister.

"Is he... Will he be in the picture?"

She shook her head, and it broke my heart. "I stopped talking to him back in September, maybe... It was a while ago. I didn't know I was pregnant, so he definitely doesn't know about the baby.

"He doesn't attend Blake. I found out he had a girlfriend and a child—that's why I broke it off. It was the same with his brother, who Blayke had been dealing with. The brother didn't have a baby, but he was a man whore. We blocked their numbers, and that was it. Last I heard, he moved." Glee shrugged.

"So y'all were on a two-man?"

Glee slapped her forehead. "Could you not? Please!" She giggled.

She'd been crying since she came home from the hospital, so it was refreshing to see her laugh.

Then, her smile faltered. "I really am sorry, sister. But I can't take you being mad at me anymore. Besides Blayke, you're my bestest friend in the whole wide world." Her lips trembled, and I knew she was feeling the hurt of my behavior.

"I'm really sorry, too, and I regret that he was such a jerk to take something so precious from you, knowing he had a family. Men can be the worst, but you'll be just fine. You both will be."

She began twiddling her fingers. "I don't know what I'm doing, but the internet has been helping. When she's sleeping, I'm on YouTube and TikTok. I've got the hang of breastfeeding, but she prefers a bottle, so I've been pumping like crazy. Don't kill me, but your freezer is stacked with breast milk."

I shrugged. "Not like I use it much."

Glee eyed me, but I met her gaze until she wavered. "Mama's been helping me via FaceTime," she said before averting her eyes. "She told me she called you."

"Yeah... She did," I whispered.

"And will you be okay?" Glee asked.

"Glee, you're the one that just had a baby."

"You know what I mean, Glow. I... You have been in here three days without... eating. Besides the crackers and waters I've been leaving on your nightstand while you're sleeping, I haven't seen you leave the room to eat. It's happening again, isn't it?"

"I'm fine, Glee."

"You look thin, Glow," she whispered.

I held back a grin and picked at the terrycloth robe. "What do you want to do, Glee? Tell me the truth. And not what I want to hear. Not what mama says. This is your life. Your daughter."

"I see what you're doing, but okay, Glow." She pulled her knees up to her chest and sighed. "Mama wants me to come home."

I knew that. It was the reason why I'd been tossing and turning. I'd been overwhelmed with all of the chaotic things going on in my life, and my mama calling and texting for Glee to come to Sparkling City would relieve some of the chaos. However, I'd been feeling sick to my stomach about my sister leaving since Cathy Glory suggested it. I hadn't even held my niece yet, and the thought of my sister taking her from this house frightened me for some reason.

"But... I'd like to finish my summer out here, like we planned, if you don't mind."

My eyes lit up at her statement. "And what about school?"

"I planned on driving down there to talk to my advisor before they go on their short summer break. I was going to see if she could transfer my scholarship. I love Cove City, but the memories are too painful. Plus, I think it will be best if I can be near family right now. I'm not asking you all to raise her or anything, but I just feel more comfortable—"

"Yes! I get it. You thinking about JBU or Sparkling City University?"

"JBU was my second choice outside of Blake. I'll have to get a job and get my own place or use my leftover scholarship money to put Baby Leader in day—"

"Keep the money, Glee. I work for myself. I make my own schedule. She can stay here with me while you go to school. It will give me something to do besides eating all day."

"You don't eat all day, Glow. You eat on camera for your job. Stop being dramatic." Glee rolled her eyes before smiling. "And how will Baby Leader fit into you and your *rich friends'* lifestyles?"

"Girl, boo! They have children, and they have *rich men* who pay for nannies. The nannies watch the children while we ladies have our time."

"Rich men. Fine men. Like your *husband*."

I gasped.

"What? I'm not stupid. I heard him at the hospital. I was in pain; I wasn't suffering from hearing loss. I wasn't blind either. Everybody got a ten in your clique! Whew!"

"Girl, worrying about tens is what got you being a teen mom!"

Glee tossed her head back, laughing a little too hard.

"I'm not married, Glee," I said, not meeting her eyes.

"Glow, no more lies. We are not lying to each other anymore. I get that you have to have your secrets about your assassin friends, but between us, no more lies. I told you about Baby Leader's dad... And your marriage isn't my business to share, so if you're scared about Mommy finding out, I haven't told her."

I sighed. "Tunan and I aren't together, but we are married. But it's only on paper. It was something he had to do. So, I agreed."

"But y'all were just in here working on Baby Leader a cousin?"

I tossed my pillow at Glee. I couldn't believe my once-virgin sister was trying to talk about sex with me.

"That won't happen again. Tunan is just..."

"Fine... Paid... Thugged out."

"Yeah, and no, and yeah. I-I don't know... I was stressed, and he relieved it. That's it."

"Well, I'm here for it. He has to be decent, at least. He dealt with Baby Leader that night."

My head snapped, surprise evident on my face.

"Yeap. I fell asleep after all that arguing, and you passed out after all that *stress relieving*."

I lifted the pillow at her again, but she blocked it.

"I saw him on the baby cam Pearla got me. He fed her, burped her, and went back to sleep with her on his chest. He left maybe two hours later, after I woke him up because I had to change her. He was so good with her." Glee sing-sang with a huge grin on her face as if she was saying something I'd wanted her to say.

"He got the magic touch, too, because she was knocked out. She didn't wake up at all. All I had to do was change her diaper and feed her. Three hours later, I had to feed her again, and she stayed asleep then too. She slept through the whole night that night, and it hasn't happened since. We need to call him back over here."

Tunan, the baby whisperer?

His being good with children was fitting, though. Not only did he come from a big family, but he had nieces and nephews that he adored. Clearing my throat, I shook him from my thoughts. Tunan was not my man, no matter how legal our arrangement was. Glee would have to find her own tips and tricks because I was not calling that man and asking him to come over here.

"Anyways, you need to eat." She grabbed the bag. "I got our favorite. Italian!"

As she pulled the containers from a plastic grocery bag, the food smell filled the air, but my mouth didn't water. My body knew it needed the food, but I could easily go a few more days on crackers and water. I knew I had to get myself together, though, so not eating and gluing myself to the bed wouldn't work any longer. Grabbing a fork, I wrapped noodles around it as Glee did the same. We stuffed our faces, and my taste buds burst with each contact of the garlicky, creamy noodles.

"Good, right? And you'll still be beautiful after eating all of this up."

"So, when do you have to go to school to talk to financial aid?" I asked, ignoring her comment.

"I know I'm still healing, but the sooner the better. I asked Mama if she could come watch her on Thursday so I can leave on Friday, and she said she would."

I nearly choked on the fettuccine. I loved my mama, but that was only three days away. I wouldn't be able to pull myself together by then. My mama would see right through me. I knew I couldn't deny her grandchild, but I needed some time before she showed up in Jagoda Bay.

"Oh, I can keep her for you," I said quickly.

"No, Glow."

"Glee. Tell Mama she can come the weekend after next. I need some one-on-one time with my niece, anyway. I gotta make up for neglecting her arrival home. Just show me what you've learned while I was hibernating and being in my feelings. Also, you should get you a hotel. Don't make that drive in one day. Your body needs rest."

"How about this... If you eat three times a day and keep it down from now till Thursday night, I'll tell Mommy no."

Glee held her pinky out. We hooked fingers, and I stuffed my mouth again. Small cries had us detaching, and I tried to get up, but Glee's arm pushed me back on the bed.

"Nope. Finish up."

Glee stood and ran out as I forked pasta into my mouth. The pasta was heavy, but after days without food, I needed this— well, my digestive system needed it.

Picking up my phone while chewing, I checked my call log, finally in a better mood. Tunan hadn't called once. He hadn't texted either.

"Leader, meet your TeeTee."

Pushing my plate aside, I held my arms out. Glee raised her brow at the food being pushed away.

"I'll eat and hold her. Gimme!" Tears sprang to my eyes immediately when I looked into her small face. "Oh my God!"

She was the tiniest, most beautiful baby on the planet. She was so pink, and her features were so vivid for someone so new. She looked like Glee's twin, but I could also see the father's DNA swirling in her features. Whoever he was, he was handsome, for sure, because she was a doll. I knew in that moment that this was my baby just as much as it was my sister's.

"I get so mad at myself, but then I see her, and I don't regret a thing. I don't regret him. I don't regret her. She's so perfect to me." My sister smiled, and the room got brighter.

"I love her name, too, Glee. She's perfect."

"She is... Now, finish your food. I have milkshakes in the freezer."

I shook my head, knowing our stomachs were about to be fucked up.

CHAPTER 6
SHIO CUPPACIO

"As you can see, it's a clean break." The doctor held up an X-ray so we could clearly see the skeletal arm.

Sure enough, the bone was broken. A whimper from the left made me refocus my gaze from the middle-aged, pot-bellied doctor to a tear-faced Bahati. She was no longer holding her arm to her chest; it was now in a sling. Her dirty clothes had been replaced with a silk pajama set, thanks to the flight attendant who helped Bahati take a shower after I declined to help her. Solana had toughened it out with the rest of us and was sitting in her clothes while caring for the small toddler, my daughter. I still hadn't seen her directly. With so many thoughts racing through my mind, I had to disassociate myself before I could give her my attention.

We'd landed four hours ago, and while I needed a shower, a gym session, maybe one or two blunts, and a triple shot of the finest whatever was in my collection, I was accompanying Bahati to see the doctor. She'd been screaming her head off during the latter part of the plane ride after the liquor wore off, so I had the doctor meet us at the hangar. He took one look at her arm and told us she needed a hospital. He wouldn't even be able to help her at his private practice. She needed X-rays to determine where the break was, because, according to him, there was indeed a fracture. His colleague had proven him right. I pressed my head into the wall since I was standing near the door with my hoodie pulled over my head and arms tucked into the black hoodie I'd gotten from the trunk of my Maybach, which was also waiting.

Bahati looked up at me for answers while the man, who could ease her pain, stood there in a white coat. Since we'd killed a slew of motherfuckers in Mexico, we were ushered through the private entrance of Jagoda One. Due to the excessive money we'd poured into this bitch, she'd been seen without ever being processed into the system. It took a few rounds of X-rays and assessments I hadn't expected, but there was nothing I could do but wait it out. Thankfully, the baby slept through the whole flight, more than likely due to being shaken up, and the doctor had also looked her over and determined she was fine.

"So... Do I need surgery?" Fat tears slid down Bahati's round face. Her voluptuous lips were trembling, but I wasn't sure if she was crying from the pain. Something about Bahati was rubbing me the wrong way. I was trying to shake the shit off because I knew I was pissed that she'd held the child from me. Still, I wanted to be anywhere but near her.

"Not at all. I'll get you put in a cast for about six weeks. You'll be somewhat restricted and experience some itching, but you'll be as good as new in no time. I can get started on the cast as soon as I gather the supplies. In the meantime, I'll have a nurse start you on an IV for a small dose of morphine. I know the Lortab has more than likely worn off."

The doctor stuffed the black-and-white X-ray into a folder and tucked it back under his arm. It would be discarded, just like any footage of us caught on camera walking the halls once we left.

"I have to advise that the morphine does come with side effects. Dizzi—"

"Dizziness, nausea, drowsiness, itching, hallucination, vomiting, oh... and constipation." Bahati finished.

The doctor was impressed.

She shifted on the elevated bed, letting her head hit the pillow. "I'm a pharmacy technician."

My eyes cut to Bahati, knocking the smirk off her face. This doctor was recommended by someone on our payroll, and her volunteering information was unnecessary to this unfamiliar doctor. It could very well put us in a position to get jammed up. I didn't know if someone had reported her being kidnapped or what. The last thing I needed was the fucking laws buzzing around, especially since Don had revealed that some already were. It hadn't been too long since we killed a detective, but we'd decided to avoid doing so again. We didn't need any pigs veering on our trail, making us renege on our plan to keep everything cool in Jagoda Bay.

Kicking off the wall, since my leg was folded behind me with my foot resting on it, I reached into my pocket and grabbed a stack of rubber-banded money. I could feel Bahati's eyes on me, but I kept my eyes on the paper as I counted out the usual amount. Placing the twenty thousand dollars on the bedside table next to the apple juice Bahati had been sipping on, I put the remaining bills back in a rubber band before stuffing them in my pocket.

"Get her right, doc."

Turning, I headed out of the room. The antiseptics were burning the fuck out of my nostrils, and the sterile aroma was making a nigga lightheaded. You'd think I'd had some fucking morphine the way I felt myself getting dizzy.

"Wait! Are you about to leave me?" Panic was in Bahati's voice.

My back was facing her, and I didn't bother to turn around as I said over my shoulder, "No. Get fixed up, Bahati."

I pushed through the wooden door, my eyes adjusting to the bright white lights of the hospital corridor. It was late morning, and normally, hospitals would be bustling by now. But we were on the private floor the mobs had secured months before, and there was only one other patient here besides Bahati.

With my shoes squeaking on the waxed floors, I moved to the far end of the hall. Walking past the empty waiting room, I briefly glanced at the Gucci backpack leaning against the far left wall. I nodded at one of the security guards hired by the mob and pushed into the room.

"Pia know yo' ass here instead of in summer school or some shit?"

Neltz had the controller in his hand, slouched in a chair he had placed in front of the TV. It was nearly too high for him to connect his gaming system to, but the dangling extension cord showed how he'd made it happen. The TV was too loud for such an early morning, but with the entire floor reserved for us, he wasn't disturbing anyone.

Neltz flicked his eyes at me. He'd been rocking his braids lately, but now he was back to his usual ponytail. He wore black basketball shorts, a red Nike shirt, and black and red Chicago 12s. The little nigga had Rio's whole face.

"She still cussin' Daddy Number Two out... Damn! I tried to do that combination."

His player was kicking the shit out of the opposition in the warrior fighting game. After looking at the screen for another minute, I realized that the player wasn't fighting back at all. Looking behind me, I spotted the other controller and shook my head.

"Lil' nigga, you in here playing a fucking coma patient in Mortal Kombat?"

Neltz shrugged while tapping a combination of buttons. "He be helping me get my skills up. Plus, Baby Shower Shirt don't get many visitors outside of us Cuppacios and his mama." He smirked at the latter part of his sentence.

"The Cuppacios are enough. I'm sure he 'bout tired of all y'all asses, and why you smirking?"

Neltz shook his head with a chuckle. "Bro mama be going so ham on him. She worse than Pia with her words. Then, after cursing him out, she will kiss him and get him together."

"Yeah, that sound like Pia for sure." I agreed while looking over Grind, who had yet to make much progress.

He still hadn't awakened, and there was little to no brain activity. We all remained hopeful, especially since his connection to Pearla was delicate. Matteo was mean as hell. I couldn't imagine his attitude if Pearla started walking around, moping the way she had been a few months ago. Grind had round-the-clock care, and I've seen God perform miracles. He'd just done one by helping us survive that war back in Mexico, so I wasn't doubting Grind's chances on waking up.

My chest tightened as I thought about how the Rodríguezes were still out there. I inspected the feeding tube taped to Grind and the breathing mask before I pulled out my phone. Though Grind had been blessed, and I believed he would come out on top even with the odds not in his favor, I couldn't imagine being in his position. I had too much to handle, too much to oversee, and too much shit to check off my list to be down bad for a few months. Some people even take years to come out of a coma, and it was a big "fuck that" for me.

"You coming to see 'bout him... That's what's up, Neltz."

Neltz slid his chair back to the bed, pressed a few buttons on Grind's controller, and then moved back to the front of the TV. "Yeah, well... My auntie not fuc—I mean, *fooling* with him, so I figure I'd come on her behalf."

I fucked with Grind, but I was glad that Pearla was standing her ground. She was clearly heartbroken, but she was too damn young with too much of a bright future ahead of her to be tied up with Grind. If it was meant to be, things would happen in the future. For now, I was happy she was living in her youth.

With my head still glued to the phone, I focused on the screen.

"I been hoping to catch that whore of his, to tell you da truth. Oh! He beatin' sum!" Neltz hammered away at the game as if his opponent had been a real challenge. I noticed he'd kept the same character but switched Grind's. He was now fighting the opposite sex.

"And why you in that man's business?" I asked Neltz while staring at my phone.

"Ohhhh! Nah... Not in his business, but I ride about my Tee Tee."

"And what's the plan if she shows up? His wife?"

Neltz turned his neck to look at me and jutted his chin to the screen. "You see this?"

His character looked as if he was slapping the opponent. "Gonna slap fire from her ass, that's what I'm gonna do."

"Nah, what you gone do is catch a domestic violence charge, and then I'm gonna have to square up with your young ass for putting your hands on a woman. We don't do that."

Kill the fuck out of them? Yeah. But beating? Nah.

I was going to have to have Tunan sit down and talk with Neltz about the consequences of fighting women. My teeth scraped against my bottom lip when I thought about how just hours ago I'd lost control and roughed up Solana.

Solana.

She had me ready.

I genuinely was ready. I was prepared to do whatever I had to do to ensure I was the only one in the race for her. Then, once I got rid of Felipe, I planned to court her and make her my wife. She just had to fuck it up by being a cokehead. Now, I didn't want her. I would've left her ass right in Mexico if it wasn't for Don.

Don.

That nigga didn't know when to quit. He had given me an ultimatum where Solana was no longer the prize and now a contender. She or Bahati would be my wife, and the fucked up part was that I didn't have my bet on either of the women.

Pinching the screen to zoom out, I slightly moved the camera, then zoomed back in. We had dropped Solana and the baby off at my house, but Bahati protested until Nel volunteered to stay with them until we got back. Bahati had made it clear that she wasn't fucking with Solana at all. I wasn't really fucking with her either, or at least, I wasn't trying to. Nel was in the living room, knocked out, and since viewing the cameras, it was clear he'd volunteered to only get some sleep because he hadn't bothered Solana and the little girl once since he walked into my house.

My reasons for wanting him to stay and Bahati's reasons were completely different. I didn't know what headspace Solana was in after the night we'd had, and leaving her alone with the baby wasn't an option.

Watching her in real time, I waited to feel that tingling I'd grown accustomed to pertaining to all things her. However, there was none, but I still stood, staring at the screen. She was curled up in bed, her butt cheeks hanging out of the shorts she was wearing, while the baby slept next to her, at a safe distance. Shya had been changed into dry clothes and fed, but Bahati insisted on bathing her herself, so Solana skipped the bath. Although I had a bone to pick with Bahati, she was still Shya's mother, so I didn't protest her request. However, caring for the baby was going to be tough with a broken arm now, but I figured we'd take it day by day.

Solana's hair was tangled all over her head, and her shirt had ridden up, exposing her flat belly. My desire sharpened at the sight of her. I was clearly out of her league, and I could say that confidently. Seeing her hit those lines sealed the deal, and it was a shame because, baby was a fighter. She fell into the routine today without question or fear. As a cartel daughter, there was no telling what she'd seen, but that didn't mean she was automatically supposed to have heart. She proved that she did today, and I was surprised because the Solana I'd gotten to know was lost and in need of direction. Today showed me she had buried her true nature under all the bullshit she'd been on since she touched down in America. She'd been with the baby since we rescued them, and even though Bahati was nasty to her, her nurturing Shya hadn't stopped. If I didn't have the image of her high out of her fucking mind, I would've enjoyed seeing her with the little girl that was supposed to be my daughter.

I didn't need my woman to be a "Bonnie," though. All I needed her to do was fuck me, suck me, and spend my fucking bread. When she revealed that she was going to give herself to me, it didn't move me. I would have politely turned her down because we weren't ready for all of that. I'd meant what I said when I said I wasn't pursuing her until I was the only nigga in the race. I wasn't pressed to fuck on anything, including Solana, who was untouched. As much as I loved the feel of a woman, I could go longer than most without it. Pussy didn't run me.

But, again, that was over with. Solana's virginity was no longer a concern of mine.

Watching as her arm crossed her face, she shifted her legs and revealed more of her stomach. Then she stilled, sat up in a frenzy, and reached over for Shya. Placing her hand on Shya's back, she listened and laid back down. I wanted to like what I was seeing, but I couldn't. The dancing, the white nose, the smeared makeup, the uncontrollable laughs—Solana couldn't be my wife.

Pretty little fucking sinner.

"Shio, I'm ready."

Locking my screen and pushing my frustrations aside, I turned to see Bahati standing beside me. Her tears had disappeared, and her eyebrows were raised. They must've given her the smallest dose of morphine possible because she was coherent and looking at me with questioning eyes.

Neltz looked over at her, then at me, then back at Bahati, and then back to the TV. "I choose Mexi-Mami."

"Hunh?" Bahati asked.

Ignoring her and him, I walked to Grind's bed. Bowing my head, I inhaled. "The Lord will sustain him on his sickbed and restore him from his bed of illness. Psalm 41:3."

"Amen," Neltz responded as he kept pressing buttons on the controller. "You know he can't look up the verse in the Bible, so telling him the chapter is pointless while he sleep, Unc."

Taking one last look at Grind, I turned to see Bahati smirking. She dropped her expression as soon as she realized I had noticed. Her arm was in a green cast that went from her knuckles to the crease of her elbow. It was unfortunate that she had broken bones, but things could have been much worse for Bahati. She was blessed, as we all were.

"Aye, let me take you to the crib."

Neltz shook his head at my suggestion. "My grandfag nearby. He gone scoop me in a few hours once he's done handling business."

I shook my head and ran my hand over my face. Neltz said whatever came to mind, and although most of the shit shouldn't be coming from his mouth, he was funny as hell. He and Nel were so much alike that it was scary. You'd think that Nel was his biological daddy, but as handsome as Neltz was, I could still see some of Hobo's ugly ass in him.

"Besides, Daddy Number Two said we on that Selena later, so I'm gonna go home after my grandfag take me to the mall and then shooting."

I smiled to stop my laughter as Bahati looked like she had too many questions from Netlz's few sentences. Ruffling his hair, he snatched away before I dapped him up and walked out of the room. Bahati was on my trail, of course.

"Shio... Back in Mexico, who—"

"Not in here, Bahati!" I gritted my teeth as I kept my stride.

Hitting the elevator, even though I preferred the stairs, I let her enter first. Once the doors shut, I pressed the "G" button that led to the underground garage. We made it to the Maybach, and I skidded out of the tunnel and onto the Jagoda Bay streets. Turning the music up because I wasn't ready to talk to Bahati just yet, we rode to my house as she gazed out of the window. Jagoda Bay was beautiful, and judging by how Bahati was tuned in, she had never been.

After about ten minutes of driving, she turned the music down and faced me. "Shio. We have to talk."

I knew we did. I was just processing everything and wasn't in the fucking mood. My night went from thinking I'd found my wife to finding a baby mama and a daughter.

I kept my face toward the road as I replied, "And we will Bahati."

"When?"

"Soon."

"But our daughter—"

"She's safe, fed, and dry."

"Thanks to your *girlfriend*, right?"

"Bahati, we were just in a fuckin' shootout. I went on a suicide mission to get you and Shya... One that could have resulted in all of us being killed, and since you've touched down, you've been tight about Solana when she ain't did shit to you but make sure Shya straight."

Defending Solana felt like the right thing to do, but the words tasted vile leaving my mouth.

"Don't do that, Shio. You only came because they told you about Shya. Had it not been for her, you wouldn't have come. Let's be real."

Her African accent was still strong and deepened when she was worked up. If we were in any other circumstances, I would've enjoyed hearing her speak with such passion. Shifting in my seat as I scanned the road for anything unusual, I tossed my eyes at her, finding her already eyeing me. Bahati was supposed to be dead to me, yet she was here because of my decisions.

Or was she?

What a fucking coincidence that when she popped back up, the chess pieces were knocked all over again?

"But I came, Bahati. You sitting next to me, right?"

"I wouldn't have gotten kidnapped had it not been for you!"

I rubbed my hand down my face and squeezed my eyes shut as we approached a red light. Every vein in my body was twitching. It felt like a dark cloud had been looming over my head lately, and that it was only a matter of time before the rain poured. Everything felt wrong. My life had been intentional, strategic, and calculated. I'd made sure of it. So much of my world had been controlled by the men I came from that it nearly drove me crazy. Then, the Cuppacio men were killed. I went into tactical mode. Life still didn't feel like my own when my cousins and I were grinding to feed our family, so I started creating more structure. Religion, fitness, reading—those helped center me in the chaos. I was grounded by routine and discipline.

Then, I got with Bahati, and shit started looking up for my family and me thanks to her pops. We had a stable plug and a stable income. Both were a first for us, and we were eating. Then her feelings drove her actions, and she started fucking with my paper, so I had to dead that shit.

That's what I did—I handled shit.

I wasn't a man of immediate action unless I'd assessed the situation. Back then, you would've never been able to convince me that I'd be given an ultimatum about who I was marrying between two unfavorable women. Bahati may have seemed like the obvious choice to Don's ultimatum, but she was just as far from it as Solana was. I had issues with both women, and constantly comparing and contrasting them wasn't something I took pride in. But I couldn't stop. In a way, it was necessary.

Don putting me on a time clock to marry one or the other was some goofy shit. Another man putting me, Shio Cuppacio, on a timer was fucking laughable. I did shit on my own fucking timing while making my own fucking choices. Those choices, though, had Bahati sitting next to me, seething because I wouldn't answer her questions. My choices had her out in the world, taking care of a little girl as a single mom. My choices had failed to allow me to see Solana for who the fuck she was. All that shit had me questioning every fucking thing.

Slightly turning my head, I could see that Bahati was still pouting. If nothing else, she was beautiful, but within hours, she'd proved that she was still an emotionally driven woman. That was a "fuck no" for my lifestyle. She didn't know how to read the fucking room, and when she did, her first move was to figure out how to get ahead of whatever so that her outcome was advantageous. The shit was selfish, and I wasn't marrying a selfish woman. In a perfect world, I wouldn't be marrying either of the women, but I couldn't say no without fucking up my cousins and my brother.

"Bahati... I didn't mean for you to get dragged in this shit." *I didn't think I'd ever see your ass again. Damn sure didn't want to. But that's what happens when you spare a motherfucker.* "But you got my word that no harm will come your way ever again," I said, keeping some of my thoughts to myself.

"And Shya?"

Shya.

The light had turned green, so we were back in motion, but I still glanced over at Bahati. She was slightly turned in her seat, legs folded, and staring at me. Her big lips were pouty, and her eyes were wide with wonder. But Bahati wasn't *her*, and she definitely had some shit to her.

"You willing to get a DNA test to prove she's mine?" I asked, glancing at the road, then back to Bahati.

She blinked but then nodded. "Yes. She looks just like your mother, Shio."

I watched her for signs of deception as I countered, "You don't know my mother."

"I don't, but you've watched your stepfather enough on YouTube for me to know what she looks like."

Silence. That's all I could give her before switching the focus of our short conversation.

"You should have told me you were pregnant, Bahati."

"After you tried to kill me? Shio, I was happy to walk away with my life. I don't resent you because I knew how important feeding your family was to you, so instead of imposing on your life, I counted my losses."

I shook my head at her foolish words. "A baby, though, Bahati? I would've fucking been there."

"I know, Shio. I'd always said that I was going to come find you, but I hadn't mustered up the courage." Her eyes fell. "I'm sorry."

Damn.

I didn't need another damn thing added to my plate, but I'd never turn my back on my child. Plus, when problems came my way, I didn't shy away from them or complain about shit being tough. I wasn't prepared for Bahati to be a permanent fixture in my life, especially since she was only supposed to be there temporarily back then. Her time with me had ended, and I didn't like to hold onto anything past its expiration date. Still, here she was, and with a plus one. I was a man first, and family was everything to me, so I'd have to adapt as needed.

"Shio, I know you don't want to talk. You've never been one of many words, especially, considering..." She glanced out of the window and grabbed her broken arm. "Why was I kidnapped? I must know."

It has always been us—the Cuppacios. We've gone through what most men could never survive. The mental, physical, and psychological abuse from our fathers that we endured together created a bond that no man or animal could break. Then, we had to merge with the Rinaldis, exposing men and women who didn't share our blood to our secrets. After that, Solana entered my world, and thankfully, she hadn't been privy to all things Shio. Now, Bahati was here. However, baby mother or not, she was only getting what I was willing to give.

Don was right about one thing tonight: I'd been letting too many people into the circle.

"To be honest with you, ion know. Why were you kidnapped, Bahati?"

I cocked my head as I merged from the highway, passing a shopping center that was a few weeks away from opening. Some of the buildings didn't have signs, but the biggest one was a Shopway—a brand-new store that was a cross between Walmart and Target. It was the store Ezio said he'd shopped at when I sent him to buy everything he could for Shya after we'd gotten back from Mexico.

Her broad nose wrinkled, and her mouth slacked.

How did the Rodríguezes know I had a child before I knew I had a child? Solana had only been in my home for less than two months. Granted, it didn't take long to get information on a person, especially if the price was right and your reach was long but the shit just wasn't adding up.

"I don't know! It is why I am asking you! And what is all of this, Shio? Are you rich? Is that bitch that's obsessed with our baby your girl? Why were we kidnapped by Mexicans?"

"You were kidnapped because they believe I'm in possession of something that belongs to them."

"What does he believe belonged to him, Shio?"

She was met with silence as the car glided atop a speed bump.

"Is she your girl—"

"No."

"Okay..." She sighed with relief, and for some reason, that made the veins in my neck pulse.

She ran her tongue over her straight teeth. "Are they some type of gang? They didn't speak English."

Bahati hadn't been the type to sleep around, mainly because she would do anything to prove that she was my one and only and that she was down for me. Even though this shit was hitting me left field, there was a good chance that her baby was mine. That meant she would be around, and if she was going to be around, she was going to easily be able to put shit together, even if I didn't tell her.

Still, I'd be getting a DNA test, and if the baby wasn't mine, I'd just handle her, silencing her and everything I was about to tell her.

"They are a huge Mexican cartel."

"And you didn't kill the ones who were in charge. I saw them, Shio. Only one was at the building, and he got away. Will they come back for us?" Her eyes widened, fear present as she waited for my assurance.

"Aye... I just told you, I got you."

She nodded curtly. There were so many questions swirling through her mind, I could tell from the way she was biting the nail of her thumb. I didn't want her in my business, but she'd already witnessed my folks and me murder before fleeing the country after said murders. We'd broken a plethora of laws, and she'd been there for many of them. I had to pivot this because the family's safety would always be a priority, and now, two women were under my roof that I did not trust. But since Bahati was going to be around because of Shya, I would rather tell her what she needed to know from my mouth than her to be digging around for shit.

"My father—"

"Your dead daddy?"

I nodded once. "He was a part of a mob. The Cuppacio Mob."

"I thought that was just a rumor." She chuckled.

There had been whispers all over Chicago about the Cuppacios. It was probably one of the reasons we got so much respect when we were first trying to figure out how to take care of everyone. We didn't pay any attention to the rumors; we couldn't afford to. We also didn't give a fuck enough about our fathers to glamourize the tales floating around Chicago.

"Nah. It wasn't a rumor."

"But people in the mob are rich, and when I got with you, you were—"

"Trying to come up, but you interfered with that because you were constantly in your fucking feelings."

She recoiled and cleared her throat. "Shio... I—"

"It's cool. I'm past that."

And I was, truly. I didn't dwell on shit. It didn't do anything for my mental.

I'd made it to the gated subdivision of my home—a home that was once my peace, where I resided alone. Now, I was sharing my roof with three other people. The magnetic key attached to my dash allowed access without having to speak to the guard.

"Our fathers didn't leave us shit. They fucked off their bread. We built our shit from the ground up. We ended up merging with another mob—the Rinaldis—and that's why I'm here in Jagoda Bay."

"So, you're a mobster?"

"Look, the only reason why I'm telling you this shit is that we're all close, and we don't filter our words. Everyone has wives, and they're *always* around. You'll hear shit, and instead of you trying to play detective, you're getting your information from the horse's mouth."

"Everyone in the mob has a wife... All of your cousins are married now? But wait... I didn't see rings on anyone but the light one, Ezio, I think. Oh, and the mean one, with the braided dreadlocks. Plus, the man with the nice suit. I don't remember either of them, though. Are they the ones who you moved here for?"

Bahati was playing coy. She knew almost everyone in my family. We were never a couple, but sometimes, they stopped by her apartment to pick up our product or drop off money. The conversations were brief, but she made sure to know who they were.

"And you were able to see all that with the pain of a broken arm, through them tears you was pouring out?"

With the way Bahati had been carrying on, one would think inspecting my cousins would be the last thing on her mind.

"What else was I going to do? I was scared, confused, and just trying to figure my surroundings out."

Instead of calling her nosey ass out, I continued. "Matteo isn't blood, but he's family. He's married to our cousin, Scarlett."

"Scarlett... Scarlett... Wait! Is that the one who—"

"Disappeared? Yeah. She was living here, though."

I was so lost in my thoughts that hearing about Princesspa didn't even bring a smile to my face as it usually did. I wasn't going to detail

Nel's and Vello's arrangements because, if she stayed around long enough, she'd figure them out. I didn't understand how baby mama's operated in the mob, but I knew Bahati wasn't going back home, pending the DNA test. She wouldn't be staying with me, but she'd have to live here long-term with my child.

If you marry her, she'll be here forever.

I quickly pushed that thought out of my mind as soon as it came.

"Our organization is built on family, bonds, and loyalty. Anything pertaining to my business dealings won't be your concern, but I didn't want you in the dark. I apologize to you for the kidnapping, Bahati, but had they not done that, I wouldn't know I had a child out here."

She shifted in her seat.

"I know you had your reasons, Bahati. I ain't gone hold that shit over your head. What matters is what we do going forward. Decisions don't have to be made today. Take a few days to clear your head and call your people. I don't know if they have a missing persons case out on you or not."

Bahati blinked, picking invisible cotton off her cast. "My father... He died about a month after... You know."

"I didn't kill your pops."

"I know." She rushed out her response. "It was business and... greed."

I couldn't say that I was surprised that her father's side hustle had caught up to him. He was a cool dude when he wasn't letting his hot pussy-ass daughter get in his head and withholding product.

"My mama and sister went back home shortly after. They were upset that I didn't want to go with them, so we haven't talked in years. Part of me didn't feel right raising her on the other side of the world. The other part couldn't imagine giving birth in Kenya. The quality of life there is just... different. I didn't want that for my baby."

I didn't have anything to add, so I didn't. Death was a part of life, and we all had to go one day. But as close as Bahati was with her mom and sister, I wouldn't have ever guessed their relationship would sour, creating ten thousand miles in between them.

"Shio... Are you rich? You didn't answer that."

The two and three-story homes that made up my subdivision lined the streets. Neighbors were walking their designer dogs, and cars that cost just as much as the houses were parked in the driveways. The neighborhood was quiet, but it screamed wealth. It was one of the reasons I chose the house over building something brand new.

"You're sitting in the passenger side of a four-hundred-thousand-dollar car, you were on a private plane, and we were snuck into the hospital on a floor my people bought out, and because of that, you were able to be serviced under the radar."

If that didn't answer Bahati's question, I don't know what would.

"Okay, Shio. I'm just trying to get an understanding of this. I'm so confused right now."

So the fuck am I.

I turned onto my street, stomach churning. The whole time we were at the hospital, my mind kept drifting back to Solana. Fuck.... She'd lied to me. She'd been hiding her habit right under my roof—right under my nose. I didn't know what the hell I was supposed to do with Solana. My first thought was rehab. But no matter how expensive one was, I knew there was a real chance that if I took her there, the Rodríguezes would find her. As a man, I couldn't pretend I didn't have feelings for her. She'd grown on me, and even though I wanted to wring her damn neck, her safety still mattered. I also knew Don wouldn't tolerate her being checked into a facility, although I could give two fucks what that nigga wanted. However, I knew my money would be wasted because she'd probably turn up back at my place hours later if I dropped her off anywhere outside of my grasp. Knowing Don, he'd fuck around and chain her to my fucking ankle—the nigga was hellish.

We finally pulled up to my home, and instead of parking in the garage, I left the car in the driveway next to my pickup truck. After helping Bahati out of the car, we trudged down the walkway to the front door. Entering the code for the smart door, I let Bahati step in first.

"Wow! This is nice. It smells good in here too."

Her eyes scanned the dark and moody space. There was a candle lit on the entryway table, and it smelled of smoke, spice, and vanilla. I was going to have to have my cleaning lady order more of those. I loved all the scents they left around my home, but this one was becoming my favorite.

Bahati kicked the slippers off at the door, compliments of the flight attendant, and continued to look around from where we were. I loved everything about my home. I'd hand-picked and arranged most of the décor. I wanted it to feel like me, displaying where I was currently in life with a sense of where I'd come from. Pictures of my guys and me floated around the space, as well as portraits of staples of our hometown, Chicago.

"Come on, right through here."

Walking through the foyer, I allowed my tall legs to leave Bahati, who was taking her time as she examined everything we passed. By the time she caught up with me, I had been in the living room for a few minutes, just staring at the wall.

"Shio. Your home is really gorgeous."

"'Preciate it. The kitchen is through there. Solana is feeding Shya. You two can take the fourth room to the left. Solana can show you—"

Bahati frowned. "No! I can find my own way."

She turned on her heels, but my voice had her stopping in her tracks. "Aye..."

She jumped.

"That baby mama drama shit has never been cute. I'm not the nigga that's gonna deal with that, put up with that, or play with you about that. If this shit ain't gonna work, you can toss out a number, and I'll pay you for my child and send you on your way. I hate that I wasn't there, and I plan to make up for lost time as a father, but if you come into my life causing problems for me or those around me, I'll end you for real this time, Bahati.

"I'm not going for that shit. Tighten the fuck up."

Bahati licked her lips, ran her good hand down the back of her neck, and nodded. When she disappeared in the direction of the kitchen, I listened to see if I could hear some bullshit, and when I didn't, I focused back on the task at hand.

Kicking Nel's foot, he mumbled in his sleep, stuffing his hand further in his pants. Vello was the spitting machine when Discover was pregnant, and Nel hibernated in his free time now that Pia was pregnant.

Kicking his foot again, Nel peeled his eyes open, still slouched on the couch. "Nigga, what?"

"Just letting you know I'm back."

Nel closed his eyes, mumbled some smart shit, and then stretched his legs out in front of him, bumping against the side table.

"Oh, and you might wanna pick up your junior from the hospital. He's up there tearing Grind's ass up in Mortal Kombat."

Nel rubbed his knees like an old-ass man, lifted his arms out, not stopping until his elbow popped, turned his head to each side, and then stood to his full height.

"I'm not picking his ignorant ass up. When Renello is with his fruity-ass grandpa, Pia and I pretend we ain't got no kids."

Rio was in Patty's face so much that he had to have been delivered and wasn't gay anymore. Still, the homosexual jokes were a constant.

We slapped hands, and he was on his way. My family had come through for me in a major way in the last twenty-four hours, and I knew as soon as shit settled down, I was going to do something extra nice for them. They'd talk their shit about it because it was understood that we rode for each other, but risking your life for me without blinking is some shit I would never toss aside. I loved those boys. Matteo's ignorant ass even got cool points for tagging along. I still didn't fuck with him or his cousin like that, though. Them niggas got a kick out of torturing my cousins and me.

Rubbing my hand down my mouth, I did a scan of the living room, ensuring Nel didn't leave shit behind. I didn't have to worry about locking the door behind him because the door automatically locked, and in the instance that it didn't, a buzzing alarm sounded off.

"Shio."

The moment I entered the kitchen, Solana's eyes were on me. Her hair was back in a ball on the top of her head, and she must have washed her face because it looked clean and held a glow on her dark skin. Bahati was dark, maybe a shade or two lighter than me. Solana was a deep, dark chocolate. Both women were beautiful, but there was just something about Solana. Too fucking bad she'd fucked up, and now all I saw was a coked-out problem when I looked at her.

Her feet were crossed Indian style as she sat on the kitchen island. She was still wearing her shorts, so I avoided looking down because I was sure I would see her panties through the thigh opening or her pussy if she wasn't wearing any. She'd pulled a sweatshirt over the baby tee she'd slept in. The word "Alo" was stitched across the pineapple-colored top that matched the shorts. Her round eyes peered up at me while she held a mug in her hand and sipped from it. She was sitting there, all innocent looking, enjoying a cup of joe like she hadn't been snorting that white girl less than twenty-four hours ago.

"Wassup, Solana?"

"The mailman brought the envelopes to the door… Says your mailbox was too full." Her eyes went from me to the mail stacked in a pile in front of her.

I rarely checked the mail unless I was expecting some shit, and most of my shit went to my PO box. This house was bought in cash, and I didn't have car payments. My cards, utilities, and insurance were all on autopay, and most of my miscellaneous bills were set to paperless. There had been more than once when the mailman brought the mail to the door. I knew he used it as an excuse to be nosy and chat. He was a lonely, old widower who got his grandchildren the last week of summer and again on his birthday.

I had 20/20 vision and still used glasses when I read, so I didn't fault my sight. From here, I could see the name on the first piece of mail, and I chuckled.

"Aite," I replied, moving toward the fridge.

"There's fifteen envelopes. Only two are addressed to you."

"So, you can read. Congratulations, Solana."

She opened her mouth, but I shot her a look that had her clamping it back shut. Steam rose from her mug, kissing her chin while she stared at me without blinking.

"This my shit, Solana. You don't get to question me about anything."

She blinked just as her eyes began to mist. "Can I ask what your daughter's name is?"

"Shya."

"Shya… Pretty. She's a good baby. Sleepy baby. *¿Crees que ellos… hicieron algo?* (Do you think they…. did something?)"

Heat crept up my neck. Solana had voiced one of the thoughts that had been swirling in my mind. My trigger finger itched, and my eye twitched. The doctor had cleared her at the hangar, but he'd only done a quick assessment of the small toddler.

"Si ponen la mano sobre algo que esté ligado a mí, acabo con toda la línea de sangre. (If they lay a hand on anything attached to me, I'm ending the entire bloodline.)

The mug Solana was holding tilted as the hot coffee spilled onto her sweatshirt. The ceramic mug slipped from her hand, but I caught it, not caring that it was burning my hand. Solana's body jerked forward into me, so I caught her too. Her eyes were round, and when she jerked back, only then did I realize what was happening.

"Bitch! You got me fucked up, hoe!"

Bahati had snatched Solana by her hair. Her hands shot back to Bahati's grip, trying to break the hold she had on her hair.

"¡Déjame ir, maldita sea! ¡Suelta mi cabello! (Let me fucking go! Let go of my hair!")

"Aye, watchout!" I fussed at Bahati.

Grabbing her hand, I pulled her fingers from Solana's hair. Solana was trying to push her, but since she was on the ground now with her back to Bahati, it was difficult.

When I had them apart, Solana crawled away from Bahati, shock still evident on her face with a bit of confusion.

I faced Bahati. "Aye, what the fuck? Didn't I already tell you I ain't with that drama shit?"

Bahati's chest was heaving as she almost blew smoke out of her nose. She bent down, and once she was upright again, Shya was in her arms. Now that I was seeing them together, I didn't see any resemblance between Bahati and Shya. Baby girl had my same skin tone, and her hair was in two puff balls like I'd seen on my baby cousins. However, even though a head full, she didn't have as much hair as the little girls in my family. Her doe-shaped eyes were bright with wonder, and her pouty lips were pressed shut as she clung to Bahati's shirt. She was a little beauty.

"Shio!"

Snapping out of the haze of adoration that Shya had me in, I snapped my head toward Bahati. She was deadass wrong for attacking Solana. This was the shit I didn't have time for.

"This bitch needs to die! Kill this hoe before I do! As a matter of fact, get the fuck out of my way. We can't stay here!"

Bahati inched forward, but I held my hand up. She paused but was still shooting daggers at Solana behind me.

"Your arm broke, you don't have a phone, and you have my daughter." *No fucking money either.* "You not going nowhere. Now, tell me what happened."

"Yes, I am! I'm leaving! If I stay here, she will have me in jail, and she's the one who had Shya, so I know it came from her." Bahati pointed her fingers between Solana and Shya before trying to lunge forward again.

"Chill, you got the baby in your arms."

"Fuck that! Look!" Shya opened her hand just as Bahati pointed to the baggie in her palm. "She keeps her hands balled up; it's a comfort thing. Once she opened it, this fell out on the bed."

Blood flooded my ears, each pulse causing my head to throb. My hands clenched into fists, my nails making crescent-shaped marks into my palms. It wasn't just anger that I was feeling because Solana was a fucking cokehead; it was the immediate surge of protectiveness I had for Shya. DNA test be damned, a three-year-old having access to drugs in my house was a fuck no. I felt my chest cave in as I struggled to find my next breath. Every muscle in my body had tightened as if I was ready to actually beat Solana's ass. When I gained the courage to face Solana, she scoot back, having already seen what was in Shya's hands.

Solana began shaking her head. "*Shio, te prometo que eso no es mío. No me queda más. Tienes que creerme.* (Shio, I promise you, that is not mine. I have no more left. You have to believe me.)"

"This bitch a fucking Mexican powder head. I'm 'bout to beat your ass, Columbiana!"

Bahati tried hopping over me, making the baby squeal.

"Aye, chill out!" I placed a hand on Bahati's chest.

"Shio, do you realize had she ate this bullshit, I would be in jail? *We* would be in jail! I'm not about to have a CPS case because your bitch plays with her nose! This is what the fuck kind of bitches you like now? Cokeheads? You prance off with a druggie, but you nearly choke me to death for nothing?" Bahati screamed so loud that I was sure the house windows had shaken.

"Is she good?" I asked.

Bahati was still shouting threats.

"Aye!" I yelled. "Is she fuckin' good?"

She nodded but kept her eyes on Solana as she mumbled under

her breath.

"Aite, go to the back.... Now, Bahati!"

Bahati squinted her eyes, not moving. "Stay out of my way, bitch. It's a wrap! Every time I see you, your ass is mine!" She then looked at me and snarled. "Handle your whore. Junky bitch."

Once Bahati switched off and slammed the door, I turned to Solana. Grabbing her by her arm, I pulled her up from the floor and damn near dragged her to the garage since it was the closest exit from the kitchen. The summer heat hit us instantly, adding to the warmth already boiling in my blood. I stalked to the passenger side of my Mercedes.

"Shio..."

"Shut the fuck up, Solana. You worried about Uriah's name being on the fucking mail, but my daughter could have overdosed due to your careless ass? Just get in the car and don't say shit else."

Shoving her into the passenger seat without hurting her, even though she deserved it, I looked to the sky to calm my anger. Once I was in the driver's seat, I felt suffocated. Ten minutes of what I assumed would be normal for us—at least until I figured some shit out—had been shattered. Slamming my car door, I put the car in reverse and backed out of the driveway.

"Where are we going?" she whispered, her fear slipping into her tone.

Phone in hand, I made a call and waited for an answer. When I heard, "Waddup, big cuz?" I sighed in relief. Sometimes, it was hard to catch the youngins in between their plays.

"Meet me at Jisei's townhouse."

I didn't have any words for Solana. I wasn't answering any of her fucking questions. There was nothing I could do for her. I wanted to kill her, but something inside me wouldn't let it happen. When I was done with her, though, she was going to wish she was fucking dead.

CHAPTER 7
CALISTA GLEE

Swiping sweat from my forehead, I looked both ways before walking to my sister's car. Four hours into my drive, I had to stop for gas. I'd already paid at the pump, but I still had to go inside the gas station to buy bottled water, some gum, and a bag of my favorite chips, jalapeño Baked Lays. I also had to use the restroom and was thankful the RaceTrac had been clean.

Opening the door, I placed the black bag on the center console and pressed the button to open the gas door. I was floored watching the numbers go higher and higher to fill Glow's Lexus. My Sentra would have still been almost half full by the time I reached my destination, but Glow's car needed the extra stop. Seeing sixty dollars on the pump screen instead of the usual thirty dollars it took to fill mine, I scoffed. This Lexus only took premium gas, and her tank emptied too quickly. Closing the gas door, I made a mental note to never get a luxury car unless I was making a mid-six-figure salary.

It was seven in the morning, and the sun had already risen, making it hot and humid outside. It had only taken a few weeks for me to forget how unforgiving the sun could be in Georgia. There had been many days of walking from building to building at Blake in this very heat, which was why braids and ponytails had become my best friends.

Climbing back into the car, I locked the doors and picked up my phone. My mother and sister had already called me several times, and by the time I was an hour into my drive, my mother decided that me driving to school alone was a bad idea. Her suggesting I turn around and let her take me was typical of my overprotective mother, but my mind was already made up. Glow, on the other hand, had pushed me out the door, eager to spend time with her niece-baby, as she'd been calling her for the last few days. She insisted I take her car since her tires were brand new and it had been serviced just last month. I wasn't turning down the chance to drive the Lexus, so I practically ran out of the house.

MOMMY

Are you okay? Have you been doing the speed limit right? You haven't been texting and driving? Have you pumped? If you don't stay consistent, your supply will drop.

I SMILED because I'd already pumped three hours ago. I'd learned that if I waited four hours to drain my boobs, they would get painfully hard and soak through whatever shirt I was wearing, especially if I wasn't wearing nursing pads.

Yes mommy. I pumped three hours ago at the rest stop. There wasn't a gas station that looked safe nearby so I pushed it out until that RaceTrac right off the state highway. I just filled up and now I'm headed out.

SWIPING out of my mommy's text thread, I went to my sister's. Cool air blasted from the vents, tossing around all the hair I'd straightened last night like an idiot. My sandy-brown strands had grown like crazy and naturally brightened from the sun, but humidity and straight tresses didn't mix. I was sure my roots would start shriveling up in no time.

SISSY

I was tracking your location. What happened? Are you okay?

Yes. You know how these small towns can be. By the time I get to the school, I should be fine. But don't panic if I don't have service. It's iffy here. I just gassed up.

A BUBBLE APPEARED, and then an Apple Pay payment of $120 came through. I still had money in my account, so I didn't necessarily need the funds, but now that I had a child, I wasn't in a position to turn down anything given to me. Driving my sister's car hadn't been my original plan, so I was thankful she'd replaced the gas money. Between gas and food, I'd told myself that I wasn't going to spend more than eighty dollars on this trip, but that plan was unrealistic in this car. Driving the Lexus was fun, but it was also expensive, and I knew that now.

Thank you! You didn't have to send this. I appreciate you so much for everything. I promise not to burden you with Baby Leader.

MY SISTER and I had made amends, but I was still treading lightly. When I walked into that hospital in the worst pain of my life, I saw hurt, disappointment, and anger on her face. For her to discover my pregnancy in front of all her friends was embarrassing. She'd been bragging about me to everyone, including her followers, not knowing I was stuck on Leader like white on rice at school. Being the smart, driven girl who got pregnant the first time she had sex was something from a Lifetime movie. I hadn't given Glow all the details because I didn't want to trigger her.

I still hadn't shown Baby Leader on the internet, and I'd been a mom for three weeks. I didn't think I'd ever tell the internet, especially since her daddy knew nothing of her existence. I wasn't ashamed of my baby, although I was at first. Those first few days, I felt overwhelmed and confused about my life. One day, I was a college student on summer break, and the next, I was a mother. It was still mind-boggling to even admit the shift in my life to myself.

Talking to the nurse, Pearla, and her friends made me feel so much better about being a mother. I still hadn't spoken to Blayke since she was taken from the hospital. I tried calling her, but her phone went straight to voicemail. I knew she didn't have me blocked because I called from *67 and got the same result. I was scared, confused, and needed my friend, but I also knew how her parents were. I couldn't do anything but hope and pray they would forgive me and let Blayke back into my life. However, judging by how religious they were, I wouldn't hold my breath.

SISSY

You're welcome, Glee. Again, I'm sorry, and you know I got you forever. No matter what. I'm still kinda mad, but my beautiful niece is making up for it.

BUBBLES APPEARED, and soon after, there was a picture of her holding a swaddled Baby Leader. I'd been having trouble swaddling her with the swaddle cloths. The nurse had shown me how, but I still wasn't doing it correctly. After hours of Glow and me watching tutorials, we gave up and ordered some pre-made ones with Velcro from Amazon. Baby Leader loved being swaddled and was less fussy that way.

I love you.

SISSY

I love you too. Buckle up.

SISSY

Oh! I meant to ask, you still not bleeding?

THAT'S why I'd stopped and used the restroom at RaceTrac. I hadn't been bleeding all week, and after two weeks of heavy bleeding the first week and lighter spotting the second, it had completely stopped. Yet, while I was driving, I felt something rush out of me. When I checked, it was just clear, odorless discharge soaking my panty liner. After removing it and washing my hands, I did a quick Google search while standing in line. According to the internet, some women only bleed for five days after giving birth. Still, I had pads in my purse just in case.

The air conditioning was starting to make my eyes water, so I turned it down before texting Glow back.

Nope. Still no bleeding.

SISSY

Okay. Make sure you get on birth control at your six weeks check up!

ROLLING MY EYES, I texted her "bye" and exited out of the text messaging app.

Turn left at the stop sign.

Siri startled me, continuing to give me the directions to Blake's financial aid office. Looking straight ahead at the green mass of land, I turned and looked at the only two ways I could go. No matter which turn I took leaving the gas station, the destinations were the same distance from here. I had stopped in the small, rumored-to-be-racist town of Elmet. I'd heard horror stories from many of my peers at school about Elmet, and how it was common knowledge to not be caught in the small town past dawn. The people at the gas station seemed friendly enough, but I had no plans to stop here or anywhere else once the sun set.

Instead of following Siri's directions to the school, I let my fingers swipe around until my social media page appeared. I shifted uncomfortably in my seat and wince at the physical pain. I was no longer bleeding, but I was still very sore from the birth of Leader. I opened my direct messages and scrolled to the message I'd received and accepted over a week ago. I had read it maybe a thousand times, and the words still made me heated. The sender's profile picture was a solid black circle, and at first, I ignored it because the username was unfamiliar. **Number_1**. I hadn't thought much of it, but then it clicked. I nearly dropped the freshly made bottle when I realized who was requesting to send me a message. I remembered how my hands grew moist as I ignored the alarm bells ringing in my head—it was the same bells sounding off now. The cold knot that formed in my stomach didn't halt my thumb from tapping on the "approve" button.

Number_1: I'm putting you on my visitors list. Visitation is Friday from 7-11. This ain't a request, Pretty Mama.

The message ended with him sending the prison's name and address. Reading it again, I looked up from my phone at the intersection. If I went left, I'd be heading to the school to start my transfer process. Blake University had been the only school I imagined for myself throughout high school. Cove City had always been a dream, but the dream was over, and I needed to make something shake in Jagoda Bay for my daughter and me.

If I went right, I'd be on my way to see her father as he'd requested. Leader wasn't the dream—he hadn't even been a thought until he was. And then he turned into my everything... until he wasn't.

The financial aid office closed at eleven today due to faculty training, according to the secretary I spoke with the other day. I couldn't do both today—time wouldn't allow me to. Handling my financial aid today would put me in a better position to get everything transferred and keep me from being stalled when it was time to enroll at JBU. Seeing Leader, though, would be a painful reminder of what I'd lost and force me to tell him about his little junior.

Staring at the open road, I felt my breathing pick up, unsure which way to go.

Holding the phone in my right hand, I brought my left to my

mouth but stopped myself. Lately, anxiety had been getting the best of me, and whenever it spiked, I gnawed on my nails. Opting to leave them alone today, I swiped to the Maps app before placing the phone back on my sister's mount. I shifted the car into drive, hoping the direction I chose was smart. As I rotated the steering wheel, I felt like I was in a mental tug-of-war between my past and my future, but neither one would feel like a win.

"WAIT IN HERE," the man, suited in a security uniform, said after guiding me into a conference room.

The ride here was smooth until thirty minutes after I left the gas station. I was experiencing separation anxiety now, missing my baby tremendously. It had only been six hours and some change without her, but it felt like I wanted to vomit. I'd left my phone in the car, so I couldn't call her until I handled this. If this was how it felt to be apart from a child, I didn't know how I'd get through the next eighteen years of her life. Now, I understood why my mommy cried her eyes out when she dropped me off at BU last year. I couldn't imagine leaving my baby and not seeing her again for months at a time. *Then, when she finally comes home, she's pregnant.* Just thinking about it made me grip my stomach and reach for the door handle. I thought I was over the self-loathing, but I guess not.

I needed my baby girl. I needed to go back to Jagoda Bay. I needed to be close to her. I needed to smell her. Then, I would be done feeling sorry for myself.

Gosh, they weren't lying when they said newborns have the best scent.

"No! No, no, no, no!" I gasped, feeling my breast grow heavy. It was terrible timing, and I was hoping Baby Leader's milk supply didn't overflow into my bra. I'd found this to be a common occurrence anytime I thought too hard about my daughter.

Walking around a table that was built to seat four, I took a seat on the brown plastic chair with metal legs. I didn't see any cameras in here, but I still hesitated to check my bra. With my back stiff, I glanced at the pale walls and attempted to calm myself. No school mascot, no campus rules, no semester schedule—there wasn't a poster in sight. It felt like I was sitting right under the vent, as a blast of cold air made goosebumps cover my skin. Silently cursing myself for leaving my denim jacket on the back seat of Glow's car, I rubbed my arms as if that would do any good.

Boom, Clank, Clank

I nearly toppled over in the chair at the sound of heavy metal on the other side of the door. You'd think I was locked in a vault with all the loud noises clamoring around.

With my eyes widened, skin fully covered in chill bumps from the air conditioning, and a bouncing knee, I breathed in shallow, quick pants. I was like a dog in heat, but I couldn't stop the feelings swirling inside of me. The door swung open, and the same man who'd escorted me in grabbed it to stop it before it could slam against the wall.

"Cali Glee..."

A long, dark chocolate figure, covered in a forest green jumpsuit, stood opposite the table. His dark brown eyes, that could turn my insides, glared at me with an intensity I hadn't felt in months. I blinked once, twice, then two more times, and by the fifth time, I was silently praying to God that this wasn't a figment of my imagination. His hair had grown out, a stark contrast from the low, sharp haircut he usually kept. Given the state of his hair, one might think his face would also be covered in the same new growth, but his mustache was thin, and he had a trimmed goatee. He looked to have gained a bit more muscle, but not too much to where his clothes back home wouldn't fit. He was still the finest person I'd ever laid eyes on.

As I finished taking him in, I frowned at the chains shackled on his wrists and his ankles. Leader may have been dangerous to the world, but to me, he was everything but. I'd pushed him aside in my mind as someone I didn't need, but the truth was, I craved him on the hour, by the hour.

Before I could respond to him saying my name, the security guard stepped inside. "Leader." The short, stocky guard held up a key. "I can give you ten minutes until normal visitation hours are up."

Leader kept his eyes on me but raised his arms. The guard took off the handcuffs from his wrists, but that still didn't ease my pounding heart. In court, he hadn't been chained. He was escorted inside wearing a suit and left the same way he'd come in. But seeing him as a prisoner made pity swell in my chest.

The guard placed the cuffs in his pocket. "I ain't got the key for the feet. I tried—"

Leader cut him off and stepped around him, as if he was signaling him to leave. "You straight."

The security guard nodded and hurried out of the room, looking both ways before the same mix of sounds made coming in followed him as he left. Once the clinking and clanking stopped, a loud silence took over. He was standing, and I was sitting. He seemed calm, almost relieved, while I was trying hard not to lose it.

Only this man can make jail look this appealing, I thought to myself.

His eyes roamed over what he could see, while I sat, not moving. "You look good, Pretty Mama."

With a lick of his lips, the chains around his feet scraped the floor as he walked to my side of the table. He was moving as if his feet weren't chained, proving that he'd grown accustomed to them over the last few months. With the length of his legs, it didn't take him long to be standing at my side. Instead of turning in my seat, I continued facing forward like an awkward idiot. My heart was beating so fast in my chest, it felt like I would need a crash cart soon. He didn't carry the same scent of saffron, jasmine, amber, and cedarwood. But he still smelled like Leader in the absence of the Baccarat. His natural aroma was clean, masculine, and reminiscent of what we'd done in the full-sized bed of my dorm room and *who* we created.

Dropping my head, I felt tears streaming from my eyes as my shoulders shook. Before I could inhale, I was being lifted from the chair and pulled into the arms of the man who had been my first everything. My first crush, my first male friend, my first love, my first lover, my first heartbreak, and the father of my first child. His arms wrapped around my waist as I buried my face in the scruff of his jumpsuit.

"I missed you, Pretty Mama."

I choked out a sob that was not only embarrassing but also expressive for the pent-up emotions I'd been holding inside. Before I gave birth, I was hurting over my first love spending ten years behind bars, and I cried myself to sleep many nights after the judge handed down his sentence. Before that, I had been crying because he'd broken my heart into a thousand pieces. The only reason I'd gotten through it was because Blayke's trauma was identical to my own, and we sulked in heartbreak together. However, Blayke's trauma was possibly worse because she had decided to abort her child. If I had known I was also pregnant, I would've thought to do the same.

Since the day I arrived at the hospital, I had been crying silently at the thought of my plans being altered and having to raise a fatherless child. I hadn't been honest with my sister when we made up this week. During those days she had been locked in her room, I nearly lost my mind. I didn't know what the hell I was doing with my daughter, and there weren't enough YouTube or TikTok videos in the world to guide me. I was drowning, and seeing Leader like this—having him hold me—gave me the comfort I sought, which was crazy because he was the root of all my problems.

"Aye..." He gently held me back at arm's length so he could inspect me from head to toe. His eyes, filled with admiration now, traveled from my face to my neck to my breasts, where they lingered a moment. When they got to my stomach, they rested even longer before moving down the rest of my curvy frame.

"Freshman fifteen," I said in a teasing way, while rubbing my damp face with my hands.

Just tell him.

"Shit, you look good as fuck. At this point, you can do a sophomore sixty and still be the prettiest baby." He squeezed my waist.

"If you say so..." I continued to sniffle and wipe my eyes.

The Leader before me wasn't the man I was used to. Gone were the designer threads, the bulging pockets stuffed with what made the world go round, and the look of destruction I used to see in his eyes. Leader had always been his own worst enemy. He had allowed this, which was proving to be his biggest downfall. As pissed off as I was at Amaya for being so careless and spiteful with her actions, jail for Leader was inevitable. It was inevitable because he believed it to be the rightful place for him. He believed it was the only way out for a man of his caliber.

Jail or Hell, he would say.

I'd told him time and time again that the tongue was powerful, but it had gone in one ear and out the other. He'd broken my heart, no doubt, but I was grateful that jail had come up on the docket instead of a pine box. Still, his eyes held a glint of something different that I couldn't quite read. Instead of leaning into it, because I knew my emotions were all out of whack, I blinked slowly before meeting his gaze.

He towered over me, legs chained, with crisp white sneakers on his feet, contrasting the green jumpsuit that looked as if he'd had it pressed at the cleaners. I'd caught a glimpse of a few inmates while being escorted back here, and none of their uniforms or shoes were as sharp and clean as Leader's. His glare was beginning to make me uncomfortable. My thoughts jumped all over, the first being if he could tell I'd had a baby. My heart hadn't slowed down since I made the turn to come to Iron Kinser Federal Prison, and I had no clue what I was doing here.

When I made my decision to come instead of going to BU, I hadn't thought about what a visit with Leader would be like. In my mind, we'd be in a visitation room, filled with people and guards posted around, watching. I had a four-by-six picture of the baby—one of her hospital photos—that arrived in the mail some days ago, but I'd left the photo in my bag. I would've been more open and prepared to tell him he had a daughter if I'd known we would have this alone time together.

Baby Leader was the cutest baby, and I was so happy with how the pictures had turned out. She wore a crochet, fairy outfit in mint green—a gift from Pearla—with a matching hat and booties. Her silky, straight hair framed her forehead, and she smiled for the camera, even in her sleep. The photographer said the photo was award-worthy, and after getting the prints, I agreed. I paid a pretty penny for them, but they were worth it for my baby girl.

I knew Leader would've appreciated the photo of his newborn, but I couldn't form the words to say the picture existed. I couldn't form the words to say he had another child now. And since I didn't have the photo, I coward and let the silence linger.

"I half expected you to walk in here with a big-ass belly."

Leader's words brought me back to the present. Stepping back out of his embrace, his facial expression neutralized, while I felt like I was about to pass out. My palms grew clammy, and my stomach churned. I didn't need a mirror to know that my skin was flushed bright red.

"Hunh? Wh...Why you say that?" I stuttered.

My breasts had grown two to three cup sizes, and the only bras that fit were the nursing ones. They were the most comfortable, too, being that the breast milk came and went. My face was still obnoxiously round, and my lips remained slightly puffy. In the months I'd spent with Leader, I'd learned how observant he was. However, his being able to sense childbirth would be another level of awareness.

I met his eyes, waiting for his response, and when he shrugged as a smile stretched across his handsome face, my chest deflated with relief.

"You've been dodging my people, baby. I thought maybe it was because you were hiding something, but I knew I'd just seen you in court a few months ago, so I don't know why that was even a thought now that you're here." He rubbed his chin as if he were piecing something together. He didn't know how right he was, and I wasn't in my right mind to tell him.

"Leader... Everything was just a lot. I had to pack up the apartment to move back home, and then I got really sick—"

"Sick?"

Shit, Glee.

Concern was etched in his tone as he closed the small gap between us and gently grabbed my chin to lift my face. I shuddered, not bothering to hold it back. His touch was electrifying—magnetic. Just like that night on my balcony where we shared a platter of overpriced seafood, he had me.

I paused, searching for a plausible illness. "Y-yeah. A, uhh... summer cold."

He tilted my head ever so slightly so that he was able to inspect every crease of my face. His thumb swiped across my chin, and my breathing heightened.

"You good now?"

Blinking, I nodded.

His eyes hooded as he kept looking at me as if I were the Mona Lisa. There were two chairs in the room, but we ignored them and just stood close to each other. He was studying me, and I was doing everything I could to hide what he was searching for.

Just say it, Glee. He deserves to know. Tell him you had a baby! Tell him he has a daughter who looks just like him and you, I was screaming to myself.

"You know out there… Outside of these walls, a nigga barely slept. I didn't dream. I saw no point in the shit. I was a doer 'cause nigga like me couldn't afford to dream."

He licked his lips as his eyes dropped to mine. Involuntarily, I licked mine too.

"But now, all I do in this bitch is sleep, Cali Glee," he admitted.

"Are you depressed, Leader? I mean… How's your appetite? Do you have difficulty concentrating, any… wild thoughts, like of harming yourself?"

I needed to know. It was crazy how I was diagnosing him as if I didn't have my own issues to resolve.

"Yeah and no. None of those symptoms, though. I just enjoy sleeping now. And not 'cause I'm locked up either. Jail was inevitable. In my position, it was either jail or death. I'd been lucky to go as long as I had without being jammed up." He preached the same song and dance while I sighed.

"I'm fucked up because of you, baby. I go to sleep because it's the one place I see you constantly. I'd never dreamed until the first night here. Shit scared the fuck out of me too." He chuckled, his minty breath tickling my face. "It felt so real, so right. I woke up the next day, on a hard-ass cot, mad at the fuckin' world 'cause I had no way to get to you, Pretty Mama.

"You ain't gotta talk to a nigga. As a matter of fact, you're too fuckin' good to be caught up with a nigga that's doing all this fuckin' time. But, shit… Let me be a man, baby. That's the one thing the law can never take from me. Let me pay for your schooling, and if scholarships doing that, let me pay for you a high rise or some shit. That way, you can study with the city underneath you. Show all them muthafuckas you one of one. Buy you a new whip so you can ride to campus in luxury and shit. Let me keep your pockets full, Glee. And so that my mama can quit stressing me the fuck out, unblock her number, please, Pretty Mama." He chuckled again, but my lip were trembling too much for me to join him.

My body struggled not to shed more tears as Leader's words seeped into my heart. I had a full scholarship that covered housing, but there was a condition: it had to be on campus. I didn't know of any housing that accepted single mothers, and if there was, I was sure my scholarship wouldn't cover it. A condo sounded nice, and so did a new car, even though mine barely had any miles on it since I couldn't take it to BU last year as a freshman. However, the idea of living alone with my daughter terrified me. The thought of driving an expensive car with valuable cargo in the back seat scared me even more. It was all overwhelming. I was still trying to get used to being a mom, and I'd only had a little over three weeks to cope with my new reality.

"You know what's crazy? I haven't talked to my son once since being here. I've been going through drastic-ass measures to locate you, but haven't attempted to find ole girl."

"Amaya?" I asked, although I knew who he was referring to.

He nodded before licking his lips as he went back to looking me over.

Tucking my feelings into my back pocket, I thought about my daughter's brother.

Brother.

My baby girl had something Glow and I never had. I'd always wanted an older brother growing up, but just the two of us had been good enough, especially with the dynamic happening in our childhood home.

"How is Leland? I mean... Has your mama or sister seen or spoken with him?"

The thought of Amaya left a terrible taste in my mouth. I knew Leader was content with his circumstances, but the bitter part of me resented her. Had she not gotten into his car with drugs, being spiteful, he'd be free.

And Baby Leader would have her father.

The thought of Amaya finding out I had a daughter made me tense. She'd been so nasty to me. I could only imagine how she would act toward my child.

Leader kissed his teeth, snapping me from my thoughts. "Nah, but it's straight. I know it won't be long before Amaya pops back up. She can only *mother* for so long. My lil' homie gone be straight. He a soldier like his daddy."

I said a quick prayer for Leland. Amaya had no right to be cruel in a situation she created. Keeping his child from him and his family wasn't the right move. It was childish, and at her big age of twenty-eight, she knew better.

I have no room to talk about maturity.

"Cali Glee?"

"Hunh?" I stammered, Leader calling out to me and pulling me from my thoughts again.

"Where you keep going off to, baby?"

"I... I—"

"Don't even sweat it. I know being here is a lot." Leader pulled me into his chest again. "I'm so proud of you, Pretty Mama. I know I came in your world and fucked up your plans. I know I broke your heart. But I was never on no fuck nigga shit, Calista. I didn't touch Amaya after laying eyes on yo' pretty ass. I would have never entered you knowing I was still fuckin' off. If I was still out there, just know... you'd be endgame for me."

He bent down, and I naturally met his face as it came closer to mine. He placed a kiss on the left side of my mouth, making me shudder at how soft and plump his lips were. He felt just as I remembered, and I couldn't stop the heat rising from my torso to my neck.

"If I was out, we'd have to gone and get married and shit. I don't give a fuck about being a husband at twenty-two... As long as you're my wife, that's all that would've mattered."

He kissed the right side of my mouth, making my knees buckle.

"I miss the way you poured into me constantly. I miss your drive, your determination... I miss checking your work and fixin' your incorrect answers 'cause you was too busy being fast." We both chuckled, and then his voice lowered, and no sooner than his thumb grazed my lips, he licked them. "I miss the sexy-ass fuck faces you made when I munched on that pretty pussy every night."

My mouth opened, letting his tongue enter. He'd taught me how to kiss, but I let him take the lead. Our tongues slithered around together, and his hand slid around the back of my neck underneath my ponytail. He gave it a light squeeze, and my already flooded panties was now a gushing mess. I tensed, praying it wasn't blood even though I hadn't bled in days.

He broke away from the kiss, licking my lips as he did so. Moving his hand from the back of my neck to the front, he pressed his body against mine and pushed the chair out of the way. Picking me up with one arm, Leader guided me to the table as I panted. My kitty thudded like it had its own drumline, and once I was settled on the table, he lowered himself. Letting my neck go, Leader hovered over my face as I grabbed onto his shoulders for support. I couldn't express how sore my body was without explaining why it was sore, so his shoulders would have to do.

"We good, baby. I got this room for another five minutes. It's meant for lawyer meetings, so it should be straight, but I had the Rock Man clean it real good, just in case."

"The Rock Man?" My right brow rose in confusion as he stood between my legs.

"Jail shit, Pretty Mama. Let me taste it, and I promise I'ma let you be. Just let me feast..."

Lord, Jesus.

I wanted Leader in the worse way. But I'd just had a baby, and the doctor was clear on no sex for six weeks.

But he is so damn fine, and he has a decade in jail. He needs this. He needs me.

"I'm spotting, Leader. But... you can put it in."

Around Leader, I could never believe my own words. I often became a person I didn't recognize, but I didn't feel bad about it. He awakened something in me. It could've been because he was my first or because he was so damn attractive, but I was putty in his hands. It could've also been that I was itching to feel something. I needed an escape from my reality. I thought I wouldn't see this man again for at least another eight years if paroled, and now, he was right in front of me.

"As bad as I want to, I can't. I ain't got no rubber." He sighed as he kissed all over my face. "Plus, I'm so fuckin' backed up that I ain't trying to slip up and make you my baby mama. That shit would *end* me, baby. I fucked up the first time, but I'll never jeopardize your future again. I can give you all my fuckin' money but raising a baby on your own without me would fuck me up."

My throat tightened, but my girl below kept pounding. Leader didn't even know he'd already fucked my world up. He also didn't know I was ready to let him do it again.

"Cali Glee?" he said, waiting for my eyes to find his. "Promise me you're not gonna let a nigga "baby mama" you. You're wifey material, baby. The thought of another nigga touching you—shit just fucks with me. But if you do let somebody that close, make sure that nigga know you ain't nobody fuckin' baby mama."

I've already been "baby mama'd, I thought as he rubbed my thigh and palmed the other.

"Shit, man... I'll never tell you to stay down for me. I want you to go be happy, Pretty Mama. Date. Do all the shit eighteen, soon-to-be nineteen, year olds supposed to do. Shit, let me sponsor a summer trip for you, Blayke, and your sister. Do some spontaneous shit, like jumping off a mountain or some other wild shit.

"But don't be nobody's baby mama. Make a nigga strap up. Get on some birth control too. If I have to come home and play step-daddy, a nigga gone be mad at me 'cause I'ma shoot him first for playing with you."

He smiled, but it didn't quite reach his eyes.

I was horny and guilty, and the two feelings were rushing over me like a tsunami. I needed to feel him. I needed to feel Leader one more time before he found out what I'd done, and the information crushed his whole world. I wanted to feel him one more time while he still saw me as innocent-ass Cali Glee.

I knew when he found out he was a father of two, our worlds would change forever. I knew the same heartbreak I'd felt over him would hit him in the same way, tenfold. He already felt bad about missing time with Leland, even though he hadn't verbally expressed it. I could see it in his eyes that being away from his family and me was tearing him up inside. At least he had time with Leland before this prison sentence. He had witnessed his birth and cut his cord; I'd seen pictures at his mama's house. He'd been present at four of his birthdays and had captured those early milestones. With our daughter—his namesake—he had already missed the birth and wouldn't see her until her eighth birthday, if he made parole.

Doing what I've been doing since I walked through the loud door —I lied. "I'm already on birth control. It helps with my period cramps. And I'm not worried about boys, Leader. It's you who occupies my dreams too."

"Good..." He licked his lips as his hands inched further up my legs. "Don't worry about me, either, Calista. Dream about that white coat."

His lips crashed into mine without another word. A burst of heat rushed through my body as he used his lips to show his yearning for me. The kiss was slow, deliberate, and thoughtful yet hungry. Shivers of delight tugged through me as he removed my sweatpants without even lifting my hips. I inhaled sharply as he unbuttoned his jumpsuit, keeping his lips locked on mine. I wanted to help him, but I was afraid. He'd explored my body more times than I could count within a short span, but I still felt like a young girl allowing a boy to explore her body as she prepared to lose her virginity.

He pulled from the kiss to push the green jumpsuit down, and it hit the floor, causing a soft clank from his ankle chains. He stood before me in a muscle shirt that displayed his tattoos that I loved and a pair of pure white Ralph Lauren briefs. Leaders' influence had afforded him certain privileges in the jail, and although I wasn't fluent in prison culture, I knew brand-new sneakers and name-brand boxers weren't given out freely.

But it wouldn't be Leader if he didn't keep himself up.

His large hand took my face, slightly squeezing it as his lips pressed against mine again. He mumbled something, but I was too turned on to comprehend anything beyond what we were about to do. My panties were still on, and feeling his finger hook them to the side had me spreading my legs wider. Letting my face go, but still exploring my tongue, he pushed his boxers down. Hooking his arm in the crease of my back, he lifted me, and my legs locked around his waist.

As I inhaled, Leader exhaled and lowered me onto his tool.

"Fuckkk! You so perfect. Like a fucking dream, Pretty Mama."

Soundless for a moment, I struggled until an "Ahhhhh!" was released from my throat. I grabbed his shoulders as he filled me by pulling me closer and closer to him. I was still sore, but I was so wet that I could hear my lower half sputtering.

"Fuuuuck, baby... This pussy still the best. Shit, you feel so good!"

He took a step back, chains clanking against the floor, as I sat on his waist, his tool fully embedded in me. I bucked my hips, ready for more friction, which caused him to moan.

"Hol' up, baby.... Hold up. Let me just sit in it. I gotta savor this pussy."

Resting my head close to his, I pressed my chest into his face as my hands rubbed his back. He nibbled on my breasts through my shirt, and I felt them swell up. It was time to pump, and I didn't have any nursing pads on, so I sent up a prayer that the bra's built-in pads would stop any leakage. As if He was striking me down for praying while committing fornication, I felt my left breast leak into the bra. I tensed as my worry spiked, and it made my vagina tighten involuntarily. Leader groaned from the feeling, and just like that, I didn't care about the leak or fornicating. I wanted and needed this so bad.

He pulled my ponytail, his passion taking over. I helped by rearing my head back and giving him access to my neck, as he moved from my breasts to sucking on my flesh. He began to slowly pump in and out of me, and each time he eased in, I whimpered. He was so long, so hard, and so thick. I was beyond sensitive down there since I was still healing, but that didn't stop me from being so damn horny. I wanted this to happen, but I also knew this was sympathy sex. I knew another opportunity to feel Leader inside of me was slim pickings. I also knew Leader having access to women he wanted to have sex with was unlikely.

"Goddamn, baby. What you do to this pussy? Shit so fucking fire. Fuck, girl!"

His pacing increased as he sucked all over my neck.

I was beyond overstimulated as I bounced up and down in his arms. My breasts were leaking, my kitty was clenching, and my nails were digging into his back and shoulders. My neck was hurting from its position so he could continue his assault of sloppy kisses, and my stomach was caving as my first orgasm was making its way through my body. It was a lot going on, but I couldn't stop the orgasm that was building if I tried. His pumps were now faster but still long due to his length. They hurt, his girth stretching a place that was trying to shrink, but I took it.

I took it like he'd taught me to on that full-sized bed at Blake University.

"Oh, God! Leader!"

"You 'bout to come, baby? Come for daddy, Pretty Mama. Let me see that face I been dreaming about."

Shit!

"Shit!" I screamed in my head and out loud.

My jaw relaxed, and my legs tightened around his waist. He placed a kiss on my jawline as he worked through my release. I was seeing stars, moons, and all the other whimsical stuff that made me go crazy for him the first time. This was why Glow had been on my case. I was hotter than before now. My daughter had flickered something in me.

"Fuck, baby! I'm 'bout to nut. I'm so happy you on birth control."

My eyes shot open, and before I could hop down, I felt his cum spray my walls. I could never forget the feeling of his warm ejaculation inside of me.

"I fuckin' love you, girl. I love you so much, Cali Glee."

"I love you, too, Leader," I whispered.

Our hearts were beating in sync as he throbbed inside of me. His arm strength was something serious because he stood there for a while, holding me up in the same position, his tool never leaving my insides.

Boom! Boom! Boom!

The hard knocks startled me as he bent to grab something from the floor while keeping us connected. When I looked down, and my face dropped at the makeshift knife he was picking up.

"Fuck... It's the guard, baby. I hate to end our time like—"

"It's okay."

"It's not. You deserve more than being fucked in a nasty-ass prison. I just... I-I fuckin' need you, Glee. I want you to live yo' life, but my heart needs you."

He eased out of me, and even that was painful. My panties went back into place, and I could feel his nut hit the seat once he let me down. I would have to stop at Walmart and pick up more underwear and take a hoe bath somewhere. I would have to stay in the same clothes, or Glow would trip on my changing. She told me to get a room in Cove City, but I was heading back to Jagoda Bay tonight. I needed my baby even more now that I'd visited her father.

He picked up my pants and helped me put them on. This man was chained at the feet but had fucked me silly as if he'd done this before. I started to ask him if he had, but I wouldn't be doing anything but hurting my own feelings that were already torn up due to our circumstances.

Once I was dressed, he pulled on his own clothes and tucked his shank back into his pocket. He pulled me into his chest and kissed the top of my head and forehead. I was praying my shirt wouldn't be stained with breast milk from the pressure applied on them.

"Glee?"

"Hum?"

"Thank you for making me dream again."

"Don't stop dreaming, Leader. I... I love you."

The heavy metal churned, and the loud clanging started again.

"Sometimes, I wish you didn't, Pretty Mama."

The guard came in, but Leader stayed in place. He jutted his chin toward the door.

"He's going to walk you out, baby. Then, he'll come back and get me."

I wanted to kiss him one last time. I wanted to tell him how much I missed him. I wanted to tell him he had a newborn daughter that we'd created the first time we did what we'd just done. Instead, I blinked, nodded, and turned to walk out behind the guard.

Everything was a blur after I made it to Glow's car. Getting in and driving off was a blur. Sending Glow a text, saying I was coming home and what my ETA was, was a blur. It was all one big blur that felt heavier and heavier as I drove away from Iron Kinser Federal Prison. Then, I felt a rush of liquid fall into my already soiled panties. I gripped the steering wheel, my hands clenching to ground myself, but the attempt was failing. The car was sounding off because I hadn't put on my seat belt, adding to the already loud noises in my head.

Boom! Clank! Clank!

My heart rate sped up, and my legs jittered. I stared straight ahead and kept driving, although everything in me was screaming for me to stop the car. Unfortunately, those noises were on replay as I felt as if I was back in the conference room, waiting for Leader to come out.

It took no time for reality to hit me. My heart went from pounding because of the orgasm to pounding because I'd fucked up. I hadn't told him about Baby Leader. I hadn't told him he was a father of two now. But I wasn't freaking out about what I hadn't told him; I was freaking out because of what I had told him.

A wicked black fear swept through me. I felt the panic overcome me as I tried to hold on to my fragile control. We'd had sex. My six weeks weren't up. He thought I was on birth control. He'd come inside me.

Vomit rose up into my throat, and as I tried to stop it, I pressed harder on the gas pedal. As it came up, I let go of the wheel and tried to prevent it from getting everywhere in Glow's car. My foot was planted on the gas pedal because I couldn't lift off due to the shock. It felt like stone—my toes were bricks that had been laid and cemented.

Then I saw a bright light, and a loud horn blasted through the prison sounds that would not go away. Before I could act and correct the Lexus, everything went black.

CHAPTER 8
GLOW

"Come on, my pretty girl. You're doing so good," I cooed as I poured warm water on my niece's hair, watching its silkiness turn slick.

Her eyes were open, looking at me with much more trust than I deserved. Her pink baby tub was inside mine, and my back was on fire as I kneeled beside it. Making sure the water didn't go inside her ears, I looked her over one last time before sitting back on my heels, drying my hands, and pressing play on the phone screen.

"Next, place a dime-sized amount of shampoo in your palm, lather it, and apply directly to the baby's head."

Nodding, I repeated the directions from the video. When my hand was lathered with Baby Dove's Head To Toe wash, I applied it directly to her scalp. Baby Leader still had a soft spot, so I avoided it as best as I could. When she began sucking on her fists, I knew it was time to speed up the process. Her bottle was already prepared—I had done that before bathing her. A few hours earlier, she had vomited, and it had run under her neck and into her hair. She needed a bath, but she had fallen asleep before I could give her one. I used that time to edit content and open PR packages. It had been over a week since my last upload, and my followers were growing tired. I'd received hundreds of messages asking if I was okay, while others simply joked, asking for the fine Memphis nigga with the fine brothers to "unhand me." Ironically, his unhanding me would mean a divorce attorney since I'd accepted his hand in marriage.

Just as I was about to upload a pre-recorded video of me trying a new Pho restaurant not too far from my townhome, Leader was waking up. I nearly panicked because I'd made plans to wash her and didn't know how. As a big sister, I didn't have a big enough age gap to have had that kind of responsibility with Glee. When she was born, I was nearing five, and while I remember begging my mom to hold and feed her, those maternal tasks never occurred in my adult life.

I could have easily called my best friend, who had a baby only a few months old at home, but I hadn't responded to any of their messages for days. I couldn't call my mom, either, because she'd be quick to get in her car to come and check on me. I'd lost weight since she last saw me in person and didn't feel like answering a lot of questions. Plus, my mom was already stressed enough about being a grandma at a moment's notice, and I didn't want to add to that. She had a cancer scare once, and we were trying to keep her healthy and stress-free so nothing else would trigger a recurrence.

Lee-Lee was bathed, and I smiled at the new nickname for her. After ten minutes of rummaging through the packages delivered that morning, I chose the perfect outfit. The pink sleeper with bears all over it was open at the bottom, resembling a long nightgown, which made changing her diaper easy. Her mom was supposed to visit BU to handle transferring business and stay overnight, but she had texted saying she was coming back home. I wanted to protest, but Leader was so adorable that I didn't blame my sister for wanting to be with her sweet baby.

I ran my hand down the side of her face as she drank from the bottle, her eyes fixed on mine. I started rocking back and forth as if I were in a nursing chair instead of my living room sofa. Glee had done a great job with packaging and labeling her breast milk. In three weeks, she already had a small stash in my freezer. I'd read somewhere that breastfed babies tend to be more cry-prone, so I was thrilled that my niece took the bottle instead of a nipple. Glee still had school, and although we could afford childcare, I knew I would be the one to babysit when my sister went to class. She was too small, too precious, for me to trust a stranger with the first baby in our family.

Leader was tiny but greedy; she'd nearly sucked the entire bottle down, and before I could burp her, her eyes that had little spiked lashes were closing. Placing the glass bottle on the table, I tossed the burp cloth that matched her outfit over my shoulder and began patting her back once I had her in place. I didn't know how to bathe a baby, but I did know how to burp and feed one. I'd gotten plenty of practice on Baby Ezio with that.

Nuzzling my nose against hers, the sweet, powdery smell almost reminded me of warm laundry. I could sniff her all day. That newborn baby scent had magic in it. If Dasani could bottle this up and sell it for one of her perfumes, she'd strike gold. And I'd buy it by caseloads.

Ding Dong

Groaning, my eyes shot open. I'd just dozed off, figuring I would get a nap in while the baby was sleeping. I stretched my neck toward the bassinet I'd pulled into the living room and relaxed, seeing that the baby was still sleeping peacefully. That bottle had put her in a food coma, and even though I'd burped her, she still puked. I had caught it with a birthing cloth, avoiding another bath being needed tonight. I was going to have to talk to Glee about how much milk she was giving her. We were probably overfeeding her, according to my Googling. She had an appointment next week, and I didn't want the doctors to tell us she'd picked up too much weight for her age.

Sticking my feet into the tan fuzzy house shoes Amazon had sent months ago, I switched past the broken-down boxes, half from PR and the other half from the stuff I'd been ordering for Leader. It would be easier for me to haul them out the front door and place them on the curb for the recycling crew that came every Sunday. Instead, I'd been putting them in the garage or against my living room wall, and for now, that is where they would be.

"Coming!" I announced with a yawn.

I'd had enough sleep during the days I was locked in my room, but caring for a newborn was hard work. Still, I'd been enjoying Lee-Lee. She was beyond beautiful and a pretty chill baby. By the time my hand reached the knob, I hesitated. I could have easily checked my Ring camera from my phone before getting off the couch, or I could have looked through the peephole. Unless Glee was back, which I doubted since it would take her hours to get here, it had to be either

Jisei or Tunan. Jisei, I could handle. She would curse me out, accuse me of hogging the baby, and all would be well. But Tunan, I was indifferent about.

I still hadn't heard from him, and while a part of me felt slighted, I was also relieved. Things were getting too heated between us. I'd gone from being celibate to becoming a leaky faucet every time he was nearby. A few weeks ago, I hoped Shio would choose me so I could be fully accepted into the circle of mob women, and now, I was married to his brother. I felt embarrassed by the whole ordeal. It was clear Shio wasn't checking for me, and seeing that chocolate beauty on his arms was a sign that I wasn't his type from the start. It wasn't my business since I had married his brother, but if this was Jisei on the other side of the door, she'd better be ready to spill the tea—after cursing my ass out, of course.

Pulling the door open, I was taken aback by the person, or people, on the other side. Tugging at the Victoria's Secret lounge set I was wearing, I adjusted my shorts and ran a hand through my hair. I had gotten my hair done yesterday—a silk press cut into a blunt, chin-length bob—but suddenly, I felt like I'd made the wrong choice.

"So, you *are* alive?"

Placing her hand on her round hip, she smelled of her perfume, which wrapped around my head like a boa constrictor. The halter top with the sweetheart bodice was perfect for her small breasts, making them sit just right. Her neck and shoulders were exposed, leaving her light caramel skin bare. Her hair was long and in bedhead curls, flowing down her back. There was no part in dividing the hair; instead, it was tossed backward, showcasing her perfectly placed makeup.

Denim jeans covered her lower body, and strappy heels adorned her feet. Her bracelet stack probably cost more than my townhouse, and her ring likely cost more than the neighborhood. Dasani Rinaldi was the definition of a bad bitch with a rich nigga who ran shit. Every time I saw her, she looked and smelled better than the last time.

"Da-Dasani?" I stuttered.

"Yeap. It's me... and my boo, Nelsa."

Dasani didn't wait to be invited in. She stepped up, prompting me to move out of her way. "Hello, Glow. Thank you for answering my text message about coming over."

I cringed at her sarcasm but threw my second unexpected guest a small smile. "Hi, Nelsa."

I locked the door behind Dasani and her housekeeper and followed them into the living room. Nelsa was in her work uniform, as usual, and considering how much they paid her, I'd eat, sleep, and breathe in that baby blue and white dress too.

"Ohhhh! The babyyyy!" Dasani switched to the bassinet, tucked her hair behind her ear, and bent down to get a better look at Leader. "I'm not going to hold her because I'm too doused in my perfumes and oils. You know they are still in the testing stages, and she's too new and sensitive, but Glow! My goodness, she is so damn gorgeous."

Leader was the prettiest baby ever. Just looking at her made me feel so ashamed that I'd said and done what I had to Glee. I was just so damn mad, and I'd be lying if I said I wasn't mad still. But my baby sister was human. She'd made a mistake, and the baby was here now. I knew there was no point in being upset anymore because I would be here for whatever they needed.

"Ahhh. She got me ready to say fuck it and give that stupid-ass nigga another baby." Dasani shook her head and stood upright. She then pulled her phone out, snapped a picture, and then locked her screen. "Just too pretty."

"Ain't she?"

"Umm humm..." she said, tossing her eyes from the baby to me.

Dasani looked at me, no judgment in her eyes, but I still felt exposed. Every time she'd seen me, I'd been put together. Granted, I was matching, but I wasn't wearing any makeup.

"Before you try to make an excuse, Glow, I know you're babysitting because Pearla told Pia. I brought Nelsa over to keep the baby since Delicate and little Ezio are with their grandmothers. Go get dressed." She pursed her glossed-cover lips. "I'm not taking no for an answer."

She turned her back to me, admiring the baby once more. Shifting my attention to Nelsa, she shrugged, so I knew there was no getting out of this. Turning on my heels, I hurried to my room. As happy as I was to see Dasani, I wasn't in the right headspace to leave the house. I'd been enjoying my time with my niece, especially after being furious that she was alive for the past few weeks. Glee was on the way home, and although I trusted Nelsa, I didn't want to alarm her by leaving Leader with someone she didn't know. Nelsa had been with the family for years, having had a hand in raising Demise. She was not only kind but also trustworthy, so I hoped Glee would trust my opinion on letting her babysit and not be upset with me.

I stood in front of the full-length mirror, assessing my outfit, reluctant to leave the safety of my walls. It took me three minutes to assemble the butter-yellow backless bodysuit with the matching skirt made of the same fabric. Dasani was wearing heels, so I slipped my feet into a pair of thong-sandaled kitten heels in the same soft hue as the outfit. A monochromatic look was the best I could manage on such short notice, and the ten-minute makeup I applied using the Rare Beauty new skin moisturizing tint turned out well, given the limited time. I'd planned to record myself using the product since it was a paid promo, but since it had been sitting on my vanity, I grabbed it.

Before leaving my room, I went to check Glee's location.

"Must be still in a bad service area..."

Her location kept saying *Not Found*, which happened a lot because Glee refused to upgrade her phone. Most teens were eager to get the latest model, but not my baby sister. As a content creator, it was my job to get every new iPhone that came out, which meant upgrading each year. I'd offered to buy her a new iPhone many times, but she always declined.

I'm telling you now, your birthday gift will be a new phone.

My message didn't send but that was to be expected since she was in an area without service.

Anywho. I'm headed out with Dasani. Ms. Nelsa is here with Leader. She's safe with her. Trust me.

That's the nanny by the way

I WAS certain I'd never told my sister who Nelsa was, but I had mentioned the plethora of nannies available to my rich friends. I hadn't shared much about the mob wives, but from the looks of it, she would be around now, so she'd find out things even if I tried to protect her from them.

I waited a few seconds to see if the messages would send, and after a minute of it just sitting there, I tossed my phone into my white Dior handbag and hit the light switch. Leaving the lingering scent of my Dolce & Gabbana Light Blue perfume in my bedroom as I walked to the living room, I couldn't help but feel a bit better with myself. Nelsa was finishing a diaper change while Leader sucked on her fists. It wasn't time for her to eat yet; she still had an hour and a half to go.

"She's greedy. Don't give her another bottle until at least another hour, Ms. Nelsa."

"Baby is okay with me. You two go ahead. Besides... It's nothing wrong with giving her more milk. At this age, all they know how to do is sleep, get cuddles, and eat."

"I—"

"Goodbye, Ms. Glow." Nelsa dismissed me, and Dasani turned toward the front door with a smirk.

Taking another look at Nelsa, I sighed and followed Dasani. She stepped aside once we reached the door to let me open it, and when I did, I came face-to-face with another person I wasn't expecting to see.

"Heyyyyy, Pearla girl!" Dasani greeted from beside me.

Pearla had her phone in her hand, with boho braids pulled into a half-up, half-down style, wearing Gray Alo shorts and a matching sweatshirt. Her thick legs were on display. She'd lost a little weight, but she was still a round, pretty girl.

Pearla's eyes swept over both Dasani and me. "Y'all look so pretty!" She beamed, her smile almost perfect, even with the braces.

"Thank you, boo. You look cute too," Dasani said as she beamed back at Pearla.

I gave thanks for her compliment also before saying, "Glee isn't back from Blake just yet."

"Yeah, I just tried to call and text her. I would have ridden with her, but I overslept." Pearla held her phone up. "You mind if I stay over here until she gets back?"

"I don't mind at all. Come on in." I opened the door wider for Pearla to enter, and she hugged us both before she stepped inside. "Bella and Mahzeyah may pull up too."

"That's fine. If y'all get hungry, have Glee order food on my Uber Eats account."

Dasani hit the alarm on her G-Wagon, and I turned to follow her. I had to carefully climb up into the passenger seat since my shoes were new and slick. It had been a while since I'd seen her drive this truck, and I wondered what motivated her to choose this car to cruise in today. She had so many cars that she could switch them out for two weeks straight and still have a few left over. Dasani was so spoiled that if she even complimented a car, Demise had it delivered to their home before the day was over.

"Glee had a pretty-ass baby." Dasani shifted her focus from the road to me.

She ran over a speed bump, and the truck wobbled since she was going ten miles over the speed limit. I'd always liked G-Wagons because they sat up high, but when I found out it wasn't a smooth ride, I scratched them off my dream car list.

"Yeah, she did." I didn't mean for my response to come out as a whisper, but I was consumed with uncertainty.

"I don't do house calls, Glow."

I sighed, the elephant in the car being called out. "I know... I didn't mean to ignore y'all, but it's been a lot going on."

"You disappointed?"

"Very. As beautiful as Leader is, I didn't want this for my sister."

"Okay. What do you want for her, Glow?"

"I..." I paused and exhaled so I wouldn't sound so small. "I want her to finish school, Dasani. We sent her to school a virgin, and I expected her to come back home one. At the very least, I didn't expect her to get pregnant. Then, the baby daddy is a no-show. She says he moved away or something. That tells me he's probably someone that she had no business messing with in the first place. The good girls always love the bad boys, so I know he's trouble, wherever he is. Had she gotten with someone who was on her level, she probably wouldn't have come home a single mother.

"I just want her to be a college student. A teenager. I want life to be easy for her because mine is already hard enough."

Dasani merged onto the freeway beside a truck bigger than the G-Wagon. I wasn't surprised when she passed it; she was driving this Mercedes truck like it was a Toyota Corolla.

"Daylani was always the quieter one of us. The sensitive one... The good girl. While I was the hot-headed, career-driven sister, she was love-driven. Daylani wanted to love and to be loved. I was so caught up in my own mess, chasing hours at the hospital and stacking up as many hustles as I could, that I missed it.

"See... I was protective of my sister, but in my mind, I knew she was a smart girl. I knew she would make the right decisions. She wasn't attracted to the kind of men I was. So when she said she was dating a law student, I let her do her. Lawyers make good money, and I figure the worse he'd do is cheat on my sister."

Daylani and Rut were so madly in love that I couldn't imagine her being in a relationship with a man besides him, but she had—they both had. Their daughter was proof of it because, while Daylani loved Rich as her own, biologically, she wasn't her mother.

"That nigga, that I thought was harmless because he wasn't the textbook bad boy, was actually putting his foot in my sister's ass. I had to lie down and serve six years for trying to protect her. He'd beat the fucking baby out of my sister, Glow. You hear me? That *safe lawyer*... the good guy, was putting his hands on my sister and doing her so wrong."

I often forgot about Dasani doing six years in jail for attempted murder. The way she carried on in life, you would never know there was a time she was locked up behind bars.

"So when you say you want her with the lame, just know them niggas be the worst type. Got chips on their shoulders and shit because the world ain't been kind to 'em. You want your sister to be with that kinda man, but I'm the bitch that's gone tell her to run away. Lace up your Nikes, Glee baby. Run from them goody-two-shoe niggas!"

We'd parked in front of a huge building, in a park reserved for "Her" according to the sign. Dasani leaned back in her seat, slightly turning her body to face me. I saw her flick her tongue across her teeth before smearing her lips together. She was so perfect looking that I struggled not to be subconscious in her presence, even now as officially one of the mob wives.

"Why did you agree to marry Tunan, Glow?"

I choked on air. "Hunh?" The question had caught me off guard, and I didn't have a prepared answer.

"I said, why did you agree to marry Shio's brother?"

"I... I..."

"You agreed because you see the lifestyle."

I huffed, my shoulders falling in defeat. "Dasani—"

"No. It's cool. You see the lifestyle. The way we live. The way these men love on us. How we're able to get up and do what the fuck we want when the fuck we want to. You wanted to be a part of that. I get it..." Dasani cocked her head. "Excluding you was never on no "mean girl" shit, Glow."

"I know—"

"Nah. You don't know. You're cool, and I fuck with you the long way, but when it comes to Demise Rinaldi, I'm forever guarding him.

"You're best friends with my sister-in-law, and by default, that made you get an in. What our men do may look glamorous on the surface, but this shit gets dark, twisted, and deadly underneath it all. I wasn't risking mine nor my daughter's life for a bitch that could walk away with all our secrets whenever she felt like it or one that may or may not have been pillow-talking to another nigga."

I sighed because she was right. I may have been desperate to be officially in with the women, but I wasn't that green to the parameters. Being an affiliate versus being a wife to a cartel member was like the difference between $99 and a big face—close, but not equal.

"I get it..."

"This shit... This mob shit? I know you didn't want in because of the money. Nah, you're an internet sensation. You got your own bread. You wanted in because you felt like you were missing out. You had FOMO. Just thinking you were missing the core parts of this mob shit.

"Now imagine your sister. Sheltered, at college, seeing what everyone else was doing and feeling like she needed to do the same or she wouldn't belong. The same way I saw you get the long face every time we excluded you, and didn't judge your ass, is the same way you should be with your sister. Now, I'm not telling you how to sister, because I wish a bitch would tell me about mine..." She chuckled as if she'd just told a joke. "But what I will say is... Give Glee some slack.

"She is still the college girl. She's still the young woman she was when she left for Cove City. All of her dreams can and will still come true. When you have a disagreement with your sister, don't ever let it get you out of your body, especially in the company of muthafuckas you want to be down with. Had I not known you, I would've been ready to fuck you up myself for how you was acting in our hospital."

Dasani reached above her head, pressed into the roof, and a compartment popped out. She grabbed oversized BVLGARI shades and placed them on her face. I'd seen the shades in Saks Fifth and knew the cost was in the four-digits. They weren't my style, but they looked badass on Dasani.

"I like you, Glow... I really do. I don't know what you and Tunan got going, but we won't have to wait too long until we figure it out. Especially with the passion I saw displayed at the hospital... Um. My girl, you in trouble."

Dasani wriggled her eyebrows, and I couldn't stop the giggle that escaped my lips.

I'd told Tunan that we couldn't have sex again the last time he was over. After that conversation, I didn't leave my room for days. It was reassuring to know that he could follow directions and let me be. He needed a wife, and I wanted in. Now that we'd both gotten what we wanted, the shit didn't feel as rewarding as I thought it would.

"What I will say is all the shit that you fantasize about when it comes to being one of us—a lame nigga ain't got a finger in it. Stop wishing green dick on your sister. I don't know Glee's business, but I do know real niggas sniff out innocent bitches like bloodhounds. Glee ain't had a baby just by anybody. And with the way she be watching our pages, she's taken some notes, I'm sure."

Dasani winked, put on her shades, and hopped out of the truck. Turning around before she closed the door, she leaned in. "Oh, and Glow... Welcome to the Rinaldi Mob. We all have a job to do. It's about time you chat with your husband and find out what yours is."

When I realized Dasani wasn't waiting for me after she slammed the car door, I rushed out, making sure my shoes didn't cause me to slip. I wasn't sure where we were, but as always, Dasani strutted confidently across the short distance to the double doors. I took a moment to scan the lot, seeing that the valet line at Demise's elaborate parties was currently present. Six-figure cars were plentiful, but with no signage or obvious labeling, I was still lost on where we were.

Keeping pace with Dasani, I walked right past the giant troll guarding the entrance. Once the door shut behind us, the dark, moody atmosphere put me on alert. Dasani continued her stroll, stopping at the elevator and pressing a button. It opened with a ding, and I stepped in behind her. The descent was short and quiet; only the elevator's hum could be heard. The elevator opened to a large space that mimicked a luxury hotel lobby with another set of double doors in front of us, with the same guard standing in front of it that we'd just passed on the ground floor. I learned early on not to question things, so I kept following Dasani. When the guard opened the door for us, the buzzing, ringing, and rattling of machines filled the air instantly.

A young, pretty girl switched by who looked to be no older than Glee, but I knew she was because the mob didn't play games when it came to the youth. Dasani stopped her with a genuine smile on her face.

"Hi, Mrs. Rinaldi."

"Hi, Mottie. Can you have my favorite bartender make me and all the wives an array of cocktails?"

She nodded. "Will that be all?"

"Yes. That's it."

Dasani reached into her rose pink, ostrich-skinned Hermès Birkin 25, pulled out three one-hundred-dollar bills, and handed them to the waitress. She smiled at both of us after thanking Dasani.

Continuing behind Dasani, I was trying my hardest to focus forward instead of on all the buzzing around me. This was very much an underground casino, and I was floored that I'd never been invited here. Marble floors, printed carpets, wood grain surfaces, skimpy waitresses, rich niggas, Kush-filled air, and expensive alcohol blended throughout the open space that housed every machine and table you'd find in Las Vegas. The way Dasani spoke to the waitress and how she hadn't been checked or questioned by the guards, I automatically knew this was her husband's business.

There was just so much happening down here that I couldn't stop looking around. I wasn't much of a gambler, but the machines were so loud and pretty that they were inviting. Men of all nationalities and backgrounds filled the space. I had even spotted a rapper when we first came in when Dasani stopped the waitress. I could have sworn I saw the governor, too, and with the way Jagoda Bay hid their scandals, his being underground was on brand. Street guys, CEOs, and law enforcement all under one roof was unheard of. However, people of different sectors were mingling, but for the most part, everyone was doing their respective gambling, making Demise even richer. It would also mean jail time for many, affecting hundreds of lives. I'd never compromise those around me. I didn't even like cheese like that.

This place was a gold mine for content. If my viewers only knew where I was right now, they would want a tour, some interviews, and some food reviews. With the size of the venue and the goal being to get people to stay and gamble, I knew this place probably had some amazing food.

"Look who I dragged from the house."

I was expecting to be reunited with the women, but what I didn't expect was for everyone to be sitting in their husbands' laps. The whole inner circle was here, except for Vello and Discover. Three men had empty laps; well, two, since Demise had reached for Dasani's hand and pulled her onto him. That left Tunan and Shio as the unoccupied seating choices.

All eyes were on me, and the ladies didn't look too happy to see me. Missy was the only one who offered me a small smile as she sipped her drink while Essex squeezed her thighs.

Demise looked from Tunan to Shio, who sat next to each other. This area was arranged almost like a VIP section, with an extra-long, curved sectional that fit everyone. It was also roped off, but it was positioned so that not many could see over a small wall, yet Demise could see everything from his spot in the middle of the comfortable sectional.

"You messy as hell..." Demise told his wife with a chuckle and a kiss on her lips.

"I get it from you, Messy Boots."

"Hi everyone." I simpered.

Jisei's spoiled ass folded her arms and turned to face her husband, as if she wasn't already in his lap. Mocha wasn't sitting on Zo's lap, but she might as well have been, considering how she was leaning on him. All she did was snicker at our friend without looking my way. I could feel Tunan's eyes on me, but I refused to look at him or Shio's. When we first approached, they were engaged in a conversation that didn't look heated but also didn't look pleasant. I was hoping it wasn't about me.

"Well, well, well... If it isn't the brother fucker herself. What's good, Glow?"

Leave it up to Nel to crack a joke. I rolled my eyes and threw a tight-lipped smile his way. I could feel my skin heating and knew the tinted moisturizer wouldn't hide the embarrassment on my face.

"Stop, bae..." Pia playfully hit his chest.

"Glow know it's all love. These niggas just found out they were brothers three days ago, so it don't count. But I will say... You chose the right brother. T.D Jakes here come with too much shit. I'm talking... long-lost daughters, Mexican princesses, grenades—"

Matteo grunted, which I knew was his way of telling Renello to shut up, but the whole conversation further embarrassed me.

"Nel, shut the fuck up," Shio said as he stood. "Glow ain't fuck us both. She ain't on no Jerry Springer shit." Shio turned and slapped his brother on the back. "Congratulations, you two!"

As he swaggered past me, I stilled. He looked and smelled good, even though he looked like he had a lot on his mind. He winked at me, and shamefully, I had to swallow the saliva that had formed from the gesture. Shio was undeniably fine, but Nel was right. I married the right man because there was just something about Tunan that made me want to come from just looking at him. However, I was standing on business about our arrangement. He was my play husband and nothing more.

"Ain't no need to act modest now. Y'all done fucked and took vows before God."

"Nel!" Pia laughed. "Please leave Glow alone."

Wishing I could ball up in a corner and die, I avoided Tunan's gaze and took the now-empty seat next to him, ensuring I left some space between us. I wasn't particularly upset with Tunan. He'd done what I asked, but the woman in me was not happy that he could easily let days go by and not feel an urge to even check on me. I knew I had some sorting out to do when it came to my feelings for Tunan, but in the meantime, I wanted him to want me. Play husband or not, I was still a woman who liked to be desired.

The waitress from earlier came over and handed out drinks to all the women. I took the cold glass and nodded curtly in thanks. There were two more waitresses behind her, passing out bottles to the men. I couldn't see the labels, but they looked expensive from the shaped of the bottle and the deep color of the liquor. It was early in the afternoon, but that didn't matter to this crew. There had been plenty of days when the ladies got drunk at brunch, and most of the time, it was early morning. The Rinaldi Mob was made up of young, rich, and flashy men and women. They had a lot to celebrate, and most of the time, bottles were flying, and blunts were in rotation for even the smallest occasion.

With my hand gripping the cold glass, I sat stiff as a mannequin. Nel wasn't letting up as he peered at me from behind Pia, whose belly had grown even more in my absence. She hadn't gained any more weight in her face, so that was a plus.

"Damn, it's trouble in paradise already? Y'all just got married last night."

Only then did all the ladies snap their heads our way. I could feel heat creep up my neck, so I placed the cold glass to my lips and took a sip. I needed something to take the edge off. I also wished Nel would shut the hell up.

"Aye."

Peering at Tunan with my peripheral vision, he was removing weed buds from a clear baggie and dumping them into the wrapper held in his left hand.

"Glow." His voice was stern.

Turning my head completely, I licked my lips out of nervousness. Tunan, as always, had a hat propped on his head, but it sat sideways. The short-sleeved Fear of God T-shirt hung from his broad shoulders, but I could see his biceps and chest muscles through the fabric. On his lower half were the matching shorts in the same gray color, and on his feet, a pair of white and gray Nike Air Maxes. He looked too damn good. He looked like his last couple of days had been well spent, unlike mine. Jealousy shivered down my spine thinking of who he'd been spending his time with, but I shook it off just as it appeared. I have a whole baby in my house now. My business needed my attention. I had content to post, money to make, and a sister to look after. That was all I needed on my mind at the moment. Still, my pussy didn't get the memo because she was thudding to the point I had to squeeze my thighs together. To make matters worse, our gray and yellow complemented each other nicely.

Ugh, I thought until we locked eyes.

His brown, lid-covered orbs bore into mine, stirring something in my chest. I had to fight the overwhelming need to be next to him as he silently assessed me. He liked what he saw, just like I did, but if we didn't stop this now, it could crash and burn. Tunan was fresh out of jail, probably for selling drugs. Truthfully, I didn't care why, but it was clear he was trying to get his life together now. He hadn't bought a car, he lived with his sister, and he'd bought my ring off the street. This setup was meant to help him get on his feet and fix his life. I supported that, but I didn't want to participate. I couldn't keep falling victim to the weapon between his legs because, just like he had things going on, thanks to Glee, I had my own issues now.

"When the last time you ate sum'n, Glow?"

Tunan licked the blunt closed while waiting for a response.

Tightening my grip on the glass, my hand was numb from the temperature now, while my heart pounded like a fist against my chest.

"I...I—"

"Don't lie, Glow. I know you've been over there giving Glee hell, forgetting to eat, and throwing up and shit. You need to put sum'n on your stomach before you get to drinking."

He ran the lighter down the length of his blunt, still eyeing me. I visibly relaxed. I didn't know where he was going with that question. I'd thought he'd known for a second, but there was no way he could know what I had been up to the last few days.

"I'm good, Tunan. And I haven't been giving Glee hell. Not that it's any of your business, but I was babysitting for her today since she had to go to school to handle business."

Tunan's brow rose. "School business in Cove City, huh?"

I eyed him because I heard the questioning tone in his words. "Yeah. She was at BU, remember? I told you this."

"Oh, I remember, my baby... I remember what you told me 'bout Lil' Glee."

His tone still had me uneasy. Glee had already snuck a baby on my ass, and I would hate to find out she was keeping more from me. From Tunan's tone, he knew something I didn't, and I didn't like that. When it came to Calista Glee, I needed all the details. The last thing she needed was another baby on top of the one she already had.

"What you been on the last couple days?" Tunan cleared his throat and drove his back further into the couch.

I watched as his legs gapped, smoke flowing from his mouth and dancing into the air. I could still feel the cold stare and cold shoulders of my girls to the right of me, and I felt terrible about ghosting them. Still, I kept my attention on Tunan because my eyes couldn't concentrate on anyone else here, even if I tried.

"Had you called, you would have known," I blurted out before I could catch myself.

Tunan hadn't been a thought—not while I was locked in my room. But the moment I got up and realized he hadn't reached out, I felt a way. There hadn't even been a "hey boo" text. We'd gotten married, had that fiasco at the hospital, had breakfast on Mother's Day, and then he came and fucked me into a coma. I was conflicted because I wasn't sure if I was madder about him being M.I.A. or that he looked like a fucking God, even simply dressed. Before I pulled myself together, I looked like death. Even when Dasani showed up, the lack of care I'd given myself over the past week was evident.

"Come 'ere," he ordered, but his voice was smooth and weed-induced.

I hated the way my body reacted around Tunan. He was walking temptation, and I didn't know if it was some shit he picked up while being locked up and deprived of pussy or if it had been on him his entire life. Since I'd met his family, I concluded that they'd been little charmers since the day they slid out of their mother.

I didn't sit on his lap like the other women, but I did scoot closer to him. Still in his relaxed posture, he wrapped his arms around my waist and pulled me in further until we were hip to hip.

"Is dis shit on paper, or are we puttin' dis shit in motion, Glow? Lemme know, cuz... I ain't gonna be tussling with yo' pretty ass."

Before I could respond, he placed his lips inches from mine and blew a gun. The herbs entered my system, calming my nerves but igniting my hormones. His lips were always so soft and moisturized, and with how tough he was and how much weed he smoked, you would think they'd be crusty.

"Aye, Essex! You gotta put me and Tune on the track. He was coming just like me with the rhyming." Nel cackled from whatever conversation was being had on the other side of the sectional.

I was still locked in Tunan's embrace while he waited for an answer, ignoring Renello. I opened my mouth while searching his face, but nothing came out. I was sure he could feel the drumming of my heart with us being so close. His brown skin was moisturized and blemish-free. His Cuban chain was just the right size for his ensemble. He wasn't wearing his grill today, but that didn't matter. He was fine either way.

"Yeah, I thought so, impossible wife."

"I'm not impossible, Tunan."

He smirked, making me melt. "You are. But it's cool... I'm gone let you make it. When you want dat pussy itched, I'll fall through, even doe I should make yo' difficult ass fein for it."

The thought of him holding out on dick had me sweating. I'd just said I was done with this man, but I couldn't help the way he made me feel.

He saw the horror in my eyes, making him laugh. "You must want dat pussy itched now, my baby."

"I can wait on that, but I wouldn't mind being... licked?"

He locked eyes with me, moistened his lips, and then pressed his lips to mine. "You want me to eat dat pussy, Glow?"

I nodded feverishly. Tunan's pussy eating skills were a twenty out of ten. Having him eat before beating my girl would be a dream come true after this week.

"If you act right, I just might." He pecked my lips again and then let my waist go.

I was so flustered that I was ready to take him to the restroom and let him bend me over. I was sure there were some available rooms in this building from Tunan to make me scream. I sighed quietly, more frustrated with myself. I folded way too easily when it came to this man. I talked so much shit but did nothing to back it up.

"Who got the baby if Glee gone and you here?" he asked, pulling me from my thoughts.

I pulled my phone from my Dior bag to see that my messages still weren't delivered to Glee. She should've made it home by now. Without looking up, I answered, "Dasani's nanny."

"Aite. She bring you?"

I nodded, trying to play with my phone settings to see if my phone was the reason the messages weren't going through.

"We gone dip in a bit," Tunan said. "I'm gone take you to put some food in yo' belly, and den we can chill at your crib, if dat's cool with you."

I had gotten frustrated with the messages still showing green, so I threw my phone back in my purse and looked at Tunan. His eyes were swallowing me as they scanned my frame up and down slowly. The way his lips pulled on the blunt and inhaled the smoke before releasing it a few seconds later had me clinching my crossed legs tighter together.

"You look pretty as fuck, wifey."

I blushed and sat up straighter. "Thank you."

"Aite! Hold y'all shit up," Demise announced, not giving Tunan or me time to say anything else.

He tapped Dasani's thigh, stopping the conversation she was having with Pia, who held up her bottle of water.

"We gone toast to the new comers. Congratulations, Tunan and Glow. Welcome to the fuckin' mob. Glow, you can call me Don." Demise tilted his bottle at us, while everyone took a sip of their drinks.

Tunan hit his bottle and then held it to my lips. I tilted my head back, startled when I felt the champagne about to spill on my clothes.

"Hol' the fuck up! Don, you ain't never toasted to us, nigga! Let me find out you're replacing Rut and Matteo and making Tunan your favorite." Nel turned to Matteo. "How you feel about that, teacher's pet?"

Matteo leaned up and shot daggers at Nel with his eyes. "Man, shutcho bitch ass up!"

"I ain't never toast to you niggas because you niggas ain't married yet." Demise, or Don as I was now to call him, shrugged before popping the cork off his bottle.

"Shit, I'm married," Ezio spoke up. "And yo' ass ain't never toasted shit to me and Jae Bae."

Don's eyes squinted. "Barely, nigga. You know what the fuck you did."

"See... Y'all love bringin' up old shit. My fav is a changed man," Nel said, defending Ezio.

"Fuck yo' fav!"

"Man, you doin' too much around the shorties, Don," Ezio said as Jisei placed her hand on her husband's chest.

She poked her lip out toward Don. "Brother, pleasseeee. Not today."

"Aite... I'll chill." Don relaxed immediately.

"Oh, really, Demise?" Dasani stood while Daylani giggled with Rut.

We all watched as Don rubbed his hand down his face. "What, Dasani?"

"She just blinks, and you do *whatever*. I get the third degree, though."

"Lies." Don waved his wife off.

Dasani folded her arms underneath her breast and huffed. "I asked for that Birkin, but I see Jisei with it."

Jisei danced in her husband's lap with her tongue hanging as Ezio grinned as if this was an everyday occurrence.

"And? You got the bag, too, childish—"

"Don't you dare call me that today, Demise." Dasani's tone flattened. "I got that bag after her!"

Don chuckled. "A day later cuz the color you wanted took longer... Stop trippin'."

Dasani looked at Don with her face scrunched up but didn't say anything else. However, the group wasn't silent for long.

"You mad or nah, Dasani?" Jisei teased.

"Big mad, hoe!" Dasani admitted.

"How you know her husband didn't buy it?" Rut asked.

"Cuz that bitch was two hundred grand. Jisei spend my money like she print it enough as is." Ezio took a swig from his bottle.

"And it's a problem?" Jisei frowned.

"Never, baby. Spend this shit up. It's yo' world, Jae Bae."

"That's right. You hear that. It's my world. Ain't it, brother?"

Don took another swig from his bottle as Dasani stared a hole in the side of his face.

"Answer so I can bop yo' ass in the jaw."

He sucked his teeth toward Dasani before throwing his hands up. "Man, it's all y'all world. You, my mama, Jisei, and Delicate Mafia."

Dasani rolled her eyes, but then smiled when Jisei stood, walking toward her.

"I love you, sister," Jisei said as she eased down onto Dasani's lap, who was back sitting in Don's lap.

He just shook his head as some of the men clowned him. He had them both rotten, and I loved that for them. Their entire dynamic could be a Tubi movie that people actually rewatched.

"As a matter of fact, Glow... Pick out a bag you want. From here on out, any wife added to the team gets a six-figure bag," Dasani announced with a wink.

Don chuckled but didn't protest, and I smiled back because I wasn't sure how to respond.

"What?" Nel shrieked. "Yeah, we need to move the wedding date up, ASAP, Pia Baby. My girl like bags and shit too. Y'all just implementing all types of new shit for this Memphis nigga and his Mukbang-ass lady."

Don ignored Nel's antics and whispered something in his wife's ear. She nodded, then whispered in Jisei's ear. Don then gave all the men a look, and they tapped their women in a way to indicate a need to separate. All the women were now on one side of the couch, while the men were on the other. Essex wasn't mob, but he might as well have been since he was always around and included.

"The baby so pretty." Jisei picked invisible cotton off her tennis dress as she handed Dasani her phone back.

"Fucking gorgeous!" Missy backed her up and turned to ask Pia, "Friend, you still ain't found out what you're having?"

"I find out next week. I was going to let you come so you can throw the gender reveal, but you'll be on *tour*." Pia rolled her eyes.

"I can still come, and I can still throw it while being on tour, so stop that."

"My daddy taking care of it. But... I still expect you and everybody else there."

"Ahhhh! Can't wait!" Daylani said, along with murmurs of excitement from the other wives.

Once the chatter died down, silence took over. Over a dozen eyeballs fell upon me, and I sighed.

"How long y'all gonna give me the cold shoulder?"

Scarlett tapped her chin. "Hmm... Let's see. How long were you married before we found out?"

"Only a few hours," I blurted out quickly. "I was about to tell y'all when Solana had run out, but then Vello started, and then Discover's water broke."

"Where the hell is Solana anyway?" Dasani pulled out her phone.

"I'm not sure," Jisei said a little too fast, and when Dasani gawked at her, she shifted her eyes back to me. "Anyway. You been ignoring us, Glow. You know we don't rock like that."

"But it's cool for you all to be in group chats and have side huddles without me?"

Everyone's face fell except Dasani and Missy's, who was still sipping and averting her gaze between all the women.

"Friend... We don't exclude you on purpose. You weren't a—"

"Mob wife. I get it." I took another sip and gave Jisei a closed-mouth smile.

"Did you marry him to be included, Glow?" Scarlett asked, grabbing my knee as if she was concerned.

"No. I... I don't know." I sighed and looked up at the open industrial ceiling. The visible metal pipes and wooden beams mirrored how complex I felt.

"But you like him... You got to because y'all's chemistry got me hot." Missy fanned.

Mocha grinned and agreed. "Tunan is fine as hell. Memphis niggas remind me a lot of Chicago niggas!"

"And yo' Jagoda Bay nigga gone knock yo' head between the washer and the dryer if he hear yo' ass!" We all laughed at Dasani.

"But for real... I don't know what Tunan and I are doing. But I do like him." I looked at Scarlett and Jisei. "I'm sorry for ghosting y'all. I had a lot going on, but that's no excuse. It's just... I'm an auntie. I'm married. My inbox is overflowing. It's a lot, and I don't do well under pressure."

Pia leaned back and rubbed her belly. "Well, drink up, hoe. You a mob wife now. Pressure is everybody middle name."

"You know we got you, boo. Just don't hide away because we don't do well with being ignored," Scarlett said before hugging me.

"Correct. All is forgiven, friend, but don't do that shit no more." Jisei wiggled her finger at me before hugging Scarlett and me.

"I won't! I promise."

The remaining ladies all rolled their eyes before breaking into laughter.

Just like that, we were back to our old selves, and I was relieved. I would need to talk about what to do about Tunan to somebody. All of the mob wives had their chaotic story on how they married into the mob or married because of the mob, but no one had married for personal gain in the way Tunan and I had.

As I tuned back into the conversation, I smiled, realizing I'd finally gotten what I wanted. I wasn't just friends or affiliated, I was in. I was happy that Dasani understood my position because I wasn't thirsty to be a part of mob life. I was just determined to be included with the women I admired and loved. A group of beautiful ladies dazzled in the most expensive clothes, fragrant with exotic aromas, with their handsome, wealthy men drooling across from them was what this was. Pinterest, Instagram, and an all-black casted movie had nothing on us.

"And don't think we didn't realize you skated over explaining what's going on with you and Tunan." All eyes were on me after Missy's comment.

I shifted in my seat, preparing for the line of questions that were about to be fired off. Tunan and I hadn't talked about what to say to anyone regarding our marriage, but these were my girls, so I planned to be as honest as I could.

"When I saw y'all talking at the Sniff-and-Sip party, I knew it was something between you two." Scarlett grinned.

"I—"

"Fuck that!" Mocha smirked. "I knew when you went live at the steakhouse, you was gonna fold. Granted, I didn't know who he was, but the way you were cheesing in that camera... Yeah. He fucked that night, didn't he?'

"Now, Moke!" Scarlett bumped shoulders with her, but the look on her face said she wanted the tea.

"Girl, if you let that nigga buss that pussy open, so fucking be it. All that waiting shit is overrated. I mean, what's the difference between a man getting it now versus later? The pussy is the same." Missy winked.

"Ion know, Missy. The sooner you let 'em fuck, the crazier you make them. Then, it's like… When they become mob-affiliated, these niggas automatically get fertile. Like, damn, is a fertile dick and a suit a part of the recruiting package?" Dasani scoffed.

"See, I'll take my rap star for 3000, Alex. So glad my man's dick went infertile when he met me. I'll take being a stepmama any day. I love on them, spoil them, and send them back to their mammy's."

"But don't you still have the boys?"

"Girl…" Missy took a swallow of her drink. "We do. She's supposed to pick them up before Essex goes on tour with G Herbo. The boys aren't a problem at all, and I would never tell my man his kids aren't welcome, but I don't have any fuckin' children.

"If Viv can be all over Instagram, arguing with fans over Essex, accepting interviews like she the main bitch, and shaking her ass at them weak-ass bookings, she can get her sons. If she doesn't want them, cool. But she gonna have to let me tag her ass again *and* sign over her rights. I'm not about to play with that hoe. I haven't even figured out what it is I want to do with my own life. I'm not her built-in babysitter."

"No lie, I feel you, bestie," Pia replied. "Either she's going to remove herself from the equation, or step up so y'all can come up with a co-parenting schedule. Being a mama is hard, but being a mama to someone else's kid, while their mama act ignorant, is tough."

"Right. I still gotta go through the properties Ms. Covington left me. Shit, I'm still grieving that crazy-ass lady. Ain't had a second to be alone so I can cry about the shit. Shits just been moving so fast that I haven't had a chance to process it." Missy blinked back what I assumed were tears. "But anyways… Enough about me. Glow, tell us about this *husband*. Since you ain't let us be bridesmaids, walk us through the day." Missy urged.

"Yes! And that ring looks so good," Dasani complimented. She was being nice because if she knew my ring had been bought off the street, she would probably smack Don for letting Tunan do that.

Glancing down at it, I smiled faintly, ignoring the pounding in my chest. I was crazy as hell to still be wearing it. But for some reason, I didn't want to take it off. Our wedding had been a hot-ass mess. That damn preacher and that God-forsaken church lived rent-free in my damn head. I was happy to have met some of Tunan's family, but Memphis was a wild place. It had been nothing but theatrics from the moment I got off the plane.

"We basically went to a courthouse. Then, I got on a plane and came back here for the engagement dinner."

"Booo! Tomato! Tomato! I can tell from that live of y'all on the porch it was more than what you're trying to make it seem." Jisei squinted at me.

"Right. Only good pussy can make a nigga have his whole family out there taking ya fucking braids down. Especially in that hot-ass Memphis heat." Missy fanned herself as if she could feel the warmth.

"I can't stand when a nigga's whole family is fine. I'm so damn glad Lorenzo ain't got no siblings. I know Tunan 'nem gave their mama hell growing up," Mocha whispered.

The men were right across from us, but the sounds of the gambling machines around us drowned out our conversation.

Sister. They were raised by their sister.

"So, y'all didn't consummate the marriage?" Scarlett asked.

"We..." I smirked, thinking about Tunan fucking me in the old-ass car when I thought he was Shio's worker. "We'd done that already prior to getting married... And, after."

"Ha!" Missy clapped her hands together. "Fuck you talmbout! Glow, I knew you had it in you, my girl. Put that pussy on him and had him marrying you, ASAP. That's like a Rinaldi record, ain't it?"

Dasani placed her glass to her lips in a teasing smile. "Hell yeah, it is! Demise had to trick me, with his ole ugly ass." Dasani shook her head in disgust but then grinned again.

"We've had sex. But it's more of a business transaction, y'all. He needed a wife." I shrugged.

"And what the fuck did *you need*? You already paid, you're famous on the net, and you fine as fuck. You can get any nigga you want, friend. So, what was it?" Jisei cocked her head.

"Shit... I married Matteo because I was flat on my ass, Glow. My mama was a crackhead, stealing everything from my baby and me. And I'd just gotten fired from my job. A man offering to pay me to be his wife sounded crazy, but it also sounded like a plan that I didn't have."

"I had Zo's baby. He needed a wife, and there was no way he was marrying another hoe."

"My brother owns all this shit and told me I had no choice. It worked out, though. I love me some Ezio Cuppucio," Jisei added.

All of the women had married for a feasible reason, and hearing what I already knew out loud had me feeling more and more like a fool. Dasani had her legs crossed, swirling the ice cubes in her glass as she held it up.

"I... I wanted to fit in, I guess. I wanted y'all to see me as an equal."

I felt so stupid. The words burned as they slipped out of my mouth, and the way everyone looked at me with confusion, then realization, made me sink further into the couch.

"I outta slap the shit out of you! What the fuck, Glow!" Jisei screeched.

"Umm hmm. I done told her... I done told her. Then, she had the nerve to hide from us, like Glee having a baby is something to be ashamed about."

"I don't know what for. At least Glee's eighteen and in college. I was sixteen without a pot to piss in."

"I was underage too. My daddy was pissed but, shit... look at me. I finished school and everything." Mocha reminded me of the degree she earned, which had been collecting dust.

But Glee didn't have the resources Mocha had. She also didn't have a rich mobster as her baby daddy, nor was our daddy "street rich." Still, I kept my thoughts in my head.

"I hear you, Mocha. It just caught me off guard. I was not expecting a baby."

"And I wasn't expecting my sister to kill a car full of niggas for her boyfriend. But it happened, and the most I can do is support her. That's all Glee needs from you. She's got all of us. She won't be alone in this. She will still be able to go to school. We got nannies and shit, and we got school, housing, and food money. It's okay to be disappointed, but be easy on her. That postpartum shit is no joke." Pia rubbed her own belly.

"Yeah... I feel bad." Jisei stared at me with a shake of her head, causing me to groan. "Whattttt?"

"Oh, nothing. I just can't believe you did that crazy shit... Married a man you don't even know. You wild as fuck, Charisma Glow. But it wouldn't be the mob if all of us didn't have a crazy-ass story. Who would have ever known my cool-ass neighbor would be locked in this shit with me?" Jisei chuckled.

"Well, is the sex even good? I know you ain't marry into an organized crime for mediocre dick..." Pia's brow rose.

My cheeks burned, and I looked across at Tunan. He was enthralled in conversation with the other men. It didn't take long for him to lock eyes with me. We held each other's gaze, and it caused my breathing to hitch. Nel, grabbing Tunan's shoulder, broke our stare, and I focused back on the women around me.

"Hell yeah!" all of the women replied in unison, followed by loud shrills.

Tunan could fuck. I didn't know whether he had gained the skill while in jail, due to being so deprived, or if it had been in him all along. But it was a wonder that he didn't have a baby mama or a crazy ex sniffing about. His dick game was that phenomenal.

The attention was off of me when Pia started talking about the gender reveal and the girls discussing Discover. I was grateful as the women fell into side conversations. The liquor had loosened my nerves, but I knew I was going to pay for this tomorrow. The way liquor made me feel sluggish the next day, plus the guilt of the extra calories, nearly had me groaning out loud. Glancing around, the women were all smiling, rings glistening, even Missy. She and Essex weren't engaged, but he had iced her out from head to toe. I smiled at how within the group of women, everyone had their someone or two. The sisterhood had me thinking about Glee.

Searching my purse again for my phone, a frown appeared on my face when I saw all the messages were still green and hadn't delivered. With my brows knitted together, I tried calling Glee and twice more afterward when she didn't pick up. Pulling up the outdoor Ring camera on my phone, I checked the driveway, and when the Lexus didn't show, I switched to the inside cameras. Both Nelsa and Pearla were standing over the baby, smiling. I received a notification that someone was in the driveway and sighed with relief.

However, when I didn't recognize the car, I frowned again. Bella and Mahzeyah hopped out laughing, and I pulled my head up from my phone.

"Pia...."

She was laughing with Missy, but when she noticed the panic on my face, she stopped. "What happened?"

"Can you call Pearla and see if she heard from Glee?"

I knew she hadn't. Still, for my sanity, I needed to double-check. Glee should have made it back from Cove City by now. And even then, her phone should have been working hours ago. Something wasn't right.

Pia stood, dialed Pearla, and placed her on speaker.

"Hey, sister. You heard from Glee?"

"Umm, no. I been trying to call her, but the messages aren't sending. We been at Glow's house waiting for her. Is something wrong?' Pearla's voice grew more and more shaky as she spoke.

I shook my head at Pia. There was no reason to alarm the girls until we knew what was happening.

"Everything is good, Pearla. Lemme call you back."

I tried calling Glee several more times and got the same results. I even checked the location, powering my phone on and off, but it kept saying the location was unavailable.

I panted. "Oh my fucking God! I should have never let her go."

Squeezing my eyes shut, I could feel the veins pulse in my neck. My mouth was dry as sandpaper, and my stomach felt full as if I'd just consumed a whole feast when I hadn't eaten anything today.

"Demise!" Dasani called out.

I was still trying to call Glee and had even stood up, beginning to pace.

I should have never let her go.

"What happened?" Don was no longer popping bottles or passing insults between the men. He was front and center with his wife.

"Glee... Glow's baby sister. Nobody can get a hold of her."

"Hunh? Where was the last place she was at?" Don turned to me.

"What's going on? You good?" Tunan placed his hand at the top of my back, and though his presence was welcoming, I was still going haywire on the inside.

The bells and dings and laughter and chatter around us faded into a dull hum. I was staring at the location again, and nothing had changed.

"She... She went to BU in Cove City to transfer. She was supposed to get a room for the night, but she told me she was coming home when we last texted. Her phone is going to voicemail now, the messages aren't sending, and I can't get a hold of her."

A cold fist clenched around my heart, squeezing until I couldn't breathe. Panic clawed at my throat, a silent scream trapped inside. Every instinct yelled at me to do something, but I was frozen, paralyzed by fear and uncertainty. The world seemed to tilt on its axis, and the vibrant colors of the casino faded into a dull, blurry haze. This couldn't be happening.

What if she's hurt? What the fuck happened? Where is my sister?

"Tunan," Don called out, all of us turning our attention to him as if he'd called us.

Tunan was doing that thing he did when he ran his hand down his waves, making my heart fall to the pits of my shoes.

"What do you know?" Don asked, confusing me because, as far as I knew, Tunan didn't know my sister beyond their meeting after he'd fucked me into a sleep coma.

"Look, I don't know what's going on, but I might know where we can find her."

That didn't make any sense—not even a little. Tunan knowing Glee's whereabouts was puzzling, but I didn't care about the how. I wanted answers on where she was. Pushing down the urge to slap Tunan until he told me what I wanted to know, I steadied my breathing and did what the rest of the mob wives would have done—let Don handle it.

CHAPTER 9

SOLANA DAMITA LEDESMA

I'd been struck breathless. As I struggled to take my next breath, it felt like I'd been punched in the chest. Along with my throat, my skin, my bones, and my eyes—all felt raw. It was as if I'd been dragged through the pits of hell, and the trail was never-ending. Except there was no devil. There was no dragging. There was no fire. Well, there **was** *fire in the dark eyes of the man I'd come to obsess over.*

Popping sounded in my ears, and puffs of air fluttered my nostrils. I didn't know how long we'd been driving, because I'd been in my head, trying to make sense of it all. The date. The drugs. The shootings. The child. The woman. The plane. The mail. Then, I was removed from the home for the second time in twenty-four hours and stuffed into the car. And like yesterday, Shio hadn't said a word to me.

The truck came to a screeching halt, jerking my body forward. My heart leaped in my chest, pounding against my rib cage. My hands were shaking, my feet were bare, and I was wounded in pride. I shook my head and grabbed Shio's arm as he put the truck in park.

"Shio. ¡No era mío! Te lo juro. No era mío. ¡Jamás haría eso! ¡Jamás! ¡Jamás podría! ¡Shio! ¡Por favor, mírame! (***Shio. It wasn't mine! I swear to you. It wasn't mine. I would never do that! I would never! I could never! Shio! Please look at me!)*** *"*

Shio, instead, got out of the truck, leaving it running. With my eyes wide, I glanced around. I wasn't familiar with this neighborhood. It was suburban, but instead of homes like those in Shio's area, these were casas adosades (townhouses). All the yards were neatly manicured, and the only other person outside—from what I could see—was an older gentleman across the street, checking his mailbox.

Mail. Less than an hour ago, Shio's mailman had knocked on the door. Nel was dead asleep, so I answered and took the mail. The baby was still sleeping, so I walked it to his office. Instead of leaving the pile of mail there, I began reading the names. Why Uriah was receiving mail at Shio's residence was baffling to me and stirred something in my chest.

The summer air brushed my side and shook me from my thoughts. The passenger door had opened. Shio, in all his glory, stood. He'd changed. A hoodie—black. But the look in his eyes hadn't. Scary and very unsure.

He took a step back, instructing me without a word. With my head bowed, I stepped out of the car, barefoot, feeling the warm concrete beneath my feet. Saliva flooded my mouth at the thought of the bag of cocaine Bahati had found in the baby's hands. I'd wished I had grabbed it, even though I had no idea what Shio was about to do to me.

He trudged behind me as I trekked up the sidewalk toward the front door. The attached houses on the street looked identical, but porch décor and flowerbeds gave each one its own personality. Shio's arm brushed my shoulder as he reached around me and twisted the front door's doorknob. I stepped inside, enamored by the décor. No matter how this place looked or smelled, I didn't want to be here, especially if Shio wasn't staying with me. From the urgency to get here, I knew he wasn't.

Turning on my feet, I faced Shio. I hadn't gotten the chance to plead my case when my feet were dangling in the air, and I was being carried out over his shoulder. I could feel his face on the side of my bottom with each thump of his steps. I knew better than to fight as I watched the world around me upside down. He descended a set of stairs, which made my stomach sour. We were in a basement—that much I knew because I'd frequented one multiple times per week to work out with this man.

He flipped me back over, setting me on my feet. The carpet felt comforting, a stark contrast to the hot concrete outside. Towering over me, Shio swiped his nose with his thumb, something he seemed to do when he was upset. My eyes pleaded, begging him to hear me out. His were fiery hot; the uncertainty just moments ago, gone. I knew in that moment that there was nothing I could say or do to make him believe me. Still, I had to try.

Reaching up, I palmed his face, my panties flooding as our skin connected, even though arousal was the last thing my body should have been feeling.

"Shio. Por favor—"

"Solana, baby..."

My heart sped, and my eyes widened. "¿Si?"

He grabbed my arms, but not in a way that would hurt me. Holding them up, he squeezed them, then released the pressure before placing my wrist to the side of his face. With his eyes lowered, he took a long sniff of my skin and closed his eyes. My chest was going haywire. It was nearly impossible for me to stay still.

"Yo no hice eso. No te haría daño... a tu...(I did not do that. I wouldn't hurt your... your...)

He removed my wrist from his nostrils but kept them in his hand, and I understood now that it was to stop me from touching him.

"My what? My what, Solana? I want to hear you say it. Dilo. (Say it.)"

"Tu... Tu... Hija..." Spilled out of my mouth, and the admission was like a dagger to the chest—painful.

"Say that shit in fucking English, Solana. English, baby. My what?" He gritted his teeth, and at the same time, he was backing me into a wall. Well, it couldn't have been a wall because it was cold and slick like a metal. Like steel.

"Your daughter," I said, exasperated in my voice. Saying it nearly knocked the wind out of me.

"My fucking daughter. You so gone off that shit, Solana, that you can't even see what the fuck is in front of you."

"Shio. I... I, please. I don't comprehend."

"What the fuck do you want from me, Solana?"

"I... I..." I felt defeated.

Truly, I didn't know what I wanted. I wanted Shio, but I didn't want to bring him down with me. My father didn't seem to want me. He'd just admitted he couldn't protect me, and that he would ship me off to the next criminal as soon as he found someone and the coast was clear with Felipe. What I wanted clearly didn't matter even if I did know. It had never mattered—not then, not now, not ever. What I wanted didn't make sense because it had never been my reality in México. The only thing that made sense was the guy I met at the party, and again at the club. He had what I wanted and needed. He had what would make me forget the pain of being unloved by every man in my life.

Cocaína (cocaine).

Shio reached inside his pocket and pulled out the clear bag of drugs. My eyes lit up, and my mouth watered. He had what I wanted. Nothing else mattered in the moment. I couldn't truly have Shio anyway, at least not with deaths and pain to follow. This was the next best thing. In a perfect world, I would have both, but since I couldn't, I would settle for the one that faithfully made me feel without consequences.

"You too fuckin' good for this shit, Solana. You lettin' this shit win. You been lettin' it win. When it ain't in you, you sleep. When it is, you party. You don't know who the fuck you are or what the fuck you want cuz you doped up all the time, and when you not doped up, you thinkin' about dope. But since you can't seem to get your head right—"

He grabbed my chin, lifting my head as I ceased breathing. His touch was only to my face but had traveled down below.

"I'm gonna do that shit for you," he mumbled.

He reached around me again, twisted another doorknob, and the wall behind me moved. Shio caught me around the back, tucking the drugs in his pocket. I wanted to claw them out, but I knew that was another battle I would never win. I knew his strength, and I knew my limits.

He'd backed us into a room where we were now standing. It was smaller than the one back at his home, but it had the same necessities. A bed, a TV, dressers, a nightstand, and an en suite bathroom. A white duvet covered the full-sized bed, and the décor was calming yet girly, though neutral. I could tell someone had just cleaned the bathroom from the aroma of cleaning products.

"I can't have you in my home, Solana."

I felt a momentary panic as my mind jumped on what he'd said. "Shio! Please!"

"Don't fucking beg." He spewed, a vein jumping in his neck. Even that was sexy.

"Shio, baby. I... I can stop. It's not that bad. I can stop. I just want to be with you! I do. I just don't want to get you hurt!"

"Me and hurt don't even belong in the same sentence."

"Shio!"

"I'm gonna hold onto yo' phone. But here..." he tossed another cell on the bed behind me. "Don't call yo' bitch-ass daddy either. It ain't shit he can do for you. And don't put the fuckin' police in my business."

"I wouldn't do that!" I looked at him as if he were the one on drugs. I'd learned very long ago that my life was meant to be off the policía (police)

radar back home. I knew this to be true for America too.

"I know you wouldn't, Solana, baby..."

Shio backed out of the room, and when I tried running after him, the steel door shut.

"Shio! Shio! What is this!" Using my fist, I pounded at the door, connecting with the cold metal. "Shio! Don't do this. Papi! Papiiii! Don't do this!"

Glancing around, there were no windows. I ran to the bathroom, and again, there were no windows there either. I was locked in—locked inside of a fancy prison with a mouth that craved only two things that I knew I couldn't have.

Shio and cocaína (cocaine).

I had no idea how long it had been since I'd been locked in the room. Among other memories, the one of Shio leaving me here this morning replayed in my mind. Unlike Shio's house, where I had access to the windows and could tell when it was night and day, this room was void of them. I could have turned the TV on to get the time, since I knew no more than a few hours had passed, but I opted not to. I'd been in bed, curled on top of the covers, since he'd left me here.

My nose was stuffy, my eyes were puffy, and my nerves were completely in disarray. I was locked inside a room, not knowing how long I was going to be here. I'd gone from barricading myself in back at Shio's to now being barricaded in by Shio. The steel door was in place to keep someone from getting out, and I couldn't stop the questions about why he had this room.

Was someone here before me? Why would he need a room to lock someone in? Had he created this room knowing he'd lock me away? Was this meant for me from the beginning, but he opted to keep me in his home instead? What was the purpose of locking me away? Was this supposed to be a prison? I had so many questions, but I knew that if Shio were standing here, I wouldn't ask them. *Insegura.* (Insecure.)

The bed was soft, and the pillows remained cool. The one my head was propped on hadn't warmed at all, and at first, I thought it was another mind thing happening, but after an hour or so of constant coolness, I figured out something inside the pillow kept its temperature. I needed it, so I was grateful. The headache that was beginning to brew would have come on full-fledged had it not been for the relief the pillow provided.

I wasn't sure whether it was the drugs that kept me oblivious to the predicament my father had placed me in, or Shio's good looks as we spent so much time together over the weeks, but while lying here, I'd come to the realization that my head had been in the clouds. I was in a foreign country with foreign people. I had no allies, no friends, and the man who had opened his home to me had now locked me away.

At least he gave you a cell phone.

But who would I call? Who? I had no one.

Tightening my arms around my stomach, I couldn't fathom how much had gone down in the last twenty-four hours. The shootout wasn't what had me on edge the most. It was knowing that Shio was now sharing his home with Bahati, alone. The beautiful African woman who could bring any man to her knees, even with her broken arms and tattered clothing. Bahati should have been the least of my worries, but I couldn't help myself. She was gorgeous. When she tossed her arms around Shio's neck, my heart sank. I wanted Shio to be with me, but Bahati looked like she should be his companion.

I cringed at the idea of who my companion would be. My father had attempted to rationalize his thinking, but the disappointment grew with each word he spoke. I should have been more affected by my father's revelation about owing Shio's Don, but I wasn't. I'd never known my papa to have an issue with pesos, but I knew my father was not a competent man. We'd been well off my entire life, and I never understood why, because my father was not a smart man. I'd seen his decisions for twenty-plus years, and they never showed a man of honor and discipline. For him to trade me, knowing he'd already agreed to my betrothal to the Rodríguezes was the most reckless thing he could have done for his organization. It was as if my father was saying "fuck everyone" as long as his hands were cleaned.

Now, in this room, I was beginning to feel something I should have felt the moment Shio placed that gun to my head: *miedo* (fear). I wasn't scared of what would happen to me. I wasn't scared of what not having the drugs would do to my body. I was scared that I'd lost Shio forever.

I heard the sliding of something and peeled my eyes open. I was facing the door, so light spewed in through a small opening. My knees were pulled up to my chest as I hugged them and waited. I wasn't being let out, and I knew that because the door didn't open. Also, Shio was done with me. The look of finality on his face when he called my name was one I'd never forget. Whatever we had ended before it began, and as painful as it was, *maybe* that was for the best.

It *was* for the best.

"I got you some food. I know you hungry." A scruffy but youthful male voice that I didn't recognize drawled. At the same time, a thank-you bag with a food carryout tray was pushed inside. "It's a mini fridge in there. We stocked that shit with water and shit. Snacks too."

The aroma of spices, steam, and deep-fried food filled the room. Although it excited my senses, it did nothing for my belly. I wasn't hungry. I wasn't anything, actually. I'd cried to myself for hours. But I was fresh out of tears, fresh out of pleas. The only thing I wanted right now was *cocaína* (cocaine).

"Thank you." I rasped. I had no plans on eating, but I appreciated the gesture.

"Solana... That's yo' name, right?"

"Yes." I squeezed my knees to my chest.

"How you get on that shit? Cocaine?"

With my eyes closed, I moistened my dry teeth with a swipe of my tongue. I was craving the feeling. I could go days without the drug, I really could. But now, my body felt like it couldn't go another second without it.

"I... It just happened."

It had. It had just happened. I wasn't force-fed drugs. My parents didn't introduce it. I didn't stumble upon it. It simply just happened. A night out turned into the most fun I'd ever had. And once I realized that my problems were non-existent while inebriated, I'd taken *cocaína* (cocaine) ever since.

"Well, I hate to break it to ya, but you gone have to *unhappen* that shit. It ain't a good look, Mexi-Mami."

My head snapped up. "Neltz?"

The voice sounded too mature to be Neltz, but my mind was so foggy that maybe I just didn't recognize him. After all, we'd only had a single conversation, and that wasn't enough to commit it to memory.

"Nah. That's the lil' cuz. I'm Italian."

Italian.

I tried racing my brain to see if I remembered him. I'd heard his name but couldn't fathom if I'd seen or met him.

"Shio is my big cousin."

"Oh..."

"Yeah."

We both sat in silence. It was long enough that I'd closed my eyes.

"My cousin... He fucks with you."

My response was a chuckle. Shio didn't *fuck* with me. It was safe to say Shio hated me now.

"Real talk, he do. He got us watchin' you and shit... round the clock. If he didn't give a damn 'bout you, he wouldn't have gone out of his way to make this shit happen."

"Yeah, well... I'm no good for Shio. He has a family now. That's where his focus should be."

Bahati, the beautiful. Her skin was as dark as mine, though our nationalities differed. As soon as she emerged from the closet, I detected an African accent. Even after being kidnapped, with us not knowing what the Rodríguezes had put her through, she was still so pretty. Not a blemish was on her face, and her high cheeks and chin were rounded. The braids fit her face well, and they were done to perfection. Her lips were plump, and her eyes curved upward at the corners in a seductive manner. Even I could see her body was to die for under both the torn clothing and the silk pajamas. She'd carried a child and done it well. A child for Shio. She was the mother of his baby, a baby I hadn't known existed. A baby Shio hadn't known existed.

But the Rodríguezes had known, and it made me wonder how long they'd known about me living under Shio's roof.

Bahati and Uriah were proof that Shio had a type. Both women carried a certain confidence, confidence that I'd never possessed and probably never would. I'd only been in the same room as Uriah once, but the power she possessed in simply existing was compelling. Bahati had a different kind of confidence—one that screamed I'm beautiful, and I know it.

Her attacking me was strange in the sense that I hadn't been in situations where I'd had to fight a woman. However, I knew how to fight. My brothers and I had countless physical fights. She had a right to be upset, but I preferred questions over reactions. She'd found drugs in her baby's hand and automatically accused me. While I was upset, I did understand her plight. I, being caught on drugs by Shio, didn't help my pleading of being innocent. But even being childless, I knew that if it had been my child, I would have attempted to fight me too.

"So, you a quitter?" The voice on the other side of the door—Italian—asserted.

"I'm a—" I thought of the best word to use in English. "I'm a realer."

"The word you lookin' for is realist, Mexi-Mami." He corrected me, but not in a mocking manner.

"Si. We don't belong."

Silence again.

"Besides cocaine, what do you wanna do with your life? What are you? Twenty-five?"

"Twenty-six," I corrected.

"That's still young as fuck, Mexi-Mami."

"Yeah. But it does not feel that way... I... I have been told that I would be a wife since I was a child. There had not been time for me to think otherwise," I confessed.

"So, just thinking... and I'm talkin' thinking hard as hell about it, what you wanna do? It's okay if you need time to think or if you change your mind later but tell me what comes to your mind first."

Running my tongue across my teeth again, I felt a tingle in my veins. I needed a hit. I couldn't have a hit, though, so I thought about what it was Italian was asking me. I didn't understand why he was asking me this, but he was placed here to "watch" me, so the least I could do was engage in conversation.

"If you could get out today, no cravin' drugs. What is it you wanna do?"

I could still feel Shio's daughter's head on my chest. The silkiness of her hair felt like it was still in my fingers. The calm I felt from just holding her and having her in my presence centered me. Grounded me. Satisfied me. I was the same way with my baby brothers; I loved caring for them and teaching them and protecting them—giving them what I never had.

"I partied a lot, but it was only because I was chasing the numbness. The high, Italian—it stops all the worry and doubt. I meet new people, and even if I'm never going to see them again, I almost live my life through theirs. The newlyweds that are on honeymoon and are overly friendly because they are high on life. The group of women who are on a girls' trip and are sloppy drunk, leaving the stress of their day-to-day lives in their home countries. It's all fun for the moment. It helps me forget my future... My present.

"But, if I had my choice, I'd still be a wife. Not only a wife, but a mother. Some days, I say I don't want it, but deep down, I do. I just would like it if I had my choice in who I chose to be the father to my children. But since I do not, I can own a business, maybe. I can go back to school to maybe care for children or become a teacher.

"I really do not know. Everything seems hard for me."

I could hear Italian shift before his voice clearly spoke. "As a woman, and shit... a man, too... But we ain't talkin' 'bout niggas right now. But muthafuckas be sayin' you supposed to have goals for yourself. Goals that will help you live the life you deserve and desire. But I believe women have options, so I believe you have options too.

"It's like this... If you wanna be a professional with a fancy degree and booming career, you know you gonna have to put your all into schooling. You gotta study. You gotta show up to class every day. If you want to be a high-earning entrepreneur typa of bitch—my bad, typa girl—you gonna have to have a vision and hustle your ass off.

"You gotta push yo' shit like crack in the eighties... Awl damn! My bad, no pun or no slick shit. But yeah, Mexi-Mami. If you want to be kept, be a rich nigga's Barbie, then you gonna have to invest in your appearance and your mindset. I ain't saying you gotta have a slim, Coke bottle figure or a BBL or no shit like that. It's niggas out here that love BBWs and odd builts, just the same. But you gonna have to keep yourself up to even attract that type of nigga that's gonna keep you. Looking good, smelling good, dressing well, even if the clothes and shit are from the clearance aisle... You gonna have to be that man's version of a walking dream.

"Now, what do all those women have in common, regardless of their goals being different? I'll answer it for you—discipline. They have fuckin' discipline. I ain't here to judge you or no shit like that, but you lack discipline, Mexi-Mami."

I swallowed the thick saliva that had built up in my mouth during his speech.

"Ain't shit wrong goin' either route. The men in my family have always provided for the women—that's just how it is. That's how I was raised, and that's the typa nigga I'ma be when the time comes. If you wanna be a wife, you gonna have to walk like a wife and talk like a wife. You gonna have to act like a wife, even before you're officially a wife. Especially if you're tryna be a wife to a nigga that ain't gone require you to do nothing but be his."

I'd said it already, but now, after listening to Italian's words, I could not see myself having a job or owning a business. I had never been led to believe that I could be that type of woman. To me, being a wife was the easy way out—I just did not like having to be the wife of the man my father had chosen for me.

My father revealing that he did not purposely match me with Felipe was a short-lived relief. It made me feel like my father had not gone too far off the deep end, and that he did love me in his own way. But what was the use now? When a Rodríguez had their claws inside of you, there was no letting go. As quickly as I'd praised my father, his name alone soured my stomach. He did not think Shio was good enough for me. He wanted me with my own kind or someone with fair skin. My papa had some nerve. Shio was good enough to hide me until he got a plan together, but that was it. My father had audacity. He was continuing to prove my thoughts about him to be factual.

"My cousin gone eventually have to marry. So you can sit in this bitch and sulk and rot. Or... You can fight back. You can fight that fuckin' addiction. You can fight whatever is in your head saying shit that ain't true. You can fight all them demons that's up on you.

"Shit gonna be harder than a bitch. It's gonna be painful too. It might damn near kill you. But seeing him walk another bitch down the aisle gone kill you for sure—no mights about that shit. You gonna be wishin' you had of gotten your shit together so you can be the one. On foe 'nem."

I heard a lighter flick, and then he pulled on what I assumed was marijuana, and seconds later, the potent funk confirmed it was.

"I looked up online that the best way to get a person off drugs was to not do drugs around them. But, shit... If you can't handle a lil' weed smoke, you ain't gonna make it in this family anyway. We all get high as fuck, but on that green only."

Weed didn't bother me, nor did it make me crave *cocaína* (cocaine). I'd been craving it since before he slid open the door hatch, anyhow.

"You too young to be a powda head, Mexi-Mami."

"I'm too young to be alone too," I whispered.

"But you ain't alone, though. Me and my cousins gonna be here with you every day, makin' sure you straight. Ain't nobody gonna violate you or mistreat you. We just want you to get better. We want you to get right. And when you get yo' shit together, you just might have a chance to be with Shio."

The burning of his weed sounded, and then the exhale of his lungs. "But sometimes, being alone ain't a bad thing. It's when you alone that you can truly hear your fuckin' thoughts. Your wants. Your needs. Shit... God."

"Si..." I choked as my eyes watered.

Closing them, I refused to let more tears fall. I was feeling so much and nothing at all. Lost, afraid, empty, craving, exhaustion, heartbroken—it was like feeling many terrible things at once and not being able to do anything about it.

"So, I'm in prison? I'm a... prisionera (prisoner)."

I could hear what sounded like him standing to his feet.

"We don't fuck with twelve, Solana. Just think of this shit as a real nigga rehab."

"*Rehab*?" I asked in a panicked tone.

I did not need rehab. I just needed to get one last hit and go back to only doing the drug when I partied. I only used it when I was stressed or when I felt that ache in my stomach. I was not addicted to the drugs.

"Don't worry, our cousin Ezio had to go through this same shit. You gonna do better, though, cuz you got the younger generation watchin' out for you. We gonna get you right, So-So. Eat up and get some rest. You in for a mean-ass rollercoaster."

The door shut, and I stood up from the bed. Something hit the floor with a thud, and seeing that it was Shio's cell phone, I snatched it up. My mouth went slack, and my head spun. They wouldn't keep me in here, hoping I no longer craved the drug, would they? I could get sick. I will get sick. They were not professionals. He sounded younger than I. What if I coded? I was locked in a room in a basement and could die if I coded!

Needing to feel something, I stumbled to the bathroom. The tile, cold beneath my feet, grounded me the way the pillow had. I flipped the light switch and stared at myself in the mirror. My hair needed brushing, the lazy ball I'd knotted at the top of my head leaning to the side. My eyes were puffy, my nose a reddish hue, and my lips cracked. Turning the faucet knob, water flowed from the spigot. Cupping my hands beneath, I filled them with water and splashed my face. Shio thought I was an addict. He had said it, too, but locking me in a room to cleanse the drugs from me wasn't going to do anything.

I was not an addict.

I liked to use drugs when I was feeling stressed and when I needed to relax. That was it. It was no different than a person having an occasional cigarette or the *canabis* (cannabis) they all smoked.

The water should have cooled my skin, but I was hot now. Feeling like I was suffocating, I removed the hoodie from my body and tossed it to the floor.

"Ahhhhhhhhh!"

Screaming did not help. Nothing would help. Removing my shirt didn't make me feel any less warm. Pulling at my shorts, I plopped down on the toilet to relieve a bladder that was not full to begin with.

How long would he keep me here? A week? A month? A year?

Imposible. Él no lo haría. (Impossible. He wouldn't.)

Looking down, I saw something brown sticking out of the sweatshirt I had just removed. Still planted on the toilet, I reached for the object. A withered, worn leather notebook that did not belong to me sat in my hands. I'd watched Shio write in the bound book many times. I wondered what he wrote about on the days he said no more than two words to me. Now with it in my hands, I could see how worn and old it truly was. I flipped it, looking to see if a name was engraved or if the book was not bound to the leather covering.

When I had gone into Shio's office to place the mail, the leather book called to me from his desk. I halted and thought quickly before leaving the office with the book and the mail. I did not know why I had put his notebook in my pocket, but I had, and now it was here, locked in the room with me.

Lifting the cover, I immediately slammed it back into place and tossed it back onto the floor. I did not care what was in the old notebook anymore. Shio's thoughts no longer matter because I no longer matter to him. Italian made a good argument, but he hadn't seen the fury in Shio's eyes when he dragged me here. All I cared about was getting out of this room. I would figure everything else out when I was free.

Grabbing the phone from the vanity, I went to the text messaging app. He had either cleared the phone or had never used the phone because it was bare. Typing my number into the sender box, I clicked to send a message.

You can't keep me here!

Shio! Just let me go back to México! I'd rather be with Felipe than to be locked here!

Shio you can't do this!

I knew he had viewed the texts because the read receipts were on. Instead of making myself look and feel worse than I already did, I tossed the phone in the same direction as the notebook and sat there, staring at the wall straight ahead.

Italian was right—this was going to be a *montaña rusa* (roller-coaster).

CHAPTER 10
TUNAN "TUNE" PAYNE

After giving my dick a shake, I tucked it into my briefs and pulled my pants up my waist. Don had handed me the keys and given me an address. In the Ferrari, the six-hour drive had taken only four. I'd been needing to pee for the last two hours, but I wouldn't dare stop. I'd been shocked that Glow had even accompanied me on the drive. The ride was quiet as we trailed behind a line of sports cars, carrying the rest of the mobsters and their women.

Outside of an occasional sniffle, Glow hadn't said a word. Don had insinuated that I'd known more than I'd given Glow, but she still hadn't questioned me. I knew we had to have a serious conversation—this just wasn't the time or place for that shit. Not knowing where Glow's head was at, I couldn't tell if she even cared to talk about that or anything else.

With washed, damp hands, I pushed the door open and paused as a group of surgeons in teal scrubs rushed past me. I kept walking, and the vinyl floors squeaked beneath my Nikes from the fresh wax. The walls were uncomfortably white, and the ceiling was covered with white acoustic tiles. The waiting area was empty of the people I'd walked in with because seconds before I went to the bathroom, we'd been called back after waiting an hour. Glow had paced the entire time, with the women trying their best to keep her sane.

"Third floor," the receptionist called out.

She sat behind a desk, chewing gum as if she didn't witness death and disappointment all day. Her long lashes fluttered, and though she wasn't all that in the face, her body made up for it. I'd seen it when we first rushed in, while she was bent over, shuffling through a cart of papers. She hadn't read the room when she turned around, giving us all fuck-me eyes. It didn't matter that we'd been tense. The men I'd come in with had dispersed, and with only me left behind, she hadn't changed her sentiments—ole girl was looking to get fucked.

"Which room?" I inquired.

She swiped her tongue across her glossed lips. They were too small for her face, and the ashy pink color didn't suit her for work. It didn't look good on her skin tone at all. Still, I kept a neutral expression and waited for her to tell me Glee's room information.

"Can I get your number first? Or better yet... I can show you why taking my number would be good for your fine ass."

She shifted her eyes to the supply closet across from us. I scowled, looking toward the closet, then back to her face, now sporting a big-ass smile, showing all her teeth. I'd never gotten my dick wet in a supply and hadn't planned on it happening today either.

"Room numba?"

"Is that an accent? Sound like you from Memphis. I love Memphis niggas." She bit her lip, and I sighed.

My patience was as thin as her edges. Instead of cursing her ass out, I went the easy route. "You'n know if I just finished takin' a shit and barely wiped my ass, bruh. But you ready to slurp me up in a germ-infected-ass supply closet?"

She shrugged and sniffed the air. "You smell fine to me and look even better." She grinned, and there was pink gloss on her coffee-stained teeth.

"Miss lady, I'm married. Now, if you can tell me da room numba to my sis-in-law, I would greatly appreciate it." I gave a tight-lipped grin.

Her smile fell, and her eyes went to my hand that was crossed at my waist.

"Ion see a ring. That's my bad. Can I see your ID? You know... So I can print you a pass?" She smirked.

She was really working the nerves that I didn't fucking have.

"No, heffa, you can not. Room?"

She frowned, scoffed, and waved me off. "Room 336."

"'Preciate you."

The elevator opened when an old, white couple walked out. Seeing them triggered the fact that I hadn't seen one black person besides that receptionist and us. This was a small, racist-ass town that I avoided like the plague anytime I traveled from Memphis to Atlanta to Jagoda Bay.

The ride was short, and as soon as I got off the elevator, Nel was ushering a crying Pia back onto it.

"Room 336. She's gonna be good. This shit is just too much for Pia. I'm gonna get a room in the next town over. I refuse to stay in Klanville."

I nodded, agreeing with him and hoping Pia would relax so she didn't go into labor so far from home. A few steps later, after rounding the corner and inhaling a whole lot of antiseptic air, I was in front of the room. Don, Matteo, Zo, Ezio, and Vello were huddled a few feet away. All their eyes shot up at me, but I kept going, pushing the door open to the room.

"Fuck, Glee..."

Various tubes and cords ran out of my sister-in-law as she lay in the bed. Both arms had IVs, and her leg was propped on a stack of pillows, with a fresh cast on it. The women surrounded the bed, two of whom were comforting Glow. Everyone peered at me with red eyes after my comment. Glow had her hands on the sides of her face as she cried so hard that her body shook.

Glee's face was damn near unrecognizable. Her eye was busted and sealed shut, her bottom lip had stitches going straight through it, right down the center, and there were purple welts all over her neck and arms. I didn't have the details, but it was clear she'd been in some sort of accident.

"Gleeeee! Oh my God. I'm so so so so so sorry!" Glow blurted out through her sobbing, her shoulders jumping with each word she spoke.

Excusing myself to get through the ladies, I pulled Glow from Dasani's embrace. She didn't push me away, crying into my chest. Dasani gave me a look and quietly left the room. Now it was just

Glow and me, standing over Glee as the low hum of machines bounced off the walls.

"She... She... She was in a wreck. Her car flipped over, ejecting her. They found her phone ten feet away, shattered. She... She... She has a broken leg, bruised ribs, and... And so many cuts and bruises, Tunan. My... My mom is so upset that our father is having to pick her up and bring her. She's too distraught to travel, and they can't stand one another. Glee... She just had a baby. Just had complications with labor... I... I feel like I'm losing my sister, and it's my fault."

"Aye! Aye..."

As I pulled Glow back, I stared into her eyes. She was so pretty and fragile. She looked tired, and her eyes had sunken in. Glow hadn't been taking care of herself, and once we got back to Jagoda Bay, I was on her ass.

"You ain't losin' yo' fuckin' sister, Glow."

"But they had to put her in a coma. There is swelling on her brain and—"

"Medically-induced coma, my baby. She gon' pull through. Look, I know shit is fucked up. Life do dat. Shit be all good, and den a series of problems just overloads ya. You gon' have to thug it out, doe, my baby."

Rubbing her shoulders, the way she looked up at me had me ready to put on a fucking cape and solve all her problems. Glow was blessed. She was gorgeous, had a thriving career, adoring fans, her own everything, and was baby-free. She'd been holding on to her version of a perfect world for no telling how long, and now that shit had hit the fan unexpectedly, she was shutting down. When I was hit with that fucking charge, I was fucked up, but a nigga like me was prepared for the worst. Girls like Glow couldn't handle the worst, but I was gone help her get through this shit, even if she gave me pushback.

"I was so mean to her..."

"Cuz she'd fucked up. You were angry, but you made it right. You gon' have plenty more chances to make it right as soon as she gets up outta here."

"You think she will?" Glow's eyes widened as she looked up at me again, as if I had all the answers.

My heart beat wildly in my chest, and my stomach churned. I

nearly took a step back because the feeling was foreign, but I stayed planted right there.

"I know she will."

Glow peered at me while I tried to dismiss the brewing in my chest.

"What do you think I'll be... I'll be—"

"Glow? Glow!"

Her body went slack in my arms as her eyes fluttered. I held her up, ushering her away from the bed and the machines. Her breathing sounded odd, and her body was slightly convulsing.

"Aye! Ayeeee!" I called out for help as I tapped Glow's face.

"Glow. Wake up, my baby. Wake da fuck up! Glow! Come on, baby. Fucccck!" Scoping her up, I carried her out of the room and ran into a doctor, who looked like she was making her rounds. "Aye, mane! Ion know... My fuckin' wife, she passed out, and her breathing is fucked up."

Glow's body was now almost weightless as she continued to convulse. I was on the verge of tweaking out seeing her like this. Between shock and fear, I looked from the doctor back at Glow. The doctor pushed her chart into a nurse walking by, and everything started moving in slow motion.

"Get me a bed! What's her name?" the brunette doctor asked me as a team came out with a bed and a crash cart.

"Gl—Charisma. Charisma Payne."

"Okay, let us take her. Charisma, can you hear me? I'm Dr. Brani."

Two nurses, one a man and one a woman, ran to me and tried to remove Glow from my arms. I was squeezing her face, trying to wake her up, as her eyes rolled back into her head. I could only see the whites of her eyes, and it looked like she was possessed.

What the fuck, my baby? I know you ain't on that shit.

"Sir, let us take her!" The doctor grabbed my arm.

I snatched away, and Glow's head bounced almost unnaturally. "Dis my... She's my fuckin' wife. She was just fine. She was just—"

"Tunan." Don walked up. "They gone take care of her. Let 'em take her." He nodded to assure me.

I glanced around, and the doctors were impatiently waiting while the women cried. Jisei was trying to get to us, but Ezio was holding her back and trying his best to calm her down.

Glow's body was still jolting, her weight growing heavy as if her body was giving up. The nurses reached for her again, but I shook them off and laid her on the bed that had been rolled out. As soon as I did, they pushed me aside and wheeled her away.

~

RUNNING my hand down my head, I watched Glow as she slept. A feeding tube lined her throat, and watching it made my stomach turn with nausea. When we first walked into this hospital, I had no idea she'd be assigned a room in the ICU. She'd had a scary night—four seizures, one nearly fatal. The room was just two doors down from her sister. When their parents arrived, their mom cut up so badly that their father had to take her to a hotel room. Everything was bad, but both sisters made it through the night. Glee was still in a medically induced coma, while Glow was merely exhausted.

There were two knocks on the door before it swung open. I expected a nurse, since they'd been rushing in and out all night, but it was Glow and Glee's twin. They'd gotten their coloring from both their mother and their father, but Glow resembled their mother more, while Glee took after their father. She was average height and weight, and pretty as hell. However, if my worry lines matched hers, I knew I was in bad shape. I hadn't slept a single wink and kept alternating between standing and sitting by Glow. My phone had been ringing all night and wouldn't stop until I told my siblings and mama I'd update them later.

When Glow seized, I panicked and called my sister, who three-wayed my mama onto the phone. I was on the verge of tears, not realizing how much I cared for Glow until the thought of her being gone was a possibility. Tuscany and my mama wanted to take the ride here, but I assured them it was enough of us motherfuckers walking around this bitch, making sure the girls were getting the best care.

Closing the door behind her, Cathy wrapped the black and gray cardigan around her waist, shivering. I wasn't sure if it was from seeing her oldest daughter in the hospital bed or the Alaskan temperatures that kept flowing through the hospital. Her hair was styled in a pixie cut, showing me that if Glow ever did a big chop, she'd still look good. She stood on the opposite side of the bed, gazing down at her firstborn.

A comfortable silence surrounded us. I hadn't met many mamas before and wasn't sure how to converse with the woman who was now my mother-in-law. Stella had been my only serious relationship outside of some high school shit before Glow.

"Glow had been trying to retire me for over a year now. She offered to help me sell the house and suggested I come stay with her. My baby girl, Glee, was accepted into the college of her dreams, so I had no reason to stay in my home. I've worked for twenty years, and it was about time I sit back and enjoy a calmer life, but I couldn't do it.

"I told my baby 'no' because I was selfish. Jagoda Bay is too painful for me. I was happy there once with my ex-husband... their father, but then I wasn't. Our arguing was constant because he wasn't a faithful man to me." She chuckled while rubbing on Glow's arm gently enough not to wake her.

"Pretty Tony... That's what they called him. Back then, the ladies liked light-skinned men with curly hair. Everyone wanted a Prince or an LL Cool J, and Pretty Tony had 'em going wild. And it drove me crazy as hell." She paused again, this time laughing. She sounded like Glow, which brought a small smile to my lips.

"I stayed because no woman was gonna break up my happy home. But our arguing started affecting the children—especially Glow. Then, words turned violent. After our first physical fight, Glow didn't eat for a week. I didn't notice she hadn't eaten; it was her father who had. We promised not to let it get that far again, but then, it happened again. And again, and a few more times until I realized I was failing my daughters—failing my damn self too."

Swallowing down the breath that seemed to be stuck in my throat, I watched their mom while she watched Glow, pain and shame etched on her face.

"Me holding on to my marriage sent my daughter deeper into a hole that I didn't know how to pull her out of. And when I finally left their father, the hole had been made. It was there for her to climb in and out of at her own doing."

She reached for Glow's left hand and swiped her thumb over her ring finger. They'd tried to remove it, but I wouldn't let them, and I wasn't even sure why. I was surprised that she was even wearing it to begin with. But seeing her walk into The Dungeon, rocked up, caused a stirring in my chest.

"I'd always thought Glee was going to be the first one married, and now... She has a whole child, and this one is a wife. Glow had always said she would never get married. My marriage did something to her that changed my baby forever. I've been running from my past so much that I missed pivotal milestones for both of my daughters."

"Glow and I.... It's a marriage of convenience. She's doin' me a favor."

I didn't want to lie to her. When Glow woke up, she would see firsthand that we weren't the doting newlyweds we should've been. We barely talked, and when we did, it was so full of sexual tension that much wasn't accomplished outside of me folding her firstborn up like a pretzel. Unless Cathy were a fly on the wall while I was buried deep inside of Glow, she would never see us close in nature.

Unless something changes when Glow is back on her feet.

Before I could sit with the thought, she said, "A husband of convivence doesn't stand up beside a bed all night. And they don't have that look on their face either."

She gave me a look that was calling my bluff. I had no rebuttal because she was right; I had been up in this bitch like I was Glow's ride or die. My feet were numb, my legs were stiff, and my throat was drier than a Popeye's biscuit. Still, there was no place I'd rather be than at Glow's bedside. Paper husband or not, I was man enough to know I needed to be here.

They were still running tests on Glow, and a doctor hadn't come in and given me a full report yet. What I did know was that she was dehydrated and malnourished, hence why she was being fed by a tube. But malnutrition didn't usually lead to a series of seizures, from what Google was talking about. What I knew now did nothing but lead to more questions—one being how a fucking food vlogger was malnourished to the point of fainting. Glow was on the slim side while being thick in all the right places. Even with the recent weight loss I noticed at The Dungeon, she was still curvy and fine as fuck, so malnutrition was a mystery and threw me all the way off.

Rubbing my hand down my face, I peered down at Glow. She was smaller than when I'd first seen her sitting under the dim lights of the steakhouse. I'd seen her naked just last week and hadn't paid enough attention to the difference. Now that she was vertical on a bed with IV cords and shit running in and out of her, the change was evident.

"I… I don't know how to help her," I stated truthfully. "I knew she had a thang with food. She's a vlogger, but she only takes two bites for da camera, and dat's it. Errtime she 'round me, she cringes at da food on da plate. I thought it was just some girl stuff. Like, she not wantin' to eat in front of me. Now, I see dat was some deeper stuff. Ion know how I hadn't before, but I see it now."

Glow's chest rose and fell. Her face was flushed and pale, and her neck was pinkish. She'd scared the fuck out of me. She'd scared the fuck out of all of us. The men had to force the women to go to a hotel a few hours ago. They didn't go without a fight, without going to the gift shop in the lobby, and without cashing out, filling the room with bears and floral arrangements. As dramatic as the gesture was, the gifts brought light to the dreadful atmosphere in the room.

"She probably ain't ate in days. I haven't been 'round to check on her. I been havin' so much shit—I mean, stuff—goin' on. I… I really ain't know da do's and don'ts of a fake marriage."

One minute, Glow was crying out, "This is just for the paperwork," and although I agreed, I still caught myself wanting to pull up on her. The truth was, Glow and I didn't know shit about each other. All the banter and flirty shit remained surface, and the glimpse she got in Memphis wasn't enough for her to really get a feel for who I was as a man. I assumed she had her life together, not needing me to play a huge role, but social media wasn't real. Glow looked like the total package on the outside, but her lying in this bed, hooked up to machines, told a different story.

"Son…" Glo's mama solemnly smiled at me. "Nothing about your marriage is fake. It's a lot of things I don't play about, and my girls are included, but God is at the head of the list. Y'all took up vows, sealing you two as one. This is *your* wife, no matter what type of agreement you have. And you being here all night tells me it's more than paperwork… No matter what your mind is telling you."

The door opened, and in stepped a white, blonde, green-eyed doctor who didn't look any older than my sister.

"Good morning. I'm Dr. Milton." He smiled, then shifted the clipboard from one hand to the other.

"Good morning, Dr. Milton. I'm Glow's mom, Cathy, but you can call me Glory. This is—"

"Glow's husband," I answered for her. "Tunan. Nice to meet you. Dem her papers?" I asked, nodding to the clipboard. I'd been waiting for an update all night. "What's goin' on with her?"

"Nice to meet you both. Glow's test results came back. Given the number of seizures she had, we had to rule out neurological issues before updating you all. I was able to get her medical files, and given her history, I believe the seizures are a symptom of hypoglycemia. Now that we have stabilized her blood sugar and rehydrated her, she should not experience any more episodes."

Dr. Milton stepped closer to the same machine that the nurses visited. I'd figured out quickly that they were watching her vitals, and I made sure to watch for their reaction to know what was happening. When the doctor stepped back with a nod, I knew he was good with what he was seeing. Before I could ask another question, he pressed the clipboard into his chest and cleared his throat.

"If we cannot get Glow to maintain a better diet with supplementations, we'll need to come up with a better plan to manage her eating disorder."

"Eatin' disorder? Fuck you talmbout, doc?" I said, looking from him to Cathy, whose face showed she was aware of what was a revelation to me.

"Glow has anorexia nervosa. Unfortunately, because she is not incapacitated and you are not listed to receive medical information... According to HIPAA, I cannot say more. However, her eating disorder is why she is here. The malnutrition and dehydration are mere symptoms. Again, you both are critical to ensure Glow manages this medical illness. It may seem like a lifestyle choice to those of us who do not struggle with this condition, but that is not the case with your wife, sir."

Anorexia. That fucking word knocked the wind out of me. The doctor was still yapping about how we could support Glow once she was discharged, but I had tuned that motherfucker out. I looked over at Glow, as if she would wake up and give me answers, but she couldn't, not in her current state.

"But... She ain't skinny, doc. I mean, she's slim, but Glow got curves. Ain't dat not eatin' shit white people shit?"

I looked at Cathy and mouthed "my bad" for cursing. I didn't mean to sound ignorant, but I was annoyed. I felt stuck—more so stunned. I associated anorexia with those young snow bunnies who looked like skeletons—sunken jaws, ribcages showing, and constant vomiting. Stepping back, I chuckled. She had thrown up. I saw it when I brought her the money. I thought she had just made herself sick from arguing with Glee.

"Damn," I mumbled, shaking my head. "Dis shit throwin' me for a loop."

"I knew, Tunan," Cathy stated.

She tightened her cardigan around her waist again in a way that she was hugging herself. She'd done that at least three times already. I wanted to be pissed at her, but it was Glow who hadn't shared the information I deemed important to know before we'd gotten married.

After sniffling, she continued. "It's something she's struggled with since childhood, but we'd gotten it under control. She started eating more and had done well with managing her stress and her need to control everything. When she began eating on camera and turned it into a hobby, I thought she'd passed it. I even researched that it was possible for people to outgrow the disorder. Of course, I had concerns when the online hobby became more of a career."

She reached up and moved a strand of hair out of Glow's face. My eyes hadn't left her since she was my only source of answers right now. Ole boy was talking about HIPAA, but I knew if I hit the receptionist off with a fake number, she would slide me whatever information I wanted on Charisma Glow Payne.

"I'm not the savviest person when it comes to social media, but her rise to success and some of the mean comments did worry me, Tunan. Still, she seemed to be handling it well. I... I... I should've moved in with her like she'd asked. The moment I found out Glee had a child, I knew it was going to trigger her stress."

Cathy wiped a tear from her face. The woman was barely hanging on. Both of her children were in the ICU. I didn't know how she was standing here, and it was proof that she was a strong woman. From everything she'd told me, she had the evidence to support that she was.

"It's not your fault. I'm sure you've done all you could," Dr. Milton assured her before I cut in.

"Uhh... So, whatchu sayin', doc? I really don't know too much 'bout dis shit."

In the hood, we didn't see people walking around with eating disorders. Hunger? Hell, yeah. Rejecting food? Hell, no. The only reason I knew what anorexia was was because of the movies Tuscany used to watch on Lifetime and shit.

The doctor set the clipboard at the end of Glow's bed and stuffed his hand into his white coat. "Again, anorexia nervosa is a serious eating disorder, Mr. Payne. It's more mental than anything. I can tell you all the things, but I'm sure you'll gain a better understand through conversing with your wife about her struggle and how you all can support her. From her file, she's lost a significant amount of weight. It's important she maintains a weight that is necessary for her to function so that she doesn't end up in the hospital again, back home."

"So you sayin' dis shit ain't got no cure? Give her some meds or sum'n so we can be on our way. Money ain't an issue."

"Unfortunately, there is no cure, and until Glow can prove to her primary physician that she can do her part, medicine will not benefit her."

"No cure?" I asked in disbelief.

"Correct. With this disorder, food is truly the only medicine. And in my professional opinion, she won't ever need the meds if she takes control now. Mrs. Payne needs to eat three times a day, plus snacks. Whole foods, protein, greens, and a carbohydrate with every meal. She's going to need someone with her daily to ensure she isn't vomiting. If we do not get a handle on Mrs. Payne's disorder, she will be opening herself up to dire consequences later. Cardiovascular issues, bone health, hormonal changes, even death. Her lack of nutrients can affect her menstrual cycle and cause infertility too. To me, she is a very lucky young woman to be alive. I've seen more severe cases, but again, the weight loss is a key indication that she can worsen if not supported to overcome her current circumstance."

My mind spun with all the words he'd said. Glow needed help, and she wasn't well. The concern on his face showed me this shit was serious, but the only thing I could think about was that I'd done this shit before. Not exactly this, but I'd done the hospital sits and hourly checkups because my last bitch was sick as fuck. After nursing that hoe back to health, and her dogging me the fuck out, I vowed never to do that shit again. Glow just wasn't my bitch, though; she was my wife. And for some reason, the Big Nigga upstairs kept putting sickly motherfuckers in my path.

"In short, we just need her to keep the food in. I want to monitor her for another day. I also want to consult more with the neurologist about the seizures, to be sure no damage occurred. I'll have the nurse remove the feeding tube in the next hour. Let us know if you have any questions."

The doctor said a few more encouraging words to Cathy, who was crying harder than before his update. I squared my shoulders and nodded at the shit the doctor was saying, not letting my worry show. I'd said cost wasn't an issue because we were mob now, but I still hadn't been told what my source of income would be within the organization. I had some bread and a mean-ass hustle, so Glow would be good. Still, I was struggling because I'd agreed to trick on Glow as my wife, and the thought of spending my bread on her health issues was triggering my ass like a motherfucker. The last thing I should've been doing was putting my all into another woman who could heal and then burn me the same way the last woman did.

But Glow ain't Stella, Tune, I thought to myself.

All this shit was a lot to take in, and since Cathy hadn't stopped crying since the doctor walked out, I took the moment to walk out too. I needed some fresh air to settle the thoughts in my head. Glow didn't deserve to be compared to Stella and the bullshit she put me through, but shit... I was human, and this shit felt like déjà vu. I had some shit to me, but Glow should've mentioned that she had an eating disorder. Of all the people I could have married, I ended up with someone who was fucking insecure about her body—someone who looked perfect from head to fucking toe. I never would have thought Glow had a damn eating disorder, and I couldn't stop the word "anorexia" from circling my brain. I know it wasn't some shit you can just come out and say, but fuck, she could've let a nigga know something.

I stepped into the hallway, giving her mom some privacy to cry in peace for her daughter. Inhaling the stale-ass hospital air, the elevator across from me dinged, and Don and his wife stepped off. Don was in a damn three-piece suit, a stark contrast from his street clothes yesterday. There was a presidential Rolex on one arm and a baby carrier in the next.

Dasani was dressed differently, too, in a navy-and-white athletic set, a huge Chanel bag, and Chanel sneakers. No matter what she wore, the shit always looked expensive, and today was no different, even with her dressed down. I didn't know if they'd gone home in a copter or were wearing some shit they'd found at the nearest mall. It hadn't been long enough for them to drive to Jagoda Bay and back unless they went by air. Knowing Don, he'd gone by air.

Dasani nodded at me as she walked past and went straight into Glow's room. Don headed toward Glee's room, so I followed. When I got inside, she had get-well-soon flowers and balloons that flooded the space. Don placed the baby carrier in the reclining chair and pushed it next to Glee. She was still banged up, but her skin had cleared up some. Shit was all fucked up, and I was wondering if I was in over my head.

Don stood in front of the carrier and folded his hands at his belt line. "You straight?"

Rubbing my left hand down my head, I sighed. "Yeah."

He looked back at Glee, as if he was checking to make sure he could speak freely in front of her. If I weren't in such a mood, I would've laughed at his nonsense because Glee was in a fucking coma. There was no way she would remember anything she heard him say once she woke up.

"I'm giving you a few days to settle in with your wife in Jagoda Bay, and then it's time to get to work."

"I think she gettin' discharged tomorrow, so I won't need a few days."

Now he was speaking my language. I was ready to get this paper so that I could get my fucking life in order.

"I know when she's getting discharged. Ain't too much, I don't know." He watched for my reaction, but I was so fucking exhausted and drained that I didn't have one to offer.

"So whatchu sayin'?"

"I'm saying, take care of your wife."

I was going to make sure Glow was all right, but the money was and always would be the motive. It was the reason I'd joined this shit to begin with. I wanted "easy" after finding myself in jail. I'd join my brother's mob because it seemed like easy money with work that aligned with my natural grind. I'd picked Glow to help secure my joining because she was an easy catch, not in need of much from a nigga. Now, here I was, finding myself dealing with shit that wasn't easy. I had a good mind to take my ass back to Memphis, although I knew that wasn't a real option.

"It's a reason I tell you niggas to get married—" Don cut in while I was mentally assessing how I ended up in this situation again. That Big Nigga upstairs was playing with me, but I was deadass when I promised Leader that I wasn't coming back to jail, so I was trying to keep my shit P.

"It ain't just because I want a crowd of married muthafuckas around me. Marriage offers emotional stability, Tunan. I can't have a bunch of unstable creatures running amok. It offers support and companionship. If you can't stand to be around your wife, how the fuck are you good with being around niggas all day? Shit gay.

"Commitment. Responsibility. Loyalty. If you can't be loyal to the woman who's draining your dick and rocking your last name, you can't commit to my shit nor be responsible for your tasks within your position. It's about financial advantages. A real woman gone spend your shit, no doubt, but she gone help you manage it and possibly grow it, or she gone do what she do so good that you gone want to earn more just to keep her.

"The social recognition is important too. My men being married enhances our societal positions when we up against these rich-ass white folk. They already skeptical cuz I'm having more paper than them, so I'm not giving them shit to pick at. Married, faithful, about their business, busting guns before being busted-ass men."

Here I was thinking you just had to be married because that's how mob niggas operated. Had I known we were building off our marriages, I would have put more thought into whom I gave my last name to. I wanted to be in so I could get this money. I wasn't financially or mentally prepared to be a real husband. I fucked with my impossible-ass wife, and I'd pay her bills and fuck her good from time to time, but running a fucking household? That hadn't been part of the plan. I didn't even have a fucking household to run, nor did I have the luxuries of obtaining one.

My fucking credit was shot. I didn't have any assets, and I damn sure didn't have the proper documents to start the process of getting a spot. That wasn't shit to do, though. I could find the nearest fraudster to get me some paperwork, but still, when I got my own spot, it was going to be on some type of shit to lay my head and know that it was mine. Don was talking about some real structured, foundation-type shit. When Shio brought me in, this nigga should have been clearer about what the fuck was required of me. I was just a hood nigga from Memphis, fresh out of jail. Being the head of a fucking household wasn't some shit I was interested in. But I was in now and knew that since I'd given my word, there was no backing out.

Not having a rebuttal that wouldn't have made me sound ungrateful, I crossed my arms and bit my tongue. I had some shit with me, and Glow had some shit with her. After a year of my life had been snatched from under my feet, I was ready to get to the money. This nigga was talking about being a dutiful husband, and Glow didn't even see my ass in that way.

"Settle in with your wife, honor her, and everything else will fall into place. You about to be very fucking wealthy, nigga. Be ready."

Heavy boots had us shifting our attention toward the door. A stocky nigga in an olive green and black uniform with cuffs, a pistol, and mace attached to his holster appeared. My face contorted into a mug. I'd seen this pig every day in the pen. He was the only nigga in the jail who didn't have an off day. There had been a few of his colleagues I would've loved to beat the shit out of when I caught them in the wild, but fortunately for him, he was cool as fuck. I still didn't fuck with pigs, though.

He jutted his chin at Don, prompting him to move toward the hallway, and I watched as the door closed. I didn't know what kind of business Don had with a correctional officer, but since that fucking pig was crooked as a motherfucker, maybe his ass was helping with a job.

The blanket covering the carrier shifted. It was the baby. She was fully covered, peacefully sleeping, with her silky black hair peeking out from under the pink hat on her head. Her little hands were clutching the burping cloth to her chest. Her mouth opened, exposing her gums, and then her nose wrinkled, indicating she was about to put those lungs to work. Her mama and auntie were out of commission, her grandma wasn't in the right frame of mind to get her, and this hospital was too fucking filthy for a newborn. She'd been born in one just a few weeks ago, so hopefully, she'd be good. Before I could take a step in her direction, the door opened again. It wasn't my business, but I was about to ask Don what was up with him and Officer Steroids when I staggered from who was walking in.

With a look of confusion on his face, he looked just the same as the day I told him to keep his head up. I hadn't had any sleep, so I could very well be fucking hallucinating, but judging by the look on his face, I was certain he felt the same. I watched as his mug contorted from haze to fear to sorrow.

He hadn't looked my way, the source of all his emotions lying in the hospital bed. From the moment he walked in the door, his eyes were on Glee.

"Wha...Wha..." He stumbled backward, chains clanking as he did so. He looked as if he were about to pass out; his dark skin had turned ashen gray.

"Leader," I spoke up, staying in position.

I knew he hadn't seen me when he first came in. His attention went to the young woman who'd been haunting his dreams, simmering his thoughts, and holding his heart since he'd been placed behind bars.

"Tune?"

Confusion had him coming my way, and I was able to resolve some of mine by him coming closer. A shackled Leader had walked into the damn room, and I was done for.

"I'm married to her sister," I informed him.

His world was already shook up, so I didn't need the nigga putting two and two together and coming up with zero. He paused midstride but remained locked on me. When his eyes watered over, he broke contact and dragged his feet to the bed. As he stood on the side of her, he inspected each and every part of Glee, letting his eyes linger on all her bruises and cuts.

"Baby, baby, baby, baby. Fuuuuuuck!" He sputtered his words as his chest heaved. "H... How? What the fuck! How the fuck?"

Had it not been for the machines, there would have been a long, black, brittle silence. Leader's eyes were wild, and the chains' vibration let me know his hands were shaking.

"I should have—" He sucked in a wad of air as if he was fighting to breathe. "I should've never told you to come see me. I should have fucking never... Baby... Baby, you can't do this shit. Who the fuck did this shit! Hunh?" Leader yelled as he shot daggers at me.

I didn't have any answers for him. As badly as I wanted to let him know everything, I didn't know much of anything. He'd have to get those answers from Don. He's the one who knew it all.

"This is my fuckin' heart. You hear me, nigga? Hunh! This is my fuckin' baby!" Leader took his attention from me and bent down with his face just inches away from Glee's. "You so fucking pretty, Pretty Mama. You know that? You so fucking pretty, baby. I need you to get up. I... I need you to get up. You gotta finish school. You gotta finish what the fuck you started, baby. Baby, baby, please. I-I won't make it. If you don't make it, I won't fucking make it... Get up, Glee... Keep giving me a reason to dream."

He placed his forehead on hers, not caring about the tubes and cords. He continued whispering words, and when I heard the word God, I knew he was praying.

Waaaaah... Wa... Wa... Waaaaah

"Shit." I rubbed my hand down my face.

Instinct had me taking a step toward the carrier, but I paused. I didn't want to overstep. Leader kept his head on Glee's, but his eyes traveled across the bed. He hadn't noticed the carrier sitting in the chair. He hadn't noticed shit outside of Glee lying in that bed.

He watched the baby for a beat as she began sucking on her hands, soothing herself.

"Whose baby?"

Rubbing my hand down my face again, I grunted. "Uhhh... Shit, yours."

"Nigga, what?"

Leader stretched to his full height, brows crinkling as he looked at me like he wanted to knock me the fuck out. I fucked with Leader, but I'd hate to have to box his ass out while he was chained up.

"Look, I'm new to this shit too. Me and her sister got married on some business shit. Apparently, Glee came home from school and went into labor the day I got married. Her sister didn't know, her mama didn't know... Shit, I don't even think Glee knew. But I do know that's your jit."

Leader kept his eyes on me like he expected a second head to sprout from my neck. Then he took a step, tripped on the edge of the bed as he rounded it, and caught himself before the chains made him hit the ground. He now stood directly in front of the baby carrier, but was just out of reach. I could see she was still sucking on her fist, but I knew from that night I stayed at the townhouse, she would need some milk soon.

When she opened her eyes, Leader dropped his head. His shoulders began to softly bounce, and I knew he was crying. I looked away to give him some privacy; I knew this shit had to be hard as fuck on him. He was serving a ten-year bid, and the girl he loved and respected was lying in a hospital bed and had just given birth to his daughter. That would be a second child whose life he'd miss for a decade.

"Pretty Mama," his voice croaked. "What the fuck did I do?"

"Aye, Leader. This ain't on you, mane. I mean, the baby all you, my G, but—"

"I... I kept my distance until my people said they couldn't contact her. So I pushed myself back in her life. I told her to come see me... No, I demanded that shit. She stopped everything. Knowing she'd just had a baby... I... We...Yesterday at visitation. Fuck!"

He shook his head as the silence swallowed us. I didn't want to say the wrong shit, so I stood quietly as the machine and his daughter made their natural noises.

"I come around, and she just does what I say. She was good—perfect. My baby was untouched... She had a future, Tune... And I... I fucked it up. Fuck!"

Leader lifted his head when she began fussing again. His chains jangled as he reached for the baby, but he was restricted by the way his hands were chained.

"Fuuuuuck! I... I can't—"

The door opened again, and Cathy stepped inside.

"Goddammit," I mumbled.

Her squinted eyes roved from me to Leader to her daughter to her grandbaby, then back to Leader. His eyes had not left the baby, and tears still flowed down his face while his hands remained in the restricted position. Her face grew red, and when I thought she was about to lay Leader's ass out, she stepped further into the room, added foam sanitizer to her hands, and went to the side of the carrier. Without moving Leader out of the way, she lifted her grand-baby from the carrier, closed her eyes, and hoisted her onto her shoulder.

I stayed put because I wanted to see how this shit was going to play out. Cathy had proven to me to be a reasonable woman, but people acted funny when it came to black men being in jail or having a record. She didn't know about my stint, but Leader was standing here decked in Iron Kinser's finest, so there was no hiding his shot.

"I'm sorry. I... I fucking ruined your daughter. I stole her future. I-I should've left her alone. I'm... Fuck. I'm—" He lifted his hands, pulling the chains. "I can't even fucking hold her. I... She's..."

"Hey." She closed the space between her and Leader, gently grabbing his chin and lifting his face. "What's your name?"

"Leader."

"I see... Leader, you did not ruin my daughter. Does she look *ruined* to you?"

He didn't answer, but the look in his eyes showed he was not letting his rationale go.

"She looks perfectly fine to me. A few bumps and bruises that will heal, but she's perfectly fine. You didn't ruin her. You just gave her much more purpose. I don't know your situation, Leader, and right now I don't care to. What I do know is that Glee is going to be just fine. She has a mother, a father, and a sister who will make sure she and your daughter are well taken care of. And when you are in a position to step in physically, we will release them to you."

She let his chin go and turned the baby so that she was facing him. Even I had to blink away my own emotion as Leader broke down again.

"I knew something was off... Something was different about her."

"Leader. It's okay."

"She's... She's so fucking beautiful."

"She is. I think she's a perfect mix of you two." Cathy smiled, and for the first time since Leader walked into the hospital room, his face relaxed.

"Just when I thought Glee couldn't drive me any crazier, she goes and make a mini her. Shit..." He shook his head.

"Leader, lift your crown. Both of you,"—She nodded at me—"God makes no mistakes. Y'all were brought into their lives for a reason, and it's not a slip-up or unconventional timing. They are both stronger than the two of you think. Trust me... My daughters are built to handle the magnitude of men that you are, but now you have to prove that you are built for them."

Damn.

Leader bent down and kissed the baby's forehead. "You just gave me another reason, pretty baby. I love you... so fucking much."

He stood and kissed the top of Glee's head and the side of her mouth. I gagged a little due to the feeding tube because the whole setup was nasty as hell in theory. It was sentimental as a motherfucker, though, and I respect Leader for his love for Glee.

"Take care of them, please. I'ma... I'ma figure this shit out. She won't be a single mama. I'ma find a way out of this shit. That's on my life."

Leader took another look at the baby as the door opened. Officer Steroids nodded, signaling that it was time for him to go. I was guessing that Don had gotten him a special furlough. That nigga's reach was so long that I was beginning to think it was nothing he couldn't do. When I thought back to how he'd put us in a whole-ass Biblical setting, I knew there was nothing he couldn't do.

Leader began to shuffle toward the door but stopped just shy of it. "What's her name?"

Don had now come back in but stood to the side, watching the scene with an unreadable expression.

Cathy chuckled lightly. "I never knew girls could be juniors. But she is. Her name is Leader... Baby Leader."

Leader tensed, rubbed his hand down his face to dry it, and then looked at Don. "Aye, Demise. Can I holla at you alone for a minute?"

Don nodded and stepped back out.

"Aye, G...."

"You ain't even gotta ask. Dey gone be straight, Leader," I assured him.

He took one more look at Glee, then at his baby, before stepping out. Though he was no longer in the room, I could feel the heaviness he'd left behind. Just a while ago, we were both in a cell. Now, we were connected by sisters.

Rocking the baby as she rummaged through a diaper bag I hadn't seen Don holding when he brought the carrier in, Cathy pulled a cooler bag out. When she maneuvered the milk so that the baby could drink it, I figured she had the baby duty shit on lock.

My phone vibrated in my pocket, so I retrieved it just before telling Cathy I'd be back and stepping out.

Leader was being led to the elevators while Don was further down the hall on a call. Bringing my focus back to my phone, I swiped the screen to access my text messages.

TULSCAN

Address you sent checks out. Stella lives there. We sliding on this scandalous bitch or nah?

KNOWING Stella was in Jagoda Bay had been fucking with my head for the last week. Just like God had come through on her beating cancer, he'd proven she was on his favorites list once again. Glow and Glee had saved her scamming ass, but her luck would soon run out.

CHAPTER 11
DON DEMISE

"So, what the fuck is this shit with Ines? We in bed with the Mexican cartel now? I thought we was straight with the Navarros?" Rut asked as he stroked his chin.

Standing at the head of the round table, all of the seats were vacant except for two. One occupied by my left hand, Rut, and the other by my right hand, Matteo. We were at the Dungeon, and although outside the double doors to enter and exit the room was buzzing with motherfuckers making illegal deals and losing all their money, it was quiet enough in here to hear an ant struggling to make its away through the window seal cracks. The Dungeon was one of my smartest investments. It stayed packed with the highest of the high to the lowest of the low. I didn't discriminate when it came to making my pockets fatter. As long as motherfuckers came in and acted like they had some fucking sense, they stayed alive enough to be in debt to my ass.

I looked at Rut in his four-piece suit, dressed like we were headed to a funeral. I would've cracked a joke on him, but I had a five-piece suit on, like I was about to marry Dasani's ass again, but this time in a full-blown wedding. Matteo was suited up as well, but I could tell he was ready to take his suit off. The nigga was mean as shit, and I was already annoyed with the situation we had going on, so I planned to finish this conversation quickly so we could all retreat to our business. There were a billion other things I could be doing besides this bullshit here.

I nodded to Rut. "Yeah, we got the Navarro Cartel, and Goal my nigga and all, but Ines is in Mexico, whereas Navarro is Colombian."

Removing the remote that was in the inner pocket of my jacket, I rolled my neck to relieve the brewing tension. I was too damn young for the bullshit that came with being the head of this organization, and lately, it seemed like shit had been spiraling. I knew it had to be due to that dead-ass nigga whose nutsack I'd spawned from. That soft, incompetent bitch boy was cursing me from the grave. But he'd have to conjure up every spirit burning around him to stop this motion. I would handle this shit as I'd handled everything else: fall in line or die. It was simpler than a lot of motherfuckers made it.

"Ledesma is a failing cartel. He's in our debt—a debt that I can't ever see him getting out of," Matteo added, and the glimmer in his eyes told me he was ready to play exterminator.

He hated that our daddy's had put that jacket on his back, but the nigga was a better shooter than me, although I'd never admit it to him. Matteo was a closet killer who only liked to come out and play when he felt like it, which had been too fucking often since his daddy fucked up and he found out Pearla was his sister. I had to shut the shit down before he brought unnecessary heat to my organization. Family or not, everybody had a role to play.

"Exactly… If the nigga can't pay, then he gone have to fork some shit over." I shrugged.

Turning back to the overhead projector, I pressed the remote, and the nigga Shio had the standoff with at the club appeared.

"Felipe Rodríguez. Firstborn son of four to Vicente Rodríguez."

I clicked the remote again, and an older, heavier Felipe appeared. They both had the same tanned skin and would have been twins if it weren't for the tattoos on Felipe's neck. I didn't know what it was about older Mexican men and weight—those motherfuckers ate too many taquitos, churros, tacos, and shit. He was getting too much money to be so fucking big. The nigga's neck was so thick that I wasn't sure how his ass was able to breathe.

"They have been wreaking havoc for years. But this lil' muthfucka,"—Pointing my laser beam to the mugshot of Felipe, I circled it—"Is a menace. According to what I was able to dig up, he was able to take over Mexico, not by drugs, but by fear. What the fuck they do in their country, I could give a fuck about, but they're littering here... Jagoda Bay to be exact."

I pressed the remote again, and over two hundred missing person cases appeared on the screen. The cases involved women and children, but mostly women. The mayor deserved a serious ass-whooping for keeping this quiet. Considering Jagoda Bay's population, the triple-digit number of cases wasn't many, but those were innocent women and children who had just vanished with little investigation happening to find them.

"I guess their own women weren't good enough for him or weren't selling high enough, so he had his people come snatch and grab on our turf. I can give a fuck 'bout what he does in other cities, but this one is off-limits."

Matteo scoffed. "And the mayor been keeping the news outlets off this shit? Greedy-ass, bitch-ass, muthafucka. Want me to go—"

"Damn, Teo," Rut laughed. "Princesspa ain't draining yo' nuts or sum? You uptight as fuck."

Matteo sneered at him before sitting back in the oversized chair.

Instead of sitting, I paced in front of the images of the Rodríguezes. "You know that nigga don't want his precious city to be painted in a bad light, Teo. But that's also a win for us because when we take these muthafuckas down, we ain't gotta be worried about the wrong muthafucka sniffing this way afterward."

I wasn't worried one way or another, but we'd been doing a good job of keeping shit diplomatic since coming to Jagoda Bay. Rio had been right when he said connections could be made without violence, so I typically only resorted to killing niggas if there was no other resolution. When it came to the police in Jagoda Bay, I'd done my due diligence over the years. I didn't like the laws sticking their nose my way, and we'd shared our wealth with the city well enough to have them mind their fucking business. However, I had the money and influence with the force and those associated to end any investigation into anything or anyone Rinaldi-affiliated. Whoever was bold enough to build an investigation on me would go down before I did. That, or end up in a premature grave.

Still, I'd spent more than enough years of my fucking life behind bars and didn't fuck with the police at all besides anonymous payroll personnel and disguised donations. I didn't even like talking to them pigs, but it was necessary to keep my business running smoothly. I had them in my back pocket, but the money I poured out for information and for them to look the other way was given right back to me. So many of them motherfuckers were frequent flyers here at the Dungeon, especially the chief. He, too, needed to lose some fucking weight because I needed him to live a long and healthy life. He was my type of crooked, and I wasn't in the mood to be trying to convert a new chief to the winning team if he died. I'd fuck around and keep killing the newly appointed chiefs while trying to get them motherfuckers to get with the program. I'd have Rio and the other Don's on my ass then, and I ain't feel like dealing with that shit either.

"So, what now? When the killing 'posed to start?" Matteo huffed.

"Slow down, Jason Voorhees. Ever since y'all's showdown in Mexico City, they've gone underground. I can't locate them, and Ines haven't even heard from his bitch-ass son either, so y'all killed him, or *they* killed him. Either way, chances are the nigga dead."

"I don't like not knowing." Rut folded his arms on the table. "Them niggas somewhere plottin' and plannin'. They know our land because they've been here snatching up women and children right under our noses without us knowing. How do we get in front of this shit?"

Taking a seat at the table, I shook my head. "I agree, and I'm workin' on it. The good thing is, them niggas have gone underground so the snatching folks up has stopped. But it also means them muthafuckas are still alive, and if I don't find them before they start movin' on whatever plans they makin', a lot of people will be vulnerable.

"I want to bring them niggas down, immediately, but I also want to try and locate as many of the women and children as I can before people start dying. And then that border shit is tricky, especially with that orange balloon in office now."

"So basically, we ain't got no fuckin' plan. And not only is Ines in our debt, he ain't no fuckin' help." Matteo pointed out.

I clicked the screen again, powering it off. "Basically. And on top of all that, Shio is growing impatient. He want them dead for his own reasons."

"Maybe I can head out there and put my ears to the streets."

I shook my head. "Nah, Rut. It was a blessing that Teo got out with them Cuppacio niggas. I ain't trying to send you over there, especially since they are probably expecting us. They may be hiding, but we don't know what other organization or militia they are working with. Fuck 'round and walk into an ambush.

"Nah... We gone have to wait this shit out, just like I told choir boy, we need to monitor then adjust. Plus, Daylani going into her busy season, and I know you be holding down the home front."

Rut sat back in his seat. "Nigga, fuck you think this money for? The nannies can hold the home front down, and if not them, my mama and sister are more than happy to step in. Let me help where I can, Don."

Shit still felt funny when my best nigga called me Don. Rut and I had done hard-ass time together. I was "Ize" to him, and although he still used my nickname sometimes, in business settings, I was Don.

"So, we wait it out..." Matteo tapped the table.

"Yeah. And if Unc get wind of this shit, he gone have a fuckin' field day." I chuckled.

Uncle Reuchie was still on ice, orders of his firstborn. Matteo wasn't playing with his ass about stepping down and being a fucking father and grandfather. He called it "retirement," and I supported it, but in times like this, I could use Reuchie. He was the one to help mold me for this Don shit. I didn't learn shit from my daddy but what not to do before I killed his ass. Uncle Reuchie set up moving the Rinaldi Mob to Jagoda Bay and helped bridge connections with the Mecanio Mob and the surrounding mobs.

Now, he spends his days chasing behind Pearla and Princess. When they weren't paying his ass no mind, he was on the golf course, or auntie was dragging his ass across the globe to shop. Unbeknownst to Matteo, his daddy was texting me every fucking day trying to get back in. But what my cousin said went because, although this was my shit, I respected Matteo and Rut too much not to consider their stances on certain shit. They were some real day ones.

"What about that Cuppacio nigga? He gone stay low until we get what we need to make a move?" Rut asked as he tapped his fingers on the thick wood.

Shio Cuppacio. Choir Boy. With his slick but not-so-slick ass.

Before I decided to merge mobs with the Cuppacios by letting

Ezio marry Jisei, I had to think really hard about the possible consequences. Through all the years that I'd considered bringing the Cuppacios on, my hesitation wasn't because I'd killed their fathers. It was because of one Cuppacio—Shio.

The nigga was calculated, intelligent, efficient, and God-fearing. Niggas that feared God were a different type of crazy. He was the type that knew he was going to Heaven so anything fucking went during his time on Earth. I always had to be extra careful around the nigga because, unlike his duck-duck-goose-ass cousins, he had some type of love for his pops, and vengeance was real. I didn't know Solana was on that bugger sugar, but knowing that she was had me smiling. It served his one-step-ahead ass right to have some turbulence in that mind of his. Giving him an ultimatum almost felt as good as busting a nut in Dasani.

"Fuck you over there smirkin' 'bout?"

"Shio... He'd be a good asset. A good replacement for Reuchie, actually. But he gotta pass the assignments I gave him. We know that nigga is just as bull-headed as the rest, but he thinks he's smarter than a fucking fifth grader, so he might go against the grain just because he feels like he can."

Matteo grunted. "That's cuz that black-ass nigga *is* smarter than a fifth grader."

"Facts. I fuck with the other Cuppacios, but it's a damn near a shocker that they share blood with him. The nigga is like a fuckin' sponge. All he do is sit back and soak up shit... Be playin' the background like he don't know we know his ass playin' the background. How you think the others gone feel about you possibly pulling him higher up in the ranks than them? Cuz, technically, if we're going by rank, Ezio is supposed to get that spot."

"Would you want Ezio's pill head ass to take Reuchie's spot?" I asked, already knowing the answer.

"Hell nawl!" both men replied in the same tone.

"Exactly. Besides, my sister wouldn't go for that shit. Reuchie's position requires more time from the crib. It will have to take a special type of man to be able to juggle all of it. It's going to take a man of discipline—a go-getter. One that not only knows how to communicate and problem-solve, but the nigga need to know how to handle being stretched thin. If I give Ezio that seat, I won't hear the end of Jisei complaining."

"I'm with Dasani... Jisei really the one runnin' shit." Matteo smirked, trying to get under my skin.

Rut kissed his teeth and chuckled. "And Pearla's young ass don't run shit? She got all y'all niggas goin' crazy, and while y'all worried 'bout her, she was somewhere worried 'bout Grind."

I looked at Rut. "Nigga, hush. You just mad you'n got a sister."

"Nigga, yo' mind going bad. Yo' ass done met Reesh. My sister solid as fuck," Rut replied, but he wasn't getting a response out of me until I made Matteo eat his words. Besides, Rut may have had a sister but she wasn't up in the mix.

"I can't help that i'm the one the ladies call on. They know *Big Don* gone come through in the clutch when the rest of you niggas somewhere mean mugging and mad at the world and shit."

"You thought you *ate* that?" Matteo mugged me. "Nigga, you want Pearla to be yo' sister so bad... Be more worried 'bout *my sister* than me. Fuck is you sayin'?"

This time, I kissed my teeth. "Yo' big grown ass talmbout some *ate that*. You be in they faces just as much as me, nigga!"

"Y'all both crazy 'bout y'all sister and each other sisters. We got that shit established. Let's move on," Rut stated, trying to diffuse the situation, but it was too late.

"I'm the better big brother. Just face it. Don't get mad at me cuz yo' lil' high-school-ass sister boy crazy."

"Fuck outta here! Pearla ain't studyin' these niggas. 'Least my sister gangsta. She bussin' shit. Only thing yours doin' is runnin' through yo' pockets."

Matteo loved hitting below the belt, but I had something for his black ass.

"Aite." I pulled my phone out of my pocket. "You call Pearla, and I call Jisei, and let's see whose sister gone pick up first."

Matteo picked his phone up from the table, accepting the challenge.

"And put that shit on speaker, nigga," I said while clicking on the phone keypad.

I knew Jisei's number by heart, so I typed it in while Matteo was doing the same thing. We both placed our phones on speaker and set them on the conference table. When they began to ring, we watched each other until both lines went to voicemail.

Rut roared in laughter. "Mane! Y'all ridiculous. They might be busy."

"Busy doin' what? They ain't got no jobs or no fuckin' bills." I spat, picking up my phone and ending the call. "Aite, now you call Jisei, and I call Pearla."

"Aite, childish-ass nigga. You just wanna get yo' feelings hurt today. And Jisei do got a fuckin' job. A career actually," Matteo informed. Like he was telling me some shit about my own sister that I didn't know.

"And when the last time she clocked in at that fuckin' career you so speak of? Exactly."

We dialed the numbers out again, both of us knowing them by heart. The phones stopped ringing at the same time as we heard both women speak.

"Hey, cousin!"

"Yes, Teooooo? You must got a new bag for me?"

I grinned, and Teo shook his head.

"Pearla, what you doing? Where you at? Who you with?" I asked my new favorite cousin.

"Ummmm, can I answer one question at a time?"

Matteo was so busy listening to my conversation that he hadn't replied to my sister.

"Pearla..." I warned.

She sighed. "I'm leaving my dad's. I'm alone."

"Goin' where?"

"To get my hair braided, Demise."

"Aite send me the location." I grinned at a brewing Matteo.

"You already got my location, cousin."

"Yeah. I know... Just makin' sure you on yo' toes. Send me a picture when you get finished. I wanna make sure they ain't played in yo' head."

I was talking, but my fingers were moving on my screen. I sent her a thousand dollars via Apple Pay and disconnected the line after she squealed.

Jisei sighed loudly into the receiver before screaming, "Matteo! Why did you call me just to hold the phone?"

"Why you answer for this nigga and not me, Jisei?" I spoke up as

Matteo's mug started morphing into a creepy-ass grin.

"Ummm... Brother?"

"Nawl. It's our dead-ass daddy. Answer the question!"

Jisei coughed. "I haven't gotten no call, brother. I swear..."

Matteo's ugly ass was smiling the hardest he's ever had as I scowled at his phone.

"You a lyin' fool! And ion see yo' location no more either. Jisei, don't have me come to that gaudy-ass, pink festival-looking house you got."

Matteo's smile dropped as if he'd had a revelation. "Why the fuck you got my sister's location, nigga? Ion got her location."

"Same reason you got my sister's, nigga." Our sisters were clearly playing us, but Jisei knew I'd put my foot in her ass. Matteo was still getting to know Pearla, so he had to tread carefully. "Jisei, I'm 'bout to call you. Hang up on this nigga."

The screen lit up, indicating that she did as I asked.

"See, I can't even call yo' sister without her begging. I miss when she was poor and grateful for a wave."

"Like I ain't just send yours a stack." I huffed.

"Nigga, cuz you a duck. I gave her the money for her hair yesterday, and the shit only cost three hundred. You done paid for braids for the whole squad."

I shrugged. "It's all good. If the three musketeers want braids, then braids it is. It's plenty more where that came from."

"I ain't runnin' out over here either, nigga."

"Yeah, aite. That's why my house bigger than yours." I smiled at Matteo because he had yet to expand onto his house since moving there from the condo.

"Y'all stupid, yo. I got shit to do so let's get back to Shio... Is your mind made up, Don? He gettin' Reuchie seat?" Rut swerved the conversation back on topic.

Instead of responding, I was watching Matteo with a smirk. With the rate his fingers were moving, he was more than likely texting Pearla to turn on her location for him or a realtor to find a house bigger than mine. He had to accept that we were both close with each other's sisters, but I was the more likable person with more disposable money. Matteo was rich, but he was mean as fuck. Money, marriage, or Lil Gas Station—as he called Princess—hadn't made the nigga any less mean.

Turning to face Rut, I finally replied, "Nah... Ain't shit set in stone. We gone see how this shit play out. If he handle everything how he supposed to, he got the position. If not, then I'll do the job myself."

"Respectfully, Don, we need a person who has the... intellect—finesse. We ain't no dumb-ass niggas, but we more so the muscle. The enforcers. Killers. We need a thinker that's a doer too."

"Damn, Rut, tell me how you really feel." I stood and buttoned my jacket.

Both men stood, Matteo still texting.

"Ain't shit but love," Rut said while pushing in the big-ass chair. "I'm here to keep it real, and that's what I'll always do. That finessing shit ain't our lane. We would've never been able to build this shit if it wasn't for Reuchie. I respect why he had to step down, but we need somebody better than him to step in his role. Someone that can bend but won't break. Someone who can see what the fuck we can't."

"Facts," Matteo replied, not taking his face out of the phone.

If his ass found a house bigger than mine, Dasani was going to be mad as fuck because I'd promised her I was done expanding the house after the current build was finished.

I nodded. "We gone see how this shit play out. I'll keep my ear to the streets with the Rodríguezes. It won't be long before they show their faces or make some noise, making it easier to find where they're hiding. No matter the race, niggas get tight when it comes to a bitch, and Shio got theirs under lock and key. Had I known they were behind the fuckin' kidnappings, they would've died in the fuckin' club that night. But at this point, ion just want a few... I want to eliminate the whole line. Another Cuppacio and Rinaldi massacre by a Cuppacio and a Rinaldi. It'll be nice to kill some other muthafuckas than our own this time, huh?"

When Rut and Matteo chuckled, I grabbed my phone and walked to the double doors. "Meeting fuckin' adjourned."

~

"BABYYYY!" I called out, removing the tie from around my neck.

I'd made it home and was tired as fuck. Admiring all the changes made throughout the years as I walked through my home, I was proud as fuck of my estate; it had become my oasis because I wouldn't stop adding whatever I wanted in this motherfucker. I'd expanded onto the mansion more times than I could count and was running out of surrounding land. Dasani asked me to stop so we could still have open space for Delicate, but shit, I'd just buy whoever house was in my way and knock their shit down. We didn't need this much space, since we only had one child, but why not? A mega mansion for a Don, his queen, and their Delicate Mafia sounded normal to me. One day, I'd pass this shit down to my daughter, and hopefully my son, but that shit was in the air because my baby mama wasn't budging on having a second child right now.

"Baby!" I yelled again.

My Prada loafers squeaked against the spotless marble as I rounded walls to make it to the main living areas. Every inch of my home was immaculate, but Dasani and her team of designers made sure it never felt cold or overly perfect. Every room was warm and inviting with expensive furnishings and decor. I'd never admit it out loud, but I liked to host. Dasani had finally picked out the starting fragrances for her perfume launch, and as soon as the bottles were done being designed, I was going to throw some ole extravagant-ass shit again.

Delicate was with my mother and grandmother at a fashion show in Milan, so we were baby-free for the next few days. I knew Dasani was home because her security detail had alerted me since she had me blocked. She was still mad about that weak-ass purse that Jisei had gotten before her.

Stepping into our bedroom, my dick hardened at the sight of her.

"I don't give a fuck what that bitch said. She know better than to say that shit to me. I keep telling Demise we not kissing no ass!"

She was standing in front of the TV, remote in hand and phone to her ear in a Skims nude high neck bra and thong set. Her tanned-colored skin was oiled as if she was headed to the beach, and the way her ass was swallowing the thong had me kicking off my shoes.

"You so two-faced."

She jumped, holding her chest as her neck snaked to look at me. When she realized it was just me, she scoffed and rolled her eyes.

"I'ma call you back, Daylani. This nigga just came home."

She disconnected the call and slapped the phone in her palm.

There was a Hermès case on the phone that I knew had cost me an arm and a fucking leg. Her hair was hanging in a long ponytail with her signature bangs. It was low-key my favorite style on her because it brought out her Asian roots with her slanted, hooded eyes. Even with her Filipino roots, my wife was all black and had the body and attitude to prove it.

"How I'm two-faced, Demise?"

She was ready to pick an argument, but I was imagining which way I wanted to give her fine ass this dick. My money had nothing to do with the way Dasani looked. She was fine before I met her, and over the years, she just kept getting finer. Hell, it was in her blood, and I knew so because her sister, Daylani, was a workaholic, running a seven-figure business, and she got better looking every year too. Their mama had done fucking good, and I wished I could've met her because I'm sure she was fine as fuck too.

"Because you stay talking shit about me. I'm yo' husband, Dasani."

Taking a step in her direction, I didn't stop until I could smell the wine on her breath. She was so fucking pretty that I loved and hated that shit simultaneously.

"Okay... What that mean?" She frowned.

"It mean"—I ran my finger down her belly—"You supposed to uplift yo' nigga, not talk down on yo' nigga."

There were visible signs of childbirth on her flat stomach, but I loved that shit. It made her look even better, and it was a plus that Dasani wasn't shy about her imperfections. Hell, she'd spent six years sharing showers with other bitches before having Delicate, but even after becoming a mom, she still flaunted her curvy figure without a care.

"You must not know who you married to. We gone be talking shit until the grave."

"Hell yeah, 'cause we gettin' buried *right* beside each other. I already bought the mausoleum."

"Ion know why for? You ain't gone be gettin' on my fuckin' nerves in the afterlife."

"Bullshit." I pecked her lips, and she pecked me back.

Dasani loved to talk shit in public, but within all these fucking walls, I ran shit. I let her have her moment in public, but in the guise that at night, that pussy was swollen from the beatings it endured. She was the biggest freak I'd known, and I'd fucked a lot of freaks in my day.

Wrapping my arms around her slim waist, I pulled her into my body. She fit like a fucking puzzle. These days, I found myself falling deeper in love with Dasani than ever before. There were days when I woke up and couldn't believe she was my wife. The old me would've thought I was a simp, a fucking buster over pussy that was plentiful. But the old me didn't know that I could have chaos and peace—Dasani, our daughter, and this home was my peace.

She was perfect as fuck, even with her being rough around the edges. She'd done time, just like me. She had a chip on her shoulder, just like me. She had a way with her words, just like me. She fucked good, just like me, and she was a go-getter, just like me. She didn't need no fancy fragrance line; she'd probably lose money before she made it in the world of parfums, but she wanted to do the shit, so I was going full-throttle behind her. I didn't give a fuck if that shit lost a hundred thousand a month. Whatever my wife wanted, she got.

"You missed me, didn't it? Ugly ass."

I kissed her soft lips again. "I missed that throat. Eat this dick."

"Nigga—"

"Now, Dasani," I asserted, and her expression changed instantly.

She pulled from my embrace, dropped to her knees, and unbuttoned my pants. Even with her pointy nails, it took her no time to set my dick free, making sure to hold my gaze the entire time. She wrapped her hands around it, and I would never get over how good her hands felt on my shit.

"I want it slow and sloppy."

Here sleek-ass eyes went slant as she twisted her mouth, lathering up spit.

Pwuah!

"Shit! Feels good as fuck, Sani baby."

Her saliva began to drip from the head of my dick, but she caught it and used her thumb to smear it in with the precum. She rose on her knees and licked the tip, sending tingles from my dick to my stomach to my shoulders before circuiting down to my socked feet.

She took me in her mouth slowly, and when she stretched it wide, letting me feel the back of her throat, I couldn't help but to grab the back of her head and hold her in place. I guided my dick down her throat, not stopping until her nose was in my pubic hairs.

"Goddamn, Sani baby. You suck dick so fuckin' good."

She pulled back, slob dripping down her chin, letting my dick go with a "pop" sound. I was so fucking hard and long that I barely recognized my shit. It was a wonder that she could even get this big motherfucker down her esophagus. She was one of a fucking kind.

Licking all over my dick, she sucked my balls into her mouth, juggling them with her tongue and jaw.

"Oh shit! You eatin' balls today?" I said between grunts.

My hand went from her head to the side of her pretty-ass face. She was so fucking perfect and looked even better gobbling my dick. I prayed that when I was old and gray, I'd still be able to get the mouth service from her. I'd hide her fucking dentures if that's what it took because this shit was incredible.

She tucked my dick back into her mouth once she had her fill of ball soup, and the way she was throwing her fucking neck had me holding up gang signs with my fingers and toes. Whoever had taught her this shit, I needed to find the nigga and dig his ass up so I could kill him again. Yes, I'd gone down the list of every nigga Dasani had fucked, down to the corny-ass nigga who took her virginity in high school. I went through a manic episode a couple years ago where I felt like killing, and her body count had to go. With dick sucking skills like this, it was no way I was letting a nigga walk the earth saying he'd had my bitch. One of the nigga's mama had the nerve to reach out to my wife on Facebook to invite her to the funeral, and I doubled back and killed her ass too.

Sometimes I wanted to kill Rut, too, because he married her sister, and they looked too much alike. Them basically being twins meant the nigga damn near knew how it felt to fuck my wife. I fucked with Daylani, but Dasani should have been an only child. She was one of fucking one, and that was the only thing keeping me from murdering my nigga. No matter how much they resembled, Dasani was made specifically for me. Daylani was too soft and sweet. I told Rut to tread lightly, though. I wasn't all the way right in the head, and I was a selfish nigga when it came to this one here. I'd kill the innocent and the guilty for her.

Holding her head in place, I began fucking her mouth, daring her to gag. But, like the freak she was, she vacuumed sealed her jaws, mimicking her tight-ass pussy. Looking down at the mess we were making on her face, I almost bust at how sexy she was. She began making gargling sounds, and that shit had me thrusting harder. I knew that pussy was wet because I could smell it. Snatching her head back before I could bust, I held it there and slapped my dick across her face.

"Aite now, nigga. You pushing it." She had a face full of dick juice, talking about I was fucking pushing it.

"Shut the fuck up."

Yanking her up, I grabbed her by the waist, and her legs immediately locked around mine. Snatching her panties off in one motion, I slid her down onto my dick.

"I get... so... sooo... Ahhhhhh! Sick of youuu... ripping my panties."

I widened my feet to fuck her standing. "I don't."

She had a billion of these fucking Skims thongs. One day, I called her out about wearing the same damn underwear until she cursed me out and showed me her drawer. I thought she was on some nasty shit until I seen all the different shades of brown underwear.

Biting down on her chin, I bounced her up and down on my dick as we stood in the middle of our bedroom like there wasn't a perfectly made bed a few steps away. I didn't have time for all that, though. I wanted this pussy right where the fuck I stood. Her pussy felt so good as it swallowed my dick. It was like wet silk on a scorching hot day. Each time she lifted, her ass slapped against my balls, and I sank further into her. I never got sick of this shit and probably never would. At first, the thought of marriage petrified me, but having a dime with good-ass pussy at my disposal was the fucking dream. Dasani not only made me look good and feel good, but she made life so much fucking better. I don't know why these niggas don't want this shit or was having a hard time securing the same for themselves.

Dasani grabbed my face and pulled my lips into her mouth. Our tongue-kissing was just as nasty as the tussling our body parts were doing.

"You love me?" I asked as we breathed into each other's mouths.

"Yeap, even though... Ahhhh, fuck... Your breath stankkkk!"

"Lie again." I slapped her ass and drilled into her harder.

"I love your pretty ass. You gonna unblock me?"

She closed her eyes and shook her head as she chased her nut. I could feel her pussy tighten around me and couldn't stop myself from rounding my hips faster. I wanted to fuck with her and stop moving, but I didn't want to fuck up my own nut.

"It's all good 'cause I love yo' fine ass... Even though yo' titties little as hell. Shiiit, Sani baby."

Squeezing her ass, I held her in place as we both came. Hers was so powerful that she nearly pushed my dick out. Still, I managed to stay planted firmly within her contracted walls as I released buckets of cum inside of her. Her eyes opened, she pecked my lips, and climbed down. She removed what was left of her panties around her waist and turned to walk into the bathroom. I spanked her ass hard before she had gotten far. Now standing, with my pants wrapped around my ankles, I lusted after my wife.

"You so fuckin' fine, Sani baby. I swear to God, I wish you was kinda ugly."

She held up her middle finger, but that shit didn't do nothing but make my dick hardened as I watched her hips sway.

"That's because you' s a hater and that's why you're staying blocked."

"Yeah, aite." I rubbed my stomach. She was saying that now, but once I ate her pussy, she'd be unblocking me again.

The bathroom door slammed, but a few seconds later, she was sticking her head out the door.

"You ready for round two?"

She scrunched her wide lips up. "Eww, no. Can you approve that transaction?" She smirked. "Now. Thanks." The bathroom door slammed again.

Stepping out of my pants, I scooped them up and removed my phone. I had a missed call from Jisei, a text from Pearla, and a notification from American Express.

Did you attempt a charge in the sum of $1,000,542.76 from Xing Gao Labs on your Card ending in 83508. Was this you? Reply YES or NO. Reply STOP to opt out.

"AYE, Dasani! You 'bout to have to suck a lil' mo' dick for a million dollars. Fuck you buyin' on a weekday?"

CHAPTER 12
SHIO CUPPACIO

"She straight, though?"

Tunan was swirling his glass of Hennessy while hunched over a plate of hot wings. We were at The Bottom Spot Bar and Grill, and although he hadn't touched his food, I'd fucked up my burger. I had a lot of shit going on my damn self, but food was one thing I wasn't going to deprive myself of.

The waitress came over and removed my plate with a grin. I returned the gesture to the brown-skinned cutie with hair so big it resembled an afro from the seventies. I hope the smile was enough for her to keep all the flirting at bay because the last thing I was up for was smiling in a woman's face.

"Yeah. She's up," Tunan replied. "But she ain't tryna leave the hospital until dey release Glee. When the brain swelling is down, dey said she can be discharged too."

"And the baby?"

I remembered the hurt and shock on Glow's face when it was revealed that her sister was in active labor. Shorty was straight up trying to lay her ass out in that hospital until Tune stepped in and de-escalated the situation. The fact that both were hospitalized was fucked up. I was going to send an extra prayer for them tonight because I knew how much Glow meant to the wives and how much Glee meant to Glow. The way Tunan was staring off every few words, it was safe to assume Glow had come to mean something to him too.

I wasn't judging my brother for caring for her in a matter of weeks. I'd begun to care about the little sinner in a matter of days.

"Cathy 'nem been rotating schedules at the hotel across from the hospital with the baby... You remember the nigga I was locked up with?"

On many of our outings and rides through the city, Tunan and I chopped it up about minor shit, and his cellmate had come up a time or two.

"Yeah. The one that got a book?"

He swirled his glass again. "Yeah, him. Leader." He paused before turning to look at me. "That's Glee's baby daddy."

I whistled. "*Damn*... I wasn't expecting you to say that shit. She must've met that nigga at school?"

When Glow and I were conversing, I'd looked thoroughly into her. When I first caught sight of her pretty ass while visiting Jisei back when Ezio was in the basement, I had to make sure she was fit for this life if I'd so happened to bring her in. That's when I found out about her sister, who was in high school.

"Yeah. He from 'round dat way. Nigga used to be deep in his feelings about his lil' college junt. I would have never thought that she was Glee, and I damn sho' didn't think he'd get her pregnant."

"Shit happens, Tune. Just because she got a baby now don't mean her life has to stop. She just gotta go harder."

I had no fucking plans on getting Bahati pregnant. But my having a forgiving heart spared her life and made me a father in the process. I, now having a child, was about to go ten times as hard, but I needed to see what my next move was about to be first, and this conversation with Tunan would certainly help my decision.

"Yeah. Well, tell dat shit to her sister. Glow gone be ready to kill my ass when she find out 'bout Leader, especially dat I know the nigga." Tune finally picked up a wing, dipped it into the dressing, and took a bite. "Dis shit ain't got nuttin' on Memphis wings. As a matter of fact, they need to switch that BBQ shit to hot wings. We got the best wings, hands down."

"Ion know. The Chi got some good-ass wings and fasho the best food. Let Bella show you them TikToks everybody be making about Chicago being the best food city."

"Chicago? Fuck dem videos. Y'all got that mild sauce shit. Dat shit ain't hittin' on nuttin'. Y'all best known for dem hot dogs."

"Deep dish pizza, nigga... Hot dogs up there with it too. But I have heard Memphis BBQ is undefeated. Y'all can keep that."

"You gotta pull up at somebody grandma's or uncle's crib for the fye shit. None of them food spots on Beale is gon' getchu right. And if the uncle ain't got sandals on with his crusty-ass heels exposed, shit gon' be slaw." He took another bite of his wing. "These aite doe."

With my back turned to the brick wall that lined the bar top, I glanced at the entrance as Tunan smacked on the wings. The gloomy weather outside did nothing to slow traffic. While the bar wasn't packed, it had a steady crowd. I turned back, facing the TV mounted above the bar. Highlights from the NBA playoff games flashed in a series of videos with Shaq and Charles Barclay arguing as usual. I was going to make it my business to catch a few games this upcoming season, but I also planned to catch some local games at the high schools.

I'd been in Jagoda Bay for a few years and hadn't gotten the chance to really enjoy the city or my paper. I'd been on a constant run to stack my money, keep up with Don's demands, and a keeping shit in line with my cousins. The day I could sit still and enjoy the fruits of my labor was the day I'd sleep like a fucking baby. I was hoping I'd have someone to share that time with, but I wanted someone worthy —someone intelligent.

"I fucked up."

I turned to see that my brother had finished half the wings and was now looking into my face again. "Tune—"

"Nawl, G..."

He picked up the almost empty glass and downed his Hennessy. His tone implied he was about to say some shit that needed my full attention, so I didn't look away.

"When you first approached me and you bought dat high-ass painting, I purposely taxed yo' ass cuz I didn't give a fuck 'bout the nigga we came from. But den you were outside the jail, and ever since, you been showin' up. The least I coulda did was asked you if it was okay to go after Glow."

He rubbed his hand down his head but held eye contact. Tunan looked like the rest of his siblings, but it was times like this when I saw our father in him. Each time Sandro made his appearance in one of my features, it threw me off, especially because I saw the shit when I looked in the mirror every day.

"Dat shit was flaw as fuck, Shio. When you sent me to stand in for you, and I saw Glow sittin' there..." He hung his head low for a second and then chuckled before looking back at me. "All I could think 'bout was how fuckin' pretty she was. I'd just told myself I was done with dese bitches. I was gonna focus on my come up and keep my dick to myself. But den, dat shit just happened. Den I needed a wife. Den I couldn't stop thinkin' 'bout her.

"I realized I wanted in with the mob more than I needed your approval. The fucked-up part of me feels like I mighta married her before you could, and if dat's the case, you shouldn't wanna fuck with a nigga like me—blood or not."

"You're right, I shouldn't. But Tune... You ain't come looking for me, it was the other way around. You don't remember because you were too young, but our father loved you. He was fucked up, no doubt, and some days I questioned if the nigga even loved me."

I chuckled as I thought back to my first time seeing Tunan. I was only youngin' and hadn't completely given up on Sandro.

"You need to leave!" the woman I'd never seen before yelled at my dad from behind a screened door.

She was different-looking from my mama. My mama was thin and always well-dressed, and this woman was heavy-set and wore a house gown with discoloration all over it. Her hair was wrapped in a scarf, and my mama kept her hair flowing down her back. The tired look in her eyes was the one thing she had in common with my mama, and from the look on her face, my daddy had done something to disgust her.

My head bounced from her to my dad. I was confused. When my dad put me on the fancy airplane, where the nice flight attendant gave me cookies and juice, I thought we were headed to Disney World. But when the plane landed, and we walked through the airport, and I saw the Welcome to Memphis sign, I knew then, we were a long way from Disney World.

"I'm just trying to see the boy. I can give him a better life—"

"A betta life? A betta life! Are you fuckin' crazy!"

The sound of people moving closer to the door could be heard, and about four boys varying in ages, two of whom were wearing diapers, appeared behind her. They all shared identical features, but one stood out among the rest. He had his eyes on my daddy, whereas the other boys were looking at their mama.

"Listen, baby—"

"Baby?"

I was just as shocked as the woman in the dingy dress. I looked at my dad with the same bewildered eyes as her, except he wasn't paying me any mind. His focus was fixated on the woman, and the pleading in his eyes was the same he'd shown to my mama when he knew he'd done something wrong, which was most of the time. Still, I loved my daddy, and that's why I was standing here, waiting for an explanation as to why we were here instead of on rides at Disney World.

This neighborhood was filthy, the houses were tiny, and this particular one looked too small for so many children to be living in it. They all looked so poor. I didn't know where my daddy had found these poor people. I didn't understand why we were here, and he was showing so much urgency and care toward the unkempt woman.

"The boy—"

"You can't even call him what he is! He's not **the boy,** *Sandro! He's your boy! He's your son! A son I wouldn't have had had I known your ass was married!"*

She began shooing the children behind her back as she whispered that last part of her sentence.

"I know... I know he's my son. That's why I'm trying to make it right. You won't take money from me. You won't let me move you away from this city. The least you can do is just let him come with me."

I blinked as my eyes shifted between my daddy, the lady, and the boy, who was still standing there, watching my daddy. The other children, who looked to be his siblings, had gone further into the house. I studied him and saw that what made him different from the other children was what made me Sandro's son.

Was he my brother?

But how?

My dad was married to my mama. Could men have children with other women when they were married? And the other boys looked like him, too, so does that mean they were my brothers as well?

"You don't think I know who you are and what you do? Hunh? My

cousin told me 'bout you. About who you're associated with. Dat wife of yours? Did she marry you willingly, Sandro?"

My dad didn't respond, which made me stare at him for answers too. My mama loved my daddy. Why would she not marry him willingly?

"Look—"

"No, you look! You were a fun time. Okay? An escape when I visited my cousin. I shoulda left your ass at the bar I met you at! But what's done is done. You're dangerous, and ***my boy*** *will not be tied up in your world." Her eyes dropped down to me, and her face relaxed a bit, sort of in a nurturing way. She looked like my mama did when my cousins and me went off with the men in the middle of the night. "I feel sorry for your son. He doesn't know the hell he is facin'. You're the devil, Sandro. You're the devil, and you will not turn my child into a demon."*

She went to close the door, but my daddy stepped closer and said, "So, you'd rather him be poor? Share a two-bedroom home with twenty other children? Sleep on the floor? Depend on welfare? He has Cuppacio blood in him. He can handle ***anything*** *he may encounter while I raise him!"*

"Oh, yeah? Dat means he can use dat ***Cuppacio blood*** *to survive the ghetto. Fuck you. Take dat boy home to his mama. He looks like he's ready to go have fun, and you're hauling him across state lines to your mistress's doorstep!" She scoffed.*

"Wait!" My daddy pulled on the door that was locked, and it was so raggedy that I was sure I could open it. "Let me just... come in. I need to... I need you."

For some reason, those words knocked the wind out of me. Why did he need a woman who wasn't my mama?

She folded her meaty arms across her large breasts and squinted her eyes. "I ain't got no pussy for you. My last baby daddy ate it all. Goodbye, Sandro. Don't ever contact us again. As long as you are affiliated with dat mess, you can never see my son. I'd rather us starve than be a part of dat."

Boom

The door slammed. My dad sighed and turned on his heels. His legs were so long that I had to run to keep up with him. Before we reached the car, another car pulled up behind it, and seeing my dad's body tense, I knew it wasn't anything good. The window rolled down, and the piercing blue eyes that stared back gave me the creeps. I knew it wasn't godly to hate people, but I hated Niccoli.

"What the fuck are you doing here?" my dad yelled.

"I could ask you the same thing, cousin." Niccoli's eyes traveled from my daddy to me. "Don knows you took the nigger out of state? That's right... Just because you waited until he was on a business trip to sneak away doesn't mean he doesn't have eyes everywhere."

"Shut the fuck up, Niccoli! I don't need permission to take my son on a trip."

"But you do need permission to bring him to your mistress. Why isn't the bitch and her child dead? That's the rule, right? Kill the outside children. Why is she still breathing, Sandro? Why is **he** *still breathing? I guess I'll bring this info to my brother."*

"Don't, Niccoli. I'm just trying to do the right thing. Look at their living conditions..." My dad gestured behind him to the house that looked as if my cousins and I had built it.

"Leave the bitch and her son! What are you not understanding about the way we are running things now?" Spit flew from Niccoli's mouth, landing on the steering wheel that he was banging his fist on.

My dad waved him off and continued his trek to our car.

"You come back here!" Niccoli screamed while pointing at my daddy. "I'm going to kill her, her bastard, and this bastard if you continue to do things your way! Get your ass back on the plane and have that nigger ready for a mission. Now!"

My daddy stopped and looked at Niccoli, his eyes colder than I'd ever seen. "You scared her, didn't you? Stay the fuck away from them, Niccoli! You want me to do things your way, fine. But stay out of Memphis. Leave them be, or this will get ugly."

Niccoli didn't reply. He drove off, making marks in the street as they did on the cartoons.

"Come on, Shio." My daddy sighed, finally taking my hand.

"Wait. Daddy... Is that my brother? What's his name?"

My daddy slowed, knelt in front of me on the dusty ground that dirtied his suit, and grabbed my shoulders. "No matter what, come back for your brother. Okay?"

I nodded.

"I'm serious, Shio. I know it's wrong to father a child outside of your marriage, but I can't change the past. You're going to be a great man one day—both of you are. You're special, though. I know you'll do the right thing when given the opportunity. Wherever your brother is then, go get him. Go get him and help him, okay? Always do right by your brother."

"Okay, Dad. But how am I supposed to get him if I don't know his name?"

My dad rubbed my head, stood, and grabbed my hand again. "His name is Tunan. Tunan Payne Cuappacio. Come. We must leave."

As my daddy dragged me to the car he had rented at the airport, I looked back at the house and saw Tunan standing in the window, watching us. We held eye contact until I was buckled into the car, and before we pulled away, I promised Tunan under my breath that I'd be back for him.

"I AIN'T TRYNA CHANGE your perspective of Sandro because, most days, I'm conflicted 'bout him myself. It's like... I want to hate the nigga, but I can't. At least, not fully. It's a constant struggle. I know you went through it as a youngin', but the best thing that happened to you was growing up exactly where you were. We suffered. We were abused. We were exposed to way too much shit for our age. That's why even though I'm still years away from thirty, it feels like I'm double it. I had so much anger and hate in my heart that it was destroying me. That's why I had to turn to God and invest in my health."

"Yeah. I feel you." He signaled for another drink, and the big-haired bartender bounced over, her eyes on me. "I still feel flawed as fuck. I backdoored you, and somehow, somehow, I'm gonna make it up to you. No homo."

"You don't owe me shit, Tune."

"I do. You blessed my pockets fresh out. Shid, I ain't even paid a fuckin' phone bill since I been out. I ain't used to another man doin' shit for me outside of my brothers, and I know you my brother, too, but... You ain't have to do none of the shit you did and still doin' for a nigga. Real shit, I appreciate the fuck out of you for bringin' me in. I ain't no pocket-counting-ass nigga, but I see how y'all livin'. I see the respect y'all get—the way the city bows to y'all. I was in dat cell not knowing what my next move would be. If worst came to worst, I was gonna ask my bro-in-law to have Goal put me on. But seeing how y'all livin', I wouldn't want to do nuttin' else but this, and I haven't even started doin' what the fuck I'm supposed to be doin'."

"Man, I keep my word. I told you I was coming back for you, you just ain't hear me. And when it comes to Glow... She's a diamond. I knew she was something special, but at the same time, I knew she wasn't for me. I never had any dealings with your wife outside of casual conversations. She's a good one. You did good. We good, Tune."

Tune was my brother, but I knew how men could get behind pussy. Plus, Glow was a beautiful woman. I was being truthful, though. We'd had a few conversations, but there was never a spark. I never even got close enough to smell her. I wanted to ensure Tunan understood that because I didn't need to become a cloud in their marriage. No matter how much they screamed that their shit was just on paper, an emotionless motherfucker could feel the connection, and a blind motherfucker could see it. Tunan didn't know it yet, but he loved Glow, and sooner than later, they would be okay with the reality of falling in love.

As for me, I was in the wildest fucking predicament. I was so in my head about the two women Don said I had to choose from that I'd been avoiding them both.

Tune bit into a wing, and from the look on his face, I could tell he wasn't enjoying it. Turning to me, he asked, "What's been goin' on with you, doe? Y'all ain't dial me up for dat impromptu trip to Mexico."

"You got a passport?" I asked the question I already knew the answer to.

"I do. But ain't no tellin' what dat thieving-ass hoe did with it." He snarled, throwing the bone on the plate.

I had never encountered a woman like Stella and prayed I never would. She took my brother for everything he had, literally. From my understanding, Tunan was doing really well before he met Stella, and when he got with her, things started going downhill. That was the price for fucking with any and everybody. I learned quickly that women enjoyed a good trick, especially if he could be tricked.

"Mexico was indeed impromptu. I didn't even want them niggas to come." I lowered my voice because there were too many ears around. "That was Don's doin'."

"So... You got a baby and a long-lost baby mama." Tunan smirked.

"Nel needs to stop tellin' my fuckin' business like his shit wasn't a fuckin' disaster just a few months ago."

Lifting my hand, the big-haired bartender nearly tripped over her foot to come our way again. She had all of her teeth on display as she waited for my request. I smiled to be polite—I was more than uninterested in women right now.

"I need another." I pointed to the empty glass that had housed a triple shot of Sullivans Cove."

"Triple shot again?"

"No. I'll take the bottle."

Her smile dropped, making her wide nose the focal point of her face. It went well with her bone structure, and she looked cute as hell with the perplexed expression on her face. I loved women in all shapes and sizes and didn't have the expectation that all women needed button noses to be attractive. Wasn't shit wrong with a bell pepper nose as long as the rest of your face matched that shit.

"The bottle is two thousand dollars..."

Crossing my hands as they rested on the bar top, I shot her a cheeky grin. "I didn't ask the cost, Brook, but if we're talking numbers, the bottle actually costs eight hundred. Your owner gotta get his profit, though, so I ain't tripping." My grin widened. "The bottle, please."

Brook's posture relaxed, and if it wasn't for the alcohol, deep-fried foods, mix of cheap and mid-range perfumes and colognes hanging in the air, I would have been able to smell how relaxed she was.

Brook turned, her ass—which was small but had grip—hanging out of her black shorts. When she reached for the brand-new bottle, I clicked my tongue.

"This the Sullivans Cove." She looked over her shoulder, big hair blocking her view.

"It is, but no need to pop a seal. I'll take what's left of that one."

She pointed to the bottle that had a fourth of the whisky left in it. When I nodded, she sucked her teeth with a smirk.

"But you'll be paying for a bottle that's nearly gone. That's silly."

Holding my hand out, I took the bottle and poured it into the glass without responding. That was her cue to go back to servicing her other customers. I wasn't up for conversing with her about what I was doing with the money in my pocket. She'd be tipped well, and since the bar usually put a twenty percent gratuity on every ticket, she should've been trying to upsell me a second bottle.

Ditzy broads.

Tossing back the glass, I tasted the tea leaves, dried pineapples, and fresh pine layers of the whiskey as the flavors scratched my throat. I hadn't tasted this flavor profile, but I knew that with the single casks, you never knew what you were getting until you tried it. I was going to enjoy the last of this bottle from the Australian company, but I'd be running an extra three miles tomorrow to burn this shit off.

"You gonna leave me hangin', or you gonna fill the gaps on what Nel hadn't? I still don't understand how he told me the play but still left shit out—like I ain't already married. Shit, I beat dat nigga down the aisle. I'm more certified than him and his brother, actually."

Tunan laughed, and I chuckled with him because he had managed to marry before all of us except Ezio. Don was sure to rub that shit in every time he was in our space too. He definitely made it a point during our conversation on the plane coming back from Mexico.

"Bahati and I fucked off for years when I was livin' in Chicago. There was... *advantages* to our relationship. Her pops was a pharmacist."

"Was? Shid, we can do sum'n with dat." Tunan's brow raised.

"Yeah. That nigga dead, bro."

Tunan's brow rose even higher.

"Not my body."

"Oh, aite. Continue."

I poured more liquor, watching the syrup-colored liquor splash into the glass.

"Bahati was too deep in her feelings, fuckin' up the money, so I let her go. Solana's fiancée found her and, apparently my toddler, and now, I'm here."

"And dem niggas?"

"MIA. But not fo' long."

I left out the details of Don's plans and would fill Tunan in when we didn't have such mixed company in our space. Openly talking about mob business at a bar was just plain stupid, and I knew better.

"So now you got baby mama and Solana at the crib?" Tunan

asked, his smirk appearing again.

I took the shot, and this time a sigh followed it. "Not exactly. Solana, since she on that shit, she's in rehab."

"Rehab? Like a facility?"

"Nah. Real nigga rehab." Italian had given it that name, and I could barely say the shit without laughing.

"How you feel 'bout dat?"

Picking up the glass, I swirled the ice around. "To be real, bro, I feel a lot of shit that I'm still sorting through. Solana should be dead for the shit she pulled. But then, Bahati was supposed to be dead too."

"So dat's why you drankin' that old-man-ass liquor? Both yo' hoes got yo' mind gone!" Tunan laughed.

"Old-man-ass liquor cuz I'm old. Just told you I'm double my age. Life ain't been consistently sweet."

"Oh, I feel you on dat shit. But on the real... What's next? I ain't tryna tell you some shit you don't already know, but you still gotta find a wife. I know you tired as fuck of hearin' dat shit, especially from Don. If dat nigga gave me a deadline, I'm sure his ass 'bout to light fye under you. You got baby mama at the crib, and Solana being watched by yo' people. How you gonna bring somebody new in dat?"

Picking up the bottle, I twisted the pour spout, and it came off with a pop. I filled the glass halfway and placed the bottle back down beside the glass. "I ain't, Tune."

"Hunh?"

"I ain't bringin' nobody new in."

"Wait... You sayin' you... Naw, bro. One on dat shit and the other been playin' hide and go seek. Fuck you mean you not bringin' nobody new in?"

"I gotta marry one of 'em."

"You ain't gotta do shit but stay black and die."

"Yeah, well, according to Don, I gotta stay black, die, and marry either Bahati or Solana."

Tunan dropped the chicken wing he'd just picked up back onto the plate and twisted his lip. "On God?"

"On foe 'nem."

"The fuck? Heeeeelllll nawl. What's the alternative? I ain't finna believe dat shit yo' only option."

The alternative is leaving the fucking mob and making my own way. But if I leave, you ain't in. If I leave, I'm leaving my family behind—my blood. I can't watch their backs if I ain't in. I can't make sure everything is running smoothly on the front and back end if I ain't in. Me leaving is going to cause a whole domino effect of shit. Plus, as easy as it sounds, no one just walks away from the mob.

"No alternative so believe it. In thirty days, another Cuppacio will be added to the family tree."

Tunan was dumbfounded with his mouth wide open as he stared at me. If the shit wasn't so fucked up, I'd be laughing.

"Don done lost his fuckin' mind. I mean, I knew his mind was gone when we got dumped in the desert, but damn! Now I really feel fucked up behind marryin' Glow. You coulda had her."

"That's all you, bro, and the desert really ain't the hardest challenge we've been on. Just be glad you came in when you did."

"I would say, it ain't worth it, but it most *definitely* is. I know you'n want nan one of dem, but shit... if it's gonna keep you on top, just do eeny, meeny, miny, moe."

"You childish as fuck." I chuckled while shaking my head.

"Real shit, you gonna have to spin in a circle and cover your eyes and point, and whoever you land on, dat's the one. The baby mama may sound like the obvious choice cuz she got yo' daughter, but from where I'm from, niggas hate dey baby mamas—especially the first one. Number two is always the sweet spot. The fact dat she hid the baby from you, no matter the circumstances, is questionable as fuck. Now, Mexi-Mami, her being on dope can cause a whol' bitch of fuckin' problems. She could get clean and you could marry her, but dere's dat possibility of her gettin' right the fuck back on drugs. She could get so sprung out dat she take you for errthang you got!" His ass shivered, and I knew he was thinking about ole girl who cleaned him out. "Den we got dem niggas she was promised to... I mean, ain't no bitch in my blood, but you know Mexicans be deep. Dey don't die, Dey multiply. Shit, I'd hate like hell to be you."

I was indeed in a fucked-up spot, but there was no sense in dwelling on it. I could walk away. I'd thought about walking away more than once since I'd been propositioned on that plane, but I knew it wouldn't end well for my people. We'd wanted this for so long to secure our family and reinvent the Cuppacio name. We didn't give a fuck about the mob; Don killing our fathers was a gift. But when Ezio saw how Scarlett and the Rinaldi Mob were living, we all agreed our mamas and aunts deserved the same. Merging was the better move for our family, and the wife requirement was simple to me—so simple that I'd been on Ezio and my cousin's asses about finding wives and doing what was necessary. Now, I was in the same position. The difference was that I had two beautiful women as options, and I wanted nothing to do with either of them.

Bahati was the obvious choice, but my gut was telling me to pay Bahati dust. Something about her rubbed me the same way as Solana doing drugs, and that was saying a lot since I was strongly against cokeheads. She hadn't faltered at all, even agreeing to the DNA test without attitude. When the nurse showed up at the house to do the DNA swabs of Shya and me, Bahati stood by with no emotion or expression indicating deceit. Shya, however, had completely shown her ass, not wanting the nurse to even touch her to collect the skin cells needed. She already cried nonstop, so I felt bad about forcing her to let the lady swab her cheeks. The way she bucked and screamed, you'd think the few seconds were hours of her having the long Q-tip in her mouth.

"So what you gonna do, Shio?" Tunan asked, pulling me from my short-term memories.

"Shit... I'll figure it out. I have a month. I'll pray on it, fast, and hopefully have some insight before Don chooses for me."

"Fuuuuck no! Don't let dat nigga choose. Ion trust none of his decisions, and I haven't even been 'round long."

"Shio?"

Turning my neck, my eyes fell to Uriah standing behind Tunan and me. My dick bricked at the sight of her, which wasn't a surprise. For one, she looked good as fuck in heeled sandals, a backless denim dress that stopped mid-thigh, and a silver clutch that matched her silver accessories. Her surgically-enhanced breasts spilled from the sides. There was some type of red gloss on her lips, and her hair was in loose curls that I'd more than likely paid for. It hadn't been long since I broke her off when I fucked around and called her Solana's name. I hadn't seen her since, and from all the shit brewing, it would be a long time before I even entertained the idea of calling Uriah up.

"Damn!" Tunan whistled, making Uriah blush.

She eyed me, the small smile playing coy on her face. "I knew that was you. I know your back from anywhere."

Turning fully in my seat, I chucked my chin. "Wassup, Uriah? You look nice."

I had no qualms about telling a woman they were pretty. The compliment didn't mean I was ready to fuck, even though my dick was saying something totally different.

"Thank you." She cocked her head. "I've been calling you."

"I've been busy."

"You're always busy."

"I am." I grabbed the glass and sipped from it while holding her stare.

"Too busy for fun, though?"

Running my hand down my mouth, I called for the bartender, who was back on my side of the bar in seconds. "Brook... Add Uriah to my tab. Whatever she wants, it's on me."

Uriah's eyes bounced to Brook, but I didn't detect any jealousy. Brook was cute, but Uriah was a twenty on a light day, and today was a light day. Uriah probably wasn't threatened because, in her mind, she knew the type of women I craved, and Brook didn't fit the criteria. Unbeknownst to Uriah, I'd take Brook down without hesitation if I were on that. Pretty women were pretty women. I didn't have a type. My dick did, however, have its limits. It didn't pump for just everybody.

Uriah kept her composure, but I could see the disappointment in her eyes when she looked back at me.

"Got it." Brook was back across the bar after realizing my need had nothing to do with her and me. You'd think she was wearing skates with how fast she walked away.

"You can at least say you'll call me when you're free, Shio. Give a girl some hope." Uriah smiled softly.

"You know I can't do that." Licking my lips, I gave her one more onceover. "But you enjoy your night."

Uriah nodded, glanced at Tunan, and then turned on her heels. The dress didn't do justice to her ass, but she still looked good in it. To a random man, Uriah looked thick, but because I'd seen her naked, had her bouncing on my dick, and had her riding my pelvis, I knew the true nature of her butt's size.

"One thing fasho, you got a type."

"Really?"

"Fuck you mean, really? Mane... You like 'em dark. You was just wastin' my wife's time."

I laughed at Tunan's ignorant ass without agreeing or disagreeing.

"You should let Don add her to the lineup. That's wifey material, for sure."

Uriah was a divorced mom of two. Don would never let her in. But I held her personal business in.

Tunan slapped my back. "You a smart man, bro. Calculated as fuck. I know you already know who you gonna marry, even if you tellin' yourself you don't. Whoever you choose, I'll be the best brother-in-law since we missed out on our childhood bondin' and shit."

"'Preciate that, Tune."

"No sweat. Now, when can I meet my niece?"

"Soon."

I wasn't ready to bring Shya around the family just yet. I still had some shit to sort through. I needed to verify she was mine first, and we'd done the test already, so it was a waiting game now for the results. I was also still processing the fact that I could be a fucking daddy. I always thought that when I had a child, I'd feel like a father. But I felt the same as I did before learning about Bahati and the kid. I felt an urge to protect her, but shit, I felt that way about all kids.

Reaching inside my pocket, I pulled out a wad of cash, tossing two hundred-dollar bills on the counter, and Tunan reached in his pocket and pulled out a fifty to add to it. My card was already on file, so I knew she'd charge the meal, the bottle, Uriah's tab, and the gratuity to that. The cash was solely for her pockets. If she were smart, she wouldn't report it to her manager. I knew they liked to cut off the tips to pass out equally among the other staffers, like the cleanup crew and security.

Leaving the bottle, I stood as Tunan pushed his plate away, closer to the edge of the bar top.

"I was gonna pay the tab, but fuck dat. You got dat high-ass, half-drunken bottle of liquor, and I can tell ole Kesha 'bout to be on some petty shit and order errthang up in dis bitch since you turned her down."

"Nigga, who?"

"Kesha. From *Belly*. On God, she comin' just like her fine ass but thicker. I can't believe you aren't married to her ass off the rip. Gotdamn!" Tunan was still looking in the direction Uriah had gone off to.

"You swore you wasn't studying women, but now you married and still lusting."

"Shit... I'm still a man dat did a year. I got eyes, and dey 20/20. Dat's yo' wife. Call Don up right now."

"Uriah would never be my wife, Tune."

"You crazy."

"One thing you gonna learn 'bout your brother is, I don't do shit without intention."

"I see dat, cuz Kesha would've been somewhere with her ankles hittin' her ears."

I laughed off Tunan and his antics as we slapped hands before making our way out of the bar. He still had the Ferrari Don had loaned him, so we met here. I was past my limit of what I preferred for driving, but I'd make it. I'd driven in worse conditions.

"Real shit," Tunan pointed to the Ferrari. "Y'all keep throwin' me dese alley-oops, and I'm gonna be indebted to yo' ass forever."

Slapping him on the back, I replied, "You'n owe me shit. What's mine is yours, nigga."

"Except *her,* hunh?"

"And *her* is?" I watched as traffic zipped by while we both stood at our vehicles.

Tunan snickered, looking just like our fucking daddy. "The one you gonna give yo' last name when dese thirty days is up. Lemme find out you playin' the long game, bro."

Instead of replying, I chucked him a head nod and hopped in my car. My life may have been in disarray, but my brother was officially in the Rinaldi Mafia, and our relationship was solid. I could scratch another thing off my list that was growing by the day. If I kept it up, I'd be checking shit off like I was Nike till I was old and fucking gray.

~

As I pulled up to my home, the solitude that usually settled over me was missing. I put the truck in park and let my head fall back into the seat. Usually, when I crossed the threshold, I shed all the worries of the world. I twisted the ring on my finger with my thumb as I assessed my house. On the outside, everything was perfect. The beams hanging under the roof overhang cast enough light that I could see the windows, the shutters, the brick, and the landscaping. Everything was in pristine condition. The HOA wouldn't have it any other way, but even then, I liked my shit to look immaculate. If my home wasn't in order inside and out, I couldn't function.

At least I didn't have to worry about Solana's unorganized ass.

No sooner had the thought crossed my mind than my chest burned, and I knew it was from the combination of whiskey and beef. I turned the engine off, jumped out of my truck, and trudged up the sidewalk. The sound of crickets chirping in harmony on wet grass filled the night's damp air. Jagoda Bay was in for a rainy summer. I'd seen the forecast for the next two months, and they were predicting at least ten rainstorms per month.

Entering my home, I was greeted by the smell of home-cooked food, which made my stomach grumble. I'd eaten the burger more than an hour ago, but liquor brought on my appetite. Usually, I'd grab a sandwich and a piece of fruit because of the time of night, but with the way it smelled, my nose led me directly to the kitchen, betraying my original plan to go to my room and shower.

It had been a long day. Since things had settled and Don had asked me to stand down about the Rodríguezes for now, I was back to my regular schedule. With Ezio and Vello on unofficial paternity leave, and Nel having to take Pia to an appointment today, I'd been tasked with making sure all our buyers were straight on product and picking up money from those who owed us. I'd even stopped by the cabin and dropped off food for Hobo. He was asleep when I got there, so I left enough for him for a few days and then met Tunan at the bar. Hobo had calmed down since he realized he was there for a long time and not for a good time. His ass still tried me every other visit, so I was happy he was asleep when I pulled up. I didn't have the energy to go back and forth with his ass. I'd been liable to kill him and betray the promise I'd made to my nephew.

One thing that wasn't regular was the sight in my kitchen.

Standing at the doorframe, I watched the scene before me. A fat ass was eating up a pair of tan shorts that jiggled each time she mixed something in the pot. Loud screams broke my stare, and off to the left of the kitchen, which was way too big for just me, was an irate toddler. Baby Shya was on one. A few strides later, I was in her space. Her cheeks were dark plum, her nose was running, and her tears were endless. The little beauty was screaming like someone had stolen her candy.

"Hey. What you doin' all this fussin' for?"

Picking her up from the table that she was sitting on, surrounded by cut-up strawberries, it was clear she didn't give a damn about the fruit.

"Hi, Shio."

I could feel Bahati's eyes on me when I didn't respond and continued to move from the kitchen to the nearby half bath. Flipping the light switch, I grabbed some Kleenex and slowly wiped Shya's little nose.

"It's okay. You ain't gotta be like that, Shya."

Her cries grew louder.

"Aite, aite, aite. Come on, pretty baby." Bouncing her in my arms, I dried her face completely. Once her face was clear, I tossed the Kleenex in the trash and continued bouncing her. "You too pretty for all that cryin'. Too pretty, little Shya. Come on... Let's get you somethin' to drink."

Walking back into the kitchen, I made her a fresh cup of milk as Bahati watched me. I wasn't sure if she was watching me because I was holding Shya or if she was watching because I was giving Shya more attention than I'd given her ass since they'd gotten here.

Handing Shya the cup of milk, she turned her head from left to right frantically while pushing the sippy cup away. I placed the cup on the counter and stared at the little girl in my arms. I wasn't sure what the issue was, and I was starting to grow concerned. She was a crier. She was crying when I got up to work out this morning, and again when I left before Bahati and her emerged from the room they'd been occupying. The doctor had said she was okay, but now I was starting to believe otherwise. Giving her a visual assessment to see if there was anything missed, she looked up at me with wide, upside-down-turned eyes, long wet lashes, dark chocolate skin, and a head full of curls that were pulled into two ponytails.

She was a doll. The way her eyebrows were naturally spiky reminded me so much of my mother. The first lady never had to get her eyebrows arched or lash extensions, as she told it. She'd always get complimented on them. Shya had similar ones. She was darker than Bahati and me, so her deep chocolate skin had to come from somewhere. I was inclined to believe it came from my mother, who shared the same skin tone. They shared so many features that it was uncanny, almost. I still hadn't told my mother that I was a father. Before I made that move, I needed the results. Although now, looking at her, it wasn't really necessary. She was literally my mother in baby form.

But I ain't no dumb motherfucker.

Finally calming from her cries, she blinked, slid her thumb into her mouth, and placed her head on my chest. The cocoa butter on her skin and the oils in her hair from the style Solana had done were just as soothing to me as her thumb was to her. My heart jerked against my chest as she heaved, signaling she was done with her crying session.

I rubbed a hand down her back as I watched her in the mirror. It was a sight—me holding a baby. I felt like I'd skipped chapters in my own autobiography. I hadn't experienced the bliss of the positive pregnancy test, witnessed the pregnancy, or felt the anxiety of labor before Shya was born. Yet, I had a child in my arms who needed care, love, and guidance.

When she'd been asleep for at least twenty minutes, only then did I turn the light out and walk back through the kitchen. Bahati was on her tippy toes, reaching for a plate with her one arm, so I stopped beside her and got the plates down that she was reaching for. Her ass grazed my dick, which had just come down from the sight of Uriah. Unlike her, it didn't get hard for Bahati.

"Thank you," she said, giving a closed-lip smile.

Looking over her, my chest grew tight. Leaving her standing there, I walked to their room and placed Shya in the middle of the bed. The TV was already on *Gracie's Corner*, and I noticed how the bed was made, and nothing was out of place. Making sure Shya wouldn't wake up now that she was solo, I turned the TV down but left it on and cracked the door.

As I walked down the hall on the way to my bedroom, I paused at Solana's door. It had to be the liquor that had me reaching up and rubbing my chest. My pulse was going haywire. Grabbing the knob, I closed the door, then did an about-face and detoured back to the kitchen.

On the kitchen island was a plate and the matching cup. Bahati stood behind the counter chair that she'd pulled out. "Come sit."

Taking the offered seat, I didn't bother pushing the chair up to the table. Bahati tried and kept failing because there wasn't shit she could do with all the muscle and weight on me that held the chair in place. Not bothering to assist her, I turned and grabbed her good arm carefully, bringing her between the table and me. Her long, thick legs were on display and oiled down in a familiar scent. The matching tank top she wore did nothing to hide her hardened nipples. Bahati was a beauty—a sight for sore eyes. And if she'd kept her shit up, I knew the pussy was still good. Her braids fit her face perfectly, and back then, I loved it when she wore them.

"I cooked what you had in the fridge; salmon, asparagus, and roasted garlic potatoes."

The stuffed salmon not only looked amazing, but it smelled delightful. However, my attention wasn't on the food. It was on Bahati.

Noticing my glare, her smile fell. "What? Is it Shya? Shio, she does that. She's spoiled rotten. That DNA test scared her too. She likes to be held all day, and as you can see—" She lifted her broken arm as far as she could. "I'm not able to do so at the moment. She needs to grow out of it anyway. I take the blame. It's been her and me for so long..." Bahati blinked her glossy eyes.

"Aite, cool. I can understand that." Licking my lips, I paused, letting my eyes roam Bahati's frame again. "But what I can't understand is why in the fuck you in her shit."

Bahati drew her head back with a frown. "Who?"

Letting her arm go, I rubbed the sides of my mouth. "You know who, Bahati. Why the fuck are you wearing *her* clothes and in *her* bath oils?"

Bahati propped her hand on her hip, poking it out, which made the shorts rise. Her pussy print had that dangerous-ass V, and although it wasn't the fattest, that motherfucker used to hit just the way it was.

Used to.

"You talking about the crackhead bitch?"

My jaw flexed. Bahati's accent was always deep until she cursed. That's when the Chicago came out of her.

"How the fuck you know the drugs weren't mine?" I cocked my head.

Her frown deepened. "Because she was the only one to hold her. This is your first time acknowledging Shya, remember? You hadn't had any contact with her prior."

Bahati cocked her head to match mine. We held each other's glare until I exhaled.

"I got a lotta shit goin' on, Bahati. But that ain't no excuse. I'll be 'round more. I'll be present."

The last thing I wanted to do was be my father and create another fucked up generation of Cuppacios. No child deserves to feel unwanted.

"She looks like my mama, but we need the results from the DNA test before I can fully invest myself. But I ain't plannin' to be less to her for the time being."

I watched Bahati to see if she showed any signs of that flaw shit she used to be on. Still staring, she didn't blink or flinch.

"And we did that. I complied because I have nothing to hide, Shio. I was snatched up from my apartment. I didn't come looking for you."

"I know that, Bahati, damn."

I sat back in the dining room chair and stretched my right leg in front of me. Using my thumb, I began twisting the ring on my finger. Bahati's eyes went from my face to the ring, and then her expression softened.

"So when will we get the results?"

"Soon," I replied.

"I'm sorry about everything, Shio. I didn't want to burden you. You had enough people to take care of. I don't mean to rub it in, but I was genuinely scared of you. I... I thought it was safer if we stayed away. But had I known you were a part of the mob, I wouldn't have done it. I know how easy it is for enemies to target family and loved ones. Shya and I should've been in your care."

Letting Bahati's words simmer, I thought of the Rodríguezes Cartel. Them being across the border was a dangerous game, especially now with the trafficking, and we not being able to touch them quickly if needed. I told Don I would fall back, but that didn't mean I couldn't look into it. Jagoda Bay had over four hundred women and children missing, all in a two-month time span. The city was trying its best to keep it on the hush, which is why I hadn't been privy to it at first. When Don revealed their connection to Jagoda Bay and Chicago, he couldn't have thought I wouldn't do my own digging. The shit I'd found out needed to be displayed everywhere. Jagoda Bay didn't want the attention, though. They don't want to scare off the tourists since the city is popular year-round, especially in the summer.

I was going to continue doing my recon while I waited for Don to do what he needed on a larger scale. Either way it was sliced, the Rodríguezes had violated, and if they thought I was on their asses when Felipe tried to roll up to the club on Solana, they truly didn't understand my character when they went after Shya.

She sighed at my silence. "Shio..."

I looked up at Bahati, who placed her hand on my shoulder. Solana's fragrance hit me like a tidal wave, and I gently grabbed Bahati's hand and pushed it away. I could smell Solana, but I couldn't see her, at least not right now. The oils waft in the air, and I realized the aroma didn't let off the same pheromones as it did coming from Bahati's skin. I could tell me removing her hand hurt her feelings, but I wasn't into pacifying them. We had a daughter, who was a full-on fucking crybaby. We'd be pacifying her enough.

Bahati sighed again. "Eat. It's my peace offering. I can't do much right now because I have to figure my life out if we are to live in this city, but the least I can do is keep this place clean and let you come home to a hot meal. And I promise I won't make any Kenyan dishes unless you request it."

I looked around her and inspected the dinner. The shit looked five-star worthy.

"Bahati." Reaching into my pocket, I pulled the card I'd already planned to give her and placed it near the plate. The black metal hit the table with a clank. "Stay out of Solana's shit. It's plenty of money 'round here. Go buy your own shit. Get Shya everything she needs too."

Standing, I pushed the chair back, towering over Bahati. I licked my lips as I watched her still, the only thing moving was her chest, slowly rising and falling. I wasn't fucking with Bahati, no matter how sexy she looked. After one more once-over, I exited the kitchen.

I had a long-ass day tomorrow, and a cold shower was calling my fucking name. I should have taken Uriah down just for the hell of it, but my hands were full enough. There was no future with her, and her feelings were starting to show with her questioning my absence. I had no intention of leading her down a path that would land her nothing but a dead end and broken heart.

God first
~~*Make sure the family good*~~
~~*Eye them Cuppacio boys, the little and the big ones*~~
~~*Build a relationship with my brother*~~
~~*Get my brother rich*~~
Health and wellness (ALWAYS)
~~*Stay on top of my mob shit*~~
Keep Hobo alive (DOING)
~~*Get through the meeting with Ines Ledesma*~~
~~*House a random*~~
~~*Find the true reason Solana is here*~~
~~*Figure out if Solana is supposed to be my wife, again*~~
~~*Find a wife that isn't Solana*~~
Kill every breathing Rodríguez Cartel member (URGENT)
Fuck Bahati up (TBD)
~~*Get my fucking daughter*~~
~~*Get Bahati's arm fixed*~~
Get to know my daughter (DOING)
~~*Figure out what the fuck I'm going to do with Solana*~~
Leave the mob entirely or Marry Bahati or Solana
~~*Get DNA test*~~
Spend time with my daughter (TRYING)
Tell my mama about Shya
Keep Solana in real nigga rehab until she clean

CHAPTER 13
GLOW

"Get up."

Bright light flooded my room as my mother opened the curtains. Lifting my hand above my eyes to block the blinding sun, I pressed my back further into the headboard.

"I'm up. I've been up since my niece decided to exercise her lungs at five a.m."

My mother walked around the room, picking up dirty clothes and tossing them in the hamper.

"Well, let some light in here," she replied, not stopping in stride.

I held my iPad up in response, though the screen was set to the lowest brightness.

"Light from an electronic device isn't enough, Charisma. You need some sunlight. You 'bout pale as hell and look like a walking corpse!" She fussed as I grinned.

My mother stood up straight after picking up the remote that had fallen, and when she noticed my facial expression, she scoffed, making me drop my grin.

"Ain't shit cute or funny about that, Glow! You nearly died in that hospital." My mother crossed her arms, dropped them, and then ran her hand through her short hair. "Do you really think you're not perfect the way you are, baby?"

Sitting up in bed, I set the iPad beside me and swung my legs over the edge. I'd been home for less than a day. My mother and I arrived to my townhouse last night, and although I missed my own bed, home is not where I wanted to be. Glee needed me—she needed my presence. But I was forced to come home on doctors' orders. Apparently, I was making myself sicker, and stress was causing me to lose my appetite. At least, that's what they believed.

"Mama, I know I'm pretty. I... I don't want to talk about it."

Sighing, my mother's eyes glossed.

"Mama, I'm—"

"Charisma." She took a seat on the bed and held my left hand in hers. "This isn't your fault. It's mine. I should have left your father the first time we fought."

She sighed, and I swallowed down a thick stream of saliva. I didn't want to listen, but I knew I had no choice. "He's a good man, but he wasn't a good man for me. Our toxic ways triggered something in you. It's my biggest regret... Seeing both of you in the ICU has done something to me. It was like I had an awakening. I'll never disappoint y'all again. Without my girls, I'm nothing. So, please, whatever it is we need to work through, let's. I just want to see you healthy. You have so much to live for. You're beautiful, successful, loved, and adored. I don't want this for you, Glow.

"When somebody comments on you resembling a skeleton, that's nothing to celebrate. Anytime a person mentions weight loss, your eyes shimmer, and when they mention weight gain, you look as though you're about to vomit. We *have* to change the narrative. We must change your thought process. It's okay to have weight on you... It's okay on anyone. It's okay to gain a healthy amount of weight and sustain it, baby."

Removing my hand from my mama's, I grabbed the back of my neck. It felt unnaturally warm, and my chest felt as if it was about to explode.

"I'll try, Mama. I'm happy you're here." I gave a lopsided grin. "And don't try to get your own place. This one has three floors. If you want space, you can have the basement. I can have a kitchen built, and you can do whatever you want with it. You can even lock us out sometimes. If you leave, Glee leaves. Glee leaves, the baby leaves."

The thought of my sister lying in that hospital bed, all banged up and bruised, made my fingers tremble. If I could switch places with her, I would in a heartbeat. I nearly had. The good news was that she was recovering well, and today they were removing her from the coma. The swelling in her brain had gone down, and there were no signs of damage. I had been thanking God for sparing my sister since I woke up, and I never would stop for the years to come.

"If you want me here, I'll be here. But I don't know how your husband will feel about that." Her sculpted brow rose, but the teasing grin had me pressing my back further into the headboard.

"Tunan?" I asked, dumbfounded like I'd married someone else. He was my husband, and I had the memory of the haunted house and the marriage certificate to prove it. "He doesn't live here, Mama."

We hadn't discussed my "husband," but I knew it was coming. When I was discharged the day after I woke up and told him I wasn't leaving the hospital, he left. I hadn't dwelled on it because I'd been surrounded by the mob wives and my parents' support. My mother had to shoo the ladies home, and even though they'd gone, I appreciated them for being by my side up until that point. It meant a lot, especially when they had just forgiven me for disappearing on them. I had a newfound respect for them because they had even been there for Glee, making sure her room was stocked with fresh flowers and that she was comfortable. Don showed his face to tell me that both of our medical bills were covered, and that felt new. Glee was on my mom's insurance, and I paid my premium every month, but it was good to know neither of us would have a co-payment to cover. The intensive care unit wasn't cheap.

"I know he doesn't live here. But"—she grinned—"He's fine as hell!" she blurted out, and her light cheeks grew rosy.

"Mama!" I screeched.

"What? I'm old, not blind."

"You are not old."

"I'm old enough to be his mama. That's old enough. Where his daddy?" She was as serious as a heart attack with her eyes waiting for my answer.

"Mama, I don't know. I think he's dead. I used to talk to his brother, and I know for a fact his father is dead. So yeah, he's dead. But I think he's Italian, the dad, I mean."

"Ew! A white man produced that fine Black king? And brothers?! Charisma! Well, excuse me, Mrs. Payne. You did not—" She leaned in, whispering like we weren't the only ones here outside of the baby who was napping. The monitor was on my nightstand, and my mom had been given the other. "You did not sleep with two brothers, did you? Oh God, my daughter is living the life of my favorite FMC."

"FMC?" I asked, ignoring the fact that she'd given me Tunan's last name.

"Yes, the main female character in the romance books I like reading."

"Mama, when you start back reading?"

Cathy Glory used to have a dresser full of books when we were kids, and we weren't allowed to touch them. But when my dad started cheating, she gave up her hobby, spending all her spare time trying to keep up with what my dad was or wasn't doing.

"I was on your TikTok page one day, and when I scrolled by mistake, I saw a BookTok recommendation. I've read fifteen books so far this year." She beamed.

"That's so good, Mama. Send me your Kindle wishlist, and I'll buy some physical copies for you. It's a built-in bookshelf in the basement too."

"I would decline, but reading is an expensive hobby, so I sure will allow you to spoil me! I like reading on my Kindle, but I'd love some in paperback. I'm sure I'll put that bookshelf to good use with the few I already got. I just may set up my camera and do a few reviews too. Since I'm not going back to work, I think that will be good use of my free time."

"I think doing book reviews is a good idea, Mama. You're so aesthetically pleasing. The community would love watching you. Where do you think I get it from?" I winked while she rolled her eyes in response. "Plus, I can get my followers to support. I got the bookshelf done because they begged me to do book content, but I don't think that's my lane."

There was so much money in social media, and often I explored other avenues when food became too overwhelming. My core audience loved it when I reviewed food, though. They watched almost anything I posted, but my food videos always had the most interactions. I thought my mama would do really well on BookTok, being that it had grown tremendously over the last few years. All it took was a few likes on the ones that popped up on your feed, and then you were thrown into the world with every four scrolls.

"I'll think about it, baby. Now back to you and these two brothers. Do they look alike? Oh, you're not going to let them train you, are you?" Horror flashed across my mother's face.

"Mama, what? No!"

"Oh! Thank God. It's cute when it happens in a book, but I can't imagine my baby girl being hammered from both ends at the same time."

"Yeah, we may need to switch your genres." I shook my head, looking over to the monitor to check on Baby Leader.

My mama kissed her teeth. "Girl, how do you think you got here?"

"Not by being tossed, I hope."

"Tossed?"

"It's the same thing as trained."

"Oh." She waved. "No, but all the shit your daddy done did, I should have let his homeboys have a turn or three."

"Oh God! Mama, please... Let's not keep that portion of this convo going. But, no, I have not slept with Shio, that's Tunan's brother. We didn't get far, and I married Tunan before I knew they were brothers. And I'm not being disrespectful when I say this, but I can't give you the details of our marriage, Mama. Just know it isn't typical, and we both benefit."

"Unlike you, I know how to mind my business. I also understand everyone has to make their own choices in life and live with their own decisions. I like Tunan, and y'all can keep screaming that bullshit about it being fake, but you didn't see the way he watched over you in that hospital. But you'll see. Time reveals all."

I hadn't heard from Tunan since he left, and I hated to admit that it stung. When he was around, I was constantly reminding him that what we had wasn't real. The sex was good, and yes, he was attractive, but we were just doing each other a favor. Still, it was when he wasn't around that my mind got the best of me. I didn't know if I missed him or just missed having a man in my space and a dick in my guts. It was all confusing.

"Glee told you, hunh?" I shifted my thoughts once I realized what she was insinuating.

"Yep. And if you weren't recovering, I'd drag your ass all up and through this house for how you handled my baby. She didn't want to tell me; I had to force her because I know you. I knew you were here being mean. I knew you were in here using her life as an excuse to starve yourself."

"Mama—"

"Let me finish, Charisma... I should have been here, so I can't talk too much. But you were dead wrong. We both failed Glee to some degree. I should have stopped everything and run here, and I'll forever regret that. This city just has this dark cloud over me. I let your father make me forget how much I loved Jagoda Bay. I was the one to convince him to take the job here."

My mama and daddy were college sweethearts. They were both attending JBU before it was torn down and rebuilt. She was originally from southern Florida, and he was from here. When they graduated, he had several job offers and was about to take the one in New York, but she convinced him to stay here. She never went back home after that. When she divorced him, she took a job in Sparkling City, packed us up, and we lived out the remainder of our childhood there. She wanted to go back to Florida, but I wasn't having it. My dad wasn't a good husband, but he was a great father. We all agreed that he at least deserved to be our dad, even though my mama hated his guts for many years.

"Anyway, the cloud is gone now, and I see very clearly that I should've been here when my baby girl gave birth. I should have paid more attention to what Glee had going on at BU, and I'll forever have to live with that. But we can't be nasty to her. As much as you hate it, Glee is an adult, and she looks up to you, Glow."

My mama paused, clenched her eyes closed, and then looked back at me. "She'd looked up to you so much so that at one point, she tried to stop eating like you."

I remembered that, even though I tried to force the memory from my memory bank. That incident was when I started forcing myself to eat more. I didn't want my sister to become anorexic, so I put on a front and hid it as much as I could. Above all, I tried for Glee's sake.

"She's my baby, and now she has a baby." I wiped at my eye that was misting.

"And she is also an adult. She is free to make her own decisions. Just like you went and married the brother of your boo, your sister is free to live her life. You don't hear me calling you outside your name and trying to attack you. Besides, your sister did good. I see y'all got the taste for attractive men from me. At least they ain't light skinned." She scoffed. "I saw one at the hospital with colored eyes, and I know he's hell."

I giggled. "Mama, stop. That's Jisei's husband, Ezio. He's in love with her, and he doesn't cheat."

Don would kill him if he did, and then we would raise him from the dead and jump him.

"I should have known that was Little Ezee's daddy. I wanted to slap his ass just off the strength. But he did make a cute little boy, so I guess he's alright."

My daddy did a number on my mama. She was nearly a colorist, treating all light-skinned people with disdain, like she wasn't one herself, with two light-skinned daughters. She told us to date only men with melanin and said she wanted melanated grandkids. My mother was way too much.

"Glee can be your baby, but just remember she's *my* baby girl. She's your baby *sister*. You were madder than your no-good-ass daddy. He's actually excited to be a Paw-Paw."

She rolled her eyes.

"Mama, you and Daddy looked kinda cozy, no lie."

"Girl, I almost forgot you were my daughter and called you something real nasty. Your daddy ain't shit to me. He is always trying to be nice. He is especially laying it on thick because he wants to bring his ole lady to meet Lee Lee."

With amusement in my tone, I straightened my spine and asked, "And what did you say?"

"I said, 'hell nawl!' I ain't that damn healed. Bitch better see her from the pictures he took on his phone."

I tossed my head back in laughter. I was always guaranteed a good laugh with my mama. She threw herself into work when Glee went to BU, and we didn't spend enough time together during that time. I knew she was lonely, but she was adamant about not living in Jagoda Bay. I was so happy she was here now, no matter how much shit she talked about my dad. I honestly didn't blame my mama for how she felt about my daddy or his wife. He'd married one of the women he'd cheated on her with. The new marriage was signed before the ink dried on the one to my mama. Glee and I didn't attend the wedding because my mama was not going for it, and when I moved in with them at nineteen, my mama caused so much hell that I moved back home just weeks later.

"You can't lie. Daddy did look good."

"As fuck." She agreed with a scoff, and I was no more good. "But that doesn't mean shit, Glow. He still ain't no good. Begged me to let him sniff it, and when I declined, he still handed me his whole credit card."

She reached into her bra and pulled out a silver Amex that had my daddy's name on it.

"I'm going to spend his money because I need to pay for movers to pack my house up. The bastard owes me anyway. Other than that, he can eat dirt."

I shook my head as I eyed the card. "Y'all are too much. Let me find out us being hospitalized is bringing y'all back together."

"Keep finding out. You're gonna be searching till the end of time. Fuuuuck yo' red-ass daddy."

I was cracking up.

"But"—she placed the card back in her bra—"Stop playing my baby like she isn't her mama's daughter. She and my grandbaby will be just fine."

"So he came to the hospital when I was out? You met him, didn't you?"

"Let me ask you this... That man in the suit, with the bodyguards and the men carrying all those pistols... If Glee wakes up and wonders why she has guards at her door, will you provide her with answers about who *your* husband and *your* friends are married to? Will you tell her the truth?"

My tongue swiped across my teeth, and I pushed my back into the headboard.

"Yeah, exactly. So stop trying to get in her business. She may be young, but she will be twenty in a few days. She ain't dumb enough to let no broke nigga get her pregnant. Now, y'all daddy went the corporate route, so that gangster shit y'all into... Y'all didn't get that from me. But with the way those young men were all up and through that hospital, swaggering around and calling shots, has my taste shifting. Give me the daddy!"

Everybody's daddy was six feet under, and in Pia's case, gay, but I kept that to myself.

"So she went and got a street nigga? Oh, God. He's going to run circles 'round my sister." I shook my head.

"He is not, Glow. From what I could tell, he loves your sister something serious. He didn't know about the baby, and that's all I am willing to share. Anything else will have to come from your sister, but just like you have loyalty to you and your friends, and their men, and your man, she has loyalty to hers. Respect that."

"Okay, so he didn't know about the baby. He knows now, and where is he?" I popped my lips. I couldn't believe Glee would like some hood nigga knock her up.

"And where is *your* husband?"

My lips perched.

"Ummhmm. Get out of her business, as I said! Give your sister some credit. I would have preferred her to wait, but I don't blame her for getting pregnant. Just like I don't blame you for getting hitched to your boo's brother."

"Shio was not my boo."

"Either way, both my son-in-laws look damn good."

"But what about her dreams of being a doctor?"

"What about it, Charisma? A baby doesn't stop shit. I was pregnant with you when I received my degree. Good and pregnant, so I went through most of my senior year sick as a dog. She can still be a doctor if that's what *she* wants to do. If not, oh well. You can make doctor money in many fields these days. The great thing about life is you can start over as many times as you want. I'm proud of her and you, either way. If you pressure her, you're gonna lose her. Just be her big sister, Glow. And stop using her life as a reason to stress about shit that doesn't concern you. Glee is going to be just fine."

My mama grabbed my chin. I could smell the faint hint of Johnson and Johnson lotion from her handling Lee Lee.

"All I wanted for y'all to do was get good men who would love, protect, and spoil y'all. As much as I hate your daddy, he has always taken care of home. Except for that fighting and cheating shit, he was decent. I don't care how good a man looks; if he's mentally and physically abusive, get the fuck on. Your husband and her baby daddy don't give me those vibes."

She stood. "We gone be aite, my little gangster princesses."

"Mama, please. Go add some fantasy or something to your Kindle. You too deep in them urban streets."

"Oh, girl, please! Them dragons and vampires gets down and dirty too."

"Mama, what happens if my stepmama see them charges on Daddy's credit card statement from you swiping his card to pay for movers? If she smart, she will track it down and find out it's you using it."

"If she's digging that hard, she deserves to get her feelings hurt. I'm swiping the magnetic stripe off this card. My only advice to her is, ya reap whatchu sow! She had a front-row seat to my misery and should be glad I'm not a willing participant in her marriage like she was in mine." My mother pointed her finger. "And watch yaself. You ain't got no fucking stepmama."

Knock, knock

My smile faded when our eyes landed on the figure at the doorway.

Damn.

"Well, damn!" my mama said, voicing my thoughts aloud, and Tunan laughed.

He stood there sporting denim shorts and a graphic shirt with the sleeves cut off to show his muscles. A chain hung from the belt loop of his shorts, and he had on a pair of Jordan 1s. I could tell he'd gotten a fresh cut today, and that made me turn my nose up.

"Well, I think I hear the baby crying." My mama stood.

Liar.

The baby was sleeping peacefully according to the monitor.

"Hello, beautiful," Tunan greeted my mama as she approached the doorway.

Blush appeared on her cheeks, plain as day, as she rubbed her hand down the nape of her neck, smiling like a schoolgirl. "Hello, son-in-law. That smells good."

He flashed her that same white panty-dropping grin that had me busting it open in his old-ass car. "Dat's good to hear. I left yo' food in the kitchen."

"You're a good man. It's no food here, and I haven't gotten a chance to shop."

"I'll order some groceries. Don't trip."

I could see the hearts jumping from my mama's eyes. If she only knew that Tunan was fresh out of jail, she wouldn't be so happy-go-lucky.

"Thank you, son."

Tunan walked in right as my mama walked out, closing the door behind her.

Crossing my arms under my breasts that were free of a bra underneath the oversized graphic I was wearing, I shot daggers at Tunan.

"How you feelin', Glow?"

"You care?"

He placed the food on the nightstand, his cologne nearly overpowering whatever was in the bag. "If I didn't care, I wouldn't ask, my baby."

Shit.

I wasn't wearing shorts, only panties, and he'd already ruined them that fast, so I pressed my thighs together.

"I'm just saying... You got a haircut and all that. Looks like you've been too occupied to care about me." I sounded bitter because I was.

I didn't want Tunan, but I didn't want his ass with anyone else.

He chuckled but didn't reply as he removed the carryout tray from the thank you bag. The food smelled good; I couldn't lie about it. He tore the fork from the plastic while holding the carryout tray.

"You handling my food with nasty hands?" I asked, trying to get a reaction from this man.

"I washed my hands in the kitchen, Glow."

"You can leave the key on the nightstand."

"Aite, my baby."

I'd given him the key to check on my house when he left the hospital. It was a spare key I didn't need, but I just wanted to be petty since he wouldn't bark back.

"Where have you been, Tunan?"

"To the barbershop and den to pick up yo' food and den here."

"Stop fucking playing with me, Tunan. I'm talking about when I decided to stay in the hospital."

"When the last time you ate?" he asked, completely ignoring my question and my growing irritation.

"Why?"

"Cuz I know dey made you eat in the hospital. When you here, you be on some other shit."

"My mama cooked breakfast. So I'm actually *not* hungry."

"Well, it's past noon. *Lunchtime.*"

Flipping the container open, a mountain of food had me nearly gagging. From what I could see, there was mac and cheese, candied yams, greens, and three large pieces of catfish piled on top of the sides. Forking the greens, the juice from them dropped onto the catfish.

"Open up."

My eyes turned into slits at the request. "You think you cute?"

"Nah. Dat little puppy yo' neighbor got, who keeps shittin' on yo' lawn, is cute. I ain't nuttin' special, but I do think you pretty as fuck. We can elaborate on dat more when you've had some food, doe."

"All this food for lunch? This is too much. Perhaps a salad?"

"Mane, perhaps dis fork in yo' mouth, white chick. Either you gonna open up, or I'm gonna open dem lips up for you."

"You sound like you're into taking."

His bushy brows, a stark contrast to his crisp line, lifted. The sun had given his pecan skin a golden glow, as if that were his name instead of mine.

"Taking from dese niggas? Yeah. I may have made a muhfucka, or three, come clean, but pussy?" He pushed the fork into my mouth. "I ain't gotta take nuttin' dat's handed over willingly."

The greens on the fork were juicy and bursting with flavor. I'd eaten a lot of food. I've visited a lot of restaurants and even had quite a few soul food reviews posted on my platforms. These greens were undefeated. As a matter of fact, his mama's were the only ones that could come close. These had a smoked spice flavor, while hers had a seasoned flavor.

Looking up at him as he towered over me, I chewed the greens before allowing them to slide down my throat. He followed it up with a second helping, doubling the amount on the fork from earlier. Then, the mac and cheese was up next. He pushed the fork into my mouth, and I didn't expect it to be so cheesy and gooey.

"Good, right?"

My reply was an eye roll as I chewed. He laughed in response—a hearty, sexy-ass, fuck-nigga laugh.

After three forks of mac and cheese, he went to the yams. The candied yams were the right amount of sweet. They were my favorite, and I wasn't even a "candied yams" person. By the third serving of yams, my stomach felt heavy, and I gagged.

"Hol' it in, my baby. Here..."

Tunan put the fork in the tray and handed me an opened bottle of water. I took a big gulp, and he shook his head. "Slow sips. Pace yo'self, my baby."

"I'm full, Tunan." I groaned, taking another sip of water.

"You ain't had enough protein just yet. Eat at least one of the fish, and you can be done."

I placed the water bottle back on the nightstand and held my mouth open as he picked up a fried fillet. "You know, I can feed myself."

"Open up, Glow."

I bit down on the catfish that was fried to perfection. I could tell the grease was fresh, and whatever seasoning blend they used was a ten.

"You know, my mama thinks you're so... *everything*. You and Glee's baby daddy. Ugh, those words don't even sound right in the same sentence. Apparently, she met him. Have you?"

His eyes locked in with mine. "I know him. But you gonna have to wait till sis wakes up. Let her tell you her own shit." He pushed another piece of fish into my mouth.

"Ughhh! Y'all make me sick," I said between chews.

He chuckled and shook his head, constantly feeding me. When I gagged, he picked up the water bottle and watched me sip it slowly. He waited until I gave him the go before feeding me another piece.

"Can you at least tell me this?" I held my hand in front of my mouth as I chewed since that piece was bigger. "Is he at least a good guy? Like... Will he be a good daddy to my niece?"

"My baby, he's solid. He loves your sister too. Cut her some slack. Open."

He pushed the fork into my mouth, loaded with more candied yams. The agreement was that if I ate the fish, I'd be done, but Tunan had to do too much. My stomach was full to capacity as it was. The last time I'd eaten this much food was at his mama's house, and I felt full for days. I didn't eat for two days after that.

"And 'fore you start, it wasn't my place to tell you. It's still not my place. Besides, I really just found out myself. Trust dat yo' sister is in good hands. Any nigga I associate with is a hunnid. Haven't you been good with me?"

Still staring up at him, I swallowed the candied yams. The cinnamon was so comforting, I almost wanted to ask for more.

"Let my mama tell it, you're the best thing since sliced bread."

"You lookin' salty as fuck dat mama feelin' me. At least I know, you still gone be bad as fuck when you're of mature age."

"That's what y'all call fifty-year-olds now? Mature?"

"Dey damn sure ain't old. Fifty is the new thirty."

"If my mama be out here on bald-headed hoe shit like some of the thirty-year-olds I've seen, I'm gonna gag for real."

"Don't be mad dat mama feelin' a nigga. I got to the daughter first, so she safe." He pushed more yams into my mouth. He did it so fast that I felt the syrup drip on my shirt.

"My mama can't do nothing with a Memphis hoodlum."

Tunan closed the container and placed it on the nightstand beside the monitor so that I could still view her. "Mama find out her daughter fuckin' on a Memphis hoodlum who likes to fuck hard and deep, and she gon' be ready to take yo' ass to get prayed over."

Nah, she's going to be ready for you to put her on one of your uncles.

"You did good. Now, we need you to keep it down."

Tunan palmed my face, my breath hitching in the process. With my legs still pressed together, I watched as his eyes lowered. He swiped his thumb across my chin, wiping the yam syrup away. When he removed his thumb and ran it down his tongue, I felt a release between my thighs.

Oh God. I said I wasn't fucking this man no more.

"Come on. Let's run you some bath water."

"You saying I stink?"

He placed his foot between my legs and gently kicked them open. "Ion know. Lemme sniff and see."

Hopping up, I pushed past him as he laughed. Flipping on the light, I let my eyes adjust to the brightness while I went to the tub. Putting the stopper in place, I set the water to my desired temperature. Tossing in Epsom salt and bubble bath, I went to the bathroom closet and grabbed a big towel, placing it inside the towel warmer. It had been a freebie from a brand deal I'd done, and one of my favorite partnerships. Besides the money, I loved keeping gifts from the promotions I've done.

Tunan's cologne alerted me that he'd made his arrival in the bathroom. He was chewing on one of the fish fillets, and even that was sexy.

"Can I get undressed?"

"Yeah." He bit down on the fish that still covered my taste buds. "Go 'head. You actin' like I ain't had my whole face is yo' ass. I done seen every inch of you, Glow."

"What if my panties dirty?"

"I wouldn't judge. Why you thank I asked you to come wash yo' ass?"

"Fuck you, Tunan."

I pushed the door closed, but he was quick. Swallowing down his fish, he pulled my back into his chest.

"I'm just fuckin' witcha." Lowering his head to the side of my neck, he took a whiff. "You smell good... Like always."

"Nope. You already fucked it up," I tried saying as normally as possible, like my being in his embrace wasn't turning me on.

His nose nuzzled my neck. "Real shit."

"What I smell like then?"

"Shitt..." He took another whiff. "You smell like... positive pregnancy tests and my pockets being emptied from buyin' anythang yo' pretty ass blinks at."

Shoving my elbow into his hard abs, he grabbed my arms and held them at my side.

"I'm just fuckin' witcha, my baby."

Jokes or not, I was getting on birth control immediately. There was always truth in a joke. Lee Lee was enough for this house.

His finger grazed my thigh, sending electric jolts straight to my pussy. I had to pray this desire for this man off of me. Tunan and I didn't know each other very well, but our bodies were like magnets whenever we were near each other. I'd never been so sexually in need. I mean, I liked to get a good nut, but I could live without it. With Tunan, it was just different, and I hated it, especially since he was my play husband.

His fingers pressed into the side of my thigh, with his nose still in my neck. When he trailed it up, pushing past the shirt that came right above my knees, my legs trembled. He reached my panties, hooking them around his fingers, and pushed them down. Once they were down far enough for me to pull my feet through, I stepped out of them. He then pulled the shirt over my head. I was now standing in my birthday suit and cold as hell.

"Get in the tub, 'fore I bend yo' ass over the sink."

Please, bend me over.

He placed a kiss on my neck and let up, and a part of me cried on the inside. I wanted him, but I would never say it out loud.

"You ain't ready for dat yet. We're gonna get you on track, and den, we can resume all sexual activities."

"Tunan, please. You ain't all that."

I'm lying like Mama now.

I eased into the tub, the hot water doing nothing to put out the fire between my legs.

With my shirt and panties in hand, he went to the hamper and lifted the lid. He dropped the shirt in and paused at the panties. Placing them to his nose, he held eye contact as he inhaled deeply. If I didn't care about my hair getting wet, I would have submerged myself in the water.

"Smells good as fuck," he said before dropping them in the hamper.

"You're nasty."

"As a muhfucka, love, but you knew that." He winked.

I let my arms float in the water as he pulled a blunt from his pocket. Tunan smoked like a chimney, much like the rest of the men in the mob. He flipped the switch for the air vent before walking to the tub.

"Ma dukes mind smoke?"

"She smoked for years after she left my daddy. Stopped when she got a cancer scare."

He nodded. Instead of sitting on the toilet, he slid down the wall near the tub's faucet and planted himself on the floor facing me. My chest rose as I watched him run the lighter down the length of the pre-rolled marijuana. Soon, the funk of his drug filled the air as he pulled on it. With his legs stretched in front of him, smoke covered his face, and the way it danced in the air had me biting back a moan.

How was it that everything this man did was a turn-on?

I watched as he took puff after puff, his eyes getting lower and redder.

"Real shit. I went through some shit with my ex. I nursed her back to health, and she did me dirty. Told myself I was done with shit like dat."

My body tensed, and I was glad I was underwater so he couldn't see my reaction.

"I'm not asking you to nurse me back to health, Tunan. I've been dealing with this since I was a teen. I got this. I just let the baby and all that get to me."

His red eyes studied me. He was so damn fine when he was high.

"Ion care if you got it. I wanna help you, Glow." He pulled on the weed again and blew the smoke away from me. "I fuck with yo' mean, wishy-washy, horny ass. I ain't sayin' I'm tryna rope you in some shit you'n want, but I want to make sure you're good. You got too much potential, Glow. You're already great, baby. We just gotta get this shit behind you."

Perching the blunt between his lips, he reached for the water and grabbed my foot. Placing it on the side of the tub, he began a deep-tissue massage on my sole. My head flew back, and I could no longer fight my moans.

"You want me to fall in love with you so bad." I joked.

"Nah." He pushed his thumb into the arch of my foot. "I'm gonna make you fall in love with food first, and den we can work on us along the way."

"I'm... I'm scared of you, Tunan. Not in a threatening way, but you see what happens to me when I'm stressed. It's the reason why I avoid relationships or anything serious. It's why I never really found a career path. Any little thing triggers me. Social media works because I don't let the comments get to me, and for the most part, my Pretty Eaters are nice."

"Lucky for you, my baby, we're in a marriage. You'n got no choice no more." He chuckled. "Real shit. This is our life now, Glow. We can make our own fuckin' rules. I can't lie, I'm focused on gettin' my paper right. So sometimes, I'll be distant. I just got out, so I'm gettin' my life in order. Plus, I'm the newest mob member. I'm tryna figure out what dat means. I won't crowd your space or no shit like dat, but

I'll be here when I can. I'm gonna get you on track, my baby, because you deserve dat. It's the least I could do, especially since you did me dat solid and took my last name."

He switched feet, so I twisted my body to give him a better grip and to make myself more comfortable. Steam rose from the water as smoke still floated around from his blunt.

"So, I didn't scare you away?"

"You scared me, for sure. But not away. You see I'm here. You ain't gotta push me away because you scared of the 'what ifs'. I know now, Glow. I know 'bout yo' condition, baby. I watched you seize four times and flatline once. Ion never wanna see you go through no shit like dat ever again. I ain't gone stress you. I actually wanna make yo' life as easy as I can. Ion got all the answers, but I can feed you, fuck you, pay your bills, and let you live in dat soft life shit y'all girls talk 'bout. Hoes is the last thang on my mind. You ain't got shit to stress 'bout cuz I ain't on shit. I'm just tryna get my money right, baby. Like I said... We doin' us—our way."

"Are date nights a part of us doing us?"

"Is that what you want?"

I nodded.

"Den we gone have date nights. A couple of times a week, if you want."

"One day a week is good. I know every weekend will be too much with me working and you doing... mob things."

"Whatever you want, my baby."

We locked eyes as he massaged my foot. If the mob didn't work out, he could open his own spa for sure. With his good looks and skill, he would make a killing.

Knock, knock

With his left hand, he removed the blunt from his lips, lifted the toilet seat, and tossed it in.

"Hey! I'm headed to the hospital. Your sister just got up. No, you cannot go. I need you to watch the baby. Your daddy is about to pull up. Thanks for the food, son; it was amazing."

"You welcome, Ma!"

The door closed back, and I closed my eyes, saying a silent prayer. The doctor had already told us Glee was in the clear, but hearing that she was awake eased some of my worry.

"We gone be aite, Glow. You gone be aite. Wash up. We on babysittin' duty."

He placed a kiss on my big toe, and then sucked it into his mouth before I could snatch it out of his grasp. He stood, laughing.

"I'ma go get the monitor."

When he was out of the bathroom, I eased into the water as far as I could go without getting my hair wet.

"Dear God... Please don't let this man be too good to be true."

CHAPTER 14
SOLANA DAMITA LEDESMA

I'd been in a fetal position on the bed for most of the day, but now, I was on the floor. My gums were numb, and not because of the white powdery substance I liked to smear across them. No. They were without feeling because my teeth had been chattering since I'd awakened.

Five days. That's how long I'd been here.

I knew because Italian had reminded me what day it was every morning when he brought my breakfast. I still didn't know what he looked like, but he'd been feeding me three times a day and conversing with me, and I had cherished that up until today. Today, I had no words for him. I had no words for anyone. He'd been by twice so far, and each time he slid more food through the slot, the food I hadn't touched remained waiting.

When I first arrived at this home, I appreciated the memory-foam mattress. Now it hurts. It hurts my skin. It hurts my bones. It hurts my head. The cooling pillows? They were now too cold. I'd tried repositioning myself many ways on the queen-sized bed, but ultimately, the floor proved the most comfortable.

So, here I was, on the ground, shuddering. I wasn't cold; my body was actually burning up. Burning with regret. Burning with shame. Burning with the need to get high one last time.

Grrrrrr!

The pains in my stomach were ones I didn't wish on my worst

enemy. It felt like sharp needles were stabbing me from the inside. I knew I needed to eat, but that would mean I'd have to leave this position, and it was the most comfortable right now. For the first three days, I was fine. I wasn't, but I didn't feel like this. I missed Shio. I missed the way *cocaína* (cocaine) made me feel. But there were not many pains. By day three, I felt mind-cramping. On day four, I slept most of the day, only waking up to eat and chat with Italian. But today, I was over being in this room. I needed out. I needed *cocaína* (cocaine).

I could take the stabbing no longer. With one knee to my chest, I stretched the opposite leg out and kicked around until I felt the plastic bag. Spreading my toes, I hooked the bag between them and pulled it toward me. I didn't know whether it was breakfast or lunch, since I was reaching for it blindly, but either would do. I just needed to eat so the pain could ease. I knew it wouldn't completely diminish. The only way it would go away was if I hit a line.

Reaching down, I snatched the bag from my toes and brought it to the side of my face. My left arm was still wrapped around my stomach, hoping I could squeeze the aching away. My head remained on the hard, carpeted floor as my eyes blinked away the pain from simply moving. I used one hand to open the bag and pull out the black plastic carryout container.

It was the breakfast bag.

There was no steam rising from the food, and rightfully so. It had been hours since it was delivered and sat untouched in this pretend *celda* (jail). Three homemade pancakes, two sausage links, and cheese eggs were in the tray. Next to the eggs was a condiment cup filled with syrup. Not bothering with the syrup, I picked up the pancake and shoved it into my mouth. It was cold and soggy from the butter. The steam had settled into the bread, making it hard to swallow. I still scarfed it down, hoping it would help the pain. Once the first pancake was gone, I moved on to the next item. Scooping the eggs up with my fingers, I swallowed them in one bite, and then the sausages. The three-food-item combo was one of the best breakfasts I'd had, and it was ice cold. Left in the bag were the utensils I hadn't bothered to open and a bottle of orange juice. Twisting the bottle cap off, I tilted my head so I wouldn't make a mess since I was still lying down. Gulping half the bottle, I put the top back on and tossed it into the bag, along with the last pancake that I'd probably eat later on.

With my eyes wide open, I was able to see underneath the bed since I was facing it. Hugging my knees, I stared into the darkness. I felt empty, and in a way, under the bed was mimicking how I felt inside. Shio placing me in this room in hopes that I would get clean would be all for nothing. I'd go back to *cocaína* (cocaine). It was all I had. It was all I could have. It was the one thing that didn't let me down. The one thing that was always accessible to me. I needed it more than I needed air.

"Aye! Aye, aye! Mexi-Mami! You good in there?"

My stomach clenched as Italian's voice startled me. The pain hadn't left. The food had helped, but as I expected, the body aches were still all over my body.

"I'm... I'm f-fine," I replied through chattering teeth. I was speaking as loudly as I could without increasing the state of pain I was trapped in.

"No, you not. You ain't talking to me today."

Closing my eyes, because his words made me feel bad inside, I tried to think of something to distract myself. If I could minimize my mental pain, maybe it wouldn't hurt so bad physically.

"I-I'm s-sorry. How w-was your d-day?" I didn't know what else to ask.

"My day? Shit... Breaking niggas pockets. Same shit, different day. Aye, matta fact, how I say that in Spanish?"

"What?"

"Breaking niggas pockets."

This is how our days had been—him asking me what a word meant in Spanish, and me translating it as best I could. It was tricky because what something meant in Spanish didn't hold the same meaning once converted into English sometimes. Still, I always provided him with an answer. It pained me to think sometimes, but I would search my brain for the right combination of words and hope the translation held up if he ever used them.

"*Rompiendo los bolsillos de los negros.*"

"Ruumpiendoe las bolseeoos dey las kneegross," he sounded out.

If I weren't hurting, I'd laugh. "Sí. Sí. Buen trabajo. (Yes. Good job.)"

"Yeah, I'ma get that shit on a shirt. I be coming up so hard off them dice games. You'd think niggas would get tired of challenging me. But... Nope. They want they money took."

It sounded like he was counting money, the rustle of paper passing over each other. It took me back to when Shio taught me how to count. My eyes watered, but I blinked the tears back. I'd refrained from texting him today. Shio and I were done. We didn't belong. The best I could do was stay put until I was let out, and then I'd figure out life from here. Maybe I could find my mom's family. She was from the States and had to have living relatives. I wondered if they had *cocaína* (cocaine)?

Fuck no, Solana. That's what has you locked away now.

"You don't sound so good, Mexi-Mami. Describe to me how you feeling... But in English. I ain't that advance yet."

If he kept asking me what his slogans and insults meant without repeatedly hearing or saying them, he'd never be fluent in Español. But, then again, Shio could keep me down here forever, and Italian could become a better Spanish speaker than his older cousin.

"I... I don't mean to be a... Uhhh, a perra... No, no... It's puta in America. I don't mean to be a puta—"

"A bitch! I know that one."

"Yes, sí..." I cleared my throat as best as I could, but it was so dry. "It hurts to talk, Italian. Stabbing in my stomach... I am shaking, but I'm not cold. My teeth hurt. My arms and legs are sore. I feel pain everywhere... But you don't need to worry about me. I-I justtt need r-rest."

White-hot pain flowed through my body as I sputtered the last few words. It almost felt as if something inside of me was broken, like a blade had penetrated my skin and been wedged in between my organs.

"Man, you slept all day yesterday, Solana."

"I know..."

I could hear more shuffling and then the sliding of the door slot. Italian sounded clearer when he yelled through the slot. "Hold the... Man! Fuck you on the floor for? Shit! I need to call—"

"No... D-don't call anyone."

Especially him.

I missed him. I missed him so much. I missed our routine. I missed the subtle glances he'd toss my way. I missed his authoritative nature. I missed his intense workout sessions. I missed existing in his space, even on the days I was high and locked in the bedroom. That night in the tub—even through his foggy eyes—he looked at me in a way that said he'd do whatever it took to win me. He was ready to do whatever to protect me. He looked at me as if I were the most precious thing in the world. I couldn't face him. I wanted to see him, but not like this. Not while I was sick, hunched over, and in agony.

The sliding of the metal door sounded again, this time screeching louder than the door slot. I knew that it was opening, but the door opened in many ways. It could be opened into two halves, as a full door, or by the slot handles on the top and on the bottom half. Italian had only been using the bottom slot to get me food. I was in too much pain to lift and see which way he'd opened the door today.

"Fuuuuck, Mexi-Mami. Want me to come in? I can help you get on the bed?"

"No... No... I-I'm okay. I'll be o-okay."

I closed my eyes and counted as the shooting torture raced through me again as I sat up. I was shaking harder than I had when I first got on the bed. I felt liquid drip down my nose, and I sniffed, but more fluid rushed into my nostrils. I swiped my face with the back of my wrist, but my skin was so dry that my hand felt like sandpaper. I felt like my nose was running, yet nothing was there.

"Yo' nose runnin'?"

I could feel eyes on me, and rightly so, since Italian was peering through the slot. I didn't have the energy to even turn around and get a glimpse of the person who'd been feeding me and keeping me company, even though a steel door separated us.

"Hold up. I know what to do... Aye, Alexa. What can I do when a crackhead is going through withdrawals?"

"*Crack*?" I said, not sure he heard me until he chuckled.

"Damn, my bad, Mexi-mami. Hold up... Alexa. What can I do to help a person who is going through *cocaine* withdrawal?"

"*Did you ask what you should do if a person is experiencing withdrawal from cocaine?*" a robotic voice replied to Italian, loud enough that I could also hear.

"Yeap."

"*Okay. Someone going through cocaine withdrawal may experience fatigue, mood changes, and strong cravings. It can help to encourage rest, keep them hydrated, and support them in contacting a medical professional or addiction specialist."*

"Damn. Okay, so, she can't take no Tylenol or no shit like that?"

"Over-the-counter options like Tylenol may help with headaches or body aches, but they won't address withdrawal symptoms. A healthcare provider can offer the best guidance."

"Aye, man. Ain't nobody going to no doctors," Italian said with an attitude, then sucked his teeth. "Damn. Alexa... How long does this shit last?"

"Cocaine withdrawal symptoms can begin within a few hours after the last use and may last several days to a few weeks. Some psychological symptoms, like cravings or mood changes, can last longer. I highly suggest contacting a medical professional."

"Psychological? What you mean? She gonna start seeing shit?" he asked in a near-panicked tone.

"Psychological symptoms refer to changes in mood and thinking. These can include depression, anxiety, irritability, and strong cravings. Hallucinations are less common but can occur in some cases. I urge you to contact a medical professional. I cannot give appropriate diagnoses because I have no medical experience or clinical licensure."

"Ummmmm," I groaned as I hugged my knees. This robot was making me nauseous. I could feel my mouth begin to water, but I swallowed it down.

"Fuck all that! Yo' ass was able to tell me how to sew up my homeboy when he got stabbed." I could hear the hesitation in Italian's labored breaths. "Alexa... Let's just say hypothetically... A person is locked away to fight the withdrawal, how long should they be kept here? Better yet, how long will it take them to get clean?"

"Cocaine may leave the body within a few days, but withdrawal symptoms and cravings can last for weeks or longer. Recovery time depends on the individual. I cannot advise on confinement. It sounds like authorities are needed. I am now programmed to dial 9-1-1 at the request—"

"Hell nawl, Alexa! Don't you call them folks. I said *hypothetically*. Shit!" I heard Italian sigh in frustration as he smashed his hand against his phone. "Fuckin' phone betta not have called them people, on foe 'nem."

Still on the floor, I couldn't bring myself to move anymore.

Italian sounded so defeated, and I hated that I was the cause. My being here should not have caused any stress for anyone, especially Italian who had been nothing but kind to me.

"Aye, Solana… I got some people comin' over today—just family. We gonna be upstairs, but if you ain't up for hearing no muthafuckas stomp over yo' head, I can cancel that shit. I gotta make some moves today while the sun out, but I promised big cuz, I'd come see 'boutcha."

That robot wasn't lying. I was just thinking about how kind Italian had been, but now, I wished he would leave me alone. I didn't care who came here or what he did in his free time. He was free, and I was not. All I cared about was *cocaína* (cocaine), and since I couldn't have that, nothing mattered.

"You can have your guests."

"Aite. Aye, they ain't gonna bother you. They gonna be upstairs. Matta fact, this shit off-limits. I ain't puttin' them in yo' business."

"It's fine… I'll be fine." I did my best to say the words without shuddering. I wanted to assure Italian so that I could be left alone.

"Mexi-Mami—"

"Italiano… I am okay. Go."

We sat in silence for a bit.

"Aite. My cousin 'nem cooking, so I'll bring yo' dinner down later. And you don't have to eat cold shit. If you want me to warm up the food because it takes you a while to eat it, I will."

"*Comprendida.* (Understood.)"

The slot slid shut. I waited until I could hear his footsteps receding and then attempted to move again. I used all my strength and fought through the pain as I tried to stand. That one motion hurt too much, so I planted my palms on the floor, got on all fours, and surged my knees forward. Shio's phone was on the floor near the wall before you entered the bathroom, so I grabbed it and continued on. One knee forward at a time, I crawled, choking on my cries until I reached the cold tile of the bathroom. I reached for the toilet and pulled my body to it. I flipped the lid open and rested the side of my face on the seat. My chest heaved, and everything I'd just eaten flew into the toilet. The toilet bowl water splashed onto my lips and face, but I didn't care. I didn't have the strength to care. All I could do was continue to hurl my insides out, even though it caused great pain to my body and my spirit.

Bwwwwaaaaaaaaah

"Por favor... haz que pare. (Please... Make it stop.)"

Chunks of digested pancakes sloshed into the water violently. It smelled terrible coming out, though it was mouthwatering going in. I continued to throw up until nothing was left. The dry heaving was just as painful as the aches of needing *cocaína* (cocaine). Each time my chest caved in, I felt my body give itself to the purging.

Using the sleeve of my sweater—the same one I'd had on when I was dropped off—I wiped my face and felt around for the handle to flush the toilet. Not having the energy to move further away, I recoiled as the mist hit my face. I would need to scrub my skin, but that wouldn't be for a while; at least not until it no longer hurts to breathe.

I'm so stupid. How did I let him catch me? I should have never done those extra lines. I should have just stayed in Mexico. At least if I were with the Rodríguezes, I'd more than likely still be able to get high. I just need one more bump. One more line. God, I need some cocaine.

Shio, baby, why are you doing this to me? Oh God, it hurts. Death has to feel better than this. Yes, that's what I need. I need to just end it all.

With my face still hanging off the toilet seat, I closed my eyes, trying to silence the voices. I was hearing them all at once.

These can include depression, anxiety, irritability, and strong cravings, echoed in my head.

Those scary thoughts I'd just had proved that the robot was right again. I'd felt a lot of emotions over the years, but never had I thought of killing myself. The problem was that I was not addicted to *cocaína* (cocaine), so while the withdrawal was hurting me physically and mentally, I knew I would be fine using the drug again once Shio let me go.

Using my arms, I tried to lift myself away from the toilet. I underestimated my lack of strength because they dropped to my sides, hitting something. Lifting my head as far as it could go, I grabbed the object and used the momentum to scurry back from the toilet and dropped against the wall.

The brown, rustic notebook I'd swiped from Shio's office was the object I'd hit. I had forgotten I'd taken it from Shio's office, and because my leaving was against my will, it'd come with me inside this locked room. I'd only showered once since being here, but I'd used the toilet plenty of times without paying attention to what was on the side of it.

Opening the book, I landed about halfway through. The writing was italicized, and although it was difficult to read, I was able to make out many of the English words.

Today, I failed my son.

Stopping at that line, I crinkled my nose. Shio didn't have a son; at least not one that I knew about.

You didn't know he had a daughter either, my inner voice spoke to me again.

I shook off the distraction and looked back at the writing that resembled something my baby brothers wrote. I needed something to keep my mind off the pain, and right now, this was it.

Today, I failed my son. I've failed him since the day he was born, but today was different. I fear he will never view me the same. He will hate me forever.

Not really understanding whose words I was reading, I went back to scan the pages toward the beginning of the book. The first few pages were unclear writing, with a lot of scattered half-thoughts, lists, unfinished sentences, and sketches of people. The drawings were just as bad as his penmanship, and I wondered why Shio, or whoever, wrote so badly.

The next page I flipped to had a long list of what the author labeled, *Possible Autobiography Book Titles.* The suggestions were very specific, and as I scanned them, I questioned whether the author was drunk when writing them. Raising a Son Who Barely Understood, The Things I Got Wrong, A House Full of Loud Silence, Before He

Learns to Hate Me, and Notes from a Father Who Never Fathered were the first five, and I thought the titles were catchy. However, I was still unsure of whose book this was because it couldn't have been Shio's.

Flipping to the next page, I came across a droplet of blood smeared on it. The writing was cleaner and more legible than the first few pages I'd seen. I shifted my body to get as comfortable as possible. I was intrigued enough to read more.

If I write this, it has to be in first person. My recollections. No distance. No hiding behind the organization like I'm a stranger to my own blood and decisions. A man should stand in what he's done—good or bad. That's how I wanted to raise Shio. However, my wants fell short, and I've disgraced the family I made for the family I've come from. If I'm going to tell the truth about this life... About us... About my wife, it has to come from me, Sandro.

I gulped down the stale taste in my mouth. This was Shio's father's notebook. Flipping until I found an entry that was longer, I held the book at the best angle in my weakened state to learn as much as I could.

"Okay, you little dicks. We need you to go into town and purchase items on this list."

All four boys were lined up, scowling. They were dressed in an assortment of wrestling graphic shirts and shorts. All their gym shoes were new, and they all had haircuts. My wife had mentioned that Shio needed new shoes and a haircut, so I'd taken the boys to the mall and let them pick out what they wanted. We ended our day with a trip to the barber. We had a guy who came over and did their cuts, but he wouldn't be able to make it until next week. My wife and I haven't been seeing eye to eye, so I've been doing whatever I can to get back into her good graces.

Now that they'd had their hair cut by the black barber, who was located in the mall and had approached me to help, begging to do their hair for a low price, I'd noticed that the guy we used wasn't very versed in black hair. He'd done such a good job that there had been smiles on the boys' faces all day. Until now.

"Niccoli."

My wife must've opened the door for him. I'd been in my office going over paperwork when I heard him yelling at the boys. They'd made plans to stay the night at Ezio's and had come here so that Shio could pack a bag. My cousin's piercing blue eyes lifted as he was eye-level with Ezio. Niccoli's eyes were dilated, so I already knew what type of mood he was in, and so did the boys, since all of them stood with their little chests poked and scowls on their faces.

"It's too hot outside, and we already got permission to hang at Ezio's," Renello spoke up.

"Yeah. You always come around trying to start stuff. We're not bothering anybody," Metavello, Renello's twin brother, backed him.

I'd always admired the fact that Lombardo produced twins. I'd yearned for Shio to have a brother in the home, but it wasn't fair to plant another seed inside of his mother under this roof. Had it been up to me, we would have never procreated. It wasn't that I didn't love my son; I love Shio with my whole heart. But I wronged his mother. I'd wronged him. I didn't deserve either of them.

Niccoli stood, straightened the navy blue jacket of his suit, and lifted his hand to strike.

"Cousin! Let us have a discussion in my office. We can even have a little party," I said to him, trying to avoid issues today.

God knows Niccoli didn't need to hit another bump, but if it got him away from my son, I was all for it.

"Dear cousin..." Niccoli let one finger down at a time on his hands that were still raised until his hand was in a raised fist. "You dare interrupt the orders of Don?"

I could see Shio out of my peripheral vision. Unlike his cousins, his face was void. I could tell that he was upset, but only because I was his father, and I knew him.

"No. Never. But the boys have pizza waiting for them."

"Pizza? Nonsense. Boys, you will come with me and do as I say or... Or... I will fuck your mothers in front of you while you eat your fucking pizza. Which will it be?"

"Let's just go." Shio pushed past Niccoli to the front door. The other three boys stayed in place, all scowling at Niccoli.

"You always ruining shit. You just a shit-ruiner." Renello huffed.

"And you're a black-ass disgrace!"

Metavello gritted his jaw together, never one to let anyone disrespect his brother. "And you're a white, nasty-ass, low-level mobster. You think that racist shit hurt our feelings?"

"It don't," Ezio chimed in.

"I'll fucking—"

"Let's just get it over with," Shio called from the door. With his hand on the knob, he pushed it open and walked out. The boys, sending more daggers at Niccoli, trailed behind him.

Niccoli put his fist down and stuffed his hand in his pocket.

"I should come—" I started, but was cut off.

"You shouldn't. Don has not requested your presence. You've done enough today."

"I've done enough by making sure they have new shoes and groomed hair. Is our appearance not a part of our organization?"

"These fucking children are not ours!" Niccoli yelled at me. "They are not of pure Italian blood. They are mistakes, and that is why they are treated as such."

"My son is of my blood. One day, these boys will take over the organization, and if Benzino does not produce a male heir, Ezio will be Don."

Niccoli was the hardest on Ezio, and I knew it would come back to harm him.

"Is that some sort of threat, Sandro? You think I'm scared of a child?"

"A child will one day be a man, Niccoli."

He scoffed and brushed past me, but I caught his arm.

"Let me fucking go before I see to it that **your boy** *is punished the harshest."*

Gripping Niccoli's bicep, I leaned in and bared my teeth. "The child will one day become a man."

Niccoli snatched away from me with a flick of his jacket. The door creaked as he opened it, then slammed shut. Sighing, I turned while rubbing my hand through my hair that needed washing. Pausing, my chest thudded as Shannon peered down at me from the top of the stairs.

"Amour—"

I paused in my stride as she turned on her heels, disappearing down the hall. I had to figure out a way to get us out of this—to get her out of this. For as long as I could remember, the Cuppacios had their own way of doing things. Our fathers, their fathers, and their fathers were all in arranged marriages. But back then, those arranged marriages were somewhat agreed upon, and even if the women didn't approve, their families did. Niccoli somehow convinced his brother that there was money in human trafficking.

Our fathers were a small mob who didn't have much financially. We were established, but more ruthless than anything. When Niccoli told his brother about the possibilities of wealth from trafficking women and children, that is when my disdain for the mob began. All of the wives had been snatched from their homes all over the world. But I was only a man of one. What could I do?

Was I a monster? Yes—I owned that. But I even had my limits. Rape and kidnapping were among them.

Boom!

I jumped from my desk, where I'd been for the last three hours after pacing and praying that Shio and the boys weren't being punished too badly. I could hear the boys' voices, but instead of running immediately, I waited it out to see if Don was amongst them. I had to tread lightly with my big cousin. He wouldn't hesitate to put a bullet in my head, and although I wasn't afraid of dying, I was afraid of what would become of my son and his mother after I was gone.

"SSSSSSSSSSANDRO!"

Jumping to my feet as my wife screamed bloody murder, my shoulder slammed the door frame of my office as I exited. Ignoring the pain, I ran to the living area and nearly blacked out at the scene before me.

"Man, what the fuck!" Renello shouted as I walked further into the living room.

"It just happened so fast!" Metavello said, kneeling at the couch.

"Oh my God! Baby, what happened? Keep your eyes open!"

My wife was kneeling beside Metaello, peering into Shio's face as he lay, sprawled out on the couch. Renello had his hands placed on top of his head while he paced. Metavello, now bare-chested, had his shirt pressed against Shio's leg while Ezio was yelling all types of obscenities. Their bodies were covered in dust, and their gym shoes that I'd just purchased earlier were no longer new and crisp. They were battered and worn.

"Whhh... What... What happened?" I stammered.

Ezio's head snapped at me. "Yo' bitch-ass cousins sent us on a suicide mission. Now look what happened to Shio!" Ezio pointed.

My wife was cradling Shio's face now, placing kisses all over him while whispering prayers. Shifting my eyes to Shio's sweat-bound body, I cowered as he lay stiff as a board. He turned his head, and his eyes fluttered at me, and my heart fell.

"He... He... He was bit by a snake."

"Whaaaat!" Shannon screamed.

"Yes, a fucking snake!" Ezio's little voice boomed.

"Son—" A hand clasped on my chest before I could take a step closer. "Niccoli, move."

Niccoli's grip tightened. "That nigger will be just fine. My brother called the doctor. He's in the driveway, walking up at any moment."

Ding Dong

"See... Although I prefer he died, my brother has other plans. Now, how about that party in your office? I need something to take the edge off from these black bitches screaming."

You see, I failed my son.

The moment I decided not to stay there to ensure Shio received the proper care, or took matters into my own hands and got him to the hospital myself was my biggest failure. I'm sure there are more that occurred before this moment, but the drugs have made my memories scattered. They are never in order or clear until my mind wants them to be.

I led Niccoli to my office as my wife cried and prayed over our son. The regret hit me immediately, but it didn't stop me from shutting out the chaos in the front room as Niccoli began to spread out the white powder that made everything better.

"Children are a heritage from the Lord, offspring a reward from him" ***Psalm 127:3***

I must do better by my son. I must.

Slamming the journal shut, I placed it on the cool tiled floor and pushed it away. My body was in pain, but the hurt in my heart felt ten times worse. I should have never taken that book. I should have never read anything on those pages. Shio's upbringing was deplorable, and it showed in his way of handling things.

He can't keep you here forever, Solana. He can't keep you here forever, my thoughts raced.

Picking up the phone, I sent Shio two text messages before locking the screen and closing my eyes. My body was on fire from leaning against the bathroom wall, and I knew I had nothing left in me after reading the horror Shio and his cousins went through. From those words in his father's notebook, Shio and I were more alike than not. And then it hit me that maybe Shio felt I was more like his father.

Not having the energy or mental capacity to pull my body back into the main room, I sank further down the wall until my head hit my outstretched arm. I was empty from the vomiting and from the reading of how Shio and his cousins were raised. Once Shio showed his face, I would prove to him that I was not Sandro. I now understand how important showing him that was.

CHAPTER 15
CALISTA GLEE

I wasn't the party girl. No. God, no. That was Blayke's thing. I was the college girl. I'd worked my butt off to graduate high school early, so I could get early admittance into Blake University. And I did just that. I was awarded a scholarship that allowed me to complete the summer program, which meant I could move on campus early.

Last year, around this time, I was preparing to go to Cove City, Georgia. I had taken my finals, gone to prom, and graduated with honors, so by the time the summer's first month arrived, my mom and sister barely had time to breathe while getting me ready for college. Once June came, we were sore, up to our eyeballs in boxes and shopping bags that almost blocked my mom's entryway, and I was eager to get onto campus. Still, my sister and mom took me to get my hair pressed, my nails and toes done, dressed me in a cute two-piece set, and Glow did my makeup. Then, we went to one of our favorite seafood restaurants. Blayke had even joined. It was the best nineteenth birthday I could ask for.

Three hundred and sixty-five days later, there was no two-piece set, even though my slightly pigmented, protruding belly wouldn't allow it anyhow. My nails hadn't been done in ages. The shellac on my toes had grown out near the tips. My hair wasn't as bad as it should have been, thanks to my mother constantly brushing and oiling it. The beat face I'd sported last year had been replaced by a beat-up one with purple welts, a dark ring under my left eye, and a lip held together by ugly stitching. My face wouldn't be the same for some time, if ever. But I'd walked away with my life, and for that, I was grateful.

Movement in my arms made my eyes pop open. It took a minute for my vision to adjust, but when it did, I couldn't stop the smile on my face. I couldn't spread it wider because I didn't want to bust my stitches. My back was sweaty from the number of pillows stuffed behind me as I sat propped in the brand-new La-Z-Boy chair that had been moved next to my bed.

"Good morning, beautiful."

My baby girl's lip perked as she opened her eyes, staring right at me. In the week I'd been out, she seemed to have gotten bigger. My hand was still swollen and bruised from the IVs, but that didn't stop me from running my hand down her silk head of hair. I'd never seen a baby with as much hair as her in my life. My "new mom" online research led me to videos of other moms saying heartburn during pregnancy equaled a head full of hair.

"Yet, I didn't have any at all," I said softly, voice not yet catching up with the morning.

There was no need to check her diaper. She'd been in the same one for three hours since I asked my mom to let her sleep in my arms during her six a.m. feeding. Reaching onto the nightstand, which had been scooted away from the bed but was next to the chair, I grabbed the caddy my mommy had set up. I wasn't sure where she got it, but there was a cooling compartment where a bottle sat, keeping it from spoiling, and on the other side were wipes, diapers, a nose cleaner, nail clippers, an extra outfit, and a face cloth.

Placing her on my left leg, I lifted the gown she was wearing.

"Yep, you're wet, stinky boots."

"Glee, I could have done that." My mommy yawned and stretched her arm above her head as she sat up in bed.

She had a room set up here, but she insisted on sleeping near me, especially since I wanted my baby right next to me. I trusted my mother and sister with my life, but after nearly losing my own, I wanted my daughter's eyes and her in close proximity at all times.

"It's fine, mommy. You were with her earlier."

And all through the night and yesterday and the day before that...

I was grateful for my mommy and knowing that she was taking to Baby Leader made this whole situation a tad bit lighter. But in the few days I'd dealt with Baby Leader alone, our bond had grown stronger. Just thinking about being taken away from her had my chest swelling, and a tear dropped from my face and onto my daughter's little leg.

"Oh, baby..."

My mom scooted until her legs were able to hang on the side of the bed. She was sleep-deprived, and I could see crinkles at the crease of her eyes that I'd never seen before. My mother took good care of herself—always had. Even when she and my dad were going through their marital issues, she was a looker.

She stood, removed Baby Leader from my lap, and pulled her little gown down. With one hand, she wrapped the diaper and placed it on the bed behind her. My mom was in a pale pink nightgown, and so was Baby Leader. If I'd had to guess, I'd say my mom purchased it as a set.

"God had another plan for you, Glee. These scars will heal, and so will your bones. My grandbaby will have the best mother. It wasn't your time." She leaned down and placed a kiss on the top of my head. "I'm so proud of you, baby girl. No matter what's occurred. Happy birthday, Calista. I'm going to go start breakfast."

I reached for Baby Leader, but she playfully swatted my hand and then left the room. As soon as my mom walked out, Glow walked in.

"Happy birthday to you. Happy birthday to you. Happy birthday, dear Gleeeeee! Happy birthday to you," she sang as she held obnoxiously big birthday balloons and a money bouquet.

Multiple gift bags, stacked onto each other, followed behind her in both hands of her husband.

My smile stretched further than it should've, causing me to wince. Glow dropped her grin, let the balloons float to the ceiling, and placed the money bouquet on my lap.

"Ugh, I forgot about your stitches. Sorry, sis."

She sat on the side of the wide La-Z-Boy and lifted my face to inspect my lip. Concern etched her pretty face.

"It's okay... I'm okay, Glow."

That didn't stop my big sister's inspection.

"I gotta dip." Tunan placed the gift bags on the bed so that they were within arm's reach. “Happy birthday, Glee.”

Glow turned, finally dropping my face. “You leaving?”

He rubbed his hand down the top of his head. “Yeah. I got some moves to make, my baby.” He sighed.

Glow shifted, and her body stilled against mine. “Umm.”

I pursed my lips, watching the tension. Poor Tunan. I loved my sister with all my heart, but she was possessive—had been her whole life. It took months of Blayke coming around for her to finally share me, and she still called her “the preacher’s kid” after all these years.

The way he was rubbing his head made me hold back a smirk. He already knew how crazy my sister was. He knew his wife was going to give him hell every chance she could.

“Thank y’all so much for the gifts, flowers, and balloons. Y’all didn’t have to.”

“It’s nothing,” he replied. His eyes were still on my sister, and hers were still on him.

“Where are you going all dressed up, though?”

I looked from my sister’s slanted eyes to my new brother-in-law. Tunan wasn’t nearly as dressed up as I’ve seen him before. Today, he was dressed nicely in a Nike set with a graphic T-shirt and matching shorts with some type of Nike running shoes.

“Want me to stay?” he asked, almost challenging my sister.

“Nah... You good.” Glow recoiled. She then turned her attention back to me, a smile back in place.

My sister was something else.

“Make sure you eat breakfast, Glow. I’ll bring lunch back.”

“You straight. Be safe.” She dismissed him.

Tunan chuckled and stared at her back for a beat before saying, “You heard what I said, Charisma,” and then made his exit.

I held onto my giggles until I heard the faint sound of the front door shutting. “Why are you so mean to him, sister?”

Glow reached around me and fluffed the pillows supporting my back. “And why you so nice to him?”

“Ehh, because I’m a nice human being.”

“Nah.” Glow punched the pillow. “Being nice is what got your ass with swollen, leaky breasts. You gotta be hard on these niggas.”

We both laughed, which had me clutching my stomach. I’d

bruised my ribs in the crash. Thankfully, they weren't broken, but they were still sore.

"Let me stop making you laugh. When Mama done cooking, you gotta take your meds."

I wasn't opposed. I didn't like the way they made me feel, but I liked how they took the pain away. The Lortab I'd been prescribed worked wonders, but the pills made me high out of my mind. Now that I was home, I had to follow the instructions to a T so that Baby Leader wasn't exposed to the medicine through my breast milk.

"But no, I don't really know any other way to be with him. I don't know what we're doing." Glow shrugged. "Enough about me. It's your day! Big two-oh! I can't believe my sister is twenty."

"I wrecked your car. You shouldn't have gotten me gifts," I replied, not caring about my birthday. I felt so burdensome, especially after hearing about my sister's condition being worse than I thought.

"Girl! Fuck that car. That's what insurance is for."

"No, it's still messed up, Glow. And now, Mommy and I are about to be staying with you. Save your money, sister. I'm grateful, but"—I lifted the flowers—"Money flowers? They are wrapped in one-hundred-dollar bills. How many are there in this bouquet?"

"Fifty..." Glow quipped and grinned. "I counted. But the blue roses aren't from me, boo. Tunan brought them in this morning."

"Your husband?" I frowned.

"You and Mama with this *husband* word. But yes. And no, I don't mind. You my sister. Any nigga that calls himself fooling with me better be willing to do for my two girls. Well, three, since I'm a TeeTee now." Glow stood. "Speaking of TeeTee, let me go get my baby."

"Glow... Thank you. Seriously."

"No more tears, boo. We done cried enough. Time to get you healed so we can scratch off this summer list shit."

"Even with a broken leg?"

"Yeap! That's why that wheelchair is in the living room. We are outside, still. Baby and all."

My little baby in her cute summer fits, enjoying the sun, was a summer that I looked forward to. To be honest, I looked forward to everything now that I'd escaped death.

"Glow?" I called again before she walked out.

"Hmm?"

"Please try. I know it's hard to..." I sighed. "I know it's hard. But please try—for me."

"I will, sis. Besides... Tunan will have me at four hundred pounds in no time." She rolled her eyes.

"I'd *love* to see that."

"Girl, bye!"

I snickered at her back, pain sharp in my chest. She closed the door behind her, and I took in the silence. The bags matched the balloons—an array of pinks and yellows. A few of the bags featured printed glitter that my mom would complain about all day. The day wouldn't end without her changing the sheets, even if she didn't see a speck of glitter on them. The bags on the bed would be proof enough.

Clutching the thick, white ribbon that ran along the length of the long stems, I admired the much-needed gift. I loved flowers, yes, but I was most grateful for the money. I wasn't broke, but without a job and with my college career hanging in the balance, along with a new baby, I needed every penny. I'd made the Dean's List both semesters at BU, but I had to think about my daughter now. There was no way I was going to take my baby away from my family to try to raise her on my own while juggling school in Cove City.

Using my index finger, I traced the beautiful blue roses wrapped in crisp one-hundred-dollar bills. The blues of the money and the flowers complemented each other so well. I knew my sister said she didn't mind that Tunan had given me such an elaborate gift, but still, I couldn't believe he'd done so. Maybe that's how husbands were with their sisters-in-law? I didn't know. Glow never had anyone even close to becoming my brother-in-law. I also didn't know many people with husbands to be privy to their behavior.

Ignoring the ache in my lip, I dug my phone out from the side of the oversized chair. My sister had gotten me a brand-new one since mine was ruined in the wreck. There were a few Facebook notifications from old classmates wishing me a happy birthday. I'd reply to them all in due time. Tapping the Instagram icon, I hit the plus sign to add a video to my story. Once I had a good boomerang of my flowers and gifts, I added a happy birthday song and uploaded it to my stories. My little ten thousand followers, whom I'd only gotten because my sister tagged me in several reels and posts, probably thought I was the most boring person on the planet. I rarely kept up with my social media accounts, unlike most girls my age.

I didn't know how I'd gotten there, but I found myself in my direct messages, staring at the last message Leader had sent me.

Number_1*: I'm putting you on my visitors list. Visitation is Friday from 7-11. This ain't a request, Pretty Mama.*

Before my emotions got the best of me, I locked my screen and placed the phone on the nightstand next to the baby caddy. Closing my eyes, I rested my head against the sofa as I took in everything around me. I was alive. I'd made it to celebrate another birthday. I'd fumbled some things but had gained major with my daughter being the perfect angel she was. I didn't understand what the Big Man upstairs was trying to show me, but I could see that I was under a major test.

My stomach clenched. I swallowed a lump of saliva as I stared at the backs of my eyelids. I hated this feeling. I was beginning to think that everything connected to my first love was just bad luck. I fell for him at school and gave him my virginity, only to find out he was still having sex with his baby mama, or at least according to her he was. Plus, his brother got my best friend, so we had to go across state lines to an abortion clinic. I can still see the blood-stained pads gathered in her underwear for days.

That's one.

I went through the worst heartbreak of my life when I should've been having the best time of my life as a freshman in college. He ended up being sentenced to ten years in prison. I somehow ended up pregnant and nearly died giving birth to the baby I didn't even know was in my womb.

That's two.

I did as he asked and went to visit him in prison, and not only did I give him my body before I'd healed, but I also nearly lost my life in a head-on collision.

That's three. Three strikes, Glee. You know what you have to do.

As deeply as I cared for Leader, I had to let him go. At this point, I didn't know if it was even a good idea to alert him or his family about the baby. As soon as I activated the new phone from Glow, I blocked his mom and siblings' numbers again. I knew he'd asked me to unblock her and keep in touch, but his world was too much for me. I'd tell him he was a father to a beautiful little girl one day, but right now, I wanted to savor the fact that I was alive. I also needed to cleanse myself of all things Leader again. I felt I was completely over him until I looked into my baby girl's face. Then, I was sucked back into his world, driving toward my own demise when I should've been handling my business to continue my education. I wasn't built for his world. I could now see why he had a baby mother who was older than him. Leader was too grown up for a girl one year out of high school.

Boom!

"Now I know my best bitch is not asleep on her birthday!"

My eyes flew open before I tried hopping up from the chair, but I was quickly reminded that I couldn't.

"Blayyyykie?"

With a birthday bag held to her side, my gorgeous bestie waltzed into the room. I angled my body so I could face her, or as much as I could with my restrictions.

"Frienddddd! Happy birthday to the *baddest bitch* this world has *ever* seen!" She grinned, easing down beside me.

I blinked, making sure these weren't side effects of the medicine, but it couldn't have been because I hadn't taken any yet. Her skin was flawless as always, but her inflamed, red-rimmed eyes had me on alert. She also looked like she'd lost a little weight. Blayke was always thick in the hips, but she looked slimmer than she did weeks ago.

"Blayke..." I could hear the concern in my voice just as she had.

She shook her head as to dismiss my worry. "I'm here to stay, Calista. I already talked to your sister, and she doesn't mind, as long as you are good with having me as a roommate again."

I tucked her hair behind her ear. She was wearing her real hair, parted down the middle, and it fell just below her shoulders. I knew her mom had taken her to the beautician, who was one of the ushers at the church. Her parents only liked it when Blayke wore her real hair, but Blayke hated it because her hair was on the thin side. I loved whatever Blayke loved. To me, she was beautiful in any hairstyle, and I loved her natural hair.

"Are you crazy? Of course, you can stay! I was barely hanging on without you these few weeks." We giggled before I reached for her hand. "What happened?"

She kissed her teeth loudly. "Somebody at the church told them we were at the hospital. That's how they found out. Them people took my phone and damn near did an exorcism on me." She rolled her eyes.

"Oh, bestie. I feel so bad."

"Girl, please! For what? If anything, you got pregnant because of me. I was pregnant first. I brought them niggas around. I'm sorry for not being here, bestie. You know my parents are fucking insane." She poked her lip out, not bothering to stop her tears.

"It's okay... None of this is your fault."

"It is! Because if I were with you, we'd be bent over a table, twerking at brunch right now instead of crying like punk bitches while you banged up." She cried, chest heaving and all.

"Oh no, Blayke. If you were with me, we would've both gotten into the wreck, I'm sure."

"Well... We would be two cripple hoes together. I don't like this bestiiiieeeeeeeee." Her head fell into my chest.

"It's okay... I'm okay. See?"

She shook her head no and then popped up, wiping her face with her hand. "I'm sorry. I'm such a selfish bitch! This isn't about me, and damn, I forgot you're sore, and I'm throwing myself all over you."

We stared at each other, crying like morons through laughs.

That's what I loved about my best friend. We were opposites in many ways, but the same too. I could let her drag me into things that went against everything I stood for, and I'd still end up having the best time. We could also be curled up on a couch, binge-watching my favorite '90s rom-coms while stuffing our faces with junk. We genuinely enjoyed each other's company, no matter what we were doing. She was truly my soul mate in the form of a friend.

"Next time you almost die, you'd better not do it without me, hoe!"

"I don't plan on there being a next time for a long time, Blayke."

"Good. I'll be right there beside you when the time comes. If we die together, I have a better chance of going to Heaven. I'll be holding on to you so tightly. God will have no choice but to let ya girl in."

I laughed and grabbed my side from the sore ribs. "I'm the one who had the baby out of wedlock. He may send me down there first and fast."

"Oh, please... I'm worse. I got pregnant and killed the damn baby."

"I'm not going back to Blake U!" I blurted out.

"And neither am I. For one, I was living in your house for free, remember, so if you're not there, I damn sure ain't. And now that I'm cut off, I can't afford that damn school anyway."

My heart broke for my bestie. She loved her parents, even through all of their rules and strict ways.

"Maybe they're just upset. They need time to cool down."

"Nah... They done, and so am I, friend..." She dropped her head, and I knew she was hurting over whatever had happened during the weeks she'd been away. "I cut up so bad on them people. Mama Cathy called to let them know what had happened to you and offered for me to ride to the hospital with her. My mama had the nerve to hang up in her face! I ran out of that room so fast, I nearly took her fingers off, snatching the phone, but I didn't get a chance to call Mama Cathy back before they grabbed it from my hands. We got into a screaming match, of course, and she and my daddy basically strong-armed me into my room.

"Them people locked me in there like I was an animal for days. Well, they didn't lock me in because I was allowed to leave the room, but they guarded me like I was incarcerated, friend. I couldn't leave the house, and you know my mama can't cook so I've been eating straight bullshit. Those days I was confined to the room, I realized their ways ain't the word of God. Those people are evil, and most of them hoes that call themselves *serving* be fucking the pastor.

"The church my parents are so wrapped up in ain't of God. Them people were calling all day for prayers about me, but she couldn't offer your mother not one ounce of hope. You could have died, Calista, and they didn't even let me at least come see you... Nah. It's a wrap with them people until they realize the church is steering them wrong. And when I find that hoe from the hospital that called my parents, I'ma beat her ass and report her. She violated HIPAA laws."

I shook my head, not completely shocked since I'd heard the

stories over the years about the church. Blayke's parents had always been a piece of work. They made her high school years a living hell. She could hardly do anything and found herself sneaking and climbing out of windows to be able to do simple stuff like going to the movies and the skating rink. I wanted to go on our senior trip, but since her parents wouldn't allow her to, I opted not to go either. They took their religion to the next level, but they were still her parents, and I knew, despite it all, she loved them.

"So... What now?" I asked as Blayke reached over and tucked a fallen piece of hair back into my sloppy bun.

"I'ma live my life my way. I may finish school... I may not. If I do, I might have to suck a lil' dick to get my tuition paid, but I gotta do what I gotta do."

Blayke placed her palm on the side of my face. Her familiar scent of Japanese Cherry Blossom was comforting. I missed my best friend so much while learning how to be a mother, and I was so happy she was here. Whatever happened next, we would get through it together. And if she wanted to finish school, I was going to make sure she didn't have to exchange sexual favors with a man to do it.

"If I have to keep the baby while you go to class, that's what I'ma do. I ain't have no real passion for being a nurse. I just wanted to be at the same hospital as you, ready to check a hoe if she got beside herself on my doctor bestie."

"A patient?"

"A patient, a coworker, the cafeteria lady, or a damn hospice patient... It's whatever for you, pookie. I just wanted to work with my bestie and buy me a cute lil' Benz and lease a high -rise in the city."

I held my side, remembering this time that if I laughed too hard, my bruised ribs would ache. "Ohh, I can't laugh, Blayke."

"I'm sorry. Let me stop. Got my bestie all banged up on her birthday. You still pretty, though."

Knock, knock

"Food is ready, and yes, I already ate." Glow was patting Baby Leader on the back.

"Ahhhh! My babyyyy!" Blayke hopped up with her hands out.

"Nooooooo." Glow backed up. "You need to clean them hands, Preacher Kid."

Blayke reached into her crossbody bag, used the sanitizer she pulled out to sanitize her hands, and was back on Glow with her hands out.

With a pout, Glow passed the baby to a cooing Blayke. "Ohhh, bestie! She is just so damn pretty."

Adjusting myself in my seat, I gnawed on my bottom lip as I watched my best friend cry while peering at my baby. She was holding her as Rafiki had done with Simba in *The Lion King*. Baby Leader's eyes were closed while tears glided down Blayke's cheeks.

"Preacher Kid, you're looking slim," Glow said with that look in her eyes as she scanned Blayke's body. When she noticed me glaring at her, she cleared her throat and wore a fake smile. "*Pearla* just came by, sis. Says she wants y'all to come next door a little bit later. Fresh air will do you good. So, Preacher Kid, help your friend get dressed after breakfast."

Glow closed the door, rolling her eyes at me, and I couldn't do anything but shake my head at her. Just possessive and obsessive. I made a mental note to pray for Glow later. I was hoping that with everything out in the open about her condition, she would be forced to do better, especially with Tunan around now.

"Who is Pearl?" Blayke said, pulling me from my thoughts.

I shook my head at her tone. "See, you and Glow are just alike. Jealous!"

"And issss! Now, who the fuck is a Pearl?"

"It's Pearla." I giggled softly. "And she's nice. Our sisters are friends."

"And she lives next door?"

"No. Glow's best friend owns the townhome next door. They are all... *related*, so I'm guessing Pearla is hanging out over there today. She's cool, Blayke. She has two other friends too—Mahzeyah and Bella. I haven't met them in person yet, though."

"I've been gone a few funky-ass weeks, and you've already replaced me."

"Never! We don't have to go if you're not comfortable."

We sat in silence while Blayke stared at Baby Leader. I watched her, wondering if I looked the same way when I stared at my daughter. I still couldn't believe I was a mother and didn't know anything until the night we got to the hospital for Baby Leader to be born.

"Our babies would've been born around the same time. You think we got pregnant the same day?"

Blayke used her shoulder to swipe the tears from her face, keeping her eyes on my baby girl.

"No telling. Our periods are synced, so that means we ovulate together."

I let silence fill the air because I knew my best friend was in her feelings. After a few seconds, she began to smile again.

"I'm glad she's here, friend, but I don't regret the abortion I had. Look at my life now, Glee? I don't even have a place to live."

"Blayke, you *do* have a place to live. And you don't have to babysit for me while I go to class. You can still go to school if you want. You don't need your parents. We will figure it out together."

"And that's why I love you." She looked up from my baby and smiled at me. "I can't believe you named her Leader. It's fitting because... Whew."

"I know... I think it fits her perfectly too."

"That baby mama gone die. She wanted to name their son Leader."

"How you know?" I asked.

"Emperor's pillow-talking ass. That no-good-ass negro!" She scoffed. "Anyways... She wanted to name him Leader, but Leader said that name was for the child who came from his wife. So, the bitter bitch went and named him after the dead daddy. I really want to find that hoe and rub this beautiful baby in her face. I know it's childish, but we owe her, especially after she burst our bubble of happiness and made us look stupid in that Walmart. I think about that shit so much, and I'm mad I didn't beat her ass."

Blayke nuzzled her nose in Baby Leader's neck. "Who got the last laugh now, baby girl? Ain't that right, lil' mama? Old-ass baby mama gone be big mad!" Blayke's crazy ass laughed.

Now knowing Leader's wishes, I shouldn't have named my baby Leader, but it was already done. I couldn't afford to complain about anything that was set in stone. He'd probably be upset about the name, but it didn't matter. Nothing really mattered anymore. Leader would spend the next ten years of his life behind bars, and I'd be free, raising his daughter.

"Do you still love him?"

Blayke had now placed Baby Leader on her shoulder and was

rubbing circles around her back and sniffing her hair. She smelled so good. I was addicted to her scent.

"Emperor?" she asked with a frown, but as soon as it appeared on her face, it vanished. "I have love for him. I feel like a part of me will always have that love for him because he was my first. But I don't *love* him. I actually hate the fuck out of that scallywag-ass nigga."

"Blayke!"

"What? I'm deadass serious. That nigga is a buster, literally! That abortion hurt like hell."

"So that's why you hate him? The abortion?"

"No. I hate the nigga because..." She paused as if she were searching for the right words while still cradling Baby Leader. "I hate him because I feel like he only paid me dust because I was a virgin. I was only something new to him. A new girl in the city, hot in the ass and ready to rebel against her parents in any way she could. He sniffed that shit out like a bloodhound."

My stomach churned at her words. "You think he used you?"

"He spoiled me. So I wouldn't necessarily say he used me, but I liked him more than he liked me. He had so many opportunities to tell me that it was just fun for him. Just sex. But he didn't. He made me believe that he loved me. He made me believe I was the only one. I think Emperor liked living the double life. His college girl put away on campus, spreading her legs for him on demand, while the women he really liked were out in the streets. I was just something to do. Something to scratch off the list. Niggas love what they think other niggas haven't had. Once he got his fill, I was disposable. I just beat him to the punch by cutting him off before he was ready to dispose of me."

I could feel my skin heat. My mind raced, and I guess it was evident on my face because Blayke was now standing in front of me.

"You and Leader are different, Calista. Don't be in that pretty head of yours thinking Leader did you like how Emperor did me. Although Leader is on my 'fuck you' list strictly because he is related to Emp, Leader loves you, friend. I saw that shit with my own eyes. He probably loved you the first night when he walked in with all that damn seafood." She chuckled as I fought the smile trying to creep onto my face.

"He's not good for me, Blayke. We're so different. But I'd be lying if I said I didn't love him too. I have to find a way to unlove him, though, friend. What will loving him do for me? For us?" My eyes flashed to my baby girl.

Blayke took a seat on the arm of the La-Z-Boy. Her familiar fragrance mixed with Baby Leader's newborn smell stirred a hum in my chest.

"You can love him, friend. Look what y'all's love created. This baby is the most beautiful little girl I've ever seen. I know how you are, friend. Everything has to make sense in your world. Everything has to align. Everything has to be done the right way. But sometimes, that's not how life works. You're perfect, Glee. You made a perfect daughter from an imperfect love. Love on that black man. It's probably the only thing that's keeping him going."

"I just... I don't know. I have to tell him about her, and I really don't want to. I have to tell his family too."

"You don't have to tell his family shit. He can tell them. But..."

"But what?"

"He didn't figure it out when you went to visit him? He didn't notice that you looked different?"

"I—Wait! How do you know I went to visit him?"

"Girl! Because I know you!" Blayke rolled her eyes as if I'd asked a silly question. "When I did finally escape my parents, I called Mama Cathy, and she gave me the whole rundown, including the location they found your car. I know where that man is locked up from Facebook. Plus, I know you, Glee. There is no way you would have left the baby to go to some financial aid office! You can do that shit over the phone. You went to see that nigga."

"I can't stand you."

"You love me."

"I do."

She smirked. "You love him too."

"I do..."

"As you should, bestie. Leader a real nigga, unlike his bitch-ass brother."

We locked eyes before bursting out in laughter. Baby Leader began to stir before a soft whine could be heard.

"Shhhh. Okay, okay. TeeTee sorry. Come on." She kissed the baby's head and rubbed her back. "But for real, everything is going to work out. I don't know how, but I know it will."

"I hope so."

"I know so! Now, let me enjoy my baby, and then I'ma help you get cute so we can meet these hoes you tried to replace me with."

"Oh, God. Blayke, please."

"This baby is so, so, so, so pretty!" Mahzeyah grinned in Baby Leader's face.

"Yeap. That's how our baby gonna look. Hold her head." Italian instructed as he stood over Mahzeyah.

She leaned away from him. "Eww, never. Get out our face."

"Y'all gonna fight over the baby all day?" Bella asked while she typed on her phone.

"I'm not fighting. He just all in our mix. We chilling... Ain't that right, pretty babyyy?"I giggled at Mahzeyah and Italian's tense relationship. We'd been next door for a few hours, and they'd gone at it almost the entire time. I was nervous about coming over, but I was glad that I did. Blayke had styled my hair in a high ponytail and helped me get dressed. There wasn't much I could wear with a broken leg besides shorts and an oversized shirt to avoid aggravating my ribs, and luckily, my sister had bought just that among my gifts. I was dressed in blue Alo shorts and a matching sweatshirt. The makeup on my face hid my bruises and made me feel more normal, especially among people who were essentially strangers. Although this was my first time meeting Italian and the other girls in person, it felt like I'd known them forever.

"Pearla, tell yo' friend our baby gonna be pretty too." Italian smirked as he leaned over Mahzeyah's shoulder and tickled Baby Leader's foot.

My mommy had changed Leader into an outfit that matched mine, and the royal blue sleep set with the matching headband was adorable against her caramel skin. Many of her clothes were still too big, so she was wearing newborn-sized clothing for now. I was hoping, once I recovered fully, I would be able to try latching her again to increase my breast milk so she could gain weight faster.

"Boy, get on!" Mahzeyah said, and everyone, including Blayke and me, laughed.

The first two times Mahzeyah insulted Italian, I thought she was being mean, but once I realized he was doing small things to get a rise out of her, I understood this was their everyday relationship. We all had been sitting around the living room, enjoying each other's company. I was in a wheelchair, but when it became uncomfortable, Italian picked me up and transported me to the couch. Pearla and I were in the middle, with Blayke to my right, and Mahzeyah to Pearla's left. We sat comfortably, showing that the couch was nice in size and had been purchased for company. The way the townhouse was decorated showed that Glow's friends had long money. I knew this already, though, from looking on their social media pages. It was so nice and so pink inside the living room area, and I couldn't believe she had left this to live with her husband. I wouldn't have ever left this masterpiece. But according to Bella, her new home was pink too. Blayke was in complete awe when we first came over because pink was her favorite color. She was ready to move in immediately.

Ding Dong

"You been saved by the bell." Italian blew a kiss at Mahzeyah, pulled his shorts up to his waist, and went to the door.

Blayke leaned up and waved in Mahzeyah's direction. "Girl, he fine as hell! Why you keep giving him the cold shoulder?"

She bit into a chicken wing, almost cleaning it bare in one bite. It was her second plate of the day, on top of her eating a full breakfast at Glow's house. They must've been starving my girl, for real, when they were trying to keep her away from me.

Pearla had gone all out. There were white and blue balloons floating on the ceiling, and they had cooked wings, sliders, and Rotel dip for me. Music was playing when we walked in, but as the hours passed, conversations took over, so Italian turned the music off. Blunts were pre-rolled and sitting on the counter in the kitchen, but they left them there when they realized I had the baby. Bella said it wasn't a big deal because they had a bottle of wine in the freezer that she had found in the kitchen. I was breastfeeding, so I wouldn't indulge, but I knew Blayke would, and with the last few weeks my girl had been having, she deserved it.

"Who, Italian? Eww. Unh, unh. He alright, but I got a boo." Mahzeyah grinned.

"Who?" Blayke scooped a Rotel-covered chip into her mouth.

"Flexer."

"The rapper?" Blayke and I asked simultaneously.

"Yeap."

"Oh shit! No wonder you over there dancing in diamonds."

Mahzeyah's jewelry reminded me of my sister's friends Instagram feeds, except she wore delicate, dainty pieces. And while everyone else was dressed casually, she looked like she was about to step out in her denim two-piece skirt set and designer sneakers.

"Oh this?" She held her wrist out, her other arm holding my baby. "My daddy bought this when I was twelve."

"Oh shit. Shut me right the fuck on up, boo."

"With his fine ass. Whew!" Bella fanned.

"Bella!"

Bella sucked her teeth at Mahzeyah's whining. "I'ma stop. Your mama said she's gonna kick my ass if I keep playing with her husband, and I believe her."

Pearla snickered. "Y'all crazy."

I couldn't help but notice that Pearla was the least talkative out of the bunch. I didn't know if she was naturally quiet or if Grind had been on her mind today. Our heart-to-heart at the hospital really helped me gain some courage about my situation. I was hoping she'd be comfortable enough to open up to me if she needed an ear so that I could be some encouragement for her too.

"Damn! Rappers and rich daddies. Yeah, we in the right clique, bestie. Flexer got some flunkies that like to trick or do Daddy Warbucks got some store runners that's 'round my age?"

"Blayke!" I screeched while holding my side.

"What? I'm trying to get us some daycare money. Hush!"

"Aye."

All of our heads shot to the door except for Pearla's at Italian's voice. He had fully walked into the living room and was accompanied by two more guys. Both were handsome, and I couldn't help but realize everyone in this crew of people was very attractive. The two guys, who were here when we arrived and had gone into the basement, were handsome too.

"This my nigga, Ro." He gestured to the guy on his right.

Ro was slim, medium-brown, and toned with a low tapered haircut. He smiled, and his perfect white teeth lit up his entire face. I knew my best friend, and he was definitely Blayke's type. When I glanced over, I was right because her eyes were directly on him. Instead of her saying something crazy, she bit into another wing.

"And this is my nigga, P."

P had light-brown skin, maybe a shade or two darker than mine, with half his hair braided and the other half crinkled. Still with a half-done head, he was very good-looking. A beard with lined side-burns adorned his face, and his mustache looked as if he'd just grown it out recently. He wasn't as slim as Ro, but the weight fit his demeanor. P had on a diamond necklace, and although Ro wore no jewelry, it didn't take away from his handsomeness.

"Wassup, y'all."

We all waved at P, who probably didn't care about us speaking since his eyes were on Pearla. She had only looked up briefly before her face was back in her phone. My girl was zoned out, but I understood because while I appreciated everything, so was I.

She's probably lovesick like me, I thought to myself.

"It's Glee's birthday. Let's turn up for the one time, and then I can kick you niggas' asses in the dice."

"Shid, say less." P rubbed his chin while keeping his eyes on Pearla.

~

"Baby, that wine got me on my ass. You need anything else?"

Blayke was standing over me, smiling. She was now in her pajamas after she'd helped me shower, change, and get into mine before she lowered me onto the La-Z-Boy. My sister had the baby and was going to keep her all night, and my mommy said she was going to sleep downstairs tonight. I'd pumped already and was prepared to pump a few more times, if needed. If Glow didn't bring Baby Leader in for her late-night feeding, I'd have to pump again in a few hours.

It was after midnight, and we'd spent the whole day with the crew next door. After being there for five hours, we discover that there was a woman in the basement. The details around her being there were still murky, and I was having too much fun to question further—as was Blayke. I was going to have to enlighten my bestie on how secretive my sister was when it came to her friends since she would be living here. It seemed that next door would be a hangout spot for us, too, so it was best she knew what I knew, which wasn't much.

"You not sleeping in here? The bed is free. Mommy said she's staying downstairs tonight."

The bed was still covered in gift bags. I had opened them all and loved every single one. I received clothes, shoes, makeup, and a new designer bag. I even collected gifts from next door, with all of the guys giving me money. They didn't have to, but I was extremely grateful, letting everyone know so. Today had shaped up to be a really good birthday for someone who just had a baby and almost lost her life in a car accident.

"Girl, didn't I tell you I was drunk? And do you see how fine that nigga Ro was? I'm going to the guest room so I can put on some ebony porn and play with this cootie." Blayke grinned with slanted eyes.

"Please spare me. When you done, wash your hands and come back."

"Ummhmm. If my legs work..." Blayke was now hovering over the bed. "These flowers are so pretty."

"Yeah. My sister's husband got them. You'll meet Tunan soon enough."

"I still can't believe she's married. But how they were all over each other on that live in Memphis, I ain't too surprised."

Blayke picked up a blue bag that had been hidden behind the others.

"Look." She held up the flowers. "These match this bag, and you haven't opened it yet."

She placed the flowers and the bag on my lap and began doing the pee dance. "Open it, friend. I gotta pee."

Instead of going to the en suite bathroom, she ran out of the room, leaving the light on. Hopefully, she would come back because, if not, I would be sleeping with the light on.

Picking up the flowers again, I held them to my nose and inhaled. The earthy scent mixed with the smell of crisp new bills was one I didn't think I'd love. Placing the flowers back on my lap, I removed the white tissue paper from the small gift bag. Reaching my hand inside, I pulled out an envelope. I'd been receiving money all day, and I was sure the money wrapped around the flowers, plus everything else, was close to five thousand dollars. The weight of the envelope told me this was more money, and I was thanking God for the overflow.

Opening the sealed flap, my breath hitched as I pulled out index cards. There was ringing in my ear, and suddenly, the soreness in my body was replaced by numbness. Blinking rapidly, I took a deep breath as my eyes scanned the first card.

Happy birthday, Cali Glee. I've never been the type to receive gifts, but you gave me the best gift a nigga could ask for: the gift of dreaming and believing. So today, on your twentieth birthday, I want to do the same. Here are twenty reasons for you to keep going.

My eyes burned as I read the four sentences too many times to count. I had to force myself to shuffle to the next card.

You smart as fuck
You ambitious as fuck
You better than any muthafucka in any room you walk into
You make everyone better, including me
You have a purpose in this world
Every day the world is brighter because you're in it
It's yo fucking world and everybody else just exists in it
It's favor over your life
You are hope
You are joy
You are passion
You are love
You are light
You are resilient
You are brilliant (I know I already said you smart but I ain't as good at this

shit as you are)
You are the blueprint
You are the inspiration
You are the reason I open my eyes every day
You are my everything
You are the mother of my daughter. My legacy.

I love y'all, Calista Glee. Kiss my baby for me. I fucking love her name. We made a beautiful ass baby, and I can't wait to make more, if that's what you want. Enjoy your birthday, beautiful. Next birthday, we're going to be on somebody's island. Daddy coming home to y'all. That's a promise.

PRESSING the twenty cards to my chest, the tears flowed down my face.

He knew.

He fucking knew.

CHAPTER 16
SHIO CUPPACIO

"The Lord is my strength and my shield; in him my heart trusts, and I am helped. The Lord is my strength and my shield; in him my heart trusts, and I am helped. The Lord is my strength—"

Waaaaaahhhh Waaaaahhhhhh!

I didn't want to disrupt their flow, so I ignored the first few minutes of Shya's crying. She'd started by the time I finished my stretches and hadn't stopped. Thirty minutes of nonstop screaming was excessive, though. Pressing the pause button, the treadmill's belt slowed. My calves burned but that didn't stop me from leaving the gym and climbing the stairs two at a time. Reaching the top, I headed toward the room where the cries came from. The heavy scent of fresh lemon filled the air since the housekeepers had been by yesterday. My floors squeaked under my gym shoes, and the wood was so polished that I could nearly see my reflection. I paid the team a hefty salary, but each time they left my house squeaky clean, I found myself thinking about giving them a raise even though I was paying them much more than I was initially quoted.

Waaaaaahhhh Waaaaahhhhhh!

The sight of me didn't stop the tantrum she was throwing. Shya sat on the bed, the collar of her pajamas was soaked with saliva dripping from her mouth. With each squeal, snot poured from her nostrils, and her chubby cheeks were soaked with tears. Her hair was still in two spiral-tipped buns at the top of her head, split by a part. Yesterday, she'd worn a lime green dress from the clothes I picked up for her last week, and the matching bows were still in place. Bahati hadn't changed the hairstyle, but she'd been refreshing it, or else it would have been a fuzzy mess.

Scooping Shya from the bed, I bounced her in my arms to calm her, my clothes slightly damp with sweat. There had been so much I'd been handling that most days I was gone before she woke and home by the time she'd cried herself to sleep. I checked in on them by watching my cameras, and Shya spent most of her day crying. I had questioned Bahati a few times when I came home, and she would be in the kitchen trying to get me to eat her food, but she assured me time and time again that she was just spoiled and in an unfamiliar setting.

Bahati had the patience of a saint. Most of the time, when I looked in on them, she was either trying to calm Shya or letting her cry it out. Like now, Bahati was on her stomach, the bed cover tangled under her, with her ass hanging out of the panties she wore. The oversized T-shirt was bunched up at her waist while she slept peacefully. The phone I'd loaned to Bahati was on the nightstand, and most days, it stayed there without her touching it. I didn't want them stuck here all day without some means of communication, although I had assured Bahati that she was free to use the Range Rover to travel anywhere she pleased. She had a spare card, the keys, and her full day to herself, and the most she'd done was shopped online for her and Shya. However, most of the purchases were for herself since Shya already had plenty.

Not wanting Shya to wake her mother, we headed to the kitchen. At the halfway mark, she had begun to calm down. As soon as I flipped the kitchen light switch, the spices from whatever Bahati had cooked the night before greeted me. Shya wiggled from my arms. The moment I let her down, she steadied herself and went into the half bath. When I saw her approach the toilet, I turned and let her do her own thing. It almost looked like a phenomenon, seeing something so small on two legs and walking. We had babies in the family throughout my life, so I wasn't oblivious to the anatomy of a human being, but being that this one belonged to me, I couldn't help but be amused. It was good that she was walking, though, especially since

Bahati's arm would be in the cast for another month or so.

Bahati hadn't told me much about Shya, but she did mention that she was potty-trained along with some other shit, and I was impressed. At her age, she shouldn't be in fucking diapers anyway, but still, there were plenty of babies who needed extra time to get the shit right. Outside of the constant crying, Shya was independent.

Instead of the sound of the toilet flushing, I heard bare feet on the wood floors. Scooping Shya back up, I led us to the sink.

"When you handle your business, you gotta make sure you wash all the germs off your hands." Holding her over the sink by hooking my forearm around her belly, I soaped her hands and placed them under the water. "See? This is how you get the germs off."

She didn't reply as she watched the water rinse her stubby fingers. I placed her on the counter, patted her hands dry, wiped her face with the same paper towel, and then disposed of it.

"You good now?" I stood back, waiting for her reply. As I knew she would, she simply blinked at me. "What do you want to eat? Pancakes?"

Blink. Blink.

"You gotta speak up... Cryin' ain't the way to communicate. You cry to express your emotions or to release your frustrations. But if you have somethin' to say, if it's somethin' you feel, you gotta let it be known."

Blink. Blink.

I had noticed by day three that she simply wasn't a talker. If it weren't for her crying day in and out, I would have thought the fucking Rodríguezes had done something to her vocal cords.

Shutting the fridge with more force than necessary, I had to take a moment to calm myself. Those fucking Rodríguezes were known to cause chaos in Mexico City but had gone ghost underground. We hadn't seen any more missing persons reports, or at least their loved ones hadn't reported them yet, according to Don's police contact. I was a patient man and had somewhat agreed to Don's plan of action, but my thoughts were plaguing me about wanting them motherfuckers dead by tomorrow.

Solana's phone buzzed in my pocket, switching my thoughts from Felipe to her bitch-ass brother. I'd just gotten her phone back yesterday after it was with my tech guy for two days. He was trying to trace her brother's phone number but came up completely empty. I was hoping to at least find his location because I'd feel better knowing where they were hiding than just letting them coast in Mexico.

Shya's little chest was heaving as she watched me. I was beginning to feel sorry for my little baby. It couldn't feel good to constantly cry all day. The more she cried, the more I wanted to introduce her to my mother. First Lady Washington was a fucking baby whisperer. Solana must've had that same damn gene because Shya hadn't cried with her either. I'd even called the fucking doctor again, the one who had examined her, and he assured me she was fine. His professional opinion was that she was just homesick, spoiled, and traumatized from being in a fucking shootout. The same shit Bahati had been saying.

Pulling the phone out, I read the two text messages displayed across the screen.

SOLANA

Shio.

SOLANA

Can we talk?

I COULDN'T LET Solana get in my fucking head. Her texting me wouldn't help the buried thoughts, and I had to let her simmer for a bit if I wanted her to get off that shit. Since I was off her, I had been attempting to focus on Bahati and seeing if she and I would fit together if married. Every thought, however, caused me to stay further away from the house instead of trying to be in her space. It was just something about her that had me questioning Bahati rather than trying to build some type of trust.

She spent most of her time cooking, so I'd made sure to have groceries delivered with the things I thought she needed. She would order things but hadn't been as generous with her spending on food as she'd been with clothes. Bahati had run up some commas on the designer websites. I didn't mind because I'd given her the card to begin with. Where the fuck was she going in Prada dresses when she never left the house was a mystery to me, but fuck it—I didn't stress over money anymore.

Grabbing one of the sippy cups left drying on the island, I filled it about halfway with orange juice, screwed on the top, and handed it to Shya. Last time I made Shya a cup with milk, she wasn't fucking with it, so I figured juice would be safe. I placed the cup beside her because I figured she wouldn't take it from me. It didn't take long before she was tipping her head back and chugging it down.

Shya was one of the prettiest little girls I'd ever seen. Though she spent most of her day dehydrated from crying, she was a good toddler. From what I could tell, she didn't wander off; she ate her food when fed, and when Bahati fell asleep on her, she didn't climb out of bed or do the silly stuff toddlers do, like sticking shit in wall sockets. That fact didn't stop me from getting the housekeepers to plug all of the outlets just in case.

"Why didn't you wake me?"

Adding a pinch of salt to the second round of scrambled eggs I'd made in the last five minutes, I lifted my head to see Bahati entering the kitchen. As always, her smooth skin was as shiny as black marble. I didn't know whether it was her skincare routine or her natural glow, but she always looked ready to grace somebody's magazine cover, even back when she was just my language tutor. Her braids hung over each shoulder, and I wondered when she'd step out to get them redone. She complained that she wanted to take her hair down, but the broken arm made it impossible for her to do so. She'd swapped out the oversized shirt for Gucci shorts and a Gucci T-shirt, tying the T-shirt at the waist. Her feet were bare, showing the hot pink polish on her toes. The last time we'd encountered each other, more than three years ago, she'd been wearing the same color polish.

"With the way she was screaming, I don't think waking you would have worked if her lungs didn't."

Shya and I had been in the kitchen for more than half an hour, her watching me while I made chicken sausage, pancakes, and now the eggs. She was on the island, working on the pancakes since she'd already downed the meat. Removing the eggs from the skillet, I opened the freezer and stuck the egg-covered spatula inside. I'd seen Ezio do the same shit for his junior not long ago. It didn't take eggs long to cool, so I removed them from the spatula onto Shya's syrupy plate. She only had a few pieces of the triangular-shaped pieces of sliced pancake left. Her round, watery eyes rested on my face for a beat, then she dropped her gaze to the eggs and scooped them into her hand. She hadn't attempted to use the spoon I'd given her; I guess it was easier to go straight caveman-style.

"You not eating?" Bahati's sultry tenor broke my stare from Shya.

It was clear that designer brands weren't made for black bodies, especially ones like Bahati's. The shorts were too big at the top, so she'd folded them at the waist, leaving a gap around her stomach, while the canvas material barely covered her ass cheeks because it was too tight at the bottom. To fit her properly, she would need to get them tailored. If I'd known she was going designer, I would've just given her the name and number of the many reps who were always calling and texting me about pieces they swore I needed. I was an easy mark for them because I rarely, if ever, declined a sale.

"I had my breakfast earlier."

I'd had a protein shake and avocado toast on sourdough before my workout, and I already had my lunch and dinner ready. The owner of the company I used for housekeeping had a daughter who was a chef. She sold meal preps, and I'd used her services a few times before. I liked to prepare my own food when I wasn't eating out so that I knew exactly how many calories I was consuming, but her meals were good. I bit the bullet and decided to order for this week and asked the housekeepers to bring them when they came yesterday. Everything had been so hectic between the two women, Hobo, the mob, and the actual work runs that I'd fallen off the wagon. I'd been consuming bullshit while avoiding the house. It was bad enough I had tripled my marijuana and alcohol intake, so I needed to shake back and get on my routine again. Weed was one of the only things keeping a nigga sane, though, so the heavy food and emptying bottles had to go.

"So I'll assume this is for me?" Bahati pointed to the plate of cheese eggs with some extra chicken sausage I'd made.

I shrugged. "Help yourself."

I had cooked the eggs for Shya, but she pulled the left-right headshake while pushing the plate away. As her little face assessed the plate of cheese eggs, I assessed her and decided to try something.

Now that she was eating the eggs without cheese with no problem, I had some questions.

My eyes followed Bahati as she stood across from me. The elbow of her free arm was firmly planted on the counter as the shorts that barely covered her ass looked like they were cutting off her thigh's circulation. Instead of pivoting to warm the plate of food in the microwave, she stabbed the fork into the eggs.

The fork disappeared inside her mouth, and when she slid it out, melted cheese rested on her full lips. She licked it away with her eyes on me. Bahati was sexy *then,* and she was sexy *now*. Motherhood looked good on her, and although I should have killed her ass during our last encounter, God saw fit that she lived to tell the story.

And have my baby.

It was challenging coming home to soft legs every night and not breaking dick off in her, but I'd done it with Solana and damn sure could do it with Bahati. I still had time to pick my wife between the two, but I was no closer to making a decision than I was when Don gave me the ultimatum.

"Why didn't you tell me Shya doesn't like cheese?"

The little display of cheese seduction she was doing ended as her face crumpled in confusion. "Hunh? She eats cheese. She eats everything."

"Nah. She acts as if she's lactose intolerant or some shit." I paused to study Bahati, and when she shrugged, I sneered a little.

"Shyla's not lactose intolerant, Shio. She probably just didn't want the cheese eggs."

"And the milk the other day?"

Bahati rolled her eyes and sighed. "Maybe she didn't want the milk either. I get you're trying to get to know her, but questioning me about the very child I've raised for the last three years is off-putting."

"Almost as off-putting as you calling her *Shyla* instead of Shya. But you got it, Bahati."

Not giving her a chance to respond, I picked up Shya since she was done eating. We went back to the half bath and washed her syrupy hands. I wasn't about to go back and forth with Bahati. I may have missed the signs of Solana being coked out, but I wasn't letting up from my gut telling me Bahati had some shit to her. I felt bad about her and Shya being caught up in my shit with the Rodríguezes, but her shit wasn't clean enough for me to choose her as my wife yet. I wasn't sure if my feelings were based on our past or my current intuition, and I would need to sort through all of that first before deciding to make this situation permanent.

Once baby girl's hands were dry, she looked up at me with sleepy eyes. Pulling her back into my arms, her head found my chest, and I could see her long lashes constantly tapping her cheeks. Her lips were glossed with maple syrup, but I didn't bother with it.

"You can use the card to get you a phone, Bahati."

I kept my voice low since Shya was headed to the land of the dreamers. I could tell by the way her breathing pattern had changed. I needed the phone back that I'd given her since I wasn't about to go grab the one from Solana at Jisei's spot. I had gone from three phones and two burners to one phone and two burners, plus Solana's phone.

I looked up to see worry etched across Bahati's face as she pushed the plate away from her. "I... I don't think that's a good idea. I've been toying with getting another phone, but... *they* took my phone. If I get another with the same account, that could be a way for them to track me here."

It was like a fucking light switch had gone off in my head. I was usually the nigga to think everything through thoroughly when I was in the midst of putting a plan in motion, but my thoughts had been cloudy as of late. Bahati and the events surrounding her kidnapping had taken a back seat to the shit happening in Jagoda Bay, and it was my fault for missing the obvious piece on figuring out where them bitch-ass niggas were hiding. I'd been so busy trying to get at them niggas using Solana's phone that I hadn't even thought about them niggas having Bahati's. My tech guy had told me that if I had a phone number that was connected to them, I'd have better luck with getting their location. I knew he would be able to track them now as long as they still had her shit.

Shya had fallen asleep on my chest, so as I reached into my pocket to retrieve my main phone, I was careful not to wake her. I didn't want her to go back into a screaming spell before I had a chance to finish my workout. I swiped past notifications from Vello and Ezio. Those twins had been keeping Vello up for forty days and forty nights, and since I was the only person he knew who was up before the sun, I had become his go-to person to call in the morning.

I hadn't been answering the last few days because I didn't want to talk about my bullshit or hear them loud-ass twins. Those infants had lungs that were just as strong as Shya's. I didn't mind her cries, but them little niggas sounded like stray cats.

"What's the number?" I asked while my eyes shifted from the phone to Bahati.

"Um... About that."

My eyes slanted at her as she wore a look on her face that said she was about to say some shit to piss me off. She straightened, and one side of her shorts became caught in her crotch, but she made no moves to fix it.

"I don't know the number?"

I ran my tongue across my teeth. "Bahati..."

She rushed in front of me. The smell of shea butter and the sprays she used back then knocked me in the face. She'd ordered every damn thing she wanted and needed, down to the body butters she had imported from her homeland. Some shit had never changed, and Bahati was a creature of habit. Just like then, she still had a badass habit of throwing me all the fucking way off.

"I know that sounds crazy but hear me out. I'd been getting so many spam phone calls that it drove me mad. So I changed the number when I upgraded my phone. I'd done all of that a day before. That wasn't nearly enough time to memorize it."

She searched my eyes. With only Shya's light snores filling the tense air, I took a step back.

"Aite, let's run this shit back from the beginning." I kept my voice even. "Tell me everything."

Her chest rose and fell as her eyes watered, and I cringed internally. I wasn't falling for that white woman shit. The kidnapping may have shaken her up, but Bahati wasn't green to this life. Her dad was in the streets heavy, so she'd been privy to a lot of shit.

"No fuckin' tears, Bahati. I know the shit was traumatizing, but you're safe here. You've been in my house and not a single thing has happened since we touched down from Mexico. Talk."

"The day before... I-I went into the phone store."

"What phone service?"

"Hunh?"

"Bahati..." She knew how I felt about repeating myself.

"Oh, Spectrum."

"You had that cheap-ass service?"

She squinted her eyes and puckered her plump lips. "I went into the *Spectrum* phone store and upgraded my phone and changed my number. Then I went to the grocery store—"

"How'd you get from Spectrum to the grocery store, and where was Shya?"

"Shya was with me. She's always with me. I drove."

"What type of car? What part of town?"

"I drive my father's old car. The motor went out in mine some time ago, and since a dead man can't drive and my mother and sister have no need for it in Kenya, I kept it for myself."

Her father drove a Lincoln Town Car, navy blue. I'd had many memories of him rounding the corner in it as he gave us our pill and drank order late as fuck. I used to be ready to shoot that bitch up every time he let his daughter convince him to delay our shit because I wouldn't commit to her ass.

I nodded. "Got it."

"Okay, so, yes. We went to Spectrum, then home—"

"Old-ass Town car, Spectrum, grocery store, and then home. Keep the sequence right, Bahati."

"I'm trying to, but you're looking at me as if I did something wrong." Her voice rose an octave, and Shya wiggled. Raising my eyebrow as a warning, Bahati sighed.

"Look, a nigga ain't lookin' at you no type of ways. I'm tryna put this shit to rest. I'm comin' up with dead-end after dead-end. I looked you up and ain't shit come up."

I watched her closely for a reaction, but all she had was a look of disdain for the conversation.

"I could have told you nothing would come up, Shio. My father, when he was killed... He owed a powerful gang up in New York somewhere. He owed them the product and didn't come through, though he'd been paid in advance. Little did we know, he had a gambling addiction."

I'd known her pops had a gambling addiction for a long-ass time. It was the main reason he began stealing from a job that paid him well over six figures to begin with.

"It spooked my mother and sister, so they fled. I'd grown to love

Chicago, and I'd hoped that... I was thinking I'd at least be able to run into you again. So I paid good money to essentially become no one. No, I do not have the contact of the person I used. You know how paranoid Chicago men are. I never met the guy or girl. I just paid my fee.

"After that, I moved to the Southside, hoping to blend in. I didn't get another job because my father had trusts set up for us in the wake of his death. My apartment wasn't anything to write home about, but it was warm in the brutal winter and cool in the summer. We didn't have much because I wanted my money to stretch at least until she was old enough to go to elementary school. We lived low maintenance. I even perfected braiding my own hair. I saved every dollar."

I nodded. "Okay, back to the day. Spectrum, grocery store, drove Lincoln Town Car home. What apartments?"

"Celestial Crest. Apartment 2-9-1."

I was familiar with them but didn't really know anyone around that way. I hadn't been to the hoods of Chicago in years. I could ask Essex if he knew someone from that part of Southside because he still made moves around the city. For that reason alone, I knew it was a high chance that he did, but he'd also been on the road so much that it was hard to link up with my boy.

Chicago hadn't felt like home for me in the years before we moved. Now that we'd been in Jagoda Bay for some time, I didn't reminisce about Chicago either. When I did go to the city, it was usually just to the graveyard and back to the plane. When we were living there, we Cuppacios kept to ourselves and were only cordial to the people we served. I'd built more connections out here than there, and I knew it was mainly because the money and status had changed. When you were mob-tied, folks treated you differently—or rather, accordingly.

"I went to *Wright Way grocery*—God, it smelled disgusting that day. Shya cried her eyes out. We went home, where I bathed her as the food cooked, and after we ate, we fell asleep on the couch. The next thing I knew, I was kidnapped. They kept us about a week, but I'm not sure of the timing because they took my phone."

This was new. I hadn't bothered to question Bahati because I'd felt bad that she'd been kidnapped and had a broken arm. But if I wanted to find these hoe-ass wetbacks, I was going to have to trace her steps. I received the call about Bahati and the baby two days after that stand-off in the club. If they'd had them for one week, that meant I was five steps behind, when I was usually the nigga who was twenty laps ahead. These niggas had already snatched Bahati and Shya when they came to Jagoda Bay.

"Shio, I'm just as confused as you are. If me spending money on the clothing has you upset, then I'm sorry. I won't waste—"

"Bahati, I'm not worried 'bout no bread. You can buy fifty Gucci outfits for all I give a fuck. I wouldn't have given you the card if I were going to monitor your spending." I looked her over again. "You can buy her some designer shit, too, though. Why haven't you?"

Bahati had been proven to be a decent mother, but it rubbed me the wrong way seeing all those designer packages for her and hardly anything for Shya. I would think she wanted to do the matching-mommy-and-daughter type shit that my mama would've wanted to do if she'd been blessed with a daughter. The type of shit Dasani did with Delicate and Scarlet did with Princess.

"I... I thought you wanted to wait until the test results before I started to spend on her."

"The results are coming. Truth be told, I'd rather spend it on her over you, Bahati, and I ain't saying that shit to hurt yo' feelings. I'll make sure you straight, regardless, but she's my child."

She nodded. "Understood. You already bought her a few expensive items. She's just going to grow out of them."

"And when she grows out of them, I'll get her some more. It ain't shit."

I handed Shya to Bahati, being careful because I knew she was working with one arm. I would have laid her down, but I didn't want to chance making her upset again if she woke. All that crying couldn't have been good for her vocal cords.

"Keep the phone I gave you, but leave the house sometimes. She's probably crying because she's bored. Take her to the movies, the park, or out for ice cream. My homie has an aquarium restaurant a few hours away. I can have a driver take y'all there. Go get y'all's hair and nails done together. You don't gotta be locked away. Whoever was after your daddy isn't stupid enough to go against me, and the Rodríguezes aren't your concern."

Looking down at my Apple Watch, I realized I was falling behind schedule. I turned on my heels before I took Shya back and let her rest on my chest so I, too, could take a much-needed nap. Pausing, I looked slightly over my shoulder.

"I left the keys to the Range on the hook near the garage. You can have that truck. It's practically new. Text me all the details of what you did that day, Bahati. I want to know everything, down to the brand of rice you used and what aisle you purchased it from. I need your full address too. I can go by the apartment and get anything you need."

She'd long known my number, which was programmed into the phone. She would text me every now and then throughout the day, asking where I was, and just like I'd done to Solana, I left her on read. I would respond if it were about Shya, but none of our brief conversations centered on Shya.

"I told you, we barely had much..." she responded.

"Well, I'm sure you got important shit. Papers and mail. Shya's birth certificate and social. Her shot records. Baby pictures. All that shit. I'll go get it. Just text me the address."

She licked her lips—big-ass lips that used to be wrapped around my dick on any given day.

"Bahati, it ain't optional. Lay her down and get to typing."

With that, I left her in the kitchen and headed back into the basement. Before getting back on the treadmill, I unlocked my phone again.

My thumb hovered over the camera on the right side of the screen. My heart stilled in my chest. Thick, dark hair covered her face as she lay in a fetal position on the hard floor. Closing my eyes, I pinched my nose and counted myself down. Solana's usage had been far worse than I suspected. The drugs detoxing her system were kicking her ass. Using my index finger and thumb to zoom in, a notification stopped my motion.

OTHER PHONE

Texting everything shortly

OTHER PHONE

Any specifics you want for dinner?

OTHER PHONE

Also, a lady named Uriah keeps texting you. Should I tell her I have this phone now?

I received one more notification, but it wasn't from Bahati.

DOC2

Bad news. We'll need to do another DNA test for all three of you. I can get that second DNA test scheduled as soon as you'd like. Check your email for more info.

What the fuck? I thought to myself, refusing to let anything else deter me from finishing my workout.

I would look over the email later this evening and get back to the doctor. I was specific about who I allowed to do the test because of our predicament: mob, kidnappers, and rival cartels. Now I was starting to think I should've gone to a clinic somewhere like Nel's crazy ass had suggested. I swear, if it wasn't one fucking thing, it was another, and each day that I lived through made my list longer and longer.

I locked the phone screen, pressed play to restart my playlist, which was already connected to the gym speakers, and let the pain of the intense workout wash over my reality.

God first
~~*Make sure the family good*~~
~~*Eye them Cuppacio boys, the little and the big ones*~~
~~*Build a relationship with my brother*~~
~~*Get my brother rich*~~
Health and wellness (ALWAYS)
~~*Stay on top of my mob shit*~~
Keep Hobo alive (DOING)
~~*Get through the meeting with Ines Ledesma*~~
~~*House a random*~~
~~*Find the true reason Solana is here*~~

~~Figure out if Solana is supposed to be my wife, again~~
~~Find a wife that isn't Solana~~
Kill every breathing Rodríguez Cartel member (URGENT)
Fuck Bahati up (TBD)
~~Get my fucking daughter~~
~~Get Bahati's arm fixed~~
Get to know my daughter (DOING)
~~Figure out what the fuck I'm going to do with Solana~~
Leave the mob entirely or marry Bahati or Solana
~~Get DNA test~~
Spend time with my daughter (TRYING)
Tell my mama about Shya
Keep Solana in real nigga rehab until she clean
Get SECOND DNA test
Check on Bahati's apartment
Don't fuck Uriah

CHAPTER 17
TUNAN "TUNE" PAYNE

"I'm tellin' ya. The bitch was stupid-dumb thick, on life, nigga. Hoe was so bad, I damn near emptied my pockets of errthang includin' the fuckin' lint." Shit-talker bragged with a slur in his words as he held up a can of Miller Lite wrapped in a paper bag.

His body had a slight lean to it, and if it wasn't for the railing on my mama's porch, his ass would've been in the fucking bushes.

"Fuck you know 'bout a thick junt?" Tuden snickered while shaking the dice in his fist.

Shit-talker had come up the street just minutes ago, and the shit-talking and boasting had not stopped since he'd made his way toward my mama's porch.

"Nephrew, I been fuckin' dese bitches since way back when. Since Rosa Parks was gettin' on the fuckin' bus. Since you was still in yo' daddy's *nutsack*!" He thrust his body forward as he held his beer can to his chest while spit flew from his lips.

"*Rosa Parks*? How old you is, Unc?" Tulen asked as he exited the house, rubbing his hand down his stomach and bringing the cool air conditioning with him.

He had one more time to use that bathroom, and our mama would be on his ass about her cold air being let out from his back and forth.

Shit-talker took a sip of his beer. I was almost certain it was his fifth or sixth one today, and it was barely three o'clock. "Don't worrrryyy 'bout how old da fuck I'm is. Just know I'm old enough to been have fucked her."

"Fucked who? Rosa?" I asked with a lifted brow as I sat up in the seat I'd been slumped in.

Memphis, like every good weather day in the hood, was live. Coming back to M-Town hadn't been in my plans at all, but I was, ready to hear the shit this damn fool was about to let roll off his tongue.

He snapped at me with a drunken glare. "Dat wut I said, ainnit?"

Shit-talker was sweating profusely, and the alcohol permeating through his pores was almost nauseating. Once my mama was done cooking, he had to eat something deep-fried and drown his throat in water to help get some of that liquor out of his system.

"So, Rosa Parks was your girlfriend? The same Rosa Parks who had to move to the back of the bus?" Tulsaire questioned for all of us.

Nephew had his Nintendo Switch in hand and hadn't been paying us any attention for the most part. His curly fade was crisp to perfection since we'd both gone to the barbershop this morning. With one of his long legs stretched out and resting between the rails and the other tapping against the leg of the chair he was in, he tilted his head as he waited for an answer.

I'd been tasked with flying in and escorting Tulsaire back to Jagoda Bay. My mama had flown up spontaneously for a weekend—as if she hadn't been spending enough time with us—and it just so happened that Tulsaire got home the last day she was set to fly out. Instead of changing her travel plans to spend time with him in Jagoda Bay, she was able to convince my sister to let him fly back to Memphis with her. Tuscany only agreed because Tuden and Tulen were still hanging around Mama's house regularly. They let Mama get her two days with my nephew in Memphis, and now I was here to collect. It was better that I did it than the head of the Navarro Cartel. Goal Navarro didn't play about his baby brother, and neither did we. We all had his safety at heart and wouldn't let a curl on his head get out of place.

The sun had shown no mercy to Memphis, and in those two days, Tulsaire's toast-colored skin had gotten a shade darker. I was just glad that Nephew had been outside and had taken a break from raising hell on the games. A little hood shit and Memphis slang were good for him. Goal must have agreed because he hadn't badgered my sister about where his baby brother was yet.

"So you callin' me a lie, you lil' brown-eyed knucklehead?" He lifted his beer in Tulsaire's direction.

Tulen, who was now sitting on the rail of the porch and sealing a blunt closed with his lips, spit out a weed bud. "Aye... Dat one gone get yo' cap blown back, Shit-talker. Pipe down."

Shit-talker slapped Tulsaire's shoe, knocking his foot from the railing. I'd gotten us both the new grey Jordan 5s that had dropped today, bright and early. Wolf Chase Mall was packed as fuck. I was so overwhelmed by the time I got to the counter to check out that I could only cop us the Nike sets to match. I had planned to rack up on more shit, but I'd had enough of the bebe kids and wannabe gangsters in the mall. We were basic as fuck today, but it wasn't shit going on in the hood but the hot-ass sun, drunk niggas, like the one in front of us, crackheads, and kids playing in the fucking street. We weren't trying to impress anybody.

"Mane!" he hollered out, almost tipping the can of beer over as he swayed. "Dis lil' spoiled-ass nigga know what it is. Matta fact, what you do wit dat twenty you got off me da otha day?"

Tulsaire's smirk remained in place. "Went straight to Dixie Queen with it. Ten-piece hot, all flats, fried hard with a grape slush. It was fye too!" he boasted.

Tulsaire was well taken care of wherever he went. These ignorant motherfuckers in Memphis fed right into the "Tulsaire trap" and gave him whatever, even without his little gamer ass having to ask. The little nigga just had it like that. He was beginning to pick up Memphis slang, too, and although he was hardly in the city, that nigga was still born here and had uncles that were Memphis to the core. His accent was Jagoda Bay heavy, but his lingo was the M through and through. My nephew was going to be a triple threat when released to the world. For now, he was still under lock and key.

"Who took you to Dixie Queen?" Tulen asked as he fired up his blunt.

"Uncle Den."

"Nigga, what?" Tulen snapped at Tuden. "And y'all ain't bring me shit back?"

Tulen blew out a wad of Kush that I fanned so that it would hit Tulsaire in the face. I was sure his stepdaddy and brothers smoked around him, but it was too damn hot for him to be catching a contact. Plus, the little nigga could sing, and I didn't want him to get the bright idea of smoking, and then boom, there go his vocal cords. Nope, we couldn't have that. We smoked enough for him and all those little niggas he liked to stream with. It was inevitable, and probably too late, but I wanted to keep Tulsaire innocent for as long as I could.

"Bruh, you was out the way. Had I bought you sum'n, shit woulda been cold as fuck. You know if you don't eat it fresh out the grease, it's ova with."

"Unc, yo' fries were gon' be too soggy." Tulsaire snickered as he pressed buttons on the handheld gaming console.

"Facts, 'Phew," my brother responded, backing him up while blowing smoke in the opposite direction.

It was too fucking hot outside for me to smoke. As a matter of fact, I needed to lay off the shit. I nearly committed myself somewhere when I passed the fuck out from Athena reading me a book, and my ass woke up face down in the desert with the Cuppacios. The shit scared the fuck out of me. It felt like one of those dreams when you went to bed and found yourself feeling like you'd been pushed off the cliff. I was sore as fuck, too, when I stood from that hot-ass sand, leading me to believe Don may have pushed us out of the fucking plane upon arrival while we were still out cold.

I had asked my sister how the nigga even got access to her home, but she was playing stupid like a motherfucker. It seemed that Don was like a fucking puppet master and held all the strings on everybody around me. I was going to have to watch myself and that meant laying off the weed. I'd gone damn near a year without it; I could do it again.

We were all so enthralled with the drunken antics of Shit-talker that we didn't see my mother step onto the porch until she was slapping Tulen upside the head.

"Owww! What the—"

"Say it and watch I slap ya again."

"Ma, what I do?" He held his head while perching the blunt between his lips.

"Out here smokin' 'round my Goddamn grandbaby! Dat's what!" Mama snatched the weed from Tulen and tossed it over the side of the railing.

When it landed somewhere in the bushes, Tulen cracked a smile. "Aite, when you set it on fire, I ain't payin' fo' no new landscapin'."

"Boy, shut up! It rained last night, so the soil and plants are wet. Stop smokin' in front of him. He's watchin' errthang y'all do." Our mama then looked up at Shit-talker, who was taking a sip from his beer. "As a matter of fact, come on in until it's time for me to take y'all to the airport, baby."

She held her hand out, gesturing Tulsaire to come inside. As soon as he was within arm's reach, she grabbed him to her chest and kissed all over his face before the door slammed shut. Tulsaire was getting a version of our mama that none of us had ever gotten. He was getting the healed her, and she was more loving, caring, mentally sane now that life had turned around financially and she had more security. Tulsaire also had his brother's mama as a grandmother figure, and his stepfather's mama, Dana, as one too. My siblings and I had never had grandparents. Our mama's mama had died long before any of us remembered, and since I hadn't known my daddy, that side of the family was nonexistent until Shio showed up. According to him, though, I'd lucked up not meeting them niggas.

Tulen pulled another blunt from his pocket and grinned. "Shit-talker?"

"Wazzup, niccah?" He was staggering so much that he had taken a seat at the end of the porch.

"You always talkin' 'bout dese bitches and shit, but I thought you was married at one point? If you fuckin' hoes while yo' wife is barely in the ground, I know you was a dawg when she was alive. You probably broke dat poor lady's heart."

"I heard she was fine too. And she drove dat clean-ass Cadillac. It was long as a muthafucka, but it was clean," Tuden cosigned.

These niggas didn't have no fucking couth. I still had three hours before Tulsaire and I had to be at the airport, and since I knew my mama wanted more time with her grandchild like she hadn't had that for the past two days, kicking it with these niggas was the move. I was going to be on the fucking plane smelling like outside like a motherfucker, but I wasn't taking my ass back to the mall for more clothes.

Shit-talker slammed his can on the concrete next to him. "Yeah, I fuck dese bitches. I mean, why da fuck not? But 'bout my wife?" He lifted the can and held out his index finger, pointing it at Tulen. He seemed to be everyone's target today. But shit, that was every day. "'Bout my wife, niccah! I respected her *always*."

"How long was y'all married?" I leaned in, resting my elbows on my knees, somewhat intrigued.

"Thurty-six years, lil' nigga. We married when I was twenty, and she died four years ago."

"Damn, dat's three decades of the same pussy!" Tuden's stupid ass whistled.

"Dat's nearly four decades of the BEST pussy. Dey don't make pussy like Emora Dean's no more. See, y'all got dat stepped on pussy. The women dese days do too much of dat hookah and Julio shit. All dat hot wings and hibachi bullshit!" He waved his hands dismissively. "Dat shit got da pussy feelin' different and damn sho' smellin' different!" His top lip curled over his nose.

Tulen sucked his teeth. "Nah... Dat's cuz you be fuckin' dem old hoes down at da café!"

"Nigga, I done had some mid thurty-year-old pussy. Shit was just as worse."

"But you nutted doe..." Tuden egged him on.

"Damn right I did, Den! It's pussy, ain't it? Give a nigga a hole ina wall, a nigga gon' stick his dick in and nut as long as it got a skirt on!"

I balled over laughing as Tuden cheesed. "Unc, I'ma have to introduce you to some bad bitches. I guarantee ya... You ain't fuckin' da right ones. I'll bring you sum'n so bad dat ole Amber Dean gon' be rollin' over in her grave. Stiff-ass wig gon' wound up stranglin' her from turnin' so hard!"

"Y'all stupid as hell." I cackled some more at these fools. Between my brothers here and my new peoples in Jagoda Bay, all I did was laugh at stupid niggas all day.

"It's Emora, niccah! And I don' seent da bitches y'all fuck with. Unc can't afford dem types. I'll take a food stamp recipient dat's happy with a few hundred for a wig, a blunt, and a bottle."

"I thought chu said the lowest you had fucked with is mid-thirties?" I asked.

"And you think dem broads don't be havin' stamps? I got some in their forties dat swipe dat EBT like it's a black card. But on the real, keep yo' type away from me. I ain't buying no Coach bags."

"While you tryna be funny, Coach done got high as fuck, Shit-talker," I replied and sat back in the metal chair.

"And how da fuck you know, bruh?"

Everyone was eyeing me, waiting to answer Tuden's question.

"Cuz I got a niece dat had me in the mall a few weeks ago, coppin' her some shit."

Tulen smirked while hitting Tuden on the chest. "Awh! I thought you was gon' say you been shoppin' for da *wifey*."

"And if I was? Don't be actin' like you niggas ain't the boss at trickin'. Tuden been trickin' since he got his first job. Lil' ass check and tryna cop a bitch some Jordans."

Tulen coughed up smoke in laughter as I told the story of us going to the mall back then. I'd borrowed the neighbor's car to take Tuden to the mall and was mad as fuck when he got to the register, and he didn't have enough. He walked out of the mall the same way he went in, with sixty-two dollars. I wasn't putting in on shit back then over a bitch I wasn't fucking.

"Guess what, Shit-talker?" Tuden asked after we laughed over the dumb shit he'd done as a youngin'.

"Who don' died?" he yelled out.

"Mane, ain't nobody died." Tuden grinned, and I knew he was headed down the road of good bullshit.

"Aite, so tell me sum'n good."

"Yo' favorite hood nephew don' got married."

Shit-talker turned his body in an almost unnatural position since my chair was behind him. "You done joined the MNS?"

"The who?" we asked in unison.

"The Married Nigga Society!"

I sucked my teeth. "Bruh! You just be makin' up shit. You don't need shit else to drink."

"On God!" Tulen shook his head.

"MNS was founded by Benson Brown back in 1872. Look it up, niccahs. But, damn, Nephrew. I'm proud of ya."

Instead of replying to Shit-talker, I held up my middle finger to my childish-ass brothers.

"Fuck dem niccahs! Dey still got milk on dey tongues." Shit-talker rested his elbow on his thigh and slightly hunched his back over. He was going to be aching like a motherfucker in the morning. "Lemme ask you dis. How she look?"

Tulen grunted. "Fine as hell!"

"As a muhfuckah! Ion know how dat nigga got out and lucked up like dat. She slick famous too. Bossed up and errthang." Tuden was full-on grinning like I wouldn't lay his ass out.

I was tired of explaining that Glow and I weren't like that, so I let it rock. My brothers knew what was up but still liked to fuck with me from time to time. They acted like Tulscan and Tuscany weren't already married.

"Look..."

Tuden had pulled up Glow's Instagram page. The last picture she'd posted was from the Sniff-and-Sip party, when she was in that little-ass bow top. That fucking get-up she was wearing was the reason I cornered her ass and propositioned her to be my wife. It was crazy because it wasn't that long ago, but so much shit had transpired since then that it felt like it had been years since that party.

"Oh, damn..." Shit-talker leaned back before leaning forward and looking up to Tuden. "How da fuck you zoom in on dis box-ass phone?"

Tulen fell out laughing while I snatched the phone from Unc, locked the screen, and tossed it back in my brother's lap.

"My bad, Nephrew..." He held his hands up, the paper-wrapped beer can still occupying his right hand. "She high yella dan a mudda-fucka, but she cold as ice in da middle of da Arctic Ocean. Dese niggas gon' be suitin' up to deep dive fo' dat dere. You know how to swim, Nephrew?"

Tuden and Tulen were hollering in laughter, and the scene had a few old heads in the hood looking our way.

Shit-talker jutted his chin at my hand. "Where da fuck yo' ring at? I know you ain't out here puttin' on for dese tied-ass hoes?"

"Yeah, where yo' ring at, Tunan..." Tuden instigated with Tulen coughing on smoke again. His ass needed to put the blunt out. He couldn't be getting high because he had been laughing since he sparked up the second Backwood.

"We ain't have time for allat, Unc. Shit just happened, but she aint trippin' 'bout it."

"Lemme ask you dis, Nephrew. Is *she* wearing one?"

Running my hand over my head, I cut my eyes at my brothers, who were cracking the fuck up again.

Shit-talker took my lack of response as a signal to continue. "Den she trippin' den. I been married thurty-six years. One thing fo' sho' and two thangs fo' Goddamn certain, women don't like to be made a fool of."

"I ain't makin' no fool outta her, Unc, and nawl, I ain't fuckin' no hoes."

"Shidd, you stupid den a muddafucka if you is. Fine as she is, I'd go Ray Charles when another woman enters da room. Dat bad pussy shit..."—He pointed to all three of us—"Dat don't upply to her. I know she sittin' on a diamond mine. I ain't lyin'."

My brothers could barely breathe from laughing at Shit-talker's drunk ass.

"I'ma tell you a secret." He paused, letting out a loud-ass belch. "The key to a happy marriage is givin' her shit without her havin' to ask. She ain't trippin' 'bout a ring? Pop up with one on. Tradition say it's up to a woman to buy the man's ring, but I say, dat's bullshit. I mean... She can go buy it, but long as it's with da man's money. You pass dat shit now, too late fa all dat. Go get yo'self a nice ring and use dat same finger to play in dat cat. Don't say a bitch-ass thang... Just pull up"—He held his finger up that still housed his gold wedding band—"And thrust dat bitch in her. 'Pendin' on how tight she *ain't*, add da pinky. She gone be comin' until the cows come home."

"Mane, hellll nawl!" I couldn't stand my brothers. The niggas had turned part hyena, and had Mama coming to the door telling us to shut the hell up.

When she walked away, Shit-talker shrugged. "Real shit, Nephrew. Make yo' woman happy. Life so fuckin' short. I did errthang right by my wife. If she saw it in the paper? I bought it. If the neighbor had it, I got it. Errthang 'round the house; I took care of it. My wife ain't never known a bill. You see dese hands?" He held his left hand, which showed scars, callouses, knuckles that were double the average size, and medium-length nails that were naturally yellowed. "Dese hands look like dis so hers could look the opposite. She was in the salons and shit weekly—I ain't do dat biweekly shit.

'Pendin' on if it was a holiday or not, she went twice a week. I took care of mine."

The sun buried itself behind a row of clouds, casting shade down on us. Shit-talker needed it because he was sweating enough that a bucket could collect it. The constant wiping at his face with the white towel he had draped over his shoulder wasn't doing shit.

"You have any regrets?" Tulen had finally calmed his giggling ass down and looked serious for once today.

"I do... Two." He sat back, pressing his back into the railing. "I regret she died 'fore me. I wasn't 'posed to bury Emora. Dat ain't the natural order of things. I set our whole lives up in hopes dat she would outlive me. I took care of it all. I paid for our burial plots, caskets, da whole nine. Even bought my suit dat she was 'posed to bury me in. I didn't want her to have no worries. Shit didn't work out like dat, doe." He took another swig of his can, which I was sure was empty or either hot as hell by now.

"You said you had two regrets." I pointed out.

"Yeah..." He burped. "Me spoilin' her shoulda came with conditions. Not in the materialistic sense, doe—in the physical. I had a cleaning service. She didn't work. Hell, I even hired the neighborhood crackhead to drive her 'round when I was out makin' the bacon. I enabled Emora. Dat ain't no thang, though. Dat's what I was 'posed to do. See, since my wife had the world at her fingertips, she found herself indulging in errthang. She was partyin', drinkin', eatin' all dat bullshit! She started puttin' on weight, but I loved dat shit. She was just right. Constant years of doin' what da fuck she wanted without me dere to at least guide her in the right direction fucked with her health. Diabetes took her faster than a thief in the fuckin' night."

He used the towel to wipe his face. "So, to answer your second question, my second and most biggest regret was not being dere. I spent so much time outside the house, makin' sure she had errthang she wanted and needed dat I forgot what really mattered." He pointed to his heart. "Had I known I'd only get thurty-six years with dat woman, I woulda had my ass home more. I woulda pivoted. We woulda ate better, exercised. One thang I do admire 'bout some folk from y'all generation is dat dey make time. Back den, our time was spent makin' sure we ain't never have to go without. I'd slit my fuckin' wrist before my wife opened a cut-off notice."

"Didn't you buy a big-ass house out in the east?" Tulen's nosey ass inquired.

"Yeap. Used cold, hard cash too. Bought it five years 'fore she died. Dat was our fourth paid-off home, by the way. The other three, I was able to divide among our children to live in until dey were ready to buy their own. Now, all but one use 'em for passive income. Dat last one from my nutsack like you two,"—He cut his eyes at my brothers—"Fucked up!"

"Well, unless you want to join ole Elenora, I'ma take this." Tuden reached for the beer can, but Shit-talker was quick.

"Back da fuck up, niccah! And I done told yo' Slim Jim-lookin' ass it's Emora!"

We all laughed as Shit-talker hugged his beer to his chest.

"But you was just preachin' all dat shit about wishin' y'all ate and drank better. You four years late, but we can start now, Unc."

"Didn't I tell you dese hoes slaw? I'm ready to be with my ole lady, anyway. *If* the can gon' take me out, oh well... You worried 'bout me, but what you shoulda been learnin' today is dat time ain't on nobody side. Fuckin' all dese skeezers, by the time you meet the one, yo' shit gon' be saggin' like horse balls."

"And I'ma still get slurped up! My brother the one need to be listenin'. I need my sis-in-law 'round fo' a long-ass time. I fucked 'bout three grade-A bitches since dat live. Glow got some fine-ass followers."

This nigga.

"I learned something from today, Unc." Tulen raised his hand.

"Niccah, what?"

"I learned dat yo' ass a liar. By subtractin' your marriage years by yo' age, it would've been another fourteen or so years before yo' ass was even born when Rosa Parks was put to da back of da bus."

Shit-talker's eyes bucked. "Ah, shit. I said Rosa Parks? I meant *Rose Sparks*! She was the neighborhood headhunter. She had a mean-ass throat too! Dese hookah hoes y'all got could neva hold dey breath like ole Rose."

We all howled in laughter as Shit-talker started mimicking someone giving his drunk ass some head. Though I had to get back to Jagoda Bay, this was one of the reasons why I loved the fuck out of my city. I had no desire to move back, but being here, in the hood, surrounded by the people who made my childhood memories priceless, outweighed the suffering and the days we'd gone without. These types of moments were unmatched.

I didn't know what the fuck Don had in store for me, and even though I low-key looked forward to it, the unknown had me uneasy. Memphis was familiar. While I technically had family in Jagoda Bay, it was nothing like my roots. Outside of the money that was to be made, there was one person who was making Jagoda Bay take Memphis' spot.

Pulling out my phone while everyone continued to clown, I went to the last text thread in the messaging app.

Stay up

THE ROOM WAS PITCH BLACK, with an orange cast on her face from the laptop screen resting in her lap. I could see her perfectly because of it. Leaning against the doorframe, I watched as she cursed, banged the computer keys, and rolled her eyes at least four times in ten minutes.

"You gone stand there and watch me like a creep all night, Tunan?" Glow said, keeping her eyes on the computer.

"Yeah, the view is nice, my baby."

"The view is a mess. My face feels swollen as hell since you and my mom have become the best of friends, and she forces me to eat more than you do. I thought that was near impossible. I need to do something to my hair. I'm behind on posting, so I've been up the past few nights trying to catch up, and now, I have bags that even the under-eye patches can't fix."

The pink under-eye patches in question were stuck right under her waterline with words written all over them. Glow wasn't talking about shit; she looked pretty as fuck.

Pushing off the doorframe, I entered her bedroom. It smelled like whatever plug-in and carpet freshener combination had been used when her mama cleaned earlier. I knew because I heard a vacuum when I called her right after being cleared through TSA.

Glow's eyes jumped from the computer screen to the bag that I was carrying in my hand. Her sneer twisted into a full-on frown.

"Tunan… I've eaten three meals *and* a snack today. I didn't throw it up, either, no matter how much I was grossed out. Please… No more today."

I'd left my slides at the front door, not wanting to track germs into the house. I smelled the cleaning products before I could even turn the key that I *hadn't* left on the nightstand as she'd asked.

Stopping at the side of the bed, I held up the black plastic bag. "You had food, but you ain't have no dessert."

"Tunaaaaan." She was groaning, pressing her back into the headboard as her laptop slid off her lap. I caught it and put it back upright before it hit the floor, smirking at her pretty ass.

"At every opportunity, you gone do the absolute most. I'm not eating nothing else tonight, Tunan."

"Well, technically…" I pulled my phone out and checked the time before stuffing it back in my baller shorts. "It's a new day. Two a.m. to be exact. You ain't ate nuttin' yet."

"And I won't be until breakfast." Lifting her head, the frown on her pretty face deepened. "Where you been anyway? Why you smell like soap? Why you dressed like that? Hunh?"

I smirked harder. "You ain't gon' lemme answer da first question without followin' up with two more?"

Her response was to fold her arms under her chest. Her bottom half was hidden by her comforter, but her bare waist made an appearance when her oversized shirt rose with the gesture.

"I went to Memphis. I flew in 'bout two hours ago. I got my nephew settled and showered cuz I was fuckin' 'round in the sun all day."

Glow cocked her head. "I like Memphis."

"It was last minute, my baby. My spoiled-ass sister acted like our other brothers couldn't fly back with him."

"With the way you stay in Memphis, let me find out you got a baby mama or something out there."

"What?" I chuckled while shaking my head at her crazy ass. Glow had proven to be more possessive than I anticipated she would be. Hell, I didn't anticipate her having clingy tendencies at all with the way she screamed that our marriage was only valid on paper.

"I didn't stutter. You're out there every chance you get. I thought the motive was the money, and the money is here. Let me find out you got a secret baby somewhere in M-Town."

Her using our lingo had me full-on laughing this time. "Lemme find out y'all been runnin' off at the mouth 'bout my brother business."

Her arms fell, and so did her face. "No we haven't—"

"Y'all have, but it ain't shit. Just know, I ain't got no kids, Glow."

"So now it's *Glow*? Not, *my baby*?"

I swiped my hand down my face. "I ain't got no kids, my baby."

"You had me waiting up all night, and you went and did God knows what."

"I went from the airport to my sister house. Kicked my nephew's ass in 2K. Smoked a blunt with my brother-in-law. Rocked my other nephew to sleep. I showered, brushed my teeth, went to the store, and now I'm here."

"Well, my plumbing works just fine. You could have showered over here."

"I will next time, my baby."

She rolled her eyes and snatched the bag from my hand with her rude ass. Pulling one of the four tubes out, she held the label to her face. She then repeated the same notion with the other three.

"Tunan. These all say sugar-free. This must've been all they had?"

Scratching the back of my neck, I shook my head. "Nah. What you workin' on, doe?"

She shrugged. "Editing a video. A while back, I did a faceless unboxing but never uploaded it. My viewers like to see me eat so I didn't think this would be interesting enough for them. But it's gonna have to do for now." She sighed.

"Lemme see." I waited until she turned the computer to face me.

The editing software that she was using had a bunch of dials on the bottom and sides of the screen. She pressed a key, and the video came to life. The video was clear and ASMR coded with her peeling the tape from the packaging. It sounded satisfying as fuck just like the TikToks Tulsaire sent sometimes of barbers doing the same thing. Glow was unboxing a Louis Vuitton bag and had even added a scarf and bag charms to it, looking pretty as fuck. My dick jumped when she did a shimmy while holding the bag.

"Dey gone love dis."

She kissed her teeth and flipped her computer back around so that it was facing her again. "Tell me anything."

"Real shit. My sister 'nem stay watchin' dese kinda videos."

"See, I watch them, too, but I didn't know how my audience was going to perceive me. My whole brand is about eating." She huffed. "My people literally calls themselves the 'Pretty Eaters.'"

I could see the frustration and emotion building in her eyes. Glow had been doing good since she was released from the hospital. She'd only thrown up once, and Ma Cathy said that could have been because she made pinto beans, and Glow had never liked them. Although she was eating, she still had a lot of work to do to beat the actual condition. I was just happy that her mama was on board and holding her down when I couldn't be here. Still, she loathed eating, and it was fucked up because not only did she need food to survive, but she had found a way to capitalize on it.

"Dey gonna watch whatever you upload, Glow."

"But I need them to engage in order for me to keep getting paid."

"Dey gone engage, comment, subscribe, *and* click the link in the bio."

"See, you playing, and I'm real life about to have a heart attack."

"My baby..." I lifted her chin, seeing the worry in her tired eyes. "Ya know you can ice dis shit for a while."

"I have bills, Tunan. I know you're handling the mortgage, but I still have other expenses. My sister had a baby. I gotta figure out what we going to do about my mama's house—"

"I'll hold ya down until ya ready to get back to it. I'll hold all y'all down... Where the baby anyway?"

Glow's eyes rounded as she snatched her phone from the nightstand. "Next door. Shit, I forgot. Let me call Glee."

I grabbed the phone before she could finish dialing. "I'm sure she's fine. She got the crew over dere and her best friend. Ya know y'all mama checkin' in too. Dey good, Glow. Relax."

She sighed. "You taking care of all this wasn't a part of the agreement."

"Fuck dat weak-ass agreement. You ain't gotta do shit you don't wanna do. If it ain't bringin' you joy, fuck dem eaters. It's plenty other greedy muthafuckas dey can binge watch."

"Really?"

"Real shit. I got you. Take dis time to do mob wife shit. Get out, go shopping, go hiking, join a yoga stretch class, travel—"

"Okay! Hold the fuck up. You feed me, and then you bring sugar-free ice-cream, and *now* you're telling me I need to exercise."

I sucked my teeth. "All I'm sayin' is, you can go do what women your age do. Ain't dat what dey do? Yoga stretch?"

"Pilates, Tunan."

"Yeah, dat shit. Go do it if dat's what you wanna do. You ain't gotta do dis online shit no mo' if you ain't enjoyin' it."

Moving the laptop from her lap, I folded it down, hoping I wasn't fucking shit up. When she didn't protest, I set it on the nightstand. Kneeling on the side of the bed, I tugged at her sleeve.

"Dey gonna watch whatever you upload cuz it ain't the food dey obsessed with. It's seein yo' pretty ass. When you ain't bein' so fuckin' impossible, you a cool lil' vibe." I blocked the punch she threw. "Watch out."

"I'm not used to having freedom from responsibility, Tunan."

"Well, real shit, get used to it. You can do whatever you wanna do."

"I can't expect you to take care of me, let alone my family."

"Aye." Pulling her face closer to mine, her legs fell on either side of my chest. I pulled at her chin, our lips as close as they could be before they touched. "However unconventional dis shit is, you my wife, Glow. Upload the content or don't. Regardless, I'ma handle shit when it comes to you, and dat's errthang dat comes with yo' ass too."

"First, you gotta stay out of Memphis, so you can actually get to the money."

Going for it, I pecked her lips once, twice, and then sucked them into my mouth without letting up. When my dicked jumped again, I pulled back. I was serious about not fucking Glow until I felt she was on the right path to beating this anorexia shit.

"With or without da mob, you gotta know, I'ma get to it, my baby."

Kissing her soft-ass lips again, I squeezed her bare thighs. Glow was so pretty, even with the weight loss. I was hoping she had at least gained something since Ma Cathy and I had been stuffing her ass. I had a good mind to tell her to step on the scale I'd seen in her bathroom when I ran her a bath, but I didn't want to push her past her limit with me.

Deepening the kiss, I rubbed my hand up her soft-ass skin. As the cover fell away from the rest of her body, my dick bricked. Her arousal was strong and loud because she wasn't wearing any fucking panties. It was something about this girl that just fucking did it for me. The health shit had me questioning a lot, but every time I thought about bouncing on the marriage, a voice was loud as fuck telling me, "Hell nawl."

Fuck it.

"What are you doing, Tunan?" She squirmed within my grasp.

"'Bout to eat yo' pussy. Lay back."

Instead of waiting for her to comply, I pulled her legs so that her ass was hanging off the bed. I sat her cheeks right on my chest, putting her pretty-ass pussy right in my face. Not waiting, I peeled her lips back and clamped down on her bud.

"Ohhhhhhh!"

"Shut up. You gone wake up my new best friend."

Bringing her pussy lips inside my mouth, I watched as she drove her elbows into the bed.

"Uggghhhhhh! Right there."

"I'ma stop." I warned her, serious about not waking Ma Cathy up.

"Okay, okay! Shit... Okay. Just don't stop."

Freaky, pretty ass.

Reaching around her, I grabbed a tube of the sugar-free ice cream. Once the top was off, I scooped some out and pressed it onto her swollen bud.

"Ahhh, gossssh!"

"Too cold?" I asked as her body bucked.

"Un hunh!" She reached out and pushed my head down. "Warm me back up."

My brothers always said food could throw a woman's pH off, but I was sure Glow had some special wash to handle it. She kept all types of products on deck from that PR shit. She was the fucking product girl.

Product girl with butter pecan pussy.

Once I took a few licks, I nearly regretted doing the shit. Glow's legs were vibrating, and the pussy itself tasted immaculate, but I'd let Shit-talker's autobiography of his diabetic wife get into my head. I fucked around and purchased sugar-free ice cream, and I had even told myself I was going to watch Glow's sugar intake from now on. This shit would have been so good had I gotten my normal brands, Blue Bell or Ben & Jerry's. I fucked up, but it was too late to back out, so I ate her sugar-free pussy straight off the bone.

CHAPTER 18
ITALIAN CUPPACIO

"You finished changin' her?"

Standing on the outside of the guest bedroom that was across from Jisei's old primary one, I pulled the blunt from the pocket of my shorts.

"Yeah, I'm done. If you smell like smoke, you can't hold her, Italian."

Awl fuck.

Just as fast as I pulled the blunt from my pocket, I stuffed it back in. I'd been smoking this townhouse the fuck out; so much so that Pearla and 'nem had to lift the windows and air it out before Glee had come over with the baby on her birthday. The door opened and out walked Mahzeyah's gorgeous ass. As always, she was frowning at the sight of me, but unlike other ugly motherfuckers, her frown made her look even finer.

While patting Baby Leader's back, she faced me, not bothering to wipe the disdain she displayed.

"I ain't smoked all day today," I protested.

"It's only noon. That isn't a flex, boy."

With the roll of her eyes and a smack of her plump, glossed lips, she turned on her white ankle socks and went in the opposite direction. With each step she took, the pleated skirt of her cheerleading uniform bounced. Green, white, and yellow never looked so fucking good. She'd been complaining about cheer camp every day, but a nigga had been thanking God every time she came around in her practice uniform. Her face, her body, and her attitude were perfect for the sport—Mahzeyah was *made* to cheer.

Baby Leader's little head popped up, making me stick my tongue out at her, and before they could get too far down the hall, I was right behind them.

"You said I could hold her after you changed her."

"Don't you need to take Solana her lunch?" Mahzeyah replied as she hurried a bit, giving me a quick glimpse of her green uniform panties that the left side of her butt cheek was spilling out of.

Smiling, I had to adjust myself in my pants. Mahzeyah was only seventeen and wasn't shaped like the older women who had no business spreading their legs for me, a minor. But her body was tight and perfectly proportioned for our age. Her thick, smooth legs were toned from her extracurricular activities, and her coffee-colored skin was flawless under the little makeup she told me was necessary, even for cheer practice. Her hair was pulled into a high ponytail today with curled ends, held by a yellow bow. Some days she wore a white bow, and other days, green. I guess it just depended on her mood. One thing her mood never changed about was how she treated me. She was the cobra, and I was the ignorant motherfucker who liked to stick my hand out to test if she'd strike, and Mahzeyah always bit. I didn't mind, though. A little bite was good for the soul, and her fine ass delivering it was enough to keep me hopeful that one day—when I was ready—she'd at least let me smell her fine ass.

I liked that Mahzeyah dubbed my ass. Women were too eager and too easy when it came to young niggas like me. Not just in Jagoda Bay, but in the Chi too. Granted, when we lived in Chicago, I was only a little nigga, but I was still getting girls. One look at me, and the opposite sex was falling all over themselves. Mahzeyah, though? Mahzeyah always gave me the cold shoulder, and I knew it was because a young nigga like me wasn't nothing to her. Her daddy was the biggest boss, and her mama had motion too. I couldn't recall exactly what her mama did, but I knew she helped people grow their businesses or some shit like that. Whatever it was, her family had her set for life, and Mahzeyah wanted for nothing. The type of niggas she gave her time to were those that could do what her daddy did for her.

I respected it. I'd be looking at her sideways if she was just out here giving it out to any nigga that passed her by. She had standards, and them bitches were high. And now that I was getting older, I understood that girls who had high standards would become women who refused to let a nigga be their downfall. Mahzeyah had no choice but to be choosy as fuck coming up the way she had. Her people were not letting her fuck with no birds, which was why I didn't understand her current obsession with that rap nigga. Flexer may not have been a bird, but he gave off platypus vibes, with his ole sneaky Phineas and Ferb ass. Being fed with a diamond-encrusted spoon all her life, I'm sure she probably thought fucking with a rapper was her best bet to maintain the status quo. And, shit—maybe it was.

I fucked with Flexer's music. I wasn't a hating-ass nigga. He had bars, for sure, and knew what he was doing in the booth from what I'd seen. Had Reaper—Grind's partner—not gotten killed, though, he'd be giving Flexer a run for his fucking money. They both had a fan base in the same age demographic, and they both were some fly niggas. It was commendable as fuck when Flexer did the tribute to Reaper. He proved that he wasn't just a rapping-ass nigga, and that he was about that real-nigga shit he be spitting in his songs. Most niggas that constantly screamed they was real tended to be the opposite, so I couldn't lie and say I wasn't shocked about the nigga being a stand-up guy.

Mahzeyah was fine as hell, so Flexer getting at her wasn't a shock either. For me, right now, she was just easy on the eyes and sometimes fun to annoy. I was a young nigga who liked pretty girls, and while Mahzeyah was a pretty girl, she wasn't the only one. I was fucking anything in a skirt with a pussy these days just because I could. I was too young and still figuring my own shit out to try and bag a girl like Mahzeyah. I wasn't even about to lie like I was ready for a girlfriend. I'd also told myself that she was too close to home, being best friends with my family, so I couldn't do shit for Mahzeyah except cause some bullshit between the crew, and I wasn't doing that stupid shit.

Mahzeyah served her purpose, though, when she came into my life. Because of her, I unlocked a new fetish in me. I didn't realize it until I met Mahzeyah, but pretty, spoiled girls were my kryptonite.

When I did settle down, it wouldn't be with a hood chick. The more rotten she was, the better. I wanted mine sixty-day-old-milk spoiled.

"Solana been had her lunch, ZeyZey." I finished my statement with a tug on her skirt, careful not to touch her ass.

I had a crush, but I wasn't a creep-ass young nigga. Plus, I didn't want her to stop coming around. It was bad enough that we were all in this townhouse unsupervised. But then again, knowing Shio's fake mad ass, he had cameras all over this bitch to watch Solana like this was his shit instead of Jisei's.

Mahzeyah spun on her heels and nearly slipped, but I caught her. The baby was still secured in her arms, smiling like she wasn't about to take her first tumble.

"See, you and those slippery-ass socks. Doin' too much." I grinned.

"Nigga, get your hands off me. Nails probably dirty. Eww." She pulled back, putting space between us.

"My hands clean. My VraVra always cleanin' my nails." I held them out so that she could see. They'd even been clipped down and filed evenly. I didn't do that polish shit, though.

Mahzeyah's nose crinkled as she patted the baby's back. "Ion know who coochie you been playing in. And who is VraVra? Is that why you call me, ZeyZey? Don't be giving me pet names you give to other bitches."

"Man, lemme hold the baby."

She looked me up and down and snarled. "Nigga, no."

Turning again, skirt flapping, she continued on, not stopping until she entered the living room. The TV was playing Essex's latest video on YouTube with Bella standing in front of it with the remote in her hand. Pearla was standing behind Glee's wheelchair, greasing her scalp while bopping her head to the beat. I couldn't believe my nigga had blown up like that. Essex was like an uncle or big cousin to me. I couldn't really remember too much of a life without him. He'd done my first tattoo, and even though it hurt like hell since I was young as fuck at the time, he was the coldest with the ink gun. Now, he was the coldest in that rap game and coming for the top spot. I had over ten tattoos, but Gal and I was just saying we needed some new art. When he came back around, I was going to see if I could convince him to pull the ink gun out. He was constantly setting up shop for Big Cuz and 'nem. It had been too long, though, since he'd even did that.

"Essex, I'm telling you... The next video needs to be "Cum to Me." I got the whole concept! Listen, Essex! You and Missy should be in a warehouse, tied up in suits. She should grab you by the tie and then start dancing on a pole in the middle of the warehouse. You rap while she dances. That will be soooo hard! Everybody already loves y'all! Plus, it'll make that baby mama of yours look even dumber." Bella was talking a mile a minute, trying to tell Essex what to do.

He had hired her to handle his social media a while back, and no lie, she ran that like she was Usain Bolt's little sister. My cousin was the best at what she did. Still, she ended up giving advice about his other stuff, too, even though it had nothing to do with social media. What made it worse was that Missy backed Bella's nonsense, which gave her more ammo to suggest some of the wildest shit.

I didn't know how Essex dealt with both Missy's fine ass and Bella's crazy self all day. Missy was feisty as hell, and Bella was bossy as hell. Essex had watched Bella grow up, just as he had with me, so Bella was family to him. But Bella wasn't Baby Bella anymore. With what Essex paid her, she now had the look that matched her bold attitude. Every time she came around, she looked like new money. Plus, she was still in everybody else's pockets, too, including mine lately, and I was supposed to be the little cousin.

Glee's eyes had been closed as Pearla greased her scalp, but it was as if she had mommy senses because they popped open as soon as we entered the space. Unlike mean-ass Mahzeyah, Glee's features were always soft. Her bruises were beginning to heal on her face, and even though there was a scab running down the center of her lip, I knew it would heal good too. She was a trooper and pretty as hell, just like all the other girls surrounding my everyday life. I didn't know how much she knew about our family, but when we loved, we loved hard as fuck, and she and Baby Leader were stuck with us now.

I reached for the baby, and Mahzeyah bopped away.

"You so foul, yo."

"Boy, whatever!"

Mahzeyah sat next to Glee's fine-ass friend, who was balled up on the end of the sectional with a blanket over her head. We'd all been up all night talking shit, telling stories, and passing the baby around. I walked them home around four a.m., and they were right back over here at ten.

"Y'all fighting over Baby Leader again?" Glee giggled.

"That's him. He be hogging her, and then gets mad when I get her. You had her all night!"

"Well, didn't nobody tell you to take yo' ass to see that nigga. You woulda been able to get her some."

"For your information, I went home. I'm seventeen, negro. I have a curfew. Everybody can't be a dropout that do what they want to do like you." She rolled her eyes.

"Y'all don't start that shit today..." Bella warned while she held the phone up to her ear. "No, Missy. I'm not talking about y'all. My lil' cousin and bestie—they argue like a married couple." Bella shot us a look before restarting the video and huffing ideas into the phone again.

"Aye, watch that *lil* word."

"You heard her. *Lil' cousin.*"

I kissed my teeth. "Put the baby down, follow me to the back, and I can show you how lil' I'm *not.*"

Pearla tossed her head back in laughter, and Glee held her hand over her mouth, trying to hide hers. She complained about her ribs still being sore, so she tried her best not to do too much.

Mahzeyah continued patting the baby's back. "Never in your wildest dreams, Italian Cuppacio."

"I know..." I shrugged. "It was worth a shot, though."

"Is this y'all baby or hers?" Pearla snickered.

"Mine..." "Ours," we answered simultaneously, with me smirking about saying Baby Leader was ours.

"Oh, Lord," Pearla said as she parted Glee's hair.

Mahzeyah smacked her glossy-ass lips. "He needs some kids. The boy got baby fever."

"I could say the same 'bout you. You pushin' out a Baby Flexer soon?"

"Tuh! It damn sure won't be a Baby Cuppacio whenever I do."

"Shol' won't!" Bella chimed in, still on the phone.

"Bruh, pipe down. As long as you don't have no kids, we gucci. Me, I'm grown."

Popping my invisible collar, since I was wearing a crew neck, I laughed when Bella waved me off and continued her conversation. I was certain by the end of it, she would get whatever it was she was proposing to Essex and Missy. She constantly complained about how much work she did for Essex, yet she was always inserting herself into anything related to his career.

"She's just so pretty and so little. I love her outfit today, Glee. I love all her outfits."

We all watched as Mahzeyah held the baby in her lap while making kissy faces at her. Glee's mom had rolled a bassinet over here since they were here most of the day. It was useless because she'd maybe slept in it once.

"Facts. She be fly. That teal and gray fit she had on... What was that? Wednesday? Hard."

Mahzeyah cut her eyes at me. "You tryna be funny?"

"Hunh?" Most of the time, I did and said shit on purpose to get under her skin, but this time, I didn't know what Mahzeyah was talking about.

"I bought that outfit."

"Yeah?" I nodded. "You did good, ZeyZey."

My alarm went off on my phone in my pocket. Instead of removing it, I hit the side button to silence it. Mahzeyah could have her for now because it was time for me to do what I'd been assigned to do. When Big Cuz called me up, I was taken aback by his request. After I'd fucked up with Hobo, fucking around with Neltz, I didn't think my cousins would ever trust me to handle shit ever again until I proved myself. Getting that call and hearing the exhaustion in his voice, I knew I couldn't say no.

Jogging down the stairs, I hit the light on the basement wall. I couldn't believe Jisei had this spot deserted like this. She'd left everything in this bitch, down to designer clothes in her closets. It was girly as hell with all the pink, but the basement was more neutral. Staying here, even though I knew it was temporary, gave me a sense of how it would feel to live alone. My spot was going to be the hangout, for sure. I wouldn't have it any other way, especially now that we'd set a standard with the townhouse.

Bending at the slot that was toward the bottom of the top half of the door, I slid it open so that I could see inside the room. I used the one at the bottom to slide her food and other items she needed in, but she'd been quiet today, so I wanted to make sure she was straight. A few days ago, I put a fan in there since she was sweating like a pig, even with the air being on sixty-eight. Yesterday, I threw in a heating pad for her cramps to help soothe her since it was recommended that she not take any medicine. We didn't want her to swap out one drug for another, and I was learning by the day that this addiction shit was not for the weak.

Solana had been a trooper indeed. She was also a good listener, or at least, I was telling myself that since when I talked to her, she remained quiet most of the time. I knew it was because she was probably in pain, but being alone down here all day was not good. Even my ass knew that.

Seeing Solana was in her normal spot, balled up on the floor beside the bed, I sighed. The room was covered in clothes, and a few food bags were scattered about. I joked that she wasn't the cleanest a few days ago, but I had no room to talk because, shit, I could do better in the cleaning department myself.

"Solana."

Her lunch was still next to the slot, untouched. She was eating most days, so that was a good sign, but she'd been going through it the last couple of days. Alexa had told us it was a mental battle. The body aches, plus her mind craving something she couldn't have, was taking a toll on her. I was watching her deteriorate by the day, and I wanted to take her to a real rehab more days than not. Solana was pretty, and she was sweet. Watching her go through this was doing something to my own fucking mental.

The twins would hit me with product from time to time to get off so I could keep some money flowing in my pockets. I sold some of it to my niggas at a wholesale price and hustled the rest. I was making about fifteen hundred a week selling white, which was more than enough for a young nigga with no bills. Most of the product given was cooked down to crack. Crack sold for more in the hood and at a quicker pace too. When I made a sale, I looked at it as a dollar sign. It was new Js. It was a pair of designer shoes. It was gambling money. It was some expensive seafood boil. Not once did I think of whom I was affecting when I sold the drugs.

This side was the fucking ugly side, and I couldn't help but feel like I'd had a hand in Solana's addiction even though I knew I truly hadn't.

"Solana...?"

She didn't budge. Usually, she would wake up when I came to the door or shoo me away, at the very least.

"Aye, Solana? You good in there?"

Again, she said nothing in response. I tried focusing to see if I could see her breathing, but it was hard as hell looking through this slot with my long limbs. I wasn't as tall as my cousins, but I was a little over six feet already. We tall niggas may have been nice to look at, but we had challenges, too, like bending and shit.

"Solana!"

I was met with silence, and my heart started sputtering.

I didn't want to call Shio. I'd fucked up with Hobo, and he'd come through, fixing my mess with that. I wanted to prove to my Big Cuz that I could help Solana fight this shit. I'd read through every online article I could find and felt like I'd been doing a damn good job.

"Solana!"

Scanning her balled frame again, the sweatshirt that covered her body looked like it was wet on the sides. Getting completely on my knees so that I could get a better view, I shouted when I saw she wasn't moving at all.

"Fuck!"

Hopping up, I retrieved the key from my pocket, which I had never used until now. It took me a few twists and turns to get the key to work, but when it did unlock the latch, I pulled the heavy-ass door open as fast as I could. It had to have weighed three-hundred pounds as it swung with a heavy, rusted sound before it banged against the wall.

"Fuck! Cuz tryna trap a gorilla in this bitch? Gotdamn!" I mumbled while stepping on top of a sweatshirt and an old thank you plastic bag after that.

"Solana!"

She hadn't even flinched at the sound of my yelling. Looking down at her still body, sweat sprang along my hairline. Dropping to my knees, I hit the ground in a splat. She was lying on top of a pool of her own vomit. The smell was rancid, and I was doing everything I could not to add to the pile of vomit.

Lifting her head, the whole right side was soiled. "Hey! Hey!

Solana!"

Tapping her chin, her eyes finally fluttered. Her mouth parted slightly, throw up dripping from the side of her face.

"Solana. Solana! Wake up. Wake up and tell me how you feelin'."

I could feel myself shaking, but I was trying my hardest to put on a brave front. My fucking cousins and their damn women were going to be the cause of me catching gray hairs at fucking sixteen. First, I had to kidnap Discover's fine ass, and when my niggas and me seen that ass naked, we all had to make like Shio and have a come-to-Jesus moment. I ain't never took nothing from a female a day in my life, but that day was the day I was tempted like my motherfucking name was Diddy. However, I wasn't no creep-ass nigga. Discover was a dangerous take, and Vello chose to take a risk that my ass would never.

This one? This one was a damsel in distress, and there was nothing dangerous about Solana except that she was trying to croak out on a nigga. I didn't want to take shit from Solana. If anything, I wanted to give her ass whatever she needed to beat this shit and live her pretty life outside of this makeshift jail my big cousins had made.

My phone rang in my pocket, and I already had a feeling who it was. Retrieving it with Solana's wet neck still resting on my arm and knees still planted in her throw up, I slid my thumb across the screen and answered.

"Wassup, Big Cuz?"

Using my shoulder to hold the phone to my ear, I continued tapping her face. She was in and out of it, and I was trying to think what I could do to get her more coherent.

"She... She breathing, right?" Shio's deep-ass voice boomed into my ear.

"Yeah. She's breathing... Solana?"

"Hmmm?" Her eyes shut close, and then she clenched her stomach.

I could hear Shio sigh with relief at hearing her voice.

"Solana..." I called out to her again.

"E... Es... Estoy bien... Solo duele... Estoy bien," she said groggily.

"Hunh?" I asked, not knowing what the hell she was saying, but she was talking so that was good enough for me.

When Big Cuz whispered, "English, baby," I tuned back in to see what he was talking about.

"Whatchu say, Big Cuz?"

"Have Pearla and Bella help her in the bath and wash her hair... I'll send somebody to come clean the floor."

"Or you can come put her in the bath yourself? It'd be good for her to see you, Big Cuz."

The line grew quiet. I watched as Solana struggled to open her eyes again. She may have been trying to adjust to the light, but either way, I was just happy her ass didn't die on me.

"Have the girls come help her, Italian."

Click.

"On God, bruh... My future wife bet not put me through half the shit these mob wives have been doin' to the Cuppacios. Shit gotta be a curse or sum'n."

Solana's body jerked, and I thought she was coughing or about to throw up some more. When it happened again, I prepared myself to be covered in it. When nothing happened, I looked down to see a slight smile on the damsel's face.

"Italian... We finally meet."

Solana's breath smelled of the throw up we were both covered in, but it felt good to see my girl smile. She'd been in this bitch going through it, and taking my ass right along with her.

"I done seen you a few times, but a nigga like me be playin' the background. So, I guess you can say we finally meetin'." I took a breath and watched her blink a few more times. "You scared me, yo," I admitted.

She opened her eyes fully for a brief moment and then closed them again. Solana reminded me of a doll, and not just any doll, but one of the ones that would be put in an antique shop or something. Even though she was a powder head, she was the finest one I'd ever seen. She was a rarity, and so far, the Cuppacio men had gone four-and-oh when it came to bagging the baddest as wives. Hopefully, us littles, as they called us, got just as lucky but without all the damn baggage. Jisei, Pia, and Discover had all come with some type of bullshit.

"I hope she does..."

"Hunh?" I asked, trying to understand what she was talking about. It wasn't in Spanish, so she had to be saying something directly to me.

Solana opened her eyes again. I hadn't noticed that they were so round and just as dark as her skin until now that I was knee deep in her throw up.

"*Chico guapo*... Handsome boy. You're handsome. Too handsome. I hope she puts you... *Pasar por mucho*... a lot... I'm struggling with translation."

"So you sayin' you hope she gives me hell? Damn, I been in here takin' care of you good. We eat good all day, errday, and you want me strugglin' when I find my wife."

As I engaged with Solana, I was texting with my free hand. Bella hadn't texted me back, which I figured, since she was on the phone with Essex, and I'd seen Pearla's phone on the fireplace mantle, so she probably wouldn't respond fast either. The next person to text was Mahzeyah. I'd had her number for some time, stealing it from Bella's phone, but I had never used it.

Aye, put the baby down and come to the basement. Bring Pearla and Bella too.

MAHZEYAH

Boy! How you get my number? You know what? Blocked!

Mahzeyah, I'm serious

MY LAST MESSAGE didn't send, which meant her mean ass had blocked my number for real.

"That was him, hunh?" Solana's smile, as slight as it was, fell. Her eyes were back closed again.

"It was."

"He has a child."

"Solana, don't even worry 'bout that right now.

"She's pretty..."

"I wouldn't know. Secretive ass hasn't brought her 'round the family."

I didn't know what the fuck Shio was doing with this secret baby, and he hadn't even told his mama. My guess was that he was waiting for a blood test, but shit, them bitches didn't take long according to some of the homies. You could even get them shits from Amazon and get the results in less than forty-eight hours. That's why I wasn't fucking shit without a rubber. Shio was playing house with one female while the other was locked away like she'd committed a triple homicide. She ate well and had a soft bed, but, damn, even prisoners got let out at least once a day.

"She's pretty," she repeated.

"Do she look like Shio?" I probed.

I was deadass wrong, but shit, we all wanted to know. The twins had met her, and so had Ezio and Teo, but there hadn't been any more conversation about her. It wasn't like them niggas would tell me shit anyway. At this point, I was coming like Neltz. I couldn't wait till I turned eighteen so they could let me in on some shit.

"*No, ella no lo hace.* (No, she doesn't.)"

I grinned. "I don't know what you just said, but I heard the word no. Y'all females kill me. Petty as hell, even on yo' death beds." I kidded.

"Stop calling us females. That is degrading as hell. Do we call y'all negros, males?"

Looking back, Mahzeyah was standing in the doorframe in that little-ass cheer skirt. "Mahzeyah, I told you not to bring the baby down here."

"Boy—Oh my God!" Mahzeyah ran into the room.

"Aye! Get out of here with her!"

She paused, blinked, and rubbed the baby's back as she was hoisted on her shoulder. "Don't yell at me, stupid-ass, lil' ass boy! Now, is she okay? Hey, ma'am! Are you okay? Did he do something to you? I have my tas—"

"ZeyZey... I ain't yelling at you, sweetie. But can you *please* get the baby out of here and grab my cousins so they can help her get in the bathtub?"

Mahzeyah finally looked at me like she had some sense and backed out of the room. She paused at the door, keeping her eyes on Solana, then they snapped at me. "And I told you, stop calling me your hoes name!"

I watched as she stormed off, skirt bouncing and ass poking out. I had to look away. The last thing I needed was for my dick to get hard while I was holding Solana's head up.

"I didn't have to hope for it. She's already giving you hell." She smiled again.

"That's just my baby mama, Solana."

"You have a kid?" she asked, her voice a mixture of concern and pain.

"Sum'n like that. Can you stand?"

It sounded like a stampede coming down the stairs, and I knew the chivalry had arrived. Ironically, Bella was the first to enter, and Pearla right after.

"Ohh, boo boo!" Bella tsked.

"Solana! Are you okay?" Pearla gasped, both coming to her side. "Move, Italian!"

"I'm tryna keep her head up just in case she throws up again... Solana. I'ma help you up."

Standing, I helped her to her feet, feeling bad as fuck because she winced the entire time. There was a red spot on the back of her shorts, and I'd been with enough women to know what that meant.

"Does she have some tampons in here?" Bella asked as I led her to the bathroom.

Not waiting for a reply, Bella started rummaging through the dresser drawers. Pearla ran ahead and started the water for the bath. Solana was taking baby steps, but it was cool. As long as she was moving, I was fine with helping her do so.

"No... No tampons. *No puedo usar esos.* (Can't use those.)"

Bella and Pearla shot each other a look that I couldn't figure out before Bella sighed and continued to look through the drawers. Not even a second later, she sighed again in relief.

"Okay, here are some pads. Let me find some clean clothes for you, boo boo."

Once we made it inside the bathroom, I sat Solana on the side of the tub.

"Italian."

"Wassup, Mexi-Mami?"

"Is... Is Shio well?"

This lady had bigger fish to fry. She was bloody, her hair was matted, she had throw up smeared all over her face, and she was locked in this bitch, detoxing from drugs. Right now, Shio was so far out of reach that even if she had arms the length of a giraffe's neck, she wouldn't be able to touch him.

Yet, I nodded.

She smiled. "Thank you, hell seeker."

I winked, washed my hands, and then walked around Bella, who was entering with a gown and underwear. Pearla was talking to Solana gently, so I closed the door behind me to give them some privacy.

Mahzeyah was bent over, her backside out, picking up clothes from the floor. Leaning against the door, I watched as she snatched up piece after piece and tossed them into the hamper. Today was a good day to wash Solana's clothes since the hamper would be full. I'd slid so many clothes to her through the bottom door slot that had miraculously appeared. It seemed as though Shio didn't care if they were washed—he'd just buy more and have them delivered for her.

"You so fucking weird, dude." Mahzeyah snatched the last bit of trash up and then grabbed the vacuum.

"You so fuckin' fine, *dude*. And you ain't gotta do that. My cousin sending somebody to clean the floor."

Rolling her eyes, she grabbed the cord, plugged it into the nearest socket, and poured carpet freshener onto the floor, which instantly covered the vomit smell with a fresh, linen scent.

"I'm not doing anything now that Glee got Baby Leader. I can clean it. I don't mind."

The vacuum came to life with a low hum. It was another expensive-ass gadget Jisei owned. Mahzeyah ran the vacuum back and forth while I watched her. When her eyes met mine, she didn't frown, but her face showed a look of disapproval.

"Y'all just going to keep her locked in here?"

"That ain't my business to tell, ZeyZey."

"She's in pain, Italian. And while these physical withdrawal symptoms subside after a few weeks, she's going to have a long road ahead due to the psychological cravings, plus the depression. That could take months, or even longer sometimes."

"How you know?"

"I plan on taking up psychology in college, but my emphasis is going to be on addiction and recovery. I want to open my own centers, maybe."

"Damn... I ain't know that."

"Well, now you do."

"Maybe I'll get high on my own supply so I can get admitted to yo' center."

She ran the vacuum in the direction of my feet, and I jumped back. "Man, watchout."

"Stop playing. This is serious, Italian. She really needs professional help."

"But can she beat it on her own?"

All of the vomit was gone, but she kept the vacuum on, more than likely trying to mask our conversation. With her hand poised on her hip, she looked at the wall past me as if she were thinking.

"She can... It will be hard, but she can. Everything is horrible the first few weeks, but then it gets better. She'll still fight the addiction for many months or years after. Some people fight it for the rest of their lives. If she gets clean, she will still be an addict. That's important to remember."

"When."

"Hunh?" she asked, looking up from the somewhat clean floor. Whoever Shio was sending needed a carpet cleaner to really get the smell up.

"*When* she gets clean. Solana gonna beat this shit, ZeyZey. And you gone be my date to their wedding?"

She rolled her eyes again, making me laugh out loud.

"Nawl, Flexer gonna be my date. Make all y'all have to go through security clearance at ya own people's shit." She smirked as I chuckled at her thinking Flexer had some type of rank over my cousins.

"That nigga ain't bigger than our program. We'll make that rapping-ass nigga come perform for free at errbody weddings. On foe 'nem!"

She laughed like shit was sweet. I'll do that nigga so dirty and have Gal and 'nem upload that shit on YouTube. Bitch-ass nigga will go viral for getting his chain, his money, and his girl took.

My phone vibrated on the bed behind her. She must've picked it up while she was in here being Mrs. Clean. Now she'd unlocked a whole other fetish: a cheerleader acting as a maid. I was going to have to have one of my cougar hoes act this shit out for me. The young ones weren't ready for the role-playing just yet. I'd played eviction with one last week where I was the landlord, and she was the tenant. She sucked the skin off my dick so I wouldn't take her to "court." I thought role play was kinky until I was able to act out some crazy-ass shit while ending the scene with some of the best nuts of my life.

VraVra with hearts displayed across the phone screen as it continued to ring. Mahzeyah turned off the vacuum and glanced at me with an evil glare. Before I could grab my phone, she snatched it and answered it.

"Who the fuck is this?" She was rolling her neck, popping her lips, and shoving the vacuum away from her as if she was still cleaning with it.

I was smiling ear to ear watching the whole fiasco.

"VraVra, don't answer her, love."

"*Love*? Do this bitch know you be in here flirting with me even though I don't want yo' ass? My nigga famous, and his money real long in real life. Hunh?" She drew her head back.

"Little hoe, don't worry about who this—"

Mahzeyah's face fell. She then looked like she'd seen a ghost as I started cracking the fuck up while hearing my VraVra go off.

"I am so sorry, ma'am. He be calling me ZeyZey, and I thought... Oh my God. My daddy raised me better than this—my mama too. I am so sorry, ma'am. You have a good day."

Mahzeyah tossed me my phone and snatched the vacuum up, running out of the room. I was laughing so hard my stomach hurt.

VraVra, aka Ginevra, was my Afro-Italian mother.

That's what Mahzeyah's smart mouth ass got. Now she was about to walk around looking sad all day.

"Hey, Mommy." I was still laughing as I attempted to calm down so I could talk with my mother.

"Italiano? Who was that?"

"That's just my baby mama."

Between ZeyZey and Mexi-Mami, I could feel the gray hairs growing already.

CHAPTER 19
SHIO CUPPACIO

With my foot on the brake, I shifted the gear into park on the stone driveway. The house in front of me was absolutely stunning. The modern-style build with contemporary and classic architectural elements could easily be featured in one of those home styling magazines. I'd been inside numerous times, but the exterior features were hands down breathtaking. A symphony of textures with painted brick in a clean, off-white hue, complemented by muted green siding, made the house pop in a neighborhood full of equally impressive custom houses. The huge windows were framed in dark trim, adding a touch of contrast where it was needed. The roofline was complex-looking, with multiple gables in a combination of dark gray shingles and metal accents.

The landscaping around the house was well-maintained, giving the house the curb appeal that matched the home's impressive look. The lush green lawn, carefully tended, extended into a massive backyard where we'd had many gatherings. A winding walkway led to the front door, lined with neatly trimmed shrubs and smaller decorative trees. The garden beds were filled with a variety of colorful flowers and greenery, adding vibrant accents against the off-white bricks.

It only took one call from Shannon Washington, and I was on my way. It was rare for my mother to call me, but when she did, I knew I couldn't delay my appearance on her doorstep. I also knew to dress comfortably because we would either be lounging or moving at a rapid pace—there was no in-between.

As I stood from my truck, I noticed the open garage was empty. It usually housed the pastor's Benz, which meant he was gone for the day. My mother's two cars, a Range Rover I had gifted her, and a Mercedes coupe were in the closed garage. She'd given her BMW to Italian two years ago. Her husband's Lexus was parked in the wide driveway that would be perfect for a basketball goal, but they didn't need one. Timothy Washington had been career-focused, which left him without children. By the time he married my mother, I was already an adult and so involved in street life that a father figure was the last thing I wanted. The pastor respected that and kept his distance. His lack of interfering is what led me to the doors of his church not long after. He allowed me to come on my own terms, and that changed my life.

Ringing the doorbell, I chose not to use my key. My mother had a key to my house and had never used it, so I wanted to show her the same respect. Besides, I wasn't the man of this house, nor had any hand in helping secure it. When we first moved to Jagoda Bay, we bought everyone homes with help from the mob, but once the pastor got his church up and running, he had us pass the house we gave my mom to another family member and bought my mother her dream home. She enjoyed decorating the five bedrooms with my money, and I wouldn't have it any other way.

"I thought I was going to have to come find you..." Shannon Washington's tone was condescending, but her smile told me she didn't mean what she'd said.

"Of course not, beautiful."

Stepping inside the house, I pulled my mother into a hug, towering over her and kissing the top of her head. Her perfume was an intoxicating aroma of velvety dark roses and a hint of saffron. She must've just applied it because it hadn't settled into her natural odor yet. I knew because when it did, it would reveal a warm blend of rich amber and creamy vanilla, adding to the comfort I felt whenever I was in her space.

Her hair was free from the lace wig today, so her natural tresses were pulled back into a low ponytail. It must have been time for her salon appointment because that was the only time she wore it like that. I could also see her bright hair color peeking from the roots. When asked about my ancestry, I always claimed Black. I was a nigga, through and through, and no one could tell me different. However, with my mother being a mix of multiple races and my father being a full-blooded Italian, I low-key was a mutt.

My mother's father was Somali and Black American. His Somali mother was brought to America and married the first man she could find to survive. Her mother was Melanesian and Black American, and those genes were strong as hell because my mother looked Melanesian when she let her natural hair grow out. Both of her parents were born in America, giving up their culture for various reasons since here, if you looked Black, you were Black. Because of my complex ancestry, I had a thing for languages, but I was born in America and looked like a Black man, so there was no use in denying it. My mother's blonde-hued brown hair denied her the same simplicity, and she often had to explain why she was a beautiful Black woman with the brightest natural hair.

"Come on in, son. You just missed the pastor."

Stepping back, my mama held me at arm's length to get a good look at me. Her hair might have been in a ponytail, but she was still dressed to the nines. Instead of a pantsuit or dress like her typical first lady attire, she was in green pants that stopped at her calves with slits on the sides. The fabric had a gloss to it, but it wasn't leather or silk. She wore a fitted white polo-style shirt with a small Chanel emblem in the corner. Loosely tied around her neck was a floral sweater of some sort, and on her feet, she wore pastel Chanel slides.

"You look pretty."

"Oh!" She swatted my arm. "This is nothing. It's just something I threw together to see my favorite son."

Closing the door behind me, I followed her into the home. My mother didn't have a specific decor style, but somehow, each room flowed together nicely. The walls were white, but the paintings brought life to the rooms along with her arrangement of furnishings and vases. If I had to put a name to it, it would be a mix of homey, garden, cozy glam. The pastor had no say, but like me, he just let her have her way.

"I'm your only son."

"And don't you forget it."

She took her seat on the extended peach-hued sofa that sat in the middle of her living room. The large area rug it sat on had hints of peach, but the other colors were pulled from the various decor throughout the space.

"You want something to drink? I won't ask about food because I know you've had your meal prep." Sitting on the sofa as if a queen resting on her throne, my mother radiated opulence and wealth.

It had been a long time coming. Shannon was living the life she was meant to now, and I loved every second of it. I'd empty every dollar from my account if it meant making her happy, but Shannon wasn't wired that way. She let me spoil her until she didn't. There were always limits with my mother—always reasons why she felt she didn't need to spend so much of my money. It had gotten to the point where she would sic her husband on me for sending large amounts to her account or leaving rolls of it in her purse. My time was limited, but I was and always would be my mama's baby. The Cuppacios liked to clown me about it, but them niggas were just as bad over their mamas as I was mine. Shannon just so happened to be a first lady.

"How have you been, son?"

Making myself comfortable on the sofa across from her, with a chest-like table separating us, I let my back sink into the furniture. No matter how much I spent on my own, it never felt quite as comfortable. I'd slept in two of the guest beds here and had the best sleep of my life. Never mind that I rested my head on a ten-thousand-dollar mattress and three-thousand-dollar sheets, my mama's Tempur-Pedic mattresses and Martha Stewart sheets did the trick every time.

I once complained about it to the pastor, and he told me, "It ain't the bedding, it's the spirit. Your mama's ambiance is just that invigorating. Got the best sleep of my life our first night under the same roof too."

From then on, I believed his theory and escaped all the mob bullshit when I could to sleep at my mama's house.

"I've been good, Mama."

"Haven't seen you in church in a while."

Not since Solana popped her lil' demonic ass up.

"I know. It's no excuse. But I catch the word every Sunday,

though. Last week, that message about discernment was right on time." I bopped my head. "Beloved, do not believe every spirit, but test the spirits to see whether they are from God, for many false prophets have gone out into the world. First John, chapter four, verse one."

My mother rocked. "Ummhmm. Are you feeling like he was speaking to you?"

Every Sunday, I felt like the pastor was speaking to me. My cousin's 'nem swore I told the pastor their business because every time they'd accompanied me to church, let them tell it, he was talking about them too.

"I do."

"That's because he was!" She sassed, making me laugh out loud.

When I saw her eyes water, I shot up and sat down next to her, pulling her in my arms. "Mama, what's wrong?"

My heart thudded, and my words came out shakier than intended. My mind went into overdrive immediately. I needed my mama to always be okay. There wasn't a world where she and I weren't in there together. She would bury me—that's how I'd always imagined it, and that's how I needed it to be.

"Oh, Shio..." She pulled from my embrace, swatting my chest. "I'm okay, baby. Sometimes, you do things that... That makes me realize that you're no longer a baby. No longer *my baby*. The tenor in your laugh was deep enough to shake the whole room. You've been a man for a long time, longer than the age of maturity, but—"

"I'm still your baby." I flashed her a smile.

"And forever you shall be. Don't mind me. I'm just an old lady with too much time on her hands that's obsessed with her child."

"You sure dat's it?"

"Yes, baby. I'm sure." She placed her soft hand on my cheek. The vanilla in her perfume was finally settling, bringing me the comfort that I yearned for. "You're so handsome, son. Tell me something good."

I chuckled. I knew my mother better than anyone else on the planet, including my damn self. "Who told you, Mama?"

Her smile broadened, and the combination of that, plus the wet tears that stained her face, was cinema-worthy. "Um. Don't worry 'bout *who* told me. I want to know why *you* haven't told me."

She tapped my cheeks twice, and once she released me, I leaned my body back so that I wasn't all up in her space, crowding her anymore.

"You know if I keep it from you, it's for a reason, Mama."

"I do. I don't ask you about the business you do out there in them streets. But I'm not oblivious to it, nor is the pastor. But only God can judge you, son, and even Timothy knows your heart enough to know God is there.

"You were born into this life, so I keep my nose out of it. But a child, Shio Cuppacio? I thought you would try and make me a Glam-Ma once you calmed your life down, son."

The downside to us Cuppacios being all we had for so long was that everybody talked too fucking much. If I had to guess, it was Nel who'd run his mouth. I knew he'd told Tunan, and I'd bet a million that he'd told Auntie, and Auntie told my mama. However the whispers went, I knew it had started with Nel's ass.

When I ran my hand down my face and looked back at my mother, she was staring right at me. "A baby girl, um? Who is her mother? Pretty little sinner?" She lit up when she mentioned Solana.

"Mama, that math wouldn't math. Solana and I haven't known each other long enough to produce a child."

"Hmph."

"I didn't know about her—the baby. She and her mother were... caught up in...sum'n. I'm still processin' myself. I wasn't gonna hold it from you for long, I just wanted—"

"I don't mean to cut you off, son, but I understand. And you don't owe me an explanation. As bad as I would love to meet her, I trust your judgment first, Shio. Always have."

"I 'preciate that, Mama. But I was sayin', I wanted to get the DNA back first. We did a test, but we had to do another one cuz the first one was incomplete. Baby girl cut up so bad that the tech that came by the house didn't get enough skin cells or whatever to complete the test back at the lab. She didn't act no better at the hospital. Me and ole girl had to hold her down."

Waiting for the second DNA test results had me more anxious than the first time. They did a blood test on all three of us at the same hospital we used for everything mob-affiliated. Convincing Bahati to bring her ass there with Shya had me seeing red the other day, but she finally caved and used the Range Rover I had basically given her. Had Bahati met me at the lab the first time instead of acting like Felipe 'nem bitch asses were going to jump out of the bushes at the hospital, we would've had this whole thing solved by now.

Shya started showing her ass as soon as Bahati walked in with her. Even I couldn't calm her down like I'd been doing at the house. She didn't want anyone touching her, but the phlebotomist had to draw her blood in order for me to get the answers I wanted. Bahati and I had to hold her down, and that shit had hurt my feelings. Now that the lab had what they needed, I was waiting for that email telling me Shya was mine, and then I'd make the familial introductions. I told the doctor before I left that there better not be any more bullshit with the test results because I was not putting Shya through that shit again.

"And how do you feel about what the results may be, son?" my mama asked, shaking me from my memory of what happened the other day.

"I don't really know," I replied truthfully. "I been busy while trying to find a good medium between gettin' to know the little girl but also not gettin' attached, but I ain't gon' lie. She looks like you, Mama."

My mother beamed before a small smile settled on her face. "Son, it's okay to be scared. It's also okay to not know *everything*. Sometimes, things happen without us understanding the details surrounding it, and sometimes it's not for us to understand."

"I hear you, Mama."

"You always do. But I want you to understand me, Shio. Understand that God makes no mistakes, baby. I won't ask you any details because that will only make me want to meet her more now that you say she favors me. I'll find out everything I need to know when she's crossing my threshold, or I'm crossing yours."

I heard my mother loud and clear, and I also understood her words for what they were. However, there *was* a logical explanation for everything. As a man, I'd learned that to be a fact. The Rodríguezes getting to Bahati and knowing she and Shya existed before me couldn't have been a case of them having one up on me. If it had been, then I was losing my fucking edge.

If Shya wasn't mine, there wouldn't be a crevice on this Earth where Bahati could hide. I'd kill her, have my doctors resuscitate her, and kill her ass again. But if she were mine, it meant I had missed years—pivotal years—of her life. Shya was so put off by being in my home that she cried and didn't talk to anyone, not even her mama. If she were mine, I'd be sick to my stomach because of our predicament and the hand I played in it.

I missed her birth, Bahati's pregnancy, Bahati's belly kicks, and the initial finding out I was becoming a father before actually becoming one. I'd missed the late-night snack runs for Bahati's cravings and taking the night shift so Bahati could sleep. I'd missed doctors' appointments, cutting the cord during the birth. I'd missed the chance to soothe her after her first shots, hearing her first words, and seeing her first steps. I'd missed one of the most vital places for a Black man to be present, knowing how important representation was in the delivery room. Mortality rates are highest among Black women because of a lack of village and the stigmas in healthcare surrounding Black people. Bahati could have died bringing a life into this world that was connected to me. The entire situation sat deep in my soul, and I kept it there because I was afraid of acknowledging all of it.

My mama placed her hand back on my face, this time, having to lean in since I was further away from her. "It will all work out as it should, son. Trust in the Lord and more than that, trust yourself. Take as much time as you need. I'll be here... I'm always here."

"I know, Mama."

"Good." She grinned. "Now..."

"What else, Mama?"

"Where is my pretty little sinner? She taking this okay?"

"What makes you think Solana's opinion in the situation matters?" I chuckled with the shake of my head.

"Oh boy! I changed your damn diapers. I know *things*."

"Yeah? What do you know?"

"I know that Solana is special. But before she can be special to anyone, she needs to get right."

"With the Lord?"

"No. With herself, and then the Lord. That baby is fighting big demons." My mama patted my cheek again and then stood. "Now, come on. My favorite son is taking me to lunch and then dropping me off at the hair salon. I have two hours to spare before my appointment, and I want to eat at that Asian fusion spot on the bay."

I wasn't dressed for lunch, but what the first lady wanted, the first lady got. If I'd known this would be a visit that required us to go out, I would've at least thrown on a Nike Tech suit.

Towering over her, I popped my back as I stretched. "You just wanna go to that restaurant because it's next to the Hermès store."

"Yeap! And I may or may not have a leather appointment in the next hour. That gives us twenty minutes to get there and forty minutes to eat. That's plenty. The Lord don't like gluttony no way."

"I may have a couple dollars to spare."

"You gonna need more than a couple to buy this bag, son. Or should I go get Timothy's Amex?" Her brows lifted.

"I think I got enough, First Lady Washington."

"Ummhmm." She side-eyed me. "I know you do. I was going to settle for a Celine, but since you hiding my grandbaby from me like ya name Drake instead of Shio, I gots to charge ya."

"That ain't Godly, Mama."

"It ain't, but who gone check me? Alrighty then."

My mother had me laughing my ass off. That lady, as sanctified as she was, played no games.

"Mama," I asked as she gathered her purse, a tangerine-colored Chanel that I couldn't remember if I'd bought or her husband.

"Yes, son?"

"On the drive, can you tell me how you knew Solana was on drugs and I didn't?"

"Oh, baby... I know you may sell it, but I dealt with your father having that monkey on his tail for a decade. I can spot the signs with my eyes closed." She reached for my hand. "You know it's nothing you can do but let her fight it, right? You can't force her to get clean. She has to want to do it for herself."

I didn't have a reply, so I remained silent. Solana should've been an afterthought now that I didn't have to see or deal with her every day. That shit didn't stop me from watching her ass on the cameras during the majority of my free time. Whenever I had a moment where my eyes didn't have to be on swivel, I planted them bitches on my phone. Solana was in bad shape, but it wasn't enough for me to show up at Jisei's townhouse. I needed to steer clear and let her battle that shit.

I grunted, finally acknowledging what my mother said. "I thought they said men go after women that are like their mothers? Must've meant fathers."

"Shio. She is not your father. I can see that clear as day too. Give it time."

"What if I don't want to give it time?"

"Then you let her go. But make sure you make peace with that before you do it. She seems to be just as stubborn as you."

I kissed my teeth quietly before switching gears. "How is it you bring up Solana but not my child's mother?"

"How come *you* ain't brought up your child's mother?" We stared at each other, the silence loud and telling. "Exactly. Now, come on. We now got thirty-five minutes to eat, and you still have to park."

STARING at the PDF on my phone screen, my thumb hovered over the bolded word "inconclusive" as the doctor explained why a third DNA test would be needed. I'd already cussed his ass the fuck out because I'd told him I wasn't making Shya go through another fucking test. Baby girl was already traumatized from all the bullshit in Mexico and living somewhere she was unfamiliar with. Now, he wanted me to bring her back to the hospital to draw more blood because the results couldn't verify that I was her father. He ran down multiple reasons for the yielded results, but he was sure there was some type of contamination or insufficient DNA collected since Shya had acted as she had during the blood drawing.

After my mother ran up a tab in Hermès, getting a bag, sandals, and accessories, I was expecting to get some good news when I saw the lab calling. Spending the five figures on my mother had put a smile on my face that I was hoping would continue throughout the day. I just knew I was going to open his emailed document and see that I was the father and the test was 99.9% sure.

I was ready to let my mother meet Shya after spending time with her since learning I was possibly a father. I was ready for my family to love on her so that I would feel okay about loving on her too. Shya needed family, and I was ready to share mine with her so she could warm up to being the newest Cuppacio in Jagoda Bay. I couldn't do any of that until I knew for sure that my blood ran through her little veins.

"An inconclusive DNA test simply means the results didn't give us a clear answer. While it doesn't happen often, it does happen more times than you could imagine, Mr. Cuppacio. Shya was upset. With her mother working with one arm and you and she holding her down, and the technician trying not to overstep boundaries while the phlebotomist drew the blood, it is my belief that the sample was either too small or contaminated from the start. It could also mean that the technology couldn't analyze certain genetic markers well enough to give a definite answer."

"So what other options do we have, Doc? You sayin' the collection process is causin' the results to be faulty... I can't make the little girl sit still for the fuckin' test." I could feel a headache brewing and tried to steady my breathing.

"I understand your frustration—"

Attempt failed.

"Doc, I pay you—and not just crumbs—I pay you big fuckin' bucks. Ion need you to understand my frustration. I need to know if this little girl is my child. Ion know why the fuckin' technician didn't take more dan one fuckin' sample! She was so busy tryna get my info, so I could ram my dick down her throat dat she couldn't even focus on doin' her fuckin' job!"

I could feel the nigga jump through the phone, so I dialed it back, rubbing my temple after swiping out of my Gmail app.

"Check it, I have a child under my roof that has a fifty percent chance of being mine, and I'm holdin' back from being a damn daddy cuz I've trusted you, not once but twice, to first confirm I'm the daddy! I could've gone to any DNA center in the city and had some answers by now. Probably could've gotten my shit back the same day. Fuck, I coulda done the over-the-counter shits at this point."

"None of those are one hundred percent accurate, sir. They are all gimmicks and money grabs."

"From the looks of it, your lab is too."

"I'm going to get this right, Mr. Cuppacio. Just give us one more—"

Disconnecting the line, I granted myself entry into my home. I was done listening to his ass, and beyond irritated that I still didn't have the information I needed about Shya being my child. I usually kept a level head, but I was no saint. I was bound to go off on somebody since I'd been up to my neck with bullshit for weeks.

Sliding my shoes off in the foyer, I placed them on the wooden shoe rack and padded through the house barefoot. The housekeepers hadn't come this week, but the house was spotless. Bahati was like me in that way. She kept the house spick and span, and although I didn't need her to, I appreciated the gesture.

It was late, nearing ten o'clock, so Bahati wasn't standing over the stove. Instead, she was nursing a glass of wine with her good arm. The silk robe she wore hung lazily off her shoulder, covering a matching nightgown. It was a mix of sexy and comfy, with lace lining the curve of her breast. As soon as she noticed I was in the kitchen, her nipples did as well.

She'd been complaining about her arm itching in the cast, so a wire hanger sat on the counter next to her elbow. I knew she was using it to scratch against the doctor's wishes. He'd prescribed her some anti-itch pills that I had gotten for her days ago, but they mustn't have been working as well as they should have. If his ass didn't get this DNA shit right, he was going to need the itch pills and every other pain medication for his damn self to heal from the bullets I was going to riddle his ass with.

The only reason why I was dealing with him to begin with was that he was vetted with the mob, and with how much illegal shit we did on a daily basis, we needed to be under the radar with everything, including DNA tests. I especially didn't need my DNA floating in anyone's database now that the city's police were sniffing around according to Don. There was no telling what body or crime scene it could be linked to, even though I knew I'd been careful with everything I'd ever done over the last twenty years. I knew I had to let the nigga do his job, I just didn't know if I could stomach making Shya let another technician swab inside her mouth or draw more blood from her little arm.

"You're home early." She placed the wine glass on the countertop and pulled her robe closed. Bahati's attire had been getting raunchier by the day. The shorts were damn near panties, and the gowns were classy versions of lingerie. Still, I steered clear. Busting a nut right now was nothing but temporary satisfaction, and I didn't need temporary—I needed indefinite. Without the DNA results on Shya, I wouldn't be able to trust myself to make lifelong decisions, including sticking my dick in Bahati. I didn't have much more time to pick a wife between her and Solana, but my mental was exhausted, and I was tired of fucking thinking at this point.

And that's some shit I never thought I would feel.

Before the doctor fucked up my head with the inconclusive results, I'd been having a good day. I ended up hitting a couple of blocks while my mother got her hair done. When she was finished, she insisted I come inside to see all of the ladies in the salon, many of them members of the church. The owner's mom was on the mother-board and was fine as hell, but she was a married woman, so all she got was a smile from me because I didn't do those. The very taken women, smiling in my face, turned into women who'd gotten their hair done on my dime. That was twelve women's hair services I'd dropped a bag on just because my mama suggested I do so. I had even given the three stylists hefty tips. It felt good seeing women happy, and when we got back to my mama's house, I drank a glass of Scotch with the pastor and chilled with them until both of them began to yawn.

After spending a full day with my mama, I didn't want to see a brick, dirty money, or Hobo's ass, for that matter. Shannon was pure, and after being in her space all day, my sins felt nonexistent. I felt clean, and I didn't want to taint that, so I decided to take it to the crib for the night. I still felt uneasy pulling up to my house knowing Bahati and Shya were inside. I went from feeling guilty about the kidnapping to feeling suspicious about everything every thirty seconds. The shit was draining me. I'd questioned Bahati numerous times about the day she was abducted to ensure her answers wouldn't falter, and no matter how I rearranged my questions, her answers stayed the same. From the looks of it, Bahati truly could've been a casualty, but my brain needed a clear pathway to see things as they were—to see things beyond what they appeared to be.

Leaning against the counter across from Bahati, I grabbed an apple from the fruit basket and bit into it. The pastor had brought home steaks, and of course, he didn't give a damn about my fitness goals, so I wouldn't need a meal prep tonight. Bahati eyed me with lust, some shit she'd been doing even when her arm was dangling on the plane. It seemed she had one agenda since she'd stepped into my home, and I'd had another. She needed dick. I needed answers. And she wasn't getting what she wanted until I had what I needed.

I needed to know how the Rodríguezes knew I had a child before I did. I needed to know how they knew how to find Bahati. It could very well be through her father, but dead men couldn't talk. I knew because I'd paid a hefty fee for a grave that I stood at periodically, and the corpse buried underneath it didn't talk back no matter how much I prayed that he would. As much as Bahati's father was in the streets, you would think he had friends, but he had no true friends who could tell me anything that I didn't already know.

The apple crunched between my teeth as its refreshing juice hit my tongue after the bite. I preferred my fruit cold, but apples were one that I could deal with lukewarm.

"How long Shya been asleep? I thought I was gonna catch her before she went down."

Bahati swirled the mahogany-colored liquid in the glass. I'd given her free rein of my home, so I expected her to enjoy the wine cabinet. What I didn't expect her to do was open a three-thousand-dollar bottle as if we were celebrating. Little did she know, we had nothing to celebrate after the call I'd just gotten.

"About an hour. Since you've been spending mornings with her, she's been less fussy. Thank you."

"She'd be a whole lot less fussy if she got outta this fuckin' house, Bahati."

"Shio."

"Bahati," I replied as I swallowed down the chewed-up apple.

"I don't know this city. My arm is broken so dealing with her in public will be a hassle. You see how she acts around people... How spoiled she is. And..." She looked off. "I know you said we are safe, but I don't know, Shio. I don't feel safe."

Her East African accent intensified the more she spoke. It did the same thing when she was aroused. It was even deeper than normal because not only was she aroused, but she was tipsy too.

"You're safe. Both of you are. You can roam this fuckin' city as much as you want, Bahati. Ion know how many more ways I can assure you that ain't nobody gone fuck with you."

I knew Bahati had her reservations, but I was feeling like a fucking broken record. Every day, I was declaring that she could get out and enjoy the city. She had a limitless card and a brand-new Range Rover to go do whatever the fuck she wanted. But I was starting to get the feeling Bahati preferred something else, and her next statement confirmed my internal thoughts.

"I'd rather us go out together, Shio. I'll feel much better if you're with us."

The second bite I took was louder and nearly cleared half the apple. Bahati ran her hand down the length of her braids and clutched her glass tighter as she waited for me to respond.

"If you need some assistance to go out, I can arrange that."

"Someone from your family?" She perked up.

"Nah."

"They won't meet Shya?"

"They will."

"When?" She sighed as if this conversation was not going the way she wanted.

I shrugged. "When I allow it."

"Shio..."

"Bahati."

She sipped her wine, which was a good idea because I didn't want to hurt her feelings if she got out of pocket. "Are we a secret?"

"Yeah."

"Wait, what?" She choked on her words and the wine.

"You been a fuckin' secret for all this time. So, yeah, you a secret."

"You know why I did that, Shio."

"I really don't." I took another bite of the apple. "I get it, but then I don't, Bahati, because I know you."

"Are you mentally well? I thought we had an understanding. I answered all of your questions. I was living my life! I didn't bother you after you tried to kill me."

"I'm very mentally stable. But the libra in me... Ion know. Sometimes, while seeking balance, I become imbalanced. I have too many muthafuckas randomly poppin' up in my life, and miraculously, everybody is connected to the same muthafucka in some way. That tips the scale."

"I'm not setting you up!" Bahati clenched her jaw as her chest heaved under the robe.

"Shit. I ain't say you was. Time will tell, though, if you are or aren't."

"Shio, don't do this. I can't live around you, walking on eggshells. Either you accept us as innocent in all of this, or you let us go. I'm not going back to Chicago. I've already decided to move across the country or the continent after this. But I will not let you blame me for what has happened to me."

"You mean to you and Shya..."

Crunch.

As I chewed on my fruit, I watched as Bahati's chest heaved. She didn't bother to correct herself or respond because she was too busy watching me eat this apple as if she was imagining it was her pussy. Her robe came undone and now hung from her shoulders. I glanced down to see that her nipples were poking through the lace fabric of her bra, and from where I was standing, I could see goosebumps form on her skin.

"Come 'ere, Bahati."

With her wine glass in hand, she took a step, but I stopped her. "Put the glass down."

The glass touched the marble countertop with a soft *ting*. She invaded my space with only a hair separating us. The smell of shea butter was strong, and the way her skin gleamed was an indication that she'd lathered in it.

Good, she hasn't used Solana's shit again, I thought as I scanned her pretty face.

"I didn't bring you here for you to walk around on eggshells. You're safe to do what the fuck you wanna do when the fuck you wanna do it. But me? You ain't never safe with me. You're safe in my home. You're safe in this city. But I ain't a safe space for ya, and I mean that in every which way it can be articulated."

Bahati gulped, but the scent of her wet pussy that hit me like a tidal wave let me know she wasn't feeling what the fuck I was saying like I wanted her to. She was aroused by the danger I'd just warned her about if she was playing with me.

"You have shelter. You have wheels. You have an unlimited fuckin' credit card. Sitting in this house cookin' food that I'll never eat and cleanin' when I have a damn company that does that shit for me ain't gone up yo' ranks. And I ain't sayin' this shit to hurt your feelings, I'm sayin' this shit to be transparent so you can stop walkin' around in the skimpiest shit you can buy online."

Her lips parted, and with my free hand, I palmed her face and tilted her head back. I didn't need to run my hand between her legs to know that she was drenched. Her body language and the smell coming from her were enough indication.

"I ain't good for you, Bahati. And ion think you good for me either."

Dragging my thumb across her lip, Bahati was damn near hyperventilating. I could put her out of her misery. I didn't like seeing a woman horny when I knew I had the tools to satisfy her, but Bahati didn't do it for me. Her plump and sticky bottom lip was soft underneath my thumb, and her eyes fluttered constantly like a newborn butterfly, but I wasn't turned on in the slightest.

"I look good. I fuck good. I eat pussy good. I trick good. I talk good. I walk good."

She was panting at this point, and her silent plea sounded desperate in my mind.

"But when I'm played with..." I snatched her into my chest. "I torture good. I slice good. I shoot good. I fucking kill good." Leaning down and placing my lips at her ear, my beard scratched the side of her face. "I fuckin' bury good."

Keeping her pressed to my chest, I leaned her head back so that I could get a clear view of her. "I'm poison, Bahati. And not the instant kind. I'm the kind that slowly creeps in your veins, shutting your organs down inch by inch."

"I... I didn't do anything. I swear! I'm innocent!"

"You innocent?"

She nodded. "I'm innocent, I swear it to you, Shio. Maybe this all happened for a reason. Now that we are united, maybe we could... We could—"

"What? Be together?"

"No. I... I... I didn't say that."

She did, but in true East African fashion, Bahati was stubborn. Her head was as hard as titanium steel. She'd never ask to be with me, but she'd do shit to ensure that she was. Just like she'd never ask for dick, even though she'd been walking around this bitch twitching like she had Tourette's syndrome.

Taking the apple I'd placed on the counter, I placed it to her lip. She bit down, and I released it, leaving it in her mouth.

"*Nitakuoa,*" I spoke in her native tongue, Swahili. It was the same language that had connected us—the one she'd taught me fluently years ago.

Her eyes expanded as her body tensed as if she was waiting for me to replace the apple with my lips.

"*Ikiwa huna hatia kama unavyosema wewe ni katika haya yote, nitakuoa.* (If you are as innocent as you say you are in all of this, I will marry you.)"

She moaned, and for the first time since she'd been in my home, my dick hardened. The problem was I wasn't sure if I'd gotten hard from the thought of her being guilty and me having probable cause to kill her ass or if my body was finally ready to let her have it. Not knowing which one triggered it frustrated me more than I already was from that flawed-ass doctor.

"*Nitakuoa* (I will marry you).

Letting her go, I took a step back. The apple gagging her mouth, her hardened nipples, the smell of wet pussy, and her heaving chest had my dick on brick.

Maybe I am ready to fuck her, I thought but quickly dismissed the notion.

"The test was inconclusive, so we gotta take another one, Bahati." Her eyes widened, but before she could say anything, I kissed my teeth. "With yo' innocent ass."

I left her standing in the kitchen. I didn't like it when my thoughts were jumbled. I didn't like it when shit didn't make sense. Usually, when shit was fucked up, my mind would go to my childhood. Nowadays, the past was just that, the past. Instead of sticking my head in the room to check on Shya, I went to my room, closed the door, and then went into my en suite bathroom. The lights automatically flicked on as soon as I stepped onto the marble floor. I pulled the black T-shirt over my head and threw it into the basket sitting on the closet floor to my right.

I had worked incredibly hard on my body. I'd pushed myself even more over the last few weeks, and the sharp lines and ridges in my abdomen were evidence that the push was working. Stepping out of my pants, they hit the floor with a thud. I grabbed my cell phone that was sticking out of my left pocket and opened the camera app. I'd gone from having sex with two women to having two women in my grasp, both wanting something from me that neither of them deserved. I'm not the kind of nigga who thinks I'm above women. I would consider myself soft when it came to women. Soft legs could nearly get anything they wanted up out of me. Shit, a chorus of smiles from church women could get what they wanted up out of me.

Men were put on this earth to serve women—to worship them. The female species was the only one capable of producing life. We wouldn't exist if it weren't for women, but in the same sense, women have been the downfall of many men. Still, I gave them the benefit of the doubt because I had that much love for the opposite sex. I was obsessed with women. I was disciplined, but every day I thought about the wit of a woman. I knew the benefit of having the right woman on my team, in my bed, and in my mind. I respected them, even when some of them didn't deserve it.

And the way I viewed women was a nod to how I saw my father and his fuck-ass family treat women. I didn't respect my father's actions. He was a coward. He didn't value my mother—not in the way he should have. Behind closed doors was one thing, but openly and publicly was another. I had all the qualities to be everything to the woman God placed in my life, but I couldn't understand for the life of me why I had to deal with fallen fruit.

Clicking the camera app to full screen, I placed the phone on the counter, placed my hands shoulder-length apart, and leaned over. Swiping down on the screen, I turned the volume up.

"This is the confidence we have in approaching God: that if we ask anything according to his will, he hears us. And if we know that he hears us—whatever we ask—we know that we have what we asked of him." Solana was on her knees, a towel wrapped around her body and another one on her head as she read from a Bible.

"First John, five, fourteen," I recited.

Exiting the app, I swiped to the call log. She hadn't texted me for a few hours. Although I never responded when she texted, I worried when she didn't.

I shouldn't worry.

Dropping my head, I closed my eyes to try to quiet the chatter. It was no use. I hadn't known peace since my first visit to Mexico City. I had, but it was temporary. Short-lived. The only time I'd had peace since then was in this bathroom, not even that long ago.

Craning my neck to the left, the porcelain tub reminded me of the night everything went wrong. It was the night that I promised myself I would pursue Solana. I promised it to her. Now, I had just vowed to marry Bahati if she was innocent. I didn't like to make promises I couldn't keep. I'd already broken my promise to Solana, and I knew in my heart there was a chance I'd have to break my promise to Bahati.

My mind wasn't wired to believe a person's word. I believed their actions. I believed their energy. And my mind hadn't been settled since I became a father, or at least since I was told I was a father since neither DNA tests could confirm it. The broken promises were just that, broken words—broken words of affirmation. However, that wasn't what made me toss more than I should've at night. What made me unsteady was that a part of me knew I'd probably have to kill one or both women before or after I made it down the aisle with one of them.

God first
~~*Make sure the family good*~~
~~*Eye them Cuppacio boys, the little and the big ones*~~
~~*Build a relationship with my brother*~~
~~*Get my brother rich*~~
Health and wellness ~~(ALWAYS)~~ (Shake back)
~~*Stay on top of my mob shit*~~
Keep Hobo alive (DOING)
~~*Get through the meeting with Ines Ledesma*~~
~~*House a random*~~
~~*Find the true reason Solana is here*~~
~~*Figure out if Solana is supposed to be my wife, again*~~
~~*Find a wife that isn't Solana*~~
Kill every breathing Rodríguez Cartel member (URGENT)
Fuck Bahati up (TBD)
~~*Get my fucking daughter*~~

~~Get Bahati's arm fixed~~
~~Get to know my daughter (DOING)~~
~~Figure out what the fuck I'm going to do with Solana~~
~~Leave the mob entirely or~~ marry ~~Bahati or~~ Solana
~~Get DNA test~~
Spend time with my daughter (DOING)
~~Tell my mama about Shya~~
Keep Solana in real nigga rehab until she clean
~~Get SECOND DNA test~~
Check on Bahati's apartment
Don't fuck ~~Uriah~~ ANYBODY
Get to the root of Shya's constant crying
Get THIRD DNA test or say fuck it
Marry Bahati IF she is innocent

CHAPTER 20
PEARLA

"So, you mean to tell me, you wouldn't fuck Chris Brown?" Blayke asked as we all sat on the sectional, nursing wine coolers.

Gallery had carried in two cases that he'd bought off the street, and we'd been tearing into them. Glee was the only one not indulging because she was breastfeeding. Her mom had taken the baby to meet Glee's dad, so she wasn't with us today, and although Mahzeyah verbalized she was missing Baby Leader every five minutes, Italian was the one with the attitude as if no one should be enjoying themselves without Baby Leader being here. You'd think he was the father and Mahzeyah was the mother with the way they'd been carrying on today.

Having a friend with a baby was a different experience for all of us. Glee was so sweet and smart, and she was so pretty and petite. She was the girl you wouldn't think had had sex, let alone would have a beautiful little baby girl. Lately, Baby Leader had been the best part of my days when I was with the crew. If she could talk, I knew she would tell all of us to get the fuck up out of her face. We were forever playing hot potato with pretty little Baby Leader.

"Bitch, hell no!" Bella frowned.

She had her laptop propped on her legs, her phone in one hand, and her wine cooler in the other. None of us were old enough to drink. Bella was the oldest of us, going into her sophomore year of college, and Italian and his boys weren't old enough to be smoking or shooting dice, but they were down in the basement doing both.

"Chris Brown! Y'all all lying! I know I'm not the only one who would take him down!"

"Uh..." Mahzeyah took a sip from her cooler. "I think you are, Blayke. I mean, Chris Brown is attractive, I give him that. But the nigga is like my daddy age. Ew."

Mahzeyah shook her head before taking another sip of her drink. She didn't have cheer practice today, so instead of being in her uniform, she was in an orange Alo skort with the matching tank, looking so cute. Her gold Bottega sneakers were somewhere along our feet, being that she kicked them off before getting comfy on the sectional.

"And Ezio look identical to the nigga. It's hard to look at Chris Brown and not see Ezee." Bella gagged. "Saying I'd fuck him feels too much like... *incest*."

Bella cut her eyes at me. I was on my third wine cooler and was feeling a slight buzz, so it took a while for me to catch on. When I did, I grabbed the decorative pillow beside me and launched it.

"Girl, fuck you! Y'all better fall up off my sister and her fiancé! They are *not* related."

Everyone burst out laughing, including Glee and Blayke. We'd run down most of the family drama because we didn't want them to feel left out when we threw jabs at each other. We'd left out the mob stuff we knew about and me catching those bodies months ago to avoid incriminating ourselves and our people, but they pretty much knew everything else. Glee took it all in stride, and that damn Blayke was fascinated.

"Ezio is the one in that picture, right?" Blayke pointed.

On the mantle, there was a photo from their engagement in front of a horse and carriage. Being a Bridgerton fan, I thought they'd had the best wedding so far, although my sister and Renello's engagement was the best proposal by default. I couldn't wait to see how the other weddings panned out. Pia was still planning hers, and I'd heard Discover was starting soon. I felt they should have double weddings since they were marrying twins, but I understood wanting your own day too.

"Yes, you saw him at the hospital when I was having Leader,"

Glee answered before shifting on the cushion beside Blayke.

When Glee was released from the hospital after her car accident, she was in so much pain. Today, she looked more like herself, and although she was still using the wheelchair, she was learning to hop around without it. Her face had completely healed, with the exception of her lip, and she didn't complain as much about her ribs. There was still a dark line on her lip where the stitches were, and it almost looked like it was an upside-down heart, but she was still pretty as hell.

"Girl, I saw 'bout thirty niggas at the hospital, and *all of them* was fine! You was in labor with a baby I knew nothing about. I didn't get a chance to really look in nobody's face like that. But yeah..." Blayke skimmed the picture again. "They do look alike. Ezio is finer, though, especially with those eyes.

"If I was his wife, I wouldn't let his ass go *nowhere*. I'd even go to the bathroom with that nigga 'cause you won't be texting bitches while on the toilet! That man is *fioneeee*!" Blayke wiggled her toes as she bounced in her spot on the couch.

"My ears are bleeding!" Bella was beginning to turn red in the face. She looked physically unwell with her dramatic ass.

"They have all become like family, and Lord knows I am afraid of grown men, but Shio? That Shioooooo! He is so fineeeeee!" Mahzeyah snickered, and Bella gagged again.

"Y'all do know these niggas y'all speak of were once dusty and broke, right? That's the only reason y'all crushing, cuz they rich."

Mahzeyah smacked her lips. "And they were still fine when they was broke too. I saw the photo album that the twins' mama keeps around. The men have always looked good."

Mahzeyah told no lies. Auntie kept the photo book in rotation.

"Since we're talking fineeee..." Bella folded her laptop and placed it on the seat beside her. "*And* since we're talking grown-ass men..." She turned so that her body was facing mine. "Matteo."

"*FINE AS HELL*!" Mahzeyah screamed.

I groaned and took another sip of my wine cooler. Never in my life did I think I would have a big brother—like, ever. I had Pia and Neltz and was content with that. Patty was so full of surprises with her lineup of baby daddies that my dad had a wife, a son, and a granddaughter, making me an aunt times two—well, two and one pending.

Matteo was my dog. We talked and hung out just as much as Pia and I, if not more. Even being in the mob, Matteo managed his time well, juggling me, his duties, and his household. Most nights, when I didn't feel like going to Pia's or my stepdad's homes, I ended up at Matteo and Scarlett's place. Hearing the girls gush over my big brother was disgusting, and I started to fake gag like Bella.

"Matteo is the meanest man of the bunch. Why the hell do y'all even see him in that light? He is only nice to like... three people. One is me, with the other two being his wife and child." I shook my head, but the girls didn't seem to care.

"Girl, I love a nigga that runs a strict-ass program! He stay with a stank face. Like, yeah, let these bitches know that this ain't *that*. Matteo looks like he don't hold the door open for another bitch. That's my type, fasho!" Bella clapped.

"I get so confused on who is related to who, but I know one person we can all relate to that we want to take down to the ground." Blayke twisted open another wine cooler.

"Who?" we all replied in unison.

"That fuckin' Essex!"

"Oh, boo!" Bella waved her off.

"Chile, I have my rapper. Ion need another," Mahzeyah stated matter-of-factly.

"Essex is *very* attractive," Glee added, shocking the hell out of me.

I giggled and then decided to tease Bella. "So, you saying he don't look good, Bella?" I had to get her ass back from salivating over my brother and taking jabs at my sister.

"Of course, he looks good. But that's Essex. He like family."

Blayke half-laughed. "He's *like* family to you. He *ain't* family."

"Girl, no. He's family. Besides, as Mahzeyah said... That's a grown-ass man. Even I have my limits. Plus, I love me some Missy."

"Girl, Missy is down with the get down too. You be seeing the way she be all over Mocha. I know they done did the nasty before and nobody can convince me otherwise!" Mahzeyah pointed out, and although I wouldn't back her statement, her point was valid.

My sister's best friend had always been sexually liberated. But I couldn't see her trying anything with Bella. We were kids in their eyes, even though Bella was nearing twenty.

"Essex is my boss." Bella drove her back into the cushion.

"And when you let him fuck you one time for keepsake, y'all can go back to being just boss and employee." Blayke stuck her tongue out, and Glee giggled.

"Sometimes... you do gotta fuck a nigga just to get him out your system," Mahzeyah ranted.

"Again, gross. Essex isn't in my system, friend. That is a grown-ass man."

I sat up and cleared my throat. "Before we change the subject, can we address the pretty-ass, Spanish-speaking *elephant* downstairs?"

Solana.

When we put her in the bathtub the other day, I was crying right along with her. She was so beautiful—so young. I didn't know her full story, but she was fighting a drug addiction, and it was taking its toll. We gave her the best bath, shampoo, and conditioning she'd probably ever had. When she was dressed, Bella gave her an Ibuprofen that her doctor had prescribed for her period cramps, and Solana was out like a light. I made it my business to check on her every day. Earlier today, she was in much better spirits. The guys were down there shooting dice now while we ladies held this floor down. I was sure she was entertained, listening to Italian and his friends talk shit to each other.

"She's pushing through..." Bella said.

"She is, but I wonder why he didn't take her to rehab?" Mahzeyah asked herself more than anyone else.

She understood why he couldn't take her there, but she didn't agree with her rehabbing alone in the basement. Between her, Bella, and me, we didn't know all the details, but we understood it wouldn't have been safe for her to be in a facility because of mob-related business.

Solana, as beautiful as she was, had appeared out of nowhere. One day, Neltz came home and couldn't stop talking about his *Mexi-Mami*. Seeing her up close, I understood why my nephew was so smitten with the Afro-Latina. Even in chaos, with vomit on her face and clothes, and her hair tangled enough to take us two hours to comb through, she was still gorgeous.

It was quiet until Bella spoke up. "I'm rooting for her. Maybe she can teach me some Spanish. I been thinking about learning another language."

"I'm rooting for her too. I'll give her a pass for having her claws in my *sugar daddy*." Mahzeyah fretted, fake rolling her eyes with a smirk.

Bella shook her head. "Her and Shio aren't together."

She left it at that, not attempting to divulge more. I shifted my eyes from my phone to her and then to Mahzeyah, seeing the silent conversation they were having. Bella would probably go into more details when it was just her, Mahzeyah, and me. For now, speaking on Shio and Solana was over.

My phone vibrated on my lap as I took another swig of the wine cooler. Seeing that they'd talked my brother up, I let it go to voicemail. I didn't feel like talking today, especially since my brother never wanted to answer my questions.

I'd been trying to get to know our father, but Teo was still at odds with him. Whenever I asked him about our father, he had little to say, but he kept encouraging me to spend time with him. The problem was, I had been spending time with Reuchie Rinaldi, and he was every girl's dream. I wanted to know how Teo felt about our father, but I got nothing. I trusted my brother, and without him being more forthcoming, I had my guard up.

I'd been a little envious of Pia and her father's bond, even though Rio took great care of me when everything was finally out in the open regarding him and my mama. Everything happened so quickly that we all had no choice but to adapt. My sister went from working security and struggling to pay her bills while running a household to being given cars, trucks, and boats. Our mother suddenly could talk, and Pia fell in love with her childhood best friend. It was something out of a movie, and it was hard to make sense of it all. I'd be lying if I said I wasn't struggling. Financially, life was much better. My sister had gone from rags to riches, and she had a man madly in love with her and a dad who was smitten with her. Pia's life was perfect, and the new baby would be loved immensely.

But me, I was stuck trying to find my place. I knew I was surrounded by people who loved me, but I didn't feel like I belonged to anyone. I didn't feel like I was anyone's number one priority.

MATTEO

Pearla

I KNEW my brother well enough to tell that the text was a warning. As mean as Teo was, he had a sensitive side too. He hated being ignored, and while I wasn't trying to do it on purpose, I was just chilling. If I answered for him, he'd guilt-trip me into coming to his house by saying Princess wanted to spend time with me. I loved my pretty niece, but the last time I was over there, I had the worst stomachache ever from eating cereal all damn day. For some reason, Princess was addicted to it—all different kinds too—and my brother was sure to keep the various cereals in stock.

It was hard for me to appreciate my own wins because life just didn't hit the way one would think it would in my position. From what I've seen, my daddy was a good man. His wife hadn't displayed any hurt about my being her stepdaughter, but I didn't know them well enough to read the situation accurately. I'd stayed the night at their house a few times and had my own room there now, but I always found myself back under my sister's roof within a few days of leaving. Everybody wanted me around, and while the attention was nice, I knew it was because they were scared of where I'd go mentally if alone for too long.

"Pearla... Who do you think looks good? You can judge the Cuppacios because, like you said, y'all are not related. I'm just trying to see what your type is," Blayke asked, probing. She reminded me of Bella so much.

"Ion know..." I shrugged. "I guess I'm gonna have to go with what Mahzeyah and Bella said. They're too old to look at like that."

Blayke kissed her teeth. "Oh my God! They like... mid-twenties! Maybe late, but they not too much older than us."

"We're seventeen," Mahzeyah gestured to me. "You're nineteen. To us, mid-to-late-twenties is a *long way* from seventeen. And it's nothing against girls that like men in their twenties, but I'm a lil' too girlish for them."

I agreed with Mahzeyah, so I just nodded my head. Flexer was twenty, but she was nearing eighteen, so they only had a two-year age gap. Blayke's eyes bulged, and she took a big swig of her wine cooler, nearly finishing it off.

"Hold up! You fucked with a nigga in his twenties?" Bella asked, almost screaming.

"I mean... yeah." Blayke picked invisible lint from her biker shorts.

Bella perked up, being nosy as hell. "How old?"

"Not *that* old. He was early twenty-ish."

"Oh, that ain't too bad. These niggas y'all lusting over are damn near thirty. Early twenties is still young. He was probably childish as hell," Bella said with a shrug.

Blayke shrugged too. "He wasn't childish, just was an ain't shit nigga. I think early twenties, it depends on the type of life a man lives. You can be a childish twenties, or you can be a mature-ass twenties that lives life like you're thirty. The nigga I was fuckin' with was somewhere in between the two. But fuck him and may he rest in hell!"

Glee rubbed her forehead and groaned at her friend's protest.

"Wait? He died?" I asked, heart thudding, waiting for her response.

"Yep! Walking 'round here looking like the living dead since I left his ass alone."

"Blayke!" Glee gasped.

"Fuck him! The nigga dead to me."

Bella cackled. "Helllll nawl! You stupid, Blayke."

"You know how you be so in love, and then boom! You wake up from that dick coma?" Blayke asked, and Glee groaned again, throwing her head back on the sectional.

"Yes, indeed," Bella responded.

"Kinda sorta. I think Flexer's the first boy I liked-liked. My first? I was just doing something." Mahzeyah chuckled.

My first time was with a boy, I was very much "in like" until he told the whole school and embarrassed the fuck out of me. I still laugh at the day Neltz got on his ass. My nephew always rode for his TeeTee. But I didn't respond to Blayke's question, and neither did Glee.

"Well, that was my first. He was everything until he wasn't anything. It was fun when I was in the moment, but the aftermath?

The aftermath... I wouldn't wish that shit on my worst enemy. Now, I'm just thugging. I'm thugging and figuring my life out. I don't have time for a nigga unless he willing to finance my *whole* life. But I know I'll have to be careful with those type of men, too, because I can fall in love, and then boom! I'ma dumb ass all over again. I can't have that —ever."

We all let the silence linger after Blayke's spiel. I was lost in my thoughts, and I figured the others were too. R&B songs played on the TV, with Keyshia Cole currently screaming at us about love. Love was a strange thing to me. I had never understood that heartbreak felt exactly what it was called until I went through it. There were still days I couldn't eat, still days I couldn't sleep. It had been six months since that night—the night that changed everything. It was almost hard to look at my sister's engagement ring because it brought me back to that day. I could still feel my own screams in my throat—the guttural cries scratching my vocal cords, almost cracking them and leaving me hoarse for days. The broken glass. The gunshots. The blood—so much damn blood—as the look of life slipped from a person's eyes. And not just any person, but the one you thought was everything, only to find out they weren't anything at all, as Blayke said.

"Pearla!"

Blinking, I'd noticed Italian had come back up the stairs, and behind him were Gal and the others.

"Hunh?" I asked Italian, who was looking at me as if he was awaiting an answer.

"I said, 'If y'all mind if my nigga, Ro, come over?' He's from the block.... And my dawg, P, walking over too."

"Walking?" Bella asked.

"Yeah, his grandpa, Mr. Joe, live 'cross the street. Jisei knows Mr. Joe... He's a cool dude. I've been rockin' with his grandson for a lil' minute. Matta fact, y'all already seen them both, at the party for Glee." Italian rubbed his head. "Shit, I gotta stop smoking."

The house had been the hangout spot for weeks, but Solana was still going through something extremely vulnerable downstairs. Italian had been careful about whom he brought around, so if these P and Ro characters were cool people, I didn't mind. I couldn't remember too much about who he had at Glee's party, though, because my mind was elsewhere.

I shrugged. "If everybody else is cool with it, I am too."

"Aite, cool."

The doorbell rang, as if they knew we'd just finished discussing them, and both Italian and Gal went to answer. Mahzeyah bumped shoulders with me, and I gave her my attention. We'd both been wearing the same perfume today, which was totally a coincidence. That happened a lot between her, Bella, and me. If it wasn't perfume, it was clothes, shoes, or bags. We spent way too much time together, and I wouldn't have it any other way.

"I know you are cool with it..." She snickered.

"Mahzeyah... I don't know what you talking about."

Everyone had fallen into side conversations, so they weren't paying us any mind. Crossing my arms, I watched as Mahzeyah's smile grew big as hell, like she knew something I didn't.

"I saw the way that P dude was looking at you the last time he was here. He's fine as hell."

"Oh, girl! That's what you're talking about..." I waved her off. "I didn't notice."

Mahzeyah's smile dropped, and her eyes rounded. "I know he's going to wake up one day, friend, and give you some answers about why he hurt you, but you are allowed to live your life. You young, fine, and having your way with two rich-ass daddies. We going into our senior year... The best high school year of our lives. And then prom. Then graduation. Then college! We still gotta decide if we doing JBU or Miami U or NYC. Wherever we go, we're doing it together, and Bella is transferring too. It's gone be plenty fine-ass boys over the next few years. We are not sitting around moping."

Before meeting Glee and Blayke, it was just us three, and we had plans to go to college together. My plans hadn't changed, even with our hospitalized friend. I was going to finish school and open my own private practice in psychiatry. It was crazy that I wanted to be a psychiatrist, and my own mind was all out of whack. But as Mahzeyah said, time was on our side. I'd get my mind right eventually.

"Sooo, you saying you gonna cheat on Flexer?" I asked.

"Oh, I ain't stupid. Flexer is a rapper. He has grown-ass women with BBLs and large followings chasing behind him. I haven't even had sex with him yet. Plus, we don't really have a label on us.

"Am I madly in love with him? Yeah, but Avenue and Millionaire didn't raise a fool. Wherever we go, I'm having my fun. I'm not tied down to no nigga that ain't tied down to me. He gonna be on the road getting his dick wet, and I'ma be in our skyrise getting dicked down. He ain't shit, and I ain't gone be neither. Right now, though, I'm chilling."

We all chuckled before Blayke said, "I know that's right, Mahzeyah."

I shifted my eyes across the room to look at all the girls. I was down bad behind Grind, and I'd been trying to save face, but these were my people. I knew no one in here–not even Glee and Blayke—would think I was stupid for being so caught up on Grind. Truth was, I hadn't even looked at another boy because there was no vacancy in my head. Grind left no room for it, occupying every cranny. He was the tenant, and although his lease had ended, he was still there on a month-by-month basis.

"Aye, y'all these my niggas, Ro and P. Y'all remember the girls? That's Glee, even though I ain't fuckin' with her today since she gave away me and Mahzeyah's daughter."

"Boy!" Mahzeyah scoffed.

"That's her friend, Blayke, my cousins, Bella and Pearla, and my baby mama, *Mahzeyah.*" Italian grinned.

"You gone stop putting that 'baby mama' word on me. I ain't having no kids, especially not yours."

"It's cool, baby. We got one already. Her name is Leader."

Mahzeyah flipped Italian off while Glee laughed. I was happy to see her not grab at her side to support her ribs. Once she got her cast removed and didn't have to use the wheelchair to get around, she would be good to go.

Bella dismissed Italian before he could continue. "We remember these niggas from Glee's birthday. No need for the intros, cousin."

My girl was hard as hell on boys, in general. There were a few dudes at JBU who had been vying for her attention, and some rookie pro athletes had been in her DMs, but Bella paid everyone dust. She'd been so caught up in her role as a social media manager that she had to squeeze in time for us. As long as she kept making time for me, I was in support of whatever she did. If she decided to get a boyfriend, that was cool, too, as long as he knew I needed my Bella. I needed all of my girls, actually. They'd gotten me through the toughest part of my life, and for that, I was forever indebted.

I could feel eyes on me as I scrolled my Instagram timeline, but I didn't care. Mahzeyah bumped my shoulder while clearing her throat, and I finally looked up. The guy named P was staring at me, and I had to do a double-take. Mahzeyah hadn't lied—P was cute. He was cute as hell. Both boys Italian introduced were attractive, but P was different.

I could see ink etched into his light-brown skin, peeking out from the teal Nike hoodie he wore. His skin tone reminded me of wet beach sand, but it looked smooth as butter. I dropped my eyes to his lips that was surrounded by a full goatee, his mustache fuller than when he came to Glee party. His beard was perfectly lined on his face from his hairline to his chin. His downcast eyes were lined with short, spiked lashes that I was sure he hated. He had a square-shaped face that looked as if it rounded underneath his beard. His hair looked as if he'd just taken out his braids with it being crinkled all over. Just like the first time he came over, he was wearing white Air Force Ones as white as his teeth. Unlike Italian and them, who were dressed comfortably, he was a mix of comfort and fashion in Nike shorts and the matching teal hoodie. I could also see diamonds peeking from underneath his hoodie.

I *had* noticed him at Glee's kickback; it was hard not to notice him. He was cute, and his rugged presence made him stand out. He was a mix between hardcore and pretty boy. Maybe it was the hair. Maybe it was the eyes. Maybe it was a combination of everything. Whatever it was, P screamed trouble to me. It was fitting that he was friends with Italian and the other guys because they were the poster teens for havoc.

"I brought food." He held up three boxes of pizza that were in his right hand. My eyes didn't leave his, although they should have, as he lifted his left hand. "I also brought a bottle of D'Ussé."

A smile spread across his face, showing his teeth were perfectly straight. I was sure he'd had braces with how perfect they were, and I got jealous because mine were still on, giving me hell. My mind did a poor job of disguising my thoughts because I ran my tongue over my own loose wire. I was due for a tightening during my next appointment and was looking forward to it. Ironically, I had planned to request teal bands this go-round.

"Now you're talking our language!" Bella hopped up, pulled her leggings up on her waist, and grabbed the pizza boxes from his hands without saying thank you.

He didn't seem to care as his eyes were still on me. Once Bella turned, Gal's eyes went straight to her backside. He had it bad, but unlike Italian with Mahzeyah, Gal kept his feelings to himself. He usually didn't say shit unless Bella got to running her mouth and talking crazy. Only then did we hear how he felt. He could pop shit back, and sometimes he left Bella looking crazy.

I finally diverted my attention from P to Mahzeyah, who was watching Flexer's story with a smile on her face. He seemed to be at a festival on a beach, given the view of the water in the background, and if it was the same festival where Essex was performing, he was in Southern California.

"You drink?"

Mahzeyah lifted her head and then elbowed me.

"What?" I asked her.

She tossed her head in P's direction. Looking up, I met his eyes again as he held a bottle out to me.

"You drink?"

Running my tongue over my lips because they were suddenly dry, I lifted my wine cooler in response. This third bottle was doing its job, and I would be lying if I said I didn't feel it.

"You call that drinkin'?"

His mouth lifted into a half-grin. There were no dimples. No boyish grin. No Burberry shirt.

Pearla, please stop.

"I'm not twenty-one..." I clicked my tongue with a cock of my head.

"Yeah, the liquor stores be discriminating hard! How the fuck do they let the boys buy alcohol and not us?" Bella stated as I smirked at her usual antics.

"That's cuz y'all lil' ass don't need to be drinking no way, unless you with me," Italian said with a sneer. I hadn't noticed that he had left the room until he walked back in holding a stack of red cups.

"If that's the case, give me a Sprite!" Mahzeyah put her wine cooler down on the ground next to her foot.

Italian softened his face and turned to look at her. "Man, here... Take this cup."

He handed her an empty cup, and she hesitantly took it. He then proceeded to pass out cups to the rest of us.

"This pizza so fye! I loves me some Hunts Brothers!" Bella bit down on a slice, taking her spot back on the sectional.

She passed a plate to Glee, ignoring her protests of not wanting any. We'd all been making sure Glee had what she needed, even though Blayke was always ten steps ahead for her bestie. A broken leg and a newborn baby had to have been tough, but she was handling it well.

Once everyone had a cup, including Glee this time, P cracked the top on the D'Ussé. Taking three strides, bringing his weed and Versace cologne with him, P was in my space before I could blink.

Shit.

"A shot or three?"

"Three?" I asked, dumbfounded.

I'd drunk before but not much. Bella had gotten us drunk once at a college party, but it was cheap punch. This was premium liquor, and I knew one shot would have me on my ass.

"I'll take a half shot."

"Nah, you gettin' a full shot..." He derided and waited for me to lift my cup.

The brown liquor flowed from the neck of the bottle so fast that I had to push it away. "That's enough!"

Everyone snickered, including P. His voice was mellow-toned but deep. It had a ruggedness to it, and it matched his appearance to a T. Instead of pouring everyone else's shot, he passed the bottle to Italian, and after Italian poured Mahzeyah and Bella's shot, the bottle was passed to Ro, who poured Blayke and Glee's. The bottle went through a few more hands before we all lifted our cups. Once Italian said something I didn't hear over the pounding of my heart, we all took the shot. The burn in my chest made me slap at it. I wasn't the only one because all of us girls, except Bella, were either coughing, had sour expressions, or gagging.

"Another round!" Italian announced.

"Hell no! That shit is nasty!" I hollered.

"Right, I ain't tryna be sick... Especially being up early with Baby Leader! Hell no," Blayke all but shouted.

"My baby can come over here with me." Italian poured himself another shot and took it to the head.

"When you're not able to sleep, you'll be knocking on the door and bringing her back. My baby likes to be up playing at three a.m." Glee smiled.

"When he realize he don't have a nipple for her, he'll be knocking!" Mahzeyah chuckled, then chased her shot with her wine cooler.

Italian kissed his teeth. "Man, chill out. Glee pump... I can just make a bottle for my little baby."

He passed the bottle back to P. I could still feel his eyes on me, but I stared at the TV, watching Usher and R. Kelly cry about the same girl. I zoned everyone out, hearing the murmurs of Mahzeyah and Italian argue while Bella and Blayke discussed celebrity gossip.

"Ohh! Let's play a game!" Blayke shouted, and Glee and I flinched.

She had made the statement in general, but her sights were on Ro. He was the quieter one of the bunch. Like the last time he was over, his sock-covered feet were stuffed in a pair of Nike slides, and he kept his fit simple in black joggers and a clean white tee. However, he was just as handsome as someone dressed in designer clothes and jewels. As he lifted his cup, he glanced at Blayke over the rim before looking away and pulling his cell phone from his pocket.

"A game? Really, Blayke?" Bella's mean ass scoffed.

"Yeah, a game. You in college so you know how it goes. Truth or dare."

Glee groaned. "Blayke, nooooo."

"Truth or dare?" Mahzeyah asked.

"Yeah. So, boom... When it's your turn, you're asked either truth or dare. Truth, you answer a question. Dare, you have to do whatever the person asks you to do. If you don't do the dare or answer the question, you have to take a shot."

"Of that nasty-ass liquor?" I probed.

"We ain't drinkin' no Kool-Aid!" P held up the bottle that we hadn't even put a dent in.

Sucking my teeth, I sank further back into the couch, feeling P's eyes on me again.

"Aite, but let's turn this shit up..." Italian reached inside his pocket and produced a dice. "If you roll an even number, it's a truth, and an odd number, it's a dare. Two shots to the person who declines, and if the opposin' person accepts and complies, the other has to take the double shot. Gal, hand me that tray."

Behind Gallery was a sofa table with a wooden tray that held a candle. Gal removed the pink candle and handed Italian the tray. We girls remained on the sectional while Italian placed the tray on the centered ottoman, and the guys surrounded it and us. P placed the bottle in the far corner of the tray so it wouldn't block the dice when it rolled.

"We gone go boys against girls." Italian turned to Gal. "Keep that shit cute, nigga."

"Fuck you, nigga!" Gal laughed.

"I'm going to sit this out, y'all." Glee placed her cup down, and no one objected.

Italian shook the dice in his hand, and when a mischievous smile covered his face as he looked at Mahzeyah, she slapped her forehead.

"You can do the honors, ZeyZey." He held the dice out to Mahzeyah.

"Boy, please! You roll first."

"Say less. You gonna blow the dice?"

"Roll the damn dice, Italiano!" she hollered, and I laughed. These two never let up.

He shook them in his fist and released them onto the tray. We all sat up on the couch to see what he'd rolled. A five showed on one, and a two showed on the other.

"Sev'n."

"Okay..." Mahzeyah pondered while gnawing her lip. "I dare you to call the last girl you contacted in your phone, and tell her you love her."

He chuckled. "That's it?"

Her face fell. "What you mean, that's it? You claim you don't have a girlfriend, so this is called stirring the pot. Oh, and it can't be a family member." Mahzeyah nodded, satisfied with her dare.

Italian reached into his pocket, swiping past notifications.

"And don't cheat, boy! You doing too much typing."

"I cleared my screen. I'm goin' to the call log now."

"Nope, nope. We young, we don't really talk on the phone like that. Go to the last text thread of the last girl."

Italian sighed but complied. "Am I sending her a text, or am I calling her?"

"You seem eager..." Mahzeyah folded her arms.

"I am. She's pretty as fuck. And I *love* pretty girls."

He and Gal slapped hands and did that stupid boy laugh.

"Whatever. Call the bitch!"

"Damn, why she gotta be all that, ZeyZey?" he asked while grinning.

"Italian, stop aggravating Mahzeyah and just call," Bella said.

Keeping his focus on my friend, he tapped the screen.

She rolled her eyes. "Put it on speaker too."

He tapped the screen again, and the phone rang once and went to voicemail.

You've reached Mahzeyah. Leave a message.

We all roared in laughter as the phone beeped to indicate the message recording had started.

"Damn, I forgot you got me blocked. But I love you, baby." Italian ended the call and blew Mahzeyah a kiss, making her cheeks turn a deep burgundy. He lifted the bottle to pour her a shot while everyone laughed.

She snatched the bottle from him. "I can pour my own shot!"

"Make sure it's a double shot. Rules are rules, baby. I told you, you're the only girl I'm worried 'bout. Round two, spice shit up. You shoulda dared me to take you to the back and lift that lil' skirt up so I can kiss it."

"Oh, Lord! Pass the dice!" Bella blurted out.

Mahzeyah poured her shot, held her nose, and tossed it back. She then flipped Italian off as she put the bottle on the tray and passed the dice to Bella.

"How 'bout we go boy-girl, boy-girl, and then swap the next round. That way, the other person has time to come up with their truth or dare," Blayke suggested.

Mahzeyah nodded, her face showing the double shot was just as nasty as the first one. "Yeah... Period. Go 'head, Bella."

"That's fine... But I'm on yo' ass when it's yo' turn," Italian whispered to Mahzeyah, but we all heard him.

Mahzeyah swallowed hard and turned her head to ignore him. Bella sat up in her seat, and I giggled because Gal looked like he was holding his breath.

He was really handsome, being the darkest one in the bunch. His skin tone resembled Shio's a lot, although they didn't look anything alike. He always smelled good, dressed nicely, and kept a pocketful of money. Still, Bella paid his ass dust.

She rolled the dice, and it landed on a four and a three, giving her a seven too.

She rolled her eyes and cocked her head to Gal. "Don't be on no weird shit with yo' young ass."

He stood back in his spot on the wall while glaring at Bella as if her words meant nothing.

"Come on... I ain't got all day!" she fussed while Glee and me shook our heads.

"You talk so much shit!" He snarled as he pushed off the wall.

"I shol' do, nigga."

"You know you white, right?"

"But you want to fuck this *white girl,* though."

Everyone was silent as the two went back and forth, our heads going from Bella to Gallery.

"And I am. I'm patient, though..." He cheesed, and even I had to look away because Gal was too fine.

Bella huffed. "Anyways! I'm black. I can say nigga, nigga! So, *nigga...* What's the dare?"

"Aite. When I ask you for yo' time, you can't say no."

"Hunh?"

"I said,"—He straightened his shoulders—"When I ask you for your time one day, you can't say no."

Bella squinted. "That's not a dare, Gallery."

"It is. I dare you to say 'yes' when I ask you for yo' time. Or take yo' two shots."

"When?"

"Just gone take yo' lil' two shots, Bellz," Italian said.

Bella ignored Italian and waited for Gal to answer, but when he didn't, his eyes boring into her, she clicked her tongue. "What you gonna do with my time when you ask me for it? I'm not having sex with you."

"I asked for your time, not for your cat. And I'm prorating mine. Could be a year... Could be ten from now. But I dare you to say 'yes'."

"Hell, the world might not be here in ten years, so dare accepted. Shit, that was easy." Bella sat back in her seat and pulled her phone back out with Gal still boring his eyes into her. Bella was a tough cookie because if a boy looked at me that way, I knew I'd be scared as hell for whatever he had planned.

"Ion know now, bestie. If it's too good to be true, it normally is. You should have took the shots!" Mahzeyah spoke up.

I smiled. "I think it's cute. It sounds like the start of a ghetto, interracial love story. Make sure we around when you cash in on that dare."

"Nah, Pearla. But I'm sure Bella will share the news." He matched my smirk before his eyes shifted to another handsome boy. "Ro, yo' go."

Ro walked up, slides flopping underneath his feet. Blayke did a cute little dance in her spot on the couch. She was feeling Ro hard, and although I'd seen him eye her a few times, it was hard to tell whether he was interested or his mind was just elsewhere. I knew mine was.

Ro released the dice, and Blayke was the first one to sit up. A nine and a two showed, making another odd number.

"Dare!" Blayke clapped her hands.

Ro licked his lips and grabbed the bottle from the tray. Blayke's body stiffened, and my stomach sank. I could tell from the way the room had gone silent that everyone had felt bad for her.

"Hey... Let's go in the kitchen and get more pizza," Glee recommended.

Blinking, Blayke nodded and pushed herself from the couch.

"What's the dare?" he asked, his voice deep enough to make my stomach sink again in another way. Italian had too many fine friends.

"Hunh?" Blayke's head reared while stopping mid-stride.

Ro took a sip from his red plastic cup. "What's the dare?"

"But you drinking."

"Oh, shit. I'm just drinking. I ain't rejecting the dare. What is it?"

Blayke's body relaxed as she sat back into the sectional, and Ro's face morphed into a seductive smirk.

"Come to the back, and I'll tell you..." she said, crossing her arms.

All of our eyes were bouncing back and forth between the two just as they were when Bella and Gal were going back and forth. Ro took another sip and glanced over at Italian. When he nodded, he took the rest of his liquor to the head and set his cup on the ottoman.

"Don't come to the back with all that playin'." His voice went lower, and even though we shouldn't be in their business, we still were since it was unfolding in front of all of us.

"Boy, you don't know me at all if you think I play games." She turned to Glee. "You good best friend?"

Glee nodded, and Blayke stood. "Cool. Let's go."

She walked around the ottoman, grabbed Ro's arm, and dragged him out of the living room. When we heard the door shut, we all fell out laughing.

"See! That could have been us, ZeyZey, but you made me do that weak-ass dare."

"Boy, in your fucking dreams. I'll never ever."

Italian pulled his pants up and smirked. "I know."

I watched Mahzeyah roll her eyes for the fifth time today before she turned to Glee, asking her if she was okay again.

"Aite, Pearla. You up," Bella said with the biggest smirk I'd seen today.

P picked up the dice, and for a minute, I forgot he and I were assigned to each other. All of a sudden, I wasn't into the game anymore. The air in my lungs evaporated as P drilled a hole through me with his eyes. His hair brushed his shoulders as he shook the dice in his hands. He had a look as if he were a lion stalking his prey.

Please, let it not be a dare. Please. Please.

He was cute—no, scratch that—he was fine, but I didn't know him. Italian had given Gal a warning not to do anything weird, but he hadn't given P the same rules when it came to me. I could easily take the shot, but I was already buzzing. My sister and mama didn't really trip about anything I did, but I didn't want to go to either of their houses smelling like liquor. I could spend the night here, but as soon as my brother caught wind, he'd be here wreaking havoc on everyone.

Matteo had never even raised his voice at me, but he was stern. I hadn't given him a reason to either, but being sloppy drunk would more than likely bring it out of him. Demise had even pulled up on me a few times. As a cousin, he was cool as ever. He wasn't as intimidating when he was playing Don. I had too many people who could randomly pop up on me, and their seeing me intoxicated wasn't what I wanted. I'd gone from only having my sister, mama, and nephew to now having a whole family with overprotective men. Did they spoil me rotten? Yes, but I didn't want to take advantage of their trust. Another shot wasn't going to happen. Plus, a small part of me was intrigued and wanted to comply. I was eager to feel something yet scared to feel something.

"Don't we gotta check on *that* downstairs?" I turned to Italian.

"Nope. It's already handled." He jutted his chin to P. "Roll the dice, Pearla."

P opened his hand where the dice sat about two inches apart. Swallowing, I leaned over and grabbed them. There were no sparks, no butterflies, no thudding heart as my fingers grazed his palm. The attraction was there, but that was about it. Breaking our eye contact, I shook the cubes in my hand and prayed that whatever it was, it wasn't bizarre enough for me to take another shot. Letting the dice go, they slammed against the liquor bottle and then the walls of the tray before coming to a stop.

Nine.

My breath solidified in my chest as Italian called out the obvious. I'd rolled a dare. There was nothing stopping him from asking me to go to the back like Blayke had done with Ro. I was so tired of sitting in hurt and pain that I probably wouldn't take a shot if he had. I needed to feel.

To feel wanted.

To feel accepted.

To feel lusted after.

Grind had pulled me up on a cloud top where I felt so good that nothing could convince me that the cloud could evaporate at any moment. Because I was not prepared and didn't open my eyes to what he'd been preaching to me all along, I fell. The cloud had completely disappeared on my ass.

I had these rich men who cared about me. They cared about me and wanted nothing from me other than to love me and spoil me, but it had been hard for me to bask in it because I was heartbroken. I couldn't be excited about my family because I was sick. I was literally sick to my fucking stomach. I was hurt to my core. It was hard to eat, hard to sleep, and hard to fucking breathe knowing that the boy I loved had played me like a fiddle, and instead of letting nature take its course, I was holding on to him.

And for what?

"I accept."

P glared at me, intrigued.

"Friend, he didn't say what the dare was just yet." Mahzeyah touched my arm as if she thought I'd zoned out again.

"I don't care... I'm not drinking no more liquor. So... I accept whatever the dare is."

P rubbed his hand down his hairy chin. "You sure 'bout that?"

"Positive," I assured with a slight head nod.

"Awl, shit!" Italian pulled a blunt from behind his ear and sparked it. "This gone be good."

Widening his stance, P crossed his chest with one arm, resting the elbow of his other arm on it as he cuffed his chin. He looked immaculate doing the subtle move. There was something sexy about it.

"Pull down on yo' nigga right now and tell him it's a wrap. Tell him you're with me now."

"Ohhhhh weeeeee!" Bella fanned herself while tucking her lips into her mouth.

"Oh, Lord..." Glee sighed, grabbing at her side for the first time today.

"Friiiiiieeeend. Why didn't you take the shots?"

"I'm cool... It's fine," I said to Mahzeyah while still watching P.

We were in a stare-off, and although I'd rather he asked me anything else other than this, I was game.

"I've been drinking. I'm not driving my brand-new truck."

"That pretty-ass Beamer out there?" he asked with raised eyebrows.

I nodded. "That's me."

"And that's one of three! My bitch got whips!" Mahzeyah bragged as if almost everyone in the room didn't have some type of access to money.

My people had blessed me. The car Nel had bought me was riddled with bullet holes, but I appreciated my baby. He'd bought me another since the insurance paid him, and my father had purchased me one, too, while Rio had purchased the other. I rarely went anywhere, so I didn't need three cars, but I was grateful. A year ago, I didn't have even one car and was living in an apartment in the hood.

"Oh, yeah? You lit, huh? I can take you in my car, though. That way I can know you really 'bout it." He challenged.

"Unh, unh!" Bella sang.

"This shit crazy..." Italian blew smoke in the air. He'd have to open all the windows and clear it out before Baby Leader came back over. "Pearla, I'll just take you. Y'all ain't 'bout to have them niggas barking at me over her," Italian stated.

"No..." I stood, stuffing my feet in the Ugg Tasman slides I'd worn today.

My outfit was simple with jean Aeropostale shorts, a white graphic tee, and a jean jacket that I'd left in my car. My hair was braided in small stitch braids that fell to the side of my shoulders with boho pieces added. I'd gone to the black-owned shop that Glow had recommended, and they hadn't disappointed.

"You have to stay here. P can take me." I turned to P, scanning him from head to toe before walking past him.

"Fuck it! I'm going too," I heard Bella say.

"Me too—"

"Nawl. Sit y'all asses down. It don't take all y'all to go."

"Boy, fuck you!" I heard Mahzeyah yell.

"The baby on the way back. Don't you want to get some time with her before you have to go home?"

That must've been enough to convince Mahzeyah to stay because, as I walked out of the townhome, I heard her say, "Open the windows."

I hit the locks on my truck and heard the front door close.

"I'ma get my truck," P called out.

Keeping my back to him, I opened the driver's door and grabbed my jacket and my Gucci coin purse. "I'm just getting my jacket."

"Looka all dat assssss!" Bella slapped me on the butt just as I was lifting out of my car.

"Now, what if I had pooted?" I joked, even though my heart was beating like an African drum.

"Then, I'll just be a pooted-handed hoe."

I giggled as I closed my car door. I stuck my arm into my jacket and faced my friend. Bella was so damn pretty. She didn't have an ounce of melanin in her, but one wouldn't know that with her mannerisms and lingo. She was my favorite white sista, but calling her white did nothing but rile her up. She identified as Italrish: Italian and Irish. I didn't even know that was a thing.

"He fine as hell, friend, I will give him that. I don't even do light-skinned. He could get it, though."

We both stood in the yard watching P jog across the street. The sun was beaming down on us, but where we were going, I'd need the jacket. P hit the locks on a black Jeep Wrangler sitting on huge tires. When he pulled in and reversed, the red brake lights were not as vibrant as the shiny paint job. I gave a silent nod of approval for his choice of car.

"You sure you doing this?" Bella turned my shoulders so that we would be forehead to forehead. Her greenish, brown eyes stared through mine, and I nodded with knowing.

"I'm sure. P's cute."

"P's *fine*. But so is Grind."

"Grind has too much going on, Bella."

She sighed. "He does."

"Yeap."

"If my cousin deals with P, you know what that means, right? He's in the streets. Plus, look at him. Jewelry, swag, Jeep... He ain't no broke nigga, and he don't have the mannerisms of a spoiled one. He's a street nigga, Pearla. You ready for that again?"

"Everyone around us is in the streets, Bella. It's probably better that way. I don't think it would make sense to not deal with boys in the streets. How can we bring a regular dude around *all this*?" My arms waved in the air before flopping to my side.

Bella let my shoulders go. "You know I'm with you with whatever. Mahzeyah, too, and from the looks of it, Blayke and Glee, too, now." She rolled her eyes.

Bella liked the girls but had put out some stank energy when they first came around. She was territorial as heck. We learned quickly, though, that so was Blayke. Again, those two were so alike that it was scary. Mahzeyah said that Glee and I were alike, too, so the group was even more balanced now.

Bella gave me a once-over before conceding. P was parked on the curb, waiting. He hopped out of the truck, opened the passenger door, and then the back seat.

"Ohhh... The liquor man is a gentleman." Bella climbed in the back. "And it don't smell like roaches or nothiiiiing in here."

Her door closed, leaving me standing on the curb.

"You still got time to take them shots." P rubbed his beard before pulling at his pants near his crotch. I knew it wasn't a sexual thing but more so something men just did. My brother and Don had done it several times when talking to their wives. Nel had done it with Pia, too, and Italian when he was running after Mahzeyah.

Walking past P, I grabbed onto the door and hoisted myself up. "Let's go."

He closed the door behind me and walked around the back. Looking through the rearview mirror, I could see Bella staring at me, still apprehensive. Blinking, I looked off. P climbed into the driver's seat and pulled his phone and some money from his pockets. He threw both in the cup holders and shifted the gear, pulling out of the townhouse driveway. His truck smelled like the black cherry scent that most guys had in their cars. His seats were smooth leather, and the interior was clean. He took good care of his truck, if it was his.

"This yours?" Bella asked the question before I could.

"Yeah."

"How much the note on this running you every month?"

Ole lord, Bella.

He chuckled sexily. "Nothin'."

"Hmm..." was Bella's reply.

"It's nice," I complimented.

"'Preciate it. Where we headed?"

Turning in my seat, I eyed P. "So just like that, you ready to pull down?"

"Shit, why not? I want you, Pearla. So if we gotta pull up on that nigga and tell him it's a wrap, I'm for it."

"What if I'm bringing you to a setup?"

A chortle escaped P's slightly discolored lips. "I ain't worried 'bout it. Where we going?"

"Period. Mr. P said he ain't never scared."

"Here." P grabbed his phone and handed it to me. "Plug in the address."

Looking down at his hand, I noticed in addition to the phone that he threw in the cup holder, there were two more phones resting in the dashboard tray.

"Three phones?" I pointed out.

His eyes never left the road, nor did he blink. "Yeah. It's a work thing."

"What type of work you do to where you need *three phones*?" Bella called from the back seat.

"I do bodywork."

"Like... who did the body? You work at a funeral home?" I asked.

He chuckled. "Sum'n like that. Here." He was still holding the phone in my direction, but his eyes were on me now.

Instead of taking it, I pulled the seat belt across my body and turned away from him. "You know how to get to Jagoda One?"

"The hospital?" He drew his head back.

"Yeap." I clicked my seat belt. "That's where we going."

~

"WHY WE AT THE HOSPITAL?"

P, Bella, and I stood in the parking lot of Jagoda One. The ride was a quiet one with only the bass from the music P was blasting, which ironically had been Reaper, Grind's deceased rap friend. It wasn't a shock, though, because Jagoda Bay loved Reaper's music. Had he not been killed, he would have had the city on lock by now. The day I went down the Reaper rabbit hole, thinking Grind had been his killer after discovering the contents in his backpack, I was put onto his music, turning me into somewhat of a fan. P was rapping every song word for word, causing the tension in the car to thicken.

I sighed, not answering him. "Come on."

We all began to walk ahead, and before we got through the doors, Bella grabbed my hand.

"Not yo' new nigga rapping to yo' coma nigga's lyrics."

"Bella, please..." I scoffed.

I hated that I told Bella and Mahzeyah about Grind writing lyrics for Reaper. Mahzeyah already knew that Grind could write because on the day in the studio, he had written a few songs for Flexer. Rappers weren't ashamed to use writers these days. If I had been an artist, my ghostwriter would stay a ghost. Flexer could rap, though. I'd seen plenty of his old freestyles. I guess he just wanted something fresh, and according to Mahzeyah, during her and Flexer's pillow talk, Grind was the best writer for rap, but he didn't like to take on clients. Flexer was the first to get him to break since Reaper's death, and he told Mahzeyah to thank me. I didn't understand why—Grind working with him had nothing to do with me.

Swallowing hard, I caught up to P's long-legged ass and fell in stride. Bella kept a few paces behind us, I guess to give the situation some space. We entered the lobby, bypassing the receptionist. I didn't have to check-in. My brother and cousin had the entire wing upstairs bought out. P was looking around, curious as fuck as to why I brought him here, but I appreciated him not asking questions. He'd see since we were here now, and it was no turning back.

We rounded the corner, and I stopped on my heels. A hard body crashed into me, and before I could fall forward, P's arm wrapped around my waist to hold me upright.

"My bad. You good?" he said.

I nodded, although I was mad that I couldn't relish how good it felt to be this close to a boy because I was stuck on the scene in front of me.

Grind's mama had her arms folded while six girls stood on the opposite side of her. One person, the ringleader, in pants so tight I could see the thread stretching, talked a mile a minute. Kaylee noticed me immediately. She looked from me to P, who still had his arm around my waist, to Bella. She smirked and went back to looking at the person talking. I knew that hourglass shape from anywhere. Her long, black weave damn near went to her knees.

"I don't know what to tell you, Kaylee. But I gotta go. You take care," Shus told her.

She walked around Kaylee, leaving her standing with her friends, and came toward me.

"Heyyyy, baby boo!" Gracious stopped in front of us.

Like the first time I'd met her, she looked like she was around our age in a black Lululemon athletic set, which featured a tank top with a sweatshirt tied around her waist and Jordans on her feet. Her eyes went from me to P's arms that were wrapped around my waist. He let me go, and the hardness that was pressed against my back disappeared.

She swallowed me in a hug, one that I needed as I closed my eyes and inhaled. Shus had become something like a friend to me these last few months. We talked weekly, and I appreciated her not bringing up Grind during those conversations. She was a mess that I loved so much. I'd missed a few of her calls because, some days, I just wanted to be left alone, but it was all love, and I knew that she knew that.

"I wasn't expecting you today. Hey, Bella," she spoke to Bella quickly and was back on me.

I'd told her all about my friends, and she had met them on Face-Time. When Shus and I did talk, we usually gossiped about the music industry and trendy things on TikTok. She was my girl when I was in the headspace to talk to her.

"Hey, boo. You look cute," Bella complimented.

"Thanks, y'all do too—"

"Really! You dismiss me for this fat bitch!" Kaylee stood at the head of her crew, who all looked busted up in comparison to her, yelling.

While she was looking like a slut, her jean shorts were cute, swallowing her thighs, hips, and ass. Her crop top, that her breasts were spilling out of, worked for her because she had the body. With her long nails, she tossed her black tresses behind her shoulder.

"Who the fuck you calling a bitch? Bitch! Fuck wrong with you, hoe?" Bella tried stepping around me, but I held her back.

"It's cool, Bellz. I got it." I stepped around Grind's mama, but they both were right on my heels.

Kaylee was pretty. She was pretty the day she pulled the marriage certificate from her ass, breaking my heart, and was still cute now. But the bitch's attitude was stank.

"Wassup, Kaylee?"

"You mean, Mrs...?"

"Oh, my bad. Wassup, Mrs. Bardin? What... You think me

addressing you as his wife gone hurt my feelings? You his wife." I shrugged. "Okay?"

"You think you so fucking smart and so fucking funny! I can't see my own husband at all! I can't even go up to the floor he's on! We have a family! We have bills! He's up there half-dead, and me and my niece going through shit!" she screamed.

"Bitch, pussy selling, all day, every day. Put it to use. Grind can't do nothing with it right now," Bella commented, making Shus snicker.

Kaylee's eyes snapped to Bella. "Who the fuck is this white bitch?"

"The one that's gone beat yo' muthafuckin' ass. Keep on!"

"I'm his wife. You not supposed to have more rank than me! And you foul, Shus! You know this shit wrong."

"Ain't shit foul about me. Like I told you, you gotta pay the cost to be the boss. And Pearla is the fucking CEO, baby. Take that shit up with my son when he wakes up because make no mistake, he will get up."

"Fuck this shit! We'll dog you in here, hoe!" one of the girls behind Kaylee spoke up. She, too, was wearing shorts, and I knew I wasn't the smallest girl, but her apple-shaped body looked terrible in them.

"Facts! Mop this hospital with both them bitches."

"Nawl, it ain't gone be no jumping. Kaylee, take these dirty bitches away from here. I don't know why you came up here anyway. You gone have to do like I did. Get a fuckin' job!"

"Why the fuck I gotta get a job when my husband is rich? He gets all my sister's baby daddy royalties! My niece needs her money! It's her daddy's money! Not Grind's."

I stepped up into Kaylee's face. "Shut the fuck up! Why are you blurting out his business in this hospital?"

"Fuck you! Do I look like the type of bitch to work a job, fat-ass hoe?"

"No, and that's the problem." I smirked.

"Bitch!"

Three of Kaylee's friends ran up but stopped dead in their tracks. P came up beside me and lifted his shirt. I'd felt it on him when he held me against his front when we spotted these hoes.

"Ain't gon' be no fuckin' jumpin' 'round this bitch."

"Who the fuck is you?" Kaylee asked.

"A nigga that's ready to *pay the price*. Like I said, first bitch waddle in this water, gon' die like a fuckin' duck. Call my bluff."

"Period!" Bella co-signed.

"Now, if you act like you have some sense, maybe I can see what I can do for you, *Mrs. Bardin*. As you can see, I'm not an enemy you wanna have."

"Hoe, you ain't got more rank than me! I'm his wife! The last pussy he dipped off in before he was shot up! He just feels sorry for your big ass! He fucked me and took his ass right to you! How the fuck my pussy taste, bitch?" Kaylee swung and missed.

Not giving her time to retaliate, I threw a punch, ignoring the racing in my heart from her revelation. Her soft nose crunched under my fist, but I kept throwing blows. I could feel her scratching my face from the stinging of her nails, but my adrenaline wouldn't let me let up.

"Whoop that hoe, Pearla!"

"You bet not let her get you on the ground!" Shus screamed.

With everything that had been pent up in me, I threw punches left and right like Neltz had taught me. My nephew was lethal with the hands and had told me I needed to learn when he was around six. Plus, my sister didn't have any bitch in her blood. If nothing else, we could fight, although I didn't like to.

"Get this fat bitch off me!" Kaylee yelled as she wildly swung but was missing my face.

That was too bad for her because I wasn't nearly finished. It wasn't her that had broken my heart, but she was getting the ass-whooping as if it had been. She should've left well enough alone because I had no plans on beating anyone's ass today.

"Aye, get the fuck off my sister, bitch!"

Kaylee was suddenly snatched up by her hair. Her titties were free, and her nose was busted from my fist. Matteo stood there, mean-mugging, and had her dangling like a rag doll. The wig peeled from her edges, dropping her to the ground. He tossed it in her face, looking at his hand as if he was disgusted. Knowing my brother, he really was disgusted.

"Get y'all dirty ass from up here. And you,"—He pointed at

Kaylee, who was looking like a hot-ass mess with the bald cap on her head and backing up on the floor—"Put yo' hands on my sister again, yo' mama gone be buryin' her second daughter. You know who the fuck this is, you in here tussling with?"

"Matteo, it's okay..." I grabbed his arm.

He grabbed my chin and inspected my face. "How was this hoe able to scratch yo' face?" His frown deepened. "Bitch, I'll kill you in here—"

Matteo turned to Kaylee, but I grabbed him. "Brother, no. It's fine."

Kaylee screamed and cried. "You wrong, Pearla! I'm his wife! His fucking wife!"

"And you tried to pull the plug on your husband! What kind of wife does that?" I screamed. "You tried to fucking kill him! Before the doctor could even give us his stats, you were ready to pull the plug, and for what? For money? Insurance? That's all his life is worth to you?" I screamed so loud that my voice cracked.

Her friends helped her from the floor. Our guards, who had been blending in with the staff, were now surrounding us and had been the reason the police hadn't been called.

"He's gone, Pearla!" She pushed her friends off her. "He is gone! She knows he's gone." She looked at Shus. "The doctors know he's gone. Everybody knows. They are only keeping him alive because of *your* people's money!" She scoffed at my brother.

"You don't know that! Stop speaking that shit into the air!"

"Speakin' what? Facts! It's facts! He's gone. Let's face it. We both loved that nigga! He don't let too many people get near him, but since he let you, you gotta face the truth. Grind was a hardbody! It's been months! Six months! You don't think he would have woken up by now? To come back to me and Rein? To you? We love him, and he loves us both. I've accepted that. It hurts but it's life." Her arms flopped.

"He would have woke up by now! He knows this shit he created is a hot mess! You holding onto a corpse! Let him go so I can put my husband away the proper way, Pearla!"

"Bitch, go eat a dick 'fo' I spatter yo' brains all over this bitch. I can help you get to them pearly gates and see if that nigga up there waitin' on you. And when I bring my gun out, I'm usin' it."

Kaylee's eyes expanded at Matteo before she and her friends ran out of the hospital, bumping into each other on the way out.

Matteo faced me again, ignoring everyone else. "Don't listen to that bitch, sis. Bitter, sour pussy-ass hoes say anything. I know a prostitute when I see one, and that's one."

I chuckled as my brother wiped the tears from my face using the bottom of his shirt. His cologne burned my eyes, but I didn't stop him.

"You're too pretty to be fightin', Pearla."

"But she was asking for it."

"And I could've had some hoes come up here and beat them bitches to a pulp. Now we gotta get you a technical shot. Come on, I'll have the doctor come to the crib."

Bella giggled at Matteo saying tetanus wrong. If my adrenaline wasn't still pumping, I would've laughed too.

"Teo, nooooo. I'm with my friends. I gotta do something first."

Matteo looked at Bella, P, and Shus as if he was noticing them for the first time. My brother, cousin, and daddy always gave me their undivided attention when I was in their space. The only person who could distract them when I was around was their wives. That was the love I yearned for, but from the man whom I'd just been fighting over.

"That's Gracious, Grind's mama. This is P, Italian's friend, and you know Bella."

He jutted his chin at Bella and frowned at P before pointing to Shus. "I'm gone beat yo' son ass when he wakes up."

Shus chortled. "Good. I'll be right behind you to get my licks in."

Matteo then turned back to me. Sticking his hand in his pocket, he removed a wad of cash and stuffed it in my jacket pocket. He then pulled me into a hug, hooking his arm around my neck.

"Pearla, I'll kill these hoes behind my blood. Answer the fuckin' phone when I call, even if it's just to say, 'Leave me alone, bitch-ass nigga.'"

Laughing into his chest, I felt my emotions well up but held them in. If I started crying, he'd take me with him. "I'm sorry, brother. We were having fun at Jisei's."

"You ain't sorry for shit. And stop drinking'... You ain't grown." Matteo stepped back. "Aye, lil' nigga. Get my sister back to the spot safely. Matter fact, do twenty miles an hour, that's royalty right there."

P stroked his chin. "Heard you."

Matteo narrowed his eyes. "You gone *feel me* if another hair is outta place. You was supposed to spray this hospital as soon as a bitch ran up on mine. Strike one." Matteo held up his index finger as he backed out of the hospital.

Bella was covering her mouth as she laughed while I shook my head. Dating anybody was going to be a hassle that I had already accepted.

"Come on up..." Shus pulled me into her side, her, too, checking my face.

"Next time, I got that Kaylee hoe. You beat her ass, but I owe that bitch too," Bella vented as she mashed the button to the elevator. We all piled on and took it to the private wing.

Once the doors opened, my heart fell to the soles of my ass. The cold air stung the cuts on my face, and as soon as I got home, I planned to clean my face with peroxide.

"You go 'head and go in. We gone stay out here." Shus ushered P and Bella to the waiting area.

P didn't object. I knew we were beyond the bet now and that he had questions that I would answer to the best of my abilities without incriminating my people, Grind, and myself.

I waved to the guards at the door, and both of them eyed my face before opening the heavy door that kept Grind safe. There was a chair and a game system at the foot of the bed, and I already knew it had belonged to Neltz. I'd called him once and had heard the machines in the background. I didn't mind my nephew visiting Grind, I just wasn't going to.

It had been six months. Six months since I'd been the happiest I'd ever been. Six months since my sister got her fairytale ending. Six months since my tires had prompted Grind to pull over to the service station. Six months since he told me to climb over into the driver's side and to drive off if something went down. Six months since I heard the deafening pop of the first shot. Six months since I didn't pull off like I was told. Six months since I caught my first body. Six months since I held Grind as he struggled to stay amongst the land of the living.

The tears rushed from my face as I stood over his bed. Tubes and cords ran out of him in all different directions. There was a joystick resting underneath his hand. I watched as the machine pumped oxygen into his chest. His nails were cleaned, his skin still had his brown color, and instead of the hospital gown, he was in a Ralph Lauren pajama set with the chest exposed. He didn't have bandages on his chest but the bullets left scars.

"Niggas like me make money so Pretty girls like you can do all the things pretty girls do.

"Pretty girls, pretty girls, pretty girls! Fuck you, Grayson! Fuck you!" My chest heaved.

"Fuck you!" I punched his chest, not caring if I was fucking something up.

"You don't deserve my mercy!" I punched him again.

"You don't deserve my fuckin' protection! You don't deserve my body, and you damn sure didn't deserve my heart!" I punched him again.

"I... You hurt me! You fucking hurt meeeeeee! You hurt me so bad! Why? Why meeee?"

I hiccupped.

"I... I didn't want to live anymore. I wanted to die! I wanted to fucking die! Do you hear me, Grind! I wanted to die! I have people who love me. I have people that care about me, and I wanted to fucking die!"

I punched him again before collapsing onto his chest. With my face against his bare skin and the smell of Dial soap creeping into my nostrils, I cried. I cried hard. I cried for the hurt. I cried for the pain. I cried for the time lost. I cried for Rein. I cried for the unfortunate situation Grind had put Kaylee and me in.

"You're so wrong, Grind. You're so wrong. Your... your wife," I spoke into his chest. "Your wife says you're gone. I saw the look on your mom's face. I think she believes it too. Still, no matter how much you hurt me, I... I c-caaan't. I can't let them pull the plug. You have so much potential. You have so much left to do. I can't let you die."

Rolling my head on his chest, I bawled.

"I'm so stupid. I know I'm stupid. I should hate you. I should hate you, Grind, but I can't. I'm hurt, but I still love you... I love you so, so, so, so, so fucking much."

I wiped my face, hoping the tears were done.

"I love you, but I'm not no nigga's second option. You choose Kaylee, and now you gotta live with your choice. I'm intelligent. If this was for paperwork to protect Reaper, you should have said that. But you didn't. You kept it from me because... *I'm just the pretty girl who needs to focus on school so niggas like you can chase the money and fuck the girls like Kaylee.* No!"

Sitting up, I placed my hand on his chest. His heartbeat was steady.

"I'm Pearla Rinaldi. I can and will have any nigga I choose. But I need you to wake up so you can witness this shit. When it's all said and done, you will feel this shit in yo' chest!"

Leaning down to his face, I planted a kiss on his chin since his lips were taped. Now that I was closer to him, I could see a tattoo on his chest right where my palm had been. Unlike the other spots on his chest, this one didn't have a wound. It was a clam—a clam with pearls dangling from it. "Prettiest Pearl in the Clam" was underneath it. That broke something in me.

Using the back of my sleeve, I wiped my face. "You gone regret the day you hurt me. But when you wake up, you better divorce that hoe faster than you can blink. Find another bitch to be happy with. She ain't the one."

Turning my back, I walked out of the room. P was leaning against the wall, looking up at me with his brow raised. P and Bella both paused their conversation. I walked over to P, pulled him into my chest, and kissed his lips. He was caught off guard, but he didn't pull away.

"You aite?" he asked when I let him up for air.

"Yeap. Where is your girlfriend?"

He licked his lips, my lip gloss now on his tongue. "She packed up and left me a while ago."

I wasn't expecting him to keep it real. I was so used to niggas selling me a dream that it was refreshing to hear the truth.

"You still love her?"

"I do. You still love him?" He jutted his chin in the direction of Grind's room.

"No."

He smirked, knowing I was lying like hell. I'd probably never stop loving Grind.

"I completed the dare. Can I at least know the boy's name that I just ended my relationship for? I know it's not just P."

He licked his lips, and the sight of him licking my saliva off caused a thudding in my panties that only Grind had produced.

"It's Price, baby."

"Price..."

He pulled me by my jacket until my front was pressed to his, the gun still on his waist and poking me in the stomach.

"Two muthafuckas that's still in love with their exes. Sounds toxic, baby." His voice was so sexy, and the adrenaline was still coursing through me, along with the emotions I was feeling from what had just happened in Grind's room. I was ready to jump his bones at this point.

"I'm not in love—"

He cut me off, his grin broadening. "You ain't gotta lie to kick it, Claressa."

Biting down on my bottom lip, I grabbed him by the arm so that we could leave. I wouldn't be back.

Price.

Pearla and Price had a nice ring to it.

Fuck Grind.

CHAPTER 21
SOLANA DAMITA LEDESMA

I hadn't slept in two days. I knew because Italian had brought me two breakfasts, two lunches, and two dinners, and I had yet to close my eyes. A normal person would have hardly been able to open their eyes by now. But I wasn't a sane person. I was actually the opposite of sane. Yet, insane wouldn't be enough to describe what I was feeling right now. With my back pressed against the wall, the bathroom had become my solace. In here, there was water, and the floor stayed chilled. As my skin shifted from itching to burning to agony, the water was the only thing that could soothe it. But today, I wasn't feeling pain on my skin. Today, I wasn't feeling pain at all. As a matter of fact, I was in such a state that it was hard to focus on exactly what I was feeling physically.

But mentally? Mentally was where the chaos lay.

I wanted cocaína... Shio... I craved cocaína... Shio... I didn't want cocaína... Shio... I didn't need cocaína. Shio... Shio... Shio...

I was losing my fucking mind. One minute, I wanted the drug and the man, and the next, I was disgusted with myself for not being able to shake it or him. We'd only kissed. We'd only held each other. Why did he have just as much of a hold on me as the drugs did? I felt that if I could at least get him out of my mind and only have to battle the drugs, then my days would be much easier—much smoother.

How was it that getting on drugs had been simple? It was actually the easiest thing in the world as long as you had access to them.

But getting yourself off them was the real challenge. I was over it. I simply didn't care what happened anymore. I didn't care if I got out of here and did a line the second I crossed the threshold. I didn't care if I went back to México. I didn't care if I married a stranger. I just wanted to be done with this.

But what I did care about was if Shio ever looked at me with longing again. I cared if he was disgusted by me. I cared about what he was doing, and who he was doing it with. I cared more about Shio and his well-being than I did my own, and the fact that I was locked in here and couldn't do anything about it was killing me. His not responding to my messages was hurting me. His being in the same space as the woman he shared a child with was killing me.

Libérame. (Free me).

I needed to be freed. Freed from this room. Freed from my thoughts. Freed from the life my father had birthed me into, and freed from the jealousy that sat deep inside of my chest. But in order to be freed from the jealousy, I had to be freed from Shio, and I didn't want to be freed from him. Not now, and probably not ever.

Letting my head hit the wall, I swallowed, my mouth dry even though I'd already drank four bottles of water today. Lately, nothing was ever enough. My body was so needy, and the constant need for food confused me because Italian fed me well every day. According to him, I needed to move my body regardless of the pain or exhaustion, so I'd been working out diligently, doing many of the exercises Shio taught me without any equipment. He told me once that my body was a machine, so every day, at least on the days I wasn't on the floor screaming bloody murder, I worked out, or at least I tried. The water consumption for the constant thirst, no matter how much I drunk, was needed. I needed something to believe in, so I was on my knees praying, or doing what I thought was praying, multiple times a day. There was a Bible on the nightstand that I'd popped open a few times. Most of the words I couldn't decode in Spanish to comprehend what I was reading. It all sounded so ancient. It all proved that I needed Shio.

Picking up the phone from where I left it after my last message to him, I debated whether to call. I wasn't in the mood to move my fingers, so I tapped the audio button. When the recording started, I took a deep breath and stopped it. Before I could delete it, it was sent by mistake. Seconds later, the read receipt told me Shio had heard it before it changed to the word "kept." That infuriated me. He was openly ignoring me. He could have turned the read receipts off, but he doubled down and chose to keep my silent audio message. His lack of care had me seeing red.

Selecting the button again, I placed the phone to my mouth.

"*Escuchas pero no respondes.* (You listen but do not reply.)"

I paused, feeling a tingle in my gums that had me swiping my tongue across them.

"You want to break me, Shio. I did not see it then, but I see it now. You put me here, in the basement with no treatment. You gave me a phone, but you have not responded to one text message. You swap me for Bahati. You want to break me. But you cannot break a person who does not care. One feeling the drugs did to me was give me a careless attitude. This—this what you do. It may hurt my body but it does not hurt my spirit. Whatever sick lesson you try to get me to learn, save it for another. Uriah or Bahati. I do not care. You regret so badly that I was placed in your life, Shio, but so do I. When I get out of here, you will be nothing more than a memory. Actually, *una pesadilla* (a nightmare). This does not matter... You do not matter. I just want you to know."

After releasing the button and pressing send, I dropped the phone before I could see the read or kept notification. Picking up the real reason for my coming into the bathroom, I blinked my eyes because, just like my throat, they too were dry. But I knew they were dry from lack of sleep. They were dry because I'd finally gotten the courage to open the leather, brown notebook again and read.

Today, I had to convince my son that I didn't care. It's better that way. If he thinks I have no regard for he and his mother, then me not stepping up for them in the way that I should won't sting as bad. Still, each day that Shio grows, each day that he peers at me, I see the respect drifting far away. I don't know how I feel about that. I do know, but the more I convince myself that I do not care, the better it would be for everyone.

Shio stood in front of me, eyes glossed over. His little chest had filled out, and his voice was beginning to deepen. He still had many years before he hit puberty, but he'd grown from the little Shio that used to run around the house, playing hide and seek with his cousins. It made me sad that my baby boy was growing up because I knew he was only growing up as fast as he was due to the lifestyle he'd been placed in. He no longer looked at me with longing; he no longer looked to me for answers. He'd become his own man, and that hurt, but I had no room for hurt. It's why I was sitting behind my desk, void of emotion, as I stared at the boy before me. I'd lost my son years ago. The night of the snake bite had been the start, and it had only declined from there. The more Shio grew away from me, the more I used. It was a wonder I hadn't overdosed with how raw my nostrils always were from how much I used. Still, I stared at him as he stared at me. Being high helped me hide my emotions, whereas Shio was showing his.

"I don't ask you for anything. I don't even talk to you."

"Shio, what is the meaning of you disturbing me?"

My hands were on the black box that held my evening candy, and I was eager to get to it. When the drugs wore off, reality hit, and when reality hit, I was unable to sit in the guilt. Guilt couldn't do anything for me. But a bump could. I wouldn't do it in front of Shio because Shannon had asked I not.

"I know you don't give a fuck about me. But you could at least do better for my mama."

Shio and Shannon had a special bond. One that I secretly loathed, and at the same time cherished. Over the years, they had learned to lean on one another. Shannon was always so gentle with him, whereas the mob was harsh. But seeing her with him just served as a reminder that I not only did not have a relationship with Shio, but I couldn't have one with Tunan either.

"I care about you, Shio."

"You don't! You don't fucking care. If you did, you'd stick up for me."

"I don't stick up for you, Shio, because you need this. You need every lesson. The world is cruel, and one day, you'll have a position and power, and you'll need all of what you're going through now in order to navigate it. As far as your mother, I love her. But, in this life, there isn't much room for love. So, the best I can do is make sure we survive."

"There is always room for love. But you know what there is no room for?"

Instead of answering, I watched him blink down his emotion. ***That's my boy.***

"Cowards. You're a coward. You are weak, Daddy. You're weak, and

you're a coward, and I hate that my mama ever met you. I'll take the mistreatments, I'll take the punishments. But my mama doesn't deserve this. Any of this."

"She's in this life."

"Because of you! Because of you!"

His chest heaved. The lessons had given my young son defined muscles already.

"You said I'll have position and power one day, and I will, but it will have nothing to do with the Cuppacios. Nothing to do with the mafia."

I know, son.

Instead of replying, I opened the box and my mouth immediately after as I stared at the small mountain of cocaine. Running my tongue across my teeth and gums, I could almost feel the high, and I had touched the drug just hours ago.

Clank clash

My hands flew up as Shio stood over my desk. Powder was smeared across the surface, and the black box was shattered on the floor now. My eyes met his, and the menacing glare in his was enough to make me want to concede, as if I weren't a grown man and he a child.

"There is no fear in love. But perfect love drives out fear, because fear has to do with punishment. The one who fears is not made perfect in love." He looked me up and down before storming out of the office.

Dipping my pinky in the residue, I rubbed it across my gums, shuddering at the tingling sensation. Closing my eyes, I repeated the motion.

"First John, chapter four, verse eighteen."

Boom Boom

Slamming the worn notebook shut at the sound of pounding, I looked at the locked door. "¿Si?"

Boom Boom Boom

Putting the notebook down, I stood, exited the bathroom, and went to the steel door.

"It's me, Bella. I'm sliding Walmart bags in the slot. I grabbed you a few things. I also got you some food."

"Gracias, Bella..."

The slot opened, and bags and food were pushed through. I held my breath, hoping that she would leave. I appreciated the company from the young ones some days, but today, I did not care for it. I'd been grateful that Italian had only left my food and didn't bait me for much conversation earlier. Mahzeyah had to have been here because that was the only time he seemed occupied.

"Aite, I'm gone, Solana."

The slot slammed shut, and I heard her feet ascending the stairs. Instead of looking through the bags, I went back to the bathroom and grabbed the phone. The voice message I'd sent showed "kept" as the first one had, meaning he'd listened to it and saved it.

Swallowing air, I pressed record again.

"I apologize. I do care, Shio. I care so much. The many days here, my mind is crazy. Please forgive me. I care a lot. I care so much about you. You are important to me, Shio."

Sending the message, I placed the phone on the bathroom counter. Going back into the room, I began removing the pajamas and haircare products from the bags. I was so grateful for Bella because she had gotten high-quality products, and I could tell from the packaging. Hopefully, after another hot bath, sleep would come easily.

~

Weightless

"Arghhh! Arghhhh! Arggghhh!"

Rubbing my hand into my head as my face burned, I pulled at my scalp that felt like it was on fire. A million needles felt like they were being injected into my follicles at record speed. I couldn't breathe because of the pain.

I'd gotten up to use the bathroom, and each time I took a step, it felt like I was dragging a ton of bricks behind me at the ankle. I dropped to the floor, exhaustion overcoming me, and the longer I lay on my back, the more cemented I felt. Sleep had been better the last few days, but every time I woke up, I experienced a new type of pain.

Pain mentally. Pain physically. Pain emotionally.

Reaching up, I rubbed my chest slowly, hoping to relieve the weight that seemed pressed into my cavity and robbing me of my next breath.

I'd been religiously working out and had even cut back on eating so much, but still, it felt as if I weighed a ton. I knew it wasn't physical weight. I was sane enough to see that nothing was attached to my body. I was carrying weight mentally. There was so much baggage within me that made me feel as if I were sinking from just the minor thoughts of my life.

Suddenly, everything was too much. The light was too bright, and the silence was too loud. I closed my eyes since I was staring at the white ceiling, and the stark color was becoming too much as well. Then, the darkness was too overwhelming, making me feel as though I was falling into an endless black hole. Being in this room was too suffocating. Being alone was too noisy. When I tried to use the TV to drown out the quiet, the sounds would only make my head hurt. Nothing I did could lift the weight, so my best option was to lie here and pray that I would feel better tomorrow.

~

Sssssk

I knew that sound all too well. It was one of the slots in the door opening. I felt so heavy that I couldn't lift my head to see who it was. Peeling my eyes open, I swallowed, my throat not feeling as dry as it had been in previous days. I was thirsty even though I'd drunk plenty of water today. My stomach knotted for something solid, not a liquid. My urges hadn't been as strong as they had been, but I still yearned for the drug. I didn't know who I was without it. Being trapped in this room wasn't helping the cravings, in my opinion. All it was doing was driving me mad. There was only one other thing that I felt I could indulge in to take away the feeling of wanting *cocaína*, and it was not a thing. It wasn't even an it. It was a man.

Shio.

If I couldn't have the drug, I'd settle for the man.

"I will overcome this addiction. This addiction will not get the best of me. I am bigger than my addiction. I am in control."

"Hmm?"

"Repeat it, Solana," the young feminine voice ordered.

I cleared my parched throat. "I will overcome this addiction. This addiction will not get the... best of me. I am bigger than my addiction. I am in control."

"Yes! Look at you. I didn't have to repeat it or nothing."

"I'm... good with directions."

"I don't like this for you."

Closing my eyes, I tried to place the voice.

Bella?

No, she has a bit more of an accent in her speech.

It's not Pearla's—her voice is much lighter.

Mahzeyah?

Yes, it's Mahzeyah.

"Neither do I, Mahzeyah," I responded, somewhat tired from just trying to figure out who was talking to me through the steel door's opening.

I didn't like being here either, but my days of hating that I'd been thrown inside this room were gone. There was no sense of dwelling on things I could not change, at least not in the present. I had some days ago to make the best of what this was, but my body and mind needed to get on one accord with reality.

"How do you feel?"

Horrible. "I feel okay."

"You do not."

Chuckling, I shut my eyes tightly because the small laughter had hurt. Every part of me hurt, down to my fingers and toenails. I couldn't do another day of feeling like this, and if I had to, then I'd put a pillow over my face and end it myself. That wasn't me being suicidal. It was me being overwhelmed by the pain.

"Tell me the truth. How do you feel?"

Mahzeyah—So bossy and so sassy.

She and Bella had that in common. They were both sharp at the tongue. But, like me, I could tell Bella had grown up around boys, and I was sure there were many boys. As *bonita* (pretty) as she was, she had this force in her. There was a streak as wide as a river of defiance in her. Mahzeyah, on the other hand, was bossy because she was an only child or the oldest. I didn't know the specifics, but I could almost guess their lives from simple conversations. She had the traits of an only child. I didn't have any close relationships with people back home, but when I was in school, I had classes with Valeria. We took classes together for many years, and although they were of different ethnicities, Mahzeyah reminded me so much of Valeria.

They were both confident, mature, and responsible. I knew Mahzeyah was responsible because she had been given free rein by her parents, and she was over here almost every day since I'd met all of them. Those were just a few traits that I knew to be true that children without siblings held. Self-centered was another, but I had not seen that in Mahzeyah just yet.

"Everything hurts," I answered her.

"Mentally or physically?"

I couldn't see her face since she was behind the door, and my head wasn't at the slot, but I imagined her arched brow rising. She was a little lady, much more in tune with the world than I was at her age. She also possessed things that I had not—friends that loved and adored her, loving parents, and a boy who was obsessed with her, although neither of them knew what to do with it yet.

"Both..." I groaned. "But today is all physically. My hair. My nails. My chest. I feel..."

"Heavy?"

"Si."

"I get what they are doing, and it's not for me to speak on it because, one, I'm a child. Well, almost a young adult, but I'm a child right now. And, two, it's not my place to get in their business. However, this isn't right. I get Shio wanting you to get clean, but this isn't the right way to go about it. If you're not mentally strong... or physically support... This could—"

"It could kill me... Si. I know."

We both grew quiet with Mahzeyah sighing loudly.

How did I tell a child that death was better than this? How could I articulate that being without the two things that made me feel something felt like death in itself? My body was not only detoxing the drugs, but the man too. While it was trying to rid my system of Shio, I was holding onto every bit of him that I could.

The way the sweat dripped off his deep skin as he worked out.

The meal preps he ate religiously when he wasn't prepping our meals fresh.

The way his glasses sat on the tip of his nose as he wrote in the journal.

The way his muscles flexed as he removed stacks of money from the counting machine before binding them with rubber bands.

These days, I've only been thinking of all things Shio, and when I wasn't thinking of Shio, I was thinking of *cocaína* (cocaine). So, yes, I knew this method of rehabilitation could kill me— the Alexa machine told Italian and me as much, but there were things far worse than death...

Like being ignored by Shio.

And not being able to purchase my fix from the friend I'd made.

"I need a *distracción* (distraction)."

I needed not to think about pain, the drugs, or the man who left me here.

"Okay, I can help with that."

Instead of letting her lead the conversation, I quickly asked, "How is cheer?"

She looked so cute in her uniform the day they had to wash the vomit from my hair. I'd always loved American cheerleaders. As a child, I thought girls in scanty dresses were only a thing on TV until I was old enough to understand it was very real.

"Cheer camp is cool. I have a few colleges looking at me."

"That is so good. Education is important."

"Yeah, I guess."

"You don't sound too happy..."

"It's not that. I love cheer. My father put me in it when I was young because he wanted me to gain social skills. It was my aunt's idea, and although I hated it at first, I'd learned to appreciate it. I've fallen in love with it. But... I don't know if I want to do it on a collegiate level. My friends and I have plans on going to college together. Bella has already decided to transfer from JBU if we decide to go elsewhere. I don't want to be stuck at cheer practice and at games when my girls are out living their best lives without me. It's bad enough that I'm missing the action over here when I'm at camp during the day. Plus, my daddy is rich. I don't really need scholarships. They can go to someone that actually needs the money for school."

I remembered when I thought the same of *mi padre* (my father). He was rich, from what I knew then. I could just get up, go swipe a credit card, and party until my knees were sore to forget my troubles. My papa had the money for me to do so. But he hadn't had it like I thought he did. Now that I knew that, I wondered how my life was sustained with his large debt to many other cartels.

"That's commendable of you... Wanting to give up the scholarship offers so others can use them to go to school."

"Yeah... And I also want to go on the road with Flexer when I'm on break. Like how Missy does with Essex. You know Essex, right, the rapper?"

"Si."

I was versed in American music. Plus, Shio worked out to his raps religiously. He was one of Shio's close friends from what I gathered when they spoke on the phone.

"Flexer is also a rapper. ¿Si?"

She'd played his music for me, and it also felt familiar. The clubs back home mostly played more American rap than Latin and Hispanic music to cater to tourists.

"Yeap. He's one of the best out. He likes me a lot. I like him too, but I'm in high school..." She chuckled. "I'm stuck here in Jagoda Bay while he's on the road, living his best life.

"I'm not saying I want to be with him all day long because I still want to be with my girls, but I want to be able to move freely. School is a non-negotiable because I will be getting that degree on time, but cheer will just take up more time from me being a rapper's girlfriend and me being my friend's wing woman. It's just... a lot of decisions I have to make."

I grinned, though it hurt. Her problems were so cute. Here she was, spoiled, rich, talented, and loved immensely, and was battling with wanting to quit cheer so she could be with her boyfriend and friends more. She was telling all of this to a woman locked in a room by a man she wanted to be with, but instead, he was ignoring her because she liked to do drugs.

"May I give my... Ooo—"

"Opinion?"

"Si... si."

"Of course. Please tell me I'm not crazy because I know if I tell my parents I want to quit cheer, my daddy will be hurt, but he will be okay with my decision. But my mama? Avenue gonna ram my head between the washer and the dryer."

"You're not *loco* (crazy)."

"Good. Good." She sighed.

"But you shouldn't quit cheer."

She groaned. "Solanaaaaa!"

"Unless it is something you really want to do, Mahzeyah. I know you and your friends love each other, and I love that you all will be going to college together. But you can still cheer and hang with them. They can sit in on some of your practices and come to all the games. At least the ones at your university. Do not ever think you are missing out on something. You are not, okay? It will be there. Your friends will be there."

At her age, I wished I were committed to a sport and a friend group. The girls were living a teen sitcom, and I'd been enjoying spending time with them, even if it was through a door.

"And Flexer?"

Licking my lips, I thought of the right words to say. "I... I have never had a boyfriend, Mahzeyah. I did not—no. I do not think I had a boy to like me at your age. I... looked different from everyone, and even if I blended, my father would have never allowed it."

I shook my worries from my head because I was beginning to fall into that deep, dark, endless hole. "I can't really speak on a subject I am not privy to, but I do understand wanting to be near someone that you like. It is almost as if not having them hurts. When you are not around him, you cannot focus. You cannot eat. You cannot sleep."

"See, exactly! Like, I need to be in my nigga's skinnnnnn! Oh my gosh! Yes."

"Umhm. But still, do not quit cheer."

"Really, Solana?"

"Yes, really. He is a world-famous rapper. Is he not?"

"Ion know about *world*, but he famous."

"He can make time to see you. You do not always have to stop your life to see him. Girls need things. Hobbies. Friendships. We need things outside of the love of a boy. Cherish your things. When all you have is the boy, as soon as he does something to hurt you, whether it be intentional or not, it will not only hurt, but it will be the worst pain you have ever felt. I do not say that to be negative because Flexer may be a wonderful boy."

"But you're saying I shouldn't be all about a boy. Same stuff my parents be sayin'."

"And they are not wrong."

"And Flexer is my mama's favorite rapper, so I know she ain't biased. Uggghhh! I'm sick."

"You need medicine?"

"No, girl, no... I'm sick, like... basically saying I'm caught between a rock and a hard place, and ain't nothing I can do about it but accept fate."

"Hmm."

"Gosh, Solana."

Maybe if I had something, anything, I would not have been so deep in with drugs and so deep in with the first man that showed genuine interest and care. She needed her things, her own things. I was happy to hear that she wanted to go to school, so I shifted the subject from the boy.

"What will you pursue in school?"

"Psychology. I'm getting into addiction studies and recovery."

"Fitting."

"Yes. I want to help people. I want to open my own clinics. And I will too."

"Si. You will, chica."

"And one day you're going to come and speak out about your recovery, but tell them I helped you, not Italian."

I chuckled. "I will. But you no like Italian?"

"No... He's annoying. I mean, he cute and all, but I got a whole rapper. What I'ma do with Italian? I mean, he ain't broke or nothing, and be calling himself buying me stuff, but he just my friends' lil' cousin. Plus, he seems like he would be too obsessed if I ever gave him a try. I'm straight. I like my space."

"But I thought you wanted to be in your boyfriend's skin?"

"And do. But he's Flexerrrrr. It's a difference."

Riiiing Riiiing

"Here. Take this."

I finally lifted my body from the ground, almost feeling lighter after that talk. Mahzeyah's pink manicured hand with gold bracelets was through the slot. When she opened her hand, it revealed a pill.

"This is another ibuprofen. They are for my cramps, but since my mama put me on birth control, I don't need them as much."

"It's okay..." I was eager to feel better, and the last pill had made me feel almost normal, but I didn't think it was a good idea after the robot said I could swap one addiction for another.

Riiing Riiiing

"Take it, Solana. It's nothing but strong Tylenol. You can't get addicted... Do you feel... full?"

"Yes." My eyes were on the singular pill as if it were my beacon of hope.

"That's the weight of the craving. The weight of the guilt from wanting to indulge. If you want to feel weightless, take this. I'll be back later. This is my mom calling."

She turned her hand over, dropping the pill before the slot closed. I got on my hands and knees, crawling toward the pill. Once I was hovering over it, I scooped it in my hand and tossed it back. Grabbing the half-full bottle of water, I swallowed it down and tossed the now-empty plastic aside. Having the urge to pee, I crawled into the bathroom, each movement sending shockwaves of pain through my limbs.

Pushing the door open with my left palm, I paused before I could make it to the toilet. My body was tired, and I knew if I didn't feel so worn down, I would actually feel the pain in my knees from crawling around. My pee would have to wait until I gathered myself before attempting to lift my body from the floor. Resting my head on my forearms for a second, I looked back up to see if there was a bottle of water near me and within arm's reach. The journal was there, as if waiting for me to get back. Forgetting about the water, I scooped it up into my hands and opened it.

I needed a distraction while waiting to see if the pill worked.

I've had bad days with my family. Awful ones. But today was downright horrific. I'm so ashamed. And what makes matters worse is the one thing that brought on the chain of events is the one thing that I've just done before writing today.

"So you're telling me no?"

Unable to stand on my feet after hitting a bump, I was leaning on the counter while Shannon washed dishes. While she was doing house chores, she was perfectly made-up in an olive green dress that flared at the calves and stiletto pumps. The wives always had to look put together, but heels weren't required. Shannon loved her pumps; that was the first thing I noticed about her. Watching the way her hair bounced against her neck as she scrubbed the dishes, my cock grew stiff in my slacks. I needed my wife now, and I didn't care if it was in the middle of the day.

She set the clean dish on the drying rack with too much force, causing it to clank against the other wet dishes. Foamy suds covered the latex gloves she was wearing, which were also ironically green.

"I'm telling you hell no. You better not fucking touch me, Sandro!"

This was where I should have stopped. I should have stopped and gone into my office, but I was high. High out of my mind, and my wife's rejection stung.

"I cannot touch you, but you fuck Niccoli. You fuck Benito. You fuck—"

"I don't fuck any of them. I am raped! I am raped by them! I am raped by them because my husband tricked me into a life that I never wanted! So, no, I have enough white men jumping in and out of my pussy. I'm not in the mood for another."

"Why?"

Tossing the dish back into the sink, I watched as the water dripped down the cabinet. Shannon gripped the ledge of the sink and dropped her head. Her sharp and bare shoulders looked good enough to suck on. It had been a minute since I tasted my wife, and despite the sinful things her body had gone through, she always tasted so heavenly.

"Why, Sandro?" She lifted her head and looked at me. There weren't tears in her eyes, no, Shannon was too strong of a woman, so she barely cried. But there was defeat in them. Still, the drugs had me seeing what I wanted, and that was a wife who was not willing to please her husband when she'd done the very thing for my family.

"Because with you, I at least have a choice in that manner. I don't have to worry about being beaten or raped against my will. I have a choice with you, Sandro, because somewhere deep down, you have some good in you. So, please, let me get back to my dishes. I would hate for your cousin or brothers to come over and see the house isn't tidy and make me suck dick before blacking my eye and forcing me to clean after. All the while you sit in the office and pretend you don't hear." She rolled her eyes and went back to washing dishes.

Standing from the counter, I placed myself behind her, moved her hair over, and licked the back of her neck. She stiffened underneath me, but I didn't care. She tasted so good. Smelled even better. Running my hand up the back of her thigh, I lifted her dress.

"Sandro, no."

"Fuuck, I love—"

My body jerked and flew into the opposite counter before I could finish my sentence.

Shio stood above me, but his facial expression was neutral. He didn't look mad or angry. He just looked like... Shio. That was him as of late. No emotion. The only time he showed emotion was with his mother and his cousins. With me, I got nothing. He barely looked my way.

"Son. It's okay. When two people are in love, things happen. How do you think you got here?"

"Don't touch my mother."

He took a step in my direction, and Shannon pulled her gloves off. "Shio, iska daa. Mar dambe ima taaban doono. (Leave it. He won't touch me again.)"

He turned his head but kept his gaze locked on me. That was another thing I was starting to despise. Shannon often spoke to Shio in her native tongue, but I never saw him speak it back. He always understood her, though, and I didn't like that. I, too, spoke in my native language, but we vowed to never teach the wives and children because it gave us an advantage—at least that is what Benito felt.

"Yes, son. Go play. I know I am." I struggled getting up as Shio walked around me. "That's right, son. Listen to your father."

Standing fully, I looked in the direction of Shio as he walked toward my office. When I started to follow after him, Shannon tried to grab me, but I shook her off.

"Shio!"

I was struggling to keep up, but when I saw him come from the office with my black box and enter the bathroom across from it, all of the high went away.

With the strength of a superhuman, I made it to the bathroom in one second flat. "What the fuck are you doing, boy?"

Shio held the box over the toilet and began emptying its contents. I launched forward and grabbed him, but it was too late. He had tossed the entire box inside the toilet. I snatched him, but he snatched back, slipping, and once he hit the ground, my feet were against his chest before I knew what I was doing. I was still high, even though I could focus more now, so I knew I was using all of my strength. Even with him struggling to breathe, he didn't squirm against me. He didn't fight against my foot either. He just lay there with the weight of a grown man, robbing him of his breath.

Looking into the toilet, my heart dropped seeing my drugs floating.

"Ti voglio bene figlio mio, ma ti ucciderò se osi toccare di nuovo le mie cose. (I love you, son, but I will kill you if you ever touch my things again.)"

I smiled while not letting my foot up, the weight still making it hard for him to breathe. His mom had her language, and I had mine. He didn't know what I was saying, and that gave me a sense of pride that I shouldn't be feeling when it came to my son. He should've been my pride and joy.

Shio blinked, grabbed my foot, and twisted it in an unnatural position.

"Arrrrghhhh!" Hot pain shot up my leg instantly.

"Se osi toccare di nuovo mia madre, non dovrai preoccuparti di uccidermi. Perché prima ti ammazzo io, spacciandoti per qualcun altro. (If you put your hands on my mother again, you won't have to worry about killing me. Because I'll kill your high ass first.)

He let my foot go with a shrug and then lifted himself up from the bathroom floor. My ankle was hurting, but I knew once the drugs wore off, it would be a lot worse.

"The next time one of your nasty-ass family members touch my mama, you gone be the one to pay for it. On foe 'nem."

He left me in the bathroom, high, confused, and now afraid. The boy was becoming a man. And I was his public enemy number one. But above all, I realized that my son, a child that had come from me, was too fucking smart and calculated for his own good, because when and how did he learn to speak Italian?

The heart of man plans his way, but the Lord establishes his steps. – Proverbs 16:9

The Lord was establishing my boy's steps. I just didn't want him stepping all over mine.

Closing the book, I did what I normally did when I read an excerpt written by Shio's father: picked up the phone.

> Shio. I... I don't know how to do this. But I'm trying. I will get better. You will see. I hope you are staying safe, and remember, today is meal prep day.

I THEN REMEMBERED a scripture from the Bible that I read yesterday and sent that.

> The Lord's curse is on the house of the wicked, but he blesses the dwelling of the righteous. Toward the scorners he is scornful, but to the humble he gives favor. The wise will inherit honor, but fools get disgrace.

I COULDN'T REMEMBER the chapter and verse, so I left that off. Knowing he wouldn't reply, I locked the screen as a tear slid down my face. I didn't know if I was crying because I felt weightless or because I was beginning to hate Shio's father with everything in me.

LIGHTHEARTED

"P issss cute, Pearla!"

I was lying on my side at the door so that I had a clear view of Pearla through the slot, who was also on her side with her eyes locked on mine. She pulled her phone back after showing me a picture of P. He appeared to be in a tuxedo at some sort of formal event, but he was handsome either way.

"Yeah... I couldn't find any pictures of him online. This came from Jisei's photo album from the wedding last year. He's worse than Grind with this no digital footprint mess," she mumbled the last sentence, and as soon as it escaped her lips, the amusement left.

"You still care deeply for Grind."

Pearla rolled her eyes and looked off past me. It wasn't much she could see from our position, just as it wasn't much I could see outside of her face, but she kept her eyes away from mine for a beat.

"I don't want to."

"But you do."

"He doesn't deserve it."

Pulling my knees to my chest, I pressed my face into them. "A lot of people don't deserve things, Pearla. That doesn't stop them from getting them. You can't just turn your feelings off."

"I wish I could."

So do I.

"So what now?" I asked.

Pearla had been excited about P. He'd been upstairs, apparently, along with another friend of Italian's for the many days I'd been here. I'd even heard them a time or two somewhere down here playing dice, but the slot was never opened when they were down here. He looked like a nice boy, which would pair perfectly with Pearla because she was a nice girl.

"I don't know... I don't want to move fast. Both of us are healing. He had a girlfriend. I had a... uh... Grind. But he's cool. And he got money." She giggled.

"You and Mahzeyah with the 'he got money' about these boys. Like you all don't come from money." I giggled.

"I don't come from money. You wouldn't believe it by looking at me, but this time last year, my sister was struggling to make my payments for my braces. Struggling to keep me at my school. Nel, Rio, my dad, my brother... They were all heaven-sent. They say a lot can happen in a year, and while the saying is one we sometimes brush over, I know for a fact it is true."

"I'm so sorry you went through that... Not having money to prosper."

Pearla had told me every detail of the shooting that had Grind in a coma, and my heart went out to her. In turn, I told her about the shootout Shio and I had been in. We exchanged a secret for a secret, and although I shouldn't have been telling that to a teenager, I wanted her to feel comfortable talking to me.

"You really like Shio."

"Si." The admission hurt. It was the only thing about me hurting today.

"I know you think you're not good enough, Solana, but you are. My nephew, Neltz, is a really good judge of character. He likes you. But, then again, he liked Grind too. Ugggh! I have to stop saying his name."

"It's okay to say his name. It's okay to love him, Pearla."

"I don't want to love him, though," she whispered.

"I know..."

She shook her head and turned onto her back. I was now looking at her side profile as she looked at what I figured was the ceiling.

"You're kind. Patient. Understanding. You're a good listener, and you're not judgmental. I know it has to be hard being here, in a whole other country, eating our foods and hearing our slang. Then, you're locked in a room and battling an addiction, and we come down here every day bothering you."

"You're not bothering me. I welcome the distraction, and I enjoy all of you."

Pearla swallowed and let the silence settle between us. I was trying my hardest not to think about Shio today. I hadn't texted him. I hadn't read the journal either. I had been feeling much better these days, and I wanted to stay that way.

"You are good enough, Solana."

Pearla turned her head to face me, her eyes glowing with tears, prompting mine to do the same. I reached my hand through the slot, and she clasped it in hers.

I smiled at her. She was so pretty and kind. I believed Pearla deserved all that was good in this country—in this world.

"You're good enough, Pearla. I will say, I think there is much more to the story with Grind and Kaylee. I have learned that sometimes, desperate times calls for desperate measures. People make decisions that you would never have thought they ever would when their backs are against the roof."

Pearla giggled. "You mean, the wall, Solana. When their backs are against the wall."

I giggled too. "Si. Against the wall."

I blinked away the tears and welcomed the laugh. It didn't hurt as much to laugh now. I thought about the deals my father signed with the devil countless times for money or power. Our entire family was either dead or incarcerated because he chose himself out of desperation over and over again.

Pearla gasped as if she had a revelation. "Oh, Lord. You're team Grind, hunh?"

I squeezed her hand, placed it to my lips, and then my face. "I'm team you. You're good enough, Pearla. You actually more than good enough."

"I don't know if you want kids or not, but you're going to make a great mom."

"Maybe..."

"You have to come to my graduation, Solana."

"Of course." I didn't know where life would take me by the time she graduated, but I'd make sure I was there.

"And prom! Oooo! I want you to help me pick out a dress and everything."

"Oh, I can see you in a pretty lavender."

Pearla snatched her hand back, her eyes wide with shock. "O.M.G. How did you know that was my favorite color?"

Her mouth was open wide, not thinking about the bands around her bracelets being lavender. She also wore lavender-studded earrings. The color looked good against her brown skin.

"Lucky guess." I shrugged with a smirk.

"I know you don't like being in here, but I'm glad you're here. I haven't been... myself. But around you, I feel... lighter. *Carefree.* Almost like my old self before everything happened. I just want to be happy again, but I don't know what happy looks like now."

"Happy is whatever feels good to you, Pearla. It doesn't have to be your previous happy. It can be a new happy."

"I know you care for Shio, just like I care for Grind, but let's make a promise pact." She held her pinky out. "We have to find happiness outside of them—outside of boys. Boys make you depressed. They make life not worth living. A boy almost made me hate this city. At one point, I hated to breathe. We can't be that way. So, us first—"

I locked my pinky in hers. "And boys second?"

"Nope. Third. Friends and family second."

We locked our pinkies together tighter.

"*Trato.* (Deal)."

"No summertime sadness. We too fine for that." She perked up her lips, and I smiled at her sass.

I nodded. "We are. No summertime sadness."

A grin spread across Pearla's face as our pinkies stayed locked. "Don't tell my sister, but Shio is going to end up with *the perfect* wife."

My body stiffened.

Pearla winked. "You."

I felt my cheeks flush with warmth. "You just said boys third, Pearla. And I'm nobody's wife, especially Shio's."

"*Boys* are third, but Shio is a man. And you will be his wife."

I had no reply, so I lay there, holding her hand via pinky, while silence settled again. After a few seconds, we both erupted into a fit of giggles. We laughed so hard that it turned into tears.

"Pearla, I have to grab a water. I'm thirsty."

She let my pinky go, and I stood. I hadn't been able to do that with such ease days ago. Grabbing the bottle of water off the dresser, I looked at the painting above the TV while I sipped. There was a black dot that I hadn't seen before. Standing on my tippy toes, I tried getting a better look, but it was no use because it was too high up.

"Solanaaaaa..."

Taking another swig of the water, I placed it back on the dresser and looked back at the painting. It was covered in swirls of white textured paint, which was why the black dot above it stood out. Shrugging it off when Pearla called my name again, I walked back to the door. Taking my place back on the ground, I lay down like Pearla and stared at the white ceiling. It wasn't an uncomfortable white anymore. Pearla went back to talking about her upcoming senior year, and I listened with glee, admiring the lives of these younger humans.

Today had been the first good day since I'd been in the room. No pain. No mental battle. No yearning for Shio. No cocaine craving. Just Pearla and me having some good girl talk that I never had before coming to the States. I wouldn't even be opening the journal today. I wanted to relish this feeling. I knew if I read Sandro's writing, I would probably revert back to summertime sadness.

I will overcome this addiction. This addiction will not get the best of me. I am bigger than my addiction. I am in control.

CHAPTER 22
SHIO CUPPACIO

Three hundred sixteen... seventeen... eighteen... nineteen... three hundred twenty.

Three hundred twenty bricks, stacked in piles of twenty, sat in front of me. The pure white cocaine that had been making us richer every day lined the back wall. I'd counted the kilos at least a hundred times, and no matter how many times I repeated my count, the number hadn't changed. The numbers wouldn't change. It had been three hundred twenty when they were delivered personally by Goal himself a few hours ago, and it would be three hundred twenty even if I counted it a hundred and one times.

There was a long list of shit weighing on me. My body was craving rest, but my mind was telling me I could do that when I was dead. This count was accurate, but nothing else in my life was aligned in the same way. For starters, bringing the product to this cabin was wrong. It was bad enough that I had a prisoner in the basement, and adding enough white to send me to the chair was a bad judgment call. However, that was all I had to work with. I was so against the shit that Goal himself insisted on delivering it. Don had been anal about us keeping shit tight with the police sniffing around about the missing women and kids, but money still had to be made. I knew better than to store the product in our stash houses. They were reserved for money only, and having both in the same places was a recipe for disaster, so the cabin was the only option.

Pulling my burner phone from my pocket, I sent a text to Ezio letting him know all was well. He responded immediately, which meant my work here was done. Nel would come to collect the product for distribution tomorrow. It would take him a span of a week, so he'd probably do it every other day, but again, we were pivoting from our usual routines to safeguard our freedom.

I adjusted the mask on my face. Goal's cocaine was straight from Colombia, and handling so many kilos of this shit, even sealed tightly, was risky. The masks we wore weren't that COVID-19 shit that was always out of stock on the pharmacy shelves a few years ago. I insisted we get specialty masks that filtered the air before it reached our nostrils when handling this shit. With this type of mask, I could be in the presence of a nuclear bomb and still breathe in fresh oxygen.

Solana's phone buzzed, and going against my instincts, I removed my gloves and swiped the screen.

SOLANA

I feel okay today. The last time I felt okay was when I was with you, Shio. I know it's not right, to want you. I shouldn't replace it with you. Not healthy, but it's the truth.

Like clockwork, Solana's text message came through, following the pattern she'd created over the last few days. She'd been sending texts, sometimes expressing her feelings, other times revealing her past. She was so much bigger than the drugs. The texts she sent me were heavy. They were so fucking heavy with the spiraling and learning how she became what she was. She'd broken a part of herself, all for cocaine. A drug. The same drug that I'd counted a hundred times today alone. The same drug that had made my family and me rich. It had a fucking hold on her. Every day that she sent a text, it further proved that she wasn't ready to be any man's wife. She wouldn't have lasted a day with the Rodríguezes. Knowing what I know now about them, I don't think he ever had intentions of truly marrying her. Beauty like Solana's was a rare occurrence. God only sprinkled one of her every few hundred years. They were going to make a killing off of her, and her being addicted to drugs would've only made it easier for them.

The camera app had been my worst fucking enemy. I'd seen Solana nearly die at least twice, tweak out every single day, pray until her knees bled, and scream like her lungs were just as pure as her pussy. She was fighting demons. Shit, she might've been fighting the Devil himself.

Picking up the brick of cocaine, I held it in one hand and the phone with the text message displayed on the screen in the other.

I shouldn't replace it with you. Not healthy, but it's the truth.

This fucking cocaine.

Why couldn't she just shake this shit? Why did God have to place a woman in my path who was fighting more demons than all of us Cuppacios combined? Feeling my hand tense, the brick cracked down the center, not breaking through the Saran Wrap.

With my thumb hovering over the screen, I typed out a reply.

> You letting this shit consume you Solana. You letting this shit get the best of you. If you not willing to let it go then what the fuck you want me to do? I can't shake it for you. Stop fucking texting and start praying.

THE SAME THUMB that had typed the message now hovered over the send button. But instead of sending it, I deleted the entire message. This girl—this fucking girl—she wasn't good for me. She wasn't good for no nigga. Yet, here she was on my fucking brain like a tumor. The same way she couldn't shake the drugs was the same way I couldn't shake her ass.

I had some pussy lying up in my home, willing and ready, but I wouldn't even touch it. I knew part of the reason was because Bahati wasn't *her*. But I refused to admit that shit aloud, and that plagued me more.

"Fuuuuuuuck!"

Tossing the brick at the wall, I watched it shatter before powder flew everywhere.

"Fucking cocaine! This the shit that got her fucking tweaking?"

Grabbing another brick, I repeated the motion. Before I knew it, my count began drastically decreasing as I grabbed another and another and another, creating a dusty mess that would've been a dream to Solana.

"She... She ain't what I fucking need! She ain't what I fucking need!"

If it weren't for the mask, Nel would walk in tomorrow and find my ass dead from an overdose. There was a white haze in the air, and I could no longer see in front of me. I went to reach for another and nearly slipped on the residue coating the floor. Still, that didn't stop me from finding my way to the piles again, not giving one fuck that I was destroying hundreds of thousands of dollars of product.

With my chest heaving, head pounding, and muscles aching, I was furious. Furious at her vulnerability to a fucking drug. Furious that it had been weeks of her being locked in Jisei's basement.

"It could have been anybody! Anybody!" My knees hit the floor, and my arms dropped as my head hung. "Every assignment you've thrown my way. I've completed every assignment you've thrown at me. I've been obedient. I've been loyal. I've been honest. I've been disciplined. But..."

I looked up at the ceiling, needing an answer. "Why her, God? Hunh? This shit ain't funny. The same—" My head dropped again, me struggling to find the words. "She got the same fuckin' addiction my father had. She thought she was gonna love me in secret like that bitch-ass nigga? She thought she was gone be able to have them drugs and me? Had she not learned enough living in my fuckin' house? My house!"

My chest heaved aggressively, and my lack of breath were not from the tiny specks that still floated down on me.

"Why the fuck you give me a bitch that's addicted to cocaine? You gave me a fuckin' coward. Slick and sneaky. You gave me my father in female form. Why do that shit to me?"

Boom! Boom! Boom!

I could feel the tremor in my knees from the banging. Covered in powder from head to toe, I stood carefully not to bust my ass. Keeping the mask in place, I trudged across the room. Some of the cocaine particles were still floating in the air, but most of it had created a thick blanket on the floor. Typing the code into the panel that granted me access to downstairs, I nearly sprinted down them.

"Woah! Woah! Fuck you lookin' like a big-ass abdominal snowman for?"

Hobo had the railing from the bed in his hand and must've been hitting the ceiling with it.

"What the"

Grabbing him by his neck, I rammed him into the brick wall. He'd been taking care of his hygiene, so he wasn't sour, thankfully. I wouldn't have been able to smell him through the mask anyway, but I didn't want to be in no dirty motherfucker's presence. He'd been brushing his big chicklet-ass teeth, too, judging by the dried toothpaste at the crease of his mouth.

"I don't know if you know this, but you way past your fuckin' expiration date. You're fed, housed, and clothed. The way I see it, you more put up than these bitches out here."

Hobo was gasping for air, and when I began to see the whites of his eyes, I let him go. He dropped to the floor like a rag doll, coughing roughly.

"What the fuck, bruh? I was just tryna call you down here to tell you the hot water ain't working." Hobo grabbed his neck.

"Nigga, do I look like the fuckin' plumber?"

Hobo scooted backward, not having anywhere to go since the wall was behind him. "Aite, aite! Damn. You know if my people been lookin' for me? My mama—"

"Nigga, yo' mama dead!"

"I... I meant my brothers."

They were dead too. I didn't divulge that information to him, though. His mother had died when he was a jit. His brothers' demises were compliments of the mob. Neltz wanted his daddy alive; he didn't say shit about the rest of the lineage.

"Hobo." I was at my wits' end and would fuck around and kill this nigga too.

"Aite, damn. Angry-ass nigga! And is that cocaine?"

Stiffening, it dawned on me that I'd fucked up. It was bad enough that the two of them were in one place. I was moving recklessly, and it was all because of this girl in my fucking frontal.

"Go sit and think about your fucked up ways, Hobo."

"Man, you on some other shit."

Turning my back, daring the nigga to pull some shit, I ran back up the stairs. I hadn't brought him any food today, but Nel could do so tomorrow. Knowing his petty ass, he'd let the man starve, so I made a mental note to tell him to take Hobo's ass some food.

"Don't come down here mad at me 'cause the bitch done pissed you off. I know the look of a nigga in his fuckin' feelings. Get out of 'em. Ain't no money there."

"Says the nigga who in the basement because of one."

Hobo chuckled. "Why you think I'm sayin' the shit?"

Closing the door, I locked him inside, not bothering to respond. Leaving the mess, I marched out of the cabin, hearing the door lock itself behind me. Hopping in my truck, I pushed the pedal to the metal, not giving a fuck about the speed limit.

The colorful array of cars I bypassed, the streetlights, and the buildings all went by in a blur. I was in no predicament to be running red lights, ignoring stop signs, and neglecting to use signal lights, but I wasn't in the headspace to care.

Parking, I left the truck running and jumped out. I knocked on the door until it swung open. Italian's face fell and the pistol in his hand lowered. He let me in but stuck his head out the door. Not waiting for him to ask questions, I moved through the living room, which was empty—a rare sight. It was usually packed with teens, doing all kinds of shit they shouldn't be doing. But at their age, we were doing far worse. It was a blessing my cousins and I didn't end up with a bunch of damn kids.

Sticking the key in the metal door, I pushed it open. The bed wasn't made, but there was no trash on the floor. Two empty water bottles were on the nightstand, along with a half-drunk glass bottle of Coke. There were a few pieces of clothing strewn about, but that was to be expected. I stood there not knowing why the fuck I was here to begin with. The bathroom door opened, and Solana peeked her head from out of it. The camera—the camera had done her no fucking justice. She looked a mess, but I swear, she was a mess in the most beautiful of ways. Her hair was braided at the front while the rest was in a ball at the top of her head. A few pieces framed her edges, making her appear innocent, and she was anything but that.

"Shio?" She blinked multiple times before pulling her head back inside the bathroom.

I heard shuffling, and instead of kicking the fucking door down because I knew what she'd been doing in the bathroom at my house, I waited. A few seconds later, she walked fully from the space into the bedroom.

Stopping a few steps away from me, she tilted her head and asked, "Shio, is it really you?"

She squinted her eyes and then folded her arms across her chest. The oversized shirt she wore covered her torso but left her chocolate thighs exposed. My dick bricked instantly. She was still looking at me as if she couldn't believe I was standing here. Shit, I couldn't believe I was standing here.

I pulled the mask from my face, letting it fall to the floor. Her eyes shifted from my face to my arms, still covered in cocaine residue. I saw the demons dancing in her face, but I also saw the fight. It was new, something I had rarely seen on the camera. I'd seen and heard her converse with the young Cuppacios and their friends, but it had only been a couple of days of that shit. It wasn't enough to prove her being ready for the world outside these walls.

Come get it. Show me what I already know. Show me you ain't for me. Show me you ain't ready.

She approached me slowly, her perfectly arched feet softly landing on the carpet with each step. A pretty little sinner who was pretty as fuck while battling a drug addiction. I held my ground as she got closer. I wasn't going to stop her. I wasn't going to ask her to fight the drug that had her by the edges. The drug was all over my body. Nothing was stopping her from running her nose all up and down my arms because I sure as hell wouldn't stop her. If she wanted to get high, I'd stand there and let her see how much she could inhale from my skin. If she wanted to rid herself of this shit, like my mama said, she'd have to do the shit on her own.

Her soft hand grabbed my wrist, pulling me toward the bathroom. She led me straight to the shower, keeping my arm in hers while she set the temperature. Steam covered the ceiling immediately, and I knew Hobo would've nutted up at the sight.

She pulled my shirt over my head. Once my shirt was on the floor, I snatched her into my chest, grabbing her face.

"Sh...Shio, please. You have it all over you." Her eyes roamed my face and then dropped down to my thumb that was running across her cheek.

"Want me to put it on your lips?" I ran my thumb underneath her bottom lip, which trembled in response.

"Shio," she whispered.

With my thumb, I pulled her chin down, opening her mouth. "Want me to rub it across your gums?"

She huffed and snatched away from me. My arms dropped to my side while she took a beat before looking back at me, slight annoyance on her face.

"*Déjame terminar de desvestirte.* (Let me finish undressing you.)"

She squatted, reaching for the waistband of my pants. Her soft, trembling fingers brushed against my skin as she lowered them, and it felt good. With my pants and underwear down, my dick sprang to attention, sweeping against the side of her face.

I could see the top of her eyelashes fluttering as she stared at the one thing I knew without a doubt she wasn't ready for.

"Aye..." She lifted her head but shifted her eyes back to my dick before I could finish my statement. "Don't start speaking that shit. Aite?"

Her eyes looked so round from this position. I watched her lashes sweep against her cheek before nodding. I stepped out of my boxers and got into the shower. I watched her through the glass as she stood from the squatted position and grabbed the back of her neck. Her shirt rose up again, and I cursed under my breath even though I couldn't stop looking at her. She did a quick pace and then shook her head before stepping to the vanity. She bent over, opened the cabinets, and grabbed something. When her hand came into view, she held a new bar of soap and a loofah. She walked over and stuck her hand in the shower, wetting the loofah as hot water cascaded over me. She pressed the loofah to my chest and began rubbing in circular motions. Before the suds could form, I snatched her into the shower completely, being careful not to hurt her. She was fully clothed in an oversized T-shirt and some mint green panties that her ass ate up underneath. I'd gotten a glimpse when she bent over, and it was now implanted as a core memory.

"Shio..."

I wanted to be at home. But when I was home, I wanted to be anywhere but there. When I wasn't there, I was in my fucking phone watching Solana like some creep-ass nigga. She was in my thoughts, in my prayers, and in every move I'd made since her ass showed up in my fucking house. God knew I didn't want her to be, but that was just what the fuck it was.

Pressing my forehead to hers, I inhaled her scent. The Dove was strong, but Solana's fragrant odor was stronger.

"Shio."

"Don't. Talk."

She nodded her forehead against mine and proceeded to wash me. The water poured over my skin and onto her. The exfoliant of the loofah and her wet shirt clinging to her curvy body all caused different feelings. The heat was loosening my tight muscles, making them heavy and relaxed, but the water pouring onto Solana's face made those same muscles tighten back up. Water droplets from her lashes shouldn't have been as sexy as they were. The loofah running over my shoulders and down my back shouldn't have felt like a match, burning a trail beneath my skin.

"Why... Why, Solana?"

"Shio—"

Grabbing her waist, I flipped her body around, pressing her back into my naked frame. "Shut up. I said don't talk."

The loofah was still in her hand, so she began to run it up my thigh. Grabbing the hem of her soggy shirt, I pulled it over her head and flung it, and it hit the glass with a *thwack*. She was braless and now in nothing but her mint green panties.

"Why?" I ran my hand across her chest, going from shoulder to shoulder as water bounced off her round, proportional titties. "Speak."

"Why, what, Shio?"

I wanted to be mad that she couldn't read my mind, but I'd be confused as fuck if I'd been begging for someone to talk to me and they show up the way I had. I moved my hand over her wet skin up to her neck. Wrapping my fingers and squeezing just enough for her to let out a soft whimper, I pulled her closer to me, her ass planted firmly against my dick.

"Why you need to replace the drugs, Solana? Why can't you just not need shit?"

"I...They make me feel good, Shio."

Keeping my left hand around her neck, I ran my right hand down the middle of her breasts. She tensed against my body, ass still pressed against the tip of my dick.

"How good?" My hand was now groping her right breast, my fingers purposely missing the nipple.

She gasped. "Y...Yeah!"

"That didn't answer my question, Solana. How good does cocaine make you feel?"

"R-Real good..."

"You've barely experienced life, baby. You don't know what good feels like. You think it makes you feel better than I can?"

She nodded and then shook her head to change her answer to no. I gave her left breast the same attention, again purposely missing the nipple.

"Shio..."

"Shut up."

Squeezing her neck, I waited until I could feel the faint beat of her carotid artery before I dove into her soiled panties. Using my foot, I kicked her legs apart as my fingers found her bare lips. She had shaved probably more than a week ago because her hairs were razor sharp, showing the new growth. Still, I split the lips and began rubbing her clitoris while holding the pressure on her neck with my firm grip.

"Oh God!" The loofah dropped, and she dug her nails into my forearm as I dipped down and pressed my face against the side of hers.

"If I made you come off a kiss, imagine what I could do with my hands. With my mouth. With my dick."

She was so fucking wet, and I hadn't gone anywhere near her pussy hole. Her bud was hardening as I flicked it back and forth. Pressing her head into my shoulder, she panted through the small breaths she could take.

I squeezed her neck again, cutting the last one short. "You think that shit can make you feel better than this?"

Her knees began to buckle as I sped up my movements.

"No... No! Nooooo!"

"I don't think you're being truthful. Just a pretty little fuckin' liar."

"Shioooooo! I'm... I—"

"Let that shit go!"

Her body bucked so much that I had to tighten my grip on her neck again to prevent her from falling forward. Letting go of her neck, I didn't give her time to recover before I flipped her around and lifted her up. Wrapping her legs around my waist, her tingling pussy sat on my stomach, panties still in place. If they weren't, and she'd been any lower, I'd slip inside. She rested her arms on my shoulder as I hoisted her higher. With her breasts in my face, I ran my tongue down the nipple of the right one.

"Ahhhhh!" She tossed her head back as steam rose around us. Spreading my hands across her back while her ass rested in the bend of my arms, I drew the pebbled nipple into my mouth.

"Ohhhh!"

I began french-kissing her nipple as she tightened her legs around me, as if they were steel cables being pulled taut. Letting the breast go with a pop, I blew on it before sucking it back into my mouth. Rolling her nipple between my teeth, I enjoyed the sound of her hissing as her middle heated my stomach. When I was satisfied, I gave the other breast the exact same treatment, not missing a step.

Lick. Suck. Pop. Blow. Suck. Nibble.

Her legs began to shake.

"Release it, Solana."

"Ahhhhhh!"

Her weight leaned us forward, but I didn't move much. I benched twice as much as Solana. I could hold her up in this position for at least an hour. I watched as she came undone, her nipple still in my mouth, not letting go until her legs stopped shaking. When I felt she could stand again, I put her on her feet and swooped up the loofah. I turned her around, her ass back to my front, and grabbed the bar soap. Lathering the loofah, I began dragging the sponge across her skin. Lifting her right arm, I ran it down the front and then the back, leaving a trail of soap. When it ran down her armpits, she shuddered.

Ticklish.

Doing the same with the other arm, her breathing heightened. I rubbed it across her belly and the top of her thighs.

"Ummmmm. Feels good."

"Solana, you have no fuckin' idea, baby."

"Shio... I... I want to know."

"No you don't." I continued dragging the loofah over her body slowly. The more I washed, the shorter her breathing became. "If you wanted to know, you wouldn't have done that shit in my fucking house. Now, release it."

"Ohhhh, Shiiiioooo!" Her head hit my shoulder while I grabbed her across the waist as she came again. A fucking loofah had her coming out of her body, and I could do nothing but shake my head.

"Talkin' 'bout *it* make you feel good."

Pushing her top half forward, I kept her ass pressed against my hardened dick. She looked so fucking good bent over in front of me. Squeezing her hips, I circled my pelvis against her ass twice.

"You three-and-oh, Solana, baby."

"Shio... I—I'm sorry."

I squeezed her waist. "You not, but you gone be. Get out."

She trembled as she stood upright and stepped out of the shower. I turned the dial on the shower wall, stopping the water. When I stepped out, I snatched one of the two towels from the hook and handed it to her.

"Dry off."

Solana's eyes were heavy with lust and worry as she rubbed the towel around her body. She then wrapped it around her and stepped out of her panties once she was fully covered. She nodded and turned, but before she could get far, I pulled at her towel.

"Hmm?"

"Face down. Ass up."

She gasped as I let her go, and she all but ran out of the bathroom. Closing the door, I wrapped the second towel around my waist and leaned over the vanity. With my hands planted on the granite, I couldn't see myself clearly due to the fog.

Just leave, Shio. The drugs. She won't be able to let go of the drugs.

Ignoring that voice in my head, I stood, pulling open the drawers of the vanity. Once all of them were open and all I saw was toothpaste, floss, and hair scrunchies, I closed them back. Going to my pants that were still covered in cocaine, I emptied everything onto the counter and tossed them into the shower. Turning the water back on, I left the pants to soak before stepping to the sink. I grabbed one of the items that I pulled from my pocket and walked out of the bathroom. Solana was on the floor, and she was face down and ass up, but in a worship position.

This girl.

"Are we praying, Shio?"

"Solana... On the bed, baby."

Holding my hand out, she placed hers in mine, and I helped her onto the bed. Of course, she kept the towel tied together as I positioned her body on the bed. Her hair was soaked, but that didn't matter as it fell around her face. The towel couldn't hide anything as she bent over the bed, her round ass stealing the show. Her pussy was glistening, and her asshole was winking at me. Just weeks ago, I was looking forward to seeing her just like this.

Not able to help myself, I slapped her fat ass. The ripples her cheeks made had my mouth watering. She tried to lean up, and I smacked her ass again.

"Face down. Ass up, Solana, baby."

She resumed the position, and I kneeled behind her. I ran my tongue down the crack of her ass, and she flattened on the bed. I folded my arm around her waist and brought her back upright, using my other hand to arch her back.

"Stay in position."

Grabbing the bottle I'd brought from the bathroom, I sprayed it over my head and again over her back, letting it mist on her skin. My dick was already a brick, but I swear, it got harder. Her dark skin and the curves along her back were sexy as fuck. The soft hum she made as the mist rested against her skin sent a shiver through me. Solana didn't understand her power, but it wasn't for me to show her. She could probably bring many men to their knees—a modern-day Judith, but I refused to let her ass behead me with her nasty ways. I needed her to shake the drug habit before I even considered her being more than the woman I had locked in Jisei's basement. Until then, I'd give her a little push to get her shit together.

"Shio..." she whispered. She didn't move, but the whine in her voice told me enough.

"I need to smell you, Solana."

Placing the bottle on the floor next to me, I swiped my tongue up her ass again, making her body jerk. I lifted her body abruptly as if she were a barbell, fell back onto the bed, and then lowered her so that my head rested under her moist pussy. I pulled the towel away, and she stiffened. I'm sure the cool air, plus the new view she had of my dick, sent her into a temporary shock. We were in a position as if we were about to sixty-nine, but I wasn't expecting Solana to do anything; I just wanted her to see what she was doing to me. Although we'd never gotten this far before, she smelled like déjà vu, and this situation felt like fate. She smelled like everything I'd ever craved had been wrapped up and stuffed inside of her ass, and this situation felt like it would happen again before it truly even started.

Deciding to leave her asshole alone for now, I pushed my entire face into her mound. My nose was between her ass crack as I lapped up her juices. I had no plans of ending my night with my face in her pussy, but we were here now. My mouth moved with precision as my tongue slithered in between her slippery folds. I was rotating between licking and sucking, swirling and plunging, all while holding her up, so she didn't plop down on my head.

Solana was making the kinds of noises I expected from a virgin, and I so wanted to stuff my dick in her to hear her take it up a notch. But she was already running from the pussy-eating I was doing. If she was running from my tongue, then she damn sure wasn't ready for the dick.

"Shioooo," she moaned.

Wap!

Her ass cheeks rippled before she flinched downward, nearly crushing my nose.

Wap!

My hand came down hard on her ass again, and she bucked against my mouth. She quivered at the tenderness of me devouring her mixed with the pain inflicted on her ass from my hand. Her pussy was warm, creamy, and clean, and outside of them sharp-ass hairs, fucking perfect. She was perfect against my fingers in the shower and perfect against my fucking mouth. I could eat her for hours, and that was the fucking problem. I could do everything for hours when it came to Solana, including watching her on my phone as if I were binge-watching a newly released Netflix series.

My thoughts spun as pleasure poured from her pussy, and the

silky feel of her nearing her breaking point shot straight down to my dick. I swallowed a wad of her gooeyness and continued my slow and steady pussy-eating. She tasted better than I thought she would.

"Ohhh! ¡Esta sucediendo! (It's happening!)"

Her legs vibrated against my head as her arms gave way, with her torso falling forward onto my stomach. I felt her hair fall over my dick and the sensation had me precumming. I thought Solana was about to start running again, but this time, she began to hump my face.

Good, Solana, baby. Chase that fucking nut.

"Come, Solana. Let me taste you," I said between slurps.

"¡Se siente bien! It... feeelss... sooooooo... Ahhhhhh!"

Spreading my mouth as wide as I could, I covered her pussy, not wanting to miss a drop. My dick was hard enough to dig up cement, and when her cum hit my tongue as I lapped away at her vagina, I swear, I wanted to bust a nut myself.

Solana would be a fucking creamer, and her release was enough to fill a pill bottle. I drank that shit happily, too—happy she didn't spray that shit out. My cousin Vello loved that shit, but I wasn't into women squirting. It was too messy, and for some women, embarrassing.

When her knees spread wider, I rolled her body off mine onto the bed so she could relax her limbs. Standing, I watched as her chest heaved and her hands rested at her navel. Solana's body was perfect. The working out we'd done in the short time before shit hit the fan had her stomach and arms toned. Looking down at her messy pussy, I licked the remnants of her from my lips as if I missed having my face in it already. It was fat. Her chocolate pussy was reddish pink on the inside and plump. Not being able to stop myself, I bent down and placed a kiss on it, causing her to jerk. Her smooth, plush thighs felt good against my head while I continued to place soft kisses on her pussy. I kneaded the flesh in my hands, causing her to moan. The moan was enough to cause me to stop and pull away—my dick was hard enough as is.

Leaving her on her back, I went to the dresser drawers, pulled out a pair of sweats, and stepped into them. I didn't replace the clothes here because I knew Solana would be able to fit everything we'd left when Ezio was here. Bella 'nem had been bringing her more girly shit lately, though, so I knew she wouldn't be wearing the T-shirt-and-sweatpants combo anymore.

"So those weren't for me?"

Grabbing a crisp white T-shirt next, I left it sitting atop the dresser as I grabbed the edge. Instead of replying, I turned back around and watched as she pulled the bed cover over her body. Her long, curly hair had fallen over her shoulders and that properly-fucked glow women had after nutting covered her. Her eyes locked on mine when she realized I didn't respond.

"You're still not talking to me, Shio?"

Crossing my arms, I licked my lips, still tasting her pussy. "What you want me to say, Solana?"

She scooted to the headboard, the covers now shielding her body. It was too late, though. I'd seen her bare, and the visual was stuck in my frontal now.

"Why did you come here if you won't speak to me?"

Because while I don't want you, my body craves you.

I sighed. "You need to focus on getting clean."

"And I have not?"

"You tell me."

Solana's eyes were downcast, and she brought her knees to her chest under the covers. "What else can I do, Shio? I'm locked in here. I have no access to the drug. Haven't seen it at all until you came in here covered in it. And even then, I didn't take a hit! So, yes, I've been ridding myself of it."

"Aite."

Picking up the shirt, I pulled it over my head before going into the bathroom. Grabbing my stuff from the counter, I placed it in the pockets and stuffed my feet into my shoes. Deciding the clothes were wet enough, I turned the shower off, looked around the bathroom one last time, and turned the lights off.

"So, that's it. You're leaving?"

"I am. Ion need real nigga rehab."

She scoffed at my snarky reply, and I felt like a fuck nigga for a second before I shook the feeling. Solana may have been something I craved, and I was fighting to keep my hands off of her, but I wasn't too gone to forget she was just snorting cocaine in my house weeks ago. I watched as she brushed a damp strand from her face. Her eyes squinted, and the attitude on her face wasn't as intimidating as she thought.

"Well, what *do* you need, Shio?" I didn't respond, letting my eyes roam her face as she continued to grow frustrated with me. "You only need to make me feel good? Like you do Uriah? Is that what brings you joy?"

"I don't eat Uriah's pussy, Solana."

"Okay, *Bahati.* She's in your home. Seems like you *love* housing girls straight out of México City."

"You want to argue, Solana?" I cocked my head. This was new, coming from her.

"I want understanding. I want to know what is next? For me... For us?"

"There is no us, Solana. It's a *you*. It's a *me*."

"Then why did you come here?!" Her voice cracked, her emotions coming forth.

I rubbed my hand down my face. I wasn't trying to upset her. "Because..."

"Because, what, Shio?"

"Because I fucks with you. I shouldn't... I damn sure ain't got no room to fuck with you. But I do. Aite?"

"What does that even mean?"

"Solana, baby... Your English ain't that fuckin' broken. I fucks with you means just that. I fucks with you."

"Do you fucks with Uriah? Bahati?"

"I do."

"Well, I don't want you to fucks with me then." She turned her face away, and her profile was just as perfect as the front view.

Chuckling, I ran my hand down my face again and internally told my dick to calm the fuck down. Everything about this fucking girl had me ready to nut up. Closing my eyes for a second, I reminded myself why Solana was down here. That was the only thing that was stopping me from dropping dick in her.

"Unfortunately, Solana, baby... You don't get to decide that," I said, widening my stance in the middle of the room.

"I do! It's my life, Shio! That's what you and my father do not understand! I can decide what I want for my life, and I have decided I do not want you to fuck with me." She crossed her arms. "¡Vete! No quiero que me jodas. (Go! I don't want you to fuck with me.)"

I clenched my jaw before swiping my nose. "Aye. Be clear, me and yo' bitch-ass daddy don't belong in the same sentence."

Silence surrounded us, and I started to walk out, but my feet wouldn't move.

"Look, Solana. I know it's your life. But—"

"But, what? But, because... What's with all the... ehh, clauses?"

"*But* you can't decide my feelings." I stared her down as she finally dragged her eyes to look at me.

"So you have feelings for me, Shio?"

"Your pussy still on my lips, Solana. What you think?"

"That means nothing."

"You lived in my house."

"Si, before you dragged me out. Bahati lives there now. Uriah has her mail addressed to your home."

"You giving Uriah way too much power."

"I saw you with her! You love her."

"I don't love shit! You saw me gettin' my dick wet! That's what the fuck you saw. And her fuckin' mail is addressed there because her husband used to own the house. I bought the house from her ex-husband. She was the one who gave me the house tour. Stop assumin' shit. Sometimes, things aren't what they appear to be. Lesson number five, remember? Ask, but don't beg. You know how to communicate... In two languages."

"But you prefer I do so in English, and sometimes, it gets confusing." She shrugged with her smart ass, knowing damn well she wasn't confused by the languages. It didn't take Solana long to catch on to shit. I had learned that about her within the first few weeks that she was in my house.

"I could say the same about you, you know..." she said.

My brow rose after her words settled. "The same?"

"Si... Stop assuming. You give me these lessons, but none of them apply to you. Just ask, Shio. You never *asked* me if the drugs were mine. You assumed." Her eyes watered, and I could feel my body growing heavy. "I would never put your daughter in harm's way."

I threw my head back and sighed. All these feelings were too much. My day had been shitty since I learned that Goal was going to bring the product to my cabin. I needed to hit up my cousins to let them know I had fucked up at least a fourth of those bricks. I kissed my teeth when I realized I was going to have to pay for that shit so that the count wouldn't be short.

"Stop crying, Solana. I know you wouldn't harm my daughter intentionally."

She slapped the mattress. "You know those drugs were not mine, but I am here!"

"Ion know shit except yo' ass need to be here! You need fuckin' help! I can't take you to a facility because that shit not secure enough, and I can't..."

"There goes the clauses again. You can't what, Shio?"

"Nuttin'."

She huffed, tears slowly falling down her face. "Shio. You give me nothing."

"These days, outside of materials, I got nothing to give."

"You have your time!"

Barely. I spend half my time watching your ass, so you won't die.

Solana slapped the bed again when I didn't respond verbally. "Go home. Go home to Bahati."

"You mean go home to Shya cuz that's the only reason I go home."

She huffed and threw her head back against the headboard. Her face softened, and her round eyes found mine. She didn't deserve to be so fucking fine and a cokehead. Those two things should've never crossed over into one woman.

"How is she?" she asked, her tone even.

"Solana, is this an argument or a conversation?"

"*Tal vez ambos.* (Maybe both.)"

I crossed my hands in front of my waist. "Spoiled. She's fucking spoiled. She's not talking."

"Still?"

"Still."

"What did the doctor say?"

"That she's good."

"I would like to see her."

I squinted my eyes at Solana. I trusted her with my child more than I trusted her to leave the basement. The shit had my mind fucked up because it didn't make any sense. I'd have to sit on the idea of her seeing Shya, even though baby girl was the most calm she'd been on the plane with Solana. She was also okay with Solana on the bed when Bahati and I were at the hospital. The flashback had me scrunching up my face. When I looked back at her, her face matched mine.

"What is it, Solana?"

"Are we not going to..."

"What... Fuck?"

She nodded all innocently and shit.

I grabbed my crotch, glad that my dick had calmed down. "Nah..."

"Why not?"

"Because I don't want to. That's not what I came here for."

"You still haven't said why you're here."

"Solana, baby..."

"Shio..." She matched my tone, and instead of responding, I just stared at her.

I need to bounce.

"Shio?"

"Is Italian sneaking you cocaine, Solana?" I asked, and she drew her head back, offense written on her face as if she wasn't in here for being a cokehead.

"What? No! Why would you ask me that?"

"Why you always in the bathroom? At my crib, you were always in the bathroom and the closet... And we know what went down in there."

"Wow, Shio."

"A few days ago, you went in the bathroom and was in there forty-nine minutes. When you came out, you were walking funny, and your eyes were red."

"Wait! How do you know that?"

I stood, not saying shit.

"Shio. Are you watching me?"

I flicked my nose before crossing my arms.

Her arms flew up. "*¡Estás violando mi privacidad!* (You're violating my privacy!)"

"You don't have no fuckin' privacy!"

"That's a camera. Right there! Am I wrong?" She pointed toward the painting right above the TV, and although I could feel my body rise in temperature, I played it cool.

"You think I'm gonna bring you 'round my people and not keep watch?"

Her tongue clicked, and she swiped the tears from her face. "Okay."

We sat in silence. She wouldn't look at me, but I couldn't avert my eyes from her face. Watching her in person was so much better. I wished like hell I weren't attracted to her pretty ass.

"Shio, I am tired..."

Shit, me too.

"When... When all this is done, can you help me find my mom's living family? That is all I ask. Then, I can make my own way from there. I will be out of your life forever."

Hell nah, I ain't helping you find shit. Damn, I sound like my fucking cousins.

I ran my fingertips through my beard. "What you want from me right now, Solana? Not on no future-type shit."

Those dark, round eyes met mine again.

Pretty-ass, good-tasting-pussy-having little sinner.

"Even if it is selfish?"

"It's okay to be selfish sometimes."

"I don't want you to go home."

Pulling my pants up on my waist, I walked over to the door. I needed to leave before I went against my word. I needed to get in the truck and call the pastor because the voices in my head were not aligning when it came to Solana.

Without giving Solana a backward glance, I grabbed the handle to the door that was keeping her from the outside world.

"So you are going home?"

"Nah. I'm not going home if going there is going to cloud your head and fuck up your recovery efforts."

I opened the door, realizing I had never locked it. Stepping through it, I closed it. Fishing the key from my pocket, I stuck it in and turned until the lock clicked.

"Shio...?"

"Yeah, Solana, baby?"

"I'm not your father."

The fuck?

The first thought that came to mind was that Italian had been down here talking too fucking much. Instead of replying, I walked away from the door before I went against my better judgment and unlocked the motherfucker. No sooner than my feet hit the main floor, my phone rang. Retrieving it from my pocket and seeing Essex's name, I wasted no time answering. Getting lost in Solana was perfect for the moment, but now that I was out of that room, business was back at the forefront.

"Aye." Essex's tone made my ears perk up.

I nodded at Italian and tossed the mask to him. "Get that to Ezio for me," I said as I continued moving toward the front door before replying to Essex. "Wuz good, E-Block?"

"That spot, yo?"

My nerves tensed instantly, even though I knew he was calling about Bahati's apartment. "It checks out, right?"

I knew it had. I'd already spoken with the leasing agent, who had confirmed that Bahati and Shya had been tenants of the apartment. I'd even paid the lease up, telling them they were just out of town on an extended vacation. I didn't have many boots on the ground in the city since my people were here in the bay with me, but Essex did. Not only did he have a business that was still very much booming out there, but he also had people. Not many, but he had enough. He'd sent one of his customers, a robber who had turned stealing from niggas into a whole business. He did credit and shit now, but I wouldn't trust a thief who used to take shit with my information. The hood did, though, and they'd turned the nigga into a business mogul.

"Answer ya FaceTime, G."

As I opened the door and stepped outside, I pulled the phone away from my face and answered the call. Essex's face appeared briefly before he flipped the camera around.

"What I'm lookin' at, E-Block?"

My truck was turned off, and the keys were on the driver's seat. I would send a couple of stacks to Italian for looking out because I had left my shit running, trying to get to Solana's ass.

"Shit, nothing." He moved closer. "My nigga, Clutch, pulled up to come run through it for us, and when he called and told me the building was on fire, I had to get on a plane and see this shit for myself."

The giant pile of rubble where the apartment building should have been covered the entire camera. I knew the building was supposed to be exactly where Essex was because when he shifted the camera to the left and then to the right, I could see that the other two buildings were still standing that it was supposed to be standing between.

Essex rotated the phone again so that I could see the remnants from the fire. There wasn't shit left.

"Even the fuckin' leasing office gone, G. They said that shit was in the lobby of this building, so all the paperwork and computers and shit gone. Hopefully everybody got out, but you know how it is in Chicago." He shook his head.

Alarm and anger rippled through my spine as I hopped inside my truck. Some shit wasn't adding up, and a lot of shit was just too coincidental. Not having the mental capacity to deal with the shit tonight, I turned the car on and drove in the direction of downtown. It wasn't shit popping in Jagoda Bay tonight, so I should've been able to get a room at one of my favorite hotels. I'd have to deal with Bahati's slick ass another day because something wasn't adding the fuck up.

God first

~~*Make sure the family good*~~

~~*Eye them Cuppacio boys, the little and the big ones*~~

~~*Build a relationship with my brother*~~

~~*Get my brother rich*~~

Health and wellness ~~(ALWAYS)~~ (Shake back)

~~*Stay on top of my mob shit*~~

Keep Hobo alive (DOING... Barely)

~~*Get through the meeting with Ines Ledesma*~~

~~*House a random*~~

~~*Find the true reason Solana is here*~~

~~*Figure out if Solana is supposed to be my wife, again*~~

~~*Find a wife that isn't Solana*~~

Kill every breathing Rodríguez Cartel member (URGENT)

Fuck Bahati up (TBD)
~~Get my fucking daughter~~
~~Get Bahati's arm fixed~~
~~Get to know my daughter (DOING)~~
~~Figure out what the fuck I'm going to do with Solana~~
~~Leave the mob entirely or~~ marry ~~Bahati or~~ Solana
~~Get DNA test~~
Spend time with my daughter ~~(DOING)~~ (ON PAUSE)
~~Tell my mama about Shya~~
Keep Solana in real nigga rehab until ~~she clean~~ (TBD)
~~Get SECOND DNA test~~
~~Check on Bahati's apartment~~
Don't fuck ~~Uriah ANYBODY~~ SOLANA
Get to the root of Shya's constant crying
Get THIRD DNA test or say fuck it
Marry Bahati IF she is innocent
Pay for that cocaine
Decide if Solana can see Shya
Find out what happened to Bahati's apartment building

CHAPTER 23
SOLANA DAMITA LEDESMA

Today, I was reminded that I'd trapped my wife. I'd trapped her in an unfortunate and unconventional situation, knowing it wouldn't be the fairy tale I promised. I write these words, the only reason I'm not as upset as I was earlier is because I've had my fix...

"This isn't right! This isn't right, and you know it!"

Tears flooded Shannon's face, but only one eye was producing them. She began pacing back and forth with her hand on her lower back, and if it were possible, she would've worn a hole in the floor.

"Siana, please calm down!"

With an abrupt stop, she faced me, and I had to hold back my cringe. Her left eye was swollen, purple, and dried blood surrounded the creases.

"How can you say calm down? Look at me!"

"Siana—"

"My name is fucking Shannon! It's SHANNON!" she shouted.

"I know your name, baby. I know it."

"Well, stop calling me Siana!"

"You know why I call you Siana."

She knew why. The wives were all here against their will, and many of them had active missing persons cases, so in order to keep us Cuppacios out of prison, everyone had been assigned a new name.

"I'm tired. I'm so, so, so tired, Sandro."

Her hands dropped to her sides, and air deflated her chest. Every time we had this conversation, I felt the urge to go numb. The only reason I hadn't killed myself was because of cocaine. What started as a recreational drug turned into a coping mechanism for me. I knew I wasn't doing right by my wife or my son, so the drugs became my escape. Plus, if I killed myself, I'd have to kill my son and wife too. I'd have to kill them both because there was no way I was leaving them here to fend for themselves against the other Cuppacios.

I knew she was tired. She had every right to be tired. Her eye was swollen shut. And I'm sure if she lifted her shirt, there would be bruises all over her abdomen, but this wasn't at my hands. It was the work of Don. It was rare that he put his hands on the other wives, but it wasn't uncommon for him to unleash his wrath, not only on my wife but also on the others. There was no rhyme or reason as to why he did it, but he did.

Shannon had taken too many beatings. She'd taken too many rapings too. Above all, she'd taken it all in the name of love. Because, unlike the other wives, she did love her husband. She did love me.

"I'm tired of pretending. You need to tell them."

"I can't."

Shannon shook her head. "You need to tell them, or I will!"

"And then what, Shannon? Huh? What will that change? What will telling them change?"

"It will change everything, Sandro! Our son can be safe, and we can move away. We can start a new life. I can get a job, you can get a job. We don't have to live like this. I can find my family, and they will help. You promised me—"

"I know what I promised! I... know!"

"Well, you need to tell them."

"How? What would I say?"

"'Hey, family. I didn't actually kidnap my wife. She is the love of my life. I brought her in under the guise that I kidnapped her.' That's what the fuck you say, Sandro."

I really wanted to, I truly did. But Shannon didn't understand. The only way she and I could be together in the way we are is if the Don believed I had kidnapped her, or if they thought she was trafficked. All of our wives were trafficked—every last one of them. They had been kidnapped or sold to us. Many of them were sold out by their own families. The rest had been snatched up without even knowing. They already had questions when I showed up with Siana—well, Shannon. I came up with this big story that I crossed state lines and took her. That was a lie.

Shannon and I had been dating for over a year. She didn't know that I was affiliated with the mob at first. By the time she found out, we were already in love. I'd already asked her to marry me. She was already wearing my ring. Not only did she not know that I was a mobster, but she also didn't know I was six years older than her. She was a minor. I was an adult. But she was the love of my life.

I somehow convinced her to go along with my story about me snatching her up so she could be brought in. However, I left out the part where the rest of my mobster family members were evil, vindictive, and abusive. Shannon thought she was being brought into a loving, close-knit family, but in reality, I led her into her own personal hell.

"Shannon, baby, listen. We cannot move away. We cannot move away and start a new life. They will find us. They will find us, and they will do unthinkable things to us. There are things out here that are far worse than death. I'm sorry that I dragged you into this. But it's our reality now. We have to get through it as best we can. That is why behind these doors, I make sure to create a safe, loving, and secure environment."

"How secure is it really? How? They come in here and snatch my son and me up. It's inhumane the way they treat our baby! We live like animals! Like fucking stray dogs! Your family is not only sick, but they are racists! They are fucking racists, and the things they are exposing these children to aren't right. None of this is right!"

"I know it isn't right. But there is only one of me and so many of them! This mob life is for life! It is my birthright. It is my son's birthright. I do not agree with how they handle you, but Shio will need the lessons. He will need the lessons in order to be great."

"You are just as sick as they are! He is a child. What he needs is love. He needs love and a stable home environment! He needs his father to love him out loud! He doesn't need a coward for a father!"

"Baby—"

Shannon lifted her hand, silencing me. "Do you think I want to be constantly beaten? Do you think I want my son to be abused all the time? Do you think I want to be forced to sleep with the other man as if I took vows with them and not with you? Do you think I want to be loved behind closed doors and treated like I'm nothing but a slave in front of your people? You did this, Sandro!" She pointed at her eye.

"You may not have been the one to put his hands on me. You may not be the one who rapes me. You may not be the one who puts our son through

all this strenuous stuff that his little body can't even handle, but it's your fault because you could have left me alone. But you just had to drag me into this situation because you didn't want to be miserable and alone!"

"Baby, that's not true. I love you. I can't live without you."

"So that means you can't live without Tunan's mom, either, right? What, you don't think I know? You don't think I know you took my son to Memphis? I'm not stupid, Sandro. What I am is tired. What I am is fed up. What about everything you promised me?"

"I remember everything I promised you."

"No, you don't know. You don't, you don't, you don't at all."

"I do!"

"You don't! ***Walks on the river. A city of my choice for forty-eight hours. Visits to wineries. Take me back to where you come from in Italy, remember? Dinner at the best steakhouses on random days, not just on weekends****. You promised me all of this, and the only thing that you've delivered is heartache. I hate it here. I hate you. I hate my life. And if you think for one minute that our son won't resent you for this for the life you've given us, you can think again. You hide behind the drugs and behind the Bible, but you're no man of God. You are the Devil. I hate the day I met you. And one day, my son will make sure we escape this hell. And when that day comes, you will be burning in the real Hell. You won't get a chance to see us happy, and you damn sure won't put your demons on my child. He's going to be the opposite of all of this."*

"Shannon, baby, let's just talk."

"I'm done talking. I'll talk when all of you motherfuckers are dead."

"WALKS ON THE RIVER?"

I remembered seeing that written somewhere in the journal. I just couldn't remember where, so I flipped through the book to see if there was a connection. I was about to give up until I came across Shio's handwriting. I knew it was his handwriting because it was so different from his father's, and I'd seen it on many of the papers in his office.

Things to Do with My Wife

Walks on the river

A city of my choice for 48 hours

Visits to wineries
Take her to where I come from
Dinner at the best steakhouses on random days
Lo

Boom Boom Boom Boom Boom

The book slipped from my hands, falling on the side of the toilet.

"Shit!"

The banging on the door startled me, and my nerves rattled. Swiping the book from the floor, I closed it, opened the cabinet underneath the sink, and stuffed it behind a bottle of cleaning solution.

Boom Boom Boom

"Who is it?" I yelled from the bathroom.

Standing in front of the mirror, I gave myself a quick once-over. Ever since Shio had come by, I'd made more effort with my appearance. The closet wasn't full of clothes like it was back at his house, but the drawers did have plenty of lounge wear, and many of them still had tags. I washed my hair after Shio left and plaited it into ten braids. Once the braids dried, I took them out, and my hair was now puffy and wavy, instead of my usual matted ball. Today, I wore a green-and-tan striped tube top and matching pants. I went braless because it was more comfortable, and the tube top worked fine without it. I could use a pedicure since the Shellac on my toes was beginning to grow out, so I had on a pair of tan fuzzy socks. Satisfied with my look, I turned off the bathroom light and entered the bedroom, which was still tidy from when Mahzeyah had cleaned it. The trash was overflowing with food bags and needed to be taken out, though. The bed wasn't made either, but everything else was in place.

"Who is it?" I asked again.

It didn't matter who it was, anyway, because I couldn't let them in. The door was locked from the outside, and only two people that I knew of had a key. Remembering I had the perfume Shio brought over, I picked it up from the dresser, drenched myself in it, and turned around to spray the sheets. I then fanned the air so it wouldn't look like I'd just sprayed it. As soon as the mist settled, a shudder ran down my spine in memory of the day Shio came into my makeshift rehab.

Would he use his mouth again? Would he let me use mine?

The moment I had stopped craving Shio, he did things to my body that made me crave him worse than before.

"Italian! Italian?!" someone shouted on the other side.

Drawing my head back, I walked to the door, pressing my ear against it. It wasn't Shio, but the voice was muffled. The steel was cool on my face, but I stayed still, trying to recognize the voice as they yelled again.

"Italian! Open this door!"

"Yeah, open the door!"

"And why it smell like smoke in here? Who been sleeping on my couch?"

The door groaned before the lock clicked as I stepped back. When it opened, a rush of cool air spilled in. I knew the voice wasn't Shio's, but he wasn't standing with the crowd staring at me. My heart hurt at the realization.

"Dasani?" I asked.

Dasani was hopping around while hunched over.

"Damn, that's all you see?" Pia turned her nose up.

"Right! A bitch done come to rescue you, and you talkin' 'bout some *Dasani*! It wasn't even her idea!" Mocha shifted her legs but grabbed the wall as she nearly fell.

"Hi, Solana. How are you?" Scarlett asked, sincerity in her voice.

"I'm... Wow. I wasn't expecting you. Any of you..." I responded, baffled that the girls were even standing here right now.

"Yeah, well, move on out of the way. I gotta piss. Ain't it a bathroom in here?" Dasani pushed past me.

"Yes. Right through that door," Jisei called behind her while still grilling Italian, who had his arm around her shoulder.

"We ain't fuck up the couch. We ain't been doing nothing we ain't 'posed to be doing, Auntie. Ain't that right, Mexi-Mami?"

Italian's handsome face mischievously grinned while Jisei gave him the cold shoulder.

"Umm hmmm. This ain't no fucking clubhouse. So it bet not be no fucking going on."

He cackled. "Tell Shio that..."

My face heated as Jisei playfully punched Italian, who was trying his best to dodge her fist.

All of the ladies filed in, and Italian closed the door behind them, winking at me. I'd hoped I wasn't loud that day, but from his response, I must have been.

"So, this where you been this whole time?" Mocha slid out of her gold strappy heels while Pia set her light pink Christian Dior bag on the dresser.

Jisei was already barefoot and was pointing the remote at the TV while Scarlett was still looking at me as if I were a sick puppy. The door to the bathroom opened, and Dasani came out, drying her hands before placing her purse on the nightstand. It was a gorgeous blue Birkin 30. I had a couple of Birkin and other Hermès bags back in México, but I preferred Chanel.

"Whew, shit! Them mimosas ran right the fuck through me," Dasani said before plopping on the bed and crossing her leg over her thigh. She attempted to unbuckle the strap on her blue heels without putting her shoes on the bed.

"You shol' been pissing a lot. Let me find out..." Jisei murmured as she typed into the YouTube search engine.

Dasani successfully removed one heel and worked on the next one. "Let you find out the fuck what?"

"That my brother put that son in you that he won't stop whining about." Jisei snickered.

"Yo' brother trapped me once, and I gave him that. But he gone have to pay me to have another baby."

"Oh God, really?" Scarlett giggled.

"Hell yeah, *really*! That nigga may be Don to y'alls niggas but he ain't shit to me. Having his baby ain't no muthafuckin' privilege. The one we got barely fuck with me as is."

"Girl, please! Delicate crazy as hell about you." Pia waved her off, taking a seat on the bed but on the opposite side. She even peeled back the covers and fluffed a pillow to get comfortable. Her belly had grown since I'd last seen her, and I said a quiet prayer she didn't go into labor down here.

"Yeah, that is my baby. But she's enough. Scarlett, you can't talk. When you having another one? Give Matteo's crazy ass a son."

"Matteo is constantly saying that when Princess asks for a sibling, he will give her one." Scarlett shrugged. "She hasn't asked yet, I guess."

Dasani scoffed. "And you just gonna let him nut in you and make it happen?"

"Yes, I am, Dasani. I mean... What choice do I have?"

My eyes kept bouncing from one woman to another. They were all dressed up, just like they had been every time I'd seen them, but I was still trying to process the fact that they were actually here.

The room went silent as everyone pondered Scarlett's last statement.

"I mean, you got a point, best friend. I'm still scared of Matteo's ass. If he say, 'It's baby time,' that means—"

"It's baby time!" the woman chanted in unison before bursting out in laughter.

Jisei settled on something to play on YouTube, but a phone ad came on before the actual video could play. She also took a seat on the bed, curling up near Mocha. Scarlett climbed in soon after, leaving me the only one standing. As I looked over everyone, I could feel the burn in my eyes. Blinking, I took a deep breath and steadied my hands that felt like they wanted to tremble. I could feel my nose running, but I knew it was phantom drops, so I refrained from swiping them.

The women were all comfortable on the queen-sized bed and had fallen into conversation as if these circumstances were natural. They were acting as if I were a part of them, and it was one of our typical girls' nights out.

"Solana... You—Solana!" Scarlett hopped from the bed as tears rushed down my face. She gently grabbed my shoulders before pulling me into her. "It's okay. It's okay. You're okay.

"I-I... I can't believe you're all here."

I didn't know how the next time I saw them would go. I had somewhat accepted that I would never see them again with the way Shio had isolated me from the world. These women were not only beautiful but also bosses. I didn't think I fit in with them and knew they would have nothing to do with me once they found out about my nasty habit, as Shio called it. It had crossed my mind more than a few times because they inspired me.

Pulling back from Scarlett, I let her lead me to the bed where there was a spot left in the middle for me. Grabbing a pillow, I crossed my legs and hugged it into my chest.

"I... Thank you all for coming."

Dasani scoffed. "Girl, we've been trying to get to you for days, but them niggas have been being all secretive and shit."

"I told y'all she was okay!" Jisei fussed.

"That's because your pillow-talking-ass brother kept you in the loop. Case in point, why I barely fuck with that nigga now. And y'all talking about *a baby*. As a matter of fact, I might need to have another one just so the nigga can be stuck. He got way too much time on his damn hands."

"He runs a whole mob, Dasani," Jisei defended.

"And he gone be running from my foot up his ass if he keep thinking he bigger than my fucking program. This. My. Shit." Dasani clapped with each word.

"Girl, whatever. He didn't tell me anything. This is *my house*, Dasani. I have access to the cameras, and I have neighbors who keep me in the loop. Mr. Joe texted me as soon as she came."

"Yeah, whatever." Dasani rolled her already sleek eyes from her Asian features.

Pia chuckled. "Y'all be coming like real-life sisters."

"And do. But how you been, Solana? They treating you good in here?" Mocha asked.

"Not you asking her like she been locked up." Jisei shook her head.

"Shit, she have been. Real Nigga Rehab. Look around, Jisei," Pia said with a wave of her arm.

"Real N—?" I asked but was cut off by Scarlett patting my thigh. I'd heard Italian use that more than once but shrugged it off.

"Yeah, Real *Nigga* Rehab. Let us say it, boo. But that's what the sign say outside the door."

"He has a sign?" I asked Scarlett, grabbing my chest.

"Italian 'nem childish as hell. Don't mind them!" Mocha waved both hands.

"I can't wait to tell Neltz I saw you today. Between you and Grind, y'all keep my boy stressed."

I faced Pia to respond. "Grind... That's Pearla's ex? Right?"

The girls had sat outside the door plenty of days, just having girl talk with me, and Grind had come up in conversations a few times. I knew he was in some sort of a coma, and I knew he'd hurt Pearla, who, might I add, was a sweetheart.

"Ex... Current. I don't know what my sister has going on these days. She spends most of her time over here." Pia sighed while also giving me a look. "But, yeah, that's him."

"Well, I love Pearla. I love all the girls." I changed the subject.

Pearla has been giddy about one of the new boys, Price. I had only seen Price on photo but hadn't seen the other boy. I'd heard them on the other side of the door plenty though. Italian had only brought them down with my permission. It didn't matter to me if they were here or not. I was locked behind a door. They couldn't see me unless Italian granted them access.

"So, when you asked us if we were doing more than drinking that night at the studio, I guess you meant powda."

"Mocha!" Jisei screamed.

Pia shook her head. "Mocha! Girl!"

"Really, Mocha?!" Scarlett said, sounding genuinely upset.

Everyone chastised her except Dasani, who was laughing really hard.

Chuckling, I picked lint off the pillow that was now in my lap. All eyes were on me, waiting for an answer, despite them telling Mocha off.

"Yes. I'm... I'm a adicta a la cocaína..." I corrected myself before they even asked. "Oo, sorry. Cocaine addict."

That was the first time I'd admitted that out loud, and I felt lighter—lighter than I'd ever felt before.

"Damn, you so pretty. I would have never thought that about you. Shit, you even make being on powda sound sexy. Co-ky-eee-nahhh!" Mocha dragged out.

"Yeah, you may feel sexy while doing the drug, but it's nothing sexy about it. I never looked at myself as an addict. It was just... Um, something to do to take my mind off my reality."

I took a breath. If I were going to tell them about my addiction, I might as well have told them where it stemmed from. "My father promised me to marry an evil man. An evil man who comes from an evil family. They are no good for my country. Drugs became an escape. I was on drugs before I was promised to Felipe. It got worse? I think that's the word I'm looking for. Sometimes English and Española blur."

Mocha grabbed a pillow and propped her chest on it. "That dude from the club? The fine one?"

I nodded. "As attractive as he may be, he is a very bad man. Still... I was willing to go with him. I never wanted to bring him to your doorstep. To Shio's doorstep." I swallowed.

"I was willing to go back home and face the consequences. I'm sorry, Jisei, for taking residence in your home."

"Girl, please! Mi casa es su casa!"

I grinned. "Very good, Español."

"Yeah, well don't get to trying to speak it to me because that's all I remember from taking it in college. But I don't know if you know this or not, but not long ago... Not even a year ago, my husband was battling an addiction. Why do you think Shio had this room set up? It was for Ezio."

Jisei tossed her silky tresses behind her shoulder and pulled on her halter top before continuing. "He stayed in this room until he was clean. It worked too. It worked, and now look at us. Happy ever after. A cute lil' baby and everything."

"My fat man so handsome!" Mocha cooed.

"I... I don't know if that will be my ending. But I did not know Ezio battled addiction."

"He did. He still does. He still craves a pill here and there, but he refrains. A bitch gotta thug it out when it's that time of the month because I don't even keep Tylenol in the house. At least not the pill version." Jisei shuddered and then shook her head.

"You won't have to worry about him, Solana—your fiancé. You also don't have to worry 'bout nothing coming to our doorsteps. My husband ain't gone let shit infiltrate what we've built. They so evil but them niggas have gone underground. They shook."

Dasani shot the rest of the women a look, and that told me that there was more she could say, but she wouldn't. At least she wouldn't in my presence.

I sighed and changed the subject. "I have my days where I feel as though the drug will make me feel better, but I am happy the craving is no longer there. It's a mental battle. A very hard one, but I am taking it day by day."

"So... How long you gone be in this basement? I mean, it's cute and cozy and all, but shit, we got malls to hit, couches to stand on, and mob niggas' pockets to run!" Mocha wagged her tongue and bucked her hips.

"I... I don't know. Italian and I just figured until I get over the craving."

"So that's the plan? Or what is the plan?"

"I guess so. But I do not know what my future holds. I do have dual citizenship. If I decide to stay, I will get a job so that I can support myself. I do not know if I want to be back in México."

I was still upset with my father. There were so many lies that I didn't know if I could ever trust him again. He had played chess with my life, and it could have ended badly. The Rinaldi Mob could have been just as dangerous as the Rodríguezes, but I knew no matter what he had said, he didn't care anymore because he needed money. It also made me think that Maura turning off my credit card wasn't about punishment, but more likely because he couldn't afford it anymore.

"Girl! You don't have to get no fucking job!" Dasani looked at me as if I was *loca* (crazy).

"Dasani, Shio and I... We never..."

"Y'all never fucked?" Pia asked.

I grew coy. "No."

"I just gotta know. You ever fucked your fine-ass, evil fiancé?"

Scarlett sighed. "Mocha!"

"What! Y'all know that Migo fine!"

"Mocha, I've never had sex with him." I squeezed the pillow to my chest. "I never had sex with anyone."

"What!" everyone screamed, except Pia, who jolted awake.

"You... a virgin?" Jisei asked.

"Bitch! Stop acting like you didn't know!" Dasani yelled at Jisei.

She held her hands up. "I didn't! I swear!"

"Yo' talking-ass brother didn't tell you that? Ha! I'm shocked."

"Wait! You ain't never had no dick, for real?" Pia squirmed around after falling asleep.

I shook my head no.

"Hell nawl!" Pia yelled.

Mocha laughed while the others said something, giving me looks of pity.

"That's crazy!"

"Oh, wow, boo."

"Um, um-um, um."

With everyone's attention on me, and me sitting in the center of the bed, I was completely exposed. My body was flushed with embarrassment but this was my truth.

"You was living in fine-ass Shio's house and ain't never gave him no coochie?"

"Si."

"Si? Si, si a bitch like me would have bust it wide open. That's why I'm a teen mom now."

"Mocha, you grown now." Jisei tittered while shaking her head.

"Yeah, I am now. But I wasn't then. But, girl! A virgin! How the hell you taking cocaine up the nose but not dick up the ass?"

"Questions that need answers." Pia yawned before trying to reach me with her hand to pat my arm but couldn't. "Respectfully, of course."

"No offense taken, ladies. But, yes, I am a virgin. My father wouldn't have it any other way. I am to be pure. A pure bride meant better deals for the father handing me off."

"That's some bullshit!" Dasani grunted.

"It is our way. I've been arranged since I was a girl. That didn't bother me. What bothered me was who I was being arranged to and the different adversaries I faced in my father's household. That is a different story for another time."

"Well, shit. How does it feel?"

Turning to Mocha, my brow rose in question. "To be a virgin?"

"Yeah. I lost my shit so long ago, it seems that I can't remember life before King Dingaling."

"Ha! You stupid." Pia cackled.

Mocha shrugged. "I'm for real, Pia."

I pondered before I shook my head. "It feels... normal? Yes... normal. You can't miss... what you haven't had, I guess."

The swipe of Shio's tongue on my bud and him sucking me into his mouth flashed across my mind, causing a shockwave in my underwear. I swallowed down my desire, not wanting to share the intimacy we shared with the girls.

Dasani rubbed her forehead. “See, I’m too damn drunk for this shit.”

“I most definitely had one too many.” Scarlett plopped back on the bed, chest facing the ceiling.

Mocha kissed her teeth with a grin. “A whole-ass virgin. No wonder Shio put yo’ ass in here. He ain’t studying no damn cocaine. He wants to lock you away. You a diamond, boo. Nah, fuck that! You a unicorn. My daddy would be so proud if I was a virgin at this big ole age.”

“Nah, because LJ wouldn’t be here. Don’t try to wish my nephew into nonexistence.” Jisei chastised.

“Okay...” Pia rolled more on her side and rubbed her protruding belly. “Do you want to wait until marriage is the question. Not what your daddy wants but what *you* want? You’re way in another country. You ain’t gotta do shit he says. And I know right now you battling addiction, one that *you will* overcome, so leave that out of your response and thinking process.”

I panted softly. My mind was languid and without hope. Shio had come over, and he’d made me feel good—really good. But he was back to not responding to my texts. He had not made any effort to show the intimacy he’d shown me when he came here.

My head shot up in the direction of where the camera was. A towel hung from it, and the burn in my chest returned. How dare he? How dare he watch me and never respond to my messages? That was a violation of my privacy, and I was pissed at myself for not feeling as violated and turned off as I should’ve.

“I don’t want to wait until marriage.”

“But I would,” Scarlett stated. “You’ve waited all this time. What’s the rush, Solana? Me... I sold my virginity.”

I looked up into Scarlett’s pretty face and then grabbed her hands. “I’m so sorry.”

“No, don’t be. It’s done. But I sold mine, so if I could go back, I would have waited and given it to my husband on our wedding night. But then, my baby wouldn’t be here. And that very thought makes me feel guilty.” She squeezed my hands. “What I’m saying is, all of our endgames lead to, or are leading to, marriage one way or another. We know for a fact that you will not be going back to Mexico. That's done. We like you too much and—"

"You know too damn much." Dasani finished with a straight face that had me stiffening.

"Yes, that's true," Scarlett softened Dasani's words, but I knew what Dasani meant. "It's nothing wrong with giving it to your forever person. For me, sex is a beautiful thing. Women process sex differently. But sex with my husband is just... *different.* Matteo has a way about himself that... I don't know how to explain it except the nigga can fuck. Like he can *fuck,* and in the same breath, he can make love so good that it brings me to tears. If I didn't have him, I wouldn't want to have sex at all."

Pia nodded. "I enjoyed sex with the other men I slept with, but Nel is definitely the best I've ever had."

"Yeah, same with Ezio. You'd think he was still on the percs the way he be having my ass folded like a pretzel every other day."

Mocha clapped her hands. "That's how I got my fast-ass pregnant, so you know Lorenzo is definitely *that nigga* in and outside of the bedroom."

"See! The man you marry is definitely going to make all the other guys irrelevant." Scarlett smiled, and I swear she was one of the most beautiful women I'd ever known—inside and out.

"Bitch, please!" Dasani stole my attention. "Demise a beast and all, but I done had some good-ass runner-ups! I was running through them ballers that brought their asses in the emergency room. Them niggas was stuffing my pussy and my pockets. Ion know what these bitches talking 'bout, but for some people, hoe is life. I met my husband being on some hoe shit." Dasani shrugged.

"Emergencia room?"

"Yeah, I used to be a nurse before I got locked up, girl."

There was so much I didn't know about these women, and each time they opened their mouths, I was more intrigued.

I shrugged, not willing to ask Dasani to elaborate. "I think what worries me the most is... Um, not knowing what is next for me. When I was at Shio's home, I had just started to get comfortable when I was kicked out. Now, I am comfortable here and can't help but feel like the same thing will happen. I don't know what my next plan is."

"Well, this is my muthafuckin' house. Can't a soul put you out. When you're comfortable, you can come out of this basement and take over my primary bedroom. I still have clothes and stuff up there with the tags on them, and though you're thicker than me, you can do something with a lot of them clothes, I'm sure.

"As Dasani said, you're here to stay. I can't tell you if you and Shio are endgame... I really wish I could. But what I will say is, you don't have to worry about not one of those Mexicans coming for you. We gone make sure you good. We got money and connections just like our husbands, and for the bitches we love, we don't mind tricking!"

"Yeap! Just like our tricking-ass husbands." Dasani pointed at Jisei.

"Oh my God! He is my brother! Long-lost brother, at that. So he can't buy me shit, Dasani?"

"Rare bags? Hell nawl, he can't. You got a husband!"

Jisei rolled her eyes. "I never thought when I finally got a sister she'd be a hater."

"That's why you ain't expected to think. Just look pretty, *Jae Bae*. But, anywho! I have to start adding this disclaimer now."

Dasani sat up and looked me directly in the eyes. "Solana, you are not a wife, so there are things that will be filtered around you. There are times that you will be excluded. There will be sidebar conversations only because the big dicks we ride every night come first before anything and anybody. I fucks with you, and although Demise Rinaldi irks my soul, I will not see my nigga back in jail. As long as you cool with that, you in the clique."

"Really, Dasani?" Jisei folded her arms as Pia and Mocha giggled.

"Yes, really! I ain't going to go into details, because I ain't no fake-ass bitch, but I *thought* it was common knowledge that if we are around you, you are in our circle. It's plenty of niggas that work for my husband, and we don't fuck with their wives like that, at all. Not because we are some mean girls, but they have their own lil' cliques like we got our own. The fact of the matter is... We bring women in *without* being married, which lets them know we fuck with them the long way. So, please... Don't do anything drastic to fit in with us because you're already in. Okay?" Dasani blinked at me with a smile.

"You messy." Mocha laughed, and Pia wiped tears from her eyes from laughing.

"I'm real!" Dasani spat. I noticed a slight shift from Scarlett and Jisei, but I knew not to ask.

Dasani clicked her tongue and shifted back on the bed to get comfortable again. "I know you're on cocaine and all, but what was the breaking point for Shio? Did he really not *know*? How did you hide it? I'm sorry, there are so many gaps in the story, and I'm a nosy bitch. My husband don't pillow talk to me like he does to his *sister*."

Jisei picked up a throw pillow and tossed it at Dasani, who caught it and tossed it back.

Wringing my hands, the day I was brought here came back to me. It was one that I tried not to think about. In less than twenty-four hours, I'd been put out and was looked at by Shio with so much hate that I felt his emotions in my gut.

"He'd just come back from taking Bahati to the hospital. I was in the kitchen, sitting on the countertop."

"Uggh! Weird-ass, back-from-the-dead-ass baby mama." Scarlett scoffed.

Her name-calling made me smirk.

"Her arm was broken—is broken..." I paused, unsure of what I could share, so I skipped past the entire kidnapping-rescue situation.

"Her ass should've been broken! Like... Shio should have put his whole foot so far in her ass that it should still be stuck. Who the fuck hides a baby?"

"Right!" Mocha backed Pia's statement.

I didn't understand why she hid Shya, but she was very much unhidden now. Shya was at Shio's home, being raised by both of her parents. The thought of them being a family made my chest burn.

"They came in, and she accused me of being careless with drugs. Before I could get an explanation out, she attacked me."

When Bahati snatched me from the counter with her one arm, I was in complete shock, but hours later, my back was on fire.

"That bitch put her hands on you?" Pia screamed.

"All, hella nawl!" Dasani spat, sitting up on the bed again.

"I was so surprised... I didn't have much time to react. I was trying to explain to Shio that I would never do that. I have smaller siblings back home. I would never leave drugs around. I didn't have much left, and what I did have left was in the closet on the island. Not in some baggie."

"You didn't fight back, Solana? The bitch had one arm so you was supposed to mop her ass all up and through that fucking kitchen! When I got done with the hoe, she would've had two broken arms!" Dasani fumed as Mocha agreed.

"Sadly, no… I did not want to fight with the mother of his child. And the baby was there."

"Man, fuck that baby!" Mocha punched her fist to her palm. "You mean to tell me you didn't at least pinch the bitch? Shio would have just had to kill me because I would have dog-walked that hoe! Ohhhhh! See, we should've been there!"

"I can't believe she put her hands on you," Scarlett said. "What did Shio do because now I'm about to forget he's my cousin and curse him the fuck out!"

"He broke it up. But then, he put me in his car and brought me here. I've been here ever since."

"And your first course of action when you get out this bitch is whooping that hoe's ass! See, Demise didn't tell me this!" Dasani was growing red in the face, and I warmed to the fact that she really cared for me.

Jisei tsked. "I heard the baby doesn't talk. She's probably too traumatized."

I didn't want to discuss Shio's daughter's shortcomings, so I didn't add commentary.

"And who told you that? See, I swear you be knowing shit and keeping it to yourself."

"My brother didn't tell me, Dasani! You know Ezio and Shio are tight. Well, not as of late because Shio been busy… I'm guessing with the new baby and all this." Jisei's eyes swept the room before landing on me.

"Okay, and Ezio and me are tight, and he didn't tell me!" Scarlett spoke up.

Scarlett sighed. "I'm gonna have to meet her. The baby, I mean. Maybe she just needs to get around Princess. You know kids help other kids get over stuff."

"Unh unh. Fuck that bitch *and* her baby."

"Dasaniiiii!" Scarlett yelled as the other women snickered.

Dasani stood, dusting invisible lint off her bottom. "What? I'm team Solana. Until DNA proves he's the daddy, fuck that baby. And even if or when it does, if Solana ain't on that, I ain't either. *We ain't either.*"

"You shol' ain't do all this with Glow." Jisei smacked her lips.

I tensed at her name. I wondered where the beautiful woman was. Since Bahati had come into Shio's life, I had forgotten about Glow.

"Girl, boo. Glow *been* my bitch. You think I'd allow her in my house and in my space if I didn't fuck with her? I just don't fuck with the way she went about shit, and I told her that to her face." Dasani nodded at me. "And what the hell you tensing for? Glow is married to Shio's *brother*."

"Oh..."

"Yeah, *oh*. We don't need no tension in our circle. Leave that shit to them other wives and girlfriends. Glow ain't stuttin' Shio."

"You so damn messy." Mocha snickered.

"My husband had some food for us delivered." She held her phone up, revealing a text thread that I couldn't read. "I'm going to go upstairs and get it, and y'all settle on a movie. Looks like we having us a sleepover! Them drinks at brunch put me on my ass. I ain't trying to go home and deal with no nigga or no baby."

Dasani nearly tripped on her heel but recovered and sauntered to the door.

"Awl shit! We done locked ourselves in. Solana, come over and do the call or whatever you do when you summon the grown-ass littles. Jisei talking about sex, knowing damn well they be fucking all up and through this townhouse."

"Girl, please. They better not be." She pointed the TV at the remote, shifting through apps. "Y'all, let's watch *Selena*!"

"One of my favorite movies." I stood from the bed and stretched.

"Oh, God. Yeah, you'll definitely fit right in. I'm so damn tired of Neltz and Nel with that shit. And I hope like hell ain't no fucking going on over here. Them littles get pregnant, and I swear, the twins gone start a war."

"Um... Y'all trying to have us crying. We already drunk and sad that our bitch is locked away and strung out," Mocha said before the loud sound stole our attention.

Boom boom boom boom

"Open this damn door!"

Dasani had asked me to come help, but she was already beating on the door by the time I made it next to her. "My thing is, what if you gotta pee, boo?"

She continued to beat on the door as I stood uselessly. I never called for anyone because I had everything I needed here or was given to me routinely.

Jisei huffed. "Girl, you just peed in the bathroom!"

"Jae Bae, please!"

The locks turned, and just as she slammed her fist on the door again, it was snatched open.

"Who the hell is you?" Dasani asked with her normal attitude and tone.

Instead of facing Italian, there was another boy in his place. My mouth began to water, my nose itched, and my fingers twitched. The tall, slim, brown-skinned boy shifted his eyes from Dasani to me, and when realization set in, his face fell. Ours expressions nearly mimicked each other.

You can fight this, Solana.

"Umm... Hello!" Dasani snapped her fingers. "Who are you?"

His eyes stayed on me. "I... Italian is upstairs putting the baby to sleep. He asked me to open the door for y'all if y'all knocked."

"Okay, what's your name? You look familiar."

"I... I... I do valet for your husband from time to time, ma'am."

He finally focused on Dasani while I was trying my best to control my breathing. Control my craving. Control my mind to overcome the feeling of need. I could feel the heat creep up my neck. My mouth was full of saliva, and my senses began to spin.

"Okay... What's your name, though?"

"Oh, Ro."

He shifted his gaze back to me, bushy brows furrowed. I was trying my hardest to focus on the present instead of the yearning. It was him. He had what I needed. He had what would put me out of my misery.

"It's Sorrow." He cleared his throat, visibly shaken by my presence, it seemed. Or it could have been Dasani's, but I had a feeling it was me.

"My, uhhh, name is Sorrow."

"Well, Sorrow... Keep this door open and come help me bring this food back down."

Dasani moved past him, and after a few seconds of him holding my gaze, he trailed behind her. When he was out of view, the craving left. My senses returned to normal, and three blinks later, I was back to myself.

"Come on, Solana. We about to start the movie. Wait till Dasani finds out the only reason my brother ordered food is that I texted him." Jisei snickered while Scarlett shook her head.

Pia sat up and rubbed her eyes after dozing off again. "I'm with Mocha. You *and* Dasani so messy."

CHAPTER 24
SHIO CUPPACIO

Staring at my text thread, there was nothing there. No messages waiting for me. While I shouldn't have cared either way, I was on edge, which is something I couldn't afford to be. An on-edge Shio Cuppacio lost sense of routine, and things like working out, eating clean, and catching the pastor on Sundays were skipped. I found myself reacting immediately, and my thoughts were being eroded because of *her*.

I had been at the hotel since the night I ruined hundreds of thousands' worth of cocaine and got a taste of Solana. It wasn't because I didn't want to face my responsibilities at home. I just didn't want to be around Shya with my head so fucked up. Between Solana's wants, the DNA test not confirming Shya was my child, and Bahati entering desperation when I was there, I just needed a fucking minute. But tonight, I was going to have to pull myself together and take my ass home. By trying not to become my father, I was slowly turning into him, and Shya didn't deserve that. My plan wasn't to leave Bahati with Shya now that I knew of her existence, but considering Bahati's ability to get her ass up every day and cook full-course meals—lifting heavy pots filled with chicken broth and all that—holding a fifteen-pound toddler should've been easy. She didn't need me, but that didn't mean that Shya didn't either.

"First, you went on a drug binge, and now you're standing out here like you lost your best friend." Nel shook his head as I lifted mine from the phone in my hand. "Fuck you on?"

Nel's lip curled over his nose as if he smelled something foul when I knew that shit was a damn lie. The only thing that nigga smelled was Imagination by Louis Vuitton and money—a whole fucking lot of it.

"You had us moppin' and sweepin' and shit like we was Cinderella, cleanin' up your dope. You still ain't gave us no fuckin' explanation." Nel had lowered his volume, but his voice still held a judgmental flair.

I looked at him before focusing back on the phone. "And you not getting one."

That shit was days ago, and he hadn't let me live it down yet. I'd already sent the money to Ezio so that the supply wasn't short. I appreciated them setting that shit right at the cabin, but as much bullshit as I'd cleaned up for them over the years, them mopping and sweeping wasn't shit.

Today, the entire family, along with the members of the mob and their significant others, was standing on the lawn of the Mecanio Estates. Rio had finally removed that Gay Boy Mansion sign Don put in his yard years ago. I guess he had no choice since there were close to two hundred people standing about. In true Rio fashion, cocktail bars lined the yard to keep us entertained while we waited to be let inside the house. The gender reveal started at five, but Pia had purposely put the wrong time so that everyone would show up on time. What she didn't anticipate was her father not allowing anyone inside, including her, until exactly five o'clock.

"You hear this nigga, bae? W. E. B. Du Bois has a fuckin' thesis statement for everything except why he had cocaine strewn every fuckin' where at the cabin."

"Nel..." Ezio warned but it was no use. Once that nigga got started, he wasn't letting up.

Pia and Vello snickered as if he'd told the joke of the century while I shook my head. Nel told her ass every fucking thing so it made no sense in scolding his ass about discussing mob business in front of her.

"Yeah, chill, Twin. It's mad people out here. Ion remember half of these muthafuckas pulling up for my party," Vello said, his eyes on his fiancée.

He had been listening to what we had going on, but Discover had his undivided attention. She was standing a few feet away with the other women, and although this was her first time popping out, she looked good. Motherhood suited her well. Her face was still slightly rounder than normal, but other than that, Vello's woman was holding her own.

Pia nodded and looked around. "Yeah, my dad contacted everybody he knew. I don't even know some of these people."

"Twin just hatin' 'cause his party was cut short, baby. Them twins said, 'Fuck yo' plans, daddy.'" Nel was on a roll, this time getting laughs from everyone.

He and Pia had already made their rounds to everyone on the lawn, assuring them that the party would start soon. We were the first stop, and forty-five minutes later, they were back in front of us. Now, we were all just standing around, getting sweaty. It was the middle of summer, so it was hot as fuck outside, but the bottled water I'd downed minutes before had done well enough to keep me hydrated. If Rio didn't open the doors soon, I would be tempted to go sit in my truck for a minute to get some cool air.

"I'm gonna go talk to the girls," Pia said, trying to excuse herself.

We'd been instructed to wear brown if we thought the baby was a girl, black for those predicting a boy, and white for those who were neutral. I was neutral about their baby's gender, so I was in a white Louis Vuitton shirt and shorts set. I wasn't normally a matching set type of nigga unless I was working out, but since I hadn't been home, I had to go to Bayside Shops and get whatever I found. Luckily, my sales rep was in the store and brought this fit straight off the truck. On my feet were white Louis Vuitton Skate Sneakers, and although I had a full bottle of the Imagination at home, I told the sales rep to throw that in the bag too.

Pia was looking stunning in a brown dress that was long, tied around her neck, hugged her belly, and flared to the floor. She had some type of shimmer lotion on that had her glowing even more than the pregnancy did. Her signature hairstyle was always some type of ponytail, and today was no different. A heavy side bang and a long, Barbie-like ponytail that fell to the middle of her back completed her look. When the glam team called me this morning, I didn't even answer because I knew they were asking if I needed to get Solana on their list since the other wives probably were. Once the call went to voicemail, I sent the trio a text asking them to pull up at my mama's house to get her right. She'd hugged me the moment I got out of the car and was somewhere amongst the rest of the mature women. Of course, those expensive motherfuckers did a good job making my mother look even more beautiful than she already was.

Nel tightened his grip on Pia's hand, stopping her from moving.

"Sprung ass." Ezio cackled as we all either watched the two guests of honors or shook our heads at Nel's foolish ass.

Ezio and his junior were in matching black Casa Blanca sets. Lil' Ezee was getting too big and was spoiled as hell by everyone, especially Ezio's mom. She had Lil' Ezee now, holding him hostage somewhere with my mother.

"Nigga, don't be mad at us cuz you can't love on yo' wife out loud *cuz yous sceed of Masa.*" Nel used his best slave voice, and that shit had us all laughing, including Ezio.

"Fuck outta here! That nigga ain't my masa, nor do he regulate shit 'round here."

Nel kissed his teeth. "Oh, yeah? Well, why yo' money gettin' low cuz you be too scared to tell Jisei no? You know if you say no, she going straight to the big dawg!"

"On foe 'nem! I ain't never runnin' out, nigga!" Ezio reached into his pocket, popped a rubber band from a wad of money, and began spreading straight blue faces between his ten fingers. He had his diamond grill in, and was sure to flex that, too, as he glared at Nel. "Mine can have *whatever* the fuck she like, no interference needed."

He then smirked at Pia, who was still being held at Nel's side, her eyes jumping from the other wives back to our crew, standing together.

"Aye, Pia... You got the latest Chanel collection?"

Pia looked to Ezio and smiled, placing her finger to her chin. "Hmm. As a matter of fact, I don't think I do. You tricking?"

Ezio smiled right at Nel before saying, "Big trickin'! I'll have it to your door 'fore this nigga wakes up to shake the piss from his dick. Don't act like you'n know who *yo'* big homie is." Ezio directed the second statement to Nel.

"Nigga, you think we turnin' shit down? Hell nawl, we ain't. And don't be out here on that light-skinned shit, tryna show out. She better have the whole collection before the sun rises. Money flashing don't impress us... It's the spending that do. Ain't it, bae?"

"Facts!" Pia was always backing Nel's bullshit. It had been that way since we were kids.

"Shit, I can have it delivered tonight. How long this baby shower last?"

"It's a gender reveal, hoe-ass nigga."

"Same thang, bitch. But I got you, *Pia baby*." Ezio winked after mimicking Nel's voice, making Pia giggle.

She'd been hard as nails when she first popped back up. Between her father and Nel loving her and allowing her to rest in her womanhood, she'd turned into a version of herself that most women yearned for. And it hadn't taken but a few months for it to happen.

"Aite now, clear-ass nigga. Pipe the fuck down, joe! You spendin' now, but was cryin' when it was time to pay for that Medieval Times-ass wedding." Nel put his hand up, mimicking a phone, and pressed it to his ear. '"*Don, what you said you was covering? Yo' sister keeps adding shit.*' Crybaby-ass nigga."

Ezio looked around before staring at Nel. "And who paid for this?"

Nel looked at Pia, and she tucked her lips in.

"Exactly! Daddy Dickemdown did, nigga."

"Ezio!" Pia squealed as she held her stomach, trying hard not to laugh at her father being cracked on.

"Fuck you." Nel sneered.

"Fuck you, nigga. That's why you dressed like a basic nigga. How we shuttin' yo' shit down?"

Nel was in a black polo-style Burberry shirt, with the signature Burberry print at the collar. He had on black jeans, even though it was hot as fuck. My nigga looked fly, though. The jewelry, fresh retwist, and Aura cologne added to his look. Above all, the woman on his side boosted his shit times twenty.

"Neltz told his ass he was dressed like a YN, but he wouldn't listen," Vello revealed, his focus still on Discover.

"On foe 'nem... Sometimes, ion like you. You don't know if you my sac mate or my opp."

Vello shrugged. "I was just sayin'."

Nel waved him off and pulled Pia in front of him. "Pia baby... Who paid for this? Me, right?"

"Renello... No, baby."

We all laughed so loud that everyone turned our way. Nel was too hot as he dropped her hand and crossed his arms over his chest.

"My daddy asked to throw it, so I just let him, baby. I let him handle everything. The flyers, the vendors, and the decor... Everything. I been too tired to care about this stuff."

"What about the wedding planner? Daylani? She couldn't do it?"

"She's planning about twenty weddings, including ours, your brothers and Discover's, plus our baby shower. I didn't want to add anything extra on her plate."

"Baby, she got a whole team. She making six figures every time we book. She could've handled it."

"Is it a problem that I let my dad throw it, Renello?" The way Pia asked the question, I knew Nel had to tread lightly with his answer.

"It ain't no problem, baby..." Nel grabbed Pia and turned so that his back was to us now. He tried whispering. "But, damn... You should've asked me. I coulda let my mama do it."

"Your mama! Did you see the way yo' mama had your house decorated? Hell nah! Wasn't gone have my baby shit country as fuck!"

We was no more good from laughing at these two fools. I'd told Ezio that Nel had met his match when he decided he was going to marry Pia.

"Okay, Pia baby. You right. What's the theme, though? I thought at the gender reveals, you supposed to wear pink and blue?"

"Renello... Let's be real. You didn't care nothing about no theme until you found out he was in charge. My daddy is a man of opulence and class. He knows how to throw a party. You saw how nice Discovery's party was."

Silence followed her statement. She wasn't lying about Discovery's party being laced.

Nel's shoulders relaxed. "Aite. You right, baby."

She stood on her tiptoes and kissed his lips. "I know. Now, I'm going over here with my girls. And Shio?"

I looked up from my phone. I was waiting for Italian to text me back. "Wassup, Pretty Pia?"

Nel turned around and sneered at me. "Don't push it, nigga."

Ignoring him, I watched Pia cock her head, her bang falling over her left eye. "We missing Solana..." She blinked sweetly at me as my face remained unchanged.

"That man got a whole baby mama who ain't Solana," Vello inserted.

Pia snapped her neck to look at him. "Take a look around... Do you see her anywhere? News flashhh! You're not gonna. The fuck!"

"Aye! You got it, sis." Vello held his hands up.

"Umm hmm. I know. We're full anyway. No new bitches allowed. Ion give a fuck if she got a baby by the pope." She faced me again, protruding belly round as fuck with her hand resting on it, the rose diamond ring gleaming in the sunlight. Pia took a few steps toward me and then patted my chest, her powdery perfume tickling my nose. "Don't count my girl out."

Instead of waiting for me to respond or giving Nel the opportunity to block her from walking away, Pia glided between Ezio and me toward the circle of wives and fiancées. I didn't bother to look over my shoulder in that direction because, although I loved all the wives, no one over there belonged to me.

Ezio kissed his teeth, gaining our attention. "I'm just saying... How the women still be side-eyeing me, but you lock one of their friends away, and they be nice as hell to you?"

"Nigga cuz you nearly *killed* Jisei. I ain't holdin' it against ya. Just know, them pills had you by the balls, my boy." Vello shrugged.

"I'm starting to think Shio could fuck all the women if he wanted to, except mine. He 'bout can even fuck Don's."

Instead of arguing against what Ezio said, I flashed a smile and winked. I had no desire to fuck anybody's wife, but I enjoyed seeing these goofy-ass niggas nut up about something. For so long, these three had no plans to be one-woman men. Now, they cried and complained about their significant others all fucking day.

"Yo' ole Gerald Levert-looking ass. I wish the fuck you would try Pia." Nel stuck his middle finger up at me.

I laughed while pocketing my phone. "You been talkin' a whole lot of shit to be a nigga that let a gay man plan his gender reveal party. I cannot wait to see this shit."

"Yeah, Twin. You slipped up on this shit," Vello added.

"Fuck yo' boring-ass-event having ass. What the fuck was yo' shit? A baby shower slash engagement? Well, I did both, *separately!* Lazy, cheap-ass nigga. Yo' bitch came with a whole dowry, and you still took the basic way out."

Ezio and I were laughing hard as fuck, but Vello must've had enough because he finished his water bottle and scowled at his brother. "You got the cheapest ring of us all. Fuckin' costume jewelry. Got Pia walkin' 'round like she Bell from *Beauty and the Beast.* One last rose petal-ass boi! Don't be mad that Daylani did ours. You know... rich nigga shit. We didn't need a *daddy* or a brother, bitch. I'm the daddy."

"Nigga, that's cuz you engaged to Little Orphan Annie. She ain't got no fuckin' daddy."

"You ain't got no daddy neither, nigga," Vello countered.

"And may his bitch ass rest in hell. I know what Discover do got, though."

"Nigga, what?" Vello challenged.

"Baby daddies. Several, and we standin' on the turf of her ex-husband. Yous a strong fella, Twin. You competin' with a rich mobster and a rich rapper. Shits tough for you, my boy."

Ezio had fallen onto me, laughing through a choke, while Vello seethed at his brother. He hated for anyone to bring up his Lil' Chef being Essex's child. Discover didn't have any kids by Rio, but since he had financed her life so she could raise Discovery with no worries, he was just as much of her dad as Essex and Vello.

Before anyone could say anything else, the crowd had quieted, and when I shifted my attention to see what was the cause, Rio Mecanio was standing on his doorstep with Patty.

"Good evening, ladies and gentlemen."

He was team boy, dressed in a black linen set, and Patty was matching him with the same set but form-fitting to her body. Pia was a perfect mix of both her parents. Just like Nel had his fingers intertwined in Pia's earlier, Rio held Patty's hand the same way. I didn't care to know their business or what they did behind the walls of his mansion, but she was always smiling, and so was he. The jokes were never-ending because we'd all seen that nigga get gobbled up by men, but we let them be.

"Children—that includes you, too, grandson—please board the

train. You will be escorted to the guest house on the west side of the property," he said into the mic. "Parents, the west side is properly staffed."

A kiddie train, like the ones at amusement parks, rolled up on wheels, pulling six individual carts, all a different color of the rainbow. I watched Neltz mumble some shit under his breath as he climbed onto the last cart. He was in a brown Jordan hoodie with khaki pants, standing clear on wanting a baby sister. Auntie Erni boarded, too, with Little Ezee. Vello's twins were still too small to be outside, so Auntie Irie had stayed at Vello's house with them. Once Pearla and her crew piled on, including Bella—although she was considered an adult—the train honked and pulled off. It was deep as fuck with kids since other members of the mob had brought theirs too.

"Now that that's settled, I must say you all look beautiful in your brown, black, and white. Daughter, you look amazing. My heart is overfilled." Rio pressed the hand that was holding Patty's hand to his heart and kissed.

Pia fanned her eyes, and the ladies consoled her as she became emotional.

"This is my first time hosting a gender reveal, but I had the most fun putting this together for my favorite couple."

"Fake-ass nigga!" Don's childish ass yelled out, sending laughs across the yard.

He'd been standing off to the side with Big Zan, Matteo, Rut, and Lorenzo. He hadn't come over to fuck with us, and we made no moves to walk over and chop it up with them. I wasn't running from the nigga or no shit like that, but there were only a few days left before my thirty days were up, and I was about to tell that nigga to go fuck himself. I'd had two failed DNA tests, no answer on if Bahati could be trusted, Solana was still detoxing, and his ass hadn't said shit about making a move on the Rodríguezes.

Giving in to my desire for Solana had fucked my head up. I was texting Italian more than usual because I couldn't watch Solana on the camera anymore. It was powered on so I could hear her, but she had something covering it now. I should've been thanking her mad ass for forcing me to stop watching her. The lack of access would help me make my decision on who to marry based on pure strategy rather than lust. I couldn't see myself loving either one of these women, but thinking back to that night, I knew Solana could definitely feed my sexual appetite if we were married. I'd only tasted her pretty ass and was fucking obsessed with the pussy. But, that shit wasn't enough.

Then, when Essex hit me and showed me the burned-down apartment building I'd just spent close to ten thousand on for Bahati's rent and utilities, I was frustrated as fuck. I hadn't mentioned her shit being burnt up, but she hadn't inquired about trying to get her and Shya's belongings either. The whole situation had me uneasy, and coincidences never felt like coincidences to me. Humans were the coincidental factor in everything, so the apartment building burning down days after I had inquired about Bahati being a tenant felt intentional. But Bahati had somewhat proven the way life would be with her being a wife. She would be a wife and mother, and nothing more. I kept telling myself that she would be enough, but I didn't trust her. I had to trust the woman whom I would be tied to for the rest of my life.

So, I wasn't ready to choose a wife, and Don would have to deal with that shit.

"Demise, you and the lovely Dasani are my second favorite couple. No worries, my friend." Rio faced the crowd again. "Welcome, everyone!"

The door to his home opened, and black and brown balloons spilled onto the walkway, followed by smoke.

Ezio clapped his hands. "Aw shit, Nel! Daddy-in-law did the damn thing."

Nel held his middle finger up as he walked over and grabbed Pia's hand. The crowd parted for them, letting the two walk in first. Once they disappeared within the fog, I let a few people go ahead before joining the end of the line. My phone vibrated in my pocket, and I pulled it out to see that Bahati was calling me. Silencing the screen, I placed it back in my pocket. Just as I got to the threshold, it was ringing again, and this time it was a FaceTime. I slid my thumb across the screen, and she appeared instantly. I'd be lying if I said she didn't look good, but Bahati always looked good. Looking good wasn't the issue I had with her.

"Wassup, Bahati?"

There was a frown on her pretty face as she looked from me to my background. She couldn't see anything but the smoke and balloon arch outside of my face.

"You haven't been home."

"I know."

Lifting my head in response to a slap on my shoulder, I pulled Zodiac, one of the last mobsters to get married before Tunan, in a brotherly hug.

"Shio."

Putting my attention back on Bahati, I moved from in front of the door and off to the side. "Where is Shya?"

Bahati flipped the screen, and Shya was napping. I could see dried tears on her face, indicating she'd cried herself asleep for the umpteenth time. My heart fell and guilt consumed me. Baby girl was still struggling with being here. I didn't have a solution, but something would have to give soon.

"I'll be there tonight."

"You sure?"

"Yeah."

Bahati grinned and then ended the call. I rounded the balloon arch and entered Rio's mansion in search of my cousins.

"Man, what the fuck is this?" Nel poked a balloon as I walked up behind him, Ezio, and Vello.

Looking at the balloons, I shifted my eyes around the space and nearly walked out to be sure I'd walked into the right house.

"Bae..." Pia had her hand over her mouth, trying to hold back either her tears or laughs. The women behind her had their phones out and were tickled pink.

"This is yo' in-law daddyyyyy!" Vello sang out, mimicking Mr. Brown from the Madea movies.

Lining the massive hallway to enter the living areas were black and brown balloons. The grand staircase also had the same balloons on a garland. It wasn't the balloons that had the men either looking uncomfortably or laughing with the women, but it was the theme that was splattered everywhere.

Hanging in the middle of the balloon arches were long Black dicks. Rio's ceiling was at least twenty feet tall, but with how long the dicks were, you'd have to walk around them to prevent them from slapping you in the face. At the ends of the marble staircase and on the tables scattered about were pairs of breasts, just as big as the dicks.

"Daddy! Oh, my God! This is hilarious!"

Rio stood near the stairs, sipping from what I knew had to be rare bourbon. "How did your old man do? Every inch of the space is decked in the theme, Pia. Look in the backyard."

Lo and behold, more tables were set up around the pool with titty and dick centerpieces on them. This was some wild shit.

"Dicks and tits is the theme for a gender reveal? The fuck, fav!" Ezio grabbed Nel's shoulder and shoved him forward, laughing hard as hell.

Nel tried shoving him off, but Ezio wasn't letting up.

"I know how you men can be when it comes to your sexuality. Never open-minded."

"Hell nawl, we ain't open-minded. This shit suspect as hell!" Don yelled as people around us were either taking pictures of the decor or laughing amongst their circles.

"Guests, please join me in the backyard."

Pia grabbed Nel's hand to lead him back. Nel was pissed, but he kept his mouth shut and followed Pia knowing if he said anything, Ezio and Vello would be on his ass.

Everyone filed into the backyard, and my stomach growled as we bypassed the kitchen where chefs were working around each other. I could smell the seasoned meats and seafood, and I knew it would be good if it was the same vendors from Discovery party. As I finally stepped into the backyard, I watched as the guests took seats at the black and brown clothed tables. The tables with a titty centerpiece filled faster than the tables with tall-ass dicks on them. A few mobsters had claimed the dick tables, but removed the dick balloons, throwing them off to the side. There was a money and gift table for guests to drop off requested items, and I knew that was Nel's doing. The nigga loved free shit. Before taking my seat, I grabbed a money bag from the table, pulled a knot of money from my pocket, shoved it inside the bag, and grabbed the permanent marker to write my name on it. There was a spot to scribble the amount, but I didn't know how much it was. I knew it was more than five thousand, though, and I knew Pia would spend it on some shit that was unnecessary, just like the other women. But that's what they were supposed to do. I made a mental note to do even better for the baby shower. I didn't have much on me outside of my credit cards.

Taking a seat at Ezio's table, I turned to find Jisei smiling at me. I tilted my head to her before looking around at everyone else. Missy and Essex were at the table, and she had been all in his face, removing invisible stuff from it. I reached across the table and dapped him up since people had him cornered in the yard, asking for autographs and pictures. We had already chopped it up on the phone after he showed me the rumble of Bahati's apartment building. I was happy for everything Essex had going on, which was a fucking lot. Missy seemed to be good for him, though, helping out with his boys and keeping his dick drained.

I scanned the rest of the table, realizing Tunan was MIA. He'd claimed he was coming to the reveal when I hit him up yesterday, but he was a no-show so far. I caught sight of his wife standing with the rest of the mob women on the lawn, so I figured he'd show soon enough. Rio escorting Nel and Pia caught my eye. The elevated brown platform he was helping Pia onto was fully decorated with balloons like the rest of the yard, but they had two black throne chairs waiting for them to sit. Nel still had an attitude, but he took his seat, and I laughed knowing his ass was biting back his words. Don was at a table across from me, and the nigga had the nerve to raise a glass. I just looked at his ass, not returning the gesture. He'd better be glad it wasn't the time and place because I'd be on his ass, picking his brain about the Rodríguez situation. I was ready to find them niggas and kill everybody, and he was trying to be all diplomatic. The one time I'm on his type of time with his unhinged behavior is the one time he is on my type of time with strategic planning.

"Now that we are all seated... Come on out!" Rio announced into the mic.

"I swear... this bet not be no gay shit." Ezio groaned before Jisei hit his chest.

The door to the pool house opened and, immediately, all the men sat up in their seats. Women filed out, covered in nothing but black or brown body paint. Their entire bodies were covered except their faces. There had to be about thirty naked women exiting the pool house in two even lines, brown bodies in one and black bodies in the other. Titties bounced and hips swayed as they switched in heels. When they were close enough to walk past me, my neck twisted and my assessment of seeing it from the back confirmed I'd been right. Their asses were on swollen.

I whistled. "Gotdamn! Where Rio get them from?"

"On God," Tunan, appearing on my side in black, grunted. We slapped hands while both of our eyes scanned the women.

"Some of them from Club Vintage. There go Passion. And look at my bitch White Chocolate!" Missy slapped a white girl on the ass, who was just as thick as the Black women, and she bent down and gave Missy a quick hug, titties dangling all in her face before getting back in line.

"Whew! So fucking glad I brought ones..." Missy opened her purse and pulled out stacks of ones.

Essex grinned. "What can I say? My baby be prepared."

"What the fuck kind of freaky-ass gender reveal this is?" Vello asked out loud.

"Ion know, but I like it, y'all!" Jisei nodded with glee in her eyes.

"Shit, me too!" Ezio revealed.

"Fact's!" Tunan agreed before slapping it up with the rest of the men before joining his wife at her table.

The music started, and the painted women all took a spot, distancing themselves apart but still in straight lines. Poles shot up from the grass and once they reached their full height, the dancing began. Waitresses came out, holding stacks of dollar bills on trays, and men and their wives began waving them down to trade out their larger bills for ones. Missy was already prepared, so she was on her feet, walking in front of the girls of her choosing and raining down. Essex was behind her, rapping since one of his songs was playing.

Jisei held her hand out, and Ezio pulled bills from the stack he'd been flashing on the front lawn. "Where the fuck the food at? We 'posed to watch pussy on an empty stomach?" he asked, and I nodded in agreement, hungry as hell.

"We can't handle money and food at the same time, baby. It's coming. Want me to go into the kitchen and find you something?" Jisei asked as she received her bills from the white-gloved waitress.

"Nawl, Jae Bae. Come on." He pulled Jisei from the table.

A waitress came up beside me like I'd summoned her, her body well-proportioned. Looking around the yard to see if I spotted the first lady, I handed the waitress money from the other wad in my pocket when I didn't see her. These waitresses weren't naked, but the way their white dresses clung to their skin, you'd think they were. She handed me the two stacks of ones, me deciding that would be enough in this mixed company setting.

Under the open sky, dancers moved with fluid grace around the poles while adults, old and young, surrounded them and threw money. The grassy ground didn't bother them at all as many of them dropped into splits as if they were floating in the air and gravity suddenly paused. Sunlight shimmered on their dark-painted skin, which I knew underneath varied in all shades matching their flawlessly made-up faces. Flipping their hair and winding their bodies, the strippers moved with strength and elegance. They leaped, twirled, and played Twister with the poles, putting the guests in a trance.

I had to give it to Rio; this was a damn movie. There were two cameramen: one at the end of the yard, filming Pia and Nel who had their own two strippers dancing all over them, and the other was filming Essex and Missy's faces. This scene would be perfect in one of his videos, the uncut version that could be released on YouTube, and if Bella's ass caught wind of it, she'd find a way to get the video on prime time TV too.

I felt eyes on me, and when I looked up to see Don had pulled two girls from the pole and was pointing to me. I'd gotten my ones but had yet to move. This nigga was always trying to control some shit. I mugged his ass before watching the two thick-ass women switch my way, abandoning their pole. Both were perfect, dark chocolate on their face as the brown paint adorned their bodies. This time, when he lifted his glass, I raised one of the stacks of money. Pushing my chair back away from the table, one of the girls lifted her leg, popping her pussy right in my face.

No smell. Good start.

Her partner bent her ass right over in front of me, close enough to sit her ass on my lap. She began wiggling her legs, creating a wave of brown Jello. Popping the rubber band on the first stack, I was slumped in my chair as they were dancing in my space. The one that had lifted her leg did it again, but this time, she twirled and landed on my lap. Her titties grazed my Jesus piece as she grinded on my dick. The other stripper was still in front of me, and as I watched her ass jiggle with fury, I peeped the garter belt on her upper thigh. Leaning over with the stripper still in my lap, I grabbed the other's waist and pulled her closer. Now with her beside me, I pushed her back into the position and stuffed some money in her garter belt. It was so close to her pussy that my finger was inches away from grazing it as I stuffed as many ones as I could.

The song had switched to Tory Lanez's "The Cry," making the girls slow down a bit.

My dick was hard as a rock because I was a man, and I hadn't busted a nut in well over a month. I had two of the baddest naked in my lap, and I refused to be ashamed about my dick being harder than a brick.

"We can take this party to the pool house..."

The women had switched places, and both of their garters were stuffed with my money. I was out of ones and was hella tempted to rain straight hundreds on them because they had been putting in work. Her arm was around my neck while her friend was beside me, playing with her pink pussy. This shit had turned triple X-rated, and I no longer wanted to look and see if Shannon was somewhere around the yard.

"Beautiful, I'm going to have to respectfully decline. But..." I jutted my chin back at Don. "He might be up for it."

They danced until the song ended, and by then, the one beside me had come all over her fingers. They both walked away and went onto the pool house after thanking me. Minutes later, they emerged and returned to the sender. They'd cleaned up, and I fucked with that because grinding wet pussy from an old nigga on a new nigga was foul. Don mugged me as the women approached him, but I paid his ass no mind.

Two songs later, the strippers took a break, and Ezio's greedy ass was able to eat. That nigga had lost his dad bod weight, but he still ate like Jisei was carrying a baby. She'd been adamant that she wasn't having any more anytime soon, but I knew he was fucking her with no regard for the shit she was spitting. Plates of lobster, steak, creamed spinach, and sweet potatoes were piled in front of us. I was acting like Ezio today and wasn't ashamed as I stuffed my mouth. Champagne began to flow, and I declined the offered glass, taking sparkling water instead. I'd been eating all kinds of shit lately, so I was limiting my alcohol intake. The strippers were back in the pool house, and everyone talked about how much fun they were having as they ate.

"They got Rio fucked up. Dicks or Tits been the best reveal I done been to. I fucks with Daylani, but he need to plan the baby shower too."

Jisei snickered at Missy's statement. "Maybe he can plan yours."

"Who?" Missy cut into her steak, feeding it to Essex instead of herself. "We got three. You know how hectic it is having three kids on tour? Baby, no. Thank God for Discovery because chile..."

"I thought y'all had the nanny?" Ezio asked.

"You know Josephine is loyal to Discover. She back here, helping with the twins. She recommended her niece, so we shall see if she works out once she starts."

Jisei shook her head. "I'm sorry, boo. I'll send you someone that I turned down. I interviewed a few who were all great, but I could only choose one. I think two were willing to travel."

Once most people were finished eating, guests were pulled from the table one by one to give their guesses on video of what we thought the baby would be. By the time I got back to my seat, I was excusing myself again. I went inside, bypassing the hanging dicks, to the first available bathroom to wash my hands. Locking the door, I pulled Solana's phone back out, and saw she still hadn't sent any texts or audio messages. Pulling my phone from my pocket, I went back to the camera app, and still, something was covering it. I hadn't known Solana's ass was that strong to launch some shit at the camera to cover it. I guess I had myself to blame for those intense-ass workouts.

Locking the screen, I stuffed the phones back into my pocket, opting out of texting Italian to give me an update. I dodged two more hanging dicks, grabbed a water bottle on the way out, and took my seat again. The plates had been cleared from the tables, and the money waitresses were handing out white towels and spray bottles full of rubbing alcohol.

"Thank y'all so much for being here! Most of all, thank you,

Daddy, for this! I would have never thought this is what you came up with when I asked you to plan. But it's perfect."

Nel grumbled.

"I have been told that the reveal is about to happen so here we go, everyone!" Pia passed the mic to Nel, who declined. She shoved it into his hand anyway, and he simply said, "Thanks for coming."

A loud engine rumbled to the right of us, and seconds later, there was a plane with a banner attached. Pulling a phone from my pocket, I went to the camera app and pressed record. The plane neared us, and the people seated at the far end of the yard began cheering. Once the plane was directly over us, we all could see the banner, which revealed the gender.

It's a girl!

The entire backyard erupted in cheers at the pink sign with brown letters as the plane flew away. I panned the camera to Pia, who was jumping up and down, and Nel, who was smiling so big, I could see every tooth in his mouth.

Hearing another plane, I turned the phone back toward the sky.

It's another girl!

"What!"

"Twins?"

"I fucking knew it!"

Everyone was making comments on the fact that the two banners were indicating that Pia was having two babies. She was no longer jumping up and down, now looking at Nel in confusion. I was smiling hard as fuck for my cousin. He could act like he was shocked, but we all knew it was a possibility.

Another plane sounded, and I heard the gasps from the elder tables. Not wanting to miss the third banner, I panned the phone back to the sky and made sure the red button was still lit, not wanting the recording to cut off.

Identical Twins!

Pink glitter fell from the third plane, raining down on the entire backyard. Nel was smiling, but Pia looked pissed. Ending the video, I sent it to Nel's phone and stuffed it back in my pocket.

"When I found that shit out, I was too happy *and* mad for my friend!" Missy cried, wiping her tears, recording her own video. She'd been the keeper of the gender, so she must've known a while.

"How the fuck did she not know she was having twins?" Ezio asked.

"One of the babies was hiding behind the other. They told her they found something, and Pia asked if the baby was healthy, and when they told her yes, she told them not to tell her nothing else... Just write it down and put it in an envelope. That's how I ended up with two envelopes."

"Oh my God! These fools can't produce anything but twins!" Jisei shook her head.

A few tables over, Discover looked mortified. She was probably having flashbacks of her chaotic delivery. Vello had undoubtedly fucked up his chances of having more kids in the future.

"Congratulations, my daughter. Let us finish the party. When it is done, I'd like to take you to the airport for your final gift."

"Daddy, you got me a plane? I was just playing when I said I wanted one!"

"Well, you have one now, darling."

Ezio whistled. "Yeah, ain't shit Nel can't do shit with Big Rio. A fuckin' jet!" He then turned to Jisei as if he had a revelation. "Aye, Jae Bae. Don't ask your brother for no shit like that, aite."

We all laughed, and everyone cheered when the strippers brought their asses back out. Tunan came back over, kicked shit and rotated a few blunts. When he dapped me up, he said he was headed out because he had something he had to take care of tonight. I offered my help, but he told me it wasn't nothing before taking his leave.

I watched the party, accepting the fact that none of these women had what I wanted. Looking at all my family enjoying themselves, I knew there was no way I could leave the mob. When I looked over and saw Rio's sister, Arianee, talking with Dasani, I chuckled knowing she was probably inquiring about Daylani's plans for Pia's baby shower now that we'd seen what Rio did for the gender reveal.

When I glanced over and locked eyes with Don, I sucked my teeth at the sight of him tapping his finger on his watch.

Fuck this nigga. Can't nobody move me but me.

~

STANDING in the entryway of my home, I scratched my face as I peeped around. Everything looked the same. From my position, there was no sign that a woman or a child had been living here for weeks. My home looked exactly the way I had left it the other day when I headed to meet Goal for the drop. Dark wood, green textiles, one painting, furniture varying from leathers to fibers, with not an item out of place. I chose the color scheme because it felt warm and invigorating. But standing here now, it felt as cold as the fucking Tundra. There was no life in this motherfucker.

The cleaning company hadn't come this week because Bahati requested that I call them off. I hadn't been here any fucking way so I obliged. Where my home would have been smelling like fresh lemons and the other fragrances that had become therapeutic to me that the cleaning company used, I smelled nothing but scents that reminded me of Bahati. The same shit she used to clean her apartment back in the day now lingered in the entryway. It wasn't bad, but I wasn't a Fabuloso and Awesome type of nigga.

Pulling my shirt over my head, I held it so that it wouldn't hit the floor. Marching to the side of my house where the guest rooms were, I passed the closed door and stopped in front of the room Bahati and Shya had been occupying. Bahati's eyes fluttered toward me appearing as she patted Shya's back with her good arm.

"Aye."

"Yes?" she answered, her breath caught in her chest.

I could see the shit as her chest inflated and stayed that way. I never cared about the power I had over women, but more often than not, women acted as if they couldn't handle my presence. Bahati had known me for years and still acted as if she were seeing me for the first time anytime we were in each other's presence.

That's how ole girl be having me feeling, I thought to myself before shaking her off my mind.

Licking my lips, I gave Bahati another once over. Bahati was perfect. Her skin, her facial features, and her body were a packaged deal many men would happily pay for. My eyes landed on her bare, arched foot that was hanging from the side of the bed, suspended in the air while the other was folded in the covers.

"If you want some dick, gone and put her to sleep."

Bahati's eyes bulged and she began choking on her own spit. She sat up, placed Shya on the bed fast as fuck, and tripped out of the covers. Before I could witness her ass hitting the floor, I left the room's doorway. Crossing the house and entering my bedroom, I left the door open for her. I emptied my pockets onto my nightstand and then walked toward my bathroom. Tossing the shirt into the hamper, I removed my shoes and walked them into my closet. Placing them near my other Louis Vuitton sneakers, I then removed my necklaces that hadn't seemed to leave my neck in days. I immediately felt naked without them, the missing weight feeling foreign. When I walked from the closet and back into my room, Bahati was standing there in her bra and panties. The matching set was brown and nearly blended in with her skin.

"Come 'ere, Bahati."

With one foot in front of the other, round hips swaying, Bahati obliged. Cast and all, she was sexy as fuck, and if you lined Bahati up with the strippers that were at the reveal, she would have put a few of them to shame. Like theirs, I could see her ass from the front, but she didn't give me long to wander because she did a spin, giving me a view of her ass spilling out of her lace panties. It was so fucking round, and the dimples in it waved as she made it clap subtly. Bahati could have easily been a dancer with the way she knew how to manipulate her body. The way she used to move used to have me brick as fuck, and it was a plus that she could do everything on my dick as well.

"Stop all that playin' and come get this dick."

I was hard, but not to my full potential. I was just as I was when the strippers popped their pussies in my face, but as soon as she put her mouth on my dick, I'd get where I needed to be.

She climbed onto the bed, and I could feel the heat from her center since she had both her legs on either side of mine. Using her knees, she climbed up my legs, not stopping until she was in my lap. When her damp pussy hit my boxers, she moaned. Her eyes were low with lust as she scanned my chest as if looking for something that belonged to her. Using my index finger, I traced the lace of her bra. Her chest heaved as she began slow grinding in my lap. The shea butter floated around my head from her moisturized skin. Bahati was a fucking dream to any nigga with eyes that loved chocolate, and it didn't hurt that she oozed sex appeal. She knew how to use that shit too.

Leaning in, she began kissing my neck while continuing to dance in my lap. Her kisses were soft and wet, and I couldn't lie about the shit not feeling good as fuck. Letting her do her thing, I grabbed her ass, squeezed it, and slapped it hard. She bit down on my neck before sucking on the bite. My dick had now grown to its full potential, and I was impressed with her ability to get me there without her needing to swallow my shit.

Reaching over, one hand still on her ass, I opened the nightstand and grabbed a condom.

"You don't have to use one... We can have a baby, or you can pull out," Bahati stated through her moans.

Bzz Bzz

She was sucking in another spot on my neck as one of the phones vibrated on the nightstand. Reaching for it, Bahati grabbed my face and tried kissing my lips, but I turned my head so that I could read the message. She didn't let the slight rejection fuck up what she had going because she went back to biting and licking on my neck, winding her hips faster on my covered dick.

SOLANA

Shio. I have uncovered the camera so you could see I am going to bed.

THE FIFTEEN-WORD TEXT message had my body stiffening and my dick deflating.

Bahati grabbed my face again, trying to kiss me, but this time, I let go of her ass and grabbed her wrist, making sure not to apply any pressure.

"What is it, Shio? I thought we were doing this. I can't kiss you?"

Licking my lips, her essence suffocated me, but not in the way that Solana's had.

She didn't look like her. She didn't feel like her. She didn't smell like her. She didn't say my name like her. And I knew for a fact she didn't taste like her. I hadn't ever tasted Bahati, but I knew there wasn't a woman on this earth who tasted like Solana Ledesma.

Bahati tried kissing me again, and I dodged her, one hand still holding the phone and the other still holding her wrist.

"Bahati, chill out."

She snatched her arm away from me. "Chill out? It's just a kiss! I can't kiss you, Shio? And who are you texting?"

Her eyes shot to the phone in my hand, but the screen had already gone black. It didn't matter. The fifteen words were echoing in my head, and the only thing I wanted to do was swipe to the camera app to see if she had fallen asleep yet.

"Is it Uriah?"

I sighed. "Naw."

"Well, why can't I kiss you?"

Chuckling more at this fucking predicament than her question, I asked, "You want to know how her pussy tastes?"

Bahati frowned. "Nigga, what?"

"Unless you want to know how her pussy tastes, keep your lips to yourself, Bahati."

"You're unbelievable. You are so fucking unbelievable, Shio! So you can fuck the cokehead bitch, but I can't get no dick?"

Licking my lips again, I scraped my bottom lip with my top teeth and thrust my hips upward to politely gesture for her to get off of me. "Goodnight, Bahati."

She snatched herself from my lap, stood, and placed her hand on her hip. "So what am I supposed to do now?"

"Shit, I apologize." And I did.

I took no pleasure in getting a woman worked up and not putting the fire out of her little pussy. But Solana had entered the fucking chat, and, unfortunately, my ass could not compartmentalize her the way I wanted to.

My eyes were low from the blunts rotating at the gender reveal, so I was peering at Bahati with hooded eyes. My dick was semi-hard, but it wasn't shit Bahati could do for it.

"It's a rose in the other room. It ain't been used before."

"What room?" she replied with attitude.

"Solana's. She ain't gone need it."

"Fuck you."

"Good night, baby mama."

Bahati stormed out of the room, ass jiggling, slamming the door behind her. I unlocked the phone screen and went back to the text. Pressing my head into the leather of my headboard, I closed my eyes because seeing her text my name had my dick harder than any of the women who had tried tonight. Swiping to the camera app, I opened it and found Solana wrapped in the covers and watching TV with the captions on. She was so fucking pretty that I blinked a few times to break up the thoughts of taking my ass over to Jisei's townhouse.

Pretty little fucking sinner.

God first
~~*Make sure the family good*~~
~~*Eye them Cuppacio boys, the little and the big ones*~~
~~*Build a relationship with my brother*~~
~~*Get my brother rich*~~
Health and wellness ~~(ALWAYS)~~ (Shake back)
~~*Stay on top of my mob shit*~~
Keep Hobo alive (DOING... Barely)
~~*Get through the meeting with Ines Ledesma*~~
~~*House a random*~~
~~*Find the true reason Solana is here*~~
~~*Figure out if Solana is supposed to be my wife, again*~~
~~*Find a wife that isn't Solana*~~
Kill every breathing Rodríguez Cartel member (URGENT)
Fuck Bahati up (TBD)
~~*Get my fucking daughter*~~
~~*Get Bahati's arm fixed*~~
~~*Get to know my daughter (DOING)*~~
~~*Figure out what the fuck I'm going to do with Solana*~~
~~*Leave the mob entirely or*~~ *marry* ~~*Bahati or*~~ *Solana*
~~*Get DNA test*~~

Spend time with my daughter ~~(DOING)~~ ~~(ON PAUSE~~)
~~Tell my mama about Shya~~
Keep Solana in real nigga rehab until ~~she clean~~ (TBD)
~~Get SECOND DNA test~~
~~Check on Bahati's apartment~~
Don't fuck ~~Uriah ANYBODY~~ SOLANA
Get to the root of Shya's constant crying
Get THIRD DNA test or say fuck it
Marry Bahati IF she is innocent
~~Pay for that cocaine~~
Decide if Solana can see Shya
Find out what happened to Bahati's apartment building
Leave Bahati alone

CHAPTER 25
TUNAN "TUNE" PAYNE

Taking a long toke from the blunt pinched between my fingers, I let the smoke suffocate my lungs longer than needed. My chest burned, my throat itched, and my eyes watered, but I let the fumes sit. With my left hand clutching the Desert Eagle resting in my lap, I let my finger graze it as my ears began to ring. I'd made this drive too many fucking times to count. This time, I wouldn't be pulling off or scoping the scene. It was go time.

Jumping from the Infiniti, since I'd taken the Ferrari back to the Dungeon, the smell of the night hit me hard. Even if I hadn't parked the Ferrari, I wouldn't be doing any drills in a seven-hundred-thousand-dollar car, especially one that wasn't mine. Scoping the scene, I noticed that this was a nicer part of town—maybe too nice. A pipe nearby must have burst or a dead animal was lingering because the aroma was nearly sickening. I closed the car door, blunt tucked in the corner of my mouth with the gun by my side. This side of the building was dark, and everyone had already retreated into their homes for the night, so I wasn't worried about being seen.

The building rose three floors total, but my destination was on the first.

Rookie mistake.

The first floor was nothing but an amateur move when you had lived the life this person had. The unit was in the building farthest back on the lot of the complex, but if it were me, I'd almost want my spot on the roof. Having an apartment on the ground floor was inviting people to target your shit. It was easy for motherfuckers to kick your door in, but I didn't need the kind of attention that came with putting my size twelve through it. So I crouched, pulled the tool from my pocket, and proceeded to pick the lock. The lighting above the door was out, and had been since I busted the light bulb three days ago, so the only glow I had was from the end of the blunt dangling from the side of my mouth.

Twist. Pull. Turn. Up. Down. Twist.

Ker-Thunk.

The door creaked open after unlocking on my first try. The air conditioning must have been set to fifty-eight, judging by how the A/C greeted me before I even stepped inside. I could see the entire apartment from the front door, proving to me that the apartments were older since the layout wasn't updated. The only light on was coming from the stove, which had a microwave built into it. The kitchen featured stainless steel appliances, an island, and fake marble. Next to that, there was a dining area with a table that was both too big and too fancy, crammed into the narrow space. There was a large mauve sofa that wrapped around the living room—again, too big for the boxed space. It sat on a pink area rug with at least seven shades of pink in swirling patterns. Across from it, there was what had to be no less than an eighty-inch TV mounted on the wall, with a floating entertainment center underneath.

My eyes glanced back at the sofa, where a little pink bow was. Stepping into the apartment, I pushed the door closed behind me and made sure to turn the lock. I walked over to the living room blinds, adjusted the gun, pulled the blinds down a little, and checked the surroundings. Once I was sure it was still quiet and sour outside, I let the blinds go and headed down the narrow hallway, the only other place I could go in this small-ass apartment. The first door was a half bath. The bleach used to clean it was strong. If anything, the leaseholder had always been tidy, and the space showed that.

The next door was cracked, so I used my gun to ease it open. The figure standing at the door made me pause. We watched each other, and when I cocked my head, the figure did too. Raising my gun, I placed my finger on the trigger, but the lack of fear in the figure's eyes kept me from pulling it. The figure turned its head again, and this time the big-ass pink bow on its head flopped and fell to the carpet.

"Ummm!"

Moans and skin slapping took my attention from the small figure, and when I looked up, I saw two more figures, one standing while the other was face down and ass up. I scooped the fearless one up and pushed on into the room. There was a chair in the corner, so I walked right past the fuck fest—sex just as sour as the air outside, skunking the room—and took a seat.

Placing the dog on my lap, I rubbed her head and watched these two motherfuckers go at it. He must've been high because there was no way he didn't feel me walking past him.

"Damn! This pussy good. I'm 'bout to nut, baby!"

Scratching the puppy's scalp, I cradled her head. It couldn't have weighed more than five pounds. I set the Desert Eagle beside her and removed the gun that already had the silencer attached. I had to make sure to thank Tulscan later for the weapons.

There was no light in the room outside of my blunt. The fact that they couldn't smell the potent marijuana was beyond me. I had heard and seen enough so I let off a shot.

"Ahh fuck!" He flew backward, grabbing his shoulder.

"What the fuck wrong witchu?" she asked as she hopped up from the bed.

"Ahhhhh! I-I-I think I been shot!"

"What?!"

"I-I-It's somebody in here. Look... The chair."

She turned, and her body stilled. Her silhouette was shadowed in the dark, but now I could see her clearly, and I couldn't be seeing what I thought I was. Nah. She wasn't that stupid to blow my bread like this.

"Get my pistol, ba—"

Placing the gun with the silencer on my lap on the other side of the puppy, I lifted the Desert Eagle.

"I wish da fuck you would. Cut da fuckin' light on."

Seconds later, there was light.

The nigga was on the ground, backed up into a black dresser, both hands grabbing his bloodied shoulder. Just seeing him had me ready to end this shit before I could get my little speech out.

"Tunan?"

Flat stomach, pink belly ring dangling from it, lace front still intact, hips poking—her body looked like she should have been fucking on a rich nigga instead of the bum bleeding on her carpet behind her.

"Tunan?"

"Fuck you keep callin' my name fo'?"

Her face didn't indicate that she was as scared as she should have been. Her nigga had a hole in him, and I had a gun that could blow her ass in half.

"I... I'm just trying to make sure that's you. Your dreads gone." She placed her hand on her hip. Her pussy was bald and glistening, the juices from that mediocre-ass fucking they'd just been doing on the parts of the lips that were visible.

Then, I remembered why I had to cut my dreadlocks to begin with. When I beat Stella's ass, the only thing she could do was pull my fucking hair. Thanks to the bitch-ass Italian nuts I'd come from, my locs were a finer texture at the root, making them more fragile. In the center of my locs, there were about fifteen dreads missing from her yanking them shits out, so I cut all of them motherfuckers off. It had taken me years to grow them shits out, and I remember sitting in jail being pissed about cutting them before I was ready.

My face was contorted in the meanest mug that I could muster. The shit had my face hurting with how tight my facial muscles were. I was looking at the bitch that turned my life upside down, and I felt nothing but pure hate for this hoe.

"How the fuck you got two titties now, Stella?"

"Tunan, when you get out—"

"Bitch! I said, when you get another titty? Last I checked, cancer ate dat shit off the bone!"

Stella jumped, her perfect porn star titties not moving at all. The way her deep brown skin was stretched over them had them looking so fucking swollen. They were too damn big not to have any type of bounce. As a matter of fact, everything looked swollen, including her cheeks and lips.

I diverted my eyes back to her pussy and let them roam to her hips.

"Turn 'round."

"Tune—"

"Turn yo' stupid ass 'round!"

Stella jumped again, along with her rat in my lap, but she stayed planted.

Slowly, she turned her body in a three sixty. Her ass was as big as the fucking sun, and although Stella was naturally thick, the thighs didn't match the ass, no matter how perfectly round that bitch looked.

"Baby, you know this nigga?" her nigga groaned against the dresser.

Had it not been for the aroma of metallic and iron, I would have forgotten his ass was there. After all, he was irrelevant.

"Get dis nigga a sheet!"

Stella jerked at my tone again, and unlike her titties, the ass moved. Leaning forward, she snatched the hot pink sheet from the bed, gathered it, and threw it into his lap. I spotted white stains on it and shook my head.

Nasty muthafuckas.

"Baby—"

"Ronnie, shut up!" Stella snapped, and it was then that I noticed her fucking chompers.

I motioned the gun from her body to her face. Her hands shot up, long-ass pink nails that looked unsanitary as fuck. The apartment was clean, but that ass couldn't have been. There was no way she could get in the cracks and crevices of her siliconed ass with all those jewels and shit hanging from the three-inch nails.

"Tunan... Just..." Her voice trembled as she forced her eyes closed. When she opened them, a lone tear hit her cheek. "Just let him go. Don't kill, Ronnie."

"Fuck you and dat irrelevant-ass nigga!" I spat.

"W-well... Why you shoot him?"

"For lyin'! The pussy ain't good... Average at fuckin' best."

Stella dropped her hands, and the fake-ass tears instantly stopped. "But you shol' didn't have a problem eatin' it."

"You think yo' stank-ass pussy the only one I ate? Hoe, you ain't special. "

"Tunan, you need to leave."

"Me? Leave? I probably bought errthang in dis bitch, includin' yo' botched-ass body! I ain't goin' no muthafuckin' where, bitch!"

"So whatchu 'bout to do? Fight me again?"

"Yup!"

"And then you goin' back to fuckin' jail."

"I'll go to jail as long as you in hell, hoe! Cuz dis time, after I beat the shit outta you, I'm puttin' a hole in yo' face and dis fuckin' mutt!" I motioned the gun toward the dog.

"Noooo!"

"Shut da fuck up, Stella!"

"I... I wanted to come visit you, but I was scared you was gonna do something to me."

"Bitch, you think? It was gonna take erry CO in dat bitch to get me off you! Now, where my shit?"

"I... I... I. Um, I have it."

"You have what?"

"Your jewelry and—"

"What jewelry?" Pulling the chains from under the collar, she damn near looked like she saw a ghost. "The fuckin' jewelry you pawned! Dat jewelry?"

"Tunan, I can explain."

"You can't explain shit! You pawned my shit, and not only dat, you relocated to Jagoda Bay, where my folks at. Dat cancer had to have ate yo' fuckin' brain cells like it did yo' titty. Do dat nigga know if yo' shit come out of remission, he gon' have to wipe yo' sour ass?"

"I-I-I'm sorry."

"Fuck you, yo' stiff booty, and yo' weak-ass apology. See, I think you thought cuz I was eatin' your pussy dat you was exempt from my wrath." I gripped the guns, one pointed at Stella and the other at her nigga in case he got froggy.

She visibly shook while trying to keep a brave face. "You not supposed to put your hands on women."

"Women? Yeah. But triflin' ass hoes is a go."

"Tunan, wait!"

Boom!

Jumping from the seat, the dog fell from my lap with a yelp as smoke filled the room. Her nigga was still on the floor screaming, so he hadn't been the one to cause the blast.

Stella's eyes went slack, and her body fell like a sack of potatoes. I lifted the guns, ready to blast whoever was coming into the room. The smoke became thicker, and before I could shoot toward the door, my finger froze. The dog's barking, which was high-pitched as hell, lowered to a slow, hard-to-make-out growl. The smoke had no smell, but my body felt light as I swayed, trying to keep my arms straight.

The dog was no longer barking. Ronnie's crying had stopped, and Stella's shiesty ass was silent. I tried to take a step, but as soon as I did, the guns slipped from my hands. My body dropped on top of something small and furry. I'd crushed the dog, but my eyes were too heavy to care. The last thing I tried to do was roll off the little mutt. I was going to take him to Athena.

Then, it was all black.

~

Whup whup whup

Whup whup whup

Whup whup whup

The sound of blades and an engine rang in my ears, but my body felt so light that it almost felt as if I weighed nothing.

Whup whup whup

Figuring I must have been asleep, I let the sounds fade as I drifted back off.

"Wake the fuck up, Joe Jackson!"

A dull, throbbing ache pulsed behind my eyes as the distant sounds became clearer. Everything was muffled, as if I were listening with my ears plugged. Before I could sit up, my body locked up under the weight of the drowsiness.

Fuck. Did I get drunk or something last night? Shit!

"Niggas these days can smoke like a fucking chimney, but a lil' sleeping gas knocks their asses out for hours. How long is this shit supposed to last, Preston?"

I felt dizzy as I drifted in and out of consciousness. It seemed like the heavy fog of smoke was lifting as a wave of nausea hit me. I struggled hard to regain consciousness, but I still felt like I was moving in slow motion, if I was moving at all. I did sense some kind of motion; it just wasn't coming from me.

Open your eyes, Tune. Fuck going on?

I didn't know what the fuck Stella had going on, nor did I know how much time had passed. My senses weren't operating well, but when I gained some awareness and was able to open my eyes, I realized that I was on Stella's funky, thieving ass. A strange, detached feeling lingered as I tried to piece together my reality.

Stella's apartment. Shot her nigga. Stanky sex. BBL. Scary-ass dog. Crushed the dog. SMOKE!

"Uuuuuugh!"

I sucked in a wad of air as I sat up straight and began swinging my arms. I felt suspended by something that prevented me from standing, but I kept swinging. My eyes popped open again, fully expecting to see that Stella and her nigga had me tied to a chair, but instead, I was met by a motherfucker sitting across from me in a deep green tailored suit with gold cufflinks.

"Don?"

There were big-ass headphones around his head, his leg was crossed, and a big-ass pinky ring, along with his wedding band, was on his left hand that rested on his knee. The nigga looked cool as a fucking cucumber with that green on while I was fighting for my fucking life.

Whup Whup Whup

My ears were ringing as the loud thumping sounds pounded in my head. Don jutted his chin to the side of me, and there were the same headphones he was wearing. I snatched them up, placing them on my head, still confused by what was happening.

"Why you like beating bitches, Payne?"

"Hunh?"

His expression was neutral, and since he didn't repeat himself, I closed my eyes. Whatever the fuck was going on was too fucking much, but the earphones helped with the loud-ass sounds, so I tried to calm myself enough to settle the lightheaded feeling.

This shit can't be happening. The last time I felt like this, I woke up in the fuckin' desert.

My eyes shot back open, and this time, instead of giving Don my attention, I looked to the left and saw nothing but clouds. The endless blue and white stretch was a terrifying void, the cotton clouds mocking my fear as they floated serenely in the sky. It was nothing serene about this shit here. Suddenly, my stomach flipped. Air rushed past the windows as a knot of anxiety tightened in my stomach while the helicopter drifted through the blue expanse. Looking down, all I could see was clouds below us.

How the fuck high up are we?

"What the fuck is this?"

I tried to remove my seat belt, but Don held his hand up. "Keep that shit on. You'll be outta here soon enough. Ion need you dying before the real fun starts."

Looking past Don, I was trying to see who was flying this big-ass copter, but past him was another seating area and beyond that nothing but buttons, dials, an empty pilot seat, and clouds.

"Who the fuck flyin' dis hoe?"

"Money."

"What?"

"Money, nigga! This is a self-flying copter. This is what the fuck money do."

"Okay, well, why the fuck am I in it? And where the fuck is Stella?"

"Why the fuck yo' married ass worried 'bout a bitch with a botched BBL? I had high ass hopes for you, Tunan, but you showed me dat you indeed got Cuppacio in yo' blood? Them old niggas had a hand problem too. They loved knockin' the shit outta bitches." He pointed at me. "That's where you get that shit from."

"Mane, ain't nobody no woman beater."

"Says the nigga with a DV charge."

"Stella deserved dat shit."

"You *deserve* to leave that shit alone. You supposed to be getting ready to work. Not goin' on quests with big-ass guns to murder bitches that ain't worth a day in jail, let alone the one fuckin' calendar year you did behind her."

"Mane, I been ready to work! I been waitin' on you."

"So is you ready or you waiting?"

I smacked my teeth in response while holding on to the seat as the aircraft turned. Looking down again, the clouds below seemed like a soft, deceptive blanket that I knew was hiding an endless drop.

"Did yo' mama get a check for you when you was a kid?" I had to know.

"Tunan, you had the opportunity to ask me when work would start the other day."

"When?"

"When you was letting bitches twerk on you and yo' wife at the gender reveal. And when you brought the Ferrari back to the Dungeon."

I was hearing Don, but I was too busy focusing on where the self-flying copter was going. How this nigga just sat there like nothing was wrong was beyond me, and I was sure copters weren't meant to fly this high in the sky.

"Matter of fact..." Don leaned forward. "Did I ask you to give me the car back?"

My head snapped at him. "Fuck you talmbout? It's yo' fuckin' car."

"Do I look like the type of nigga to drive behind another nigga? If I gave you the keys, it's yours."

"I can't take no car from you, Don."

"You already did. I'm sick of you driving that mildewed-ass Infiniti around. Shit ain't a good look. You making me look like a cheap, petty-ass Don whipping that busted shit."

"I rather work for my shit. I'll prove myself so I can earn my own riches and buy what the fuck I need. I appreciate it, but save the car-buying for the bitches."

Taking money from my brother was one thing, but another grown-ass man buying or giving me a car was out of the fucking question.

"A nigga driving a hoopty with pride. Ain't that some shit. But, shit... I'm glad you said that. You know,"—Don flicked his hand. "Proving yourself. That's what you doing today."

"Hunh?"

"You thought it was that easy? Yo' brother vouch for you, you marry his bitch, and give his blind ass directions?" Don laughed. "Nah, ain't shit easy 'bout the Rinaldi Mob. You, for sho', gonna have to work for this shit."

The door slid open, and a gush of wind entered, making it hard to breathe. I was fighting with my lungs, and again, Don was sitting there poised as a motherfucker.

"We call this, survival of the realist. Four obstacles. At the end of each one, you'll enter the next. You'll have instructions on how to navigate at each habitat."

"Habitat?"

"Yeah, nigga. Now get out."

"What? Nigga... You... Outta yo'... Fuckin' mind! Who?" I gulped.

Don chuckled. The wind was beating my ass, making it harder and harder to breathe. I'd never gotten hit the way this wind was taking me out.

"See, that's the thing. You niggas always think y'all got a choice. This my shit. And what the fuck I say, goes."

My seat belt clicked, freeing me from the seat.

"Don, I sweardaGod! Ahhhhhhh shiiiiit!"

The copter shifted, and since I was no longer suspended against the seat, I flipped out. The air rushed through my fingertips as I tried to grab on to it to stop myself from falling.

"Fuuuuuuck!"

The world flipped as my body tumbled through the cold air that blasted against me. All of my senses were heightened and tanked at the same time. My stomach lurched at the realization that I was deadass plummeting through the blue and white sky that I was just looking at. The helicopter shrank above me, now mimicking a buzzing insect. Wind squealed in my ears, and my vision blurred as I thought about the inevitable. The ground was going to meet me, and I'd be nothing but a pile of blood and guts. He should have at least let me kill Stella before I died.

"Arrrrggghhhhh!"

The world was zipping by so fast that all I saw through my weary eyes was blue. My heart was beating rapidly, and I swore I was having a fucking heart attack. Then, a violent tug that jerked my entire body slowed the fall. I was yanked upward with brutal force. The freefall had come to an end and was replaced by a gentle sway of a canopy. I looked up and could've pissed myself from happiness when I saw the parachute. The fabric spread wide above me, but my adrenaline was still surging. The loud gusting calmed, but now the silence was deafening, broken only by the whisper of the breeze. I'd never thought of this element of the Earth as a threat, but today had shown me that wind was no fucking hoe.

Blinking, I was able to see where I was falling now. The brief respite under the canopy shattered as I realized the fucking ocean loomed below. Panic clawed through my throat as I peered down at the unforgiving stretch of dark water.

What the fuck?

"Shiiiiiiiit! Stop, stop! Reroute! Re-fuckin'-route!"

I began kicking my legs, but it was no use because a mere second later, my body landed in the water with a harsh splash. The impact had me wheezing as the cold water caused a physical shock, stealing my breath as I dropped into the depths. The parachute, once my savior, was now turning into a fucking hinder, dragging me down, the cords tangling around my limbs as I fought against what I assumed was the ocean waves or lake jetstream.

"Ugggghhh!" I drew in water, choking. It was salt water, which didn't tell me shit since I knew most of the water on Earth was salt water.

I was in a desperate struggle, battling against the suffocating weight of the parachute, the icy grip of the water, and the growing fear that this was about to become my watery-ass grave. I couldn't go out like this. I still needed to fuck Glow a couple more times before I'd be somewhat okay with dying. I tried my hardest to untangle myself from the cords, but the more I twisted, the more tangled I became. Each second that passed was a fight, and each breath was a victory as I clawed my way to the surface. Every time my head bopped out of the water, I was happy as fuck to see a glimpse of the sky.

Just as I broke the surface again, gasping for air, the parachute lights tightened. A jolt of pure terror ripped through me as I pulled backward with unnatural force. I tried looking back as water slapped me in the face while my arms flailed.

"Whatdafuck?"

A dark shape breaching the surface was behind me. The few breaths I had left my body as I watched a fin slice through the water. It wasn't just any fin, but a big-ass gray, triangular fin.

"Is dat a fuckin'—"

The realization hit me like a punch to the gut. There was a fucking shark behind me. Its teeth tore through the nylon as he pulled at the parachute that I was tangled in. A white object floating on the surface made me snap out of the fear that had temporary paralyzed me. With all my might, I sacrificed breathing to remove myself from the parachute. My legs burned, my muscles screamed, and the world faded to black as my lungs began to give out. Then, I felt free. I felt free as a fucking bird but had no time to celebrate. Swimming to the surface, I sucked in the salty air that drifted over the water but surged forward. Not knowing if the shark would come back and finish me for his meal, or if he had friends nearby, I turned into Michael Phelps, arms smacking the water in the direction of the white blob, which was a boat. I'd never swam so fast in my fucking life. I needed to take Shio's advice and get my ass in somebody's gym if I made it out of this water alive.

Feeling as if I was making some progress, I made the mistake of looking back and saw the sharp-looking fin heading toward me. I sped up my strokes, praying that I would see my mama and sister again. If I did, I was hugging them first and killing Don's ass immediately after. This shit wasn't worth no fucking mob membership. It damn sure wasn't worth a fucking Ferrari that I couldn't even afford the maintenance on.

Spotting the ladder, I grabbed it and pulled myself up, only to slip back into the water. The shark was inches away, so I hoisted myself up the silver railing with all my might. At the same time, the boat nudged away from it, and the shark rammed its cone-shaped snout into it.

Dropping onto the floor of the boat and landing on my back, coughs erupted from me. With my hand on my stomach, I felt like I was hacking up every piece of intestine in my body while trying to stabilize my lungs. I'd made it. I'd fucking survived this shit.

The deck was warm beneath my wet body, so I didn't rush to sit up. The polished wood was radiating the sun's heat, and I was thankful that it was a sunny day because had it been raining, my body would've been freezing against the chilled wood. The smooth surface calmed me—a stark contrast to the chaos I'd just escaped with the cold water doing nothing but causing panic. The gentle rocking of the boat produced a soothing rhythm, almost acting like a lullaby, soothing my racing heart.

This shit was for the fucking birds. I couldn't wait to cuss my brother out for even suggesting I join this fuck-ass mob.

I inhaled slowly and deliberately as I tried to regain control of my nervous system. Above, the sky didn't look so threatening now that I wasn't falling from it. This was the craziest shit I'd ever faced, and I couldn't see how this could be topped. However, I had a feeling this was just the beginning since Don had told me habitats, which was plural.

"Good morning, Tunan!"

A voice had me sitting up and looking around. I instantly missed the heat from the wood as I looked out before me. I was on a yacht that was big enough to cast a shadow over the ocean that was serving as the boat's backdrop. Elegant wood with fancy fixtures on the deck shone in the sunlight, reflecting the sky like a mirror. Sleek lines defined the boat's silhouette, and had I not been alarmed when I jumped on this bitch, I'd be impressed with the craftsmanship given to the boat.

Still, there was no sign of anyone as I scanned every surface before me.

"I'm not here with you physically, Tunan, but I'll be your guide throughout the training."

"Who da fuck is dis?"

"It's me... Scarlett."

Scarlett Rinaldi. Princesspa Cuppacio. Ezio's favorite. Matteo's wife. My cousin.

We'd been properly introduced at the hospital, and I could see now that every single Cuppacio was attractive, regardless of the race of their mother. Many of us lucked up because our mothers were even more beautiful than the Italian motherfuckers.

"What da fuck is dis shit, Scarlett? Don ass tryna kill me?"

Wet clothes clung to my body as I stood on the sleek deck. She'd said she wasn't here, but I was still looking for her. There were steps that led to the undercarriage or probably the living quarters, but I stayed my ass planted right where I was. I needed to see where I was going.

"This is your induction into the Rinaldi Mob."

"I thought marriage was the induction?"

There was a white towel on a padded bench behind me, so I snatched it and dried my face, trying to get the water out of my ears.

"Marriage was merely a requirement, but in order to fully become a member, there are a series of survival courses that you must complete."

"I did the one in Egypt."

"Making a blind man see challenge. Yes, that was only one. You are behind on a few more, so you will complete them all today."

"By myself?"

"Yes. But no worries, cousin. I'll be here with you in spirit, guiding you, sort of like you did with Shio in the pyramid."

Deciding to sit on the bench, I placed my head in my hands and groaned.

How was it that the other niggas had a chance to space their shit out, but I had to do all of mine in one day and without a fucking team? That shit wasn't fair. Don must've thought I was fucking Captain America.

The boat rumbled and began to surge in the water. Just like in the copter, I saw no one driving the yacht as the room where the captain was supposed to be was empty.

"Dis shit ain't even worth it, on God."

"You'll do fine, Tunan. It's all a game of instinct. You use your God-given tools to get through this, and you'll come out a victor."

The yacht sliced through the water, a graceful dance of power and tranquility. A gentle hum vibrated through the hull as the engine purred, propelling the boat forward through the crashing waves. A refreshing spray kissed my face as the bow cut through the water. As good as the ride felt, I was aggravated. I couldn't appreciate it for thinking about what was to come.

"In approximately ten minutes, the boat will come to a stop. You'll then start the swinging challenge."

"*Swinging*?" My head popped up.

The only swinging I knew of was from the Don Rio nigga that Nel and Vello had told me about. I'd met him at the gender reveal, and the hanging dicks still had me side-eying his ass. I didn't know what type of shit Don thought this was, but that was where I drew the line. I'd seen enough dicks and balls involuntarily to last a lifetime while knocked during shower time. The only one I was interested in seeing now was my own. I wasn't swinging for no amount of fucking money.

"Scarlett, dey just gone have to kill me. I ain't doing no swinging."

"It's not as hard as it seems, cousin. You just have to hold your breath and let your body work for you."

"Mane, what da fuck type of shit do da niggas in the mob got goin' on? My brother be with dis shit?"

"Shio has completed all missions successfully. He is indeed with the shits. Four minutes."

Looking ahead, heart racing, I began to look for an out. All I saw ahead were trees, and there was no way this big-ass boat could go through the trees. When Shio told me about joining the mob, he didn't say shit about giving up your manhood. I was down for killing a motherfucker, robbing niggas who deserved to get jacked, and as of a few minutes ago, jumping from a fucking plane. But swinging? Yeah, no. My mama 'nem may as well get their black clothes ready.

The boat slowed to a stop, and I cussed under my breath. There were so many trees stretched across the strip of land that it was all I could see: trees and water. Various vines hung from the trees, but you couldn't see beyond that or even through it.

"Scarlett... I ain't with no gay shit. I'm 'bout to just jump back in da water. Tell my sister and nephew, I love 'em—"

"Wait, Tunan. What type of swinging do you think I'm talking about?"

"Shid, gay shit."

"Tunan, absolutely not."

I sighed with relief. I had most definitely judged the shit out of everyone in the mob in just ten minutes.

"If you look up, you'll see hanging vines."

There were brown rope-like vines hanging from the trees that sprouted out of the water. Though it was the same body of water, this end looked muggy and dark. Several bugs and insects croaked and chirped in harmony, and a stinging sensation on my skin had me slapping at it. Lifting my hand, there was a fat-ass mosquito smushed against my arm. If I caught malaria out in this bitch, I was fucking Don up, for real.

"Reach up and tug on the vine closest to you."

I didn't follow her instructions. I just stood there, adrenaline not ready since I'd been thrust into the last two disasters.

"Grab the vine, Tunan."

"Fuck!" Pulling my pants up my waist, I leaned over the boat's edge and grabbed the vine.

"Now climb the railing, hold on to the vine tightly, and let it swing you to the next vine."

"Say, what?"

"You'll swing through the trees but please try to remain as high as you can. The waters are infested."

"Infested with what?"

"Climb the railing."

Looking up at the vine, I saw that it disappeared in the leaves of the tree. I tugged on it as the boat rocked. I could feel heat creeping up my neck, so I looked back instead of climbing up. Sparks of orange glows were on the deck, and the more I watched, the faster it grew and rose.

"What the fuck? Aye, Scarlett!"

"Climb up, Tunan," Scarlett instructed. Her voice was still mellow, even though she'd told me to do the same thing three times now.

"The boat! It's on fire!"

"Yes, the boat is set to self-destruct. Climb the rail. Do not let the vine go."

It was as if we'd given the "okay" by stating the obvious because the small flames grew into an uncontrollable force, melting the far end of the boat. There were only a few inches that separated me from the fire. I knew I didn't have long to either trust Scarlett and let the vine swing my ass or jump in the water, which I'd just learned was infested.

Lifting my leg, I climbed on the rail. I could feel the fire on my back now, so I wrapped my leg around the vine and swung from the boat as it erupted into flames. Don was just doing some shit because, why in the fuck would he set a nice-ass yacht on fire? There was no logical reason for doing that shit. As I hung onto the vine, inches above the water, the fiery boat began reversing.

Splooshing sounds below me had me looking down, and I could see dinosaur-like scales and a tail of something bigger than that fucking shark. Deciding it would be in my best interest to climb, I went up the vine as far as I could go. It wasn't too much higher, but it was high enough so that I was safe from the swamp. Knowing it was a matter of time before some bullshit happened, I looked ahead at all the vines dangling from the trees. I didn't know which one to grab next because I didn't know if they could support my one hundred and seventy pounds. Spotting one that looked sturdy enough, the vine fit into my palms as I launched myself, the swamp a short drop below.

This shit is crazy.

Adrenaline still pumping from the shark's jaws and the helicopter's ejection, I gripped the rope-like vine tighter. One would have thought I was the king of the jungle himself with the way I was swinging on this plant. The swamp air felt thick and heavy, a suffocating blanket of humidity that clung to my skin. The canopy of trees blocked the sunlight, but I could see sun rays reflecting on the Everglades, making it look like a steamy cauldron. I pushed my body forward, grasping the next vine, and this time, my hand landed directly on a sharp-ass thorn that stabbed the fuck out of my skin.

"Fuuuuuuck!" Removing my hand, I slid down the vine, and an alligator jumped out of the water, snapping at me.

"Ahhhh shiiiiit!" I screamed, blood dripping from my hand as I clenched my grip tighter onto the vine.

The alligator tried to snatch me down, missing me by a few inches, and I yelled to that motherfucker that he wouldn't be eating my ass today. I couldn't see his underside, but the top half of his body proved he was massive. The motherfucker looked like he could eat an elephant for breakfast, lunch, and dinner.

Climbing back up the vine, I tried to go higher than before as the alligator splashed into the water. Two more noses peeked from out of the murky sludge, all three lined up, waiting and ready for me to fall.

"Dese da same damn gators from da pyramid?"

Forcing my body forward, the air whipped past me, a rush of humid heat with the musty scent of decay rising from the alligator-infested waters. Each swing was a fucking gamble—a desperate prayer that the next vine held me, and that the makeshift jungle gym didn't betray me. Don was a playful-ass nigga, but this shit was not a game. I'd been kidnapped, thrown from a fucking copter, swam from a shark, and now I was swinging to prevent becoming a meal to these big-ass alligators. It was like Scarlett had said: I was in for a fight for my survival. It was more than proving myself. It damn sure was more than a Ferrari. This shit was life or death, and maybe that's what sick-ass Don was trying to show me.

However, his ass could've put me in a shootout or some other shit. We Memphis niggas ain't know shit about playing jungle and ocean games.

On my new vine, now in the thick of the trees, I couldn't see anything behind or in front of me but green and brown marshland. This shit felt like something straight out of the movie *Anaconda*. Just as the thought entered my mind, I shook it away. The last thing I needed was to conjure some shit, and it came true. A snap echoed through the swamp, a chilling reminder of the danger lurking below. The vine that I was gripping shuddered violently. Looking down, I could see that one of the alligators had sunk its teeth into the fibers.

"Ohhh, fuck no!"

Panic flared within me as I felt the vine begin to tear. The plant snapped from the weight of me and the alligator pulling on it. It was too much, and a second later, my body fell flat. I tried to grip another vine, but it slipped through my fingers, scratching my hand again. All three gators had their mouths open as the swampy ground rushed up to greet me.

"Maamaaaaa!"

Suddenly, a sting shot up my back, breaking my fall. My feet were dangling, and my shirt was gathered underneath my armpits. My clothing had been caught on a thorn, and the break in my fall allowed me to find a vine that I could grasp. I wrapped my leg around a trim limb to steady my body. When I stopped hollering, I tugged the vine, making sure it wouldn't tear. Since it seemed steady enough, I pushed my body forward, and I could feel and hear the rip of my shirt from the big-ass thorn. Warm air stung whatever scars I'd accumulated on my hands, arms, and legs, but I'd rather be scratched up than gator food.

"About three more swings, Tunan, and you'll reach the end."

"Scarlett?" I heaved as my eyes searched for another vine. I wasn't trusting one vine to get me through this jungle anymore. I'd been hoping I wouldn't have to switch before the fall because my arms were beginning to burn. But that shit was dead.

Scarlett cleared her throat. "Yes, cousin?"

"Mane, where da fuck you been? I was almost gator food."

"Sorry, I took a quick break to return my husband's call."

"Aaaagh!" I grabbed another vine, flying through the trees. When I felt stable, I huffed. "A break? When my life hangin' in da balance?"

"You're doing amazing, sweetie."

I kissed my teeth but didn't lose focus as another thicker vine came into view. I prepared myself as best I could to leap onto it. An alligator thrashed upward, growing impatient that I hadn't fallen into the dark water yet. Latching onto my vine, it pulled violently, and the vine broke away quickly. It was perfect timing because I'd already jumped and landed on the next vine. I slid onto it lower than I wanted to be but not close enough that any of the alligators could pull me off. Using my legs to lift me higher onto the vine because my arms were done for, I was able to see over the lush.

Sunlight was beaming through from the other side, and I sighed in relief when I saw flat grass with a brown truck stationed on it. I scrambled to regain my grip, muscles screaming in protest. I was going to try to make it without changing vines again. Adrenaline was coursing through my veins as the alligators huddled together near the end of the water. The largest one used its powerful jaws to break through the many vine strands around me, but luckily, it continued to miss mine. Deciding I should leap once more since these motherfuckers were determined to knock me down, I used all my might to grab one last vine. There were a few more trees cascading over me, but I could see the roof of the truck clearly now. We were at the edge of the swamp now, but alligators had legs, and I didn't want them bitches to get out and chase me to the truck. I needed to land close enough or swing my ass onto the top of it.

"Shiiiit!"

I launched forward when the vine snapped without warning. My arms windmilled as I sailed through the air. I tried grabbing onto the last few vines around me, but nothing was long enough or close enough. God was the only answer at this point because I could hear the rustling of the alligators and other animals surrounding the open area where the truck sat.

Oomph!

The wind was knocked out of me as I hit the back of the Jeep. I could hear the sloshing of the muddy water as the alligators fully emerged. Seeing the size of their legs and feet would've caused my ass to faint, but my blood was pumping so fast that all I could do was holler as my back burned from falling on it for the second time today. Snapping was inches away from my feet, so I climbed up the back of the truck. I didn't think the truck bed was low enough for the alligators to jump on, but then again, I didn't know if alligators could jump. The motherfuckers could easily shock my ass since that's all that had happened today. Balancing myself while trying to steady my breath, I stood on top of the roof, looking at the ground. The alligators stopped at the opening, circling each other, not making an attempt to enter the open area where I was.

A win was a win, but I couldn't help but wonder why the bitches weren't trying to come eat my ass as they had been when I was acting like Tarzan.

"Fuck you talmbout! Ahhhhh!"

Tilting my head, I beat on my now bare chest since my ripped shirt had fallen somewhere in the swamp, and I yelled into the air. I'd made it again.

"A fuckin' hard body, baby! Y'all can't get rid of me!" I slapped my chest again, the ache not overriding the victory I felt.

"Oh shit!" The truck ascended, pushing me backward as it began moving through the grassy plain. I was able to find my footing before I fell.

"Great job, cousin. Please get inside the truck."

"Aite."

The driver's side window was open, so I slid in, damn near breaking my fucking back in the process. I was going to need two massages a day for a month once I finished playing Don's games. I couldn't wait to smack the fuck out of my brother for not warning me about this shit.

"Welcome to the savannah!" Scarlett's voice broke through my thoughts, blaring from the speakers of the truck.

The savannah stretched out before me, an endless area of golden grasslands dotted with acacia trees. The air, thick with the scent of dry mud and wild herbs, rushed in through the open window. It was a welcomed change from the swamps' suffocating humidity and vile smells of decay. The truck bumped over a rocky, uneven ground. Since the car was driving itself, I slid over into the passenger seat, with my arm folded out of the window. The sun setting in the distance painted the sky in fiery hues of orange and purple. A sense of peace settled over me as I cruised along in the self-driving safari truck, silence only being broken by the chirping of crickets and the distant call of a bird.

"There are a few things that you must know about the savannah."

My gaze shifted to the display of the truck, which was only a black screen with the temperature shown. It was ninety-nine degrees, but with all the windows down and my damp pants and shoes, it felt as if it was cooler.

"What I need to know, Scarlett?"

I was feeling like that nigga. There couldn't be shit worse than those man-eating gators, or that Olympic swimming-ass shark. Just like my brother, I'd defeated them, so I was ready for whatever now. Don had mentioned four obstacles, and I was hoping falling from the copter counted as one so that it meant I'd only have one more to go.

"The savannah is home to a wide array of animals, including elephants—"

"Elephants graceful as fuck. I'ma be straight."

"Zebras—"

"Dem black and white shits? Yeah, ain't dey like donkeys? I'm good, cuz."

"Giraffes—"

"Yeah, dey tall asses just wanna eat trees all day. Dey only fight each other."

"Wildebeests."

"Dey just some African cows."

"Hyenas—"

"Now, dem some bottom-feeding scavengers. I'll kick da shit outta 'em."

"Various species of birds, reptiles, and insects—"

"No threats to dis top dawg! I'll swat da fuck outta dem shits."

"Cheetas—"

"Hol' up, now, cuz..." I sat up in my seat, sticking my arm out the window. Cheetahs were fast as hell, and to my knowledge, they could catch me by the neck, drag me up a tree, and feast on me for days.

A herd of gazelles frolicked in front of the truck, which made no effort to slow down, but luckily, they hopped out of the way just in time. Where there was prey, predators lurked nearby. Scarlett didn't have to tell me about the laws of the savannah; those shits echoed the life I'd lived in Memphis growing up.

Roooooaaaaaaarrrrrrr!

Hairs stood all over my body as a guttural rumble shattered the tranquility, sending a shiver down my spine. I caught a glimpse of orangy-brown fur in the side mirror, but it was a blur with how fast it had moved. The roar didn't sound like a hyena, though, and them motherfuckers weren't orange.

"What da fuck was dat, Scarlett?"

"Another animal that lives in the savannah is the lion. Please keep your hands and feet inside the vehicle."

Roooooaaaaaaarrrrrrr!

A massive lion burst from the tall grass to the left of the truck. Its eyes were fixated on me, muscles rippling beneath the tawny coat.

"Lions process objects differently than we do. When they see the truck, they see a giant predator. They won't attack as long as you remain inside the vehicle."

Roooooaaaaaarrrr!

Pulling my arms inside the truck, I pressed on the door siding to let the window up.

"Where da fuck is da button? How da fuck you roll dis shit up, cuh?"

Taking my eyes off the lion for just a second, I saw there were no buttons and no way to let the window up at all. When my eyes bounced back toward the lion, it looked as if it were about to charge the truck.

"Scarlett, dis big-ass nigga 'bout to attack! Let da window up! Now!"

"Sorry, Tunan. The windows are being rolled up now."

The windows began moving at a snail's pace. I'd be fucking dead by the time the windows fully let up. My stomach was clenched tightly, and the thought of this lion eating my ass alive tore at my fucking insides. This was the craziest shit I'd ever had to deal with. All these fucking animals—I didn't know what Don's obsession was but that nigga needed help. I wish I had told Glow more so that she'd be more prepared to be a young widow. The look in the lion's eyes told me he was determined to attack and eat my ass.

"No worries, cousin. He won't attack the vehicle."

Roooooaaaaar!

"Where da fuck do you get yo' animal facts from? Dis nigga 'bout to charge and flip dis fuckin' truck ova!"

The lion began running toward me, causing me to scoot down in my seat. I clamped at the cushion while waiting for him to approach the safari truck. His head was as big as the door, so I knew with one shove, the door could possibly cave in.

"Calm down, Tunan."

"I can't! Dis nigga 'bout to eat me! And you calm and shit like I ain't 'bout to die! "

Arf Arf Arf Arf

The lion paused, and although my heart was beating like a fucking drum, my eyes followed the lion's big-ass head.

"Wait! Tunan, is that a—" Scarlett squealed.

"Puppy, run!" I shouted.

Arf Arf Arf

A white fur ball stood a few feet from the truck that was now slowing down. I was panicking because the puppy and me was in danger. When another lion walked from the grass shadows, I tried to jump into the driver's seat to get the truck to pick up speed again. The lion sauntered to the other lion, and side by side, I could see these were mating lions.

These niggas were about to tag team me.

Arf Arf

Well, they may maul the dog first, I thought as I looked back and forth between the lions and the white furball.

I wanted to shout for the dog to shut the fuck up, but Scarlett hollered through the truck speakers first. "Oh my God! How did a puppy get in there?"

"Get in here? Da fuck you mean, cuz. Somebody left dey dog out here. Probably did it runnin' from dese big muthafuckas! What I do know is dis lil' nigga betta run!"

Both lions began to walk, then trot, and then broke into a full gallop in the direction of the miniature dog. The puppy was as clueless as my ass was when I woke up in the copter, racing across the savannah. It must've thought it was vacation with the way it looped around the trees and in and out of the tall grass.

The truck began to accelerate, again, matching my racing heart. My pants felt wet, and it had to be from that salty ocean water because I knew I hadn't peed on myself. Shit, I hoped I hadn't peed on myself. The truck drove into the tree line, and when I was about to curse, it kept driving. It didn't stop, going over a bridge that went across a big-ass river. I prayed the fucking truck didn't stop or slow down again.

After dodging those lions, we rode through the fucking deserts out of *The Mummy*, and when my ears started ringing from the sands singing, I passed out. When I woke up, I was covered in sweat from the heat. I was mad as fuck that the expensive-ass truck didn't have any fucking air conditioning. I stripped down to my damn boxers and immediately regretted the shit when the truck rolled into the tundra. I had never shivered the way I was in the truck as it glided over ice. I struggled to get my pants back on, and when four polar bears spotted me, another chase began. Scarlett was still asking if I saw the puppy, and I told her ass that I wouldn't be able to find no damn white puppy on ice and snow. The polar bears were able to knock the truck across the ice a few times, and I was positive that I'd pissed myself this time more than once. Whatever money Don paid for this truck, though, was well worth it. After every tumble, the truck rolled back onto its wheels and raced forward.

When we began rolling up a steep hill, I was ready to say fuck all this shit again. We'd been in the damn Jeep an hour, and I was done being the prey to all these predators. I ain't even have my brothers or the Cuppacios to help me navigate this shit. The truck started fighting to grip the rocky terrain, the engine whining like it had been through enough, just like I had. The altitude fog started to surround the beat-up truck, too thick to see through, blinding me to the road in front of us. I knew we were ascending a winding road from the way the truck jerked from left to right, and I was low-key praying that this bitch didn't tilt wrong because I knew it'd be endgame for my ass. Just when the engine gave way, the truck dropped.

"Oh fuckkkkk! Scarletttttt!"

"I'm here, cousin. Just eating my fruit bowl. Everything is fine. You should be at the school... Right about... Now!"

The Jeep bounced as it hit the pavement, the fog evaporating as the surroundings now showed we'd made it back to civilization. Gawking at what appeared to be a school building that the truck had landed in front of, I sat still on high alert.

Did my ass just fall from a fucking mountain?

The doors to the vehicle popped open, and I slowly scanned the area, unsure of what to believe. However, I wasn't taking any fucking chances. I'd seen too much shit within the last few hours and multiple habitats.

"We have come to the end of the training. You may enter the school for debriefing, Tunan."

All I had wanted to do was scare Stella's ass, and in turn, I'd gotten turned every fucking which way but loose. I'd been the motherfucker that bitch niggas were scared of, but I was skittish as hell during whatever the fuck this shit was. I should have kept my black ass at the fucking gender reveal instead of trying to get even with that skank. Knowing Don, though, he would've snatched my ass from wherever I was, just as he'd done when Shio had to go in that pyramid.

Easing out of the truck, I scanned the areas again before pulling my pants, shoes, and socks from the truck floor. I was in my damn drawers, running into the building, not knowing what I was running to. The waxy scent of crayons and the chemical smell of markers filled the air. Cool air brushed my skin as the metal door shut behind me, causing me to jump. The lighting wasn't as bright as outside had been, but it was stark enough against the white walls. Making a left, since that was the only way I could go, I began the trudge down the hallway that was lined with mini burgundy lockers.

Sssssss

"Ahhhhhhhhhh! What da fuck!" My fucking soul jumped out of my body as I hit the ground and backed against the locker. "Ahhhhhhhh! Fuck nawl! We already been to da swamp!"

Icy fear twisted around my heart as a massive anaconda dropped from the ceiling with its mouth wide open, looking as if it could fit my entire body inside. My throat was sore and hoarse from screaming since I was dropped from the plane. I was swearing like a bitch in this school, but I didn't care. A fucking anaconda was right in front of me like it lived here.

Arf Arf Arf

I know that ain't that fucking white furball from the savannah.

The puppy trotted down the hallway, jumping in front of me as if he wasn't running through the grasslands just hours ago. Using my foot, I nudged his ass in front of the anaconda. I didn't know how he'd escaped the lion and made it all the fucking way in the same building I was in on those short-ass legs, but he'd been an offering from God to save myself.

The puppy leaped forward, and I was already gagging because I knew the snake eating his ass was going to be gruesome. When the puppy jumped onto the snake and landed on his feet but appeared inside the snake, my mouth clammed shut.

"What da–"

Clap Clap Clap

Don appeared in the snake's mouth, clapping as he walked forward, toward me.

"It's a holographic. See..." He swiped his hand, and the snake disappeared.

My eyes shifted from him to the puppy, who was looking at me as if I was the fucking crazy one.

"Dat shit looked real as fuck! Like, what da fuck is wrong witcho ass, mane!"

Don stuffed his hands in his pockets as if his ass didn't just push me off the plane hours ago. The thought of that shit had me ready to square up with his ass, but the thought of more animals appearing from the cut made me cringe, so I remained on the floor against the lockers.

"Congratufuckinglations. You have made it out alive, fuck nigga. Welcome to the mob."

"Shiddd, you already welcomed me, I thought. All dis shit wasn't even necessary."

"I welcomed your wife, nigga. You had to pass these fuckin' challenges first, like the other Cuppacios. And I added on a few other shit to test out what Preston been working on."

I slowly stood, not caring that I was only in my underwear. Finally allowing myself a moment to calm down, my body instantly began to ache and burn from all the cuts and bruises I'd gotten through the challenges, as Don called them.

He chuckled as he bent down and picked up the puppy. "I didn't think you had it in ya, but you Cuppacios gotta be made of gorilla balls because y'all continue to beat destiny. Somebody should've died by now."

"Dat shit ain't cool. I almost fuckin' died 'bout seven times."

"You know what ain't cool, nigga? You leaving a fuckin' mob event to go do some shit that could've got your black ass sent back to prison."

"I ain't know I had to clear my personal affairs with you."

"You wanna be rich?"

"Duh, nigga."

"Well, you gotta clear that shit through me. Anything you do can come back to me, Payne."

"It was a fuckin' gender reveal with dicks hangin' errwhere."

"And titties slangin' too. It was still mob shit, and you went to see bout that sour-ass hoe."

Arf Arf

The puppy barked as if it were agreeing with Don.

Leaning against the locker, I closed my eyes. I couldn't believe what the fuck I'd just gone through, and now I was standing here, damn near naked, being lectured like a fucking child.

"Aye."

"Yeah, nigga?" I said, keeping my eyes closed. I was done using these bitches for today.

"Leave that hoe alone. You 'bout to end yo' freedom for them cloudy-ass diamonds she stole and stale-ass pussy she toting. Lock the fuck in, twin."

Don turned on his feet, dress shoes clacking on the waxed floors.

Arf

The puppy was basically telling my ass goodbye because when I finally opened my eyes, they both were gone. All I could do was thank God that I'd made it out alive. Thinking back on everything, I didn't know what obstacle had scared me more, but I knew now that I had no reason to fear man. If I'd learned anything, I learned that man was prey no matter what habitat you dropped that motherfucker in. I was still mad with Shio, but I should've known after the pyramids that Don was bound to do some shit like this.

Pushing off the lockers, I limped my ass back out of the school building. The parking lot was empty, the beat-up Jeep was gone, but sitting directly in front of the doors, the engine already cranked, was the Ferrari that Don refused to take back.

"Dis muthafucka," I said, opening the door and slowly dropping myself inside. "Fuck nigga swear he dat nigga—I'm dat nigga." I adjusted the rearview mirror and got a good look at my face. Instead of grimacing at how horrible I looked, I smiled as if I had just won the lottery. In a way, I had.

"We in dere!" I was officially in the Rinaldi Mob, and I could smell the money already.

CHAPTER 26
SOLANA DAMITA LEDESMA

I didn't know if the camera Shio had been spying on me with was working anymore, and quite frankly, I no longer cared. I had also powered the phone off and promised myself I wouldn't turn it back on unless there was an emergency. Shio didn't get to spy on me any longer. He didn't get to leave my messages on read. He had broken the last straw when I texted him last night that I had taken the towel down I'd tossed over the painting to cover the black dot, and he read the message but didn't respond. This morning, I threw the hair dryer at the black dot, hoping to break it. I was sure it was broken because I'd thrown it four times. I felt better afterward and decided that one of the first things I'd do once free was go to one of those places that let you break things. The adrenaline from the throws made me feel alive.

When Dasani and the American mob wives left, they made Italian give them the key, saying I didn't need to be locked up like an animal. Jisei told me to move up to her bedroom, but I declined. I had grown to like the room, and I felt it was actually working. I assumed that my not craving the drug was only a temporary fix, and that one day the craving would return, but maybe if I stayed put longer, the likelihood of that happening would be lower. It was almost like I had been watching a clock, waiting for the cocaine craving to return. I had been passing the time with Shio's father's journal, centering my internal thoughts on him and how his life somewhat mirrored mine when it came to drugs. Anytime I wanted to read, I went inside the bathroom and closed the door, locking it in case someone came inside the room.

When I saw the boy, the one who had been my supplier, I knew I would fall back into the slump. I knew that the weeks did not change me, and I would find a way to ask him for some cocaine. But that wasn't the case. I did have a few seconds of wanting, but that quickly faded the moment he left the basement and didn't come back. Over the last few days, there had only been the girls and Italian visiting. I had yet to see the baby I knew was here from time to time, because not only had I heard her little voice, but Pearla had told me her friend had a baby.

These days, my head was clearer—much clearer—so it didn't take me long to put everything together. Pearla's friend, who had the baby everyone fawned over, was Glow's little sister, *and* Glow lived next door. A woman that Shio had been interested in at one point or another was mere steps away from where I'd been *real nigga rehabbing.* At first, I had no reason to feel any type of way about Shio and his line-up of women. But after he made my body feel *celestial* (heavenly), I had a lot of care about the women in Shio's life. And after he came over and did the things he'd done to my body, I had every right to feel how I felt. What I couldn't understand was how it was possible for one human to make another's body feel such pleasure, and that pleasure was better than any high I'd ever had. I'd been doing drugs for some time and had never had that feeling or experience. I couldn't help but wonder if the experience was like that with everyone or if I'd only felt the satisfaction because it was Shio.

Gnawing on my bottom lip, I could still feel fog surrounding me as I lay on the bed with a towel wrapped around my hair and my body. It was late because I had slept most of the day away. According to the TV, it was nearing two in the morning, and the house was still. Italian and the others must have taken their hanging out somewhere else tonight. Although the metal door was now open, Italian continued to bring me my meals because I wouldn't leave the room.

Yesterday was Pia's gender reveal party, and I had received an invitation to join them. I declined to go, scared about everything that came with leaving Jisei's basement. I was scared of the many possibilities of what could happen when I did leave. I wasn't ready to see

Shio, especially if I had to see him with Bahati. I didn't want to see the boy who made my craving come back at first sight. I'd been missing Shio's daughter and wanted to see her, but I couldn't handle seeing them be one big happy family among other people they called family. Italian had encouraged me to at least fix my own food yesterday and had left me a piece of mail with Jisei's address and a card to order food if I didn't want to cook. The credit card did not have his name on it, though. Shio's was printed across it, and it sent me into a slumber. It was still on the dresser when Italian brought down breakfast this morning, but he left it there even after I told him to take it. I had been upset all day yesterday from just seeing Shio's name, and because I was upset, I chose sleep and starvation. I happily ate the breakfast and lunch Italian brought down before falling into another slumber today—this one induced by the drug detox. Now, I was awake, looking crazy and feeling crazier.

Instead of going into the bathroom to read more about Sandro, I settled onto the bed to watch a movie about a girl who was searching for her family after believing she was adopted. I had been addicted to watching the movies on this network called Lifetime. We had telenovelas in México, but nothing this fascinating. I made sure to watch the movies in Spanish but had the American captions turned on. I'd been learning so much from that simple trick and planned to ask Italian for paper soon to practice my English writing.

The movie made me think of my own family so I turned the TV off. I knew I wasn't adopted, but I wished for some information on my mother's family so I could meet them and learn about my mother. Hopefully, Shio would help me, but if he couldn't, I would ask the American mob wives. They were adamant that I would be fine here with them, and as much as I did not want to accept help from anyone, I was not stupid enough to believe I could make it in this country without any allies. As long as the Rodríguezes didn't bother them, I would accept their friendship.

"No. I will not let my thoughts go there."

Standing, I walked into the bathroom, grabbed the vanity edge, and closed my eyes. Pearla and I had talked about triggers, and along with my father, the Rodríguezes were a trigger. Tightening the towel around my head, I closed my eyes and began the breathing exercises that Mahzeyah had taught me.

"I can overcome the addiction. I am sober. My life is bigger than the drug I am addicted to."

Water dripped down the side of my head and steadied my thoughts. I opened my eyes and repeated my new mantra. The fog from my shower was still faint even though I'd taken the shower over thirty minutes ago. I usually wouldn't shower this late at night, but while I was sleeping, a rush of liquid flooded my panties. I still had two weeks or so until my period, but it had changed before so I thought I had come on my cycle early. When I went into the bathroom to check, it was just an odorless liquid accompanied by some mild cramping.

Not in the mood to blow dry my hair just yet, I pulled from the vanity and opened the cabinet underneath it. I removed the hair dryer that was still in perfect condition even though I had launched it at the wall multiple times. I attached the comb and set it aside before grabbing the hair oil and the notebook that had become my best friend. Setting the hair items on the vanity, the notebook knocked over the bottle of perfume. Thoughts of Shio surfaced, making my stomach ache with yearning. It was crazy that these days I didn't crave the drug but a man.

Disgusted with myself, I needed to escape my thoughts. I grabbed the notebook and tucked it under my arm before picking up the perfume bottle. Removing the cap, I doused myself with it. My skin was still damp in some areas, especially my upper body, because my hair was wet under the towel. Undoing the towel wrapped around my body, I let the cold perfume mist settle over me. Once I was satisfied that I was soaked in the fragrance, I sat on the closed toilet lid, crossed one leg over the other, and opened the brown notebook. I still felt a little guilty about taking the journal, but I had gained so much insight into who Shio was that I could not regret my decision.

My entire life, I had never really known anyone. I knew what they wanted me to know, and that was usually things that didn't matter much. My papa, for instance, had never told me he didn't want to marry me off to the Rodríguezes, nor did I know he was in debt to Shio's Don. I never really knew my older brothers because their madre (mother) made sure to keep them away from me. The only reason I was allowed near my younger brothers was because she did not want to care for them. The tourists I partied with were always a one-off thing, so I didn't have any friends my age. I didn't know anyone, and before being tossed in this room, I didn't know much about myself either.

This was Shio's father's journal, but I had learned so much about Shio within these pages. I could understand why he was the way he was. And while I should have been running the other way, it only drew me to him more. Still, I had nothing to say to him. He and I simply didn't fit in life. He was not a considerate man. His choice to ignore me showed that he could also be immature. I did not want that in a companion.

Opening the journal, I flipped the page past what I had already read. Settling somewhere midway through, I prepared myself for what was to come. There was love, betrayal, addiction, abuse, and so many illegal things going on in this journal that I didn't understand how Shio's father could have ever thought he would have been able to publish this book without incriminating his entire family. It had to have been the drugs that had him thinking someone would publish this for an audience.

Boom Boom Boom Boom

Jumping, the book flew out of my hands. I caught it before it could hit the floor, stood, and put it back into the cabinet.

Boom Boom Boom Boom

"I'm coming!"

I hoped Italian's underage little self hadn't been drinking again. The last time they all got drunk, they fell asleep outside the door, talking me to death all night. Although I wasn't the happiest that they had been drinking, the group was like my babies now. I felt comfort when talking to them, the same comfort I felt from the American mob wives.

Looking around the bathroom, I searched for my pajamas and scoffed when I realized I must've left them on the dresser.

I opened the bathroom door slightly so he could hear my request. "Italian, pass me my pajamas, please. I am not decent. They are on the dresser."

Boom Boom Boom

Snatching the door open, I stuck my head out, shielding my body. "Italian! I just got out of the show—Shio?"

In a white tank top, basketball shorts, long white Nike socks, and Gucci slides stood Shio just outside the bathroom door. His eyes were low and red, and although he smelled of soap and Listerine, I knew he'd been smoking because I could smell the marijuana too.

"What... What are you doing here?" I asked with as much attitude as I could muster.

Licking his lips, he held his hand out. Snatching my pajamas from him, I remained behind the door but kept my head out, waiting for him to answer.

Whatever product he had used to moisturize his body had defined his muscles because of the sheen. His hair was lined to perfection and his face was without blemish, perfectly sculpted like his parents had carved him out of stone. There wasn't a piece of jewelry in sight besides the gold ring he always wore. He was void of all the things that would enhance a man, and yet, he still was extremely attractive. As my eyes assessed his frame, I reared my head back, noticing two large light purple welts on the side of his neck. I was inexperienced but I was not dumb. Those were marks of passion.

How dare he?

"Get dressed and come out, Solana. I'm sleepy."

"Ehhh... Okay... If you're sleepy, Shio, go to your home."

Using his thumb, he swiped his nose and looked off briefly before giving me his attention again. "I did. Twice, and left both times. The thing about houses is when it's no love in that muthafucka, it don't feel like home." He took a step back. "Lemme holla at you real quick."

I sighed. "I was about to blow dry my hair."

I thought of the first thing that came to mind to hopefully distance myself from his request. To further support my claim, I hid myself further behind the door and opened it wider so that he could see the products on the counter. He reached his long arms in, collecting the hair dryer, the brush, and the heat protectant.

"Get dressed and come out."

Closing the door because I felt like if I held it open any longer, he'd see me pass out, I slammed it harder than I intended. My pajamas for the day were simply a nightgown. Bella had brought it down the other day, claiming it reminded her of me. It was just a house dress with sombreros all over it. We both got a good laugh after I promised to wear it.

Drying my body quicker than I ever had, I slid the dress over my damp head since I also removed the towel. I wanted to skip moisturizing my body, but it would just bother me, so I grabbed the Neutrogena oil. It was another Walmart buy from Bella, and since I'd learned that a little went a long way, I poured enough in my hand to cover my body in one pass, finishing in less than a minute. I was actually way too oiled, but I didn't want to keep him waiting for too long, nor did I want to fuel his speculations that I was doing cocaine.

Opening the door, Shio was standing by the bed, holding the hair dryer. He gestured for me to sit down, and seeing the door was shut and locked again had me uneasy.

"I... I don't need you to show me how good my body can feel without the drug anymore. Thank you for that, but I'm okay, Shio," I said as I nervously took a seat.

Instead of replying to me, he began sectioning my hair. I could feel it separating horizontally, from ear to ear, and knew I hadn't given him a comb, so it had to be his fingers. They felt so good against my scalp, and I closed my eyes while squeezing my thighs together. I wasn't wearing any panties because Mahzeyah had told me it wasn't good to sleep in them, according to her mother. I was learning a lot from the littles about American life, and while I was older, I trusted them to only tell me things that would not hurt me.

Once my hair was sectioned, he took the brush and began brushing the back left portion from the bottom up. I'd been tender-headed as a child, mainly because people did not know what to do with my coarse hair or how to care for it, but over time, I grew out of it. He was handling my curls with such care that one would have thought I was still sensitive.

The brush detangling my strands and the silence that surrounded us were serene. I was grateful for him not forcing conversation because my focus was solely on controlling my breathing and the thumping between my legs.

"Your hair got longer." He pointed out as he moved to the next section.

"Yes. It normally does when I wash it regularly. Plus, I have been taking these vitamins. But you probably already know that, um."

He chuckled in response as he moved to the front right section. For some reason, the silence was no longer comforting, and I felt that

Shio wanted to talk. He wouldn't have come if he didn't because he had no problem ignoring me any other day. I wanted to return his sentiment, but unlike him, I thought of myself as a considerate person.

Swallowing my pride, I began to say something, but he said something first.

"What's on your mind?"

"You..." *Always you, Shio.*

"Oh, yeah? Well, that makes two of us, Solana."

"You should have stayed home, Shio."

"Didn't I tell you it's not a home?"

"Well, casa. You should have stayed at your casa. Your house."

His voice softened as he went to the last section. "I tried to, Solana. Last night and tonight."

My eyes quickly closed as I tried to steady my breathing again. His hands exploring my scalp triggered a rush of emotion throughout my body. My body tingled with every physical contact through his fingers, and it was driving me insane. It was too much to bear.

"Besides... I'm where I want to be right now," he said.

"Right now?"

He placed the brush down on the mattress and picked up the hair dryer again. "Yeah."

He clicked on the dryer, and before he placed it in my hair, he sprayed my hair with the heat protectant. When he was satisfied with the amount, he began running the dryer comb through my sectioned hair. I'd never imagined that Shio would be here drying my hair. In this moment, it made sense that he was a girl dad. This was not the first time he'd had his hands in my head. He'd done the braid during our first workout, but at that time, I had not known how he could use his fingers. How he could use his hands. How he could use his mouth.

Jumping from the bed, I turned to face Shio, hands folded across my chest since I wasn't wearing a bra. I couldn't handle him touching me another second because I was indeed on the verge of coming. He shouldn't hold that much power over me. He shouldn't ooze that much sex. I could still feel myself wanting to come, so I began pacing to bring myself down from the high I felt.

"Shio, y-you shouldn't be here."

"Sit down, Solana. I'm almost finished with your hair."

My semi-dry hair bounced as I paced, flowing down my back and past my shoulders, some strands falling to the sides of my face.

"I can't sit, Shio."

His tone was even, not realizing the area between my thighs was on fire. "You can, Solana."

"I can't! I can't sit, and I can't allow you to touch me. When you touch me... I just... I think you should leave."

He began wrapping the cord around the hair dryer, pulling it from the socket hidden behind the nightstand. I continued to pace while shooting him glances. When he chuckled, I wanted to hit him.

"Solana, baby... You think I need to touch you in order to make you come?"

"Shio! *Por favor* (Please)." He knew what he was doing to me, and the fact that I was begging him to leave made me more upset.

He placed the dryer on the nightstand along with the products. My hair smelled of Argan oil due to the shampoo and conditioner, but I could also smell the fruitiness from the heat protectant. He reached and tugged at my gown, but I snatched away from him.

"Shiooo. Please." I groaned.

He pulled at my dress again, and I snatched away again, but he was able to catch the other side and pull me into him. With my chest heaving, we were face to face, give or take, given the height difference.

"I don't like the way you're always pushing and pulling me. I'm not a broken toy." My breathing was coming out ragged as if I was still pacing the floor.

He eyed my lips and I folded them into my mouth. He didn't deserve to lust over me.

"You know I'll never harm you, Solana. You may not like the way I go about doing this shit, but you love when I put my hands on you."

"Shio. You are kind of—"

"Kinda what?"

"I am trying to find the word in English." I then tucked my lips back in before huffing. "It is like a chemical, but they use the word in a way to describe an unhealthy person. They say it in the movies."

His brow lifted, and when realization set in, he tossed his head back in laughter. Since I was still pressed against his chest, his boisterous, deep chuckles went right to my vagina.

"You callin' me toxic?"

I nodded once.

He scraped his bottom lip with his top teeth. "Shit... That ain't good."

He let me go, and I flew backward so fast that I fell against the dresser. Holding on to it and leaning my bottom against it, I hoped he would keep his distance now.

Widening his stance, Shio cupped his hands in front of his waist. "Solana, do you understand why I put you here?"

"Because you thought I gave your daughter drugs."

"No, Solana. 'Cause I don't fuck with cocaine. At least not in a sense of a muthafucka doing it." He shook his head before moving to sit on the bed. His legs gapped and his elbows rested on his knees. "And 'cause I fuck with you, I wanted you to shake this shit."

I squinted my eyes. "You thought it was wise to put me here without professional help?"

He lifted his head, peering at me with hooded eyes. "Did you need a professional to help you get on that shit?"

I went silent.

When he realized I wouldn't answer, he sighed. "Look, Solana. I fuck with you."

"Here we go with that word again. You know I do not like it. You fuck with everyone."

"Let me finish, yo. I fuck with you, but I don't fuck with your ways. Your habits. Your routine. It... It reminds me of my father a lot... But you already know that 'cause somebody has been runnin' their mouth."

No. I know that because I read it from the man himself.

"He had the same habit, and it made him do some shit that he shouldn't have. I'm not— naw. I refuse to go through that shit again with *anybody*."

"You really think I remind you of your father, Shio?"

He stared at me, and I shifted my hips trying to relieve the building pressure from just his eyes. He may have been right. He didn't need to touch me to make me come.

"Naw, Solana, baby... I think you remind me of me."

"Um, qué?"

"You remind me of me... Unresolved childhood trauma, that is. We both didn't have the best upbringing, and that shit followed us into adulthood. Except, I didn't become an addict. I did pills and drank, but I went cold turkey on that shit and didn't look back. It didn't affect my way of living, my decision-making, or my mental health. I fuck with you, but I don't fuck with the fact that you're an addict."

What he said was comical. It was so comical that I could not laugh. I would not laugh. Not at him. Not at his pain.

"Shio, I think you are an amazing person. You are giving. You are disciplined. You are determined. You are ambitious. You do anything for your family, and all of them adore you. You are a man of faith, strength, and courage. But you are an addict too."

He cocked his head and squinted his eyes.

I had already unleashed Pandora's box, so I forced myself to finish. "You start your mornings at four, before the sun rises. You like to run five miles after your two-hour workouts. If you are not eating your meal preps, you have one plate of said food—never any seconds, and you only eat the bad stuff until you are satisfied, never full. You have to consume two hundred and fifty-seven grams of protein a day. If you miss church, you watch at least two sermons back-to-back and overcompensate by doubling the tithes you send to your mother. When you are not working out or eating healthy or praising the Lord, you are looking after everyone in the family. You have let your childhood trauma turn you into an addict too."

"I haven't."

"You have. Miss a day of workouts. Miss a day of clean eating. Miss a day from checking in on the family. Miss a day of not consuming any fruits and veggies. Sleep in one day. Just one." I dared him before shrugging. "You cannot. You cannot because it will start the detox process. You would not even last two days before you are back at it."

I pointed to my chest. "I have lasted twenty-six! Twenty-six days without a drug that you hate so much! The one in which you have become a king from! Even when you came here covered head to toe in it, I did not relapse! Even when it was staring me in the face, I did not relapse! You watered your clothing because you thought I was going to sniff it!" I frowned in disgust when I thought back to it.

"Like... Like I am some bum? Well, you are wrong! You do not know me as well as you think you know me. When I figured out what I wanted and who I wanted to be, I did not look back. No matter how much it hurt!"

"You shouldn't have gotten clean in the premises of wanting me or the possibility of becoming my wife."

"What! I did it for me! For *me*! Not for you. Not for my father. For me! And for those teenagers who have held my hair back while I threw up. Who have washed the piss from my skin! Something you were able to see on the camera, and not once did you come. Not once!" I held up my index finger.

"I did it for me! I don't want to be your wife. Even while detoxing, I never thought I would become your wife." I scoffed. "But I know you have to choose. I know your Don gave you an ultimatum. Bahati or me, right?"

"You shouldn't have been snooping."

"I didn't snoop anything! It was obvious! The entire plane ride, the way you kept bouncing your eyes between her and me. I could see you compartmentalizing and listing why one woman was better than the other and vice versa."

"You don't know what I was thinking, Solana."

"Your not denying it tells me I know exactly what you were thinking, Shio."

"So what now... You clean? The door was open, and no one is here. Why didn't you leave? Isn't that what you planned on doin' the night I caught you stuffin' that shit up yo' nose? Fuck me and flee?"

"That was then, and this is now. I am going to take a few more days to get my thoughts in order, and then I am going to ask the girls to help me. I am in no position to turn down anything. Jisei said I could stay here so I may explore that option. When I get on my feet, I will find my family and maybe move to another state. I know how to sit still and make decisions without my emotions now. If I lived in this state, I would only be putting myself in harm's way. Maybe in the path of the Rodríguezes."

Shio kissed his teeth. "They ain't gonna fuck with you." He gritted his teeth in a growl-like manner with each word he spoke.

"That is good to know."

"And you not moving out of state, Solana."

"That is not for you to decide." I huffed and uncrossed my arms. "I am an addict to you, and you need to worry about the other things in your world. I will be just fine."

"But you said we're both addicts."

The movement was so swift and silent that I hadn't realized he had latched onto the hem of my nightgown until I was being pulled in his direction.

"Shio, no."

"You said I'm addicted to workin' out..."

I tried to back up in the opposite direction, but the gown was stretched to its capacity. I could feel the threads giving out and hear them begging to tear.

"Sh—"

"I'm addicted to eatin' clean."

I was still trying to resist as he kept pulling me toward him.

"To worship. To my family. To my grind. But you left one thing out, Solana."

Riiiiip

The gown tore right down the middle and slid from my arms. I was standing between his legs, naked as the day I was born. He swooped me into his arms, folding my knees directly on his thighs. My breasts bounced onto his face, and the smile he gave me as he kissed each one made a small gush of liquid moisten my vagina.

"You left out my most dangerous fuckin' addiction... My newest one."

"Shio, just—"

The cool air circulating in the room brushed against my skin as his arm wrapped around my thighs and he hoisted me up. My vagina was now directly in his face, and no amount of wiggling could remove my hips from his strong hands.

"You, Solana. Yo' ass my fuckin' addiction, and I'm ready to relapse."

"Shio, wait—"

He pressed his mouth onto my vagina lips while holding me upright, cutting my words off instantly. As he sucked my bud into his mouth, I could feel the back of my knees pressing against his shoulders.

Sluuuuurp

He licked and then sucked my entire vagina into his mouth, leaving me no choice but to grip his shoulders. Suddenly, the air was too hot, my skin was too hot, his touch was too hot. But his mouth was the perfect temperature. Biting my bottom lip to suppress the moans that I was too embarrassed to let go of, I made the mistake of looking down.

"Sh... Sh... Shioooo."

His mouth was full, and the way his jaws moved as he looked up at me while consuming me made the feeling ten times more euphoric. He squeezed his arms around my thighs, pulling me further into his mouth. His lips were so warm—so wet, so soft. I shuddered all over as suckling sounds filled the room. I could feel my stomach caving in and cramping as I began to quake. I had seen Shio a few ways, but this way? This was my favorite way to view him. I didn't care about my breasts hanging or my body being exposed. All I cared about was that he continued to make me feel this good.

"I'm. I'm—"

"Come," he commanded.

My legs went stiff, my stomach completely caved in, and it felt as if I had just snorted a line with the way my eyes were crossed. My body shook uncontrollably. My nails were deeply embedded in the skin of his neck as he latched onto my bud.

"Ahhhhhh!"

I went limp in his arms, falling over his head as if I'd lost consciousness. His laughs shook my body as I tried to steady my breathing. He filled both of his hands with my ass cheeks, squeezing them together and then pulling them apart before biting down on the inside of my left thigh.

"Ummmm." I could do nothing but hum from the sensational feeling that came with releasing.

"You tapped out?"

I nodded once, even being upside down, forehead resting against his back.

"Too bad."

He stood, flipped me around, and placed my back against the bed. This man's strength needed to be studied, but I expected nothing less from a person who was addicted to training his body.

"Solana?"

My eyes shot open. Shio was standing between my legs. He looked down at my hands that were covering my mound. I didn't know I was shielding myself; it was just a natural reaction, I assumed.

"I can eat your pussy all night, if that's what you want, ma."

"Why does it sound like there is another option?" I asked, chest still heaving.

"'Cause there is." He rubbed his hand down his face before grazing his top teeth with his bottom lip. "I can put us both out of our misery. But you should save yourself. You waited all this time."

"But you have already made me come. Multiple times."

"Yeah. With my mouth. With my words. But I ain't made you come with my dick."

I shuddered again at just the thought of being that close to Shio. "I am sure it is the same thing."

"Oh, baby, trust me. It's not the same thing." He chuckled.

Shio grabbed my leg, stretched it out, and took my foot into his hands. My hands still covered myself, now feeling more exposed at the idea of having sex. He massaged my right foot, holding eye contact before swiping his tongue across the arch.

"Ahhh!"

I slightly lifted from the bed, but he didn't let up. Maintaining eye contact, he snaked his slimy tongue between my toes. Using his free hand, he knocked my hand away from my mound and placed his thumb between my lower lips, directly on my bud.

The combination of his hand and tongue sent shock waves through my body. All of my hair, including the ones on my head, stood at attention, or at least that is what it felt like. As this man sucked my toes and fingered my hardened bud, I could do nothing but moan and slowly move my hips in rhythm with his. This may have felt just as good as him using his mouth to please me, or even better—I was not sure. Maybe everything Shio did to me physically felt good. Maybe it was just because it was Shio, and he was my taboo, and I liked him so much that everything felt good.

My bud became a rock, and that feeling returned to the pit of my stomach. He let my foot go but gave the opposite one the same treatment. My skin tickled, and my breathing became heavy with me inhaling and exhaling the same air. I dropped my chin into my chest with a sigh of pleasure before closing my eyes shut. I couldn't look at him. Looking at him doing these things to my body made the building pressure intensify.

"Come, baby."

"Goooood! Ahhhhhhhhhh!"

I snatched my foot from his mouth, and at the same time, he dropped down, keeping his thumb moving but covering my box with his mouth. My legs clamped shut, closing his head in, and although I felt bad, I was jerking too wildly to care.

Laughing prompted me to open my eyes. Peeling my thighs apart, Shio was still in position, but instead of his mouth still on my now sensitive vagina, he was simply gazing at it.

"What... What is it?" I asked, out of breath but slightly concerned.

Shio shook his head. "Don't make no sense how good you taste. How wet you are... You shouldn't be this fuckin' wet."

"Why not? Maybe I am just different from the others." I sassed. I didn't know anything about how the vagina worked and what different vaginas had from woman to woman.

Instead of replying, he kissed me down there again, and I jumped.

"Aite, baby. I'm done."

He stood, but I grabbed his hand. "Shio. Do not go. I want to... I want to do this."

"Nah. You ain't ready, Solana. Save that shit for the nigga you marry."

"I do not care about him. Whoever he is... If I even marry. I care about right now, and right now I want this."

He ran his hand down his face as I grabbed at the hem of his shirt. He dropped his hands and pulled his shirt over his head, causing my hands to graze his lower abs.

Dark chocolate.

Eight pack.

Biceps.

Triceps.

Tattoos. So many tattoos.

"If we do this shit, it won't feel like the other shit. It's not going to feel good to you. As a matter of fact, it's going to hurt. Even if we go more than one round, it still may hurt. It could be days, weeks, or months before you can appreciate how it feels. Plus, as fucked up as it sounds, Solana, baby... This won't change anything between us. We..."

He paused as he sighed and rubbed his hand down his face. "We just not ready for each other."

We weren't. As much as I wanted us to be, we were not ready to be anything more to one another. As put-together as Shio seemed—both how he appeared and how he felt—he had unresolved issues just like I did. My focus needed to be on organizing my life now that I'd kicked the drug addiction. But us not being ready for something permanent didn't mean I couldn't satisfy the part of my body that had been craving this. I had been yearning for this since the day I walked out of the bathroom and saw Uriah pleasuring him. Us having sex now would be no different than us doing it the night he caught me in the closet. I had plans to give it to him and then move on with my life. I could still do the same thing now.

"Will it feel good to you?"

His eyes lowered. His lips were moist with my juices, and he made no attempt to clean my cum from his mouth. "Hell yeah."

"Well, that is all that matters. You have made me feel good. It is your turn. Come, please." I patted the bed.

I knew what I was asking for. I knew it would hurt, especially because of Shio's size. When we were in the tub, when he was blind, and in the shower when he came over, I had seen how massive his penis was. I tried to block it out, knowing I may never have the opportunity to feel him, but now that I could, I was as prepared as I could be for the feeling I would have when he entered me.

I watched as his hands lowered to his waistband. I closed my eyes right before his fingers hooked inside the basketball shorts. I even kept them closed as the bed dipped under his weight, and he climbed up my body, pushing me back onto the bed.

"Solana..."

He grabbed my hands and pushed them above my head. My eyes sprang open, coming face to face with the handsome Shio. He hovered over me, nose to nose, and our lips were only inches from each other.

"Don't beg, baby. Lesson number five. You ain't ever, ever gotta beg for shit when it comes to me."

"It doesn't feel that way," I whispered.

He searched my eyes for something. I didn't know what it was, but I returned the look. "Lesson number nine. Always say what's on your mind. And pair that shit with lesson number four and say it confidently."

"Is it not a little too late for lessons? You've *been* asking me what's on my mind."

"Yeah, but not like this." His breath tickled my face. I could smell myself on him, and instead of it grossing me out, it turned me on.

"Okay. I think I am about to start my period."

"That's what you choose to say, Solana? Right here? Right now?"

"Yes. That is what was on my mind."

His forehead pressed against mine, noses merging as he closed his eyes and chuckled.

"Just listen... I felt a rush while sleeping. That is why I took a shower, but only to find it was clear... discharge? I think that is the word for the vagina fluids. Yes, discharge. But then, my stomach started cramping. It is still cramping." I breathed out.

"Baby..." He kissed my lips. "You not about to start your period."

"How do you know?"

"'Cause I know your period, Solana."

"But I am cramping."

His eyes opened. He then reclaimed my lips, crushing our chests together. His tongue explored the recesses of my mouth. His kisses were slow, drugging me, and had my nipples rock hard against his chest. I was sure to kiss him back with as much passion as he was kissing me. As our lips explored, he let my arms free, rubbing his hand in my hair.

That feels so good.

How was it that everything he did felt so good? How was he this experienced?

"Umm..." I moaned before screeching. "Argggghhhhhhh!"

White, hot pain shot through me. I was no longer seeing Shio. I was seeing the stars above. He said it would hurt. He never said it would feel like I was being split open. My body lifted but could only go so far as he was on top of me. I felt full, too full. I felt packed, like a billion needles had penetrated me from the bottom, and that pain spread all over my body. Whereas everything else felt good, this hurt.

He groaned before saying my name.

"Sh-Sh... It huuuurrrrrts."

He kissed the side of my face, and I hadn't known tears were running from my eyes until I felt them in my ears.

"You want me to stop, baby? Or you want me to put the rest in?"

"The rest?!"

How much more could it be?

"Aite, I gotchu."

I felt him pull out and ease back in, and that made me grab his back. It was no wonder my father wanted me to remain a virgin. I thought the doctors constantly checking me monthly was painful and uncomfortable. This feeling was much worse.

By the time he eased back in, I was in full-blown tears. The pain hadn't subsided, but I wasn't crying because of the pain anymore. I was crying because I was doing something I wanted. I was doing something I wanted with the person I wanted it from.

"Solana, baby."

Opening my eyes, Shio's sexual face was so attractive. He continued pumping in and out of me slowly as my legs wrapped around his waist, trying to find comfort.

"This... Uhhh. It hurts so good. But I don't want—"

"Spanish, baby. Fuuuck." His mouth covered mine hungrily as his kiss sent new spirals of ecstasy through me. "Spanish, baby. Say... That... Shit... In Spanish."

"Mhmmm, Shio!"

His pace had increased, and his body had become slick with a light sheen of sweat. I was sure my skin mirrored his, but I could not look to see because I was stuck with my eyes on him as I felt the complicated feeling of pain and pleasure.

"*Esto duele tan bien. Pero no quiero que pares.* (This hurts so good. But I do not want you to stop.)"

It hurt, but not as excruciatingly as it did moments ago. There was no way I could have endured this with Felipe. The only reason I was not shoving Shio off me was because of how much I liked him.

"*No voy a parar, nena. Te sientes tan bien. Te sientes tan bien envuelta alrededor de mi pene.* (I'm not going to stop, baby. You feel so good.

You feel so good wrapped around my dick.)"

Shio's Spanish was so good. It was so sexy. He was so fluent as if it were his first language. And his tone and accent had my middle drenching as he continued sliding in and out.

"*Todavía no he entrado del todo y se siente perfecto.* (I haven't gone all the way in yet, and it feels perfect.)"

"*¿Perfecto?*" My nails dug into his back.

"Fuckin' perfecto, baby. You so fuckin' sexy. So fuckin' pretty."

I closed my eyes, his body feeling so good pressed against mine.

"*Abre los ojos, cariño. Necesito que me veas. Necesito verte.* (Open your eyes, baby. I need you to see me. I need to see you.)"

I peeled my eyes open. His own eyes were watery, and I had to blink to make sure I wasn't making it up in my head.

"Te amo, Solana."

"Hahhh," I gasped as he continued his pace, feeling everything times a million. He was stretching me but the pain no longer mattered; his words did.

"Shhh... Shio."

"I love you, Solana. I fuckin' love you."

"*Te amo, Shio. Te he amado desde el día en que te sentaste a la mesa de mi padre.* (I love you, Shio. I loved you since the day you sat at my father's dinner table.)"

"Fuuuuck! I love when you speak Spanish, baby. Got my dick so hard. You feel so gotdamn good, Solana."

"I thought..." I was panting as his dick expanded even more inside of me. "I thought you didn't like it."

He kissed me again, his lips covering my plump ones completely. "It ain't too much about you that I don't like." He stuck his nose in my neck and placed his hand between my legs. "I'm gonna make it feel good for you, baby. You may not come, but some of the pain will be an afterthought."

He began thumbing my clit, and he was right, the pleasure outweighed the little pain I still felt. I didn't feel that budding pressure anymore; I only felt full. Very full.

"You ovulating, so I need to pull out. But, fuck!"

His body began to shiver as he began to pushed himself into me harder. I was moaning so much that my mouth had gone dry.

Licking my lips, I asked, "But, what?"

"But I can't pull out. You feel too good. Fuuuuuck, baby. You feel too fuckin' good. My list is 'bout to get even longer."

Shio's lips met mine while his movements sped up. He felt harder inside me than just a minute ago. It was almost as if a steel pipe that was covered in slime was being thrust up my vagina. I couldn't keep up with his thrusts, even if I tried. The pain and pleasure were confusing me, and I couldn't stop my body from quivering or my throat from releasing sounds of ecstasy.

"Pussy... so... fuckin' perfect. Shit." His body bucked and then stiffened, and I felt a stream of fluid shoot inside of me.

That felt good, and I couldn't help but feel whatever he was feeling. He slid out of me slowly, still trying to catch his breath, but he continued thumbing my bud. When he was all the way out, I felt relieved, but instead of him getting up, he latched onto my right breast while he continued to rub circles on my bud.

"I need you to come, baby. I want you to feel what I just felt." He bit down on my nipple, and my back arched as his thumb raced against my moans.

"Yesssssssssssssss, Shio!"

"Come for me, baby. Make that pretty-ass pussy cream."

"Ahhhh!" My stomach clenched and cramped, and as I came, I could feel some of the fluid he shot inside of me gushing out.

"Damn, ma."

"W-What?"

He placed a kiss on my inner thigh. "That was a lot."

"Is that a bad thing?"

"Hell yeah. Shit looks like octuplets."

I shot straight up, knocking him from between my legs. "Shio..."

He pulled me on top of him with a grin. "I'm just fuckin' with you. You want a Plan B?"

"Are those not illegal in the States?"

"Ain't shit illegal to me."

"It is my first time. I will not get pregnant."

Shio chuckled while rubbing my butt. "Solana.... I'm healthy, and I eat clean most days. My soldiers march, baby. Shya is proof of that, and I wasn't even up to par then. I'm probably the most fertile nigga in the family thanks to my lifestyle. You will get pregnant, baby."

"We do not need that."

He quieted as my vagina ached, coming down from the sexual high. "Naw, we don't. But let's worry about tomorrow's problems tomorrow."

"Okay..."

I listened to his heartbeat within his chest, not being able to believe what had just happened.

"Shio..." I tried sitting up, but he wouldn't let me. "I smell blood."

"You're bleeding, baby."

"I told you."

"That's your hymen, Solana, not your period. Just chill. We will handle it in a minute."

I heard a door slam above us and was reminded where I was.

I groaned. "They are going to know we had sex."

"And. They be fuckin' their damn selves."

I nudged his chest. "They do not."

"Yeah. Aite." He chuckled, his after-sex voice churning my insides.

Not knowing how else to say what was on my mind, I did what he said early and just said it with confidence. "I would like to see Shya."

Without taking a beat, he responded, "We have plans tomorrow. I was going to let Dasani's sitter watch her."

My heart fell into the pit of my stomach. "Plans with Bahati?"

"Solana."

"No." I cleared my throat. "It is okay. Bring her anyway. She can stay the night. If it is okay with her mom."

"I'll bring her. Maybe you can get her to talk."

"Good."

I yawned, feeling my eyes go heavy, although I knew I needed to stay awake. I did not need to sleep in Shio's arms like they did in the movies. I needed to create a safe distance from Shio, but it was hard to when he would not let me go. I sighed, giving up and letting the sleepiness carry me away.

Before I closed my eyes, I said into Shio's chest, "I know this changes nothing, but Shio, I am so happy it was you."

Weightless. Lighthearted. Carefree.

I was drifting off to sleep, too incoherent to hear his reply, but I could have sworn I heard him say something that I knew he wouldn't utter.

This changes everything, baby.

CHAPTER 27
GLOW

"You look good, daughter," my mother complimented, appearing in the mirror that I'd been standing in front of.

With a pink blanket tossed over her shoulder, even though Baby Leader was down for her evening nap, she inspected me through the glass. I smiled at her before focusing back on my dress.

Today had been my first day active online since I was hospitalized. I had been scrolling but hadn't actually posted anything. I had enough food vlogs that had been edited for upload and would last me for at least another two weeks, but instead of going that route, I went live. I'd been nervous about doing a get-ready-with-me because it wasn't my usual content, although I'd done it before.

My followers had been in my comments and messages for the past few weeks, asking where I'd been. I was consistent with my uploading videos or going live randomly, so my going ghost wasn't normal to them. Some had speculated that I was lying up with the "fine ass Memphian," which is what they called Tunan. Although they weren't too far off in their assumption, my disappearance had been much deeper than that.

"Glow, you look amazing."

I'd done my makeup on live, removed the rollers from my fresh closure sew-in, and shown three outfits for them to choose from. The one they'd picked was my least favorite of the lineup, but since I'd spent two and a half hours on live, I didn't have the time to change.

"I don't know, Mama. My thighs look so—"

"Nope! Absolutely not. You look beautiful. We not doing any body shaming today or for any days to come. If I had your body, I, too, would have a man waiting outside in a car that looks like it should be on a NASCAR speedway."

Between her and Tunan, I'd been eating like I was recording myself. After sharing a lap dance with him and a pretty brown stripper, who had so much butt that it should've been criminal, he made sure he stuffed me full of every food item left over from the dinner portion of Pia's gender reveal. He had shown up late, and then, when he got a call from his brothers, he left early. I hadn't heard from him since, which was two nights ago. He did call yesterday to tell me that he was picking me up early today so that we could make a stop before going to the dinner Shio had planned. My mama saying he was outside had me grinning. He had kept his promise, and he was on time—ten minutes early, to be exact.

"But is the dress too short for a dinner his brother is throwing?"

I was wearing a black bandage halter mini dress that showed the top half of my back and scooped low, revealing cleavage in the front. Around the neck and the bust were gold hardware in open circles. The hem of the dress had the same feature. I thought the dress was too short and too sexy because we weren't told the exact occasion for the dinner. I finished the look with black YSL pumps and a gold clutch. My deep, side-part sew-in was styled in very loose, vixen curls that fell just how I wanted. On my wrist, I kept it simple with my Cartier watch, and in my ears were diamond studs.

My mama eyed the dress. "It's not too short to me, baby."

"But my butt looks too big and my hips too. And I'm not talking about weight when I say this—" I started, since my mama had begun to give me chastising looks. "I'll be in the room with other men. My friends' husbands. I don't want to come off disrespectful."

I tucked my hair behind my ear, placed my hand on my lower stomach, turned, and posed. *Yeah, my booty looks way too big in this dress.*

"Yeah... That's what happens when you have a man that you love who is treating you right. You start spreading, baby."

"Mama! And love is a stretch."

"What? I know I have two daughters that be having sex. I've

gained a grandchild and a son-in-law out of the blue. You look amazing, baby. And stop worrying about taming yourself down for their men. Their husbands will be in the room, and so will yours. They knew you were a bad bitch when they decided to befriend you. If we are talking about the same women from the hospital, then you are surely dressed appropriately."

I chuckled because my mother was right. I was sure that Missy or Mocha would probably be wearing something even shorter or more revealing than this dress. I was probably being self-conscious because I was spreading, and because Tunan had taken my scale, I didn't know how much I weighed now.

Grabbing my oversized clutch from the vanity, I picked up my perfume of choice and doused myself in it again. I kissed my mother on the forehead since I was towering over her in my heels.

"Thank you, Mama."

"Ummmhmm. I need to start putting that on my resume. That 'I'm the bad bitch maker.'"

"Ha! Goodnight, Mama. Stop reading those books."

"Stop lying to yourself about how you feel about my handsome son-in-law, and then maybe I'll consider!" she called to my back, being sure to keep her voice down since the baby was sleeping.

Baby Leader would be up in three hours for a feeding, and after that, she'd sleep through the night. Glee and Blayke were next door, like they always were. They had gotten their glam done for the dinner and looked absolutely amazing. I opted out since the trio was so booked today, and I was in the mood to do my own. However, I couldn't do it quite like Bruna—or Bruno, because I'd heard his name change over the years. It was magic in those hands of his. Looking in the mirror once more, I nodded because maybe my hands did have a little magic in them too.

Pulling the front door open, I stopped in my tracks. Tunan was standing on the porch looking so fucking good that I wanted to take him in the house and let him have his way with me. I didn't even care that my mother was now living within a few walls of me. He could take me right now, and I'd be okay with her hearing. I eyed him from head to toe and shuddered internally. We hadn't had sex since I'd been home from the hospital, and the last time he was over here, I thought it was going to be the night he finally gave me the dick. He'd been holding out like I hadn't had it before. However, he had been pleasing me orally so I couldn't complain. It was good, too good, but I needed penetration.

"Fuck, Glow." He grabbed my hand, helping me step down from the doorway.

Holding my hand up, he turned my body so that he could get a three-sixty view. Tunan was salivating over me, but he was looking damn good himself. He was in black slacks that stopped right above the ankle. His top was a silk-like material and stopped right at his waist, showing the Prada belt that matched his loafers. Everything about him was immaculate, and the Ferrari resting in the driveway was the perfect backdrop. He'd been in it when we drove to the hospital, but I'd been too hysterical to care.

Tucking my hair behind my ear, I lowered my head to hide the blush on my cheeks.

"I love dis color on you, my baby." He ran his fingers through the strands of my hair.

My stylist had done a custom brown-and-blond mixture to mimic the braids I'd had in. I loved the colorway and wanted my sew-in dyed with the same mixture.

"Thank you. I'm glad you like what your money paid for."

Yesterday, while the stripper was dancing on me and I was dancing on him, he was making it rain on me instead of her. I gave her some, of course, but collected enough to pay for my maintenance today.

"Yeah, keep dis." He was still feeling the ends of my hair. If it wasn't for the material of this dress, he'd be able to see that my nipples were hard.

Stepping onto the sidewalk, my hand still in his, I walked over to my car. Price was coming out of his grandpa's house, and he, too, was in all black. However, there was a stark difference in appearance. Where Tunan was date-night ready, Price was looking like he was headed to rob someone.

I sure hope not.

When Jisei's door opened, and Pearla came strolling out, I whipped my head between the two. Her hair and makeup were perfect, making her look like a doll, but she wasn't dressed just yet. When he met her in the middle of the street and wrapped his arms around her waist, I was taken aback. I remembered vividly FaceTiming his girlfriend. I even followed her and thought she too was pretty, but she wasn't Pearla. I couldn't remember if I'd seen his girlfriend on social media lately, but from the way he was all in Pearla's face, I was guessing he and ole girl were no longer a thing. Mr. Grind better wake up soon because Price's young ass was fine, and he was a lover boy from what I was seeing. I just hoped Pearla wasn't taking a page out of Glee's book. They had way too much freedom in Jisei's house. And even though my bestie said she had cameras up, I was going to have to start popping up over there to be sure nothing too explicit was happening.

The engine in the Ferrari rumbled as we drove out of my neighborhood. His large and calloused hand took mine, and he pressed it to his lip as he maneuvered through traffic with one hand. Had someone told me a year ago that I would be in the passenger side of an exotic muscle car with my husband while he kissed the ring on my finger as I made a mess in my panties, I would have thought they were lying.

But here I was.

"You like puppies, Glow?"

I turned and gave him a side-eye. "Where'd that come from?"

He chuckled. "Nuttin'. I might have one, doe. Seein' if you wanted it, and if you did, I'd go pick it up."

I didn't know how I felt about a new dog and a new baby in the house, so I didn't reply. The music pumped through the speakers as the car glided along the streets, the day still present even though I knew it wouldn't take long for the sun to set.

"Is it da kisses for me. She like hit it for me. She like ooh... She like oohhh. Damn, baby, you get my self-esteem." Tunan kissed my hand again as he butchered the lyrics to "Self Esteem" by Lamb4oe. He didn't sound bad, but he was singing out of order.

We came to a red light, and he intertwined his fingers in mine and pulled me toward him until I was leaning into his face. "Put her ass in da eeerrr. Put her ass in da eeerrrrr."

I burst out in laughter like my pussy wasn't begging to be touched by him. He placed a kiss on my lips. Once more, and then twice more, before letting me go. Had there been more room, I would have melted to the floor. The light had barely turned, and he was going way above the speed limit. The song ended, and he lowered the volume since it had restarted.

"You look good as fuck, my baby."

"So do you," I returned the compliment.

What the hell was I feeling like? I normally gave Tunan attitude, but right now, I was completely and utterly smitten, and all he'd done was sing two lines.

He chuckled with a grin. "What up witchu, Glow?"

Keeping my face forward, pretending like I was enjoying the scenery, I swiped my tongue across my bottom lip. I'd done a lip stain and lip gloss, so I didn't have to worry about constantly reapplying my lip combo. The Pretty Eaters had also suggested that.

I turned to him. "Why you didn't come over after the gender reveal or last night?"

He licked his lips, and I could've creamed if I didn't have the sliver of self-control I was struggling to maintain. I could smell his cologne and a faint weed smell, so his low eyes let me know he'd gotten high before pulling up. It had to have been at his sister's house because the car still smelled new and like leather.

"Mane... You wouldn't even believe it if I told you."

"Hmmm. You didn't take one of the strippers home, did you?"

"Weren't all da strippers dere when I left, my baby?"

"You tell me."

He placed his finger on my bare thigh and slowly dragged it up. Stopping right at the hem of my dress, he bit his bottom lip, and I knew he could feel the heat between my thighs.

Shifting his eyes to mine, he waited until I met his gaze. "I wasn't wit no bitch last night or the night befo', Glow."

"Promise?"

Once we came to another light, he held eye contact again. "I promise, Glow."

My belly fluttered. "I want some dick."

Caught completely off guard, Tunan laughed heartily. "You always want some dick, lil' baby."

"Yeah, and I thought I was going to get some last night. I have gained my twenty-plus pounds back and everything. I'm good for a fuck." I shrugged.

His smile fell. "Mane, I know I been 'round, but we ain't really talked 'bout how you feelin' and shit."

I folded my arms under my breasts, which were nearly spilling out of my dress. "I'm okay... Better."

"Ion mean to be a mood killer, but I went through some shit last night dat got me lookin' at life differently. We gotta figure out how to permanently get you well, my baby. Ion like seein' you laid up in da hospital."

I still had days when I struggled. I still had days where I didn't want to eat, but I hadn't thrown up. I'd been keeping my food down even when I could see the weight packing onto my body.

I cleared my throat and swallowed down the need to eat my words before I said them aloud. "My daddy, as much as I love him, he, uhh... He would call my mama fat every chance he could... especially when he got caught cheating. The screams turned into fighting. And then, I began throwing up. Their arguments stressed me, and stress triggers it, I guess. Even now.

"And too much food on my stomach just feels wrong, so I sorta just don't eat. And in a sense, I can control the way I look by throwing up. I can control the situation if I can control myself. Plus, nobody wants to walk around looking as big as a house."

"So, you'n really know exactly what brought on dis anorexia shit. You'n know if it's from yo' daddy body-shamin' yo' mama, dem fightin', him cheatin', or you not likin' food." Tunan chuckled, but not in a way that he was laughing at me. "My baby, we gone have to get to da root."

He circled his finger on my thigh, and his touch was so light, but it left me burning with need. "Childhood trauma... Dat shit a muhfuckah. My mama, her birthday... dat shits in September."

I whipped my head toward him, ready to knock the smirk off his face because the math wasn't mathing. We'd just celebrated her birthday not even a full two months ago, if I wasn't mistaken.

"Yeah... She checked out on us, leavin' a house full of kids to my sister. To put it in better terms, she was triflin' as fuck. Sittin' on her ass collectin' food stamps, housing, and whatever else she could from da government. She ain't give a fuck if we ate or had decent clothes, and it was no excuse cuz she had no vices." Tunan swallowed, his Adam's apple shifting.

His mom had already told me she wasn't perfect and that she'd made mistakes, but with the way her children loved her, you wouldn't think she'd been unkind to them. I did, however, see that the boys bonded more with Tuscany. They worshipped their sister. I was still waiting for him to explain to me why we'd celebrated her birthday in Memphis, in that hot ass heat.

As if he'd read my mind, he continued. "When she finally got her shit together, after my sister popped up pregnant, she got a medical billing and coding degree and a good job in da hospital. Bought dat house we was at. We were still livin' in da hood, but life looked so much better. It felt so much better cuz my mama decided to make a change. So she celebrates two birthdays. One on da day she was actually born, and one when she got her life together.

"Ain't no rules in life, Glow. Not ones dat we absolutely have to abide by, where livin' is concerned. You can still hold on to dat childhood trauma, or you can let dat shit stop witchu. It will never fully go away. Never. Let it sit witchu so you can grow from it. Let it help shape you. Let it serve as a reminder dat life ain't perfect. Life ain't no aesthetic. No cohesive algorithm."

His low eyes swept my frame. "Dis ain't no trauma for trauma, or no tit for tat. I been through some shit, too, Glow—in my adulthood and adolescence. But if I sit *in* it instead of sitting *with* it, I'd foreva be stuck."

His words hit me like a tidal wave. I had no comeback, so I swallowed hard and let them simmer.

"You perfect to me, Glow. I'm yo' fuckin' husband, my baby. I wouldn't give a fuck if you gained a hunnid pounds, I'd still suck yo' whol' pussy in my mouth."

I sputtered a laugh but was stopped when his hand traced upward. I moaned and spread my legs, giving him complete access. His finger trailed up further, not stopping until he traced the lining of my panties.

"You bossed da fuck up. You sexy as fuck. You'n even know da advantage you have. You did dis shit without a nigga. Without an organization. You ain't got no kids, doe I'd gladly play stepdaddy if you did. I told myself when I got out, I was focusin' on my bread, but I ain't been thinkin' 'bout dat shit. All I can think 'bout is you. Yo' well-being, makin' sure I ain't eva gotta see you laid up in da hospital again. So we gotta get you right, my baby, so yo' nigga can focus on gettin' us right, aite?"

He dipped a finger inside of me, and I shook. I was so wet that he slid in deeper than he intended. "Fuuuck, Tune."

He swerved the car over to the far lane and parked right on the side of the expressway. "Let the seat back."

He pulled his hand from my snatch as I let the seat back. Once it was back as far as it could go, he hit the emergency lights and began undoing his belt buckle. I slid my black no-show panties from my legs and lay back as he climbed over. He was too tall, but we were making it work. He grabbed my leg, bringing it up to my head, and pulled my breast from the dress. Once he bit down on it, I screamed out as he slid his dick inside of me. It didn't go in as easily as his finger, and it took a minute for me to adjust to his size, but when I did and he bottomed out, my stomach clenched.

"Tunan! Shit!"

"Dis pussy so fuckin' wet. So... fuckin' tight, my baby."

He let my breasts go with a pop, pressed his chest into the back of my leg, driving himself deeper. He began caressing his hands over the curves of my hips as my dress was bunched around my waist. I squeezed my pussy muscles making him groan and drop his head to mine. He was fucking me so good as if our lives weren't in danger on the side of the road. The car rocked as passing vehicles zoomed by, but we didn't care. His hard body was pressed into mine as he rocked in and out of me, taking me where I'd crave to be.

"Tunan... My God. I'm boutttaaaa commmmeeeee!"

"Come, baby. Come on yo' dick. Fuck, Glow."

I clenched around him as my numb leg began to shake. Stars exploded behind my eyes as waves of pleasure soared through me. His tongue traced my lips before he pulled them into his mouth. His kiss was urgent and exploratory as he fucked me faster than it should have been possible in our current position. My sister had just gotten into a fucking accident, so I should've been more cautious, but good dick had me losing my fucking common sense.

"Fuck!"

He snatched himself out of me, leaving my lips throbbing and my pussy satisfied. He was coming inside his hand, raising up fully to let my leg go. His long, thick, brown dick glistened from my juices, and it was a beautiful sight as it spat up cum. My legs were still wide open while I steadied my breathing and watched him shudder as he filled his hand. When he was done, he sat back on his knees, his backside hitting the dashboard.

We both stared at each other before bursting out in laughter.

"Dis shit crazy!" He shook his head. "Where yo' bag? You be keepin' products and shit in it."

I reached on the side of the door where I'd felt the clutch drop. I opened it up, moving stuff around until I grabbed the wipes. I handed one to him and he cleaned his hand off. He reached for a second wipe and pressed it to my vagina and rubbed me tenderly. When he leaned in and placed a kiss on my lips while rubbing, I moaned out loud, ready for another round.

"We gotta go, my baby."

He climbed back on his side of the car, and with a third wipe, he cleaned his dick and tucked it away. I put my panties back on, pulled my dress down, and grabbed the travel-size perfume to spray away the faint sex smell. He checked the rearview mirror and waited for an eighteen-wheeler to pass before merging us back onto the road.

"What?" I smiled coyly when I noticed he was checking me out every few seconds. He had just drilled my ass to the leather, so if he was wondering why I was sitting over her happy as fuck, he'd have to put two and two together.

Tunan rubbed his hand down his head, and it looked as if he was blushing too. "Mane... When I was locked up, dem niggas swore up and down dat when you got a wife, dey wouldn't want sex." He licked his lips. "I thought our first time was gone be da only time, especially after we signed dem papers."

Putting my spray back in my purse, I grabbed my gloss. It was sixty dollars and wasn't a brand deal, but so far it had been worth the price tag. Flipping the visor down, I reapplied the gloss to my lips and then smoothed down my hair.

"Well, I don't know about their wives, but yours is about that life."

I flipped the visor back up and readjusted my seat belt. I could feel Tunan's gaze, so I turned slightly to meet his eyes. He was leaning in a semi-sideways position with his elbow in the door.

"Whattttt? Stop looking at me like that."

"Like what?"

"Like... that." I tossed my hands. "All *Tunanie*."

"Like I wanna pull over and put yo' whol' body in my mouth?"

Rolling my eyes, I focused back on the road in front of me. "Where we going? The dinner isn't for another two hours."

"Oh, now you ask?"

"Yeap."

"Lemme ask you dis,"—He shifted his posture and switched lanes, getting off the turnpike—"You all in?"

"What you mean?" I asked, but my heart began to patter.

"I like dis, Glow. I like you. I like us." He motioned his index finger from me to him. "Ion want dis shit just on paper. I want it in real life, my baby. I want to wake up to you, go to sleep to you, and all dat."

"Tunan. I... I..." I kissed my teeth. "We barely know each other."

"And you rockin' my last name. We know each other enough."

"But you have those days where we don't talk, and you go to Memphis, and you disappear, and I don't be knowing what you're doing."

"My baby..." He grabbed my hand again. "I got some adjustin' to do, I'll admit. I ain't been a free man dat long, so I be handlin' my business and tryna straighten out my affairs and shit. But on all da days dat I'm gone, don't I make sure you straight?"

He rubbed his thumb over my ring finger, Memphis accent just as heavy as his dick. A ring that my followers hadn't let me forget about the whole time we were on live. I didn't confirm or deny anything. Tunan was trying to establish the very thing I'd been avoiding: clarity.

"Glow?"

"Hmm?" Snapping from my thoughts, the lights inside the vehicle adjusted to a soft glow as the sun began to set.

"Don't I make sure you straight?"

"You do," I replied with no hesitation.

"Aite, den. So we doing dis?"

He made a right turn, pulling into the mall. Since it was a weekend, the lot was full. Bypassing the empty spots, he parked in a handicap spot that was only steps away from the entrance.

"But why are we at the mall, Tunan?"

He shifted the car into park. "I wanna get a ring. I can't be walkin' 'round, makin' bitches think I'm single." He winked.

"You shoulda been did that."

"Mmcht. Can you walk in da mall in 'em? Or I gotta carry yo' pretty ass?"

"Look at dis dress, Tunan. It's too much to be walkin' through the mall."

"Da jewelry sto' right past da food court. Dat's why I parked back here."

"This dresssss—"

"Look good as fuck, my baby. Ion give a fuck 'bout a muthafucka lookin'. I want 'em to look. I'm da only one touchin' so let 'em lust, my baby."

He hopped out, came around my side, and pulled me out as soon as the door let up. Tunan wrapped his arm around my waist and squeezed my ass like we weren't in a parking lot full of kids, families, and security. We looked out of place, but somehow, I felt right in place.

"If you keep lettin' me fuck you like dat, Glow, it ain't shit you won't be able to get from me, my baby."

"I thought I could get whatever already?"

He slapped my ass and grabbed my hand, leading us in the direction of the mall while the doors let down automatically. That car was just as sexy as he was.

"You can."

As we stepped through the double doors, I pulled my dress down over my backside because it seemed to ride up every few steps. My pumps clacked on the tiled floor as the scent of pretzels, fried foods, and cleaning supplies filled the air. Before we could reach the food court, we were in the kiddie section, where there was a carousel and a few more attractions, but it was practically empty on this side.

Just as we reached the carousel, Tunan pulled me into it, sitting down on it and bringing me onto his lap.

"Tunan!" I tried removing his hands from my waist while looking around.

There was also a movie theater back here, but it seemed vacant, even though the marquee was lit up. It would be my luck that a movie would end, and we would be bombarded with a group of people headed home. Shifting my eyes from the marquee, I stared into Tunan's fine-ass face.

"You ever fucked in da mall, Glow?" He began humping me from the bottom as I tried to get up, but my laughter didn't have me operating at my full strength.

"Ummm, hell no! And we not about to start. Tunan we have to goooo. You already got me in here looking like a slut."

"Yeap." He kissed the back of my neck. "My wet pussy, bossed up, pretty-ass slut."

"Tuuuune."

"I love da way you say my name, my baby."

He grabbed my face and turned it so that my lips were accessible. Right there on the carousel, we engaged in a kiss so sloppy that we should have been fined for fornicating in public.

"Glow."

"Hmmm?" I was floating, and I hadn't had anything to induce intoxication. I was on a dick high. I was on a Tunan high. I had completely dropped my guard and was agreeing to be this man's wife for real, and nothing in me was screaming to run.

"Tonight, when we get to yo' spot, I wanna talk 'bout some shit dat you need to know. If we gone do this, I wanna be one hundred percent transparent. Aite?"

I licked my lips and nodded.

"You got me fucked up!" A loud voice startled me to the point that I tried to get up, but Tunan's strong arms kept me planted.

A shapely woman, who looked as if smoke was blowing from her head, stood over us. She was cute and had curves for days, but I'd never seen her before in my life.

"Excuse me?" I asked, confusion written on my face.

I tried peeling Tunan's hands from my waist again but to no avail. I didn't like this woman, whoever she was, standing over me, especially with the way she was huffing and puffing.

"Tunan, dis what we doing?"

My head whipped around so fast that I knew my tresses had slapped him in the face. Tunan, though, had a stale expression on his face and looked unbothered as fuck.

"Who the fuck is this bitch?" she shouted.

My head snapped again, this time looking at the woman who knew who Tunan was, wondering who she was calling a bitch. She was pointing at me, as if she deserved answers more than I did.

I instantly slapped her hand out of my face. "Don't put your fucking hand in my face."

"So you can't talk, Tunan?" She snaked her head, ignoring me once she realized I was no punk.

"Who is this, Tune?" I asked, keeping my eyes on her because I refused to be caught off guard.

"Ion know, my baby."

"So you don't know me, Tunan Payne?"

"Hell nawl! Get da fuck up outta my wife's face, doe."

Her eyes went to my ring, and she looked as if she was about to blow a gasket. "Wife? So you come to my house the other night and shoot my nigga, but you out here playing husband? What the fuck did you do to me? I woke up naked on the floor of my bedroom."

Tunan hopped up carefully, moving me behind him, but getting in the woman's face. I couldn't have heard her right. Tucking my hair behind my ear, I pulled my dress down as I gathered myself.

"Bitch, you know dat ain't how it went! Stop da fuckin' cap, garbage-ass hoe!"

"Nigga, you was at my house last night and you shot my nigga!"

Tunan grabbed her around the neck and squeezed while jerking her body.

"Tunan!" I scoffed as I looked around.

"Mane, fuck dis weak-ass bitch!"

"Get your hands off her!"

He shoved her, making her tumble over a garbage can that I hadn't noticed until now. She hopped up from the spilled trash, leaving her Foot Locker shopping bag and fake Gucci purse on the floor.

"Stella, take yo' sour-ass on, hoe!"

"I wasn't sour for the year and a half that we were together!"

"Hunh?" I looked back and forth between the two.

"Yes! I'm his fiancée!"

"Bitch, you wish!" He walked in her direction, and she immediately backed out of his reach.

"Tunan, don't lie for this hoe! With yo' abusive ass! The only reason why we broke up is because this nigga couldn't keep his hands to himself!"

My hand grabbed at my stomach as the carousel began to spin, only it wasn't spinning. My senses were.

"Don't believe her, my baby." Tunan turned to my direction.

"Believe me, *my baby*! Look!" She pulled her phone from her breast and flipped it so that I could see the screen.

There was a picture of her, and she looked unrecognizable with her busted eyes, knotted head, and swollen, broken nose.

"Look!" She swiped, and there was Tunan's mugshot except he had locs that hung around his face.

I had to blink a few times to be sure that it was him, but aside from his hair, it was the same face. She zoomed in, and domestic violence and aggravated assault were listed among the charges. My mouth went dry and my hands trembled. I could feel bile rising up my throat, so I turned and let it out. Chunks of my lunch splashed all over my feet, but I didn't care. I couldn't stop throwing up, even if I wanted to.

"Glow! Dis hoe lyin—"

"Bitch!"

With vomit still flowing from my mouth, my head was yanked backward, and I was dragged to the floor. I felt a pounding on my head just as the vomit stopped, and before I could react, my head was let go with a jerk.

"Bitch! You got me fucked up!" Tunan had pulled Stella off of me and had slammed her on the ground into my splatter of throw up.

"I'll kill you hoe!" He heaved heavily as he held her to the ground.

"Police! Put your hands up!"

Four officers tackled Tunan, one slipping in the throw up, while Stella caught her breath. Backing away, I watched as Tunan was being read his rights and handcuffed, while Stella was screaming that she wanted to press charges.

Who the fuck did I marry?

CHAPTER 28
BAHATI

"So... Where did you say we're going?"

I was giddy as hell. I'd been pissed that Shio came home around four in the morning when that was usually the time he'd get up to work out. My attitude was short-lived when he told me we were going out today. Shio had driven me to a hair salon not far from his home earlier, since I still showed no interest in driving, where I'd gotten a full-on treatment. Braids were my signature, but since he'd insisted that the place where we were going was fancy, I had the stylist remove my braids and give me a weave. We agreed on a thirty-something color, and the brown was a perfect contrast with my dark skin. I'd decided on fringe bangs and thirty-inch virgin bundles. Now that I had gone this route, it was going to be hard for me to go back to braids. Thankfully, I had access to Shio's unlimited funds to afford the expensive weaves.

Shio activated the left turn signal before merging into that lane. I felt like a princess riding as a passenger. When I got home from the salon, I felt like a million bucks. I had gotten my entire body waxed, a full set, and a pedicure in the color milk bath, which was a cloudy white with hints of chrome that looked amazing on my nails. It was going to be my new signature color and design.

"I didn't." Shio's deep voice seemed to shake the car and land in the seat of my panties.

Three plus years, and Shio had only gotten sexier. Back then, I felt like I hit the lottery when I came across him. He looked so damn out of place in the library, all thugged out and rugged. I thought he was there for the second-chance program that the library hosted weekly, but I got the shock of my life when one of the librarians led him to me. He wanted to learn a new language. I wasn't fluent in the language he requested, but I knew I wanted him in my space, so I convinced him to learn Swahili. It took nine months for him to become fluent, but after about three months, he had the basic language down. By month ten, I was riding his dick. At first, he wouldn't give in. Shio was very clear on not mixing business with pleasure. He almost slipped through the cracks until I figured out what it was I could do to hook him. Sometimes during our sessions, he'd step outside, and me being the nosy girl I am, I noticed he was serving customers or his cousins were dropping off product to him. One day, I overheard them complaining about an inconsistent plug and knew that was my chance.

My father had always been into drugs. It was how he put himself through school, being a low-level dealer. It took nothing for me to convince my papa to add Shio to his list. But like all good things, it came to an end when I let my jealousy get the best of me. This time, I was doing things the right way. I'd thought Shio was going to kill me. I could see it in his eyes all those years ago. Life was slipping from my body but then he stopped. This time, I was not letting anything stop me from making him mine, and this spontaneous date was proof that I was doing things right.

There was a dress laid out on the bed when he picked me up from the salon. I'd always looked good in red. The dress was short, felt nice to the touch, and draped at the shoulders. The gold Christian Louboutin heels and gold accessories added the perfect touch. I was so excited that I dressed early and spent two hours taking pictures and videos of myself. When Shio knocked on my door, I almost fainted at the delicious sight before me. I had mostly seen him in black, but tonight, he was in tan. Tan slacks that were wide at the leg but not in a feminine or bell-bottom style, a shirt made from the same material as the pants that hugged his abs just right, and Cartier frames on his face. He looked so incredibly good and smelled marvelous. He'd been rejecting my advances, but I knew tonight was the night.

Shio's dick was huge. I knew because I'd never forgotten. Even when he was choking the life out of me while pumping his dick in and out of my pussy, I found myself fighting pleasure and the will to live. I'd never been with a man who was as blessed as he in the sex department. Tonight would not only be the night I would have him again, but tonight would solidify our future forever. He was mine after tonight, and no one could stop us.

Flipping the visor down, I checked my lipstick. The MUA at the hair salon had done her thing. The matte-chocolate lip was perfect with the dress and gold accents. A red lip was a little too bold for me, and I was going for elegant class tonight. When I was satisfied with what I saw, I went to flip the visor up and caught a glimpse of the back seat. The baby's car seat was back there, but it was empty. Now that I thought about it, he'd had her when he dropped me off at the salon, and when he picked me up, she wasn't there. I had been so happy to be baby-free for a few hours and to not hear constant screaming that I didn't think much of it.

"Where is our daughter?"

Shio turned the wheel, looking sexy as ever. We were in his Maybach, and it was fitting for the occasion. He was pulling out all of the big guns tonight, and I was so ready to end the night with him on top of me.

"Bahati, you just now noticing she's gone?"

Turning my head to hide the embarrassment on my face, I watched as the bright city lights zipped by. I could feel the heat of his glare and knew I had to turn things around before the night was ruined.

"Of course not! I thought maybe you took her to your mother for a meeting finally. I was just wondering if she was staying the night. I wouldn't mind having the house to ourselves." I placed a hand on his thigh, hoping to cop a feel, but my hand hadn't landed in the right spot.

"She's not with my mother." He looked down swiftly before removing my hand.

"Oh, okay. It's your kid, too, so I won't question you further."

I left the subject alone. I didn't need anything ruining our moment, including Shya.

Thirty minutes later, we pulled into a restaurant on the outskirts of downtown. I knew that because I could see the tall buildings in the background, and I'd seen enough posts on social media to know what Jagoda Bay's skyline looked like, even at night. Cars that were in the same price range as Shio's were being valeted as young Black couples stepped out. While Shio wore a diamond chain with a Jesus piece dangling from it, the other men wore two or three diamond necklaces stacked against their collars. It was gaudy, but since the beginning of time, that is what our people have done—wear our gold and jewels on display. When our car reached the front of the valet line, it didn't take me long to realize that the restaurant had been rented out, and the people in front of us were Shio's family and members of the mob. I recognized the twins and Ezio at once.

My door opened, and a young, brown-skinned boy stood aside so that I could get out. I turned my nose up because he was supposed to help me out of the car, but from the smell of weed wafting off his clothing, I knew this must have been his first day. Once I was out of the car, I pulled my dress down and could feel the valet boy's eyes land on my ass. The dress was almost too small for bottom, but the way it wiggled as I stepped in the heels, I wouldn't have chosen a more perfect dress.

"Gaaaaddamn, cuh! Dis baby mama?" A light-skinned boy, who I'd seen park the car in front of us, slapped hands with Shio. He looked familiar but I couldn't place him.

"Yeah. Bahati, this Italian. And this Ro."

Ro didn't speak but it was fine; I didn't like the way he was eyeing me, anyway. The light-skinned teenager, on the other hand, was drooling at the mouth.

"Wait! Italian as in your little mannish, twelve-year-old cousin, Italian?"

He grinned and rubbed his hands together. "In the flesh, love. Except I ain't twelve no mo'."

"Park the car, Italian. But aye..." Shio pulled his cousin aside, turning their backs to me. "They good?" I heard him ask Italian.

"They straight, Big Cuz. Baby cousin was chilling with my Goddaughter all day."

I mumbled under my breath. "Goddaughter?"

"You nosy..." The valet boy, Ro, interrupted my eavesdropping.

"I'm not. Why are you watching me anyway? And who valets cars dressed like that and smelling like that?"

He was in a black T-shirt and black joggers with black Air Force Ones. Given how all the guests who had entered the restaurant were dressed, he could've at least worn black slacks and a collared shirt.

"The nigga that signs my paycheck ain't complaining, love. You enjoy your night." He gave a tight-lipped smile while I rolled my eyes in response.

"You ready?" Shio came up next to me to escort me inside.

With a smile on my face, I didn't pay the peasant a second glance. African American boys were carefree and often into drugs. That is why they stayed at the bottom of the barrel. Shio was not African American. His blood touched many bloodlines with his mixed heritage. With an Italian father and a Soliman and Melanesian mother, he was a made man before joining this mob. He didn't fit the stereotype of a man with dark skin living in America. He had a work ethic that went back to his ancestral roots.

Once we crossed the threshold, the restaurant buzzed to life. The tables were empty but the lighting was dim, setting the perfect mood for a nice dinner. A piano was playing while a singer serenaded the crowd somewhere in the distance. My stomach growled from the spices permeating the air. I hooked my arm inside of Shio's and nearly melted into him as he ushered me through the restaurant. Even with my heels on, he was still taller than me, and I loved that. I knew, in due time, we would make giant babies.

We came to a door at the far end of the restaurant, and when he pushed the door open, the chatter ceased. Beautiful women sat next to handsome men, some of the men familiar and others not so much. I smiled nervously as everyone inspected me. I didn't know if I was expecting a warm greeting or what, but I surely wasn't expecting to be eyed like the enemy.

"This nigga..." a handsome man whispered loud enough for everyone to hear. Because the room had gone still, his voice echoed, making it easy to reach everyone's ears. He was sitting next to a woman who had to have had Asian roots. By the large glacier on her hand and the diamond band on his, she was his wife.

"Demise!" She scolded him as softly as she could.

They were a beautiful couple, and she looked like she would be a woman of my caliber. Looking around the room, all of the couples were a perfect pair with all of the women rocking large, unique rings and dressed appropriately and to my taste. I was giddy thinking about how I would be joining the left-hand clan.

"Aye, y'all... This Bahati. Bahati, this is the family."

"Umm, where's Solana?" a dark-skinned beautiful lady stated with attitude, and the look on her face was as if she had smelled something sour.

"Baby, please." Her husband, an attractive chocolate man, groaned.

"I'm just saying... Who the fuck is she?"

Shio either didn't care that we were getting crazy stares or was used to his people's indecent behavior because he guided us to our seats without replying.

I was seated next to Vello's woman, and knew that in order to make tonight go in my favor, I would need to say whatever to get on these women's good side.

"Hi. Your ring is beautiful... So is your dress."

She turned slightly in her seat and planted a fake smile on her round face. "Thank you. I appreciate the compliment about the dress, especially since I'm postpartum."

"Baby, I told you that you look good."

"I know, but it's different coming from a woman, Metavello."

She smiled again, this one not as forced. "You know how babies can make you feel insecure..."

"I'm afraid not."

She reared her head back. "You do have a child, right? You and Shio? You must have snapped back the same day you gave birth then."

I choked on my spit. "Oh, no! I meant, yes... We have a daughter. I just didn't think he'd told the family yet."

"They know, Bahati." Shio pushed my chair in before walking behind the woman's chair.

"You look beautiful, Discover. You carried my nephews well." Shio leaned over and kissed the top of her head, making her blush before Vello shoved him off.

"We told you 'bout all that romancing our women and shit."

"Facts!" Nel backed his brother.

I picked up the glass of water and sipped it. "But to answer your question, my labor was terrible. I gained a lot of weight but lost it by the time she was six or seven months."

"Um..."

To keep the conversation going, I asked, "You have twins?"

She nodded. "I do. A daughter, too, but she's my big baby. Here..." Discover pulled her phone out and showed me a set of twins that had Renello and Metavello's whole faces as a beautiful little girl held them while sitting on a huge sofa.

"The one on the left is Explore, and the one on the right is Adventure. Their sister, Discovery, is holding them. Although *somebody* kidnapped my baby," she said the last part out loud.

"Discover, don't start, man. She internin' with Daddy for the summer." The man across from us, next to a lady wearing a long weave, smirked. I had to do a double-take because it was Essex, Shio's childhood friend.

"Oh! Hi, Essex!" I waved as his woman mugged me.

"Hey," she spoke for him, sarcastically, causing the dark-skinned girl from earlier to snicker.

"Wait..." I turned to Discover. "You are married to Metavello and have kids by Essex? Their childhood friend?"

Discover locked her phone and turned away from me.

"Yo, you nosy as fuck. But she had Lil' Chef before she knew me," Metavello answered for his woman, and with that went the only ally that I possibly could've had amongst the women.

I would win them over before the night was done. I had no other option if I wanted Shio to marry me.

"Aye,"—The one with the half-Asian wife stood—"Gentleman, let's step out back to smoke."

All the men moved on his command, ending their separate conversations and following him out of the room. I had never seen anything like it, and the power move made my insides warm. The only indication that they had even been here a minute ago was the mix of their colognes.

"I'm not married to Metavello yet. We're engaged," Discovery divulged after a silent pause had passed.

"I'm sorry. I didn't mean any harm... I was just trying to understand."

"Girl." She waved me off. "You're fine. The only person who gets up in arms is Metavello because he *hates* sharing Discovery with anyone."

"All of you are very beautiful." I spoke up, and a few gave me tight-lipped smiles, while others gave dry "thank yous."

"Anyway... Girls, look at this footage from the reveal."

The one with the long ponytail pulled everyone's attention toward her. She'd gotten up from her chair and the pregnancy looked so good on her. She pulled her phone out and the women gathered around her. I could see the screen from my position, so my nosy self watched.

"This shit so fuckin' dumb." Nel graced the screen with a frown. I could see balloon decorations in the background, and I leaned in because it looked like inflatable penises and breasts.

What on earth type of video is this?

"You cursin' at me?" someone asked him off camera.

"No, Pia baby." He rolled his eyes.

I knew it was Nel still, and not Vello, because of the way Nel was wearing his hair. Even today, the twins styled themselves differently from hair to clothes to jewelry.

A hand reached in the frame and swatted his arm.

"Aite. Fuck it... Just know yo' pops ain't on no homo shit," Nel said clearly before mumbling, "I'm yo' daddy, and I think you're a dick."

The ladies screamed in laughter, and even that sounded rich.

"This shit so fucking funny! I love your daddy real bad for that damn party!" The Asian-looking one cackled.

The screen flashed to the next person. "I'm yo' big cousin, and I think you a dick." Ezio lifted a glass to the screen.

The one with soft waves in her hair who was wearing a navy dress today came onto the screen. She'd been sitting beside Ezio, so that had to be his wife. "I'm your cousin-in-law, and I think you're a dick. Junior is ready for a playmate."

The next person had been sitting next to the man with locs, who'd been mean as ever on the plane from Mexico. Matteo was his name, if I remember correctly.

"I'm yo' cousin, and I think you are a tit! Can't wait to meet you, beautiful."

Matteo was on the screen next and looked pissed. "I think you a girl. Ain't sayin' that weak-ass shit."

"There go me and my man!" The dark beauty pointed to the screen. She and her man were equally brown and equally attractive.

"I'll be your TeeTee, and I think you a dick."

"Yeah, you gon' have a dick..." Her husband pulled her into his side, which caused her to giggle.

The video spanned to the Asian-looking woman, whom I'd spotted first tonight. "I'm TeeTee Sani and... Come here, Demise!"

She reached out of the video screen and pulled the head man in charge into the frame. He was their Don. He had just spoken with such influence. Just as my pussy had throbbed many nights for Shio, it had done so for him too. I usually liked my men dark as night, but the power he held couldn't be denied.

"What's this, Sani?" he spoke to her, ignoring the camera.

Shit, I nearly had to stop myself from fanning, and the ladies must have had the same feelings because they were oohing and ahhing when they hadn't done so for their men.

"Don't mind him, little baby. We are your auntie and uncle, and we think you're a tit."

"Nah, you think it's a tit. We need dicks. We're building an empire, baby." He kissed the side of her face and walked off camera.

"According to biology, I'm yo' daddy too." Metavello snickered into the screen.

Discover chuckled beside me as Metavello continued his guess. "But I know they sayin' it's just one, but I ain't buyin' it. I think it's two of y'all, and I think y'all boys. Y'all gonna walk 'round lookin' like quadruplets, raisin' straight hell."

He then pulled Discover into the screen and wrapped his arm around her waist and kissed her neck. The girls ahhed again.

"Stop, Metavello! I'm going to waste my drink!"

"That was my first drink in ten months too!" Discover fussed at the screen.

"Don't worry 'bout me, just tell the camera what you think the babies are, Big Mama."

"Well, it's one baby. I don't wish twins on them!"

"I really want to beat Metavello's ass for cursing me like that!" Pia fussed in real time.

"Well, I'ma go with what your uncle-dada said. Twin boys!"

Pia cut her eyes at Discover, who was bent over laughing. "I'm sorry, girl. I really didn't know."

Pia flicked Discover off, who blew a kiss in return. The screen then panned to Shio. Now, it all came together. The day he had come home and teased me with dick, he was looking godly as fuck. I had been craving Shio so bad that I had to talk myself down from breaking into his room and taking the dick. I was pissed at his mixed actions, but he made up for it today by finally letting me meet everyone.

"I'm whatever you need me to be. Uncle, cousin, confidant." He cheesed in the video.

My God.

"Solana's man so fine..." one of the ladies tried to whisper.

"Mocha!" Don's wife laughed.

I kept my eyes forward, sitting poised and unbothered. I was here, not Solana. They could have their jokes, but I'd be the one slow winding on Shio's big dick tonight. That was something Solana couldn't say she had ever done.

My purse vibrated, and I pulled the phone Shio had given me out. I thought it was him since he was the only person who had contacted that phone outside of whoever the hell Uriah was. The screen was black, and I cursed under my breath because I knew who it was now. Excusing myself to no one in particular since they didn't care and had made it clear they preferred Solana to be in their company, I exited the room and went out the same way we'd come in.

The men must have truly gone to the back of the building because no one was outside. The two teens valeting had even disappeared.

"Hello?"

"Bahati."

I huffed into the phone. "Look! You shouldn't have called."

"Why not?"

Looking around, I covered my mouth when I saw the coast was clear. "Because he is proposing tonight. To me! He has this fancy dinner set up and—"

"That wasn't the plan!"

"I know, but this plan is better." I smiled and cleared my throat. "Look, all of the men are here. You can easily go and get her. It will be seamless."

"How the fuck can I do that when I can't find her? Unless she's back at his home, si?"

"No. I don't know where she is."

"Bahati!"

"Truly, I don't know where she is, but track the baby."

"What do you mean?"

"Track the baby! She has the baby. You can grab them both. Look, I have to go! I'm standing outside, and one of the valet boys was acting suspicious of me earlier. The women also don't like me very much."

"What the fuck does that have to do with me?"

"Everything, Felipe! Go get your bitch! Get your bitch so I can get my nigga, baby."

"You are cold-hearted to be *a mother*. Don't have any more children, Bahati." He laughed.

"Fuck you. Just go get that Solana bitch and kill her, for all I care. I didn't need her popping back up, and I don't need her popping back up again."

I ended the call knowing Felipe hated to be hung up on. I was no longer his pawn, though. I was free and under the mob's protection —under the protection of Shio.

Stuffing the phone back inside my purse, I turned on my heels and came face-to-face with a dark figure. "What the hell?!"

The valet boy that I'd just said was weird toward me was standing in front of me, blocking my path to reenter the building.

"You're the one being nosy now. What did you hear, negro?"

His hands went to his left pocket, and I saw my life flash before my eyes. I had no way of protecting myself, so all I could do was scream. He pulled his hand from his pocket and opened it.

"Aye, all I wanted was to ask you if you wanted to buy some blow." The powder baggie sat in his open palm.

"Ew! No. Get away from me."

Pushing past him, I scurried back inside the restaurant. A waitress was walking past with Lemon Drops so I grabbed one off the tray, even though she was taking it into our room. I let her walk ahead and guzzled half of it down. By the time I got to the room, my nerves and jitters were dissipating.

This was my life now. Solana would be no more after tonight, so the women may as well get used to me. That Uriah character was next if she posed a threat.

"So, ladies... Let's start over, shall we? I'm Bahati, the mother of Shio's only child."

CHAPTER 29
SHIO CUPPACIO

This changes everything, baby.

I had been planning this dinner for the past week. I would have had it later rather than sooner, but when the date became available due to an engagement cancellation, I had them charge my card for the private affair. It had been a while since all of us were together without ass and titties on display, and with the way my family had been holding down Solana, I wanted them to feel appreciated as well.

I invited not only the adults but the littles too. They, always ones to seclude themselves, were in the private room next door, so I would split my time between the two rooms tonight. Instead of being inside the building, Don had pulled us out back to smoke. About ten blunts were in rotation, and since we were at the back of the building, the only light was from the moon, our jewelry, and the tips of the blunts.

"What the fuck?" Nel jumped, causing all of us to reach for our guns.

"Joe, what the fuck you on?" His twin said aggressively, looking in the direction of the dumpsters where Nel stood.

"I know y'all just saw that big-ass rat."

"Bro." Ezio tucked his gun back into his waistband as I removed my hand from mine. "A fuckin' rat, Nel?"

"Fuck you mean, a fuckin' rat? Hell yeah! A rat."

"Maybe that should be y'all's next challenge. Who can escape the wrath of the mighty rats?" Don stated, causing Zo, Teo, and Rut to laugh before he joined them. We didn't see a damn thing funny because the challenges continued to get more and more risky.

"You know, if that is the challenge, yo' tall ass gone be in there with us, right?" I nodded at Teo.

"And just like the other shit, y'all gone be on your fucking own."

"Ain't we missin' a Cuppacio?" Don pointed out, changing the subject.

I looked down at my Audemars Piguet. I was feeling flashy tonight so I wore the bust down. "He made a pitstop. He coming through."

"Yeah..." Ezio pulled from his blunt, smoke filling the air. "Anytime one of us is missing, all we gotta do is step to Demise. He may have dumped a nigga in Thailand."

"Y'all swear y'all can take a nigga. And is smokin' good for yo' sobriety? High-ass nigga."

"Yo' sister ain't complainin'." Ezio grinned, and Don scoffed.

Nel jumped again. "Yeah, fuck this shit! That makes two big-ass rats, and those big-ass rats mean they been fuckin' and makin' big-ass babies. Shit gone spoil my damn appetite 'cause I'm gone think the restaurant got rats, and I'm too hungry for that shit."

Nel dropped his blunt and stepped on it before swinging the back door open.

"Scary-ass nigga done blew my fuckin' high." Matteo put his blunt out the same way.

Everyone else followed suit, going inside and leaving Don and me alone. I hadn't been smoking, just listening to these nigga's chop it up and enjoying the slight night breeze.

"You all spiffy and shit."

I smirked. "Just tell a nigga he fly, yo."

"You aite. Cool enough to kick shit with. But what the fuck is this shit? I hope it ain't no proposal."

Standing from the wall I'd been leaning on, I approached Don. "You said I had to marry one, right?"

"I also said you had thirty days, or I was pickin' for you. I think you got two more of them shits. You sure that's you in there?"

I laughed. Don was a fucking mind-bending motherfucker. "Yeah, we both know you wasn't pickin' shit, at least not for me."

I pulled the door open and stepped inside.

"Yeah, aite. Remember who run shit, Cuppacio."

I wasn't worried about leaving Don alone because I'd already seen the big-ass guards he had posted around the building. I shook my head because the Don ran the mob, but he didn't run me. I made my way through the kitchen, where the chefs and servers were working. Instead of lingering to see the reason the restaurant smelled so good, I continued into the ambiance of the restaurant. Stepping into the room to check on the littles, I immediately grinned at seeing the younger generation dressed up and talking shit to one another.

"Italian, please go to one of the other seats. Ion feel good."

"That's cuz that nigga was posted in the blogs with that model bitch. Don't get mad at me cuz you love-sick, ZeyZey."

I looked around after hearing Italian and Big Zan's daughter bickering, and nodded in appreciation. This group had been holding me down in more ways than one. They had all stepped up to be my hands, eyes, and ears when it came to Solana because, even though some other shit was brewing there, she was mob business at the end of the day. Glow's little sister and her friend were giggling in the corner, fitting in as if they'd come to Jagoda Bay with us from Chicago. They were very much a part of the crew now, and I made a mental note to chat with Bella and Pearla about what was appropriate to say and not say in their company. The three musketeers, Bella, Mahzeyah, and Pearla, had been busy since six o'clock this morning because I'd paid them to get everyone together, including this bunch.

"Italian, give her fifty feet."

Mahzeyah's eyes shot to me. She looked so much like her mother but a lot like her father too. "Ohh, heyy, Mr. Shio. You have to give me the glam squad information. I need them to do me up for prom, graduation, and senior pictures!"

"Yessss! They have to get us right," Pearla cosigned, and it was good to see her smiling. I knew it had a lot to do with Mr. Joe's grandson, however, but we'd be on standby if that situation blew up from Matteo finding out or Grind having a miracle and waking up, demanding her.

"I ain't trying to be messy..." Bella started, putting her phone on the table.

"What, Bellz?"

"Ion like yo' baby mama, cousin."

I chuckled. "You ain't met her."

"I saw her and that was enough! She aggy-looking."

"She fine, though," Italian said with lust in his eyes. The little nigga was getting too much play to think he had a shot with Bahati.

Mahzeyah snapped her head toward Italian so hard that it looked like she was from a scene out of *The Exorcist*. "And you fake as fuck! Excuse my language, Mr. Shio. You know we team Solana!"

"Solana my nigga for life. She already know how this shit gone go, and so do everybody else. That don't mean Brama ain't fine."

"Who?" I asked.

"Brama... Shio baby mama..."

Bella snickered. "That is not that lady's name."

"Irrelevant. That's what it needs to be. Don't mean she don't look good. Solana knows I'm team her."

"I hope this ain't no proposal 'cause I'm objecting!" Bella crossed her arms.

My cousin was in a dress and heels and had diamonds on her neck and wrist like she was a mob wife. Whatever the fuck Essex was paying her, he was doing it well.

"Why everybody thinks this is a proposal? Damn, I can't do nothing nice for the fam?"

The girls eyed me uncomfortably, and my smile fell. I rubbed my hand down my face.

"Bellz... Y'all told Solana I was proposin' to Bahati?"

Bella's eyes danced around before they landed on me, and her face answered my question before she responded. "Whatttt? We needed somebody to talk shit to, and Solana is our best Mexican biatch. She wanted to know why we were gettin' fancy."

Suddenly, my heart was pounding in my chest. I hadn't stopped thinking about Solana since I left her bed last night. I wanted to slip back in with her this morning, but with the way she was wincing, I wouldn't dare. I meant it when I told her I loved her. The fucking thought of her made my heart race. I loved the hell out of Solana, but I knew love wasn't enough. What we shared was earth-shattering, truly soul-quaking, but the fact remains that she was an addict, and she might've been right about my addiction, yet the fact remained that she was addicted to drugs. I was not. Now, the thought of her thinking I would bring Shya to her so I could dip off and propose to Bahati had me ready to break out in hives.

"Just think... You had a team to get all of us to dress up really nicely, and you rented out a restaurant. Then, when Solana told us you had plans with Bahati, we put two and two together." Bella smacked her lips and rolled her eyes. "Were we wrong?"

"Very." I began to back out of the room. "The appetizers will be out shortly."

"Favorite, cousin?" Bella sounded like she wanted to cry when I was the one ready to run up out of here and get my ass to Jisei's townhouse.

"Wassup, Bella?" I knew I wasn't her favorite, Metavello was, but I wasn't going to call her out on it because she was trying to lessen her mistake.

"Can we please have at least one round of Lemon Drops? None of us drove." Bella placed her hands in a prayer position.

"Bye, Bella."

Closing the door shut, I made my way into the other room, where everyone should've been. The men hadn't made their way back into the room yet, but I could see them in the distance, sipping from glasses as they chatted in the open space of the restaurant. I guess the beauty of renting an entire dining establishment was that we had it all to ourselves. This was actually our only option since Don was always trying to talk business. To him, business was dashing insults and talking shit, but nonetheless, business was always done. My mama and aunties had taken a booth in the back and were clinking their glasses together, which I didn't understand because there was more than enough room for them in our room. I shrugged, knowing they always found themselves a separate space at events, and it was fine with me as long as they were enjoying themselves.

Opening the door, all of the wives had frowns on their faces as Bahati ran her mouth a mile a minute. She wasn't reading the room because they all looked like they wanted to knock her the fuck out.

Listening to the words spewing from her mouth, I didn't think—I just reacted.

"Ahhh!" she screamed.

Glass shattered, chairs moved, and a very scared Bahati found herself at my mercy as my hands wrapped around her neck as she dangled in the air. Her eyes were bulging as she clawed at my arm, but I didn't give a fuck. I kept squeezing, the look in her eyes all too familiar.

"Repeat what you said!"

"I-I... I-I."

"Shio! I don't think she can repeat it with her airways restricted."

My head snapped at Dasani as she and all of the other women had gotten up from the table and backed away toward the far wall.

"Oh, I heard her. I heard her loud and fuckin' clear."

Bahati was struggling to breathe, minutes away from either passing out or passing away. This was déjà vu, but this time, her ass was dying.

"You said, she was all like, *Shio, I promise you, that is not mine. I have no more left. You have to believe me.* Ain't that what the fuck she said?" I turned my head to the women as I felt Bahati become weaker on the table.

"She said that, but you're about to k...k...kill her." Discover hiccupped, near tears.

"This scandalous ass bitch needs to die! She too fuckin' slick!"

"Shio..." Dasani warned.

"Fuck that. How the fuck does she know what the fuck Solana said when she said the shit in Spanish!"

Everyone quieted as if understanding why I was ready to kill this sneaky-ass broad. I knew it. I knew it since the plane ride from Mexico that her ass couldn't be trusted.

I leaned into Bahati's face. "Shio, *te prometo que eso no es mío. No me queda más. Tienes que creerme...* Those where Solana's exact words. You're a fuckin' dead bitch, Bahati."

I felt myself being pulled off Bahati, and before I could react, I came face-to-face with Ezio and Nel. Bahati fell to the long table, coughing uncontrollably, before sliding from the table to the floor, taking the white tablecloth with her.

"Bitch—"

"Aye!" Don boomed from the door. "Come take a walk with me... Now, Shio."

Needing to get the fuck from out of the same space as Bahati before I murked her in front of the women that I loved and respected,

I was the first one out of the room. The littles all ran from the door, tripping over each other as I exited. Instead of going toward the back of the restaurant again, I went out front. If she thought she was about to get away with the sneaky shit, she had another thing coming.

"Shio."

"What?" I barked as Don followed me outside.

I began pacing, needing to move so I wouldn't go back in there and finish her off. Bahati being able to speak Spanish changed everything. It changed so much shit and also put so much more into perspective. The loopholes in her story. Her not wanting to leave the house. The fucking apartment magically burning down that I still haven't addressed her ass about. She had some shit to her from the very start, and although I felt it, I was trying my damndest to give her the benefit of the doubt and build a relationship with our daughter.

"Don, this shit ain't addin' up."

"I know."

"That bitch can speak Spanish!"

"That I didn't know, but I ain't surprised."

I stopped pacing and faced Don. With the way I was feeling, I would flat lined his ass too. He reached into his jacket's inside pocket, and I reached down to my waistband.

"Slowdown, killa. I ain't 'bout to do shit funny." He pulled a manila folder from the jacket pocket.

"Fuck is this!" I snatched the folder. Reading over its contents, I became even more enraged. "So, I'm not the father. Yeah, that checks out. This bitch is good as dead."

I closed the folder and handed it back to Don.

"Open it back up and read again."

"Why? I saw what it said. Shya isn't mine."

"Open it back up, nigga. Read the line right before your name."

I opened the folder back up, my eyes scanning the entire page now, and I could feel the spirits of the bodies I was about to drop.

Conniving, phony, sneaking ass bitch!

"Them test wasn't readin' right for a reason. You had the doctor shook when you didn't schedule the third test, so he reached out to make sure we hadn't listed his ass to meet the maker. I told him to retest what he had. That shit wasn't faulty, Cuppacio. Whole time, that shit was accurate as fuck.

"You ain't the pappy, nigga. But the gag is, she ain't the mammy either. So who the fuck kidnapped-baby y'all over there playin' house with?"

CHAPTER 30
SOLANA DAMITA LEDESMA

The soreness in my vagina shot through my body with each step I took. Nibbling on my thumb, I paced the room. My vagina wasn't even the sorest thing on my body. Every limb ached, and the hot bath I'd soaked in using Jisei's tub didn't help. Shio was very attentive and helpful the night I gave my body to him, telling me a bath was necessary. I had yet to regret giving Shio my body last night. Everything was perfectly imperfect. I never thought I'd be losing my virginity in a makeshift rehab, but I wouldn't have wanted it any other way. From the moment he entered my body, cocaine had been more than an afterthought. There was no the drugs could ever give me a high better than when Shio touched, licked, sucked, and entered my body.

However, when the littles came down here to alert me that Shio was hosting a private dinner and they hinted at him proposing to Bahati, I wanted nothing more than to take a bump. Usually, when I felt the urge or was tired of my own body causing me pain, whether mentally or physically, I read the journal. But the metal door was open, and I was unsure about the camera working. I also thought Shio could've set up another camera before leaving in the early morning hours since I would have his daughter alone in here tonight.

The round-faced, two-foot-tall human was making it impossible for me to lock myself in the bathroom to read more of Sandro's confessions. Her round eyes watched me as I paced the length of the floor. Everyone looked so nice as they said their goodbyes and left. I'd even heard the voices of the glam team upstairs getting everyone ready. I was too afraid to leave the basement and speak to the trio although I knew seeing them would lift my mood. I didn't want to explain why I was here, tucked away in the basement with a prison-style door. Once the house went quiet, everyone gone to the dinner proposal, I sulked. Shya and I could've walked around the town-house, but I felt safest in the basement.

When Shio carried me to Jisei's bathtub before he left this morning, it felt good to get out of the basement and see how cute and feminine Jisei's home was. When I'd been dragged here, I hardly paid attention to my surroundings, so shaken by Shio thinking I'd been responsible for Shya finding a baggie of drugs. Though the home had been filled with the littles, it still smelled and felt like Jisei as I looked around when coming back down to the basement.

My mouth went dry, thinking about the girls showing up for Shio tonight. I loved them. I felt a connection to them like I never had with anyone before, but Shio had their loyalty and I understood that. They didn't owe me anything, although I was grateful for the comfort and solace they had provided during my time here. Time spent with them had healed a part of me that I hadn't known needed mending. The laughs we shared and the tears we shed were therapeutic. They would forever hold a special place in my heart once I gained the courage to leave this room and make something of my life.

Shya's eyes bounced from the TV to me as I walked, and when she took one long blink, I stopped. Dropping my arms to my side, I watched her blink again and tilt forward a bit while sitting on the mattress.

"Am I making you *mareada* (dizzy)?"

Her response was another blink.

Shio had fulfilled his promise and dropped her off earlier this morning. He walked her in, handed her to me, and then proceeded to change the sheets. He had changed them last night, but I had bled onto the mattress protector, and since he couldn't locate one, he brought a brand-new one with him. Closing my eyes, I inhaled deeply and could almost smell his cologne in the room with us. As soon as he changed the sheets, he pulled me into his chest. Sore and all, my panties were drenched, along with the panty liner. Even after soaking in the tub, I was still spotting. I was starting to believe that Shio had split something open down there.

"That pussy ain't ready for me again," he said into my hair, in only a voice that he and I could interpret.

He kissed my forehead, and then he was gone. No mouth-to-mouth. No, I love you. No confession of need. I gathered my feelings and made the best of my morning with Shya. Between playing toddler games and watching Ms. Rachel, we enjoyed each other's presence. She had a few fussy moments, but Italian had brought us all types of snacks and foods throughout the day, which fixed that. I'd finally met Glow's sister's baby also. She was so tiny and precious, a real-life baby doll. When Italian came back down to get her, I met Glee too.

Once it was Shya and me again, I changed her hair. I was on a natural high being with her and doing all the things I wished someone had done with me as a little girl. Still reminiscing about the night before while spending time with his daughter, I fought the thoughts of Shya being Shio and mine, and not Shio and Bahati's. It was crazy that thoughts of Shio having a child with another woman infuriated me, but when Shya was in my presence, it all went away, just as it did when she was rescued by her father. Shya was adorable, and she hadn't asked to be here. Plus, I knew all too well how it felt for a woman who held the heart of a father to not accept his child. I'd never be that way.

Shya didn't deserve that.

Shio telling me that he loved me felt unreal, and last night was filled with nothing less than passion. It was intense. It was necessary, and even though I was in this room losing my mind—losing a battle of needing—I would absolutely do it all over again and not change a thing if given the chance. I never thought I would lose my virginity to a man like Shio. A man who had gutted me in the best way. A man whom I was absolutely and truly in love with. His taking it was special to me, even though nothing was meant to come of it.

But that was why I was pacing the room. It is why Shya had taken her attention from Ms. Rachel on the TV to me. He was marrying her, solidifying the reality that nothing would come of us. I knew nothing would change. I had said it to him and myself as he entered me, repeatedly making my body convulse in confusion last night. Shio and I couldn't be together because I still had my struggles. I didn't have any direction in life. I was a visitor in this foreign land. I was a long way away from a man like Shio making me his.

But who was I kidding? There wasn't a man alive like Shio. I was sure I'd never have another opportunity to be loved and adorned the way I knew Shio would love and adorn me.

I wanted to cry. I wanted to scream. I wanted to yell. I wanted to fight.

Most of all, I wanted to feel.

Shya blinked those baby doll eyes at me. I eased down onto the mattress beside her, the very mattress that her father had laid me down on and made me feel like I was his. A man like Shio could tell you the truth a million times, but your mind still came up with its own conclusions because it was him. I felt myself growing mad again. I felt the delusional arguments creating themselves on why Shio should be with me and not Bahati. I had to suppress my feelings and change my thoughts because Shya didn't deserve that energy.

"Your madre and padre will become one soon."

Shya blinked in response.

"He's probably on one knee as we speak."

Picking up the phone, I checked the time and locked the screen with a huff. I didn't want to go to my text thread because I didn't trust myself. I probably would text one of the girls or even Shio. I didn't need to hurt my own feelings further by begging.

Lesson number five.

Holding my arms out, Shya looked down at them for a second before climbing into them. We were both in pajamas, having changed just before the littles left. We were supposed to have a pajama night and had even taken pictures that I sent to Shio. I knew it was risky because her mother didn't like me and had even attacked me, but I couldn't help myself. What were the odds that the pajamas Shio packed for her and me were similar? Just as I sent the pictures, Bella came down and notified me about what was about to happen. I had been pacing ever since.

He'd told me nothing would change but something had changed. We'd crossed a line I didn't want to come back from, and his first action after telling me he loved me was to propose to the mother of his child. Not only that, but allowing me to keep their child while the act was being done was cynical.

Shya rested her head on my chest as if to help my pounding heart. Her two puff balls smelled of coconut and seemed to have grown since the last time I saw her.

Rubbing my hand through her fluffy hair, I sighed. "At least I'm not alone."

My mind drifted back to the proposal. How did he do it? Did he prepare a speech? Did he shed a tear? Was she surprised, or had she had a hunch? The thought of her getting what I just had for the rest of her life did more than infuriate me. It destroyed me. Was last night sympathy sex? Was he taking a chance to get me out of his system before he got with the woman he really wanted?

Wrapping my arms around Shya, I pressed my nose into her hair. "*Sé feliz de que eres una bebé.* (Be happy that you're a baby.)"

I should never have had sex with Shio. Not because I was heartbroken, but because I was embarrassed. My giving myself to him the night before he proposed marriage to another woman reeked of desperation. My cheeks flushed warm. I must have been the worst lay of his life. For a man to sleep with a woman, and the very next day ask to be married to another—I had to have been awful.

I should have asked the wives for tips.

"*Soy una perdedora.* (I'm such a loser.)"

"You know the point of girl talk is to actually talk back, Shya."

I could feel her breathing slowly and knew she was on her way to sleep.

"Well, I wouldn't want to talk to Maura about my dad, so I get it."

Hmmmm... Hmmm. Hm hm hmmmm... Hmmmmm... Hmmmm... Hm hm hmmmm.

I began humming a tune that she seemed to love. It was the same one that I hummed to her on the plane, and the same one I hummed to my baby brothers. It was the same tune I hummed when my feelings got too overwhelming. The tune was my reprieve when there was absolutely nothing I could do about my circumstances over the years.

Click

Complete darkness surrounded us, prompting me to tighten my grip around Shya when I heard the sound.

"H-h-hello?"

The power shut off, and since there were no windows down here, I couldn't see in front of my face. Stretching my hand over the bed, I blindly felt around for my phone. Once it was in hand, I shone it over Shya's face, and her little mouth was open wide as she slept. Easing her onto the bed, I stood while navigating to the flashlight.

Hmmmm... Hmmm. Hm hm hmmmm... Hmmmmm... Hmmmm... Hm hm hmmmm.

Walking towards the door, I pointed it in front of me. I didn't stop humming, scared of what had made the sound, but also thinking it could have simply been the power shutting off. But now I wondered what had caused the house to lose power? There were no storms. Finally, at the base of the stairs that would take me to the main floor, I shone the phone's flashlight and immediately wished I'd stayed inside the room.

"Ahhhhh!"

Temptation. Craving. Feeling.

Him.

Not him, but *him*.

In the dark, beyond my flashlight, he was there, already halfway down the stairs. The one who had supplied me with what I wanted or needed the night of the Discover's proposal. I saw him again at the club just before Felipe arrived. And once more, the night when all of the ladies had come over.

He leaped toward me, and at the same time, his hand covered my mouth. I dropped the phone, fear racing through me. It must have landed on its back because the light was gone. Still, his hand was over my mouth, suppressing my screams.

"Don't scream."

I will overcome this addiction. This addiction will not get the best of me. I am bigger than my addiction. I am in control. I will overcome this addiction. This addiction will not get the best of me. I am bigger than my addiction. I am in control. I will overcome this addiction. This addiction will not get the best of me. I am bigger than my addiction. I am in control.

"Listen to me, Solana... You're in danger. I know I'm not the one you want to trust, but right now, I need you to come with me."

What were the odds? What were the chances that right when life became too much, my vice was right here? I could feel my body tremble, and so could he because he began to curse under his breath.

"Solana, we gotta fuckin' move. But if you want to live, don't make a sound."

He removed his hands from my mouth, and I indeed did not make a sound unless you counted the thumping of my heart that matched the soft panting of my breath. I could hear him moving, and when the light from his phone shone over his face, I took a step back. He was so young and so handsome. He didn't look like he sold drugs that not only made people feel good but also ruined lives.

"I will overcome this addiction. This addiction will not get the best of me. I am bigger than my addiction. I am in control. I will overcome this addiction. This addiction will not get the best of me." I moved backward toward the room where Shya was asleep.

"Solana... I just need you to trust me. You're in danger. We have to go. Now."

I whispered silently, my lips moving but the quietest sound coming out. "I will overcome this addiction. This addiction will not get the best of me. I am bigger than my addiction. I am in control. I will overcome this addiction. This addiction will not get the best of me."

"Fuck... Look... *Hmmmm... Hmmm. Hm hm hmmmm... Hmmmmm... Hmmmm... Hm hm hmmmm.*"

My calf hit the bed. I'd made it into the room without facing forward. His tune made me pause, his humming identical to mine. He took slow steps until he was directly in front of me again.

"H... how do you know that song?" I whispered.

"Because I know who you are, Solana. Well, I didn't before I sold you that shit, which is my bad, by the way. But I know who you are."

He flipped the phone around, the flashlight now pointing at his face, with his phone screen illuminating my face. My eyes focused on him instead of the phone, taking a moment to outline his features. He looked like a young adult, yet there was a softness and hardness in his face at the same time.

"Look, Solana."

I took a step back from the picture on his phone, falling onto the mattress since there was nowhere else for me to go. I blinked nonstop, trying to make sense of what I was seeing.

"¿Cómo conseguiste esa foto de mi madre y de mí? (How did you get

that picture of my mother and I?)

"*Tengo la foto porque esta es mi hermana.* (I have the picture because this is my sister.)"

He pointed to the photo, and my ears burned as my brows creased, trying to process his words.

Wait, he is speaking in Spanish.

"*Este eres tú y esta es mi madre. Nuestra madre.* (This is you, and this is my mother. Our mother.)

"You speak Spanish?"

"Yes. I speak a few languages. My mother made sure my sibling and I were fluent in most. Now, we have to go, Solana. I won't hurt you. I'm sorry for sellin' you drugs. I'm sorry for everything. But lemme fix it."

In disbelief, I just stared at him. I didn't have any siblings from my mother. My mother didn't have any more children. I was her first child, and she died giving birth to me—or so I was told. My father's words were so few about my mother that anything seemed possible, like a drug-dealing, Spanish-speaking man claiming to be my brother.

Brother.

Not like I was short of those, but my mother's son.

"Okay."

"Okay?"

"Yes, okay."

"Uh... Aite. Come on."

I stood but then stopped. "Wait. I can't leave the baby."

"What baby?"

"She's on the bed."

He shifted the light and there was a jump scare. Shya was sitting up in the bed, eyes wide open.

"Hey. I-I'm Uncle Ro. Can I pick you up?"

Ro. His name is Ro, I thought to myself, not remembering if Italian or the girls had told me his name.

"Ngisize," Shyla said while whining.

"She doesn't speak," I said as I stuffed my feet into a pair of house shoes. I didn't know where we were going, but with the lights off in the house and no one here, I had to trust him. Plus, he had a picture of me with our mother. It was indeed me in the picture because I had the same photo, except there was no sister in it.

Did I have a sister?

Ro moved toward the bed. Lighting was scarce, but from his phone, I could see enough.

Shya climbed into his arms.

"Let's go! Stay behind me."

Following behind him, I saw him pull a gun from his waistband, and then everything became real. I remember him saying I was in danger, but I never processed it because he was the danger just moments ago. Knowing now was not the time to ask questions, I stayed close as we climbed the steps.

Zip Zip

I could feel hot air go past our heads, and I instantly trusted him. He didn't lie. Someone was here to try to kill me.

"Shit! Get low, Solana."

Pow Pow Pow

He shot back in the direction of where the bullets had come from, but we kept moving, not missing a step as we climbed the stairs. Now on the main floor, there were windows, and I could see a silhouette of a person shooting from the kitchen.

Plaw Plaw Plaw

The body in the kitchen dropped, and the figure from the door had been the one to do so.

"Price?"

"Yeah. I saw the lights go out and a nigga walk through the back."

My possible brother tucked his gun and pulled me along. Shya wasn't crying, but her eyes were open. She shifted her head around, looking as if she knew what was happening. Her alertness made me breathe easier. She was unharmed, and I needed her to be. Shio would never forgive me if something happened to his daughter in my care.

"Fuccck! I appreciate you, bro!"

Price held the door open, and if I weren't so shaken up, I would throw my arms around him. I needed to praise Pearla on how good a job she'd done deciding to give him a chance.

"No sweat, Ro. Y'all go. I'ma make sure ain't nobody else in here and try to get the power back on."

Price looked the baby and me over before going back into the dark house. When we heard his gun sound again, it proved that there were other men inside the house.

"Fuuuuck!" Ro shouted quietly. "Come on. I parked down the street."

"Why so far?"

"Solana... I stole the fuckin' car."

What?

Before we could make it off the lawn, a car pulled up in front of Jisei's townhouse, causing me to freeze, and Ro to pull his gun out.

"I'm 'bout to beat yo' muthafuckin' ass! A gun, Ro?" A lady in scrubs hopped from the car, and the sight of her had me feeling a wave of emotions. The girl had rounded the car and had a menacing glare at Ro. "Who baby?"

Plaw Plaw

She jumped and tried to take cover behind the car. "Are those gunshots?"

"Yes! Look, we need to get the fuck outta here!"

He pulled his sister up, shoved her in the passenger seat, opened the back for me, and did the same. With the door closed and Shya still resting on his chest, he marched to the driver's side.

"You going to drive with the baby?" his sister asked what I was thinking. Instead of Ro responding, he shifted Shya in his lap.

"At the party I was working tonight, I heard a bitch sayin' to have her and this baby killed, so I came." He threw his thumb toward me in the back seat before pointing to Shya in his lap. He was now driving, and Shya wasn't causing any lack to his driving skills as he navigated the wheel with one hand.

Letting his words digest, my eyes rounded, realizing he had just said someone at a party wanted me dead.

"Work! What fuckin' job? You ain't got one," she said, staring at his face and head, her profile visible to me.

"Where do you think I get the money I give you from?"

"Them weak-ass drugs you be tryna sell!" she screamed as he turned, the car on two wheels.

Drugs are definitely not weak.

"And be careful, this is my client's mama's car!"

"Listen, sis. I need you to trust me. I do valet, I told you that. I'm trying, sis. I'm fuckin' trying."

"Okay, but you heard a bitch say what now that had you playing superman?"

"African girl. Sounded Kenyan, though. She was on the phone, giving instructions to kill her and the baby." He jutted his head my way this time instead of his thumb.

Ro turned out of the neighborhood, going as fast as the Cadillac could take us.

"And you decided to play Clark Kent?"

"Ngisize," Shya blabbered, and I wanted to grab her, but I was still too shaken up.

From the shooting, the revelation, and the girl in the front seat, I was sure a new wave of trauma would have me fighting the drug cravings even more.

Who wanted me killed? Bahati? No, she wouldn't order a hit on her own child.

"When it comes to my sisters, damn right, I'ma suit up. Just like I do with you."

"What?" she said, the side of her face I could see scrunched up.

"Ngisize!"

The girl turned in her seat, and my eyes bulged. She didn't look at me with the same surprise as I did her. She still seemed upset.

"What the fuck is going on? And why does this baby keep saying, "Help me." What the fuck did you do to her?" The girl whose face I couldn't stop staring at frowned at me after asking the questions quickly.

"Hunh?" I asked just as the car made a sharp turn.

"This is our mean-ass, big sister. And the baby does speak. She just don't speak English or Spanish. She speaks Zulu. Ngisize means help me."

"Ngisizeeeee!" Shya wailed as if she was finally relieved someone said something she understood.

"*Ungakhathazeki. Sizokusiza.* (Don't worry. We will help you.)" Ro's sister—my sister— said to Shya because her face fell. "Wait..."

Ro hit another turn, and the only thing that kept me planted instead of flying across the back seat was the look of realization coming across his sister's face as she stared at me.

"¿Solana?"

To be Continued....

ABOUT THE AUTHOR

Lisa Austin is an award-winning, National best-selling, independent Author who often creates tales about the grit and grind of the streets, but with a romantic twist. Born and raised in Memphis, TN, the on-the-rise Author has been penning stories her entire life.

patreon.com/LisaAustin

ALSO BY LISA AUSTIN

Yayo: The Beginning

Yayo:Riot's Revenge

Riot 3 (Yayo)

Death of a Nawf Memphis Trap King

Boostin' around the Christmas Tree

I choose you boo 1&2

Annihilate your love

You're My favorite Mistake 1&2

Peek it's boo 1-3

Bossed Up

Bayb

If Cupid was a Thug

Giving it a try with a street Guy: The Valentines

Forever Good in his Hood

Bound to a Bandit

Dreaming of Spring

Big Boss

Humbled by a Real n*gga 1-3

Humbled on Christmas Day- lani & Rut

Just like I taught you

Honey, I f*cked the Plug 1-3

Daddy's Lil Baby

Pregnant by a Muthaf*ckin Don 1&2

A Winter Crest Christmas: Pure & Luxe

A Winter Crest Valentine's: Snowy & Sphere

Wealth over riches & bad b*tches

Paradise Bay: Coastal & Bliss

Exhilarated 1-3

Put it on The Mob: Ezio and Jae

On The Mob: The Cuppacio Twins

Blake University: Leader and Calista

Hellcat Barbies: Saskia and Zodiac

The Mob: Shio Cuppacio

Join my Facebook group and mailing list for exclusive sneak peeks, prizes, book gossip, and never-before-released short stories! Also, follow my Amazon Author page for first dibs on new drops!

Made in the USA
Coppell, TX
24 June 2026

83183053R00350